The Great Hour Struck

On Eagles' Wings: Part One

Gary Varner

iUniverse, Inc.
New York   Bloomington

The Great Hour Struck

On Eagles' Wings: Part One

iUniverse books may be ordered through booksellers or by contacting:

iUniverse
1663 Liberty Drive
Bloomington, IN 47403
www.iuniverse.com
1-800-Authors (1-800-288-4677)

ISBN: 978-0-595-51787-9 (pbk)
ISBN: 978-0-595-51014-6(cloth)
ISBN:978-0-595-62032-6 (ebk)

"Lili Marlene" lyrics: Original German Lyrics by Hans Leip, English Lyrics by Tommie Connor and Music by Norbert Schultze. Used by permission of Edward B. Marks Music Company

Cover Photo Credit: Jacket with 101st Airborne Patch: © Marek Slusarczyk. Image from BigStockPhoto.com

Cover Photo Credit: Cobblestones shadowy path: © Mikolaj Tomczak. Image from BigStockPhoto.com

Printed in the United States of America

iUniverse Rev. 11/10/08

To Carol
For never doubting in me, in this, or any other endeavor.

Acknowledgements

First, I must acknowledge my best friend, wife and lover, Carol Varner, for reading the endless rewrites without complaint and for your unceasing encouragement as I pursue a dream. You amaze me.

For permitting their dad his imaginary friends, I gratefully acknowledge our children, Jessica and 2nd Lt. Clayton R. Varner.

For an advanced education in the craft of fiction writing and skillful editing, I am indebted to Jeff Gerke.

For sharing their memories—some unbearably painful even six decades later—I stand in admiration and salute the Normandy veterans who personally spoke with me. Anyone taking the time to listen to these unassuming gentlemen quickly realizes that they are, indeed, the greatest generation. I must also acknowledge the life-long labor of 101st Airborne historians—Mark Bando and George Koskimaki in particular—for their noble and painstaking efforts in preserving and publishing the legacy of the heroic men wearing the Screaming Eagle patch in 1944.

My advance readers have my heartfelt gratitude. Among them are exceptional encouragers, whose repeated and timely support assured my perseverance. Thank you Kevin, Jeff, Derek, Luke, and Ben.

Finally, *I will lift up mine eyes unto the hills, from whence cometh my help.*

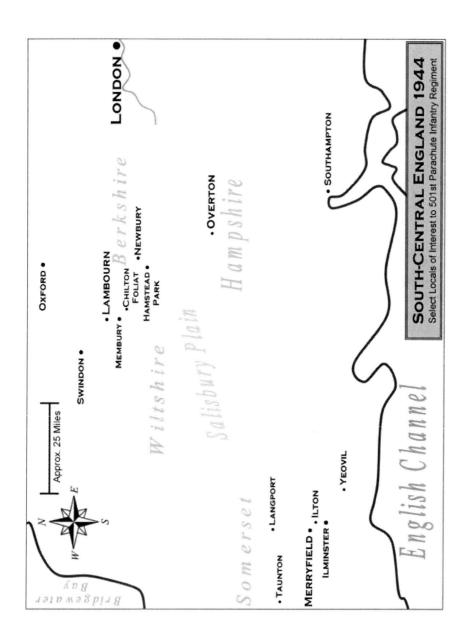

SOUTH-CENTRAL ENGLAND 1944
Select Locals of Interest to 501st Parachute Infantry Regiment

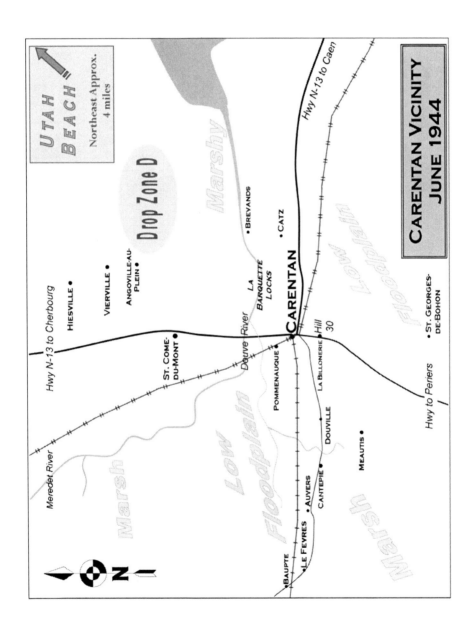

CARENTAN VICINITY
JUNE 1944

UTAH BEACH
Northeast Approx.
4 miles

Drop Zone D

Marshy

Low Floodplain

Marsh

Low Floodplain

Marsh

Hwy N-13 to Cherbourg

Hwy N-13 to Caen

Hwy to Periers

Meredet River

Douve River

HIESVILLE

VIERVILLE

ANGOVILLE-AU-PLEIN

BREVANDS

CATZ

CARENTAN

LA BARQUETTE LOCKS

ST. COME-DU-MONT

POMMENAUQUE

LA BILLONERIE

Hill 30

DOUVILLE

ST. GEORGES-DE-BOHON

MEAUTIS

CANTEPIE

AUVERS

LE FEVRES

BAUPTE

N

Then the great hour struck and every man showed himself in his true colors.

FYODOR DOSTOEVSKY
Crime and Punishment, 1866

Prologue

June 6, 2008

Believing I'd located the object of my decade-long search, I had no clue of the real treasure I'd stumbled upon.

"Has the signed *All Quiet on the Western Front* sold yet?"

"English or German edition?" My hostess's voice carried down a hallway covered in assorted portraits spanning generations. "Sugar? Milk?"

My pulse rate jumped. *English or German?* I must've misunderstood her. "Lemon, please, if you have any."

I turned left through an open doorway and entered the library. The room's size and location indicated that the architect had had a master bedroom in mind. Despite the dehumidifier and citrus air freshener, a trace of musty old-book odor hung in the air. The hand-rubbed oil finish on the oak bookshelves matched the hardwood floor. Full shelves lined three walls clear to the ten-foot ceiling. Assorted stacks of books half-covered an antique walnut-veneer table occupying the room's center. A picture window interrupted the bookshelves on the far wall. Two overstuffed recliners faced each other and lent an air of casual intimacy to the home library.

Alone for the first time in twenty minutes, I wiped my palms on my jeans. *Play it cool, or prices skyrocket.*

I glanced left. Behind an oak desk hung a poster-sized, tin-framed print of an airplane. I stepped closer and squinted to make out the words at the base of the print—"Douglas C-47 Skytrain. Workhorse of the Air Forces Is Solving Transport Problems On Our Far-Flung War Fronts." The poster's style appeared technical and dated, the colors faded. It suited this library about as much as a portrait of Gandhi suited the Pentagon.

Disregarding the out-of-place print, I drifted toward the aged volumes. The titles shelved in prime position—eye level, adjacent to the picture window—drew me in as if having a gravitational force. I pulled a book out at random and held a 1934 youth edition of Stephen Crane's *The Red Badge of Courage*—a worn reader's copy unworthy of shelf space in proximity of signed first printings that could fetch offers into the thousands. I replaced it and skimmed adjacent titles. All seemed faded, bumped, or weathered. *Odd. Where're the Erich Maria Remarques? The first edition C.S. Lewis titles that had brought this collector a measure of notoriety?* I scanned the library for a secure glass case.

Finding none, I assumed the collector had taken a prudent course and locked the literary treasures away out of sight. With nothing to do but wait for my hostess, I squatted and leaned close to the shelf. I detected a theme—Chekov, two Dostoevsky titles, Gogol, Pasternak, four Mikhail Sholokhov titles, Tolstoy, Turgenev. I reached for a faded black copy of *Crime and Punishment*. Something had warped the cover.

The book fell open to reveal a waxed paper envelope. A flowing feminine hand had scrawled "Summer 1944, Merryfield" across the envelope. On the novel's yellowed page a masculine hand had jotted in block letters "June 6, 1944" in the margin and underlined a passage, "Then the great hour struck and every man showed himself in his true colors." Faint spots stained the page as though someone had rescued it from the first scattered raindrops of an approaching thunderstorm. *Or teardrops?*

Over the years I'd stumbled upon a number of fascinating letters and intriguing artifacts tucked away in books and forgotten for decades. My curiosity begged me to peek. If the envelope held something interesting, I'd make an offer on the next-to-worthless book. I sat the novel on the windowsill and eased the envelope open an inch.

A pressed rose—most of the petals shattered and resting on the envelope's bottom—explained nothing. I spread it open more and turned it toward the light. A faded pink ribbon secured a strand of blond hair to the stem.

Memento of a special dance? Wedding? A birth? Maybe a funeral?

I looked up from the aged items and gazed out the picture window, noticing for the first time an impressive view of lush, park-like fields, massive oaks, scattered evergreens, towering sycamores, and a meandering river.

A cane punctuated footsteps on the hardwood floor. I pivoted to find my hostess carrying a steaming cup of tea—split lemon slice on the rim. Despite her silver hair and cane, she could've passed for a distinguished lady in her early to mid-sixties. Her brown eyes conveyed a mischievous alertness that made her nearly constant smile seem genuine. If her advanced years had reduced her stature, she had indeed been tall in her prime. Her blue pantsuit was made of a fabric other than the tacky polyester her generation favored.

Her glance landed on the ancient envelope in my hands, stalling her movement. Her smile vanished. Feeling like a burglar caught in the act, I scrambled for an explanation. "I'm sorry… I enjoy Dostoevsky… couldn't resist opening…"

"Really? Can't imagine anyone *enjoying* three-page paragraphs." The cup and saucer in her hand produced a stuttered rattle.

Fearing that the tea would spill, I took the cup and saucer and held the envelope out. "And this was in there."

When she took it her demure smile returned, and with it her air of composure. "A man who collects stories might assume there's one hidden in this envelope." She heaved a sigh and settled into a recliner. "You came so far—Manchester, didn't you say? Heaven's sake, it doesn't seem right to turn you away empty-handed." Gazing out the window, she began half humming, half singing an evocative melody.

I caught a couple of lines, "…give me a rose to show how much you care, tie to the stem a lock of golden hair…" A teardrop trickled down her cheek, yet her honey-brown eyes had come even more alive, appearing decades younger.

Her humming faded and she said, "I don't suppose you've ever heard 'Lili Marlene'?"

PART I

PREPARE FOR WAR!
Joel 3:9

We sometimes encounter people, even perfect strangers, who begin to interest us at first sight, somehow suddenly, all at once, before a word has been spoken.

Fyodor Dostoevsky

Chapter 1

The Paratrooper

4 February 1944
London

"You guys got to come see this! This airborne joker's about to blow his head off!"

Second Lieutenant Sam Henry looked up from his American Red Cross-furnished soldier's guide to London and turned toward the excited voice. An Air Corps corporal was spouting the news to a pack of 8th Air Force compatriots as if he'd just discovered a circus sideshow.

"Ain't pulling your leg, Tommy. The joker's got his finger on the friggin' trigger, I swear t—"

Sam tucked the London guide into his pocket and raised his voice above the crowded street noise. "Show me where."

The corporal pivoted, and twisting his lip into a snarl jerked this thumb over his shoulder. "Eighty-six it, bud—" The corporal's insolence disappeared the moment his glance landed on the lieutenant's bar shining from the center of the blue parachute infantry patch on Sam's overseas cap. The corporal squared his body and saluted. "Sorry, sir, I didn't see—"

Sam waved a sloppy return salute and narrowed his gray eyes. "I asked *where*, Corporal."

The corporal pointed east. "Past Rainbow Corner, sir. Veer back left, not far, go another thirty yards, duck down this alley, turn back east, right above this Chinese joint on the left."

Sam shook his head. "You lost me. My first time here in Gomorrah. Can you take me there?"

The corporal's friends dispersed into the flowing crowd. He glanced around, pointed his eyes skyward, and gave an exasperated sigh.

Sam raised his hands. "Look, take me to the right building, that's all."

The corporal lit a Camel cigarette. "Is that an order, sir?"

"No, it's my word."

The corporal shrugged. "Follow us, sir." He grabbed his one remaining Air Corps buddy by the arm and began backtracking.

Sam maneuvered through Piccadilly Circus behind the 8th Air Force enlisted men like a halfback following his blockers. The horde of olive-drab and khaki-clad humanity slowed their forward progress. The street level reeked of damp wool uniforms, booze, and puke. Elevated behind Sam the scrolling multistory electric ad for Guinness Ale flashed through the London fog. The four and five-story gray stone buildings darkened the mid-afternoon narrow streets.

His escort turned up an even dimmer alley. The crowd thinned. Sam found himself diverting his gaze away from working girls—or, as the *Stars and Stripes* newspaper identified them, Piccadilly Commandos—who had paired off with amorous GIs. Sam stepped over a used rubber amongst numerous cigarette and cigar butts. The feminine giggles and moans lacked sincerity.

He frowned and hurried his pace. Little of what Piccadilly Circus offered appealed to his palate, yet a morose curiosity had drawn him to the hedonistic center of the GI's London. A guy can only dunk so many Red Cross donuts at Rainbow Corner.

Earlier, at the Stage Door Canteen, he'd tolerated some "starlet" singer—whom he had never heard of—introduced as "straight from an exclusive Hollywood engagement." And to top off his day's entertainment, he'd gone in for *Girl Crazy* at the London Pavilion cinema house—and walked out forty-five minutes later. *They could've spared us yet another Mickey Rooney and Judy Garland pairing—though the Gershwin tunes were decent.* He promised himself he'd use his next leave to take a trip to the cathedral and castle ruins at Salisbury, maybe swing by Stonehenge while there.

His guide turned left and exited the alley. A woman's voice chased Sam, "Do come back soon, Yank. I be offering me special price for parachute regiment *lef'tenants.*"

Sam couldn't resist a glance over his shoulder. Maybe the dim light was playing tricks, but the prostitute looked closer to his mother's age than his own.

Across the street the store signs and windows transitioned to being all done up in Chinese writing. The corporal stopped in front of a dirty white door and pulled it open. "Up there, sir." He pointed toward a dark stairway. "Top of the stairs is as close as I got. Never really saw anything. Don't want no trouble."

As Sam stepped across the threshold, stale ammonia fumes assaulted his nose. The foul air and stains on the wall gave evidence that more than one person had mistaken the stair landing for a urinal. He scrunched up his nose and folded a stick of Wrigley's Spearmint into his mouth. "Thanks, Corporal."

The corporal and his buddy departed as if Sam carried a contagious disease. Sam removed his overseas cap and trotted up the stairs. At the top, he paused and pushed his fingers back through his medium-brown hair combed in a small pompadour. He blinked his eyes to adjust to the poor lighting.

GIs packed the hallway in a writhing olive-drab mass of shifting shoulders and craning necks. Sam stepped toward the crowd. The GIs' attention focused on an illuminated doorway on the right, three-fourths of the way down.

A bottle flew through the doorway and shattered on the brick hallway wall. The GIs erupted in hoots and applause. A high-pitched male voice howled, "Get a bucket, mop, and lots of rags, boys. You'll need it to clean my brains off everything in this whore's ratty dump!"

Three GIs nearest the door ducked away from the light. "Look out! He's pointing it this way!"

A sharp metallic click sounded.

The packed men surged toward Sam like a rushing wave. He stood his ground and two laughing GIs collided into his chest.

Sam grabbed one by the elbow to keep the GI from falling—the man reeked of booze. "Easy, big boy. What's all the excitement over?"

"This nutcase threw everyone out of a little party we was having so he could blow his brains out in privacy." The GI punctuated his report with profanity. "They should toss all them crazy airborne clowns in a cage and—" The GI's bloodshot eyes took in Sam's silver parachute jump wings and worked their way up to the lieutenant's bars. The GI gulped, said, "Sorry, sir," and made a hasty departure down the stairs.

Sam wove his way through the crowd. Just short of the door, he spotted a frowning staff sergeant wearing a 1st Infantry Division patch and Combat Infantryman's Badge. Sam stepped up beside him. "Anybody give a thought to helping this guy, Sergeant, or is this just about the fun and games?"

"I dang sure didn't start this here circus, sir." The veteran sergeant shook his head. "Some of us been a trying to help the feller, but I ain't going back in that there hornet's nest. Reckon I got shot at enough in North Africa and Sicily. Don't aim on getting killed in some Limey cathouse. Figured calling the MPs would just make it worse. Someone would get shot for dang sure."

A pint glass sailed past and crashed into the wall.

Sam lowered his voice to just above a whisper. "What's his name?"

"William Cray. Buck sergeant. Goes by Billy."

"The gun?"

"One of them big ol' British Webley revolvers, sir. He keeps a loading and unloading it, spinning the cylinder, cocking the hammer. Pointing it and pulling the trigger. Reckon that's the third time it landed on an empty cylinder."

"Does he smoke?" Sam said.

"Favors them Chesterfields."

Sam turned to the men behind him and whispered. "Chesterfields. Come on, I need a fresh pack and a lighter. Hurry."

A thin-faced private sporting jump wings and standing a tad shorter than Sam's five foot, nine inches, stepped forward extending a pack and a Zippo.

Sam spotted the 101st Airborne Division patch on the skinny private's left shoulder. "So, a fellow Screaming Eagle."

"Five-O-First Parachute Infantry Regiment, sir. Private Stephen Morton." The teen's thin lips all but disappeared with his grin.

"A fellow Geronimo, at that. Excellent. I want you standing close by, Private Morton. I may need you real quick." Sam turned to the sergeant. "Know what unit Billy's in?"

"Oh yeah, proud as the cock-of-the-walk about it. Made dang sure we all knew he's in the Five-O-Sixth Parachute Infantry Regiment."

"One of Sink's boys…that's just dandy." Sam moved to the doorjamb. *You don't need to do this. Just go find some MPs.* He ran his fingers back through his hair. *You sure you know what you're doing?*

Before he could answer himself, more metallic clicks and snaps distracted him. The rapid clicking roll of a spinning revolver cylinder accompanied an anguished moan.

Sam's pulse raced. "Someone needs to help this guy," he said to no one in particular. He took a deep breath and exhaled. "Hey, Billy, if it's OK I'm coming in."

A high-pitched tenor voice replied, "Why should I let you?"

"Thought you might want to visit awhile with a fellow Camp Toccoa man." Sam extended his leg into the doorway light.

A hand latched on his shoulder and yanked him backward.

The 1st Infantry sergeant leaned close and whispered in his ear. "Billy made his favorite chippy stay in there with him. Candace. Younger than most. Tall blonde. Good gams, but ain't nothin' compared to her b—"

"No need to draw me a picture, Sergeant. Where's she now?"

The sergeant shrugged. "Ain't heard nothing from her since Billy slapped her a time or two. Oh, been about fifteen, twenty minutes ago, I reckon."

Sam pulled away. "Billy, I'm coming in now. My name's Sam."

"Currahee, Sam," Billy said.

Sam stepped into the doorway light. The bare light bulb and open blackout curtains backlit Billy. The soldier appeared as a darkened, nondescript form sitting in a high-backed chair. Sam shielded his eyes and blinked.

Sam's eyes adjusted, revealing the cathouse flat in segments. Stage curtains dominated both the left and right limits of his vision. Through a part in the left curtain he could make out a mattress on the floor and assorted pillows. A bar stood in the right-rear corner near a window. Bottles—standing and tipped over—covered the bar's surface. An overturned table, missing half a leg, lay askew. Broken bottles adorned the half-wet hardwood floor. The room reeked of hard liquor and cheap perfume. No sign of the girl.

Steady handed, Billy pointed a large revolver at Sam's chest. The black muzzle looked large enough to accommodate a nickel.

"Easy, Billy." Sam raised his hands to shoulder height. "See, I'm unarmed. Just want to talk awhile. This is my first time in London. Having one heck of a time finding a fellow Camp Toccoa man around here."

Billy lowered the Webley revolver to rest on his knee. "If I didn't see jump wings I was going to bore a half-inch hole right where they belonged."

Sam noted the expert marksman's badge on Billy's chest. Four weapons bars hung under it. "No doubt you could. I only qualified expert on the M-One. Barely even qualified with a pistol."

Billy pointed the pistol back toward the door. "You just make the pistol an extension of your pointer-finger. Look at your target, both eyes open, and drill it. Don't let some clown make you stand all stiff and aim it like a rifle."

Sam sidestepped away from the pistol's bore and slid his Corcoran jump boots through the debris. He pointed to a second red velvet overstuffed chair facing Billy's—about six feet separated the two chairs. "Mind if I take a load off? Been walking all day. Almost got killed twice just trying to cross the street. Looked the wrong way before stepping out."

Billy's mouth bent into an abbreviated smile. "Happened to me, too." He stuck the pistol muzzle under his chin.

Sam checked the seat cushion for broken glass and seated himself with a big sigh. "Now that feels real good."

A loud metallic click announced Billy cocking the hammer.

"Ain't no way now I can walk out this room alive. Just ain't no way." Billy scrunched his eyes shut.

The hammer dropped with a metallic slap.

Sam's reflexes jerked.

Billy kept the big Webley tucked under his chin and re-cocked the hammer.

"You don't really want to do that, Billy."

A scratchy amplified hiss came from behind the parted curtains. An orchestra played the opening bars of "Lili Marlene"—the British version, featuring Anne Shelton's melodic soprano.

> Underneath the lantern, by the barrack gate
> Darling, I remember the way you used to wait
> T'was there that you whispered tenderly
> That you loved me, you'd always be
> My Lili of the Lamplight
> My own Lili Marlene

Billy covered his ears—one with an open palm, one with the big revolver. "Not that freakin' record again! Told you to play some Benny Goodman. Don't want some fat Limey dame singing the last song I hear."

A woman's hardened yet enticing face popped around the curtain. *She must be Candace.* Her bobbed hair was a shade of blond that only originated in a bottle. A red handprint highlighted her left cheek. Bright red lipstick, rouge, and eye shadow sufficed to advertise her profession. Her harsh Cockney voice shot back, "Can't find no Benny *bloody* Goodman!"

Billy cursed and pointed the pistol at Candace.

She ducked away. "Lili Marlene" ceased with a scratch.

"None of my business," Sam said, "but my first impression says she's hardly a gal worth killing yourself over."

"Good point. Maybe I'll kill her first." Billy's eyes glistened. He kept the pistol leveled on the spot Candace had vacated. "Oh, she'll tell you all sorts of lies to make a fella feel swell. She gave me nothing but a bad case of the clap."

Candace swished from behind the curtains while donning a short, fur-collared coat over a form-hugging red dress. Sam's first view of Candace's body confirmed the accuracy of the 1st Infantry sergeant's crude description.

Billy followed her with the pistol.

Candace locked a malevolent gaze on Billy. "You ask me no questions, I tell you no lies. Them's the rules to me game, Yank. Told you as much from ruddy day one." She turned to Sam. "We be closed for business now, *Lef'tenant.*"

She sauntered for the door—cheap flowery perfume rolling out in her wake, high-heels beating a staccato tempo on the hardwood floor.

Billy held the pistol steady, waiting until the door framed Candace's shoulders, and pulled the trigger.

Sam flinched.

The revolver didn't fire.

Sam exhaled. Sweat trickled down his ribcage.

Lewd comments followed Candace's clicking heels out the building.

Billy broke the Webley open, revealing six empty cylinders. "You forgot to mention you're an officer… *sir.*"

Sam considered leaping across the room for the gun. He tensed his muscles to pounce and started applying downward pressure to the velvet chair arms.

Billy reached to his lap and flicked a bullet into the cylinder. He snapped the revolver shut and leveled the muzzle between Sam's eyes.

Sam leaned back and raised his hands. "Relax, Billy. No need to call me 'sir.' We're in London, on leave, having a little friendly conversation, one Screaming Eagle to another." He tried to spot the one bullet in the four visible cylinder cavities facing him. The cylinder hole in the ten o'clock position looked different, not as dark. That put the single bullet one cock of the hammer away from the firing chamber. Or did it?

Does a Webley cylinder rotate clockwise or…? Sam preferred not betting his life on a fifty-fifty proposition.

"*My* lieutenant's one helluva first-class jerk," Billy said.

"Some sure are. Don't let my butter-bar get you all worked up. I was a buck sergeant just like you not even five months ago. OCS was all the Army's idea, not mine." Sam grinned and motioned for Billy to lower the gun. "You know, I'm a better conversationalist without a gun pointed at my face."

Billy complied, but straight away loaded two more big bullets.

"What unit you in?" Sam took out the Chesterfields and Zippo. "Care for a smoke?"

Billy nodded. "First of the Five-O-Sixth."

Sam tossed the cigarettes and lighter. "They got you guys over at Aldbourne, don't they?"

"Yeah, the digs ain't so shabby for horse stables."

"Scuttlebutt has it Sink's a first-rate regimental commander," Sam said.

"Runs us so much you'd think we're a freakin' track team more than parachute infantry."

"Sounds just like the Five-O-First." Sam noted that the hallway had gone silent. It seemed the crowd had departed for another show, or he was holding the audience spellbound. He folded another stick of Wrigley's Spearmint into his mouth and extended the pack Billy's way. "What's your best Mount Currahee run time?"

Billy shook his head. "Forty-three minutes, four seconds."

Sam gave a soft whistle of admiration. "Beats my best time," Sam lied. "By a good *minute*. How many jumps you got under your belt?"

"Twenty-nine." Billy set the Webley on his lap to light a cigarette.

"That beats me, too," Sam lied again. "If you were in my platoon I'd be looking up to you. So, tell me, why would one squared-away paratrooper such as yourself want to cash in all his chips so soon in the game?" Sam attempted a smile. "If a case of the clap was all it took, our ranks would be getting pretty decimated."

Tears swelled in his eyes and trickled down Billy's square jaw. "I've messed up things so bad. Can't ever get it all straightened back out."

"Let me guess…you got a girl back home."

The tears multiplied. "A real dreamboat. Got her a diamond and popped the question right before shipping out. She said yes. Writes me *every* day. I ain't never laid a wrong hand on her. She's precious. A true doll."

"And she'll still be a doll when you get back. She doesn't need to know a thing about all this. Unless someone's been over here there's no way they could ever understand." Sam scooted his chair toward Billy. "But I understand, Billy. All us red-blooded boys, so far from home, young and manly. Can't ignore the fact that some of us won't make it through combat, but who knows who? A guy's number could come up, so why not experience *all* of London's charms first? A guy's got needs. No one can blame you. I sure don't."

Sam inched his chair closer. Just another foot and he'd be in range to snatch the gun. "Sounds like you earned those stripes," he said. "Squad leader?"

Billy exhaled a cloud of smoke. "Yep, in a rifle platoon."

Sam wagged his head. "Your buddies are going to need you."

"They're parachute infantry. They'll do just fine and dandy without me." Billy wiped a thumb through each eye, sniffed, and dragged the back of his hand under his nose. "The brass will take my squad away anyway."

"For a case of VD?" Sam said. "Hardly. And no one needs to know about this little gunplay."

Billy grimaced. "I'm freakin' AWOL." Billy held up four fingers. "Supposed to have reported back to Aldbourne four days ago."

Sam waved a dismissive hand. "That all? No sweat. Happens all the time. They'll just confine you to barracks a couple weeks, knock you back a pay grade or two. No big deal. Bet you get your squad back in no time at all." Sam started pushing himself out of the overstuffed chair. "I'll take you back to Aldbourne personally, put in a good word to your CO. Let's go."

Billy's eyes widened, he grabbed the revolver and pointed it at Sam's mouth. "No! *You* sit."

Sam complied and forced a grin. "Let's talk about Toccoa. Did they make you dig holes for no re—?"

"Sit on your hands," Billy ordered.

Sam tucked a hand under each thigh.

Billy flicked the cigarette butt across the room and laid the Webley across his lap. "Don't you dare move." He lit another cigarette and clamped it with his teeth. "You *will* watch this. You *will* clean my brains off your face." He broke open the pistol and nimbly loaded the last three cartridges. "And then you *will* report to my jackass platoon leader exactly why."

Billy jammed the Webley back under his chin, cocked the hammer and closed his eyes tight. His jaw muscles visibly clenched and trembled.

"Then you're needing to do a better job of explaining to me exactly why," Sam said, pulling his hands free, "because I'm just not getting it, Billy. Suicide is not the answer. It solves nothing."

Billy pulled the cigarette from his mouth. "Solves plenty."

Sam bit his lower lip and forced the memory to surface. "A friend— no, more than a friend, more like a father to me—killed himself back in September. Stop and think this through, Billy. You pull that trigger and, sure, it's all over for you, but it only messes up everyone you leave behind. Feeling like they never even mattered. Like their love was never even worth your time or effort."

Keeping his eyes closed, Billy said, "Nothin' really matters." He took a long drag on the Chesterfield.

Sam struggled to sneak forward on the soft seat cushion. "I don't see how a guy in the parachute infantry can say that. A guy in the Five-O-Sixth to boot. You've chosen—chosen twenty-nine times now—to jump out of an airplane. You've pushed yourself up Mount Currahee when every fiber of your being screamed at you to quit. But you didn't. You're not a quitter. You've *chosen* to be an elite warrior."

Billy's voice raised an octave. "I've *chosen* to end it all, right now."

"No, choose the valiant way. Choose to make a diff—"

Billy loosed a string of profanity. "A difference against what?"

"Against tyranny. Against those who'd rob us of choice. Liberty. Not just in a national sense, but real personal, individual liberty."

Sam snapped his fingers. Billy's eyes sprung open.

"If you're all so set on dying, Billy, at least choose to do it in such a way that will honor your family and further humanity. We're going to fight real evil. At least take some Nazis with you first. Come on, Billy." Sam extended his hand, palm up. "Hand me the gun."

Billy pulled the revolver from his chin and thrust his arm out. The cocked Webley muzzle stopped against Sam's forehead. "Suppose I don't die in combat. Then what?"

The big pistol shook.

Sam gulped hard. "Then—"

"Then I mess it all up all over again. I find another Candace. Embarrass everyone. Hurt my girl. Shame my folks." Billy crushed out his cigarette on the chair's arm. "That's what life's about and it ain't worth living through again."

Sam leaned away from the pistol muzzle. "Pull that trigger and you forfeit any chance for redemption. Jump with your squad and you can make up for all this. Start over again, afresh."

Billy's eyes altered, as if resolved.

Sam pleaded, "Billy, come on. Think of your sweetheart. You can't choose *here* of all places. Not in some Piccadilly Commando whorehouse."

"Watch me!" Billy leaned back, kicked out so his chair scooted away, and shoved the Webley barrel into his mouth.

Sam stood ramrod straight. "Sergeant Cray, what is the parachute infantry motto?" Sam's pulse raced. "Tell me now, Sergeant!"

Mute, Billy squeezed his eyes shut. His jaw muscles went rigid again.

"Strike, seize, hold! That's what we do. We strike, seize, and hold." Sam softened his tone. "Billy, it's the same with life. Strike out for what you know is good. Seize it. Then hold on for all it's worth."

Guttural, anguished sounds rose from Billy's throat.

Sam stepped forward two steps and leaned closer. "Billy, Billy... *life*... the good stuff... strike, seize, hold."

Billy's eyes opened.

"Don't do it, Billy... do *not* pull that trigger... *live*."

Sam's instincts told him that Billy's eyes were now pleading for life.

He took a half-step, laid his hand on the huge revolver, and gently tugged.

Billy's gun hand fell away.

Sam lowered the revolver's hammer and broke it open. The bullets dropped amongst the broken glass.

Motion in the door caught Sam's attention. Men poured into the room—the 1st Infantry staff sergeant and Private Morton leading the way.

Sam's knees wobbled. He placed a hand on Billy's shoulder, as much to keep standing as to comfort Billy.

Chapter 2

Jump School

5 February 1944
Newbury, England

"Sir, with all due respect, I didn't choose to join the parachute infantry to teach non-combatants to jump."

Sam tried not to fidget as he sat at attention in the straight-backed chair. Despite the typical chill found in English dwellings, sweat trickled down his ribs. The room's simple desk, wooden chairs, plain lamp, and battered filing cabinet typified the office of every other staff officer Sam had languished in—only the desk nameplates differed. This one read: Capt. Cranston, S-1, 501st PIR.

An hour earlier the summons had irritated Sam—interrupting the momentary escape he relished in Dostoevsky's *Crime and Punishment*. On the short walk to the S-1's office his irritation had shifted to fear. Fear that he'd landed in hot water with the regimental brass over how he handled Sergeant Billy Cray's cathouse incident. His fears proved unfounded and forgotten. Forgotten due to the typed new orders before him. Forgotten and replaced by acute frustration.

In Virginia plantation owner's accent Captain Cranston said, "On that account you're quite mistaken, Lieutenant. You joined the parachute infantry to *serve*. It just so happens that we, not you, get to choose exactly where you might best *serve*." The personnel officer's eyes never left Sam's file. "Time's running short to get the 101st Airborne Division filled out. We need you elsewhere. For just a spell, mind you."

Sam leaned forward. "But, sir, my understanding was that if I came over to England early to help get things prepped for the whole regiment, you'd bump me to the top of the list for a rifle platoon."

Captain Cranston jabbed his finger in Sam's file. "One helluva outstanding jump record. Let's see…forty-one jumps, nineteen with combat gear, seven night jumps. You've graduated from the Jumpmaster Course. Served as jumpmaster for a dozen sticks." He looked up from the file. "In about every category your OCS cadre rated you just a notch below walks-on-water. A bit too free to express your opinion at times, but we can overlook a few lumps in the buttermilk. Remnants of the civilian still in you. On more than one occasion evaluators noted that you're a natural teacher. No, Lieutenant Henry, you were tailor-made for this assignment."

"But, sir, I trained to lead a parachute infantry platoon. You picked me for OCS to *lead* a parachute infantry platoon. I want to lead men on combat jumps, not *teach*—"

Captain Cranston raised the volume of his voice. "Like I said, too free to express your opinion." He stared at peeling paint on the old English manor's ceiling. "You have your orders, Lieutenant Henry."

Sam gnawed his lower lip. Boots clomped down the hallway outside the closed door. Captain Cranston scratched the fringe of hair ringing his head. Sam leaned back in his chair and sighed. "I'll give it my best effort, sir."

"Of that we have no doubt." Captain Cranston rubberstamped a page, closed the file, and stared across the desk at Sam. "I can appreciate a new butter-bar second lieutenant wanting to lead men. I'll see to it division keeps you on this training assignment for just one cycle. They've found a way to cram the four-week Fort Benning parachute school into just two weeks."

"When do I report, sir?"

"Tomorrow, oh-eight-hundred hours. The division's parachute jump school is at Chilton Foliat. Just up the road. A driver will pick you up at o-seven-thirty."

Captain Cranston tossed Sam's file into his out box. "When it comes to the One-Hundred-n'-First, we're still the new kids in town. Scuttlebutt has it that some ol' boys in the Five-O-Sixth and Five-O-Second who've been here a little longer aren't exactly welcoming us Geronimos with open arms. We must be mindful, Lieutenant Henry, first impressions are lasting impressions. Represent the Five-O-First well and you'll get your platoon in two weeks."

*   *   *

18 February 1944
Membury, England

Sam strode down the Membury Airfield tarmac with an added bounce to his step.

Two hundred yards distant a C-47 Pratt & Whitney fourteen-cylinder engine whirred and coughed before firing to life with a belch of blue smoke.

Membury Airfield was a short ride from the Chilton Foliat jump school, situated atop a plateau among the sharply rolling hills of Berkshire County. The approach to the airfield consisted of narrow and at times steep roads meandering through pastureland and winter wheat fields. Ringneck pheasants darted in and out of the low hedgerows and isolated woodlots.

He shifted his T-5 parachute harness and looked back at the trailing divisional staff officers, surgeons, chaplains, and a couple of sailors. Every pupil, except a Navy ensign, outranked Sam. He cast a smile at his graduation candidates. *One last jump and I graduate twelve out of my original fifteen. Not too shabby. Then, my own platoon.*

His pupils waddled like a line of ducklings, making Sam chuckle. This final jump required a full combat load on top of the bulky parachute harness and reserve chute. The surgeons and chaplains carried pouches stuffed with extra medical supplies, surgical tools, and communion kits. The staff officers and Navy men carried an Army Colt 45-auto pistol and folding-stock carbine. As instructor, Sam carried only his main and reserve chutes over his baggy M-42 jump jacket and trousers. All wore GI steel pot helmets, modified for airborne troops with the addition of more secure Y-straps and a football-style cupped leather chinstrap.

A fresh-faced Air Corps second lieutenant, jogged up alongside Sam.

"Little late?" Sam said to the navigator.

"Go and figure. Last-minute changes. We've been assigned a new drop zone."

Sam folded a piece of Wrigley's Spearmint into his mouth and offered one to the navigator as they walked. "Why change DZs now?"

The navigator took a piece. "Seems our Limey hosts have some big maneuvers brewing on the Salisbury Plain. Why we just now got the word, I've no idea. So, we're dropping you gentlemen about twenty-five nautical miles southeast. Just north of some village. What's it called?" He pulled a map out of his case and jabbed his gloved finger on the circled spot. "Overton."

"Why was I left in the dark?"

"Relax. I'm telling you now, aren't I?"

"What's the DZ like?" Sam asked.

"Piece of cake. Plowed hundred-sixty-acre rectangular field, long axis running east-west. Plenty big for one stick of jumpers." The navigator slipped the map back into the case. "A regular milk run for me, too. We just head in the general direction of London, hang a U-turn, bank it to kind of west-southwest, and flip on the green light."

"Navigators who speak in such highly technical terms sure boost my confidence."

"Hey, why should I waste my highly technical vocabulary—courtesy of my rich Uncle Sam—on jokers crazy enough to jump out of a perfectly good airplane? Pearls before swine."

A cold wind gust bit Sam's exposed face. He looked at the airfield windsock. It jumped and pointed straight south. "The weather?"

"Weather wizards expect a strong cold front to blow through late afternoon, maybe evening. High winds, freezing rain, sleet tonight. Don't sweat it. They say we've got at least four hours of marvelous weather for jumping." The navigator lit a cigarette. "New drop zone. A big cold front moving in… I'd just as soon wait a day or two, but our much-beloved commandant—what a gem that clown is—he wants to push your group on through to make room for a batch from the Five-O-Second."

Sam glanced over his shoulder. He preferred his brass-heavy pupils heard none of the navigator's insolence—or the weather forecast.

They reached the twin-engined cargo plane, painted with a gray belly and olive drab top. Its second engine coughed to life, making it harder to hear. Sam accepted a hand from the crew-chief to climb into the cabin. The unique combination of hydraulic fluid, burnt aviation fuel, male bodies, and assembled aircraft parts joined to replicate the aroma of Sam's father returning from a day's work at Douglas Aircraft. His father's charcoal-gray felt fedora had retained the C-47 scent as though soaked in it.

Sam followed the navigator into the cockpit. The pilot and copilot flipped switches and jabbered in aviation jargon. The array of gauges, instruments, and controls never failed to impress Sam. "Could we make this one nice and easy, sirs? Today's graduation day—no day for a guy to break a leg."

"Terrific, just what this army needs," the pilot said, "another dozen cocky paratroopers showing off their silver jump wings and blousing their trousers in their boots, looking down their noses upon the rest of us mere mortals." He scrawled an entry into his logbook. "Better head on back, Lieutenant. We need to beat a cold front."

Sam frowned. "Navigator said that'd be no problem."

"Easy for him to say, he doesn't have to fight the rudder of this beast in a stiff crosswind. I'd just as soon get in the air and get your class dropped ASAP. Don't want to put any more faith in our witch doctor weathermen than I have to."

Sam departed the cockpit, closed the door behind him, and moved down the aisle. Unlike a real combat jump, his "stick" of twelve men only half-filled the plane. Near the door, he tossed a little packet of GI toilet-paper to a youthful surgeon. "You ready for the final exam?"

The surgeon examined the packet. "What's this, Lieutenant Henry?"

"Call it an early graduation present. Turn it over." Sam had learned that the surgeon had pitched for the University of Southern California three seasons before Sam played baseball for UCLA. War or no war, Sam refused to let the rivalry lie dormant.

The surgeon laughed. On the toilet-paper package wrapper—in official looking block letters—Sam had printed: USC DIPLOMAS. "Why, thank you, Lieutenant. After graduation maybe I can return the favor and help you out with a little free surgery."

"And what type of surgery would that be, Captain?"

"A very common medical procedure on UCLA men. I remove your head from your rectum."

Sam grinned. "I suppose in one way or another all USC med-school grads are specialized in proctology."

Increasing roar from the twin engines cut the banter short. The C-47 lurched forward and taxied. For those jumping, it would be a short flight—fifteen, twenty minutes, tops.

About the time the C-47 leveled off at the prescribed altitude of 5,000 feet, it began a sweeping starboard turn. From his favorite position—kneeling in the open portside doorway—Sam could just make out London on the horizon. *London… I hope the Five-O-Six brass went easy on Billy.* His eyes strained to identify landmarks.

Before he could pick out St. Paul's or Big Ben, the plane finished its turn and flew west. He lost sight of the sprawling city and pushed thoughts of Billy aside. He scooted back from the frigid blast in the doorway. He looked forward to floating down to the relative warmth of forty-five degrees.

His attention shifted to his graduation candidates. The two Catholic priests fumbled Rosary beads through gloved hands. One Protestant reverend eyed the ceiling, another bowed his head. The divisional staff major tapped his foot at about 180 beats-per-minute. The orthopedic surgeon patted his pockets in rotation as if he couldn't find something urgently needed. A thoracic surgeon chain-smoked, his face glistening with sweat despite the cold. Sam's pupils showed a marked decrease in nervousness compared to the first jump.

The two Navy men casually smoked and attempted conversation over the flight noise. Ike's SHAEF shop—Supreme Headquarters Allied Expeditionary Force—had attached the sailors, a lieutenant and an ensign, to the 501st. SHAEF's invasion plan called for the Navy officers to radio battleships and destroyers for heavy gun support. It was the only invasion detail Sam had been privileged enough to learn.

Sam returned to the doorway. He enjoyed the irregular patchwork of hedgerow-bordered fields marked with farmsteads, flocks of sheep, glass greenhouses, or herds of cattle. The new drop zone left Sam ignorant of recognizable landmarks he could use to predict the time left, but the C-47's descent told him the jump was near. The pressure built in his ears. Smacking gum to help his ears pop, he locked his gaze on the jump lights.

The red light came on. "Stand up and hook up!" he yelled.

The twelve men rose in unison and hooked their static lines to the cable running lengthwise down the fuselage ceiling.

A wind gust knocked the plane sideways. Several wide-eyed pupils looked to Sam.

"Relax," Sam yelled over the engine noise.

He sensed the plane decelerating from the 180 mph cruising speed to around 100 mph for the jump. Sam had taught his pupils that much faster than 120 mph and the shock of an opening chute could cause a lot of painful damage—especially where the T-5 harness straps got jerked into the crotch. A chute opening at excessive airspeed could also break gear loose.

"Check equipment!" he yelled. Each man checked his own equipment and then checked the chute of the man ahead.

"Sound off for equipment check!"

In descending order, each man in the stick, starting with number twelve, yelled his number followed by, "OK."

"One, OK!" rang in his ear. Looking out the door, Sam estimated they'd leveled off higher than the planned combat jump altitude of 800 feet. They appeared to be closer to the training jump height of 1,200 feet. *Pilot's adjusting for the crosswind and air pockets. Air speed seems about right...nice and slow. Thank you.*

Another wind gust struck the fuselage. The C-47 dropped and rose. The crowded line of jumpers lost its collective balance. Five fell in the aisle. Two toppled sideways, back into the metal bucket seats.

The downed pupils leapt back up and reformed the line.

"I may need those diplomas of yours before we get to the ground," the USC surgeon—number two in the stick—shouted over the engine noise and wind.

Sam resisted giving a clever retort. One minute out from the DZ, while experiencing turbulence, called for his total concentration. "Number One, stand in the door. Close it up, tight!"

Twelve men shuffled toward the door like a contracting caterpillar.

"Ready?" Sam shouted.

"Ready!" the stick of jumpers shouted in unison.

Sam knelt aft of the door. His quick glances alternated between the ground and the jump light. If they did as he'd trained them, each jumper would brace himself in the door until the jumpmaster tapped him on the left leg and yelled, "Go!" In rapid succession the plane would empty.

On an actual combat drop, no one would wait for a leg tap. The paratroopers would pile out, jumpmaster first, in a steady stream to assure landing in a tight group. At 100 mph a C-47 could cover a lot of ground fast—no one wanted the nightmare of dropping into combat alone.

Sam had trained his pupils for the simple sequence—pivot left upon exiting the door, tuck, slowly count to three, and brace for the jolt of the deploying chute. If lacking that jolt, the jumper was to, without hesitation, pull the reserve chute ripcord.

The jump lights switched from red to green.

Sam tapped the leg of number one. "Go!" With practiced haste he repeated the leg taps and shouts, emptying the plane in under fifteen seconds.

Standard operating procedures didn't require the jumpmaster on a training flight to jump. However, regimental commander Colonel Johnson had set the pace at 130-plus jumps. Sam's pride and pure enjoyment of jumping compelled him. He rose from his kneeling position, hooked his static line, and positioned himself in the door.

Sam gave the crew-chief a white-toothed smile and jumped, the 501st's battle cry rushing out his throat. "Geronimo!"

He turned left and tucked. The prop-blast whistled through his helmet. One thousand one, one thousand two, one thou—

The chute deployed with the usual teeth-jarring jolt and sound of popping fabric. He decelerated from 100 mph to twenty-four feet per second, swinging like a pendulum.

As the oscillations lessened, Sam first checked his own canopy, then scanned for the chutes of his staggered stick of student jumpers. Twelve full canopies. He admired the new, more warrior-like camouflage chutes some had. He preferred the green-camouflage over the older white chutes. The white implied a helpless downed airman, rather than what a paratrooper was—an elite infantryman attacking from above.

The C-47's twin-engine buzz dissipated into the distance. The rectangular field looked just as the navigator had described. The breeze nudged the stick a little south, but not in danger of colliding with a row of mixed poplar and pine trees bordering the field.

Beyond the row of trees, Sam could make out the extreme northern edge of a village. *What did the navigator call it…? Overton.* The nearest non-farm structure was a large, two-story brick building with swingsets, teeter-totters, and soccer goals behind it. Smoke drifted upward from dozens of chimneys and settled over the little dell. He grinned like a grammar school boy getting away with mischief. *They'd quit paying me extra if they knew how much I loved this.*

Sam turned his attention back to his pupils. Jumper number one, already on the ground, was gathering his shroud-lines.

Number two, the USC surgeon, completed a textbook parachute-landing fall. Numbers three through seven landed uneventfully.

Sam glanced north. A wall of leaves, dried grass, and crop debris blew across the plowed ground. He realized he was watching the actual leading edge of the forecasted cold front. The same front not predicted to hit for hours.

Sam shifted his attention back east, hoping the rest of his pupils remembered how to collapse a wind-filled chute. If not, each risked being dragged across rough ground for a couple hundred yards.

The wall of wind slapped his dangling body and shoved his chute south.

He pulled down on his left shroud-lines to compensate. A seam in the right side of the white silk chute picked that instant to surrender to the forces of repeated stress. It tore.

The three-foot rip spilled air, propelling him even further south.

His descent accelerated.

At 400 feet, he knew he'd miss the drop zone.

Chapter 3

The Pitchfork

"I have splendid news, Jeremy. Today you assume the character of Fitzwilliam Darcy. So do go to the corner and put on a costume you find most befitting Mr. Darcy."

Maggie Elliott held a copy of *Pride and Prejudice* aloft and pointed toward the costume corner, where an array of old coats, hats, canes, umbrellas, and assorted theatrical props lay. Jeremy rushed from his desk as if Maggie had just told him that Father Christmas had hidden special gifts among the props. He donned an oversized smoking jacket, knee-high riding boots, and a *Three Musketeers*-style hat.

"Remember, Jeremy, as Mr. Darcy, mind you, I expect you to explain to our fellow readers why you didn't let the Bennet family know about the wonderful deeds you were doing for them."

Maggie put a finger to her chin and gazed upward. "But we need a good Elizabeth Bennet to present her side of the story…" She rotated in the center of circled desks and let her smile fall on an underdeveloped fourteen-year-old girl with a pronounced overbite. "Sally." The girl's face lit up as if Princess Elizabeth had just invited her to high tea. "I do believe you'd make a lovely Elizabeth Bennet today."

As Sally rushed for the props, Maggie directed her pupils' attention to the questions she had written on the slate chalkboard: How did Elizabeth Bennet's prejudice delay her from finding happiness? What led Elizabeth to misjudge Mr. Darcy's character so badly? What do Mr. Darcy's actions tell us about the nature of a true gentleman?

Maggie glanced at the small window in the classroom door. Someone was spying on her. The squinting little eyes sunken into a flabby face identified the spy as Headmaster Hampton. *Dear me. Time to improvise.* In a voice loud enough to carry through the door, she announced. "Class, turn your attention to the three essay questions on the board. I want a three paragraph essay for each question, due next Wednesday."

The class gave a collective moan. Sally looked crestfallen. "What 'appened to me being Elizabeth?"

Headmaster Hampton smiled and pulled his face from the door. Maggie listened to the sound of his departing footsteps. Relieved, she put an index finger to her lips and let her voice take on a conspiratorial tone. "But if everyone takes part in our playacting discussion you may each choose just one of the three essay questions."

Joy returned to the faces of her adolescent students. They were an oil and vinegar mixture of East End London evacuees and local Hampshire County children.

Maggie turned to Jeremy. "I do believe it's time to hear from our Mr. Darcy."

Jeremy stood at the row of windows on the classroom's north side and gazed outward.

Maggie suppressed a chuckle. "Oh, Mr. Darcy—that was your prompt."

Ignoring Maggie, the lad leaned closer to a window and craned his neck.

"Jeremy?" A mechanical buzzing reached Maggie's ears. *Odd, I can't recall an airplane sounding that loud from in here.*

Throwing his arm up to point, Jeremy knocked off the *Three Musketeers'* hat. "Blimey! It's a bloody Jerry bomber! A Junkers JU-Eighty-eight. Comin' from bombin' the London docks. Look how low it is!"

The class erupted from their seats and rushed the windows.

"Must be hit bad," another boy yelled. "The Jerrys are bailin' out!"

Jeremy stepped back from the window. "Bang on! There's one heading for us!"

Sally screamed. The scream became contagious among the girls.

"Class… class…" Maggie said, gently clapping her hands. "Please do find your seats. Class!" However, she maneuvered for a better view.

To her amazement, a man dangling under a white parachute was indeed drifting toward the school.

"We should give that lousy Jerry what for," Jeremy shouted.

"Let's nab him," another lad said and ran for the door. Six boys followed.

"Like ruddy 'ell you will," Jeremy said. "I saw him first!"

Maggie dashed for the door. Before the boys reached the exit, she had it blocked.

She tried to look imposing, her feet shoulders' width apart, hands on hips. She looked down at the seventh and eighth form boys, the tallest only stood shoulder-height to her. "Nobody leaves this room. Jeremy, you spotted the German plane, so you may go report it to Headmaster Hampton. Ask him to notify the Home Guard."

Jeremy puffed up, elbowed a mate, and darted out the door.

Maggie addressed the elbowed lad. "Simon, you shall guard this door. Allow no one to pass. Is that clear?"

"Aye, ma'am. No bloke gets past me."

"The rest of you, return to your seats, I'll return shortly. Work on your *Pride and Prejudice* essay." As she trotted toward the stairway, the absurdity of her last instruction struck her. Yet that mattered little. If a downed Nazi pilot was dropping into her schoolyard, she had to take action.

A German bomber at Overton struck her as pure nonsense. Yet Jeremy excelled at few skills quite like his ability to identify warplanes. He'd had over four years of experience. She had to prepare for the worst and adjust as needed. An escaping enemy pilot might instigate panic across Hampshire—starting with her young charges.

She bounded down the steps, burst through the double doors of the school's main entrance, and ran along a brick wall on her right. *I'll just keep him in sight from a safe distance until the Home Guard arrives.*

She heard glass shattering, then a hollow thud.

Over the wall a white parachute canopy collapsed.

Maggie came to a sudden halt. *Oh, blast it all! Now what?* She needed protection. Her frantic gaze landed on a three-tined pitchfork leaning against the wall.

*   *   *

A sense of helplessness overwhelmed Sam.

With mere seconds left to avert disaster, he shoved helplessness aside and willed his training to kick in. Fighting to control the chute, he tugged on the left risers.

The crowded row of pines and bare poplars passed under his feet, but did little to slow his southward drift.

He scanned downward to anticipate where he might land. A long barn stood to the left. To his right he caught a glimpse of a woman running from a multistory brick building.

The earth rushed up to meet him.

He looked between his feet. A glass greenhouse filled his vision. Panic seized his gut.

To dodge the greenhouse he yanked hard on his right-front riser. The urgent tug combined with the existing rip spilled more air than needed.

Sam's jump boots shattered a pane of glass.

He jerked his legs up and gritted his teeth in anticipation of the jagged glass slicing skin.

A wind gust yanked him off the glass roof. It also shifted his body horizontal to the ground and only slightly lower than the canopy. The laws of physics took over. He plunged the final twenty feet out of control.

A patch of plowed soil and a steaming mound flashed below.

Gritting his teeth, Sam tensed his body in anticipation of a parachute-landing fall nothing like he'd covered with his pupils.

Leading with his left shoulder, he collided with the mound. The parachute canopy collapsed.

The steaming pile yielded with a consistency somewhere between a haystack and loose mud. Incredibly, Sam felt no pain. Spitting and sputtering he got to his knees and plucked a sticky clump of straw off his cheek. Fresh cow manure, household food scraps, and soiled straw covered him.

He regained his feet and stumbled away from the rank heap. He gathered in his shroud-lines and clutched the defective chute silk to his chest.

A discomfort in his chest made him aware that he was holding his breath. He gasped for air. The all-encompassing stench overpowered him. He reached to unbuckle the muck-fouled T-5 harness.

An agitated female Cockney voice shouted. "'Alt! Get your bloody 'ands up. Don't make me 'urt you."

Sam looked up from the slippery harness buckles. The orders emanated from a well-dressed young lady. He failed to comprehend half of what she was shouting, but the pitchfork she held like a GI practicing a bayonet assault left zero doubt about her intent.

"It's OK, missy. No harm, no foul. Uncle Sam's good for the damages." Sam quit his one-handed fumbling with the harness and set off toward the opening in the brick wall. "Go back to whatever you were doing. I've got to find my stick."

She stepped into his path. "I said 'alt! You're 'ereby a prisoner of His Majesty. Your war's over."

Sam took a longer look at the brazen young woman—as tall as him, blond hair, and a face very easy on the eyes. "I'd love to oblige, missy, but my war hasn't even begun yet. Listen, you look like a reasonable girl…"

He reconsidered his words—a well-dressed, looker wielding a pitchfork failed the rationality test. He'd attempt appeasement. "Look, at most there's two broken panes in your hothouse. Send a bill anyway. Break out a few more panes if it makes you happy. Make up a number. Uncle Sam will pony up the greenbacks, guaranteed." He grabbed a pitchfork tine and attempted to fling it aside.

The woman reacted like a close-combat instructor. She yanked the pitchfork out of his grip and sidestepped to block his way. Glaring, she moved the sharp tines in circles near his chest. "You don't fool me. You flew a German bomber—a JU-Eighty-eight. If you know what's good for you, you won't move again 'til the Home Guard arrives. Hands up!"

"You've got to be certifiable. Listen to me. I'm American. Lieutenant, United States Army, parachute infantry."

"I saw the Junkers. And that's hardly American kit you're wearing. Too baggy. Wrong color."

"You don't say? OK smarty, then what's this?" He jabbed at the Screaming Eagle patch with airborne tab on his left shoulder.

"Cow dung and a bit o' eggshell?"

Puzzled, he looked where his divisional patch was supposed to be. Instead, he found a thick smear of green manure and a piece of brown eggshell. His nose informed him that he wasn't escaping the stench, because he was the stench. He dropped his gathered chute, unfastened the parachute harness chest strap, and reached inside his jacket for his military ID.

The pitchfork flashed.

"Ouch!" The back of Sam's right hand stung.

"Keep your hands where I can see them! We'll be having none o' your ghastly Nazi tricks."

The back of his hand was dripping blood. "Watch it!"

She narrowed her honey-brown eyes. "How do I know you're not reaching for a pistol? Or a cyanide capsule?"

"Listen carefully," Sam said. "I am *not* armed. And I have no suicide pills. I *am* an American!"

"That's ruddy well what I'd say too if I were a downed *Luftwaffe* pilot on English soil. Sit! The Home Guard's on their way."

Passivity seemed the prudent option. So—cold, wet, and stinking—Sam plopped down, sat cross-legged on the white silk parachute, and gazed up at his captor. Even in a rage, she presented a gorgeous package. Her bare, shapely calves dominated his line of sight. Time to relax and enjoy the view.

"Fine," he said, "we'll do it your way. Just know that my men are on the other side of those trees," he pointed over the greenhouse, "and they're on their way, too."

Fear flared in her large eyes.

The sound of multiple running feet came from the other side of the wall. A half-dozen boys rounded the corner, each brandishing a tool. Two boys led the pack—one lofting a fire ax over his head, the other armed with a claw-hammer. The ax-boy wore an oversized, purple smoking jacket and knee-high riding boots. A floppy hat with one side pinned to the crown and a large ostrich plume sat atop the claw-hammer assailant.

Sam tensed his muscles and shifted. One wacky English girl armed with a pitchfork he could handle. He had serious doubts about his odds against a half-dozen crazed boys wielding carpentry and yard tools. He figured he could outrun the boys—even clutching his gathered chute and harness. First, he had to grab the chute out of the mud and get on his feet. He uncrossed his legs, leaned on his left palm, and gathered his legs under him to spring to his feet. "I'd love to stay and chat—"

Gasping in disbelief, he watched the pitchfork's center tine enter his left forearm and exit the opposite side. His scream filled the space between the greenhouse and brick building.

The pitchfork's momentum pinned his arm to the mud.

"Ow! You crazy—!"

She pressed the pitchfork harder.

A warm wetness spread across his forearm. Crimson blossomed on his sleeve.

Sam bit his lower lip and focused past the blonde's legs. The two lead boys skidded to a halt, weapons still held high, but jaws dropped in stunned silence. The four trailing assailants piled up into their backs. Sam groaned. Blood expanded over his sleeve.

"Jeremy, didn't I ask you to get Headmaster Hampton?" The woman's voice took on a more composed tone.

"No, ma'am, you said to ask him to call the Home Guard. I reckon he didn't believe me. Seemed a wee miffed. He's looking for you now."

"Drop the ax and bring him here." She blew a blond strand out of her eyes. "And do be quick, Jeremy."

The pressure lightened on Sam's arm. "That's better. Could you—?"

The blonde took a new grip and twisted the tines with renewed vigor.

"Ughhhhh…!" Sam screamed.

The boy in the smoking jacket and oversized boots dropped the fire ax and took off running. Before leaving earshot, Sam heard the boy say, "That ain't no *Luftwaffe* uniform. What the bloody 'ell was that bloke doing in a Junkers?"

She kept the pressure on the pitchfork and glanced over her shoulder. "Simon, I'm quite disappointed in you. I'm disappointed in all of you. Drop those tools and return to class."

The boy under the floppy hat protested. "But a real gentleman like Mr. Darcy would never leave—"

"This isn't a novel! This is real life. Do as I say."

Simon dropped the hammer and retreated. The remaining boys followed, taking quick glances over their shoulders.

Pain shot up Sam's arm. "Let me up. Now!"

"Why do you bomb civilians?"

"Stop and think!" Sam grimaced. "Listen to my voice. Do I *sound* German?"

"You most certainly aren't British."

A jeep full of GIs rolled into view in the gap between the greenhouse and wall. Sam gave a feeble wave with his free hand. The driver stood on the brakes, cranked the steering wheel left, popped the clutch, and lurched into the farmyard. Four 101st paratroopers bailed out and trotted to Sam's rescue.

"You OK, Lieutenant Henry?" a corporal called in a Bronx accent.

"Oh my… Oh, dear Lord! What've I done?" the blonde asked of no one in particular. She released the pressure and began pulling the pitchfork away.

"No, stop. Stop!" Sam pleaded. "I don't need that filthy tine dragged back through."

"Oh, but I'm dreadfully sorry!" Her eyes became troubled. "I honestly didn't believe you to be a Yank."

"Only told you a dozen times."

"Then why were you in a German bomber?" She dropped the pitchfork.

"Ow!" Sam reached for his impaled forearm and twisted his body to find a position offering some relief. "You just don't give up, do you?"

The drop zone medic knelt for a closer look. "Glad I don't have to mess with this." The medic yelled back over his shoulder, "Someone go fetch me one of those surgeons, ASAP!"

Four agonized minutes later, the USC pitcher-turned-surgeon jogged up. He knelt to assess the arm and gave Sam a broad grin. "So how'd you manage to drop on a pitchfork? That's one slick trick, even for a UCLA man."

"Medic, find me another doctor," Sam said through clenched teeth. "This one can't help where this pitchfork's stuck."

"Sorry, Lieutenant, they didn't trust me with any morphine on this jump. Can you tolerate the pain?" The surgeon pinched his nose. "Because I'm not sure I can tolerate the stench much longer."

"Just get it pulled out, Captain." Sam bit his lower lip.

The surgeon opened a medical bag. "Good thing the Army had the foresight to update you on all your shots before we crossed the pond. I can only imagine the host of *clostridia* on that pitchfork."

"I'm dreadfully sorry." The tall blonde leaned back over Sam. "I do believe the nearest hospital is in Basingstoke. Might I arrange transportation?"

"That won't be necessary, miss." Using folded gauze drenched in disinfectant, the surgeon gave the tine a thorough cleaning, followed by a liberal dousing of alcohol and lingering passes with a Ronson lighter flame. As a final precaution, he dusted sulfanilamide powder until a bright yellow film covered the tine.

"What're you doing that for?" Sam asked.

"When we drag that back through your arm it might do us a favor and spread some sulfa where we can't reach." He gripped Sam's forearm and nodded at the medic.

The medic eased back on the pitchfork handle.

"It's fine by me if you did that a bit faster," Sam said through gritted teeth. It stung more going out than going in. It bled more, too.

The pitchfork removed, the medic unbuckled Sam's T-5 parachute harness. After shedding his jump jacket, Sam rolled up his shirt and long underwear sleeves. The tine had gone clean through the thick part of his forearm—missing bones—and left a small hole on each side. The entry wound already showed circular bruising.

The surgeon poured hydrogen peroxide on the punctures and let them bleed for further cleansing. "Nasty puncture. Good that you missed the greenhouse, though. Last month I put over a hundred sutures in a sergeant who did a PLF through a greenhouse roof." He pressed sulfa powder into each puncture, and wrapped the forearm with a military dressing. "After the bleeding stops, keep it open to the air." The surgeon looked over Sam's shoulder. "What'd he do to earn this, miss? Make a pass at you? You must grant him certain allowances—he's a UCLA man."

Sam twisted and found the young lady attempting to explain the whole incident to an obese man in a frumpy tweed suit.

She turned to Sam and said, "I'm dreadfully sorry, Lef'tenant. Could you please find it in yourself to forgive me? I'm mortified. My sole intent was protecting my pupils."

A gust of wind sent a shiver through Sam. "Simple case of mistaken identity. I'll live. Just do me a favor and find a deck of aircraft ID cards, then practice, Miss…"

"Pardon me, but I must return to my class." She pointed upward and removed herself as fast as her skirt permitted.

Sam glanced where she'd pointed. In the second story windows at least twenty sets of wide eyes gazed down. He turned back to catch a last glimpse of the woman.

He wanted to call her back. Yet, it wasn't just her long legs and distinct feminine curves that motivated him. It was something else. Her spunk and pluck? *Maybe I'd be hacked-off if she weren't so pretty.* He wanted to go into the school and meet her properly. *Bad idea—my odor would force the building's evacuation.*

"Sir?" the corporal said. "We still have some work to do out in the field. The staff major and a chaplain got dragged across—"

"They get hurt?" Sam folded his arms to hold in some of his escaping body heat.

"Nothing like you. Just scrapes and bruises, torn uniforms. Having a helluva time getting the chutes untangled out of that windbreak, sir."

Picking up his jump jacket, Sam said, "Let's get back to work then." Disgusted by the stench and wet filth, he wadded the jacket into a ball and tossed it on the steaming dung heap. Leaving the yard, he looked back up at the second story window. Not a single student remained in view, but the blonde was looking down. They made eye contact. He swore she blushed before jerking her head away.

The corporal was gathering up Sam's parachute.

"Leave it, Corporal," Sam said, "it's got a huge rip in it. I'm sure the farmer can find a good use for it."

After policing the drop zone, Sam congratulated each jump school graduate and waited until all personnel boarded vehicles. He found it odd that there was a new driver—the lowest ranking private—sitting alone in the jeep. Everyone else was crowding into the cab or canvas-covered back of the deuce-and-a-half truck. Sam craved the relative warmth of multiple bodies huddled together under canvas. He walked to the truck and attempted climbing the tailgate, struggling without the use of his left arm. "Hey, someone want to give me a hand here? Sergeant, why—"

"Hold it right there, jump instructor," the voice of the USC surgeon interrupted. "We took a vote. It was unanimous. You ride in the jeep. Nothing personal, you just reek."

"Ha, ha. Very funny." Sam grabbed the tailgate and awkwardly managed to get both feet off the ground, yet once again failed to climb in.

"Don't like the vote, Lieutenant Henry? We have a field-grade officer in here willing to make it an order."

"Nice try, but I'm the jump instructor. As such, I'm in command."

"Just completed jump number five," a gruff major said. "School's out. Go get in the jeep."

Sam dropped to the ground. "But, I'll freeze to—" A wadded Army blanket smacked him square in the face.

Resigned to his fate, he draped the itchy blanket over his shoulders and plopped into the jeep. Sam noted the driver's scrunched face. "Just get moving, Private, and you won't have to hold your breath. Today we both got a lesson on the privileges of rank."

The mini-convoy—jeep in the lead—left the DZ field and approached the school. Just past the main entrance, as the road veered left, at least two-dozen junior high aged Brits and their blond teacher lined the road. A number of students displayed notebook-sized pages of paper, a single letter filling each page. Like a Burma Shave roadside sign, it progressively spelled out, SORRY LT HENRY.

As the jeep passed, the blond teacher faced the class like a choir director. Following her waving arm rhythm, the class chanted in thick Cockney, "Good luck, Yanks!"

The truck paused to allow chewing gum and Hershey's chocolate bars to fly out the back. The kids darted into the road to snatch up the booty.

The jeep rolled on down the road, but Sam glanced back. The blonde stood out amongst her charges—tiptoeing and waving toward Sam.

Chapter 4

Introductions

21 February 1944
Lambourn, England

"This the best they could send us?"

The 1st lieutenant with an oiled orange peel complexion sat behind a walnut desk. His wide-set eyes challenged Sam to a staring contest. Sam obliged.

The wall clock's swinging pendulum counted the contest off—click, clack, click, clack.

Snickering came from behind Sam, from the captain seated at a desk across the room. Sam wondered how 1st Battalion's S-2—intelligence officer—could find any humor in the awkward situation. "Let our personnel officer do his job," Captain Franklin Young said. "Lieutenant Henry *is* parachute infantry qualified, isn't he?"

Sam blinked.

A smirk spread across 1st Lieutenant Nelson Pettigrew's flat-featured, round face, but his unblinking eyes never left Sam's eyes. "So?"

"*So*," Young said, "from what you showed me in his file he's got a lot more jumps than you."

Sam noted that both Young and Pettigrew wore large, blue-stoned class rings.

Pettigrew broke-off his stare from Sam, leaned over, and addressed Young directly. "My concern extends only as far as *one* jump—the one slated for Fortress Europa."

Sam shifted his gaze to the wall-hanging behind Pettigrew. It was a four foot high, hand-painted plywood oval bearing the 501st Parachute Infantry Regiment's insignia—a stylized Indian in full war bonnet holding a lightning bolt like a spear ready to thrust, under a parachute canopy. The 501st battle cry, "Geronimo," scrolled across the bottom. The insignia—red and white on a bright blue background—served as the only splash of color in the Spartan room.

This room was one of four in the expansive Lambourn Place estate that HQ reserved for offices for First Battalion officers. Sam had hoped for an English country manner ambiance. He got colorless walls, faded embroidered drapes, four utilitarian British military desks, and a half-dozen folding chairs. Aside from the 501st emblem, everything matched the drab weather. Pettigrew leaned back in his chair, stuck his jump boot heels on the desktop, and returned his attention to Sam.

Sam shifted his weight from jump boot to jump boot. Sweat trickled down his ribs. The first encounter with his platoon leader wasn't going well. Pettigrew exuded confidence—Sam's height yet stockier, wavy dark-brown hair doused in tonic, and a Clark Gable mustache.

Pettigrew scanned Sam like a car buyer searching for imperfections in a used sedan. He propped an Army personnel file open on his chest and squinted at the page. After a few seconds, he frowned and cursed. "They sent me a draftee! Does First Battalion have any other draftee officers, Captain Young?"

Young responded with an exasperated sigh. Sam thought, *Is it my draftee status or Pettigrew's antics causing the annoyance?*

"No, we most certainly do not." Pettigrew said, answering his own question. "Not a single conscripted non-com either." He returned his attention to Sam's file. "Where are you from, Henry?"

"Los Angeles."

Pettigrew stabbed a file page with his finger. "Really? According to your *official* War Department records you were born March 17, 1922, in some backwater dive called…" Pettigrew refocused on the file and in a disdainful voice read, "Banta Springs, Missouri." He looked up into Sam's eyes. "Did some *draftee* clerk make an error? You just stood right there and informed me you hail from Los Angeles."

Sam swallowed. "I consider L.A. home. My family moved—"

"No, please permit *me* to fill in the blanks. No doubt your story is a quite common and predictable American tale, yet tragic, nonetheless. Pappy's a sharecropper whose share just always came up short. He hears of jobs in California, so he loads up the family in some dilapidated truck and heads west from, in your case, Missouri. But it just as easily could've been Arkansas, Oklahoma…"

Pettigrew lit a Chesterfield cigarette. Talking around it, his voice took on a shrill tone. "So Pappy immigrates to California, a common garden-variety economic refugee. Why, you're right out of a Steinbeck novel, Henry."

Sam clenched his jaw. *Leave my father out of it!*

Pettigrew exhaled a cloud of smoke. "Be that as it may, the Henrys caught a break and ended up in Los Angeles. Which leads me to deduce that fate landed Pappy a job in the aircraft industry. Otherwise you'd be a prune picker from Bakersfield or Salinas." Grinning, he dropped his jump boots off the desk and leaned forward. "So tell me, Henry, how close did I get?"

The puncture wound in Sam's forearm throbbed. "I fail to see how this is relevant—"

"That close, huh? And good job on losing the hick accent. I'm certain that was no small undertaking. And I'd better start hearing some *sirs*. If you haven't noticed, my bar *is* a different color than yours!"

"Sir…again, I don't see how this pertains to my assignment."

Pettigrew snuffed his cigarette out in an overflowing ashtray. "I don't imagine you would, Henry." His gaze returned to the file folder. "Seems your draft board summoned you in the middle of your junior year at the University of California at Los Angeles." He smirked. "Now there's one well-established bastion of academia of global renown. It must be all of, what…twenty years old?"

Sam took a deep breath. "My profs kept me challenged enough. I was very thankful for the opportunity—"

Pettigrew leaned over to see Young. "You'll appreciate this, Captain Young. File says he played varsity baseball." Pettigrew looked back at Sam. For the first time Pettigrew's grin seemed genuine. "I lettered all four years at West Point. Catcher. Captain Young was our shortstop. Did you start?"

Sam sensed his pulse rate slowing. "Second base. Batted third."

"Hear that, Captain Young? Another middle infielder. Strength up the middle wins games." Pettigrew did another visual appraisal of Sam—this time with the demeanor of a state fair cattle judge. "It fits, Henry. You have the appearances of a middle infielder. Wiry. Bet you have quick hands. Good reflexes. Quick decision-making. All valuable traits for a parachute infantry junior officer, too."

Sam smiled. "Never really thought of it that—"

"The key to catching is calling a tactical game that keeps the opposing team off balance. The catcher is the general of the diamond." Pettigrew lit another Chesterfield. "Nothing gave me greater pleasure than setting a batter up. Call for high heat for two, three pitches. Then signal two fingers for that sweeping curveball."

Sam felt like he'd just received the same treatment, psychologically.

"Yes, Lieutenant Henry, I think the S-One officer knew exactly what he was doing sending you as my assistant platoon leader."

Sam suppressed a grin. "Glad to hear it, sir. I'd like to start by meeting the men."

"A splendid idea." Pettigrew came around the desk and extended a half sheet of paper. "And I've got just the place for you to start. Requisition a jeep and make a short run north, about ten miles, to the town of Swindon."

Sam took the paper. "I was told that all Able Company platoons were here at Lambourn today."

"You were informed correctly. I need you to retrieve my platoon sergeant, Staff Sergeant Jennings, and the Second Squad leader, an Injun named Springwater, from their unfortunate incarceration."

Sam furrowed his brow. "Jail?"

"British jail," Pettigrew said. "I let them cool their heels there a couple of days. The chief constable in Swindon refuses to release our, and I quote, 'hooligans of the first degree,' to any US Army representative other than an officer in their direct chain of command. It seems Sergeants Jennings and Springwater managed to incapacitate six RAF mechanics. Two remain hospitalized."

"How many brawls does it take to get arrested?"

"In this case, just one. Enjoy your journey, Henry. My presence is required at battalion staff to plan an upcoming field problem." Pettigrew strode out the office then stuck his face back inside. "I hope you packed your glove, Henry. I'd like to give you a tryout on the regiment's baseball team."

Sam allowed his stiffened muscles to relax.

Captain Young crossed the room and gave Sam a hearty handshake. "Congratulations, looks like you passed his little test. Don't let the *tryout* comment bother you. He'd make Stan Musial try out, then make him change his batting stance. Consider yourself fortunate you weren't some hapless West Point plebe getting inspected by him."

Sam heaved a sigh. "Does it get any easier?"

"Nelson is the third generation Pettigrew to graduate from the United States Military Academy. Graduated fifth in the Class of Forty-Two—well ahead of me, I might add. He's still a tad irked over me making captain ahead of him." Young stood six feet tall, with thinning blond hair and blue eyes set deep in an intelligent face. "Make the most of the opportunity. He's a master at small unit infantry tactics. Learn a thing or two from him before they promote him. And a word to the wise…" Young waited until their eyes locked. "Never let him even imagine—in any way, shape, or form—that you pose a threat to his authority. It's one of the few things he doesn't handle well."

*   *   *

Swindon, England

"Comes to a quid, two shillings, twenty-six pence, Lef'tenant."

Sam counted out the paper pound and shilling notes with no problem, but raked his finger through the coins piled in his palm bewildered. He picked up a small silver coin, read it, and dropped it back into the pile.

"Mind if I lend a hand, Yank?"

Sam looked up sheepishly. "I really can count, just haven't been here long enough to recognize your coins."

The middle-aged publican leaned over the bar and plucked the required coins from Sam's hand. "That be all of me shepherd's pie. Got me ol' lady peeling more spuds, but if you lads be needing more fare, then kidney pie will have to do."

Sam grabbed the two plates mounded with third helpings of shepherd's pie. Heading toward the back booth, he took in the ambiance of the most authentically English place he'd yet experienced.

The concrete and brick floor felt irregular under his feet. A fire roared in an expansive fireplace, a ready supply of split oak waiting on the hearth. In a closet-sized side room, a quartet of gray-haired men in tweed jackets smoked pipes and played cards. Red stag antlers decorated spaces between the age-darkened timber beams in the open ceiling. Two dartboards hung side-by-side on a whitewashed plastered wall. Even the publican, with his bird's nest mess of thin gray hair, fit Sam's preconceived image. Sam inhaled the unique olfactory cocktail—ale, pipe tobacco, burnt oak, and a hint of ancient mustiness—and smiled. *This is England.*

He set one plate before a broad-shouldered, square-jawed soldier in his late-twenties. The second steaming plate Sam placed in front of a sinewy, copper-skinned young man with high cheekbones, a slender nose, jet-black crew cut, and narrow, obsidian eyes.

"That's about it, unless you're fond of kidneys." Sam sat next to Sergeant Jennings. "Didn't they feed you guys in jail?"

"Just enough to make a feller hungrier, sir," Jennings said. The way Jennings combed his sandy-red hair straight back accentuated his receding hairline.

"How about cutting back a little on all the *sirs*, Sergeant," Sam said.

"Mighty tough to break a ten year habit, sir," Jennings said through a mouthful of shepherd's pie. "Besides, I get a little out of practice and next thing you know I'm catching hell from an officer not so obliging as yourself." Sergeant Jennings shoved a heap of potatoes into his mouth. "So, you were saying they had you in George Company before Officer Candidate School at Fort Benning?"

"Yeah, then after OCS they held off on giving me to a platoon and shipped me over here a month ahead to help get things ready for the Five-O-First's full arrival. Then I just did a two week stint at divisional jump school." Sam nodded at Jennings's scraped knuckles. "That happen often?"

Jennings pointed his fork across the booth at Springwater. "Them Limeys called my buddy here *chief*. That rubs him the wrong way a mite, sir. You see he's not one…yet. A chief, that is."

Springwater nodded his long head and the corners of his mouth turned upward—the most expression Sam had yet seen in the young buck sergeant.

"I'd say more than a mite," Sam said. "Enough to make you two take on six Limeys."

"We was walking away, all peaceful like." Jennings turned Sam's way, showing off a shiner under his right eye. "Ignored their request for Ted to whoop a war cry. And wanting to see pictures of his teepee and squaws. But then they went and asked my buddy if he planned on scalping any Krauts."

Springwater shook his head. "Not the Crow way."

So that's his tribe, Sam thought. *Taller than any Indian I've ever seen… but that wouldn't be all that many. Young for a squad leader. Must be awfully good.*

Jennings emptied his pint glass. "And then there sure weren't no call for them RAF boys to start swinging no table leg."

Springwater reached up and touched the scabbed-over goose egg pushing through his crew cut above his left ear.

Sam stood. "Can I get you guys anything else to drink?"

Springwater shook his head.

Jennings picked up his glass. "I could use some more of this dark 'n warm stuff the Limeys seem dead-set on passing off for beer. At least it's wet."

Sam wove his way through empty varnished pine tables and chairs, thankful that no other officers were present. Officer Candidate School had made it clear that the Army frowned on the fraternization he was engaging in—buying food and drinks, chatting it up with enlisted men. However, the Army's way wasn't his style. He bounced up the four uneven steps to the Lord Raglan Public House bar. "Another pint of your house ale and a cup of coffee."

The publican folded a copy of the *Swindon Advertiser* and patted it flat on the bar. "Another pint I can do. But nary an ounce of real coffee for a fortnight now. Will a cup o' tea do you, Lef'tenant?"

"Seems only fitting." Sam spread the pile of coins on the bar. The publican picked several out and pushed the rest toward Sam. Sam pushed the coins back. "Keep the rest." He pointed at the newspaper. "How's the war going?"

The publican flipped the *Swindon Advertiser* over to reveal the front-page headline: Leningrad Siege Broken. He tapped the front page. "Premier Stalin proclaimed the Moscow-Leningrad rails open again. Nine hundred day siege—them Russians be a tough lot. Seems your Two Corps lads be having a hard go of it at Monte Cassino. Took some key ground then got shoved right back out by some Jerry paratroopers. Reckon they could use you lads there. Give them Jerrys a decent taste o' their own medicine, one para regiment to another. Not much worth reporting from the Pacific or Asia."

Sam returned to the booth.

Sergeant Jennings nodded to Springwater. "Now's 'bout as good a time as any, Ted. Go ahead."

Springwater pushed an envelope toward Sam.

Sam gazed at the envelope, postmarked: Crow Agency, Montana. "Afraid I'm not following you two."

Jennings pushed the envelope closer to Sam. "Well, sir, it's like this, Ted here has a little problem."

"Requires an officer, sir," Springwater said.

"It may seem odd, us only just meeting a couple of hours ago." Jennings pushed his empty plate away and lit a cigar stub. "But I reckon over the past decade in the regular Army I've broken in more than my share of butter-bars—some first-rate, others not worth a tick-ridden pup that can't tell a possum from a coon. Surely enough to get darn good with first impressions. You seem like a straight shooting OCS man, not one of them by-the-book West Pointers. Ted agrees, and in the past year-and-a-half I've found him to be a flawless judge of character." Jennings sucked on the cigar stub and looked toward Springwater. "Well, go on. Show Lieutenant Henry what you done showed me."

Sam looked into Springwater's copper colored face. "What's on your mind, Sergeant?"

"Tribal Council letter." Springwater pointed a long index finger at the envelope. "A request I must pass on to my platoon leader."

Sam furrowed his brow. "That's still Lieutenant Pet—"

"Sir, please, read it first," Springwater said.

Sam put his hand on the envelope. Springwater grabbed Sam's wrist. "It's private, sir. Whether you can help or not, please don't tell anyone else what it says."

Jennings pulled Springwater's hand away. "Relax, Ted."

"Can't promise anything 'til I read it, Sergeant." Sam pulled a piece of stationary out of the envelope. *How can I help with a family crisis on some reservation in Montana?* Below the embossed Crow Tribal emblem, someone had written in flowing penmanship: "To the officer leading Sergeant Theodore Springwater."

The letter first gave a brief tribal history, highlighting the fact that the Crow had never taken up arms against the U.S. government, but rather had served the Army well since the 1860s, first as scouts against a common enemy, the Sioux. The last two paragraphs spoke of the need for Sam's involvement. He reread it to be sure he hadn't missed a single, at times bizarre, detail. Sam blew air through pursed lips. "Wow. Apart from us sitting right here, does anyone else in Able Company know about this?"

Springwater shook his head. "No sir."

"Look, like I said before, let's cut the military formalities. Around anyplace like this, call me Sam. Before too long we're going to need each other to save our mutual scalps." Sam cringed at his poor choice of metaphor. Jennings chuckled.

"Call me Springwater, or Ted. Either's fine." Springwater's expression remained unreadable.

"I took the liberty of checking out your service file—for both of you—before heading up here," Sam said. "A little recon to find what I might be walking into. Sergeant Springwater, you're still nineteen, yet you currently hold the First Battalion record for jumps. Before becoming a squad leader you were the best scout in Able Company. But..." Sam took a sip of tea. "Your fists keep landing you in trouble."

Springwater shrugged. "Fists are the only tongue some speak."

"Amen to that, brother." Jennings raised his pint glass as if to toast. "And, sir, I'm here to vouch to the honest-to-goodness gospel truth: Ted ain't never struck no officer."

Sam couldn't suppress a grin. "Glad to hear it, let's keep it that way." He glanced at his watch. "OK, we need to get on down the road. Motor pool wants their jeep back. But first, I need to understand this letter." Sam tapped the paper. "Tribal tradition says for you to attain the rank of Crow war chief you must perform four tasks, all witnessed by another warrior and attested to by another war chief, or the officer you report to."

Springwater nodded. "That's the Crow way."

"Now the first requirement listed, 'leading a war party without the loss of life,'" Sam read directly from the letter then looked up. "That shouldn't be too tough to fulfill. As squad leader you'll be leading patrols." Sam looked back down at the letter. "Now the next required task I can't promise to be so easy. 'Taking a tethered horse from an enemy camp.' Would they count a truck, jeep? Perhaps Hitler's personal staff car?"

"Horse only. It must be an *iichiili*." Nothing in Springwater's face acknowledged Sam's attempt at humor.

Sam advanced down the list of requirements. "The next one may prove a bit tricky too. 'Striking an enemy with a coupstick.' I'm afraid the Army forgot to issue that item to its Indian recruits."

"In the Great War, Tribal Council counted rifle barrel, rifle butt, or bayonet," Springwater said. "Just can't shoot pointblank or stab and count as coupstick strike."

"Thanks for that clarification. But that just leads me to a bigger concern about the fourth requirement; 'wresting a weapon from an enemy.'" Sam handed the letter across the table.

Jennings smashed the soggy cigar stub into the ashtray. "Now that's the one I'd dang sure pay admission to see."

Sam ran his fingers back through his hair. "Listen, both of you, I want this to work out. I'll do what I can. The way I see it, it's really not official Army business concerning medals or promotions, so I don't see why anyone away from this table needs to know." Sam noted relief in Springwater's dark eyes and a smile grow on his lips. "But none of this can, in any way, jeopardize platoon security or mission. Got it?"

The smile vanished from Springwater's face.

"Sir, you've got yourself nothing to worry about when it comes to Ted Springwater." Jennings drained the last drops from his glass and slammed it down. "He's dang sure the one I'd pick to stand with me in a C-Forty-seven door when that jump light goes green and we go a knockin' round Hitler's back porch uninvited."

Chapter 5

Able Company Men

22 February 1944
Lambourn, England

"I already went and told our whole platoon all 'bout you, sir."

"Had to have been one awfully short speech, Private Morton." Sam offered the skinny paratrooper a stick of Wrigley's Spearmint in hopes it might slow the First Platoon runner's nonstop chatter.

Morton flicked his half-smoked cigarette away and shoved the gum into his mouth. "Even before I found out you got assigned to us, I'd told them all 'bout you talking that Five-O-Sixth joker out of blowing his brains out. Where did you get that silver tongue of yours? Something' they teach a guy in college, sir?"

"Not exactly." Sam squinted, straining his vision toward the fog-obscured wood line 150 yards distant. Movement allowed him to distinguish human forms from bushes and tree stumps. He picked up the pace.

"One thing's been bugging the hell out of me, sir," Morton said through smacking gum. "How'd you know there weren't no bullets in that pistol?"

Sam took several paces before replying. "I didn't know, Private. I guess it struck me as the height of absurdity just standing around, doing nothing, letting fellow GIs act like they were watching some freak show. Someone needed to help the poor guy. No big deal."

"It's sure a big deal to me, sir. What a stroke of luck, I get to be the runner for you *and* Lieutenant Pettigrew."

Sam kept his Corcoran boots to the sheep path heading east through the hilly pastureland between Lambourn Place and ridge called Lynch Woods. Despite the fact that it was February, a thick carpeting of green grass dominated the pasture. The scent of sheep pellets and dirty lanoline hung in the damp air. Tufts of wool clung to the barbwire fence and scattered bushes. Subdued snippets of conversation, coughs, and laughter reached Sam's ears.

His stomach fluttered in anticipation of meeting his first rifle platoon as an officer. Nearing the paratroopers, Sam squared his shoulders, stood straighter, and made his strides more deliberate. He discretely popped a couple of aspirin for his arm. *I hope the word hasn't gotten out about the pitchfork incident.*

The first paratrooper was napping—head turned away, helmet serving as a pillow. The sandy-red hair and staff sergeant stripes identified Jennings.

Morton pointed at the prone form. "Platoon Sergeant Jennings. He can catch forty winks 'bout anywhere, out like a light in under a minute." Morton cupped a hand beside his mouth and raised his voice. "Problem is, any Kraut within a half mile can hear his snoring."

"Sergeant Jennings and I got acquainted yesterday," Sam said.

Jennings jerked to a sitting position and started to push himself off the pasture floor. "Sorry, sir, didn't know it was you."

Sam motioned for Jennings to stay put. "No need to interrupt your nap, Sergeant."

Jennings yawned and stretched his arms upward. "Good morning, Lieutenant Henry. Figured the Army could pony up enough to get you a better tour guide."

"Ha, ha. You're just a regular Bob Hope, Sergeant," Morton said, leading Sam toward the tree line.

Morton stopped near a Browning M-1919 30-Caliber Light Machinegun on a tripod. The three teenaged-looking paratroopers near it—one barefooted—started to rise. Sam waved them off. "As you were. We're in the field now. Let's get out of the habit of rising and saluting. No need to drop hints to German snipers."

"Lieutenant Henry," Morton said, "meet Harrigan, Donovan, and O'Connor. What we like to call our *Mick-chinegun* crew. Get it, sir?"

Sam shook each man's hand. When he shook the hand of the barefooted, freckled redhead, Morton said, "Corporal Harrigan's the best machinegunner in Able."

"Good to hear that, Harrigan."

Harrigan gave a toothy grin.

A rolled-up pair of socks and tin of foot powder landed in Harrigan's lap. Sam turned the direction the items had flown from and found Sergeant Springwater walking toward them.

"Good to see you again, Lieutenant Henry," Springwater said. "Harrigan gets blisters."

"Cut me some slack, Sarge. You would too, if you had to lug that thirty-cal up and down these hills in wet boots." Harrigan admired the wool socks. "Thanks for coming through again, Sarge."

Springwater looked Sam in the eye. "We just figured out that you're the same Piccadilly Circus lieutenant that Morton's been bending our ears about."

Waving his arms, Morton said, "You guys think I've just been flapping—"

Springwater cut Morton off with a scowl and spoke to Sam. "Makes our understanding yesterday feel right, sir."

Resisting the urge to grin, Sam nodded.

Frowning, Morton led Sam toward the trees. "Sergeant Springwater likes cutting me off when I'm talking. I don't hold it against him. He's a swell guy to know. Always hauls extra stuff in his musette bag. You name it—aspirin, buttons, lighter, needle and thread, toothbrush, M-1 tool, gun oil, grease pencil, paper, bootlaces—he's a regular Woolworth's, only he don't never charge nothing."

They approached a blond paratrooper sitting cross-legged with his back to a stump, rubbing wire-rimmed spectacles with a flannel cloth. He held the glasses toward the sky for inspection and went back to cleaning. He spotted Sam, put his eyeglasses on and got to his feet before Sam could stop him. He stood as tall as Springwater—a good four inches taller than Sam. Extending his hand, his whole face lit into a smile. "Sergeant Lazeski, sir. All the guys call me Laze. It's a pleasure to meet you. Morton told us about what you did in London."

Sam detected a faint accent—maybe Slavic. If so, it matched the paratrooper's round, expressive face, trim frame, and green eyes.

"Sergeant Lazeski is Sergeant Springwater's assistant squad leader," Morton said. "Only guy in the whole regiment from South Dakota."

Sam looked at Lazeski. "Never been to South Dakota myself. What did you do before the war?"

"Grew up on a sheep ranch. Dropped out of South Dakota State— animal husbandry major—to join the parachute infantry."

Sam pointed to a flock in the adjoining pasture. "You must feel right at home then. Picking up anything you can take back with you?"

"Wouldn't mind trying some of these black-faced Hampshire rams on our Rambouillet ewes, sir." Lazeski reached down and pulled up a handful of grass. "And you'd never catch me complaining about green grass when about now all we've got back home is six foot snowdrifts. How about yourself, sir? I mean, what did you do before the war?"

"University of California at Los Angeles lectures, between baseball practices."

Lazeski let his smile expand. "Know exactly what you mean. I played freshman basketball. Hope to make varsity when we get back."

"Sergeant," Sam said, "no offense, but you've got me curious. How'd they ever let you in the parachute infantry wearing glasses?"

Lazeski chuckled and unhooked his eyeglasses from behind his ears. "I wasn't about to let something like a little rule about no eyeglasses keep me out. So they stand me in front of an eye chart, I say a little prayer and rattle off letters. Must've guessed well."

A burst of laughter erupted from inside the woods. Morton leaned to see into the scattered trees. Sam caught a bit of distant conversation, "What's her letter say?"

A curse triggered more laughter. Morton moved toward the commotion. "Sir, these guys, these guys…you've got to meet these guys."

"I'm sure we'll have plenty of time to talk more, Sergeant Lazeski," Sam said. "Got to keep up with my guide." He caught up to Morton. "Seems like a real likable guy."

"Laze? You bet. Everybody likes Laze." Morton wove through the trees. "Just don't never call him no Polack. Last guy who did got a bloody nose and knocked on his keister."

Sam spotted a trio of khaki-clad paratroopers sitting on the forest floor playing cards. Morton trotted ahead. "Hey, guess what? I brought our new lieutenant so you clowns can meet him personally."

The three launched themselves off the ground and came to attention. The men stood like progressive stairsteps. The paratrooper on the left stood no more than five-five, the one on the far right at least six-two, and the one in the center evenly splitting the height difference.

"At ease, gentlemen," Sam said. "This isn't a parade ground."

"Come on, guys, I told you Lieutenant Henry ain't that kind of butter-bar." Morton turned to Sam. "No offense, sir, meant no disrespect with butter—"

"None taken," Sam said. "But in the future, *lieutenant* will suffice."

Morton pointed to the short paratrooper. "Private Vincenzo Vigiano, but you'll 'bout never hear him called anything except Pinball."

Sam shook Vigiano's hand, noting the barrel chest and thick neck that didn't quite match the cherub face and pile of black curls. "Pinball? You like to hang out at the arcade?"

"No sir, my football team hung that nickname on me."

"Yeah, we've watched the little squirt play back in the states in a game against the Five-O-Second," the middle paratrooper said. "Guys go to tackle him and instead he just bounces off and even picks up speed—like a pinball off a bumper."

"Where'd you play your football, Private Vigiano?" Sam asked.

"Southwest High, St. Louis, Missouri." Vigiano's chest puffed out even further.

"Cardinals fan?" Sam said.

"Browns, sir."

Sam shook his head and clicked his tongue. "In that case we may have a big problem." He gave Vigiano a good-natured tap on the shoulder. "Always been a National League man myself."

"Lieutenant Henry's from California," Morton said.

"Me too, sir." The middle paratrooper extended his hand. "Private Joe Silva. I grew up just outside Merced."

"Lieutenant Henry's from Los Angeles," Morton said. "Bet he knows some real-life movie stars."

Sam chuckled. He noted Silva's striking good looks, swarthy skin, and heavy five o'clock shadow—though it was just late morning. "Silva, from California. Spanish?"

Silva raised his chiseled chin and titled his head. "No sir. Portuguese," he said with flare and an expertly trilled r.

The big paratrooper raised a hand. "Don't go n' get him started, sir. To hear him tell it, his Portagee kinfolk turned this place he calls the *San Wa-Keen* Valley into a dang Garden of Eden. Goes on and on 'bout them there Silva dairies and Silva alfalfa and—"

Silva flashed a mischievous smile. "Don't forget the Silva almond orchards, you big hillbilly."

"Lieutenant, if you don't mind me asking, you got any sisters?" Pinball said.

The question seemed so random that Sam hesitated. "Three, all younger. Why?"

"Back in California, if Silva ever comes knocking on your door, whatever you do, *do not* let him anywhere near—"

Silva turned toward Vigiano. "Give it a rest, Pinball."

Pinball glared back.

Silva raised his right hand as if he was taking an oath. "Pinball, I swear on a stack of Bibles—Italian, Portuguese, *and* English—your sister made a pass at me."

Morton pointed at the massive paratrooper. "Lieutenant Henry, meet Private Tommy Collins, one of our scouts."

"Dang sorry you stepped into this little spat, sir," Collins said. "Pinball just learnt Silva got a letter from his sister yesterday and, well…" As they shook hands, Collins's grip swallowed Sam's. Collins wasn't just tall; his big-boned frame supported enough muscle to crowd his jump jacket.

Pinball stepped closer to Silva and tilted his head back. "A guy does a buddy a favor, takes him home on furlough, and how does he thank you? He slaps your face by going—"

"Pinball, it wasn't my fault. You've seen the Silva charm work its magic before." Silva spread his arms out palms up. "The ladies just can't resist."

"But my sister?" Pinball backed off. "Come on, Silva."

Grinning, Silva put a hand on Pinball's shoulder. "Like it wasn't exactly her *first* stroll down the carnival midway."

Pinball pulled away. Collins coughed into his hand and stepped between Pinball and Silva. "I reckon there ain't no call for Lieutenant Henry to fret 'bout your family business." He looked Sam in the eye. "I'm from *Missourah*, too, sir. But a different neck of the woods from Pinball— down Howell County way. West Plains. And you can bet we follow them Cardinals."

Sam remembered West Plains—mid-way across the state, not too far north of the Arkansas line. His memory flashed to when his Banta Springs Pirates played a road game there his sophomore year, just a month before he'd moved to California. He studied Collins's face but failed to recognize him—and he would've remembered playing against such a massive beast. *Must've missed each other by a year. Just as well…*

"Hey, Collins," Morton said, "you and Lieutenant Henry got a lot in common."

Sam's heart raced. *How'd a PFC runner get a hold of my file?*

"You don't say?" Collins turned his head and spit brown tobacco juice.

"Please excuse the big hillbilly's uncouth habit, sir," Silva said, as he lit a Lucky Strike.

Morton took a batter's stance and pretended to swing a bat. "Lieutenant Henry's a ball player, too. University of California. Played varsity."

Relieved to discover Morton was referring to baseball, not geographic origin, Sam latched onto the topic. "What position?"

Collins grinned big enough to expose brown stained teeth. "Pitcher. Only lost two games in all of high school. Cardinals as good as promised me a tryout when we get back. They said—"

The other three privates gave a collective moan. "Here we go again," Silva said. "They said, 'We're always looking for a big lefty that can throw a rising fastball.'"

Collins slapped Silva between the shoulder blades, sending him stumbling forward. "Well, they dang sure did. And you watch me, you rutting Portagee, someday you'll see my name in the papers."

"Sure, we will," Pinball said. "In the funny papers with Lil' Abner."

All but Collins and Sam hooted. Sam suppressed a chuckle. Morton laughed so hard the gum fell out of his mouth.

Silva stopped laughing. "What's that, Morton? Teeth falling out. Didn't you watch the training films on good oral hygiene?"

Pinball leaned forward and pointed at the ground. "It's gum. What's up, Morton? You always said you can't stand gum."

"Sure," Silva said, "but I'd bet my next weekend pass Lieutenant Henry enjoys the occasional stick. Just like how Morton only smoked Lucky Strikes 'til he saw Lieutenant Pettigrew smoking Chesterfields." Silva shook his head and mumbled, "Morton's got to be the biggest brown-noser in..."

A shrill voice rang through the woods, "Lieutenant Henry. There you are. Come on over here. Got someone you need to meet."

Sam noticed the privates stiffen.

"Right away, Lieutenant Pettigrew." Sam turned to the paratroopers. "Good to meet you guys. I'm sure we're going to work well together. You three all in Sergeant Springwater's Second Squad?"

"Yes sir," Silva said.

As Sam walked away, he overheard Morton say, "What'd I tell you guys? Pretty much a regular Joe. Got guts, too. Had that big Limey pistol poking his forehead and didn't even flinch."

Sam approached Lieutenant Pettigrew and an officer smoking a pipe. Both warmed their hands over a campfire at the pasture's edge.

Morton trotted up and slowed to get in step with Sam. "Us four, we like to joke around. Rag on each other. But we're real tight pals, sir. We can talk that way 'cuz we're like family—brothers from different mothers. You'll like them. I'll introduce you to the rest of the platoon later."

Sam offered another stick of gum. Morton accepted.

Morton got within six paces of Lieutenant Pettigrew, came to attention, and held a crisp salute.

Pettigrew stomped over to within inches of Morton's face. "This is the last time, Private. Salute me in the field again and I'll see to it you're peeling spuds until Churchill gives up cigars!"

Morton's face remained expressionless. "Sorry, sir. Thought you needed a runner."

Pettigrew stepped back. "I will need you at nineteen-fifteen hours. Until then I don't want to see you in my proximity."

Looking bewildered, Morton pulled back his jacket sleeve and studied his watch.

Pettigrew rolled his eyes. "That's seven-fifteen in the evening, Private Morton."

Morton shrugged. "Of course it is, sir."

"Look, Morton, it's imperative you instantly recognize military time." Pettigrew shook his head. "What's your time in service?"

"Nearly two years. Only have trouble with the big numbers, sir."

"Splendid. That's just splendid, Morton. I'll radio General Eisenhower and inform him that First Platoon, Able Company, Five-O-First PIR needs to knock off work by noon every day!"

Muffled chuckles from nearby paratroopers accompanied the berating. Sam looked at his boots and tried to find something to say that would diplomatically end the private's humiliation.

Pettigrew pivoted to Sam. "You need to join us, Lieutenant Henry." Guiding him toward the fire, he leaned close to Sam's ear. "You're probably thinking, *not* the best choice for runner. But let me tell you, Morton smokes two-and-a-half packs a day and I watched him run the six-mile roundtrip up and down Currahee just ten seconds off the all-time record of forty-oh-five, and then immediately just stand there and light up a cigarette. A genuine phenomenon to behold." He pulled away from Sam. "I trust you were able to get that paperwork squared away at battalion HQ."

Sam nodded.

"Splendid." Pettigrew gave Sam a slap to the shoulder. "Now we can get underway like proper parachute infantry rather than a bunch of pitiful straight-legs." Pettigrew pivoted and yelled in a shrill voice, "Sergeant Jennings!"

"Right here, sir."

Pettigrew spun back around. Jennings stood ten feet away. "Assemble First Platoon in formation. Steel pots and web gear back on. Weapons ready. We practice noise discipline as if in an enemy-held sector starting in…" Pettigrew glanced at his wristwatch "…fifteen minutes."

Sergeant Jennings walked away and shouted, "Squad leaders, on me."

Sam stepped to the fire and nodded a greeting at the pipe-smoking second lieutenant. He was slightly taller than Sam, with wavy dark-brown hair brushed straight back, and the winsome looks and demeanor of a college fraternity recruiter.

Pettigrew stuck his hands over the fire. "Second Lieutenant Sam Henry, meet Second Lieutenant Lloyd Sterling, Second Platoon Leader."

Reaching across the fire to shake hands, Sam said, "We're rooming together. You were already asleep when I got in from Swindon last night."

Sterling pulled the pipe stem from his mouth. "Do forgive me for forgetting to put out the welcome mat. You can expect the VIP treatment from the Lambourn Welcome Wagon tomorrow."

Sam gave a puzzled look.

"Please, no false modesty. News of your Piccadilly cathouse heroics precedes you, Lieutenant Henry." Sterling smiled. "I've heard a couple of versions, perhaps you can grace me with yours sometime." Sterling repacked his pipe bowl. "Seriously though, it was a *very* good thing you did. Took some intestinal fortitude."

Sam averted his eyes to the fire and said what came to his mind—a favorite quote. "All that is necessary for the triumph of evil is that good men do nothing." He looked up, not knowing what to expect. Lieutenant Sterling, now solemn-faced, was nodding.

Pettigrew rolled his eyes. "Which, gentlemen, is exactly why we're standing here in a stinking sheep pasture across the Atlantic. So I suggest we *do* something to successfully execute this field problem." Pettigrew looked to Sam. "We're to combine forces with Lieutenant Sterling's Second Platoon, divide into four groups, start dispersed, reassemble while dark, then rendezvous before dawn with Captain Tarver and the rest of Able at a road intersection to be determined. All while traversing several miles and avoiding contact with elements from Baker Company serving as our opposing force."

Sterling clapped his hands together. "Sounds fun enough. Shall we get cracking? Give her the ol' college try?"

Pettigrew frowned and lit a Chesterfield. "You two develop a plan to mix our platoons and a system to identify friend from foe in the dark. Excuse me for now, Captain Tarver plans to distribute our op order and map grid coordinates in ten minutes."

As Pettigrew faded into the fog, Sterling clicked his tongue. "A shame. All his strengths, yet the poor lad just doesn't know how to have a good time." He started to chuckle.

"What's so funny?" Sam said.

"You." Sterling shook his head and held up a hand. "Don't worry, it's nothing."

"You can't just tell a guy he's a laughing-stock and then say it's *nothing*." Sam noted the wedding band on Sterling's finger—the first he'd seen in Able Company. "We butter-bars need to stick together."

"Organize a butter-bar guild? I don't imagine Ike would approve." Sterling waved a dismissive hand. "Really, it's nothing." He chuckled again. "Just the way you came marching up that pasture awhile back. Strutting like Colonel Howard Johnson himself. I felt this urge to jump up and salute, then saw who it was."

Sam remembered his stomach doing nervous flip-flops as he approached his men for the first time. "That bad, huh? You think very many noticed?"

"Does it matter? We're all so mindlessly conditioned to jump to attention and salute any higher life form. I do believe had Descartes been in the Army his conclusion would've been, 'I *salute*, therefore I am.'"

"A second lieutenant paraphrasing Descartes?" Sam squatted to get his hands closer to the fire. "Don't suppose you were musing over Kierkegaard on your first jump out the door of a flying C-Forty-seven?"

Sterling's expression became serious. "But of course, both the literal and metaphorical leap of faith." His face shifted to a smile. "Kierkegaard would've most definitely been a paratrooper."

"I was beginning to wonder if anyone else in the Five-O-First even knew Kierkegaard from Cooper," Sam said.

"Sure, Gary Cooper's a better actor. Kierkegaard could've never pulled off the Sergeant York role."

Sam grinned. "You didn't pick up on Descartes and Kierkegaard watching Saturday matinees."

"University of Illinois, Urbana-Champaign, actually. Minored in philosophy as an undergrad. Bachelor's degree in history. Managed to get halfway through a masters in European history when this strange urge to take leaps of faith from perfectly good airplanes overwhelmed me."

"Do you miss it?"

"Academia?" Sterling snorted. "Plenty of time for that after this war plays out." Sterling emptied his pipe bowl into the fire. "My wife? Now that's another story altogether. I miss her every waking moment…and more than half the sleeping ones. She's a senior at U of I. Humanities major. We'd only been married five months when Tojo bombed Pearl."

"Tough break."

Sterling got a faraway look in his eyes, then shrugged and clapped his hands. "*Your* fearless platoon leader, Napoleon Junior, will be back soon.

So how do you propose we tell friend from foe while playing blind man's bluff tonight?"

"First, I'd—"

Sterling held up a hand. "Wait." He pulled something purple from his pocket. "This has been duly authorized and hereby awarded to you."

Sam took the trinket. It resembled a Purple Heart medal fashioned out of a tin can, paint, glue and scraps of cloth. The inscription on Sterling's version read: "For wounds received, non-venereal, while in combat with indigenous allied females."

Sam blushed.

Sterling's face broke into a knowing grin. "How's the arm?"

"How on earth did you ever find out?"

Sterling gave Sam a pat on the back. "The Five-O-First is not a large fraternity. I like to keep tabs on our butter-bar pledges. I expect about everyone will know by sunset."

Chapter 6

Disillusioned

February 1944
Krivi Rog, Ukraine

"In the mood to go hunting?"

SS Oberscharfuhrer Helmut Behr lowered his Zeiss binoculars and slid down the snow-covered brick rubble into the shell crater. *Sturmmann* Jahne followed. Behr removed his priceless Red Army fleece mittens and grinned at his counter-sniper team. "That weasel informant actually got it right. Two Ivans just ducked into the factory administration building. The first carrying a burp-gun, the second a scoped rifle."

His three men—whitewashed helmets atop their heads and white and light-gray cotton snow camouflage covering their winter uniforms—readied their weapons. Clouds of white vapor billowed from each mouth. Behr looked at the new man. "Prove Jahne wrong, Tobias. He insists I was foolish to select you from the replacement pool."

"Only because you two grew up together." Jahne smirked. "Look, the odds are against the new *bubi* surviving the week."

The replacement's eyes betrayed his fright.

Behr held up a finger. "*Ja*, but he survives the week and his odds for making it six months go way up."

"Still not a good idea," Jahne said. "Ivan kills him on one of your hunts and it makes for awkward conversation when your mother buys pork cutlets from his father." Jahne looked the replacement up and down. "Do they only grow giants in Frankfurt's Romer District?"

The replacement *soldat* bore little resemblance to the fourteen-year-old Behr remembered four years earlier. Since Behr had departed the Romer neighborhood the butcher's son had grown to 189 centimeters—almost enough to look Behr eye to eye.

A stick grenade slipped out of the new man's hand and disappeared in the snow.

"Relax, Tobias." Behr reached under his snow camouflage top, pulled out a flare pistol, and loaded it. "Watch my hand signals, never panic, you'll do fine." Behr extended the flare pistol upward. "Our Ivan sniper is attired in virginal white. Highly inappropriate." He pulled the trigger. The flare whooshed skyward between the windowless concrete and tin factory buildings shielding their position. At 100 meters high the flare burst into a violet star against the dawn light.

"Wrong color," Tobias whispered. "Violet is for enemy *panzer* sightings."

"Ivan is no *dummkopf*. He figured out the standard *Wehrmacht* flare code long ago. Violet tells only *Unterscharfuhrer* Neumann which building to scour with his telescopic sight." Behr tucked his flare pistol away. "Best counter-sniper weapon is another sniper."

Behr scaled the side of the crater and trotted off. Packed snow—underlying the four centimeters of new snow—crunched and squeaked under his 105 kilos. He wove his way through jumbled iron, bricks, and broken concrete of the Krivi Rog Octoberist Revolution steelworks. He recalled maneuvering this same path on a recon mission. He mentally cursed the inexperienced junior officers of the 5th *SS Panzergrenadier Thule* Regiment for losing this portion of the sprawling Stalinist designed steel mill, then retaking it twice—only to abandon it two days earlier. Neither side now wished to occupy the center buildings.

Behr wriggled under a collapsed conveyor belt and duck-walked three meters to the corner of a workshop. Leading with his MP-35 Bergmann submachine gun, he leaned around the corner. No tracks marred the fresh snow. No telltale cigarette smoke or clouds of breath billowed around a burned-out halftrack, building doors and windows, or a two-meter high coal pile.

A wind gust blew drifting snow into his face. *Coal is life.* He considered dashing out and grabbing a few lumps for his bunker stove. *If I were an Ivan sniper, I'd set my sights on that coal pile and just wait.* He decided to bring his own sniper, Neumann, and do exactly that tomorrow.

He signaled the team to advance. Hans dashed across the factory alley and took up an over-watch position. As soon as Hans pointed his captured Soviet PPSh-41 submachine gun to cover the gap, Behr leapt to his feet and crossed.

Using subtle hand signals he maneuvered his team in a leapfrog fashion to the steel mill's four-story beige brick office building. Behr pushed his back to the wall and scanned his surroundings. Two sets of boot prints approached the wall and vanished into a blown-out and scorched basement window just below street level.

Jahne ran up and poked his MP-40 machine-pistol into the hole. Tobias followed him, knelt next to the hole and covered their back-trail with an antiquated bolt-action Mauser KAR-98 rifle.

Hans arrived and covered the north approach.

Behr caught Tobias staring at the puckered three-point scar on his right cheek. Behr fingered his disfigurement—a wound courtesy of Bolshevik shrapnel in the Demyansk Pocket in early '42. Many stared, but few men had the nerve to mention that when Behr grew excited the scar turned a bright purplish-red. Tobias averted his gaze.

Behr craved a cigarette. His anxious gut told him to call off the hunt. *A bad harbinger.* Sweat dripped into his eyes. Each previous time he'd been overwhelmed with dread he had found precious—albeit temporary—relief from an unlikely ally. Wounds. Wounds severe enough to pull him off the frontline and give his shattered nerves the rest they craved. He deemed his cheek wound—which had also left his face partially paralyzed—well worth the temporary relief it gave him from the frozen hell of the Demyansk Pocket.

Wary of booby-traps and alarms, he led his team to another blown-out basement window twenty meters south. He leaned close to Tobias. "Once inside, stay clear of windows. I've never seen Neumann miss a mere three hundred meter shot." He unfastened and turned back two of the six covers on his magazine pouches, making two more magazines and their sixty-four rounds of 9mm ammo more accessible.

Flashlight in his left hand, MP-35 in the right, he dropped into the hole and swung through the basement window. His broad shoulders scraped each side of the frame. Hitting the basement floor, he went prone and rolled over to a vertical shadow.

Silence.

Behr blinked to speed his eyes' adjustment to the dark basement.

The next *panzergrenadier* dropped in and dashed to the pillar to Behr's left. The third slipped through the hole and knelt facing the opposite direction.

Behr switched on his flashlight and scanned the room. Empty brass casings littered the concrete floor under each of the three windows. A ruptured *Wehrmacht* helmet stood out under the far window. At the middle window, fresh boot prints marked the dusting of drifted snow.

The fourth *Waffen SS* man dropped to the basement floor and advanced with weapon ready. The distinct barrel-shroud and drum magazine of the PPSh identified the man as Hans.

Behr's flashlight beam illuminated a straight line stretched across the window the Red sniper team had entered through—a tripwire. Keeping the line in his flashlight beam, he approached. The line terminated in the pin ring of a Soviet fragmentation grenade wired to the window frame. He signaled Jahne to go guard the door the boot tracks led to and gestured Tobias to come to his side.

Grinning, Behr handed Tobias the flashlight. "Keep the light on the grenade, no matter what." In the shaky light, Behr's hardened fingers bent the grenade's straightened safety pin back to ninety degrees and unfastened the tripwire.

Behr took his flashlight back and moved toward Jahne and the door.

Jahne leaned close to Behr's ear. "Stairway's clear to the ground floor."

Behr took strips of burlap from his pocket and tied them around the soles of his hobnailed jackboots. "See to it no one goes up without silencing his boots."

Jahne nodded.

Behr shouldered his MP-35 and, careful to step lightly, advanced up the stairs.

At the ground floor, Behr peeked around the doorframe to the right.

His heart rate jumped. A soldier in a Soviet uniform was a mere three meters away.

He shifted his submachine gun until Russian mustard-tan cloth filled his sights and began squeezing the trigger. His cheek scar throbbed.

The bloated Soviet extended a frozen hand upward, as if begging for aid. The corpse was barefoot and coatless.

Behr let the pressure off the trigger.

The dead man had a narrow face, trimmed reddish-brown goatee, big eyes, and a hooked nose. The blue uniform piping identified him as a commissar.

Your comrades abandon you in death? No one wants a Bolshevik Jew, not even your lesser evolved Slav and Mongol countrymen. Two and a half years on the Eastern Front had convinced Behr that the same fate awaited him. *If this be the day, let fate hunt me down. Rodina Mat won't drink my blood like vodka without paying dearly.*

He refocused on the mission. No hallway doors or windows remained intact, allowing in enough ambient light for decent vision. At each end of the long, institutional-green painted halls, he could see outside. A long shadow marked the opposite wall. At last, a day with sunshine.

Drifting snow whisked down the hallway.

Following the fading boot prints leading left, he prowled down the hall, careful not to pause in any doorway. Behr heard muffled steps behind him and turned to find first Tobias then Hans mimicking his movement. Jahne exited the basement, pivoted right, knelt next to the dead Russian, and pointed his machine-pistol toward the north door.

Behr advanced another five meters. Above the Cyrillic letters marking the building's south exit was a rusted stairway landing. He followed the metal stairway and handrail downward to his right. It terminated in a corner. He looked back up to the rusted landing where the metal stairs reversed direction and sloped upward, and deduced that the pattern repeated itself to the roof.

He took a deep breath and stuck an unlit Russian cigarette into his mouth, hoping the thick *papirosa* might lessen his nicotine cravings.

CRACK!

A single high-powered rifle shot rang out.

Behr convulsed as if shocked by an electrical wire. He dropped to a crouch and threw the MP-35 to his shoulder.

The shot originated from outside the building. Behr guessed about 250 meters west. *Neumann, my dear friend, is that you plying your trade?*

Silence.

Sweat stung his eyes. He mopped his forehead with his sleeve and stepped toward the stairway.

Far above, rushed steps echoed on the metal stairs.

A meter from the stairway Behr halted. His closed fist shot up to ear level—a signal to halt.

The frantic steps on metal steps grew louder. Only one *kommie* was descending.

He stuck an open hand behind his lower back, signaling to take the man prisoner.

Running footfalls reverberated on the metal stairs three meters above his head.

He followed the sound with the muzzle of his Bergmann.

A felt boot bounded into view and froze on the second step down.

Behr followed the winter boot up to Russian mustard-tan quilted winter pants. Nothing above the knee was visible.

What stopped him? Behr's gaze worked down the stairs. At the end of the stairway, an elongated shadow of a rifle barrel stretched across the wall. He glanced over his shoulder. Tobias had stopped in a doorway flooded by the rising sun.

Metal creaked.

Behr jerked his attention back to the stairway.

The Russian boot lifted.

Behr rose to his full height, jabbed his MP-35 barrel against the felt boot top and pulled the trigger halfway back.

A single 9mm slug penetrated the Russian's lower leg.

Screaming, the Russian tumbled down the stairs and landed almost seated with back and shoulders wedged into the brick corner. The Russian brought a PPSh-41 to bear.

Behr ducked under the stairs.

The Russian sprayed the hall with a long burst.

Another PPSh-41 responded from behind with two short bursts.

Taking advantage of Hans's suppressive fire, Behr stuck his Bergmann out from under the stairwell one-armed, pointed it high at the corner, jerked the trigger back to full-auto and worked the spray of bullets downward until his magazine emptied.

He ducked back under the stairway and slapped in a fresh magazine. Facing back to the corner he saw Hans's PPSh-41 then head poke around the corner.

Hans's eyes darted left to right. "Clear!"

Behr pivoted to face the Russian's corner and shouldered his Bergmann. He bit his lower lip and emerged from under the stairwell.

Sidestepping right and rising to his full height, his eyes followed the bullet-pocked bricks downward. The Russian slumped in the corner, a neat bullet hole bored above each eye. Long, dark hair cascaded over each shoulder. Tiny brick chips speckled the hair like dandruff. The dark eyes—wide open and locked in fright—had a slight slant that matched the high cheekbones. A pretty girl.

A wave of nausea swept over him. *Nein! Not another fraulein!*

A whimpering groan reached his ears from behind. He looked over his shoulder. Hans knelt over Tobias. Eyes squeezed shut in a grimace, Tobias clutched the point of his left shoulder. Bright blood seeped from between his fingers.

"Hans, search this one for documents." Behr's ears rang from all the shooting in close confines. "Jahne, come with me."

Leading with his Bergmann, Behr moved toward the dead girl. *Why another pretty Eurasian girl?* He suddenly felt a sense of political shame. *No, she is not attractive. She cannot be. How dare I assign beauty to such a mongrel?* He took his gaze off the dead girl and glanced up the stairs.

He stepped over her legs and started up the steps. Jahne followed. Between the second and third floors, Behr noted light traces of bloody boot prints descending the stairs. With each of his ascending steps, the descending prints became more distinct, more crimson. On the fourth floor landing the bloody boot prints turned down a hall painted the same institutional-green, but with a parquet floor with occasional warped and loose boards.

Behr followed the red tracks around overturned office chairs, scattered desk drawers, an overturned filing cabinet, and machinegun ammo boxes. The third door on the right hung askew—the upper hinge broken from the frame. A bloody track marked the door threshold. He looked down his submachine gun sights and darted past the doorway, visually sweeping as he crossed the void.

Jahne took up a position on the opposite doorjamb. Behr took a measured view of the room portion he could see. On the floor an expanding pool of dark blood crept across paper forms and an abacus. The muzzle end of a rifle wrapped in white cloth and burlap confirmed that he'd found his quarry.

Knowing what he would find inside, Behr forced a grin. "Mind if I go first?"

Jahne shook his head. "*Nein*. Be my guest."

"Neumann won't shoot me. I owe him forty marks." Behr stepped into the room. The Red Army sniper lay face down atop two desks butted together and stacked atop another two desks. Positioned in the back corner, the sniper had been elevated for visibility yet recessed into the back shadows for concealment. "Check the other rooms, Jahne."

Behr poked his Bergmann into the window and held it for a ten count. He stepped to the window and waved his arms in wide arching motions over his head. Across the factory complex, high at the roof ridge on a massive foundry building, what appeared as a lump of snow gave a quick wave and disappeared behind a ventilation shaft.

"All clear," Jahne reported, yet stayed in the hall.

"Relax, Neumann knows it's us. Let's get Ivan's papers and get out of here before his comrades decide to investigate. This one studied his craft well."

"*Ja*. Don't they all?" Jahne entered taking a big step over the blood. "If he's the one we think, he's made eight kills in six days. Never shot from the same place twice."

Behr stomped on the riflescope and tossed the weapon out the window. At the base of the prone sniper's neck a dark hole stood out against the red stained white camouflage covering. He grabbed the dead sniper's right shoulder and rolled the body over atop the stacked wooden desks. The Red Army gray fur hat tumbled off the sniper's head.

Shoulder length blond hair fell across the desktop. Rosy cheeks and green eyes marked the feminine Slavic face. The sniper looked older than the girl downstairs—perhaps a match to Behr's twenty-six years.

He shoved the body away. "Go! We can learn everything we need from the other one." Departing the room Behr slipped in the blood. He paused in the hallway to light the Russian *papirosa* still hanging in his mouth. The harsh *makhorka* tobacco soothed his nerves but did nothing to suppress the new wave of nausea.

At the top of the stairs Jahne paused and looked back. Behr waved him on.

As Jahne bounded down the noisy stairs, Behr removed his helmet and squatted. He held his dark brown hair out of his eyes and vomited his stomach empty. He tried to stand but nausea forced him to his knees. He dry heaved until the muscles connecting his neck to his shoulders ached. Sweat beaded on the shaved sides of his head.

He rose and braced his arm against the wall, resting his head on his forearm and alternating drags on his Russian cigarette with deep breaths of sub-zero air.

At least the blonde was Neumann's handiwork. Behr's legs began trembling. He closed his eyes. Who would grieve for these girls? A fiancé? Mother? Proud papa? Commanding officer who doubles as lover? *How can I dehumanize such an enemy?*

He pushed himself away from the wall, retrieved his helmet and worked his way down the stairs—leaving his own bloody boot prints on the steps.

At the base of the stairs he found Hans bent over the girl's body. Helmet-less, Hans's blond hair fell forward, covering his eyes. A perverse leer marked his mouth. The Russian's quilted coat covered the bottom two steps. Hans's hand didn't seem to be searching her tunic pockets. Hans shifted position. His groping hand erased any doubt about his activity.

Behr shook his head at the perversity. "What shall I do with you, Hans?"

Hans continued his groping.

"I chose to look the other way last time, Hans. Go find a live whore back in the village, why don't you?" Behr stepped over the Russian, averting his eyes from her face. He bit his tongue. *Who am I to judge? Hans is but nineteen, full of repressed lust. Cheating death daily.*

He picked up her PPSh-41. Tobias leaned against the wall not a meter from where the Red Army girl had shot him. Tobias stared at Hans with unveiled disgust.

"Not something you'll write home to Mama back in Frankfurt, is it? They'd want to lock Hans up and throw away the key to protect their daughters, *ja*, Tobias?"

Tobias looked away.

Behr turned back to Hans and glared with his hardened hazel eyes. "Enough! Show some self-control! You'll find no documents there." He turned back to Tobias. "What does Papa the butcher know about the savagery and deprivation of the Russian front? About as much as my papa, the baker." He handed Tobias the PPSh-41. "She was the sniper's spotter and security. The sniper was also a *fraulein*." Over his shoulder he said, "Don't forget her binoculars, Hans. Get her ammunition drums, too." Behr took the last drag on his papirosa and flicked the butt away.

Tobias eyed the weapon Behr had just given him. "*Danke, Herr Oberscharfuhrer*."

"Keep that Mauser for inspection. We can't be misplacing valuable *Reich* property, now can we?" Behr pointed at the sunlight pouring in through the door. "I hope you learned something today. Your shadow almost got us killed."

Jahne poked his head around the corner. "We're overstaying our welcome." As he moved toward the door, he leaned close to Behr. "Did I hear you get sick?"

"Those rancid rations that Ukrainian *hiwi* cook served this morning." Behr pivoted and found Hans working under the quilted pants. "Playtime is over, Hans. Get away from the body and give me her papers. *Schnell!*"

The tone snapped Hans back to military order. "*Jawohl, Herr Oberscharfuhrer Behr*." He trotted over and handed Behr a Red Army identification booklet.

Behr's mind automatically sounded out the Cyrillic characters. *Federova, Anya Igorovna.* The instant he knew the name he regretted the knowledge. A name, in combination with a face, became a person. *A sergeant, same as me. Yet nothing like me. Just another Slav. No, she's worse. From her eyes, she had a touch of the Mongol horde thrown in. Such faces should disgust me.*

He jumped out the exit and headed west, toward German lines.

*   *   *

Behr shoved the knob-less door inward and entered the smoky hovel. The room reeked of cooked cabbage and burning paper.

An emaciated man clothed in tattered rags bent over a stove constructed from a discarded fifty-liter tin drum. The man rose, yet his shoulders remained hunched. With a blue wool shawl pulled tight over his head, the man smiled, revealing a jumble of rotting teeth. His narrow face and scraggly whiskers reminded Behr of a weasel.

Behr spoke in simple Russian. "Old fool, you forgot to mention the sniper team were *dyevooski*—young ladies."

"*Nyet?*" The weasel-man bowed submissively and, head held askew, looked apologetic. "Then please excuse my poor memory, *gospodin*."

"Do not call me master if that's the best service you can offer." Behr scanned the dim room. He took in the hoard of heating fuel on the dirt floor—a small stack of broken painted boards and larger stack of office forms. A crust of dense black bread sat atop a three-legged table. Water dripped from the ceiling. In the corner, encased in blankets on the only bed, an elderly woman pulled two children tight to her side.

Behr scowled at the squalor. "A Judas soon finds himself without friends." He raised his open hand as if cocking back to slap the old Ukrainian. The man closed his eyes to receive the blow. Instead, Behr's left hand came out of his pocket holding a pile of paper money. He tossed it up. "Your thirty pieces of silver."

Small bills fluttered across the room. A couple of bills sailed into the stove. The Ukrainian's dirty hand stabbed into the flames to salvage the shameful lucre. "*Spaceeba, Gospodin* Behr. Thank you. Now my grandchildren will not starve to death."

Behr backed out of the hovel and spit the foul taste from his mouth.

Chapter 7

Reprieved

Behr sat in a frigid meeting hall adjacent a massive steel foundry structure and savored his greasy salami, black bread, apple jam, and ersatz coffee lunch. Chewing, he leaned his head back. Through a jagged hole blasted in the roof he watched snow-laden clouds race past towering smokestacks.

He lowered his gaze to sip the tepid coffee substitute. An *oberschutze* stood timidly before him. Looking over the cup's rim, Behr acknowledged the battalion headquarters messenger.

"Herr Oberscharfuhrer, the battalion commander orders you to report to his bunker, immediately."

Behr grunted and waved the messenger away. He shoved the last gristly salami slice into his mouth and pushed himself up off the broken concrete chunks serving as his table and chair. He meandered through the half-wrecked labyrinth of a steel mill before descending a metal stairway. His jackboots rang out with each step. The sound took his mind right back to another noisy stairway. And the *kommie* girl's felt boots.

Two floors below, his hobnailed boots clicked against concrete. The lower level held scant warmth absent on the surface, but reeked of musty cement dust and coal smoke. A makeshift lamp devised from an expended 40mm antiaircraft shell illuminated three storm troopers sitting around a table. All three looked up from their card game and acknowledged Behr. At the second door on the left Behr gave two polite raps, pushed the wooden door open, and entered. The industrial storeroom now served as the lieutenant colonel's personal bunker.

Behr clicked his heels as he came to attention. Tossing a Nazi salute he said, "*Heil* Hitler! Oberscharfuhrer Behr, reporting as ordered, Herr *Obersturmbannfuhrer* Steinhaus."

A kerosene lantern lent shadowy illumination to the unpainted concrete cubicle. Seeping watermarks stained the wall behind the colonel's Soviet-made desk. A small, coal-burning stove—just offset from the center of the room—radiated substantial heat. Behr's envious gaze lingered on a cot with two blankets occupying the space between the stove and wall. *Luxurious!*

Steinhaus looked up from writing and returned the Nazi salute. "Do have a seat, Behr."

Behr pulled the only other chair in the room and positioned it so a leg almost touched the stove. Still unsure of his commander's mood, he sat.

"Care for a cigarette?" Steinhaus gave a knowing grin. "Accept my apologies, today I have only Russian *makhorka* tobacco."

"*Danke,* Herr Obersturmbannfuhrer." Behr took a fat cigarette and accepted a light from the colonel. Even expecting a reprimand, he wasn't turning down a papirosa. "I offer no excuse for my tardiness."

"Hasn't our time together taught you that I extend much grace toward my battalion's only Knight's Cross recipient?" Steinhaus let the strong Russian tobacco smoke linger around his nostrils. "I already ran into *Sturmmann* Jahne. He told me all I need to know. Three dead Bolsheviks. A sniper team and that forward artillery observer you lucked into on your way back. Just one light wound to your team."

"Did Jahne tell you the sniper and her spotter were women?"

Steinhaus slapped his desktop. "Valuable intelligence. Good news, I might add."

Behr furrowed his brow. "If I may be so bold, Herr Obersturmbann-fuhrer, how?"

"I'm shocked a veteran of your caliber must ask. Consider the Red Army's state of affairs, Behr. We're getting increased reports of Ivan using women in combat roles. Snipers. Radio operators. Artillery observers. For many months we've known of entirely female artillery batteries and a bomber squadron. I've read corroborating reports of a lady—and I use the term strictly in the biological sense—*panzer* battalion commander fighting between here and Minsk. Imagine that!"

Behr took a long drag on his cigarette. *What game is afoot here?*

Steinhaus smiled. "Signposts of abject desperation. Which makes the war all a matter of arithmetic. *Ja.* When Stalin exhausts his supply of men, we've won. The increased use of women shows that the historical moment for National Socialism may soon arrive. It's just been a matter of time the way the Reds throw away their men in those barbaric human wave assaults."

Herr Obersturmbannfuhrer, Behr thought, but dared not voice, *you're confusing desperation with dedication. How can we possibly defeat a people so determined, so motivated, that they'll sacrifice the blossoming flower of their nation's womanhood?* He thought of the dead spotter. What was her name...? Anya Igorovna Federova. Anya. His nausea returned. *I'll never survive this.*

"So we didn't do so badly, now did we, Helmut? One minor wound for three of their special, skilled *soldaten* killed."

Behr recognized a chance to massage a fanatic's ego. "One *Totenkopf* panzergrenadier is more valuable than ten Bolshevik sergeants."

"I read a provocative *Pravda* article, months ago. Claimed that one fraulein sniper at the Leningrad Front has killed over three-hundred *Reich* officers. But we all know *Pravda* is full of lies." Steinhaus chuckled.

Behr remained solemn.

"Come on, Behr, you speak enough Russian to know *pravda* means truth. Humor me and laugh at my little jokes. After all, you and I go all the way back to the summer of forty in France, when we were both green replacements—mere *fohlen*."

Behr opened the stove door and tossed his cigarette butt in. The glowing coal reminded him of flame jumping out his Bergmann's muzzle. The felt boot. The coffee colored cascading hair. The haunting beauty of Occidental and Oriental mixed.

Steinhaus leaned forward and lowered his voice to a conspiratorial tone. "Tell me, are you a religious man?" He took a deep drag on his papirosa. "Might you term yourself...devout, *Hauptscharfuhrer* Behr?"

The conversation's peculiar change of direction quickened Behr's pulse. "Begging the colonel's pardon, but I'm not a master sergeant."

"But of course you're not religious. No split allegiances allowed in the SS. If I recall, we completed the political indoctrination classes together, did we not?"

Behr remembered well the Nazi Party education he'd received while in France in late 1940. He'd believed in the causes of National Socialism well before then, but after the classes—mandatory for all *Totenkopf* men—he knew why he believed and could articulate the doctrines.

Steinhaus shrugged his shoulders as if he was giving up on an arithmetic problem. "Well Behr, either someone dear to you is very religious or..."

Behr resisted the urge to squirm in his chair. His mind flashed to a great aunt, a nun. What possible crime against the Reich could a pious old maid have committed? *And how could her crime possibly implicate me way out here?* Sweat rolled down his temples. Steinhaus's words were striking visceral fear in Behr. And it seemed the Obersturmbannfuhrer was enjoying it.

"Divine intervention may be the only explanation to account for this." Steinhaus held up a sheet of paper and laughed. "It seems you've been granted a reprieve. Come now, why the long face? Seriously, Berlin needs you elsewhere. I've fought this since September."

Behr shifted away from the stove. "I'm afraid you've lost me, Herr Obersturmbannfuhrer."

"A new *SS Panzergrenadier* division is forming in France. The Seventeenth-SS, to be exact. High Command requires new divisions to repel the impending invasion across the English Channel. Berlin has selected a number of venerable *Ostfront* noncommissioned officers as the training cadre on the *Butterfront*. They lost one in a training accident. Reconnaissance battalion. You are ordered to replace him. I'm forbidden to deny the request this time."

Relief seized Behr. A rare smile spread across his face. Steinhaus was handing him a ticket to escape the *Ostfront*, alive. And the ticket didn't cost him another wound.

Steinhaus rose and extended his hand. "*Alles gute*, Hauptscharfuhrer. *Ja*, I made no mistake about your rank. You will serve as company sergeant, effective upon reporting to the Seventeenth."

Standing too quickly, Behr's head swooned as he shook the colonel's hand.

"You found a way out of this frozen hell. Get out today, Behr. Get out before we find ourselves trapped in another Demyansk Pocket. Now if you'll pardon me, paperwork beckons." Coming to attention, Colonel Steinhaus clicked his heals and saluted Behr. "You've brought great honor to the *Thule* Regiment, Helmut Behr."

*   *   *

By midafternoon Behr was riding westward in the cab of an Opel lorry evacuating wounded. He kept a tight grip on his gasmask canister. His *kameraden* had stuffed it with an impromptu parting gift of makhorka loose tobacco and papirosa cigarettes. He sensed one of his melancholy funks coming on. With the noose snug around his neck, Berlin had granted him a reprieve. Yet the reprieve also exiled him from his Totenkopf family.

Nonetheless, he departed with a host of companions—ghosts that disrupted his sleep repeatedly. Ghosts offering no promise to cease their haunting. In fact, that very day he had obtained a new ghost to torment his slumber. Another beauty from the place where Europe met Asia.

A ghost named Anya.

Chapter 8

Returned

4 March 1944
Lambourn, England

Exhaust fumes and fresh cow manure fouled the air inside the idling bus. More Jersey cows trudged across the road. Maggie Elliott glanced at her wristwatch and heaved a sigh of resignation to her plight.

Her quest to find the battle smock's owner was proving more tedious than daunting. The Overton Home Guard had suggested Newbury as the place to launch her search for a Yank paratrooper sporting an eagle-head shoulder flash. The quest had begun on a predawn bus, Overton to Whitchurch. Followed by a longer bus ride north, Whitchurch to Newbury. There she learned her errand required a jaunt west, Newbury to Chilton Foliat.

She arrived at Chilton Foliat a fortnight late. The paratrooper she sought had been reassigned. His present battalion was billeted in the remote village of Lambourn. So much for a relaxing Saturday afternoon reading C. S. Lewis.

The cows cleared the road. The bus lurched forward, continuing the dismal journey over the steep hills and narrow dells of the Berkshire countryside.

So why go to all this bother? A sense of economy hardly motivated her—America's vast resources could tolerate a wee bit of waste. No one had suggested that the proper course of action called for her to spend the numerous unpleasant hours required to launder, remove stains, repair, and personally return the battle smock. *Why can't you just leave well enough alone, Maggie?*

Her day's detective work had uncovered that the Lieutenant Henry she sought—full name, Samuel George Henry—now served in 1st Platoon, A-Company, 1st Battalion, 501st Parachute Infantry Regiment, 101st Airborne Division. Her wartime experience told her that the information she possessed served as the military equivalent of an address.

Maggie reflected upon the odd encounter. No academic course could've prepared her to handle a foreign soldier—enemy or allied—disrupting a Jane Austen lesson. Nor had she taken a practicum on controlling a mob of rowdy seventh and eighth form boys ready to mete out justice with hand tools. She chuckled to herself as the bus traversed the green hills.

The bus connecting Chilton Foliat to Lambourn, via Aldbourne, dropped her at what promised to be the final stop. She assured herself she would then put the whole fiasco behind her. Forever.

After a short walk, she presented her identification card and explained her business to a sentry. She signed a ledger and crossed through the estate gate. Stone houses transitioned to horse stables, then neat rows of corrugated metal Nissen huts. She followed the cobblestone roadway until it terminated before the stately Lambourn manor house, now serving—as so many other British estates—as a military headquarters.

Maggie entered the building and followed the signs in the spacious foyer directing her to the offices of the 1st Battalion, 501st PIR. She took a deep breath and approached an occupied desk. Her day's experience with these 101st Airborne paratroopers had proven consistent with her past—and fortunately rare—American encounters. To a man, the Yanks came across as overly familiar and arrogant. The gum-smacking clerk she stood before served as a perfect case in point. The only difference being that this one possessed an accent that she could only match to what she'd heard in a James Cagney gangster movie.

Her pulse rate increased. *What if I have to talk to this Lef'tenant Henry? What will I say? Why does my stomach churn so? Get a grip, Maggie.*

Again, she tried to convince herself that she was merely returning property. A gesture motivated by a desire to make amends for the injury she'd inflicted. However, she couldn't reconcile her racing heart and upset stomach to her cold logic. Her musing landed upon a more truthful reason for her nervousness—fear. The fear of pain. Just speaking to a uniformed young man had the same effect as a sharp blow that reopened a deep wound.

"He's not around." The acne-afflicted clerk spoke without so much as a polite attempt at eye contact. "What's your business with Lieutenant Henry?"

Despite the room being overheated in a manner the Yanks preferred, Maggie pulled her coat closed. She couldn't ignore the clerk's eyes roaming over her body. "I'm returning the lef'tenant's property. A battle smock."

The clerk raised an eyebrow. "Never heard of one of them."

"A battle smock. It's worn over a shirt. Has an assortment of pockets."

"Oh. We calls them jump jackets. How's it you got ahold of the lieutenant's clothing?" The clerk shot her a wink and clicked his tongue.

"Actually I—" Realizing the innuendo, she lost her train of thought and felt herself blush. The soldier renewed his lustful visual appraisal. She readjusted her coat in a subtle attempt to downplay her feminine features and thwart his roving eyes.

She placed the parcel in front of the clerk as if returning a failed essay. "Excuse me, it's growing late and I can ill afford to miss the last bus." Taking on the tone she would use speaking to a prepubescent pupil caught sneaking a peak at a girl's knickers, she said, "Corporal, I find your crude adolescent behavior quite repugnant. Very poor form. Now please be so kind as to see to it that Lef'tenant Henry receives his parcel. Good day!" She pivoted to make a dignified exit.

"Hey, doll face, forget the bus. I'm off duty in a couple hours. I'll get us a jeep and drive youse home. What the heck, I'll spring for dinner. Maybe a couple beers." The clerk clicked his tongue. "Been saving some nylons for that special—"

Maggie wheeled about, her hair swung around to cover her right eye. Her uncovered eye shot the clerk a look meant to dash any ill-conceived romantic notions.

Revelation came over the clerk's face. "Youse that pitchfork dame!"

Maggie abandoned a dignified exit in favor of haste. Yet she made sure her heels hammered an angry beat to punctuate her departure. She slammed the door. It only semi-shielded her from the full-force of the profanity and raucous laughter. She headed for the Lambourn Place gate, knowing her escape route required her to risk another 300 yards of stares and unconcealed rude remarks. She clenched her jaw and resisted the urge to bolt.

Lewd comments notwithstanding, she needed to get far away from soldiers. Even though the uniforms differed and she couldn't understand the half of what some Yanks said, young men preparing to go to war conjured up dreadful memories.

She reassured herself that, aside from today's relapse, she was healing. She wasn't asking herself if the pain would ever go away but a couple of times a week. Last winter she'd asked herself that question a couple of times an hour.

Passing in front of the Nissen huts, a thought halted her. In her haste to escape the ill-mannered clerk, she'd forgotten to inquire about Lieutenant Henry's arm. Very bad form on her part. She pivoted and bit her lower lip. Any serious problem would've been pointed out by the clerk—which he hadn't. That is, if she had given him the time—which she hadn't. Lieutenant Henry might be in the infirmary. She dared not imagine what dreadful germs she might've inflicted with the muck on that pitchfork.

The late-winter wind blowing down the high valley buffeted her face and nearly pulled her headscarf off. She looked down at her feet. Retracing her steps to that randy clerk wouldn't do—she would miss the last bus. Yet, if she continued to the bus, she would feel devoid of charity.

Come on, Maggie, you detest indecision, so decide already.

Indistinct shouts of command, a fair distance to her left, snapped her out of her vacillation. She turned toward the commotion and gazed toward the upward sloping pasture behind the Nissen huts. The noise grew to include multiple footfalls and shifting equipment. Reminiscent of medieval knights, over a hundred warriors trotted into view. She had never before seen soldiers in full combat kit. The view mesmerized her. With each passing second, the knights grew nearer.

The first wolf whistle ended both the noble knight illusion and her inaction. She turned toward the bus stop and moved at a quickened pace. She chided herself aloud. "Don't look back. Ignore the caddy remarks. Eyes forward."

An American voice carrying authority shouted, "Sergeant Jennings, have the platoon fall out. Weapons inspection, one hour."

That's his voice! As shouted orders progressed down the ranks, she discounted the possibility. Most Yanks sounded alike to her British ear.

Another wolf whistle chased her. "Oh, yeah! Hey, doll face, wish I had a swing like that in my backyard!"

Eyes forward. Keep walking. Maggie took a deep breath. *I'll be out the gate and around that stone wall. Just a few more strides.*

"Will you take a gander at them legs? Haven't seen gams that long since—"

"Private Silva! Private Morton! Got enough energy left to disrespect the local ladies? Maybe you want to double-time the last two miles again."

"No sir, Lieutenant Henry!" the soldiers responded in unison.

The name jolted Maggie as her momentum carried her through the large wooden gateposts that separated Lambourn Place Estate from the village of Lambourn. Her heart urged her to return up the cobblestone road. Instead, for the second time in as many minutes, she stopped, pondered her feet and bit her lower lip. She leaned against the wall and pressed her hand to her chest—certain her heart was about to pound its way out.

She took several calming breaths and reached her decision. To return would only subject her to further humiliation. She'd fulfilled her Christian duty to Samuel George Henry. She had returned his battle smock and was now assured that he had returned to top soldierly form. She hadn't picked him out as an individual, yet the evidence proclaimed that the man she'd assailed was now fit enough to march carrying his kit and shout commands—in addition to whatever else they do to prepare men for violent death.

She consulted a scrap of paper in her handbag and glanced at her watch. The bus schedule gave her four minutes to reach the Wheelwright Arms pub. She walked on.

Maggie reached to relieve the tickle on her cheek. Her finger came away wet. She chose to believe that the winter wind had generated the tear. After all, this time she merely cried one tear.

Chapter 9

The Parcel

Standing alongside his cot, Sam eased the web gear harness off his shoulders and bumped his wounded forearm against a chair back. He gritted his teeth to brace himself for pain that failed to shoot up his arm.

He removed his soiled jump jacket and rolled up his left sleeve. The gauze looked almost fresh. The battalion surgeon—while singing the praises of the new wonder-drug, penicillin—had informed Sam that it was a minor miracle he didn't have a major infection.

First Battalion's junior officers were billeted in Lambourn Estate's cut-stone guest cottage. Sam struggled with the reality that a house at least triple the size of any house he'd ever lived in could be referred to as a *cottage*. This first-floor room housed Able Company's 2nd lieutenants. Four cots lined the white plaster walls. Spare uniforms hung in small, open wardrobes at the foot of each cot. Writing tables with folding chairs stood at the opposite ends.

Sam considered the friendly ribbing he'd endured for more than a week and grinned. The pitchfork assault ended up overshadowing the Piccadilly Circus incident. It seemed about everyone in Able Company had had something to opine about the incidents. Except Lieutenant Pettigrew. Pettigrew never so much as even mentioned either. The silence baffled Sam.

Footsteps on the hallway tiles interrupted his musing. Lieutenant Pettigrew stuck his head into the room. His flat face expressed disgust—as if the room housed a leper colony. "You've got a parcel at battalion HQ."

"From my mother. Picked it up this morning, *sir*." It grated on Sam that Pettigrew was the only 1st lieutenant that made 2nd lieutenants address him as sir.

"Some English dame dropped this one off." Pettigrew lit a Chesterfield. "You need to figure out how to more rapidly deploy that redskin's squad. The fault rests squarely on his shoulders for our failure to achieve mission objective on time."

"All things considered, I think Sergeant Springwater did a more than adequate job." Sam worked to keep his voice unemotional. Memories of the freezing creek and rain-drenched slope rekindled his anger. The field problem had given Springwater only twenty minutes—a near impossible time constraint—to get crew-served weapons to the peak of Lynch Woods, deploy his men, and provide a base of simulated suppressive fire in support of the rest of the platoon moving in assault.

"In combat, *all things considered* and an *adequate* job will equate to mission failure, Henry." Pettigrew blew a cloud of smoke into Sam's quarters. "Or were you on sick-call day fifty-four of your ninety-day-wonder OCS course?"

Sam refused the bait.

Pettigrew's voice grew more shrill. "A dozen mortar rounds and two cans of machinegun ammo were left on the far creek bank. Was he thinking he could provide suppressive fire with arrows and spears?"

"Sergeant Springwater assumed that—"

"He *assumed* wrong! And in so doing, failed to look after the critical details."

"Easy to do given he was set up to fail." Sam's temples began throbbing. "Why did you go behind his back and order his own men to leave the munitions?"

"Better now than in combat. Better a brawling Injun as an example." Pettigrew smirked. "The whole platoon learned a valuable lesson."

"OK. Fine." Sam threw up his hands. "You're the platoon leader. Now, if you'd excuse me, I'd like to pick up my parcel before weapons inspection."

With an arm casually braced on each doorjamb, Pettigrew blocked Sam's exit.

Sam took it as a sign to address the core issue. He swallowed hard. "Look, I didn't write the Army table of organization that says each parachute infantry platoon is uniquely allotted two lieutenants." He held up two fingers. "You don't like it? Fine. Next month when you make general you can change it."

Sam tossed on his dirty jump jacket and barged past Pettigrew. He'd pay later. *Life would go so much smoother if I'd just keep my mouth shut.* To burn off anger he double-timed it the short distance to battalion HQ in the main estate house.

"Got a parcel for me, Corporal Mazooti?"

"Lieutenant Henry, she was here, sir."

"Afraid you're going to have to be more specific. She…?"

"The pitchfork dame, sir. Tall. Dishwater blond. A real dish. But I couldn't tell youse much on her finer points. She was wearing this heavy coat." The clerk smacked his gum. "And spunky. She gave me a look that I ain't never seen from no Philly broad. Tried getting a date, but no dice. The nylons didn't even work their magic. She sure would've beat the hell out of them Piccadilly commandos."

The clerk's crass, albeit accurate description of the woman who'd impaled Sam got his full attention. "Get that gum out of your mouth so I can understand you. How do you know it was her, Corporal?"

"She asked for youse by name." The corporal stuck his gum on the edge of his ashtray, reached into a desk drawer, and pulled out a brown-paper parcel tied with string.

Sam took the parcel. "When was she here?"

"Couldn't have been an hour ago, sir."

Not understanding why his pulse rate just climbed, Sam looked at his watch—seven minutes until weapons inspection. She'd be long gone by now anyway. He recalled catching a glimpse of a young woman trotting down the road and Silva's racy comments about a girl's legs. Though uncouth, Silva's remarks were an apt depiction of the long legs Sam had viewed close up, at ground level.

Those long legs had just stood right there. *What am I to make of that?* He glanced at his watch. No time to dwell on it now.

*   *   *

Sam longed to collapse into overdue slumber when he noticed the unopened parcel on his cot. *Oh yeah, that blonde looker.* She brought a smile to his face. He picked up the parcel and untied the string.

Sterling walked in wrapped in a towel. "What you got there?"

"That schoolteacher who mistook me for a Luftwaffe ace dropped this off."

"Again, justice eludes me, Sammy-boy. My wife seems to have misplaced my address and you get a hand-delivered package from some gal who ran you through with cold steel." Sterling shook his head in mock disgust. "Get to talk with her?"

Sam folded back the brown paper, revealing tan material. "Nope." He shook the cloth out and held out a jump jacket at arm's length. "Would you take a look at that?" He let out a soft whistle. "Can't be. No way. It was covered with all manner of barnyard filth and blood. Reeked beyond redemption."

Sterling chuckled. "I heard that was a more fitting description of you."

Sam pulled it into his face and inhaled. "Impossible. Can't be the same jacket. She must've used the ruined one as a sample and somehow… But how? It's not new."

Sterling finished toweling off. "It's just a jump jacket. Army's got a few hundred thousand more."

"You just don't get it, Lloyd. No one has ever done anything like this for me before. Not even my own mother." Sam grabbed the left sleeve in both hands, inspected the arm and spotted the irrefutable proof—two mended holes matching the size of a pitchfork tine. "Talk about going above and beyond the call. She cleansed every trace of blood and stitched the holes closed. The thread even matches the jacket's color. Exactly!"

Sam held the sleeve close to his eyes and scrutinized a mended hole. "There's not even any puckering."

Sterling shook his head. "Had this laundry obsession long?"

"I detest laundry. That's why I can appreciate this…this amazing act of kindness." Sam held the Screaming Eagle patch up to Sterling's face. "Even the white on the patch could pass dress inspection and it was covered with cow—"

"What's that?" Sterling pointed between Sam's feet.

Sam picked up a handwritten note and read it silently.

> *Lieutenant Henry,*
> *Again, I beg your forgiveness concerning my hasty and ill-advised actions. I attempted to clean and repair your battle smock as a small, yet sincere, token of my regret over our little mishap. I do hope and pray that your arm is on the mend.*
> *Warmly,*
> *Margaret Elliott*

"'Our *little* mishap'? The gall." Laughing, Sam shook his head. "She deliberately impales me and calls it a little mishap! Can you get more of a British understatement than that?"

"How about more pertinent facts? Address? Phone number? Sorority affiliation? Suggested rendezvous?" Sterling grabbed the note and scanned it. "No such luck. At least we've got a name. Looks like we've got some detective work ahead of us."

Sam snatched the note back. "Not so fast, Sherlock. One critical question remains unanswered. And we're not playing gumshoe until it is."

*   *   *

"Go ahead. Be my guest."

Sterling stood over the slumbering, pimply-faced clerk and passed his hand over the body like a high-class waiter presenting a meal. Sam hesitated. Sterling yanked away the clerk's blanket. Sam shook Mazooti's shoulder. "Corporal, get up!"

"Get your grubby paws…" Mazooti rubbed his eyes, looked up, and blinked. "Geez, can't this wait until morning, sirs?"

Sterling gave an authoritative scowl. "Urgent matter. Outside now, soldier."

Mazooti draped a blanket over his shoulders and obeyed just as the Army had conditioned him. Outside the corrugated metal barracks, the corporal was already smacking gum. "Sirs, I'm innocent. Had no idea them dice was loaded. Besides, it was just a bunch of them friggin' Air Corps mechanics. Ain't never taken no airborne money."

"Do we look like MPs?" Sam said. "Save your confession for the chaplains. We're here on a critical S-Two matter."

"Seems you committed a major breach of security this afternoon." Sterling frowned disapprovingly. "Allowed an unidentified civilian to waltz right into battalion HQ and leave an unauthorized, uncensored, and uninspected parcel."

Sam lifted the groggy corporal's drool-dampened chin. "Wake up, Corporal."

"Why did you neglect asking for proper ID?" Sterling rapid fired his questions. "Which gate did she enter through? Did you not deduce that this was the same woman who had recently assaulted—with intent to kill—an American officer? How'd you know the parcel wasn't full of explosives?"

The corporal stood slack-jawed.

Sterling said, "Yes indeed, the regimental S-Two fears that the exact location and disposition of the Five-O-First PIR has been compromised to Nazi High Command."

Shaking his head, Sam made disapproving ticking sounds. "I'd sure hate to be in your jump boots."

Mazooti's teeth began chattering. Sam reasoned that had the corporal been fully awake, less intimidated, warm, and about twenty-five points higher on the IQ scale, he would've deduced that much of the populace of Wiltshire and Berkshire were capable of betraying such information.

Sterling stepped close to the corporal's ear. "Did you detect a foreign accent?"

Mazooti nodded enthusiastically. "You bet! She's had a Limey accent."

Sam frowned. "Hardly foreign. In case you hadn't noticed, we're in England."

"OK, let's assume our man here is worthy of his stripes." Sterling stepped between Sam and Mazooti. "Just suppose this innocent British dame decides to write her dear hubby about the wonderful time she had visiting the Five-O-First in Lambourn."

Mazooti moved his mouth to protest, but Sterling put a finger to the clerk's lips. "Shush!"

Sam stepped around his friend to deliver the scripted knockout punch. "Only her husband happens to be some hapless POW locked away somewhere in Hitler's backyard. The *Gestapo* gets ahold of her letter and bingo, they discover the exact location of the Army's best parachute infantry regiment. And before you can finish stamping weekend passes, we've got us a full squadron of Luftwaffe bombers dropping high-explosive gifts from Adolph." Sam extended his arm and pointed to the sky. Mazooti's eyes followed. Sam wiggled his fingers and brought them downward while Sterling whistled like a falling bomb.

"No, sirs! Ain't no way." Mazooti pulled the blanket tighter around his shoulders—his clouds of breath visible in the damp night air.

"And...?" Sam arched his eyebrows and turned his hand over and over.

"She ain't married." Confidence returned to Mazooti. "Ain't even engaged, sir."

"How can you be so cock-sure, Corporal?" Sterling asked.

"Simple, sir. She ain't got no ring. Ever since that beating I took at the Jersey Shore, I always double check for that ring. A ladies man like myself can't afford—"

"Excellent!" Sam's face spread into a smile. "With your keen powers of observation, Mazooti, you may be suited for Army intelligence. We'll be sure to make mention of it in our report." Sam gave the clerk a pat on the back.

A visible shiver went up the clerk's body. "May I get back inside, sirs?"

Sterling gave a dismissive wave. "Hit the sack, soldier."

Sam bit his lip to keep from laughing. As the clerk trotted away Sam couldn't resist saying, "And I want those dice at the bottom of the latrine before breakfast. Understood, Corporal Mazooti?"

"Yes sir! No more loaded dice. Not even with Limey sailors."

Chapter 10

The Investigation

5 March 1944
Overton, England

"Refresh my memory. Whose command do we fall under?"

Traveling east from Whitchurch, Sam depressed the clutch and downshifted to enter the Overton village limits. Chilly morning wind whipped over the open jeep.

"Anglo-American Joint Conflict Resolution Command," Sterling said, practicing his officious voice. "AAJCRC falls under the auspices of SHAEF. Meaning we answer to Ike alone. We investigate violent encounters between American military personnel and the King's subjects, civilian variety."

"Must say, I'm quite impressed with my new job." Sam shook his head. "And to think, right now you could be headed to London for a good time."

"My good time awaits back in Illinois. Don't need to be patrolling for Piccadilly commandos. Only gets a fella short on cash and long on a good case of the clap. Besides, it's the thrill of the hunt, Sammy-boy. Listen. I hear the hounds baying."

Sam accelerated past brick and glass shopfronts. At the town hall he turned north onto road B-3051.

Over the wind and engine noise Sterling yelled, "Tally Ho! It's the thrill of the hunt." Sterling laughed and slapped his knee. "Personally, I think you'll get shot down before we even get close to the drop zone."

Sam admired the storybook-like row of stone and brick cottages alternating between slate and thatched roofs lining each side of the road. An ancient mill hung over the headwaters of the River Test. One-hundred-fifty yards past the river a stone church dominated an intersection. He stopped the jeep. Organ music drifted out of the church. Children played tag in the churchyard. A wooden road sign for Court Farm pointed left.

"That's the place." Sam accelerated and cranked the wheel. Past a riverside athletic field, he veered right, following the narrow road uphill. After 250 yards, they spotted the sizable two-story brick schoolhouse. "Eureka!"

"Relax. Stick to the plan. Trust the pro." Sterling tapped his finger on his own chest. "Let me do the talking. You just pretend to jot notes and act official."

Sam drove past the school and turned into the farm courtyard next to the greenhouse. "Makes my arm ache just being here."

The enlarged dung heap assaulted his senses. The rising steam visually accentuated the stench.

"She handled your jacket after you landed in that? Whew!" Sterling wafted his hand back and forth in front of his face. "I've *got* to meet this dame."

They walked past the dung pile toward the double doors of a long stone barn. Sounds of cattle mooing and metal scraping concrete came from the inside. Sam followed Sterling into the barn and halted while his eyes adjusted to the semidarkness.

A youthful male Cockney voice called out. "'Ello. You chaps looking for Mr. Watson?"

Sam blinked a couple of times. A scrawny teen carrying a pitchfork squeezed around a cart of soiled straw and walked toward them.

Sterling stepped forward. "We're conducting an official investigation with the American-Anglo Royal Conflict Resolution Commission."

Sam leaned close to his friend's ear. "That's not the name you told me."

Sterling nudged Sam away. "And you are…?"

"John Needham." The boy's wild reddish-blond hair poked out from underneath his tweed cap. As the teen examined their dark olive-drab class-A uniforms his eyes widened. "Blimey, you chaps," the boy gulped, "pardon me, you sirs are airborne! I turn seventeen in three months, then I'll bloody well leave this farm to join the paras. What unit did you say you was with, sir?"

"On loan to the Anglo-American Criminal Conflict Command. We answer only to Field Marshall Montgomery." Sterling cleared his throat. "I trust we have your full cooperation."

The boy gulped again and nodded.

Sterling scrunched up his face. "Take us someplace warm where we can breathe."

"Yes, sir. Next door's the green'ouse." The boy marched out the barn with his chest puffed out, pitchfork carried as though it was military issue.

Inside the crowded greenhouse—a pleasant 70° and smelling of vines and unripe vegetables—Sterling started the questioning while Sam stood by, pencil and pad in hand.

"Are you aware of the international incident that took place on this very farm involving a certain teacher named…?" Sterling clicked his fingers.

Sam looked at his blank pad. "Elliott, a Miss Margaret Elliott."

"Yes, Margaret Elliott," Sterling said. "Seems she assaulted an American officer with a certain farm implement."

John dropped the pitchfork as if it had become red hot. "Blimey! I thought my brother and his mates was feedin' me a cock'n bull story. She really stuck that para colonel in the paunch?"

Sam coughed into his fist to conceal his laughter.

Sterling stayed in character. "We can't have allies assaulting each other willy-nilly, now can we, Mr. Needham? We must locate this teacher to complete our investigation. Do your parents own this farm?"

"The deuce, no, guv'ner!" The teen laughed. "Me mum was killed during the Blitz and me pop's a merchant marine sailor. Me brother and me, well, we got shuffled off here from London in thirty-nine to finish school and work on farms. I've had enough of books and muckin' stalls. Like I says, three months and I join the paras."

"Tell us about Miss Elliott." Sterling examined a cucumber vine. "Does she harbor any pro-Nazi sympathies?"

"She teaches me kid brother, not me. She's from London, I knows that much. Been here nigh on a year."

"Her place of residence?"

"I reckon with the other London teachers. Other side o' Overton. At Dellands Road."

Sterling pointed to the pitchfork on the gravel floor. "Is that the weapon?"

The youth took a step away. "Me brother claimed so."

"Then we're required to confiscate the pitchfork."

Sam shot Sterling a glance meant to curb his enthusiasm. "I really don't think that'll be necessary."

"Oh, but it's absolutely necessary." Sterling looked stern. "Vital evidence. Collect it and tag it, Lieutenant."

"I best go tell Mr. Watson." John started for the door. "I won't catch 'ell again for lost tools."

Sterling hooked the teen at the elbow. "That won't be necessary, just have him go to the post office and complete SHAEF Allied Expense Form Twelve-ninety-x." Sterling turned to Sam. "Write it down for the helpful lad."

Sam made a show of looking at his watch. "Isn't it time we got moving?"

Sterling pointed to the far corner. "Those roses for sale?"

"Sorry, guv'ner. Them's Lady Watson's prize stock. Her little secret, too. Supposed to keep every square foot in vegetables."

"Cut me a dozen and I'll personally put in a good word for you with Monty. Didn't you say you wanted to be airborne?"

The teen grabbed a pair of hand shears and assaulted the roses.

Sam leaned close to Sterling's ear. "Exactly how do you propose we tell Field Marshall Montgomery?"

"Not that Monty, Sammy-boy. Sergeant Monty Acres, from Dubuque. Leads my mortar squad. He'll get a kick out of this."

John returned with a dozen of the choicest red roses, twine binding the stems.

"We must insist you keep this all hush-hush, Mr. Needham. No need for further unpleasantry between our two nations. If any word leaks out, rest assured you'll be barred from the paratroops. Understood?"

The youth gulped hard and nodded. He came to an amateurish attention stance and gave a palm-out British salute.

Sterling returned the salute, reminded Sam to retrieve the pitchfork, and exited the greenhouse toting the long-stemmed roses. Sam reached for his wallet and removed two one-pound notes. Hurrying out, he stuffed the cash under the teen's cap. Just outside the door, he heard an enthused, "Blimey! Thanks, guv'ner."

Sam couldn't escape the farm fast enough. The time required to weave the jeep down the narrow road relieved some tension. Laughing, he threw a backhand into Sterling chest and pulled off near the stone bridge overlooking the River Test. "If you end up flunking out of grad school you've got the makings for one first-rate con artist."

"You're assuming there's a difference, Sammy-boy."

"So, now what, Sherlock?"

"Elementary, my dear Henry. Find Dellands Road." Sterling glanced at his wristwatch. "Ahead of schedule. I suggest we slow down, relax a little.

Never a good idea to drop in on the fairer sex unannounced too much before noon on a Sunday."

Sam turned off the engine. "And the roses?"

"Take it from a married man, they'll work wonders. A small token of appreciation." Sterling sighed. "Are you really that inexperienced with women? I'd think a guy growing up amongst all those California beaches and starlets would be more suave."

"Sorry to disappoint you, buddy." Sam felt a tinge of guilt for not being more forthcoming about his family history. He considered changing the subject to the infrequency of Sterling's name at mail call. Instead, he diverted to a neutral, yet masculine theme. He pointed to the shallow river. "Looks like a dandy fishing stream."

"Clear as gin." Sterling took out his pipe and tobacco pouch. "I've heard these rivers are loaded with trout." He tamped down the bowl of tobacco and lit it with a Ronson.

Sam sniffed the vanilla-scented smoke and closed his eyes. "Did I ever tell you your pipe smoke takes me right back to UCLA? Reminds me of my favorite professor—Dr. Rosenfeld."

"Let me guess." Sterling smirked. "Teaches philosophy?"

"Taught. Suicide. Six months ago."

"Talk about a case of physician-heal-thyself."

"Come on, Lloyd, cut the baloney. I'm serious."

"So am I. Sorry if I came off flippant." Sterling blew a cloud of fragrant smoke. "I guess that explains why you're always wanting to discuss philosophy—Kant, Hegel, Spinoza... Where does literature fit in?"

Sam smiled. "My other favorite teacher—happens to be my grandfather—teaches high school English."

"So, as our resident sage philosopher, Sammy-boy, give me a metaphysical take on what we're all about. The big picture, beyond the pursuit of mysterious women."

Sam shrugged. "If Dr. Rosenfeld couldn't find something worth living for, why should I be any further along?"

A pair of white swans drifted down the river.

"I'm not sure you believe that." Sterling pulled the pipestem from the corner of his mouth. "No purpose, no hope. No hope, no life. What might've sunk your professor's hopes?"

"Can't help but think; maybe if I'd been there I could've talked him out of it, like I did that Five-O-Sixth sergeant in that Piccadilly cathouse." Sam gnawed on his lower lip. "Dr. Rosenfeld was all torn up inside by what the Nazis are doing to his country, his people. He was Jewish. Escaped Germany just in the nick of time."

"Just all the more incentive for us to hurry the hell up and kill the lousy Nazi sons—" Sterling waved his hand. "Stop me when I start sounding more GI and less the history scholar." He pointed his pipestem at Sam. "But we've got to have purpose. Purpose combined with a moral code. Otherwise we're no better than animals."

Sam twisted in his seat and wagged a finger at Sterling. "But we are better. We can *choose*."

"So, it all boils down to choice?" Sterling said. "I was kind of hoping moral absolutes and transcendent purposes might be what separate us more from the animals."

Sam sat in silence. Ripples rolled outward from a rising trout. In the distance a train clacked and rolled down the tracks. Sam blew on his hands to warm them. Smoke drifted from chimneys. Peace pervaded the small valley. Overton seemed far removed from any war.

CLANG! CLANG!

Sam shot straight up and spun around. A large uniformed man wearing a flat British helmet stood behind the jeep, his swagger stick poised to strike the fender again.

"Do pardon me, Yanks. Never intended to give you a start. Just an old bloke trying to do me job." The man surveyed the jeep's cargo area. His weathered face frowned. "I received no notice concerning military exercises."

Sterling stepped out of the jeep. "But of course not. Investigations of a sensitive nature can hardly be conducted by publishing our intended stops. We're with the Joint Command for American-Anglo Relations." Sterling extended his hand and tilted his head back to look the Englishman in the eye. "And you are?"

"Dawkins. Alfred Dawkins, of the Home Guard." Dawkins shook Sterling's hand. Sterling grimaced. "And I dare say I've never heard of the Joint Command for Ameri...Am..."

"American-Anglo Conflict Resolution." Sterling massaged his right hand. "And you haven't heard about us because the village of Overton has only recently experienced an unprovoked assault on an American soldier by an English civilian. We're here to wrap up the investigation. I'm sure a man entrusted with your responsibility is well aware of the case."

"Case? Some daft teacher mistakes a Yank paratrooper for a Jerry pilot. End of story. Hardly a case."

Sterling turned to Sam. "See, Lieutenant, I told you the reports concerning the vigilance of the Hampshire County Home Guard were accurate. Make an official record of his statement."

Taking pencil and notepad in hand, Sam acted out the ruse.

Dawkins pointed to the jeep's cargo area. "Do explain the roses and pitchfork."

"Seized the pitchfork as evidence. And the flowers...well, the flowers are for..."

Don't choke up now, Lloyd! Sam thought, and said, "The flowers are a gift from Supreme Headquarters Allied Expeditionary Force to smooth over any trauma the young lady—a Miss Margaret Elliott—might be experiencing as a result of the unfortunate incident." Sam pocketed his pencil and pad before Dawkins got curious about his bogus notes. "Like you said, a simple case of mistaken identity."

Dawkins smiled, showing a jumble of decaying teeth. "In that case, you can find the London teachers on this road at the corner of Dellands Road, right side. Uphill all the way, nary a half mile."

"We'll include your eager cooperation in our report," Sterling said.

"Will you, now? Please, you chaps can spare me the theatrics. I can recognize airborne shoulder flashes. And I can sure smell this crock from a mile away." Dawkins pointed at Sam. "You're a handsome, young para lef'tenant, gray eyes, fine brown hair." Dawkins looked him up and down. "Even seated you look about five-foot-nine, eleven stones. She gave me an accurate enough description. And if my guess be right, under that sleeve you've got a couple nasty puncture wounds. It's all part of *my* official report. Care to accompany me to the Home Guard office to see it?"

Sam's countenance dropped.

Dawkins made ticking sounds with his tongue. "You Yanks be rank amateurs. In the future, you may want to actually know the name of the department you invent. Nevertheless, I'm inclined to excuse your ineptness. You probably didn't count on running into a chap who'd been a big-city bobby for nearly three decades."

Dawkins kept his gaze locked on Sam. "Now, you I understand. Though some may consider it daft to pursue a lass who introduces herself with a wicked pitchfork jab. Cupid has done stranger things, though. But I must admit, your mate here is a wee bit of a puzzle. What's in it for him? He's wearing a wedding ring. Not that that hinders the libido of some Yanks much."

Sterling slipped his pipe into his class-A jacket pocket. "We'll be leaving now, Mr. Dawkins. Maybe you'd like some roses for the missus?"

"Jolly well tried me own shenanigans to win the heart—and other parts—of a certain *mademoiselle* in France, nineteen-fifteen." A sly grin crept across Dawkins's face. "Me recollections of sweet Michelle are fresh to this day."

Dawkins backed away until he could read the stenciled numbers and letters on the bumper and jotted notes. "Now, if it be a local lass, you two lads would already be on your way, and your superior would know all about this before you even got back. If it was me own daughter, you two would both be finding yourselves swimming in the cold River Test. Aye, but it's one of them London teachers. So it be none o' me business. Just keep your mates away from the local girls. You know what they say the problem is with you Yanks…you're—"

"Overpaid, oversexed, and over here," Sam recited the cliché.

"A huge exaggeration where the two of us are concerned," Sterling said.

Dawkins nodded. "Splendid. Jolly well keep it that way."

"Just one last question," Sterling said. "In your description of my friend you used the word, 'handsome.' Were those Miss Elliott's words?"

"A lass don't have to say the exact words. Being a married man yourself you should know these things."

"Pearl Harbor interrupted my education as a husband."

"Aye. Now be gone with you before I regret me soft sentimental side and telephone Newbury for your MPs."

Sam cranked the engine. Sterling dropped into his seat.

"Wait!" Sterling fumbled around his feet and pulled out a musette bag.

"You out of your mind?" Sam said out of the corner of his mouth.

Lloyd tossed Dawkins two packs of Chesterfields.

Dawkins slid the tobacco treasures into his coat pocket. "Quite generous, lad. I hope you won't object if I trade these for a half-dozen packs of Woodbines." He waved farewell. "Cheerio, Yanks."

Sam shoved the gearshift into first and released the clutch pedal. Dawkins again banged his swagger stick on the jeep fender. Sam hit the brake and stalled the engine.

A mischievous grin covered Dawkins's face. "And do remember to keep to the left side like a civilized motorist."

Sam restarted the engine, popped the clutch, and swerved to the left side.

After less than two minutes of driving, they arrived at Dellands Road. Sam tried not to stare at the target house. It was a modest Tudor cottage with smooth whitewashed stucco and exposed dark beams. Two dormers jutted from the slate roof.

Sam blew into his hands. "When will this country warm up?"

"Compared to early March in Central Illinois, it has. You want to talk about the weather, or knock on that door? Remember what they said at parachute school at Benning."

"They said a lot at Fort Benning. Which week?"

"More like day one. Refusal at the door and you wash out." Sterling pointed at the house. "Well there's the door. Jump light's green, Sammy-boy."

"Geronimo!" Sam launched himself out of the jeep and grabbed the roses. Striding for the door he tried to muster a look of confidence he didn't feel. In the alcove sheltering the door he adjusted his overseas cap and straightened his tie.

With cold knuckles, he gave the door three raps.

Footsteps approached from the other side. His stomach knotted. The latch rattled. The door swung open.

Chapter 11

The Reunion

Margaret Elliott's antithesis stood in the doorway. Sam took a half-step back. The short woman exceeded Margaret Elliott by twenty years and fifty pounds. Gray streaked her brunette hair.

The woman gasped and covered her mouth.

Sam removed his overseas cap. "Pardon me, ma'am. Reckon I'm at the wrong house." He hoped Sterling couldn't hear a hint of Ozark accent slip out. "I'm looking for a schoolteacher, from London. Perhaps you can direct me?"

The woman blinked several times. "I'm a teacher from London."

Sam raised a brow. "Yes, but…"

"But you're wanting Margaret Elliott, I'd wager." A knowing smile crossed the woman's face. "Do come in." She extended her hand and pulled Sam into the house with the handshake. "I'm Mrs. Weatherall."

"Lieutenant Sam Henry. Excuse me, but my friend." He motioned over his shoulder with his thumb.

"Oh, do pardon me." Mrs. Weatherall took a step over the threshold and shouted, "Young man, please, do join us."

She took Sam's khaki trenchcoat and dropped it twice before managing to hang it on a coat tree. "You must excuse me. I've languished in semi-exile since September, thirty-nine. Rarely do I entertain guests—never American lads. No complaints, mind you. One must do one's part for the war effort."

Thirty minutes and two cups of tea later, Sam and Lloyd sat in a sparsely furnished sitting-room adjoining the foyer. Fragile looking furniture contrasted a hefty radio in the corner. The puny coal pile glowing in the fireplace knocked the edge off the chill. A framed landscape print of foxhounds on the hunt dominated one wall. The only other pictures on the wall were portraits. Sam had learned much, but hardly anything concerning Margaret Elliott.

"Our evacuee East End pupils once numbered over eighty at first," Mrs. Weatherall said. "However, many parents claimed their children back when the Blitz lightened. One or two older lads ran off, presumably to join the military. Now, the Little Blitz has picked the numbers up to forty pupils." She stirred her teacup with a miniature spoon. "Our children are quite fortunate. Whitehall shipped some children to Canada, even Australia—quite disruptive. Many of our remaining students have no home in London to return to."

Mrs. Weatherall rose to refill Sterling's teacup. "I'm somewhat the vagabond myself—a Luftwaffe incendiary bomb found our flat during the Battle of Britain." She poured a dab more milk into her own tea. "My family was already scattered by then, my husband a Lancaster bomber mechanic in Exeter at the time—been to North Africa and Italy since. My son was called-up into the infantry, special commando training in Scotland now. My baby girl mans an antiaircraft gun protecting Vauxhall Bridge, when not attending university lectures."

Mrs. Weatherall excused herself for a fourth trip to the kitchen. She bustled back wearing a stern expression. "Young man, I'll have you know your untimely parachute landing jolly well disrupted lessons well into the following week."

"It wasn't my inten—"

"Nonetheless, you must realize, having lost loved ones in the bombings, some pupils were already highly traumatized. Then the sight of blood. Well, it was quite upsetting for some."

Sterling set down his teacup. "Getting stuck by a pitchfork wasn't exactly my friend's idea of a walk in the park."

Mrs. Weatherall raised a reassuring hand. "Miss Elliott has been duly reprimanded."

Sam recognized a diplomatic opening. "By the way, when do you expect her?"

"Why, it's Sunday morning. Naturally, Margaret's at church. Today she invited another teacher, Chloe Hamlin. She's always inviting someone. I'm surprised she didn't invite you while holding you captive." Mrs. Weatherall looked at the mantle clock. "On occasion she departs for London straight from church."

Sterling squirmed and shot Sam a "what now?" look.

"If it's not an imposition," Sam said, "we'll wait."

Mrs. Weatherall smiled and bent forward to pour Sam more tea. "I do wish I could offer coffee. I understand you Yanks are quite fond of coffee."

From behind her back, Sterling rolled his eyes.

Sam pointed at an eight-by-ten framed portrait on a lace-covered end table. "Your son? Is that an infantry uniform?" The handsome soldier had dark, curly hair, a confident smile, and the pencil-thin mustache popular among British troops.

"Oh, my dear no, that's Margaret's—" Mrs. Weatherall overfilled Sam's cup and spilled tea.

The tea burned Sam's hand. He jerked and spilled more tea.

Mrs. Weatherall scurried away. "Oh, clumsy me! I'll find a flannel."

Sterling leaned closer. "Didn't that skirt-chasing clerk insist she had no ring?"

"Probably just her brother," Sam whispered with confidence he didn't feel.

"Brother? Are you blind? From your description of Miss Pitchfork, there's zero family resemblance."

"Why should you care? You're only along for the thrill of the hunt. Remember?"

"The hunt, yes." Sterling jabbed his finger toward the portrait. "But if that isn't her brother, we're not hunting, we're *poaching!*"

Outside, footfalls on stepping-stones alerted Sam. The doorknob turned. He stood and straightened his class-A jacket. The door swung inward and blocked his view. A female stepped in, turned away, and closed the door. She removed her headscarf, revealing bobbed brunette hair.

Sam's shoulders sagged.

Removing her coat, the young lady called out, "Oh, Mrs. Weatherall, there's some sort of American military motorcar out front. It's got Maggie all flustered." She spotted the two military coats on the coat tree and spun around. "Blimey!" She held her hands over her heart. "You blokes ruddy well know how to frighten a girl."

Mrs. Weatherall reentered the room. "Chloe, I'd like you to meet our American guests. Lef'tenant Lloyd Sterling of Illinois, and Lef'tenant Sam Henry of California. Gentlemen, Miss Chloe Hamlin of London."

Chloe extended her hand. "Pardon me, I'm afraid I didn't catch your name."

"Sam Henry."

"*The* Samuel Henry? Yank paratrooper whose plunge in the dung heap so thoroughly disrupted my roommate's life?" Chloe's smile held the same hint of mischief as the Mona Lisa.

"Guilty as charged, here to offer my apologies and thanks."

"And ruddy high time, I'd say."

"Chloe! Your manners." Mrs. Weatherall wagged a finger. "Please do excuse her. I fear teaching the middle forms has made her forget how to address officers and gentlemen. Chloe, in lieu of insulting our guests, perhaps you could join me in preparing sandwiches." Miss Weatherall hooked Chloe by the arm and dragged her away.

As soon as the women were out of earshot, Sam said, "What do you make of it?"

Sterling frowned. "Hard to read. Could go either—"

The front door swung open. Sam's stomach lurched. His mind fogged. *What stupidity drove me to do this?*

Margaret Elliott stepped into view. Radiant. His mind cleared. Instantly, nothing he ever attempted seemed more rational or compelling.

"Good morning, Lef'tenant Henry. I wasn't sure we'd ever meet again," Margaret Elliott directed her large eyes slightly downward. "Last time was less than smashing."

He gazed a little too long at her face. Her attractiveness surpassed his pain-clouded memory—an attractiveness not so dependent upon photogenic beauty, like an aspiring Hollywood starlet's, but rather a bright countenance that radiated outward from those honey-brown eyes.

Blushing, she looked away.

"Good morning, Miss Elliott. I thought we should meet under more civilized circumstances. And please, call me Sam."

"Very well, Sam. In light of our first encounter, we may dispense with formalities. Call me Maggie." She looked Sterling's direction. "I don't recall you."

"Pardon me. This is Lieutenant Lloyd Sterling. He wasn't there."

"Pleased to meet you, Miss Elliott. I hope you have no plans to use that again." Sterling pointed at the pitchfork Maggie held in her left hand. Maggie's face had drawn Sam's focus so intently that he failed to notice the pitchfork.

"Oh, don't worry. The Home Guard relieved me of all defense responsibilities against enemies of the Realm—real or imagined." Maggie leaned the pitchfork against the wall. "I saw this in the back of your..." A puzzled look came over her face.

"Jeep. We call it a jeep." Sam pointed at the pitchfork. "Why'd you bring that in?"

"I'll answer *if* you tell me why you took it from Court Farm. Is it the same—?"

"A souvenir," Sterling said in uncharacteristic candor.

"It's OK. I paid for it," Sam said.

Sterling shot him a questioning glance.

A look of concern crossed Maggie's face. "Oh, dear. Do forgive me for not asking sooner, but is your arm on the mend?"

"Healing nicely. Care to see?"

"If it's not too forward of me."

"Not at all," Stepping across the room, Sam removed his class-A jacket. He unbuttoned his shirtsleeve, rolled it up to his elbow, and peeled back a Band-aid.

"I dare say I expected much, much worse." Maggie leaned closer and gently touched near the wound. "An answer to prayer, most certainly. No infection?"

Maggie's light touch sent a shot of electricity up his arm and down his spine. It had no association with pain.

"None whatsoever." Sam's stomach fluttered. "Not sure about the power of prayer, but I'm a convert to the miracle of medical science. A new drug from the States. Doctor called it penicillin."

"Yeah," Sterling said, "thanks to the wonder-drug Sam won't be missing the big show—our drop into Hitler's backyard."

Maggie's countenance fell. "And that's a good thing?"

Her comment struck Sam as odd. "Pardon me?"

"Did it hurt?" She gripped his forearm and turned it over, revealing a larger Band-aid covering the exit wound. "Later, I mean?"

"None whatsoever," Sam lied.

Sterling went into a mild coughing fit.

"Good. I can't even begin to express how hideous I felt." Maggie released his arm. "Returning your battle smock—I'm sorry, jump jacket—was the least I could do."

"Now that came as quite a surprise." Sam rolled his sleeve down and put his class-A jacket back on. "And thank you very much. As good as new. Expertly done."

"Comes from years of experience. Every young lady has a role to serve in the war effort, starting in nineteen-forty. First did my part mending and altering uniforms. Nothing terribly gallant, I'm afraid."

"Oh, I almost forgot." Sam retrieved the roses off the floor next to his chair and presented Maggie the bouquet. "My way of saying thanks…for the jump jacket, I mean."

"Roses! I simply adore red roses. But where'd you possibly find such beauties this time of year?" Maggie buried her face in the blooms and inhaled.

Sterling gave a little wave. "You might say I'm the one with the flower connections, Miss Elliott."

"Well then, thank you *both*," Maggie said, but her eyes remained on Sam.

"I'm just glad we found you," Sam said. "It wasn't exactly easy."

Maggie chortled. "Wasn't exactly easy? Let's see, you with a motorcar, and just the wee village of Overton to search for a schoolteacher who's gained great notoriety for her creative use of farm tools. Sounds like a regular Sherlock Holmes mystery to me."

She smirked and cocked her head. "You want to hear about not exactly easy? Try locating a Yank junior lef'tenant named Henry, wearing an eagle flash on his shoulder. Have you any idea how many airborne chaps have invaded southern England? Furthermore, I did it alone. Using public transport, mind you. I might add that I endured an abundance of name-calling, wolf whistles, and unabashed leers—worst of all from that disgusting Don Juan clerk of yours. Now that wasn't *exactly* easy!"

Sam grinned sheepishly. "Makes me appreciate the jacket all the more."

Chloe returned balancing a platter stacked with petite sandwiches. Mrs. Weatherall bustled in carrying a second tray. "Please forgive us, this is the best we could muster, considering the short notice and rationing."

"Perhaps I could be of some assistance with dessert?" Sam produced four Hershey bars from his jacket pocket. Sterling pulled an additional five chocolate bars from his musette bag.

"Long-stemmed roses and chocolate!" Chloe ogled the Hershey bars. "Maggie, please do assault an American chap more often."

"Oh, the roses." Maggie started for the kitchen with her bouquet. "They must need water. I doubt we have a vase large enough."

"Please gentlemen, sit. Enjoy your sandwiches," Mrs. Weatherall said, waddling to the radio. "I don't mean to be a rude hostess, but I'm in the habit of listening to the *BBC Noon News*."

The room filled with electronic whistling and static as the radio warmed-up. After a minute, a distinguished British voice overpowered the electronic noise. "Heavy resistance still reported around Monte Cassino. Meanwhile the American Sixth Corps continues its courageous push inland at Anzio toward the grand objective, Rome. Allied commanders in theater remain optimistic that the Italian capital will soon fall under allied control. This has been a service of the BBC."

A haunting melody filled the room.

"Oh, listen, it's that new version of 'Lili Marlene,'" Chloe said, pointing to the radio. "The one by that American actress with the German name."

"Marlene Dietrich." Sam smiled and leaned toward the radio. "Her version's catching on fast."

No one spoke over Marlene Dietrich's smoky sensuality.

> Give me a rose to show how much you care
> Tie to the stem a lock of golden hair
> Surely tomorrow you'll feel blue
> But then will come a love that's new
> For you, Lili Marlene
> For you, Lili Marlene

"I, for one, prefer the lyrics Anne Shelton sings," Maggie said, reentering the room. "This Yank version paints Lili as some cheap tart. A regular camp follower. One soldier's gone and another takes his place."

"For most GIs it's not the lyrics so much as Dietrich's voice. More mysterious. Sultry. Like..." Sam explanation tailed off while watching Maggie survey the room holding the vase of roses.

Maggie started toward the end table with the dashing soldier's eight-by-ten portrait, and faltered. A pained expression crossed her face. She went to the opposite corner, moved a small figurine, and placed the vase on an end table alongside the radio.

"Thank you so much, Sam. What a thoughtful gift. Each bloom's perfect. East End flower vendors always throw in one or two inferior blossoms."

"It was nothing." To maintain a straight face, Sam avoided Sterling's glare.

Forty-five minutes of dainty sandwiches, Hershey's chocolate, and awkward conversation later the group dispersed. Mrs. Weatherall bowed out to write her scattered family. Chloe excused herself to wash dishes. Sterling made an excuse about exploring the local trout stream. "Motor pool wants their jeep back by 1730 hours. So I'll meet you back here no later than four o'clock." Sterling grabbed the pitchfork as he departed.

"I don't recall seeing fishing tackle in your motorcar." Maggie looked puzzled. "Perhaps your friend fishes with a pitchfork."

"I doubt it. Otherwise he would've asked you along for lessons."

Maggie smiled. "Touché, Lef'tenant Henry."

"More likely he'll find some quiet shelter and write his wife. They're virtually newlyweds. The war hasn't been kind to their relationship."

Maggie's smile vanished. "I know."

Confused, Sam considered asking her to explain. Maggie's dour expression dissuaded him.

She sighed. "Care for a walk? There's this beautiful park and woods. Part of the Laverstoke Estate. Not so dreadfully far."

Sam's heart leapt, but he tried to play it cool.

He helped her into her coat and caught a subtle hint of perfume. For the first time he noticed her attire—a navy blue wool suite with a white ruffled blouse under the jacket. Her skirt went to just below the knees. It would've remained rather unremarkable on most women, but on Maggie it accentuated her long feminine form.

And this living portrait of wit, beauty, selfless service, and spunk had invited him on a walk. At that very moment, Sam felt capable of jumping out of a C-47 without a parachute.

Before leaving the cottage, Sam discretely removed a rectangular parcel from his trenchcoat pocket, but left it hanging. He was perspiring enough already.

Chapter 12

The Walk

Maggie giggled. "And rumor has it your screams were heard clear to the town hall."

"It wasn't *that* bad." Embarrassed, Sam looked away. "And your students could've silenced me real quick armed with all those tools. What do you teach, anyway—agriculture? Carpentry?"

Maggie led westward at a leisured pace. English cottages lined the right side of the lane. A hedge fence and pastureland were on the left.

"English and English literature, actually."

"Which explains why one of your star pupils referred to Mr. Darcy." Sam swung out his arm and extended the rectangular parcel.

"My, but you do have quite the memory, Lef'tenant." Maggie nodded toward the parcel. "What's this?"

"A gift."

"Another gift?" Maggie's eyes showed a joyful fascination. She stopped walking and took the parcel. After eagerly untying the string and pulling the brown paper away, she gasped and held a new edition of Jane Austen's *Pride and Prejudice* at arm's length. "Sam, how thoughtful." She pulled the book close and parted the crisp new pages. "I've read it at least a half-dozen times. I've written four papers on it. Now I teach it. Yet I've never owned my own copy. Without reservation it's my favorite Austen novel." Maggie bowed in a playful curtsy. "Please accept my deepest gratitude, Mr. Henry."

Sam blushed at Maggie's foreign femininity. "I like Aus...Austen, too," he stammered, "just don't admit it around my fellow paratroopers. We have more in common, too, Maggie. After the war I hope to teach English and English lit."

Maggie gave an exasperated huff and frowned. "And there you had to go and ruin a lovely moment. Do not patronize me, Yank."

Sam felt as if she'd punched him in the gut.

Maggie must've seen the hurt in his eyes. "You must understand, it just seems that you Yanks make sport in deceiving us English girls. Tell us marvelous tales, anything you think we want to hear, in hopes of receiving certain *favors* later."

Sam pointed at the book. "Maybe you carry a little prejudice, like Elizabeth Bennet? But I told you the gospel truth. In fact, my grandfather teaches high school English and literature."

Maggie resumed walking. "Where'd you attend?"

"UCLA." He noted the puzzled look on her face. "Sorry, that's University of California at Los Angeles. It started not all that long ago as a teachers' college. I also play on the baseball team."

Maggie again looked confused.

"Not familiar with baseball, huh? Where do I start?" Sam looked skyward. "I suppose it's like cricket, only more…more American."

"If it's like cricket, why don't you just play cricket?"

He shrugged his shoulders. *Why can't I think clearly? She probably thinks I've never talked to a girl before.*

"Seems you Yanks take pleasure in changing things for no apparent reason."

Walking, he admired her long fingers gliding along the top of a picket fence. "I don't question the system. Not when it says they'll help pay for my education as long as I keep playing baseball."

Maggie smiled. "Sound enough reasoning."

From inside a cottage, he spotted half a wrinkled face peeking from behind a closed curtain. *Oh, great, the cackling hens will broadcast our walk to the whole town before sunset.*

Maggie also noticed the elderly face and offered a big smile and little wave. The curtain jerked closed. "The villagers regard me as daft as a brush. That pitchfork jolly well sealed my reputation in Hampshire County."

She pushed a blond curl out of her eye. "I graduated last year from Birkbeck College. That's part of the University of London. A rather forward thinking Yorkshire Quaker chap founded Birkbeck. He felt that elevating youth out of the lower classes through education might benefit all of England. Birkbeck was also the first college in England to admit women."

"Sounds American to me."

"Hardly." Maggie stuck her hands into her coat pockets. "Theological principals, perhaps. But I don't believe any American model motivated Mr. Birkbeck."

The path narrowed. Decaying leaves littered the way.

Maggie's accent fascinated Sam. He racked his brain for something witty to say that might get her chatty. "So did the good friend, Brother Birkbeck, achieve his dream?"

"Birkbeck remains the sole London college never to close during the Blitz. Received two direct hits, but never closed. Good thing, too, or I'd jolly well still be taking lessons." Maggie stared down at her shoes for five or six steps. "Which, I suppose, would've been of great benefit to your arm."

"My arm's not complaining one bit." Sam waited for eye contact. "Small price to pay for a walk in the English countryside with a special young lady."

"Please, Sam, stop it now." Maggie looked away. "What you know of me is dreadfully scant."

"But the quality of my knowledge surpasses the quantity. You stood with more courage than most men would've when facing a man you sincerely believed to be the enemy—granted, a wrong assessment, yet courageous nonetheless. Then you took considerable time and effort to clean, repair, and return my jacket. I've never met a girl like that."

"And here I was under the impression Los Angeles was *so* cosmopolitan. You really must get out more, widen your social circle."

Ouch! Sam didn't know how to respond. He glanced at Maggie. Her mischievous grin relieved him. He couldn't help but smile back. "Please excuse me. Perhaps studying hard enough to keep my academic scholarship, playing baseball, and working odd-jobs limited my social circle. Take away any one of those three and I would've been building airplanes with the rest of the Henrys."

Maggie vigorously nodded her agreement. "The only exclusive part about Birkbeck College is that it remains reserved for students that can only fund their studies through the sweat of their own brow."

"What did you do to earn your way?"

"Your jacket. Since I was sixteen, even before the War Department made me, I spent at least forty hours every fortnight mending, sewing hems, removing stains."

"If my jacket's any indication, you're quite the expert."

"Thanks, but *never* again. I'm a teacher now, and a teacher I shall remain. I must admit though, the odd occasion arises when I feel like only a daft bloke would ever choose teaching."

"I can see why. That mob that came at me looked like a teacher's nightmare."

"And once upon a time, *not* so long ago, I could be counted among them. Education is their path out of the East End slums. However, that's far from the primary reason I teach. Frequently, while I'm teaching, I feel I couldn't possibly be more alive. As if teaching might be the very reason God placed me on this planet. Have you ever felt that way, Sam?"

"When I parachute out of a C-Forty-seven." He leapt over a mud puddle and offered his hand to help Maggie.

She ignored it. Her countenance turned pensive. "But how much of your life can you spend leaping out airplanes?"

He didn't know how to answer such a question.

Maggie waved her hand. "I'm terribly sorry. That came out entirely too cheeky. I dare say I don't know you well enough to pronounce such judgments. Do forgive me."

"Nothing to forgive," Sam said. *A gal like you could make a guy forget all about jumping.* He looked around and noted the leafless trees scattered on both sides. "As fate would have it, you're the first *English* English-lit teacher I've ever met. Do you like any American lit?"

"American literature? Humph! Strikes me as a colossal contradiction of terms," Maggie said in the mocking tone of a university lecturer. She gave another mischievous grin. "Why don't you try me, my esteemed visiting scholar from the University of California at Los Angeles?"

"OK. Professor…?"

"Professor Crumpetlump."

"OK, Professor Crumpetlump, do enlighten me with your insight on Mark Twain?"

"Take your pick, either too contrived or too colloquial. I do believe an original copy of *Beowulf* would be easier to read than *Huckleberry Finn.* That is for anyone whose *native* tongue is the King's English."

"You may have a point there." Sam rubbed his chin as if in deep thought. "How about Jack London?"

"The man fails to give justice to his great name. So, are Americans so shallow and dull that one must turn to animals to create remarkable characters?"

"OK, maybe London wasn't such a good choice either." He wagged his index finger as if he'd landed upon a brilliant idea. "Now for originality, and depth, how can you beat Edgar Allen Poe?"

"What sort of nation can so celebrate a drug addict who suffered from mental illness? No, on second thought, to be fair, he did not suffer from mental illness, I do believe he rather *enjoyed* it." Maggie chuckled at her own joke.

Sam laughed, too. "Let's forget American writers for a minute. Maybe we could agree on Russian novelists. I enjoy Dostoevsky."

"Enjoy? Certainly, my visiting American scholar did not say, *enjoy?* How does one *enjoy* such horrifically long paragraphs?"

"OK." Sam held his hands up in mock surrender. "There's obviously no way I'm going to win against the renowned Professor Crumpetlump. Perhaps we could find a time when you could teach me some insights into British writers, like Austen?"

"Perhaps."

Sam read no enthusiasm in Maggie's one word reply. Her face betrayed no emotion. Mildly confused, he crossed though an iron gate that Maggie opened and latched with familiarity. As the trail meandered down a narrow valley, they neared the River Test. Sycamore trees along the river transitioned to rolling hills dotted with massive leafless oaks and the manicured parkland of Laverstoke Manor. They crossed the Test on an arched stone bridge. A stone church was nestled in a small meadow. Rather than seeming an intrusion, the church accentuated the landscape's natural beauty.

"It's quite beautiful," Sam said. "Prettier than when I drove through."

"The beauty of many things is only enhanced when you slow down. Even during this time of year—the least beautiful season."

"I think the beauty's enhanced if shared with someone beautiful." Sam cringed, certain his words rang with sophomoric flattery.

Maggie blushed and drifted down a graveled path.

"What I meant," he said, "was that this morning I came through with a dog-faced soldier. And now I'm with a striking young lady. For any red-blooded American male the contrast is remarkable."

His comment failed to elicit a clever retort he'd already come to expect. *I should've kept my yap shut.* He picked up his pace to catch up to her. "Is that the church you went to this morning?" Sam pointed to the stone chapel.

Maggie turned back to face him. "No, Sam, that one—like far too many English churches—is just for show. The occasional wedding, funeral, or baptism is about all it's used for anymore."

"Still prettier than a postcard."

"The British Isles have no want for picture postcard churches. Unfortunately, the view for most Brits remains merely the outside. The war certainly changed that for me. But it wasn't just the war…"

Sam glanced at his watch and frowned. Disappointed, he snapped his fingers.

"A problem, Sam?" Maggie folded her arms across her chest.

"Already a quarter 'til four. Lloyd will be back at your place in fifteen minutes."

*   *   *

The sight of the jeep waiting in front of the cottage came way too soon. Sterling jumped out from behind the wheel and in an exaggerated manner pointed at his wristwatch. As Sam and Maggie neared, Sterling yelled, "Sorry, Miss Elliott, but we've got to roll."

"What's the matter, fish not biting?" Maggie shouted back.

Sterling reached into the jeep and hoisted an eighteen-inch trout in each hand.

Maggie turned to Sam. "How did he?"

"Don't ask. You don't want to become an accessory after-the-fact. Let's just say that Lieutenant Sterling has his ways."

"Gave four more to Chloe," Sterling shouted. "Enjoy!"

"Destroy the evidence," Sam said. "I'd strongly advise tonight's dinner."

He escorted Maggie up the walkway to the door archway. Maggie gave a shiver, hunched her shoulders, and crossed her arms in front of her chest. Her chill baffled Sam. She wore a heavy coat. The return pace had warmed him. He felt no breeze.

"I've got to go now, but I'd really like to see you again, Maggie." He opted for a bold approach—the war's pace didn't allow for hemming and hawing. "Soon, if possible. My schedule—"

"I think that'd be a dreadful idea. Thank you for the flowers, chocolate and," she held up her book, *Pride and Prejudice.* And please express my gratitude to Lef'tenant Sterling for the fish. Good bye, Sam."

Sam stood alone, dumbfounded, staring at a closed door. Shoulders drooped, he turned toward the jeep. Halfway down the walkway he heard footsteps and spun around.

Chloe stepped close. Her toes bumped his Corcoran boots. She fumbled with his breast pocket.

"She's not quite smitten with you yet, Samuel 'Enry. But I reckon she's bloody well close." Chloe's slurred words held a Cockney ring. She looked straight up at his chin. Her breath reeked of alcohol. Her fingers stuffed something into his pocket. "No, not yet." Chloe patted the pocket. "Don't hoist the white flag, love."

Chloe pivoted, stumbled on a flagstone, and went back into the cottage. The door failed to latch and began a slow swing inward.

Sam stepped into the foyer and reached to close the door. The temptation proved too great. He couldn't pass on the chance of capturing Maggie's features one last time. He leaned forward and glanced around the door toward the sitting room. Empty. Feeling guilty for his little intrusion, he ducked out and secured the door. He jogged down the walkway and hopped in the jeep.

"About time." Sterling slammed the jeep into gear and popped the clutch. They departed as if they'd just robbed a bank.

A quarter mile later Sterling asked, "So? How'd it go?"

Sam slapped his thigh. "Turn around, now!"

"Easy, Romeo. What's wrong?"

"Forgot my coat."

"Sure you did, that's why you've got me along this time. You've got a habit of leaving your outer garments around this little burg." Sterling poked a thumb over his shoulder.

Sam looked in the back and pulled his coat from under the trout and pitchfork. He held the coat to his nose. No fishy smell. But he was in no mood for Sterling's fish tale. "How'd it go? Peachy. Like making a night jump at six hundred feet with a streamer."

"Geronimo, Sammy-boy! Such is the game of love. A shame, too, Maggie seemed like a real keeper. Oh, well, write it off to experience. Find out who Clark Gable's younger double in the picture was?"

Sam shook his head.

"What'd Chloe just say?" Sterling asked. "Looked like she was all over you."

Sam gave a dismissive wave. "Not my type. But you're right about Maggie. Now there's a rare catch. The whole package. Knockout looks, brains, sense of humor, loves good books—"

"And quite handy with farm tools."

"Yeah." Sam drifted to silence and remained sullen the entire trip back to Lambourn. A thought plagued him. *Is Maggie fair game, or am I poaching on another man's land? Doesn't matter, she as good as told me to get lost.*

*   *   *

Maggie leaned to look out the dormer window as the jeep pulled away. Her heart raced, her knees weakened—feelings too fresh in her heart's memory.

In one hand she held the portrait she'd snatched from the sitting room before dashing upstairs. In the other she held *Pride and Prejudice.* She put the gift down and clutched the portrait to her breast. "Ian, I'm so s—" Her voice caught in her throat. "I'm so, so sorry."

She opened a dresser drawer and lifted a stack of undergarments. With reverence, she placed the portrait face down in the bottom of the drawer. She let the folded clothes drop back into place and slid the drawer shut.

She collapsed on her bed and curled into the fetal position. Sobs wracked her body. "Why, Lord, why? *Please*, why? I'm not ready. *Please*, no, not again."

Chapter 13

The Cadre

March 1944
Thouars, France

"Step away, *soldat*, you're blocking the speaker." Hauptscharfuhrer Helmut Behr lit a Russian papirosa cigarette.

A smooth-faced private moved away from the portable phonograph, allowing Lale Andersen's plaintive voice to fill the auditorium with "Lili Marlene." Behr scanned the roomful of his neophyte warriors flaunting the *Gotz von Berlichingen* cuff-band. "Silence!"

All conversation ceased. Haughty Aryan faces all turned to Behr.

Behr exhaled a cloud of smoke. The nearby youths suppressed their repulsion to the malodorous foreign tobacco. None dared complain. None dared move away from their company first sergeant—the venerated Knight's Cross recipient.

The lyrics took Behr back to Russia.

> Then I heard the bugle calling me away
> By the gate I kissed her, kissed her tears away,
> And by the flickering lantern's light,
> I held her tight, 'twas our last night,
> My last night with Marlene, my last night with Marlene

"*Ja*, Lili Marlene got us through many a long *Russki* winter night," he said as the last melancholy notes faded. "Those lyrics were penned a generation ago—nineteen-fifteen, I believe—by a *landser* destined for the

Russian Front. Some things never change." Behr blew smoke out his nostrils. "Return to your seats. Where'd we leave off in *Glauben und Kamphen*?"

Scooting and scraping chairs made a racket. He raised his copy of the SS troopers' guidebook, *Believing and Fighting*. Berlin considered Behr's charges in need of thorough political indoctrination. He derisively called many, *Teilzeitdeutsche*—part-time Germans. In fact, many were ethnic Germans raised outside the Fatherland's post-Great War borders. *Let them watch a comrade's head get blown off by a subhuman, then they'll learn what this drivel is really worth.* He took a drag of harsh tobacco.

"Herr Hauptscharfuhrer Behr, could you tell us about fighting the *Kommie*?" a recruit in the front row asked in accented German. "As it relates to material found in our political guidebook, of course."

Behr understood that the soldat—all 200 occupying the auditorium, for that matter—really desired more war stories and less political theory. *I tell them the unvarnished truth and I'll find myself a common schutze in a penal battalion on the next train east.*

He allowed his mind to drift. The vision that first leapt forward was of a beautiful girl—politically speaking, a slit-eyed mongrel mixture of Europe and Asia—dying to the chatter of his Bergmann. *Nein, they want a war story, not a tale of haunting.*

"It was my honor to serve *Fuhrer* and Fatherland with the Totenkopf Division. We'd be well beyond the Volga today if our Rumanian and Italian cohorts had been more zealous in their duty."

He scanned the disappointed faces. Seeing no officers, he changed his tack. "But, I'm afraid as a noncommissioned officer my expertise is quickly exhausted addressing geopolitics. If I may digress to a more personal level—it was early autumn, forty-one." The youthful eyes brightened. "I fought in a motorcycle reconnaissance company. We raced to the very outskirts of Leningrad. My company spent the summer without a front. We advanced, conducted reconnaissance, and advanced yet again, while the rest of the division encircled and collapsed pockets of isolated Reds behind us." He crushed out his papirosa.

"Then, quite suddenly, the tactical scenario shifted. We parked our motorcycles and allowed the whole division to catch up for the final push on Leningrad." His mind's eye viewed the flat, birch and pine wooded countryside, interspersed with potato, cabbage, and beet patches, broken by dank, mosquito infested marshland. "On the southern edge of Leningrad was a low ridge—the Pulkova Heights. There I watched wave upon wave of bombers smash Bolshevism's birthplace.

"Of course our Finnish friends were just as close north of the city and even though they had just that small sector of Russia and we had the rest of the country—from Leningrad all the way to the Caucus Mountains—they failed in their duty to link with us. On a clear day, through my Zeiss field-glasses, I could view the dome of St. Isaac's Cathedral in the city center. We were that close."

He closed his eyes to refresh his memory. September 1941 felt like a decade and three severe wounds ago.

"We needed intelligence on the southern suburb defenses. My *zug* was given the honor of being the first to come off Pulkova Heights and enter Leningrad. Now, the Bolshevik propaganda charlatans claim that no German boot has trod within their sacred city. A lie. I spent a number of days inside. By day, from hidden positions, we observed—mapping defenses, estimating troop composition. By night, we'd move. When the time came to exfiltrate, we decided to leave Ivan some mementos of our visit. The last building we used for observation had communal flats billeting Russian officers. We cut the throats of five Reds in their sleep. Two were commissars. One a Jew."

A hand went up. Behr nodded and the recruit asked, "What lesson for us did you learn from that mission, Herr Hauptscharfuhrer?"

Before Behr could answer, another soldat said, "Quit being such a boot-licker, Erik. That was a different enemy. We'll be fighting Americans or Brits."

The comment spawned spontaneous murmurs across the room.

"Bad assumptions—like that one—and you'll never see your twentieth birthday." He strode closer to his pupils. "That mission taught me much that saved my life several times since, and might yet again. By day, we observed countless women and old men dig an anti-panzer ditch and construct concrete bunkers. A bombed factory continued production of artillery shells. Half-starved twelve-year-old *untermensch* Slavs comprised the workforce. Never again did I underestimate the ability, nor resourcefulness of a determined enemy. You'll serve the Reich well by doing the same."

He decided to return to *Believing and Fighting* before his mouth landed him in political trouble. "Turn to page six. Last paragraph." He read aloud, "'Why must we be vigilant in the preservation of Aryan blood lines?'" Behr grinned. *How brilliant, how age appropriate—the propagandists phrase the text just like a short catechism.*

*   *   *

The afternoon sun cast long shadows across the stone houses of Thouars. The day's lesson on motorized movement to probe enemy lines had gone well. As Behr rounded the rough cobblestone street corner, he inhaled the aroma of rye bread drifting up from the noncommissioned officers' canteen. His stomach growled. Food could wait.

He marched into the 17th SS Reconnaissance Battalion headquarters and gained access to the personnel officer. After exchanging *heil* Hitler salutes with the one-armed major, Behr placed a scrap of paper on the desk.

The major read the single sentence and tossed the paper into a wastebasket. "Hauptscharfuhrer Behr, do not toy with me. I refuse to accept your resignation as company sergeant." The major displayed a Demyansk Shield award on his empty sleeve. "So dispense with the theatrics and simply tell me what you really desire."

"At least one trained sniper." Behr turned so his own Demyansk Shield was more visible to the major. "Sir, must I complete another requisition form? Without at least one sniper, my job is untenable."

"I'm well aware of both your request and the value of a sniper." The major slapped his empty sleeve. "This shield we share has its limits, and you are now pushing those limits. How can I deliver a sniper if you stand here complaining?"

"Then I'll leave." Behr saluted and walked away. Stopping in the doorway, he pivoted. "Herr *Sturmbannfuhrer*, last week while you were away in Rennes, a unit of Russians volunteering to help us liberate their precious *Rodina Mat* passed through."

"And I regret my timing." The major frowned. "I'm completely out of—"

Behr tossed a full pouch of Russian makhorka tobacco onto the major's desk. "The only thing *Russki* I too miss."

The major rolled a cigarette with the glee of a child unwrapping candy. The major's one-handed technique fascinated Behr.

"You'll have your sniper, Behr. Though an experienced one, I cannot assure."

"Why should he be any different from the rest?" Behr lit his own Russian cigarette and exhaled through his nostrils. "They'll all have ample opportunity to gain experience soon enough."

*   *   *

Behr inhaled the bitter cordite. It smelled like German gunpowder, but the American arms produced more smoke. *I would've thought the American munitions industry to be more advanced*, he thought as he examined the firearms arrayed on oiled tarps.

He stood among the *kompanie* sergeants and junior officers on a grassy firing range, listening to a firearms expert demonstrate enemy small arms. The British offering left Behr unimpressed. All were either crude or archaic.

Excessive smoke notwithstanding, he considered the American weapons superior. The heavy slugs made the Thompson submachine gun and Colt 45-auto pistol formidable weapons. Yet Behr wouldn't trade his Bergmann for the Thompson, and the pistol bucked so much that the firearms expert failed to hit a torso-sized target half the time at twenty-five meters. The light machinegun the expert called a B-A-R was accurate, but the twenty-round box magazines could never keep up with a belt-fed MG-42. The small carbine felt light and balanced, and the semi-auto action impressed Behr. Yet its diminutive cartridge made it best suited to troops the expert said it was issued to—officers, drivers, and those manning crew-served weapons.

However, the rifle the weapons sergeant was currently demonstrating seized and held Behr's full attention like the season's first sunbathing fraulein along Frankfurt's Mein River.

The weapons training cadre passed several around. "The M-One Garand is a gas-operated, semi-automatic rifle. Accurate and effective out to seven hundred meters. In Tunisia, I was on the receiving end of a mere *truppe* of Americans—dug-in, holding high ground. Firing only this rifle from over three-hundred meters. They pinned my *zug* for two hours. Over half of us sustained wounds."

"Was this a special weapons squad you encountered?" Behr threw a captured Garand to his shoulder and sighted through the aperture sights.

"Nein. This is the standard weapon issued every *Ami* rifleman."

Doubtful grumblings and curses broke out. Behr scowled at the weapon.

"How about reliability?" Behr yanked the receiver open. "The Russian's had their Tokarev rifle, but the *muzhiek* peasants couldn't prevent it from jamming. Our own Gewehr-43 is very temperamental."

"The American design is every bit as reliable and as our bolt-action Mauser, under all possible field conditions."

The weapons expert pulled out a bundle of rifle bullets held together by a stamped metal clamp and shoved them into the top of the M-1 receiver. He released his thumb and the receiver slammed shut. "The rifle may now be fired as rapidly as you can pull the trigger, eight rounds." The expert shouldered the M-1 and aimed at a target against an earthen backstop 150-meters downrange. He fired seven shots in rapid succession. The gun bucked and climbed with each powerful round. Yet behind the target, small patches of earth and grass erupted. Each shot found the target.

The weapons expert dropped the buttstock from his shoulder. "Do not let this intimidate you or your men. Granted, my expertise is firearms, not tactics nor the will of our enemy. Nonetheless, I observed two great flaws in the Americans that tended to neutralize this rifle's advantages." The expert held up one finger. "First; the individual soldier seemed hesitant to use it. It was not uncommon to take a whole *Ami* platoon under fire and only have four or five even attempt to return fire."

He held up another finger. "Second, the first burst from our MG-42 usually paralyzed their forward movement. To be expected from conscripted and spoiled sons of democracy. Remain aggressive and make ample use of the MG-42. Drop mortar rounds on them when they cower. They can be beaten. Their premiere infantry division ran like frightened hares at Kasserine Pass."

The weapons expert raised the rifle back to his shoulder and changed his point of aim to a wine bottle seventy-five meters down-range. He released half a breath and squeezed the trigger. The rifle roared. The bottle disappeared.

At the instant of the shot, a distinct metallic ringing captured Behr's attention. Behr looked down and spotted a black piece of metal—the metal clip that had held the bundle of eight bullets together.

"Does it do that every time?" Behr picked up the stamped piece of sheet metal.

"*Ja*, of course. The empty clip is ejected and the receiver is held open for re—"

"Nein." Behr shook his head. "Does it make that sound? That metallic pinging."

"*Ja*. It may serve to tell the shooter it's time to reload."

"*Ja!* And it also tells anyone nearby that this American wonder-rifle is empty."

"They never let us get that close. Nor was one ever alone."

Behr nodded, and held his tongue. Russia had taught him that when it came to closing with and crushing your enemy, one should never fully depend upon past or normal occurrences. He turned the metal clip over and over in his fingers and tucked the pinging noise away in his memory.

Chapter 14

The New Battle Cry

9 March 1944
Lambourn, England

Four soggy days and nights of field problems spent in the chilly Berkshire-Wiltshire mud made Sam's wooden folding chair feel luxurious. Enjoying a new appreciation for the coal furnace in the Lambourn Estate guest cottage, he cleaned his carbine.

Sterling shook his head. "Say what you like, Sammy-boy. I just don't get it. You qualify expert with an M-One Garand—one helluva instrument of war, I might add—and yet you opt to carry that sawed-off peashooter."

"They no longer pay me to be a rifleman. Figure I can be a better butter-bar if I'm not tempted to get in a long-range shootout." Sam patted his folding-stock paratrooper model carbine. "Besides, when needed, fifteen shot mags make for a lot of firepower."

"Your choice, your funeral, my friend. Those bullets look like pistol rounds to me. Good luck even hitting—much less knocking down—anything past a hundred yards. And what genius decided to put the safety and the magazine release buttons side-by-side, anyway? You ever hit the wrong button and drop your mag?"

Sam gave Sterling a look that said he wouldn't dignify such a ludicrous question with a response. "I've got a whole platoon of M-Ones and Thompsons for all the knockdown power I'll ever need. And I have no plans to fight Jerry alone. Two days into the invasion you'll be tired of lugging that beast and begging me to trade."

Sterling set his nine-pound M-1 aside. "Listen to us. Two university scholars debating the relative merits and demerits of weaponry. We're regressing."

"Can't imagine why. Takes a major effort and a day's pass just to find a decent novel around here." Sam yanked an oiled patch out of the carbine's short barrel. "And here we sit, what, not even twenty-five miles from Oxford?" Sam thought of another university. "Any mail from the U of I School of Humanities?"

Sterling didn't look up from smearing gun oil on his bayonet. "Nope."

Sam hurt for his friend.

*   *   *

15 March 1944

Sam shoved open the door labeled "A Co. 2nd Lts." and hurled his helmet toward his cot. It struck the wall, causing a chip of plaster to fly across the room.

"That ring-knocker clown! *I'm* the one to blame for the lack of aggression. Or, *I'm* getting too close to the men for effective command. Or, *I'm* too independent!"

Sterling ceased dealing cards. Three card-playing lieutenants departed. Sterling gave a mock pout. "Bad day at the office, *honey*?"

Sam snarled. "Can it, Sterling! At least you get to lead a platoon."

"Yeah, and my lieutenant's bar is still the same color as yours." Sitting on his cot, Sterling gathered the deck of cards and leaned back until his shoulders rested on the wall.

"How'd you like to be the whipping boy for *First* Lieutenant Nelson Forefathers-Came-Over-on-the-Mayflower-Mother-Went-to-Vassar Pettigrew?"

"No, thanks. We should all say a prayer for Captain Tarver's good health and non-promotion every night—bless his Tennessee National Guard soul. Scuttlebutt has it our favorite first lieutenant is in line to be Able's next executive officer. That might be enough to request a transfer to a *leg* unit."

"Don't patronize me. Nothing's bad enough to become a straight-leg." Sam rubbed his temples. "Got any aspirin?"

"Just put up with Pettigrew. There's no denying he knows his stuff. West Point men don't stay anywhere long anyway. You'll be platoon leader in no time. Then some new butter-bar will be ragging about that obnoxious Lieutenant Henry."

"If there's even a platoon left to lead. He's now managed to gut morale." Sam sat on his cot and fitted the liner back into his steel helmet. "Don't they require psychology one-o-one at *any* military academy?"

"Afraid you lost me."

"OK, arriving in England, what was Colonel Johnson's battle cry?"

"One Five-O-First paratrooper is worth three soldiers," Sterling said in a passable Jumpy Johnson impersonation. "He had us repeating it to the men at every opportunity."

"And did it increase morale?"

"You bet, but—"

"But, it led to new problems, right?" Sam leaned forward. "Problems that could've been anticipated. Like every pub in Swindon and London getting busted up by Geronimos taking on numerically superior opponents from France, Poland, Britain, Canada and even our own straight-leg and Air Corps units. We had to tone it down and rein the men in before Ike caged us all."

"True, but you've got to admit, his three-to-one ratio turned out pretty darn accurate."

Sam wagged a finger. "The point is that the very concept had consequences when taken off base and into the world. Right?"

Sterling nodded as he shuffled the deck against his belly.

"Well, Pettigrew has come up with a dandy new one he thinks will somehow boost the men's fighting spirit. He's used it at least a dozen times in the past two days. It's killed morale." Sam's voice turned more pensive. "You just can't remove a man's hope and expect any good to come out of it."

"For a guy who wants to teach, Sammy-boy, you sure have a gift for losing your audience."

"Stick with me. You know how paratroopers are younger than other soldiers?"

"Only proves that as a person ages he gains enough sense to not volunteer to jump out of a perfectly good airplane." Sterling grinned at the standard parachute infantry cliché. "Is that the psychology one-o-one you're referring to?"

Sam shook his head. "Apparently Pettigrew had nothing better to do one day, so to fight boredom he dug into the personnel files. He discovered that every member of First Platoon, except for himself, Jennings, and me, are under twenty-one and will be for another six months. So, Pettigrew starts yelling in that shrill voice of his, 'You'll never see twenty-one, boys. So kill as many Krauts as you can!'"

"Ouch." Sterling grimaced. "That's his new battle cry?"

"Bingo! But today it's *my* fault," Sam said, stabbing his finger repeatedly into his sternum, "when Captain Tarver criticized First Platoon for lacking its old aggressiveness."

"Well, buddy, I'd be relieved. Pettigrew spared you. You made it to twenty-one."

"Very funny." Sam shoved a stick of Wrigley's Spearmint into his mouth. "But I can handle Pettigrew's little mind games."

"That wall and your helmet might beg to differ."

Sam twisted on his cot and fingered the gash in the wall. "Listen, it's simple logic and psychology. No one has the right to trash another man's hope." Sam punched his fist into his palm. "A hope for a future. You remove that—as Pettigrew is well on his way doing—and I'm afraid to think about how a man might act. A man with nothing to live for, nothing to look forward to but being dead and forever nineteen. How do you command and control such a man in combat?"

"Don't lose sleep over Pettigrew's new little battle cry. You've got a bunch of wholesome American boys. I bet that kid they call Pinball was even an altar boy. Jennings and Springwater will keep them in line. So don't get your knickers all in a wad, Sammy-boy."

Sterling pulled out the ace of diamonds—the symbol within the 101st Airborne for the 501st Parachute Infantry Regiment. "And never forget, one Geronimo is worth three of any other army."

Chapter 15

The Hunt

11 March 1944
London

A conductor blew two shrill whistle blasts. Yet another train rolled out Waterloo Station. More coal-tainted steam billowed to the high roof.

Sam glanced at his wristwatch for the tenth time in five minutes and folded another stick of Wrigley's Spearmint into his mouth.

Waterloo Station represented a transportation center worthy of the grandeur of its battle namesake. A dozen tracks terminated under an expansive covering supported by steel girders seventy feet overhead. Vendor's kiosks and stalls dispensed travelers' needs. Porters scurried between the trains and the imposing four-story cut-limestone and brick structure that housed ticket agents, offices, and a hotel.

Sam scanned the flowing tide of humanity and recognized assorted American, Canadian, and British uniforms. A few uniforms and languages—perhaps Danish, Polish, or Dutch—defied precise identification.

A few hours earlier he had considered his task quite simple—wait in a train station and pick out a tall, attractive blonde amidst the sea of uniforms and testosterone. He had strategically positioned himself near the train platforms and passages that served as human funnels connecting Waterloo Station to the London subway system.

An occasional paratrooper near Sam's rank wanted to talk shop. He'd met two British airborne lieutenants and a guy from St. Paul in the

82nd Airborne—a Sicily combat jump veteran. Sam regretted his aloof demeanor—always looking past his new acquaintances, distracted, not catching questions they asked.

He considered his purpose in London as no different from the average GI—except he was hunting for one girl in particular. For the other GIs about any female would do. Which is why most took the Bakerloo Line three subway stations northwest and got off at Piccadilly Circus. Sam held no desire to return there.

The debauchery and primal urges of his fellow countrymen tended to put Sam off. He viewed it akin to a colossal, yet perverted, deer hunt. Many enjoyed the deer camp camaraderie, all had high hopes of bagging their quarry, and most were equipped with time-tested bait—nylons, lipstick, Hershey bars, and plenty of folding money—needed to lure London's young ladies into range. The safety conscious hunters packed Army issued prophylactic kits or purchased condoms from enterprising newspaper boys.

An inebriated British sailor stumbled up and gave a sloppy salute. "Pardon me, Yank Captain, sir, but what time is it, chap?" The rum on the sailor's breath almost bowled Sam over.

Holding his breath, Sam said, "Nineteen-hundred hours," and pushed past the drunk. Needing a place where he could gather his thoughts and plan his next move, he wove through travelers toward platform number eleven.

He reached a lamppost away from the crowd and pulled out the crumpled page Chloe had stuffed into his pocket. The evening air, laden with the scent of steam and coal, cleared his head. A dull gas lantern allowed him to read—for what had to be the fiftieth time—the cryptic numbers and names list. The list began with Waterloo Station, followed by three-digit numbers—843, 871, 887, 903, and 937. These had proven to be trains with Overton stops. Over the past six hours, all five trains had huffed into the station and disgorged their human cargo. All without any trace of Maggie.

With each train, Sam's hopes surged and sunk. A portly conductor had assured him that all passengers had detrained 937, the last train on his list. But the conductor gave a sliver of hope when he informed Sam that 981—a train not on Chloe's list—originating in Andover, would be the last train with any possibility of carrying Overton passengers.

Yet, five minutes earlier, Number 981 had also arrived, without Sam's quarry.

Sam stared at the crumpled paper. Scribbled names connected by arrows followed the Waterloo Station train numbers. Through time spent in the train station, Sam had discovered that this portion of Chloe's cryptic note represented a schematic for the subway route, ending with Aldgate

Station. Last on the list was a street address: 47 Albert Street. Sam assumed the address represented Maggie's London home.

Do I just show up knocking on her door? He tried to imagine his own father's reaction to some foreign soldier showing up at the Henry door desiring the company of one of Sam's sisters. Sam chuckled. *Sure wouldn't want to be in that poor sap's shoes.*

A whole day's leave wasted hunting Maggie. He yanked the gum wad out of his mouth and flung it on the tracks. His inspired masterplan had called for him to bump into Maggie and make it appear as pure serendipity.

To complicate matters, his mind was still doing mental gymnastics over the handsome British soldier in the portrait. Sam was basing his hope upon Chloe's suggestion—and only a desperate man or outright fool would place his faith in a tipsy foreign girl's suggestions.

He brushed at a speck of lint on his class-A uniform sleeve. Sighing, he closed his eyes. *Time to call off the hunt? Or, stalk 47 Albert Street?*

He leaned back against the lamppost.

*   *   *

Maggie exited the empty train. She preferred to finish grading book reports over jostling down a crowded train aisle pressed between young men in wool uniforms worn too many times between launderings. Five minutes after the doors had opened a conductor cleared his throat. She looked up to find a vacant carriage. She stuffed the reports into her valise—atop her very own copy of *Pride and Prejudice*—and exited.

The platform had almost cleared. Unimpeded, she hurried to make up for lost time. A Saturday spent grading a backlog of assignments and exams, along with following up on a matter of discipline promised two rowdy students, had managed to delay her three hours. She considered herself fortunate to catch the last train—No. 981, originating in Andover and taking on passengers at Overton and Basingstoke.

She glanced at a platform clock and hoped her parents weren't growing alarmed over her tardiness. The recent rash of air raids—what some were calling the Little Blitz—tended to heighten her parents' anxiety. Fortunately, the present weather appeared too heavy to allow an air raid. However, the evening was young. Weather may change. Or, the Luftwaffe might blindly drop bombs through the clouds. It had happened before.

Three-fourths of the way down the platform she noticed a lone American underneath a lantern, head turned slightly away. His eyes appeared closed. Nearing him, she identified the screaming eagle shoulder-flash. *Perhaps that chap knows Sam.* She entertained the notion of asking, but declined. A Yank, eyes closed, leaning against a lamppost was either ill or drunk—more than likely, both.

The Yank propped a foot on the lamppost and shifted his position. She noted that the man's countenance wasn't that of a drunk. Rather, he seemed pensive.

The realization jolted her like an electrical shock. *It is Sam Henry!*

Averting her eyes downward, she veered away from the lantern light. *Just keep going. Don't look back. Did he see me?* She sped up to a subtle trot. *No denying I saw him. And I ran like a frightened schoolgirl. What do I have to fear?*

Slowing for the crowd pressing to navigate the funnel to the Underground passage, a Scripture verse came to mind. How did it go? Something from the First Epistle of St. John the vicar had quoted the previous Sunday. *"There is no fear in love..."* How did it end? *"...because fear hath torment."*

Quite to the contrary, her experience suggested that love, not fear, inflicted dreadful torment. Moreover, how could the term *love* be used in the context of Samuel Henry? Therefore, the passage was far from applicable to her relationship with the Yank. *What ruddy relationship? There's jolly well no relationship.* Nonetheless, it felt pretty much like sheer torment, so it had to be fear—an echo of extraordinary pain.

"Hey, missy, I'm enjoying the view, but you want to get it in gear? You're holding up traffic."

Startled from her thoughts, Maggie glanced over her shoulder, finding a short American sporting pilot's wings. "Oh, please, pardon me. Seems I forgot something." She struggled back against the crowd, like a fish swimming upstream.

"Let me give you a hand." The pilot winked. "I've been told I'm good at uncovering hidden treasures."

She glared down at him. "Do you have the gall to address American ladies in such a rude manner?"

Looking away, the pilot worked his way around her, mumbling American gibberish.

Repeatedly excusing herself for bumping people with her valise, she wove through the crowd. Away from the funnel, she craned her neck and looked toward the lamppost. Sam—or the Yank paratrooper she had imagined as Sam—remained, covered in an eerie pool of yellow light underneath the lantern.

She approached from behind. With each step trying to drive the knot from her stomach.

*   *   *

"Waiting for Lili of the lamplight?"

Sam spun around. Maggie! His quarry had stalked him. And she looked gorgeous.

A locomotive whistled. Steel wheels screeched.

"Not since I heard—from good authority, I might add—that the Yanks had turned Lili Marlene into some cheap tart. Or was it a camp follower?"

Maggie blushed and looked away. "Both, actually. *Touché*, Lef'tenant Henry." She looked back, smiling. "Never imagined I'd run into you in Waterloo Station."

"Just sightseeing." He feared his grin might betray his excitement. "Exploring London through the subway."

"Underground. We call it—"

"Underground or subway, it's still an adventure for a guy from California. LA's built around the car. I drove a buddy's…" Sam let words tumble out as he concentrated on the real riddle. *How in the blue blazes did she find me first?*

"Adventure on the Underground?" Maggie folded her arms across her chest. "This from a chap who enjoys leaping from flying airplanes?" she said in the tone of a teacher who'd caught a student in a bit of monkey business. "Your explanation stretches credulity, Lef'tenant Henry."

He shrugged. "Just playing the tourist."

Maggie's eyes sparkled with mischief. "Platform Number Eleven, Waterloo Station is on every tourist's itinerary." The corners of her mouth took on a flirtatious set. "Right up there with Big Ben and Buckingham Palace."

"Trying to get my bearings. And what happened to calling me Sam?" He pivoted and pointed. "That way to Birkhead College? Maybe I can enroll in a night class—"

"Birkbeck. It's Birkbeck College, University of London. And I'm afraid you Yanks are too overpaid to qualify for admission."

"Well, since I'm so overpaid, maybe I can buy you dinner?"

"How's your arm?"

"Just name the restaurant."

She made a show of looking behind him. "I don't see your friend."

"Gone fishing. Like a good steak?"

Her smile lessened. "Do you really think you can just bump into a proper English girl and make a date on the spot? Does American arrogance have no limits?"

"No on both counts. Hungry? I'm still buying."

Her smile disappeared. "You Yanks assume you can simply buy anything. My time is not for sale, Lef'tenant."

Sam cringed. Time for diplomacy. "Look, Maggie, I'm really sorry if you took that wrong. My intentions are honorable." Maggie's expression seemed to soften, so he said, "I'm also a tad nervous about any nearby farm implements, in case I get you upset."

"This is London, so you're a wee bit safer."

"Then please consider me a friend. Is there anything just friends could do? No money. No pressure. No expectations."

"Sam, meeting you like this is a bit of a surprise. I have plans. I'm already a good three hours late—"

"Who're you meeting?"

"None of your ruddy business." Maggie looked at her feet. "My parents and sister, if you must know. And I'm afraid I must—"

"Mind if I tag along? I'd rather meet a real English family than aimlessly wander London streets like the rest of the GIs."

Maggie shook her head. "Blast it all, but you are the persistent bloke, Samuel Henry." She seemed to contemplate the toes of her shoes for a minute before looking up with a weary smile. "Fine. You win. They'll have supper waiting, and even with the rationing, my mum always prepares too much. Claims I don't eat enough. Perhaps you could educate my sister on cheeky Yanks. Follow me."

Sam held out his hand. "May I carry your luggage?"

"A gentleman who jumps from airplanes! Why, thank you." She handed him the valise. "It may also help hold your compatriots at bay."

He followed her to the Underground, trying to make small talk, but the random station noise and Maggie's rapid pace made conversation nearly impossible.

"Breakfast, six-thirty to nine. Checkout, noon. Room service menus—"

Maggie looked over her shoulder wearing a puzzled expression. "Excuse me. Did you say something about *room service*?"

"You walk ahead, without speaking. I follow in uniform, your luggage in hand. I feel like a bell-hop."

Maggie's eyes sparkled. "Do behave yourself and you'll be tipped handsomely." She sighed. "I'm sorry, but we must make haste."

They ventured deep under Waterloo Station and made enough subterranean turns to disorientate his Ozark woodman's sense of direction. Disobeying his instinctive internal compass, Sam followed Maggie onto a Bakerloo Line carriage, went one stop to Charing Cross, and transferred to the Metropolitan and District Line heading east. Just as diagramed on Chloe's note, they exited at the seventh stop. Unlike Waterloo Underground Station, Aldgate Station was shallow. He surfaced to a dim and dingy world smelling like a rain-drenched bonfire.

Maggie waved her arm in an arc. "Welcome to my neighborhood, Sam. London's East End."

He followed her up Whitechapel Road, down Brick Lane, and northeast to smaller side streets. He made out dark recesses where buildings once stood. Only piles of brick rubble or an occasional charred beam remained. The faint light and bomb damage notwithstanding, he surmised that he'd never find this neighborhood on any tourist itinerary.

"Remember the lad who came at you carrying the fire ax?" Maggie asked.

"You pinned me and he got all dressed up to finish me off."

"It was his day to play Mr. Darcy." Maggie pointed to a gaping dark hole across the street. "His family lived there. Third floor, in back."

"Did they…?"

"Jeremy and his brother were in Overton at the time. His mum was taking shelter with several thousand others, yours truly included, at Liverpool Street Underground Station. Every earthly possession destroyed. His father perished last year on some far-flung corner of the Empire—irony is that Jeremy still can't find Burma on a globe."

"Why'd the Krauts bomb here?"

"Near enough to the docks. It gets worse either east or south of here. The Nazis don't care one whit if they mostly hit homes. I have three pupils who've lost parents in the bombings." Maggie twisted and pointed back toward central London. "A couple of miles behind us a German pilot parachuted from his damaged bomber. His slow descent assured a rather large reception committee. They beat him to death before the authorities arrived."

"Can't say that I blame them," Sam said.

Maggie shook her head. "I can."

"When *I* was the downed Kraut airman, your intent wasn't exactly benevolent."

Maggie wagged a finger. "To be fair, I never intended to kill you."

"My arm begs to differ."

"My point is, there is nothing particularly noble or Christian in vigilante justice."

While he pondered how to extricate himself from yet another opinion aptly shot down, Maggie trotted up a landing and inserted a key in a double door.

He looked up from the street and took in the three-story brick structure. Half the ground floor was below street level. Empty flowerpots lined the outside of the windows. At odd intervals, bricks seemed blackened, sooty. Uneven boards covered several windowpanes. He presumed bomb blasts had blown them out. Tape crisscrossed the remaining glass. No light escaped the blackout curtains. "Sure is a large house."

Maggie opened the door. "Hardly for six families."

He bounded up the steps and concluded the only way to avoid further verbal blunders was to keep his observations to himself. A diplomat might term the neighborhood as economically depressed. The less polite would just call it what it was—a slum. On their Overton walk Maggie had shared her working-class roots with him, but she seemed so articulate and classy that he figured she was fashionably exaggerating her humble beginnings.

He followed Maggie up several wooden steps and down a wide and dark hallway. Random floorboards sagged and creaked. The aroma of potatoes and pork lingered. His stomach picked that moment to growl more loudly than the floor creaks.

Maggie giggled but didn't look back.

"Sorry, haven't eaten in over eight hours," Sam said.

"And with all that Yank coin? What a shame. You're at the right place now. Mum will look after those hunger pangs."

Maggie rattled with her keys and pushed a door open. "Hello! I've brought a guest home."

Sam stayed behind Maggie in the dark recesses.

"Chloe come 'ome with you?" A Cockney accented, matronly voice advanced toward the door. A woman appearing just shy of fifty, slim, and almost as tall as Maggie stepped into the doorway, wiping her hands on her apron. "We was starting to be more than o' bit worried." The woman threw her arms around Maggie. "We was comforted only by the fact there was nary an air raid siren." The woman pushed Maggie away to arm's length and looked her daughter in the eye. "Them Yanks pester you again?"

"Not unless you count this one." Maggie motioned toward Sam.

He stepped into the light spilling from the doorway. "Good evening, Mrs. Elliott."

Mrs. Elliott gasped and threw her hand to her chest. "Blast it all, Maggie! You could've given your dear mum fair warning before I goes and sticks me foot in me mouth." She gave Maggie a swift backhand to the shoulder.

"Relax, Mum. This is Lef'tenant Samuel Henry. And when it comes to sticking one's foot in one's mouth, you two might find you share much in common."

Mrs. Elliott's expression turned even more surprised. Her gaze came to rest on Sam's forearm.

A round, middle-aged man and teenage girl arrived behind Mrs. Elliott. The man's face beamed at the sight of his daughter. He plowed his way through the doorway and hugged Maggie. Stepping toward Sam, he extended his right hand. His fingers appeared stained and plump, like burnt sausages. His pinky finger ended at the first joint. "Edmund Elliott's me name." Maggie's father stopped pumping Sam's hand. "Pardon me, lad, did I hurt your arm?" Edmund touched Sam's right forearm with a tenderness in sharp contrast to the handshake.

"Oh, no. No, you're fine. It was my left arm, and it's about all healed."

Edmund slapped Sam's shoulder. "Do come in, lad. The missus coddled some spot on bangers 'n mash."

Sam was having a hard enough time understanding the thick Cockney accent, but Edmund's last phrase lost him entirely. His expression must've betrayed his confusion.

Maggie translated. "He likes the sausage links and mashed potatoes mum prepared."

The teenage girl subtly elbowed Maggie.

Maggie scowled. "No need to resort to violence. Sam, this is my sister, Daphne."

He smiled and nodded. Daphne stood three inches shorter than Maggie, with slightly darker hair, but possessed the same eyes that would allow all but the legally blind to pick her out of a crowd as Maggie's sister.

Maggie took her valise from Sam. "Shall we eat then? Lef'tenant Henry just informed me he's ravenous."

Chapter 16

Failed Diplomacy

"It was delicious, thank you. I'm stuffed."

Careful not to again bump the loose-jointed dining table, Sam sat his chipped teacup down. Maggie's description of supper had led him to anticipate an abundance more in line with American standards. He found the bangers 'n mash long on potatoes and short on sausage. Half filled, his stomach was already expressing disappointment.

The dining and living rooms merged into one room. Gas lamps illuminated the crowded space. The blackout curtains made the flat seem even smaller. Mrs. Elliott scurried back and forth to an unseen kitchen. The noise from the kitchen suggested a space equivalent to a walk-in closet. A short hall held three doorways—fabric served as doors on two. Two prints—one of an English pastoral scene, the other of Tower Bridge— hung on the walls, along with a studio photograph of the Elliotts. Sam estimated the family portrait to be ten years old. The early adolescent Maggie appeared gangly, yet happy. A younger Edmund beamed with pride, resting a hand on each daughter's shoulder.

"What do you do for a living, Mr. Elliott?" Sam asked.

"Please, lad, call me Edmund." His eyes reflected the same mischievous joy as Maggie's eyes. "Boiler room mechanic at a clothing factory. Learned me trade in the Royal Navy during the Great War."

Mrs. Elliott—he still had only heard her referred to as Mum—scurried into the room. "Maggie told us 'bout your battle smock. Sounded like a lost cause to me, but when Maggie gets an idea in her head, heaven help us all."

Maggie stepped from the kitchen and began clearing dishes. "So, Sam, what advice might you offer my naïve sister concerning these Yanks that infatuate her so?"

Daphne shot Maggie a dirty look.

Sam had no doubt whose side he had to take. "First and foremost, don't believe a word they say."

Maggie walked away carrying dishes. "So, as an American soldier, does that apply to you as well, Lef'tenant Henry? Dare we trust your words?"

He ran his hand back through his hair. "Just offering a rule of thumb. Many are near Daphne's age, far from home, and enthralled, yet inexperienced with pretty girls."

Maggie reentered the room. "I see. And you'd be much older, closer to home, and disinterested, yet quite experienced with pretty girls."

"No, not exactly. That's not what I said." He looked across the room for assistance from the only other male. Leaning against her father's overstuffed chair, Maggie put an arm around Edmund and kissed his forehead. The grin across Edmund's face told Sam he was on his own in this particular debate.

"Daphne, you just have to be careful. Don't trust every friendly American. They have more spending money each month than most had in a year of civilian life. Naturally, they want to spend it on a pretty girl. Their intentions aren't always honorable." Feeling his diplomatic duty completed, Sam leaned back and crossed his arms—topic closed. "I understand you attend Birkbeck too. Want to be a teacher like Maggie?"

"Not like Maggie," Daphne said. "But I do want to know more about you Yanks. Do I understand you correctly? Some Yank strolls up and offers an evening at a top restaurant, he pays everything. I should beware of such a chap?"

"Spot on!" Maggie wagged a finger at her sister. "Now you're catching on. It could jolly well even happen in a train station! And remember what Sam said, the Yank's intentions are likely *far* from honorable!"

Sam held up his hand. "Wait just a minute, that's not what I said."

Maggie returned to the table. She looked at Sam with the same mischief in her eyes that Sam had seen on the Overton walk. "I've even heard that some Yanks make gifts of chocolate and roses. How about them, Sam? Dare we trust their motives? Or are such chaps no different from your common Yank?"

"Chocolate and roses!" Daphne looked skeptical. "I've not seen sweets since the Blitz, and only a blasted rich chap could get flowers now. Whoever told you that is daft."

"Oh no, I assure you, I have it on very good authority." Maggie nodded vigorously. "Please, do help me, Sam. Have you heard of any such extravagance?"

"I might know of an instance." He squirmed in his chair, yet looked Maggie straight in the eye. "But is it fair to pass a blanket judgment on the American? Maybe he was new to England. Maybe he didn't fully understand the customs, or what's been going on here for the past four years. Maybe the American should get a second chance to prove his sincerity."

"But you just said not to trust them." Daphne pouted. "Now I'm confused, how do you give Yanks a chance to prove their sincerity if nothing they do can be taken at face value?"

Sam shrugged. "Maybe invite him to meet your family. Let them help evaluate his character."

"Aye, that piece of advice may work for Maggie, but me second daughter, well…" Edmund squinted and pointed his pipestem at Daphne. "She'd be bringin' home a platoon's worth of ruddy Yanks every fortnight."

"My concern is for Daphne." Maggie leaned forward in her chair. "The whole of Britain is an armed camp. But that won't last, now will it, Sam?"

"Well, I'm just a second lieutenant—"

"Be that as it may, even the most junior lef'tenant knows you Yanks are only here a short time." Gazing at the ceiling, Maggie sighed. "And it doesn't take a general from Sandhurst Academy to know that we're mere months from a cross-Channel invasion." She faced her sister. "All these Yanks will be gone in very short order, Daphne. Then, eventually, they'll all sail back across the bloomin' Atlantic…or maimed, or de—."

"Bad form, Maggie," Edmund said with a father's disapproving frown.

Maggie's eyes locked with Sam's. "I just don't want to see my little sister hurt." Her eyes became moisture-laden. She gathered the mismatched cups and saucers and scurried to the kitchen.

Edmund shifted in his overstuffed chair and sucked on his pipestem, despite the fact that he exhausted his one bowl of tobacco a quarter-hour earlier. "So, what is it your father does in Los Angeles?"

"He builds airplanes for Douglas Aircraft," Sam said, avoiding the correct, past tense. "Cargo and transport. C-Forty-sevens. The RAF calls them Dakotas."

"Aye, must be one busy bloke then." Edmund slapped his pipe bowl rim against his palm. "He must be right proud having a lad turn out like you—an airborne officer and the like."

"I suppose." Sam shrugged, not wanting to delve into painful family matters. "It gives me a kick jumping out of planes he might've built."

Mum reentered the room and tried to hide a yawn.

Sam glanced at his watch and stood. "I've sure enjoyed the evening, but I've got to get across town. My room's at the Russell Square officer's club. Not sure how—"

"While in London you must attend church with us," Mrs. Elliott said. "I'm sure Maggie already invited you."

"Actually, no… Can't say I've ever attended an Anglican service."

"Won't be long before too many Englishmen can say the same," Edmund said. "Up to a couple years ago I can't recollect the missus and me choosing to hear a vicar since Daphne's christening."

"Did the war change that?" Sam said.

"More like Maggie," Edmund said. "She put the religious boot to me flabby arse."

Mrs. Elliott shot her husband a disapproving glance and asked, "Sam, where might you attend services in California?"

The assumption caught Sam off-guard. He ran his fingers back through his hair. "Grew up Baptist."

Joy spread across Mrs. Elliott's face. "Then you've read Spurgeon."

"Who?"

"Charles Haddon Spurgeon. An Englishman," Mum said. "Preached right here in London, he did."

Sam tried to look apologetic. "Not familiar with him. Sorry."

They set the time and place for meeting the next morning. Edmund marked out on Sam's Underground map the best route to Russell Square. Sam pretended he needed help finding the Underground. To his pleasure, Maggie volunteered to guide him. As it ended up, Maggie didn't lead him all the way back to the Underground, but only as far as the corner of Brick Lane and Whitechapel Road. A heavy mist obscured visibility and lent a sense of seclusion.

"So, Lef'tenant Henry, does your dinner offer still stand?" Maggie asked without looking at him.

"You bet." He tired to subdue his elation. "Name the time."

"Tomorrow. After church."

"I'll have all afternoon before I have to catch my train." His mind reverted to Daphne's lessons. "But can you trust me?"

"Trust extends both ways, I'm afraid. There are things…things perhaps I should make you aware of."

Sam held a hand up, oath-like. "I do hereby promise, I'll be all ears. No chocolate. No flowers."

"But your friend's trout were quite tasty. For tomorrow I think I'd prefer beef, though. That is what you asked earlier, wasn't it? If I enjoyed steak?"

"Then steak it is. See you in—"

Maggie's chin quivered. She pivoted and trotted back toward Albert Street.

Baffled, Sam stood speechless as she vanished in the mist.

Chapter 17

Pain

12 March 1944
Spitalfields, London

"The vicar was spot on today." Mum adjusted a shawl over her head.

Sam found himself more impressed by the architecture. He took in the columns and steeple dominating the front of Christ Church, Spitalfields. Fog obscured anything past thirty yards.

"Aye. But I reckon the vicar will be preachin' on forgiveness again right ruddy well soon." Edmund donned a tweed tam-o'-shanter to cover his palm oil plastered jumble of salt-and-pepper gray curls. "What 'appens after the Hun bombs us more than seventy-times-seven?"

Daphne sidled up a little too close to Sam. "What did you think of the service?"

Pushing a blond lock back into place, Maggie said, "Daphne, it's quite refreshing to hear you taking an interest."

Sam took a half-step toward Maggie. "A tad more formal than my old Baptist church. My preacher liked to shout."

"Shouting might do us a bit o' good," Maggie said. "Wake up folks just occupying pew space."

Mum's coat collar showed three obvious moth nips. "Maggie tells us she's showing you a few sights."

Sam counted off on his fingers. "Parliament, Big Ben, Westminster Abbey...whatever else time permits."

"Well, if we don't see you again," Mum said, "rest assured the Elliotts will be saying prayers for you."

Edmund removed his hat and bowed slightly. "Aye, lad, that we will. And on behalf of the Elliotts, I want to beg your forgiveness for me eldest daughter sticking you."

"Nothing to forgive, sir. In fact, I've told Maggie how much I admired her courage to protect her students."

"You're indeed an officer *and* a gentleman." Edmund hooked two fingers under his tight shirt collar and tugged. "Just see to it that you ain't as foolhardy as me daughter when you be face-to-face with real Huns." Edmund punctuated his well-wishing with a two-handed handshake. "Just do your duty, get back to California, and become a right proper teacher."

Daphne parted with her parents, leaving Sam with a flirtatious smile and wave.

Maggie led Sam down damp streets lined with three and four-story dirty brick buildings.

"Your family seemed to know a lot about me," Sam said.

Maggie shrugged. "Our initial meeting was quite traumatic. One might expect the event to be spoken of among family."

"I've been trying to figure out last night."

"What's there to figure out?"

"The corner you backed me into when I was trying to help you with Daphne." He took a deep breath. "Then alone, you tell me you want that steak dinner. Which am I to believe?"

Maggie halted with a little stomp and spun on him. "Which to believe? Surely, you don't really want to discuss *which to believe*. You…you arrogant Yank!"

He threw up his hands to signal surrender.

"Do you think me so naïve? Or is it that you think yourself so clever? Am I supposed to believe that you just happened to bump into me at Waterloo Station?"

"Wait just a minute! It was *you* who found me, not—"

"Only because you were either too daft or too blind to see me first! I tested you on the Underground. When we pulled into Aldgate Station I said nothing and you started to get off before I ever moved. You knew where I was going. I felt a bit like a hunted animal."

He winced, reached into his breast pocket, and pulled out the crumpled paper. Pinching it between his thumb and forefinger as if it was foul, he passed it to her.

Maggie smoothed it out and inspected it. "Chloe?"

"I did *not* ask for it. Nor do I regret that she gave it to me. Never intended to make you feel uncomfortable."

Staring at her shoes, Maggie bit her lower lip.

Sam took off his overseas cap and pushed his hand back through his hair. "Look, I blew it. How about I just scram?" He pivoted.

"Wait." Maggie kept her gaze on her shoes. "I said I had some things to tell you."

"Yeah, and you've said plenty. I deserve—"

"That wasn't it." Maggie looked up. Her expression had softened. "I need to talk."

"OK. Then what?"

"That steak you promised." The corners of her mouth turned upward. "I hope."

"Fine, but can we find someplace besides the sidewalk to talk? It's getting too damp and cold for my Californian blood."

North of old Spitalfields Market, he followed Maggie into a working-class diner. The white walls and tables were in marked contrast to the brown concrete floor. The room was devoid of customers. Sam's boot soles detected a tackiness associated with a thin layer of grease and dirt. The diner smelled like scorched gravy. He scrunched his nose. "Never would've guessed a place like this for a good steak. But you're—"

"No, silly," Maggie said. "That task may prove more taxing than returning your battle smock. We popped in here for a spot o' tea."

They gravitated to a corner booth. The middle-aged waitress wearing a dirty apron approached with a cigarette dangling from the corner of her mouth. Maggie ordered tea, Sam coffee. The waitress's infrequent visits indicated either poor service skills or superior social skills—either way, they had privacy.

Maggie looked him in the eye. "Sam, it would appear you're pursuing me. And I must admit, a part of me is quite flattered. But…"

Sam's heart sank.

"…I find little reason to risk my affections with a soldier. Or, more to the point, certainly not with a Yank soldier."

Bad coffee churned in his stomach. "It's not like I'm from Mars. I think we have a lot in common. I just wanted to spend some time together. See what happens from there."

"Is it worth the risk, Sam? You're in England a short time. It's the nature of your duty. So why even start?" Maggie refreshed her tea from a small pot. "Remember, in Overton, the soldier's portrait on the end table?"

"Not distinctly." He chose not to mention the tea spill it caused. Or, the awkward moment with the flowers. Or, how it tormented his thoughts daily since.

"His name's Ian Fletcher. We were engaged to be married and I loved him beyond words." A single tear glided down Maggie's clear cheek. "There, I've said it."

Sam gazed into his coffee cup.

"We met at the University of London. He was starting divinity school. Wanted nothing more than to shepherd a flock. Oh, he was idealistic. All about duty and justice."

Sam looked up to see another tear slide down her opposite cheek. Feeling like an intruder, he retreated to his coffee.

"Well, his sense of duty and justice landed him in the Seventh Armored Division." Maggie's voice gained a sarcastic edge. "Monty's favorite. His celebrated Desert Rats." She took a sip of tea and made a sour face. "Needs more milk."

Sam swirled his coffee. "You don't have to tell me this."

"March of forty-two—almost exactly two years ago—he shipped out. I begged him to marry before he left. He insisted we wait, there'd be plenty of time after the war. He didn't see marriage just then as being fair to me. He said there was the odd chance of leaving a young bride as a widow." She dabbed her eyes with her handkerchief. "Or worse, a new mum with no father for the baby. He reasoned that a young woman shouldn't be a bride of just a day or two, only to become a widow forever. He said it would hurt too much. But I can't imagine it possibly hurting more."

Maggie sobbed into her handkerchief and lightly blew her nose. "We wrote every chance we got. Oh, he was jolly well proud of his crusade against Fascism. They promoted him to sergeant. Gave him command of his own tank crew. He shepherded them like they were his wee flock and he loved them so. I'd read his letters and find myself envious over the affection he held for his men. Then he got his real prize. All the way from Detroit, Michigan—a new Sherman tank. You have heard of the Sherman tank, haven't you?"

"Sure, it's our best—"

"Well I bloody well wish I never heard of that blasted tank. He loved his crew and he loved his Sherman. Named the silly thing *Nimrod*. Painted on its side, 'Even as Nimrod the mighty hunter before the Lord.' He got a big kick out of putting scripture on the side of his new Sherman, and now my jealousy extended to a blasted machine. Other commanders named *their* tanks after their girl back home. But not Ian, no. And now I thank God he didn't."

Sam glanced up from his coffee.

Maggie stared into her tea and stirred it in slow circles. "He was killed November third, nineteen-forty-two, the Second Battle of El Alamein."

"Didn't Monty win El Alamein?" He bit his lip too late.

Maggie dropped the spoon in the cup with a heavy clank. She looked across with red eyes, tears pouring down both cheeks.

"Are all Americans as naïve about the nature of war, Lef'tenant Henry? Do you think men only die in defeat? Perhaps victors get to resurrect their dead?"

"I'm so sorry, Maggie." He gave the back of Maggie's hand a gentle touch. "Yeah, I guess in some ways I am naïve."

The waitress came halfway across the diner, then retreated.

"So, Ian's letters just stop. I hear nothing. Absolutely nothing. What am I to do? Assume the worse? Every day filled with anxious hope. Hope, but no letter in the post. Now if we'd been married I would've been the first notified. But a fiancé can't be next-of-kin, and both of Ian's folks had passed." She sipped her milk-laced tea. "His legal next-of-kin was some alcoholic uncle up in Leeds. I write him and I write him, but receive no response. So, in desperation I travel to Leeds and learn that Ian was killed November third. By then it's January sixth!"

Maggie looked Sam in the eye. He couldn't bear it and turned his gaze back into his empty cup.

"Ian's platoon leader and company commander also died that day. Nimrod's crew was scattered—mostly in hospitals. Each assumed the other had informed me. Finally, I got a letter. One of Ian's wee flock wished to tell me of Ian's heroic death. His intentions may've been noble, but his letter didn't help, not one bloody bit."

The waitress refilled Sam's coffee. She set a folded handkerchief next to Maggie's cup. "For you, love. Looks like you need it more than me."

Maggie picked up the hanky and dabbed her eyes. "Seems a German antitank gun hit Nimrod square in the front. The shell passed clean through. Ian was standing in the turret and was merely struck in the foot by a bit o' flying metal. Nothing too serious, mind you. He only needed to push his lower body out the hatch and he would've been safe. But with smoke filling the tank, he ducks in to evacuate his crew. One makes it out right away, unhurt. The one next to him, the gunner, I think, had a broken arm, so Ian lifts him out. Ian calls out again, but the two men left deep in the tank don't respond."

Maggie unfolded the hanky and dabbed her eyes. "So he drops down and finds them both unconscious and bleeding. Somehow, he manages to get the driver pushed out of his hatch. But, while Ian is still pushing the last of his flock out, the tank bursts into flames. He's caught inside. Almost got out. They could see his hands protruding above the hatch, but he only had one good foot and had spent all his energy saving his crew. The future

Reverend Ian Fletcher burnt to death as his wee flock looked on, each one quite helpless to do a ruddy thing."

Sam took a long sip of tepid coffee and sighed. "A brave man. Very heroic." He took another sip.

"Oh, absolutely. Nothing but praise and medals for Sergeant Fletcher. But for me? I'm left all alone with ghastly images and unfulfilled promises. Everyone soon forgot Ian. I refused. A year passes and well-meaning folk say it's time to move on with my life. And what exactly does that mean? Am I supposed to *move on* as if Ian never even existed? Never captured my heart? I longed to give my whole being to him—mind, body, and soul."

Sam bit his lower lip. He felt like a cad for pursuing Maggie as if she was some carefree sorority pledge. "You can't ask the impossible of yourself." He picked each word with utmost care. "Almost seven years ago my brother passed away—more than my brother, he was my best friend. A drowning accident. It haunts me to this day."

Maggie gazed toward the ceiling. "They say we all have our cross to bear."

Sam sighed. "I just want you to know that I have some empathy. You can talk openly with me."

Maggie looked him in the eye. "Sam, I am speaking openly." Her tears were flowing less freely, but her large honey-brown eyes remained inflamed and full of sadness. "One of Ian's mates said I should blame America. Said the Desert Rats took to calling your Sherman tanks Ronsons."

"Ronsons?"

"You know, *Ronson*—the cigarette lighter with the advertisement slogan, 'Just one hit and it lights every time.'"

He winced and sipped cold coffee.

Maggie attempted a weak smile over a quivering chin. "But what good does harboring unforgiveness do? Only leads to bitterness." She looked away. "But the pain of losing Ian is indescribable." New tears rolled down her cheeks. "Sam, part of me longs to get to know you. I won't deny it. Why else would I return your battle smock? But my heart screams, 'Maggie, don't you dare risk that sort of pain again.' I haven't consulted an atlas, but I do believe a very large ocean and whole continent separate London from Los Angeles. Then there's the whole unpleasant matter of this far from finished, blasted war."

Sam stared into his stale coffee.

Maggie slid out the booth.

Sam slapped a one-shilling note on the table and scooted down the bench seat.

"Please, Sam, no need to get up. I just need to visit the loo."

After a few minutes, she returned and sat, red-eyed yet looking refreshed. "I do hate this war so. The death and mayhem. Youth uprooted and rushed. You and I've been robbed of our best years." Maggie sighed. "Perhaps we could start all over? I mean just you and me—meet again like normal people, in normal times."

Sam slowly shook his head. "Not sure I would if I could. Even if you'd just turned your back on me and marched out that door. It's all worth it." He pretended to sip coffee to buy time to articulate his thoughts. "I believe that everything I am today is what my past choices have made me. Destiny *is* choice."

Maggie frowned. "Is it? Not sure I agree. I *am* a mottled combination of my own choices—both good and bad—and where God has providentially placed me. Then I must factor in my interaction with the choices—again, both good and bad—others have made involving me. Too often, it makes little sense. It's like looking at the reverse of an elaborate tapestry. But someday I expect God will show me the front and, somehow, it will all make perfect sense. And it will be beautiful."

Her philosophical statement both puzzled and intrigued Sam. Before he could ask her to elaborate, his stomach emitted a loud growl.

Maggie grinned. "Which reminds me, I know an overpaid Yank lef'tenant who owes me a steak."

"Which reminds me, I know a tall, *English* English teacher—quite handy with farm tools, I might add—who owes me a tour of London."

"I understand she requires payment up-front. Let's find that steak and we should just have enough time for some Westminster sights."

*   *   *

"Too bad about that restaurant taking bomb damage. Ended up being our best bet for a steak, too." Sam ate his fish 'n chips on a bench along Bishops Road near Paddington Station.

Maggie gathered her greasy fish 'n chips newspaper wrapping and stuffed it into a dustbin. "And Leicester Square, no less. Might have been this poor East Ender's only chance to dine like a princess. Sorry all that hunting for a steak shortchanged your tour—some ruddy worthless guide I turned out to be."

"And I've a mind to report you to your supervisor." Sam smiled. "I would too if it hadn't been for the impersonations you did of half the folks buried in Westminster Abbey. I think I've finally got a handle on sorting out all the Georges and Anns."

"That be the case, then, Lef'tenant Henry, you're a far sight ahead of most Britons." Maggie reached to brush a piece of fish breading from Sam's class-A jacket.

Sam noticed a slight indentation on Maggie's ring finger. His gaze didn't escape Maggie's notice.

"Aye, the mark remains. The ring was so blasted tight I barely got it on my hand. But I dared not breathe a word. Took every pence Ian owned to buy an engagement ring." Maggie spread her fingers and held her hand in front of her face. "In his memory I kept it on it until a few weeks ago. Yet to be frank, it wasn't purely for sentimental reasons. Served a practical purpose, too—it kept you Yanks away. The sober ones, anyway."

Maggie touched the ring's mark. "Sometimes it's like an amputee's phantom limb. I know it's gone, yet I still sense its presence."

Sam tried to sneak a peek at his wristwatch.

Maggie frowned. "Must you leave for Lambourn?"

"Afraid so. However, you still owe me a *complete* tour. And I still owe you a steak. I can get another pass next weekend. How about it?"

"No, Sam. I daresay it won't work."

His shoulders sagged. He stuffed four French fries into his mouth to hide his dashed hopes.

Maggie snatched his last fry. "No, I'm afraid London is quite out of the question."

French-fry sticking out his mouth he looked into Maggie's large eyes. Her cheery expression baffled him.

"Next weekend I'm scheduled to stay in Overton. My turn to oversee pupils. So…perhaps you can come to Overton?"

"You bet." He waded up his grease stained newspaper wrapper. "Yeah, I'll be there even if I have to parachute in and run a gauntlet of pitchfork wielding teachers."

Maggie laughed. "I'll see to it all pitchforks in Hampshire are locked away."

Chapter 18

Desire

April 1944
Thouars, France

"Nein! I refuse to accept this!"

Behr crumpled the *kompanie* inventory sheet in his hand. "Herr *Hauptsturmfuhrer* Von Gremp, we comprise half the reconnaissance force for an entire panzergrenadier division. To report enemy disposition we must be able to stay ahead of assault regiments operating at *blitzkrieg* speed." He slapped the wrinkled paper with the back of his hand. "Unacceptable!"

"I may lack your experience, Hauptscharfuhrer, but I'm no *dummkopf*. The *Fuhrer*—in his quest for certain victory—is focused on unleashing new super-weapons assured to force Churchill and Roosevelt to—"

Behr's glower cut Von Gremp off mid-sentence. "*Jawohl*, and since we would expect nothing less from our Fuhrer, spare me the political lecture." He took a long drag on his papirosa. "We must have more transport or our youthful charges will never live long enough to populate the new Reich lands with deserving Aryans."

Behr stared at Von Gremp's own whiskerless chin.

Von Gremp pointed to the inventory sheet. "What is allocated *is* what we get."

"You continue reasoning like someone driving a Wehrmacht desk and sunning themselves in Crete, Herr *Hauptsturmfuhrer*."

Von Gremp shot Behr a look suggesting that the senior sergeant had better watch his step.

Behr narrowed his eyes. "Quit acting like the Prussian general's son, you're *Waffen* SS now."

Von Gremp's shoulders shrunk and he looked away. Just over a year earlier, the Red Army had trapped the elder Von Gremp, with the entire Sixth Army, in Stalingrad's frozen hell. His father, along with nearly two-dozen other generals, disobeyed Hitler's direct order to fight to the last man, and surrendered with Field Marshall Von Paulus. If that wasn't enough humiliation, *Generalleutnant* Von Gremp became a pawn of the Soviet propaganda machine. To vindicate the family name the junior Von Gremp denounced his father and joined the Waffen SS.

"Tell me what we need," Von Gremp said. "*Need*, Behr, not merely desire."

"Being trapped in the Demyansk Pocket ended all my illusions of desire." Behr's partially paralyzed face produced a crooked smile. "We need another *Achtrad*." Behr pointed at the eight-wheeled SdKfz-231 armored car tucked away in the nearby woodlot. The leafy branches protected it against Allied fighter-bombers. A machinegun and 20mm automatic cannon protruded from the small turret. "It's fast and has the most reliable radio. If Berlin balks, point out that an *Achtrad* has little value apart from reconnaissance."

"Berlin will deny. Our battle in France will be defensive."

Behr shook his head as if he was dealing with a remedial *schweinehund*. "When the Allies invade we won't wait here entrenched. Our first clash will be a meeting engagement. Hopefully, *very* near the beach. We must have another Achtrad. Request five if that's what it takes to get one."

Von Gremp looked back to the inventory sheet. "Nonetheless, our troop transport problem remains unsolved."

"Obviously." Behr's irritation crept into his voice. "Find us four more halftracks. In one we'll mount a mortar. And get as many motorcycle sidecars as you can. Make up a reason to justify the number."

Von Gremp jotted notes. "Does the sniper have the skills you desired?"

"He could shoot the eye out of a running roebuck at four hundred meters. He also carries fifteen-kilos of baby fat. Which reminds me," Behr said, eyeing the strained tunic buttons at Von Gremp's midsection, "the *entire* company needs a five kilometer run, every day."

Chapter 19

Confusion

15 April 1944
East End, London

Daphne planted a kiss on Sam's cheek. He blushed.

"It's really no big deal. Just trade my cigarette ration for the smokers' chocolate."

Daphne's gaze locked on the pile of Hershey bars on the dining table. "It's still more chocolate than I've seen in four bloomin' years."

A haze of vanilla-scented tobacco smoke hung in the flat like a London fog. It emanated from Edmund's overstuffed chair. "May the good Lord bless you, Samuel 'Enery, for your kindness." Edmund stuck the pipestem into his mouth, a contented smile on his face. "Tobacco more fittin' a ruddy blue-blood than some East End bloke."

"Edmund, did you see the fruit? Canned peaches and pears." Mum acted almost giddy as she examined an odd shaped can. "And a dozen tins o' this canned meat."

"Spam. Like bangers, only without the casings," Sam said. "According to Mr. Hormel, it's made from a hundred percent pork. But you may want to try it before you thank me." He scrunched his nose. "A lot of GIs aren't too fond of it."

"It be more than our monthly meat ration," Edmund said. "We're much obliged."

It seemed to Sam that the whole Elliott household couldn't have been more thrilled with his visit—except Maggie. In the three hours since his arrival Maggie had acted preoccupied, her usual banter and sharp wit absent. Her mood baffled Sam. Each of the five previous dates had brought increased closeness. However, the best steak in London—or any steak, for that matter—still eluded them and had become a running joke.

Maggie reached for his dirty dishes, but avoided eye contact. He pushed his chair back, grabbed two plates, and followed Maggie into the cramped kitchen.

"Maggie, what's wrong?" Facing her, he took her hands and gently held them. "Did I do something?"

"Not at all." She stared at the warped wood floor.

"Then why the cold shoulder?"

"What?"

"Why are you giving me the brush-off?"

"If you wish to communicate with me, Sam, I must insist you speak proper English."

He lowered his voice to a whisper. "You know what I'm getting at. Something's wrong, but I can't read your mind."

"Then perhaps it'd be best if I showed you." Maggie yanked her hands out of his grasp and fled the kitchen.

The front door rattled. Sam stepped out of the kitchen in time to see Maggie depart the flat. He stood dumbfounded.

"Don't just stand there gawking like some daft Frenchman, Sam," Edmund said. "Go after her, lad."

*   *   *

Sam and Maggie got off the Underground at Paddington Station. Nearing the station's west doors, Maggie halted and stared at a mixed huddle of GIs and English girls. Money changed hands and a laughing GI walked away with two heavily made-up girls—one latched to each arm. There was something familiar about the face and hair of the one on the left. *Candace from Piccadilly Circus? Billy's Candace?*

"I pass through here often on my way for a stroll through Kensington Gardens," Maggie said. "Yesterday, just minding my own business, I was first propositioned by your countrymen, then threatened by these charming representatives of English femininity."

Taking Sam's arm, Maggie barged past the remaining GIs and tarts, and exited Paddington Station.

Strolling past colorful storefronts along Craven Road, Maggie looked toward the overcast afternoon sky and said, "It baffles me just how a morally justified war has degenerated into so much immorality. I dare say our soldiers will return to find tens of thousands of babies fathered by foreigners."

Sam's mind went back to his one visit to Piccadilly Circus. "I don't expect it's all that rampant. A few girls looking to make money. Maybe some like the lark of it all. But most English girls behave themselves."

Maggie dropped his arm. "Oh, so it falls upon us English girls to resist? Behave ourselves? You Yanks are merely innocent bystanders."

Sam shook his head. "Soldiers just want a little fun before they ship out. Shipping out knowing full well that Fate's about to roll the dice with their life. So I guess—historically speaking—their behavior's only natural, maybe even normal."

"So it's natural? Even normal, is it? Fun and games. All perfectly acceptable as long as no one gets hurt?"

"In a way, I suppose." Sam cringed. "Please don't twist my words. You have to make some allowances for wartime conditions."

"So, why don't you take part, Sam? I trust you have all the same male urges. And you're certainly not getting any of *that* sort of gratification from me." Her face contorted. "And you too expect mortal combat. So why not, Sam?"

His lips parted to answer but she didn't give him a chance.

"After all, *wartime conditions*. Thousands of miles from Los Angeles. There are no shortage of willing ladies. So why—?"

Sam cut her off with an upheld hand. "It's just not me."

"That much I know, and I'm quite thankful. But why not?" Her question rang sincere.

"Does a guy have to have a reason?"

She glanced at a pair of shoes in a storefront window and frowned. "I'd like to think a gentleman would."

"OK, then." He shoved his hands into his pants pockets. "Because, on a certain level, it's just not right."

Maggie nodded her head. "And why not?"

Sam hunched his shoulders and let them drop. "It's not the way to treat and respect others. Others you care about."

"Why not?" Maggie folded her arms across her chest. "For that group back at the station, one might argue that arrangements were beneficial to all parties concerned."

Sam shoved his hands deeper into his pockets. "Maggie, come on, I'd never betray you."

Maggie halted. "Why not?"

"Because, I really care for you." Sam tried to make eye contact. "And if the past few times together are any gauge, I think you care for me, too."

"Indeed I do, Sam, but that's hardly enough."

Sam watched her stride away on those long legs. After a half-dozen paces, Maggie looked back. "Kensington Gardens is this way."

Sam caught up.

Maggie halted and stared at her toes. "So, I must ask again—why?"

"Can you be more specific?"

"Why are you a perfect gentleman in most every regard?"

"That's a bad thing?"

"It can be if you can't give me a why."

"A why for what?"

"Sam, you're charming, well-read, intelligent, sensitive, and well-mannered. You don't smoke and never swear." She reached out and touched his cheek. "Did I mention handsome? You always take care to smell quite pleasant. Your generosity exceeds Father Christmas. My personal library has quadrupled since knowing you. My family absolutely adores you. I've never seen you drink—much less get drunk—and you've never so much as laid one inappropriate hand on me. Even at those times when, perhaps, I wish you had."

"I must've missed that." Sam let a small grin turn the corners of his mouth. "Exactly when—"

"I'd think a man of your intelligence might catch the hints." Maggie returned his grin. "I simply wanted you to hold me close. Feel your lips against mine. Maybe gently caress me. Yet you didn't. As usual, you did the right thing. But why, Sam? *Why?*"

She wanted me to kiss her? Caress her? He took a breath. "Maybe I don't want to mess up what we've got. No regrets."

"But why? I'm sorry, but you must remember where I'm coming from. In a few weeks, I pray daily that it won't be so, but in just a few bloody weeks you might end up in a grave!" Her voice cracked. "What's there to regret from the grave?"

The answer that popped into his mind first seemed best. "You getting hurt, again."

"Really? So what? You go on and on about UCLA and your Dr. Rosenfeld. If he's right that we're merely dust returning to dust—ruddy worm food—then so *what?* Why even care, Samuel Henry?"

"OK, Maggie, I give up. What're you getting at?"

"Only the dearest part of my life." Her voice cracked again. "And we don't share it. At first I thought we did." Anguish etched her face. "Maybe a naïve presumption on my part. Maybe I let myself fall for you too soon. Lord knows I tried not to. Remember that Sunday you found me in Overton?"

She's fallen for me? His heart lurched. "Right, Overton. I'll never forget it."

"My behavior was ghastly. Part of me so wanted to chase you away."

"And a part of you wanted me to stay. You didn't have to invite me on that walk."

"You're right, but not about why I invited you. I hoped that walk might uncover something in you to loathe. Something that might repulse me. To end the odd romantic fascination that had grown since the day I mistook you for a Luftwaffe pilot." Maggie halted and looked him in the eye. "We walked nigh on four miles and despite my best efforts I found nothing in you to squash my schoolgirl infatuation. In fact the exact opposite occurred. And your gift, Jane Austen no less…oh, how you frightened me that day, Lef'tenant Henry."

Sam folded a stick of Wrigley's Spearmint into his mouth. "The war rushes everything. I assumed no ring, no problem. There's no time for the whole boy-meets-girl thing…" Sam's words tailed off upon seeing the faraway look in Maggie's large eyes. "That's not it, is it?"

Maggie bit her lower lip and shook her head. Her eyes glistened.

"Then, what?"

"Sam, I've been trying to talk about it for weeks, but every time I do you seem to take things off on some philosophical tangent. Kant this or Hegel that. You haven't given me hardly a chance to say that for the past four years the central part of my life has been my faith. It provides all the *whys* I need to keep going. Please listen, I'm not speaking of dry textbook theology."

She looked down at the sidewalk. "Sam, you're searching for answers in trendy philosophy, but it will always come up short when you ask the *whys*. That's what I was driving at when I asked why you don't behave like other Yanks. You have no reason for the upstanding way you act. Morality with no foundation. Which means it cannot endure." She met his eyes. "My faith…how can I word this…"

Sam reached under his collar and jerked out the chain with his dog tags. "I was taught the Bible as a kid. Went to Sunday school 'til I was fifteen." He pointed at a metal tag. "See there. Even got a 'P' stamped in my dog tags. That's 'P' for Protestant, just like you. Maybe I'm interested in deeper answers. Maybe I'm not so all-fired sure about things as you. But come on, Maggie, it's not like I'm an atheist or—"

"Yet you entertain dangerous ideas. You carp about your silly little Lieutenant Pettigrew taking away the men's hope—and rightly so—but where's your hope? Upon what is your hope founded? Hope and faith work together. Both must have an object. My faith doesn't remove the pain, but it gives me more than merely an academic framework for the whys. Sam… you just don't get it, do you?"

Sam pulled off his overseas cap and pushed his fingers back through his hair. His gut tightened into an empty knot. His sojourn in the world of romance had been too short. In his novels it always seemed that love conquered all.

"So now what?" he whispered and cringed in anticipation of the answer.

"Let's walk."

They crossed a street and entered a gate near a storybook English cottage—an entrance to Kensington Gardens. The afternoon sunlight revealed a rolling landscape—pathways curving through green lawns, past gnarled oaks and massive sycamores. The trees budded with promises of new life. Scattered daffodil and jonquil flowerbeds bloomed. A series of pools with fountains emptied into a small lake. The fountains were still, the water fouled and moss-laden. It matched his mood better than the flowers.

Sam heaved a sigh. "Bet it'll be gorgeous here in a few weeks."

"Much sooner than that. An explosion of flowers. Roses and foxglove. The treetops full. Lush grass." She stared at a fountain. A pair of robins darted toward the water and flittered away. Maggie swallowed hard and looked away from Sam. "What's a butter-bar?"

Sam scrunched his forehead. "Where'd that come from?"

"Please, just answer me. What's a butter-bar?"

"OK. I'm a butter-bar." He tapped the gold bar on his cap. "GI slang for a second lieutenant."

Maggie stared at his jump wings. "I was right then."

"Right about what, sweetheart?"

She swallowed twice. "What compels you to take part in a suicide unit?"

Suicide! Where'd that come from? Sam ran his fingers back through his hair. "You're not making sense."

Maggie's chin quivered. "Some errands for Mrs. Weatherall took me to Oxford Circus. This inebriated lef'tenant wearing one of your eagle flashes bumps into a couple of young officer chaps with a multicolored triangular patch with a two on it and—"

"Second Armored Division," Sam said. "Go on,"

"One chap raises a fist to strike the airborne lef'tenant, but his mate stops him and says, 'Give the guy a break, every airborne *butter-bar* is just a dead man walking.'"

"Oh, is that all?" Sam rubbed her shoulders gently. "Don't worry, Maggie. Those clowns were just exaggerating. There's bad blood between our divisions going way back to Fort Benning."

Maggie pulled a hanky out of her handbag and dabbed her eyes.

"My platoon's not training to die, Maggie. Sure, we're training to fight. Fight smart as a team. And we're good. The best. I've told you about the men. Sergeants like Jennings, Springwater, Lazeski—they're tops."

She frowned skeptically.

"Really. Captain Tarver knows his stuff. Lieutenant Pettigrew was trained at West Point. And the men! Wow! We've got this big blowhard, Private Collins, a country boy. And this sawed-off little powerhouse of an Italian kid, Private Vigiano. Call him Pinball. I could go on and on, but this I know for sure, we *will* take care of each other."

Maggie covered her quivering chin. "Soon you'll get your first fight. Then what?"

Sam opened his mouth to reply.

Maggie stuck a finger to his lips. "Then they'll find you another fight. And another. And another. And yet another. Then what?"

"Then I come back. You've given me a reason to live—"

"Oh, poppycock!" Maggie threw the hanky into his chest. "Don't utter such rubbish. Pure naiveté." She leaned into him. "Sam, Sam, haven't you heard anything I've been saying? I'm not enough." She wiped a finger under each eye. "This whole off-we-go-to-war routine may be new to you, but not for me. Remember? I jolly well wasn't enough to bring Ian home."

Sam gazed at Maggie's honey-brown eyes. *A guy would never tire of looking into such eyes.* His throat tightened.

Maggie sniffled. "I'm afraid I must say goodbye, Sam. Look me up when this whole dreadful mess is ended and we'll see where it goes.'"

"I'm coming back. I still owe you that steak. Then we'll work things out, together—"

Maggie leaned over and kissed his cheek. She let it linger longer than a friendly peck. "No, Sam, I'm afraid you must work it out yourself."

PART II

STIR UP THE MIGHTY MEN.
Joel 3:9

I want to travel in Europe… I know that I am only going to a graveyard,
but it's a most precious graveyard.

FYODOR DOSTOEVSKY
The Brothers Karamazov, 1880

Chapter 20

Tumult

16 May 1944
Thouars, France

Behr shot bolt-upright in bed. The explosive blast had showered shattered glass across his blanket. Bitter cordite filled his nostrils. Moonlight poured in through the blown windows. Another artillery shell crackle-howled overhead and exploded down the street. Four more whistled past in quick succession, each striking farther away. A walking barrage.

He leapt out of bed and pulled his pants on. While ducking his shoulder under a suspender, the door burst open. A wide-eyed boy under an oversized helmet staggered in.

"Americans, Herr Hauptscharfuhrer!" The boy clutched a machine-pistol to his chest.

Behr pulled his camouflage battle smock over his head. "Which direction?"

"Every direction, Hauptscharfuhrer, dropping from the sky like a plague of locusts." The teen's knees visibly shook, the helmet wobbled.

The un-soldierly sight disgusted Behr.

Another shell howled overhead and the soldat dove under the bed. Behr cursed and kicked the boy's exposed boot. "Get up, *schweinehund!* Find Hauptsturmfuhrer Von Gremp. Tell him to meet me in the church steeple."

The boy ventured out first, one hand pressing his wobbling helmet, the other clutching the MP-40. Exiting the gray stone house, Behr found it disturbing that only the foreign chugging of heavy machineguns registered in his ears. The fast ripping of the MG-42s and chattering pop of the MP-40 failed to join in.

Reaching the main Thouars boulevard, he and the boy turned left. He bent at the waist and trotted up a cobblestone slope. A ground fog hung in the low ground. His jagged cheek scar grew inflamed.

The boy topped the crest and came face-to-face with an advancing American. The American raised his M-1 and fired twice into the boy's face. The boy's bloody helmet hurtled backward and skipped on the stones until striking Behr's boot.

He paid it no attention. Another sight stunned him to immobility. The wonder-rifle's muzzle flashes had revealed a chimera.

He raised his Bergmann and jerked the trigger all the way back to fire full-auto. There was no rapid chatter of gunfire. No reassuring recoils against his hands. He relaxed his trigger finger and pulled again.

Nothing!

The American rifle bore loomed in his face. Another flash emanated from the M-1 muzzle. The aberration confronted him a second time. This time the image appeared distinct. The flash illuminated a face both beautiful and haunting—the blended femininity of Asia and Europe. *Anya!*

Behr lashed out. His backhand smacked flesh—soft, distinctly feminine flesh.

He shot bolt-upright in bed. Sweat rolled off his brow and stung his eyes. He panted for air. He caught movement in the corner of his left eye. A naked female rolled from his bed and donned a nightgown. She spewed angry French oaths.

Half-awake, he failed to convey a name to his tongue—except Anya. The woman rushed out and slammed the door.

Too late, he called out, "Claudette!"

French profanity assaulted the closed door. Behr shook his head. A dream. He rolled out of bed, put on his pants, and ducked his shoulders under suspenders. He cautiously opened the bedroom door and stepped into the dining room. The wavy-haired French brunette sat at the table in dark shadows. She uncorked a bottle and poured one drink.

"I want you gone by morning," Claudette said in broken German. She downed the liquor, poured another glass—*calvados* by the smell—and took a slow sip. "Helmut, you harbor many demons deep inside your soul."

"Did I hurt you tonight?"

"*Oui*! But tonight was nothing. Not compared to two nights ago. When you…you, I don't know the word in German." Claudette pulled the string hanging from the bare lightbulb over the table. "You did this."

Behr squinted and shielded his eyes from the harsh light. Claudette gathered her hair to expose her long neck. His eyes adjusted. An ugly set of bruises confronted him.

"You muttered something and 'Anya, Anya.' A mixture of German and Russian, I suppose. I was too busy trying to survive to understand your babbling."

He searched his memory. *Am I guilty?*

Claudette slapped his face. "I almost die at your hand and you don't even remember!"

Shame prevented him from looking her in the eye. He lit a papirosa and inhaled.

"Why do you smoke that Russian rubbish?" Claudette lit a *Gauloise*. "You're a virile man, Helmut." Claudette took a long drag. "But you buried your soul in Russia. You are dead. Your soul just hasn't informed your body yet. I have no wish to share in your torment a moment longer. Again, I ask…no, I insist, you depart immediately."

"*Ja*. As you wish, *ma chere*," he said in mixed German and French. "And perhaps as soon as I'm gone, may I suggest you visit the library. Find a book on English. The language, that is, not the people. It would be a wise investment. I suspect the next man to share your harlot's bed will speak English as his native tongue."

*   *   *

17 May 1944
Overton, England

Maggie stared out her classroom window. The ancient glass distorted the spot where Sam had landed. The compost pile was gone—scattered for fertilizer over Court Farm fields.

Books banged shut and chairs noisily scooted as her last pupils departed for the day. The cacophony of unsupervised children in a crowed hall drifted into the classroom.

"Maggie?"

She made a furtive finger swipe under each eye before pivoting. Chloe stood in the doorway.

"Something the matter?" Chloe pulled the door closed and moved toward Maggie.

Maggie's throat tightened. She nodded and returned her gaze to the spot where she'd met Sam. She felt Chloe's arm embrace her shoulder.

"Thinking of him?"

"Feeling like some heartless witch," Maggie said. "I certainly mucked this one up. He was never anything but a real prince to me, and I go and toss him aside like so much rubbish. I fear for the hurt that may come, yet I jolly well fear that I'll never see him again even more. Oh, what I'd give for just another evening together."

Chloe squeezed Maggie's shoulder. "It's hardly too late to do something about it, Maggie."

Chapter 21

The Inevitable

18 May 1944
Lambourn, England

The flurry of activity on the parade ground between the Lambourn Place estate house and the Nissen huts made Sam chuckle. "Reminds me of when I was a kid. I'd kick a red ant nest just to take in the chaotic show that followed." He turned to Platoon Sergeant Jennings. "Phillips get the mortar loaded?"

Sergeant Jennings shifted his stubby cigar to the corner of his mouth. "Truck number five, sir."

Sam made a notation on his inventory list. "Machineguns?"

"All squared away, Lieutenant."

"Personal gear?"

"Tagged and stowed," Jennings said. "Had to promise Mazooti a Kraut dagger to store that pitchfork with your bag. That goldbrick wanted a dern Luger. Talked him down."

Sam caught sight of Private Morton picking his way through the scurrying mob. The men, overburdened with weaponry or support equipment, trudged in an ant-like procession toward a double row of deuce-and-a-half trucks.

Morton halted in front of Sam and saluted. "They said you need me, sir."

Sam made a notation on the inventory form. "They were wrong."

"If it's all the same to you, sir, I'll just stick around until you do." Morton folded a piece of Wrigley's Spearmint into his mouth.

"It's not all the same to me, Morton. Go wait with second squad. I want everyone staying put in one spot. Relax. Join a card game."

Morton trotted off looking like a scolded puppy. Sam scanned beyond Morton's bobbing head and saw the tall pair of 2nd Squad sergeants. Springwater and Lazeski stood over their squad like brooding hens.

"Pardon me, sir, but it seems to me you're the one needing to relax," Sergeant Jennings said. "We're way ahead of the rest of Able. Besides, the card playing idea ain't gonna fly. I suppose it was Collins that sent Morton over here so they could get a hand in without having to explain the rules all over again."

Sam glanced at his watch and returned to studying the forms on the clipboard. His mind registered nothing. Lieutenant Pettigrew had disappeared as soon as 1st Battalion received its warning order to prepare for departure to the marshalling area. Sam suspected Pettigrew was kissing-up to regimental staff ring-knockers. Before vanishing, Pettigrew turned the platoon over to Sam. *Anything goes wrong, I'll catch the grief. Whatever goes right, to Pettigrew goes the glory.*

Jennings pulled the soggy cigar from his mouth. "Nope, ain't nothing in First Platoon needs fretting over, sir."

"Good, Sergeant, because I've got some unfinished business in town."

"This circus ain't pulling out for at least an hour." Jennings attempted relighting his cigar. "I'll keep everything squared away here, sir."

Sam handed Jennings the clipboard and tried to look casual while walking among paratroopers. He passed through the Lambourn Place timber gateposts and picked up the pace to double-time down a slight slope, past old stone houses.

At the Wheelwright Arms pub, he jogged left and went another hundred yards until he crossed an arched stone bridge. A hammer striking metal rang out. Above the double workshop doors hung a simple sign: B. H. Alvis, Ironmonger. The double doors stood wide open. Sam entered a workshop smelling of cut iron, burning coal, and recent welding.

A hefty man with blackened hands spotted Sam and smiled. The blacksmith's girth taxed his leather apron. He dropped a heavy hammer on a metal table and moved toward Sam with a meaty hand extended. "Lef'tenant Henry. Back a wee bit earlier than expected."

"I know we agreed to a couple of weeks, but…"

"War has its way of not consulting our calendars. Aye, yours be no different from mine. The day we deployed—"

"Excuse me, Mr. Alvis, I don't mean to be rude, but we're pulling out now. Were you able to get it done?"

"Reckoned you lads might be leaving us right soon. A bloke would have to be daft to miss the signs." The blacksmith walked to a cabinet of small drawers and pulled one out. "Now, I gave fair warning, I'm no jeweler. But I did a ruddy right job of it, if I do say so me'self." Alvis held up an iron ring for inspection. "Might this be what you had in mind, lad?" The metal glistened. "Must admit, had me doubts when you handed me that pitchfork."

Sam gave a low whistle. "Can't believe how bright you got it."

"To make it fit like a proper ring, all comfortable like, I had to grind off a third of the tine's thickness on the inside. Had me missus try it on."

Sam took the ring and flipped it over in his palm.

"Does it strike your fancy? Of course it'll tarnish over time, but nothing a little buffing can't remedy." Mr. Alvis pointed his massive finger at the overlapping joint. "I like the way the tip comes around and overlaps. Looks right stylish and makes the ring adjustable to any sized lass. Well, lad?"

"Better than I imagined." Sam reached for his wallet. "How much do I owe?"

Mr. Alvis held up a blackened hand and shook his head. "Nary a pence. As a loyal subject of His Royal Highness, I figure it's owed you—being a daft English lass that put it through your arm in the first place."

"Best thing that ever happened to me."

"And you're one of them chaps that jumps out of airplanes too, aye?" Alvis let out a deep belly-laugh that might've swung the plank doors if they hadn't already been open.

"She's the most amazing girl. The whole package. Smart, pretty. Lots of spunk."

"And right handy with a pitchfork. Might you be plannin' to marry the lass?"

Sam admired the ring. "In a heartbeat. But she won't have me. Not yet anyway."

"Behaving herself like a proper lass. Waiting for the wedding night, is she?"

"No… Well, not, no! I mean, yes." He blushed and stammered. He held up his hand and started over. "Yes, she's behaving herself. But no, that's not the problem. Seems we don't hold the same commitment on—she wouldn't like the term, but let's say—on a religious level."

"I'm liking this lass. Needs lessons in aircraft identification, but other than that…"

Sam glanced at his watch. "I'm sorry, Mr. Alvis, but if we continue this conversation I'll end up AWOL."

The big blacksmith's face looked puzzled.

"A deserter," Sam said.

"Well, we don't want you facing no firing squad. Not before you get on that same religious level with your love anyway."

As Sam reached the doors, the blacksmith's booming basso voice stopped him. "One more thing, Lef'tenant."

He pivoted. It seemed moisture was pooling in the big smith's eyes.

"It won't be a bloomin' thing like the training I seen you lads do around these hills. Jolly well held me tongue, but…" Mr. Alvis cleared his throat. "I was at the Somme, summer of sixteen. Me and four of me best mates joined together. All eighteen, all full of ourselves. You're looking at the only one not buried under French sod. Don't know why the good Lord delivered me, but I haven't neglected His grace a day since. Me wife and me, we'll be keeping you in our prayers." Mr. Alvis snapped to attention and executed a perfect, palm out, British salute. His blackened hand stood out in sharp contrast to his white forehead.

Sam returned the salute and loped away.

He had a couple more stops to complete his mission. He halted near the village center and took a seat in the gazebo in front of the ancient church. Pencil stub in hand, he scribbled:

> *May 18, 1944*
> *Dearest Maggie,*
>
> *I can't stop thinking about our last time together in Kensington Gardens. Unfinished business eats at my heart. I want to work this out. I can no longer imagine life without you.*
> *I never intended to simply accept your goodbye. My full intent was to get with you again first chance I got. Never thought we'd go almost straight from Exercise Tiger into Exercise Eagle. Leaving today for the last stop. Don't know where. If I knew and told, they'd bust me and leave me behind. Probably sounds like a good plan to you, but I can't play it that way. I'm told we'll be caged until the real deal.*
> *Regardless—I will see you again.*
> *I Love You and Cherish Your Memory,*
> *Sam*
> *PS – This note was supposed to be about the gift you found in this box. Yes! It's from exactly where you guessed. That deadly center tine even! I wish I had time to explain it in person. Just*

this—no assumptions on my part. You don't even have to wear
it as a ring. Just keep it to remember me until I return.
And I will return!

He glanced at his wristwatch. Forty minutes had passed since he'd left Sergeant Jennings. He tapped a rapid beat with his foot. He wanted to write more. He wanted to tell Maggie that he wished the ring meant more, much more. However, he didn't dare risk botching his chances by rushing his thoughts onto the permanence of paper.

The obsession that tugged at his heart didn't seem to be a choice. A longing far from the volitional choice he was always going on about. Maggie drew him in much the same way as a good novel. But his love for books represented a passive, one-sided affair—outcome predetermined. He had no idea how to proceed with an affair of the heart. Another's thoughts, another's volition, another's feelings must be guessed each step of the way. And Maggie's temperament wasn't one that lent itself to easy guessing.

A favorite saying of his grandfather assured Sam's course of action: "Worthy goals are rarely easily achieved." Maggie's affections—could there be a more worthy goal? It should be difficult.

He folded the paper to fit the small box, forced the lid closed and wrote Maggie's Overton address across the top. He glanced around to assure he was alone and removed a rubber stamp and inkpad from his pocket. He stamped, PASSED BY MILITARY CENSORS on the box. Hardly a total deception. Officers were trusted to censor their own mail. His little fraud assured that no one gave the box a second look. He tied it off with a piece of string.

Fighting the urge to dash through the narrow streets to the post office, he tried to make sense of the ironmonger's emotions. He hardly knew the man. Why the moist eyes and evoking Deity? There seemed to be a deep pain in Mr. Alvis that Sam—or maybe his uniform and all its implications—forced to the surface. By her own admission, the same could be said of Maggie.

He recalled a UCLA philosophy lesson on Karl Marx. Marx proposed that religion was the opiate of the people. Now Sam had a context. Opiates killed pain. Opiates numbed. The morphine Syrette each paratrooper would carry into battle was an opiate. War had wrought deep emotional pain in Mr. Alvis and Maggie. Religion served them as an opiate. That was fine for them. Their pain was real. They needed a regular injection. Sam didn't. *I've always toughed it out through pain. I'll do it again.*

He found himself in front of the Royal Mail. He reached for the door handle and pushed, only to have his shoulder hit and rattle the glass. He pulled. The door remained shut. He stepped back. A hand scrawled note announced: Yanks departing. Popped out for 45 minutes.

"Forty-five minutes from when?"

An elderly woman walking past gave him a strange look and picked up her pace.

He looked at his watch. Out of time. He shoved the box into a cargo pocket and jogged toward Lambourn Place. At the church, he cut left to take a footpath that ran between the cemetery and high stone wall that separated the Lambourn village and Lambourn estate. He politely worked his way through four crying young ladies surrounding a low gate in the wall. Ducking through, he returned the MP guard's salute and headed straight for the Nissen huts.

Sam zeroed in on the foul language and South Philly accent coming from the hut storing overseas bags and personal items not needed in a battle zone. "Corporal Mazooti, could I speak with you?"

"Give me a minute." Mazooti looked over his shoulders and recognized Sam. His expression soured. Mazooti returned to his clipboard and growing mountain of stuffed duffels. "Youse got no beef with me, sir. My dice is straight and I ain't been sharing no war secrets with no leggy Limey dames."

"Relax, Mazooti. I understand you're interested in a Luger?"

Mazooti looked up with brightened eyes. "Yeah, I was just thinking that a Nazi dagger weren't enough rent to store unauthorized tools."

"Mail this little box for me, preferably yesterday, and I'll up the ante to a Luger."

"Make it a Luger *and* Kraut dagger. The blade should come in handy in South Philly."

"Deal."

Mazooti nodded. "Just drop it on my desk, sir."

Chapter 22

The Ring

21 May 1944
Lambourn, England

Maggie stepped off the Newbury-Lambourn train. The void of Yanks heightened her sense of dread.

She carried a special gift. She'd convinced herself that it must be given in person. The post just wouldn't do.

Exiting the Lambourn train terminal, she wove northward through the crooked cobblestone streets, hoping as she rounded each bend to spot an American khaki battle smock. She would've even welcomed a wolf whistle. Anything to alleviate her fear that the Yanks had vanished.

Nearing the Wheelwright Arms, she heard none of the boisterous laughter that always accompanied Americans. She cupped her hands on the dirty glass and peered inside. She made out two elderly chaps playing darts and a barmaid cleaning pint glasses.

A jeep holding a lone Yank paratrooper zipped past. Her hopes soared.

Passing through the Lambourn Place gateposts, her hopes came back down. The guard shack was empty. The road was deserted. The area ahead that had housed over a thousand men was as silent as her school at five o'clock on a Saturday. Venturing on, she noted that each abandoned Nissen hut door was padlocked. Fighting to stop the quiver in her chin, she turned a corner and arrived at the manor house. A jeep sat parked in front. The sign still read: HQ, 1st BN, 501st PIR. A glimmer of hope returned.

An eerie sense of tranquility pervaded the estate. She opened the door fearing the worst. No one sat at the desk. The door to the next room was closed. The hallway to her left was dark. Across the room a soldier napped on a shabby divan, his back to Maggie.

She cleared her throat and received a rattling snore in return.

"Excuse me." She hesitated, unsure how to address the sleeper. "Pardon me…"

More snores.

She walked over and tapped the soldier's shoulder.

The soldier shifted. "Would youse cut me some slack, Sarge. I'll have your friggin' inventory report done, in friggin' triplicate. And, yes, before chow."

Recognizing the repulsive voice, Maggie recoiled. Scooting backward her heel snagged the edge of an area rug. Her other heel followed and caught on the bunched-up carpet. She fell backward and landed on her backside with a loud thud.

The clerk jerked upright and rubbed his left eye. His right eye popped wide open seeing Maggie unsuccessfully attempted to push her skirt to cover her thighs.

"Tell me youse ain't no dream!" The couch's coarse fabric, combined with sweat and drool, had reddened the pimples on the right half of the corporal's face.

She failed to regain her feet or dignity before the corporal leered at her legs and worked his eyes upward. This time she lacked a winter coat to assist with modesty.

Recognition arrived in the corporal's eyes. "Not again! Last time youse was here it 'bout cost me a couple-grand. And I caught the third-degree from a couple of shave-tails. Youse ain't got no POW husband. Ain't getting no skinny off me."

Maggie got her feet back under her. "Pardon me, but I can't understand the half of your babbling. Could you please direct me to the whereabouts of Lef'tenant Henry."

"No can do, doll face. That's Uncle Sam's secret."

"Lef'tenant Henry would want me to know."

"Call me Dom." The clerk took up his official post behind the desk. "Let me spell it out—big, military, secret."

She dug into her handbag and produced a military identification card from when she repaired uniforms. She hoped the groggy corporal might fail to notice the expired dates.

He squinted at the card. "That mug shot don't do your eyes justice."

Maggie leaned across the desk and pulled her card away. "Please, just tell…"

The corporal sniffed the air like a foxhound.

I should've waited until finding Sam to apply perfume. Maggie also caught the corporal's scent. She tried to breathe through her mouth to reduce the stench of stale sweat from an unwashed male body.

Her anxiety level jumped. "Are you the only soldier present?"

"Nah, they left a squad behind to hold down the fort. We'll be back up to platoon strength when the rest take off from Merryfield. Saving some the best for the next jump."

They're indeed gone, she thought, but said, "Well a pity, but if you can't tell me, you can't tell me." She added a pout on the outside, but allowed a sly grin on the inside. *The little cretin just let Sam's location slip and he doesn't even realize it. I'll find Sam.* But first she needed to find an escape from the corporal's lustful gaze.

"Sorry, Margaret, but orders say I can't spill the beans to no one about where they're holding the Five-O-First, except to Hundred-'n-First and SHAEF personnel. Makes no sense—they already knows. But orders are orders."

"Well, far be it from me to land you in trouble, Corporal." Maggie looked at the clock and feigned surprise. "Oh my, look at the time. I must be off to catch my train. I'm dreadfully sorry to have awoken you all for naught."

"Relax, youse got plenty of time. Why, we could even *make* time." He winked. "After that I could get a jeep and run youse back to Overton."

Her stomach turned at the corporal's suggestion. Then the implication of his last words hit her. *How does the little worm know I live in Overton?* She shook her head. "Overton? You're mistaken. My ID clearly lists my place of residence as London."

"Nope, it's Overton, and I—"

"I must be off." She headed for the door. "Thank you for your time, Corporal."

"And here I thought them Jersey dames took the cake for leading a guy on."

She reached for the doorknob.

"Lieutenant Henry left a little present for you."

She froze halfway through the doorway and looked over her shoulder. The corporal dangled a small parcel by the string like a baited hook.

"That's how I knows youse live in Overton. It's written right here. Twenty-five, D-E-L-L-A-N-D-S."

Each letter drew Maggie back a couple of steps. By the time he reached 'S' she was standing at the desk.

The corporal smirked. "Can't imagine how I forgot to mail it. Must be all the rotten details they dumped on me. Yeah, them jokers run off to get the glory and I gets all the friggin' work."

She held out her hand. "Let me spare you some work."

Just out of her reach, the corporal dropped the small parcel into the desk's center drawer. Leering, he slammed the drawer closed with a thrust of his pelvis.

"Corporal, please. That's addressed to me. You have no right—"

"*I* have no right? You waltz right in and try to seduce me."

Maggie took a deep breath. "I beg your pardon! I never—"

"Oh, but you did. And you show me an expired ID that says youse live in London and now you want a package addressed to some dame in Overton. Maybe Lieutenants Sterling and Henry were right about you being a spy."

She felt her cheeks flush. "Poppycock!"

The corporal tapped his finger to the side of his head. "Then why does Lieutenant Henry get all urgent about sending youse this package just before the big invasion? I bet you've been wrapping your legs 'round his, getting military secrets and—"

Before the corporal could finish his lurid speculation, Maggie slapped his pimpled face so hard she knocked him backward. Entangled in the folding chair, he crashed to the floor.

Leaning across the desk, Maggie slid the drawer open, snatched the box, and dashed for the door. The chair banged and rattled as the clerk tried to extricate himself from the cramped space between the wall and the desk.

Maggie silently pleaded, *Lord, deliver me from this mess I've gotten—*

A forearm hooked around her waist and lifted her off the floor.

She launched her elbow backward, connecting with solid ribs. Her captor's grasp didn't slacken. She flailed with her handbag and kicked her heels backward. The grip tightened. She looked over her shoulder. A sleeve covered in stripes filled her vision.

"She come in here to seduce me, Sarge. Then she sucker-punches me and steals a box from my desk." The corporal punctuated his accusation with curses. "Never trust no Limey skirt."

"Watch your language around a lady, Mazooti. And how many times do I have to tell you, never take the Lord's name in vain around me." The sergeant loosened his grip on Maggie. "Now, miss, to sort this all out I'm going to have to let you down, but first you've got to promise to quit fighting. OK?"

Her feet touched the floor. Strong hands released her as if she were a frail animal. She faced away from the men and rearranged her clothes as modestly as the setting permitted. Turning around, she found the hormone-driven corporal rubbing his left cheek. He dropped his hand to tuck in his shirttail, revealing a red imprint matching her long-fingered hand.

The sergeant—appearing to be in his early thirties, broad at the shoulders and narrow at the hips—chuckled. "Looks like she connected pretty solid there, Mazooti. I'd like to think she was swinging for the virtue of all the English ladies who've had the displeasure of meeting you." The sergeant turned toward Maggie. "You OK, miss?"

She nodded.

"Afraid I need to see some identification."

She passed her current identity card with a trembling hand.

Mazooti puffed up. "Check them dates, Sarge."

The big sergeant examined the ID card and returned it. "Looks A-OK to me. I've heard about you, Miss Elliott."

Her face must've shown her surprise.

"Your pitchfork work is legendary. Lieutenant Henry's platoon sergeant's a buddy of mine. To hear him tell it, Lieutenant Henry is one first-rate officer. Takes care of his men. Smart in ways that count. But I guess I'm preaching to the choir. What's this about taking something from the desk?"

The corporal moved toward them. "Search her, Sarge."

The sergeant glared at the corporal and pointed to the door. "I'm eighty-sixing you, Mazooti. That's an order!"

The corporal departed massaging his face and slammed the door.

"So you won't feel uncomfortable, Miss Elliott, we'll step outside."

Outside, she took a deep breath, welcoming the fresh air. The big Yank leaned against the spare tire on back of a jeep. She opened her palm to reveal the small box.

"It's addressed to you." The sergeant shrugged. "So what's the problem?"

"A better question is why that corporal kept it." She was regaining her wits. "Why didn't Sam—I mean Lef'tenant Henry—just mail it?"

"Don't know. In the end, it could just work out for the best. All outgoing mail from the marshalling areas has a hold order on it."

"Is there any possible way I can see him?"

"Afraid that won't be possible, Miss Elliott."

"Not even for only a minute or two?"

"Not even ten seconds."

Maggie cringed. "Will *it* be soon?"

"Not soon enough for those waiting." The sergeant glanced at his wristwatch. "May I escort you to the train station, miss? I don't want you having to look over your shoulder for that sad-sack, Mazooti."

*   *   *

Halfway back to Newbury, at the Great Shefford village stop, Maggie remembered the very purpose for her trip to Lambourn—the gift for Sam in her handbag. The good sergeant might've found a way to get a parcel to Sam before the invasion. *No. I must deliver it face-to-face.* But when? It had to be soon. At Merryfield. *But where's Merryfield?*

She considered the small box from Sam. Taking a deep breath, she untied the string and lifted the cardboard lid. A folded note popped out. She studied the brief letter. Halfway through the postscript she grabbed the box and overturned it onto her palm.

The ring landed in her hand and stunned her.

The stunning effect wore off and turned to indignation. *A ring! How dare him! How presumptuous! The nerve of the Yank! Just how short is his memory?* She dropped the ring back in the box and forced herself to finish the note's postscript:

> *I wish I had time to explain it in person. Just this—no assumptions on my part. You don't have to wear it as a ring. Just keep it to remember me until I return.*

She reread the postscript three times, failing to find any possible context that didn't frighten her. She released a heavy sigh and gazed out the window. In her faint reflection, she watched tears roll down both cheeks.

How dare you, Samuel Henry. How dare you remind me of that day you took my heart captive. Granted, the use of the pitchfork was quite creative. However, he'd fashioned a ring—the one symbolic piece of jewelry that reminded her of the things about this war she most detested.

How dare you, Sam! Why did you have to make it a ring? 'No assumptions' on your part? How can I bloody well assume anything else?

Through tear-blurred vision, she reluctantly poised the ring over the tip of her ring finger. It slid into place and rested in the remnant of the groove from Ian's undersized engagement ring. In contrast, the iron band was loose. She spun it around her finger and gazed back out the window.

After a minute of absentminded rotation, she started to pull the ring off, but stopped at the first knuckle. She pushed it back down into its groove and covered the iron band with her right palm. She held her hand there until disembarking at Newbury to complete her journey by bus.

Exiting the bus in Overton two hours later, the new weight on her finger felt quite natural.

Just keep it to remember me, Sam had written. She contemplated his request as she walked uphill to Dellands Road corner. *Remember? How could I possibly forget?* The hard part—the part that she couldn't muster the faith to believe—was the last part of Sam's request: …remember me until I return.

Later that night, unable to sleep, Maggie stared at the ceiling. She touched the pitchfork ring. *How dare he make promises beyond his power to keep! How can it possibly work? It simply can't work. Oh, God, please, make it work.*

Chapter 23

Waiting

27 May 1944
Merryfield, England

SHAEF christened the grand invasion Operation Overlord. They codenamed the airborne phase Operation Neptune.

Training ceased. Only exact operational details remained unknown. The cooks served the best chow. First-rate movies played four nights a week. PT no longer commenced before dawn. Rest was even encouraged. Staff officers organized sporting events. Sam, Pettigrew, Young, and Collins played endless innings of baseball. Armory sergeants distributed live ammunition, hand grenades, and a variety of explosives.

Invasion planners sequestered 1st and 2nd Battalions and HQ Company of the 501st PIR at a joint RAF and US Army Air Corps base in a flat valley ringed by rolling hills. Sam recognized the airfield as the same they had used for the Exercise Eagle rehearsal jump May 11. Merryfield. But he could only narrow its location to southwest England, somewhere between the distant towns of Salisbury and Exeter.

The scenery appeared rather idyllic, even worthy of a picture postcard—if not for row-upon-row of C-47 Skytrains marring the landscape. The new tent city and sloppy barbwire fence surrounding the compound also spoiled the pastoral scene. British soldiers patrolled the perimeter to contain the waiting paratroopers and guard the secrets each now held. In between the airfield and the adjoining village of Ilton, white plywood signs—readable from both directions—announced in block letters: *CIVILIANS ARE FORBIDDEN TO LOITER OR TALK WITH TROOPS!*

Sam hadn't received a letter from Maggie since departing Lambourn. The communication restrictions frustrated him. The Army had placed a temporary hold on outgoing mail, making impossible even a semi-coded letter to drop Maggie hints about his sequestered location.

Melancholia threatened to engulf him. The steak dinner he'd just walked away from triggered it. His failed appetite had nothing to do with the smart-alecky chow-line remarks about the Army feeding the fatted calf to the fatted calves. He simply couldn't enjoy a steak, not without Maggie.

Only one thing buoyed his hopes. A rumor. A 1st sergeant knew a guy who'd heard about a leggy blonde hanging out near the Lambourn gates. Maggie? Maybe she received the pitchfork ring and immediately ran to Lambourn to confess her undying love for him. *Not a chance.*

Whenever hope surged, his mind returned to the Kensington Gardens episode. He remained uncertain if Maggie even wanted to see him again—at least not until after the war. Vain imaginations, all reaching the worst possible conclusions, plagued his mind. The abundance of idle hours only worsened the situation.

Sam walked laps inside the compound. As he neared the main gate on his third lap, he looked outside the barbwire enclosure toward the brick building housing the pilots' mess.

A fair-haired young woman stood underneath the lamppost.

The Wrigley's Spearmint dropped from his slack jaw. Since hearing "Lili Marlene" in line at the officer's mess hall, the lyrics had been replaying in his head. At that moment, he was convinced he was living a verse:

> Orders came for sailing somewhere over there
> All confined to barracks 'twas more than I could bear
> I knew you were waiting in the street
> I heard your feet but could not meet
> My Lili of the lamplight,
> My own Lili Marlene

Maggie found me! His pulse quickened. *And what a clever way to let me know.* He picked up his pace and headed for the barbed wire limits. His proximity to the fence was making a guard antsy. Sam's breaths came in gasps. He raised his hand to wave.

A husky American stepped out of the pilots' mess and pulled the waiting girl into his arms. Sam's initial thought kicked harder than his old mule. *Why's Maggie hugging that chubby pilot?*

Realizing it wasn't Maggie, relief washed over him. Relief turned into concern—concern over his delusional mental state.

*   *   *

An hour later, in their pyramidal tent, Sam ended his rambling dissertation on his indefinable romance. Sterling seemed attentive enough, but had only given the occasional nod or low whistle. Sitting at the edge of his cot Sam extended his hands in a plaintive manner. "Well? You're the married expert. Speak up."

Sterling reached under his cot and fumbled inside his musette bag like a raccoon—hands busy but eyes looking away. He pulled out a rubber band-wrapped stack of envelopes, peeled off the top letter, and sailed it across the room. It landed facedown on Sam's lap. Sam turned it over. The address was typed.

"Got that right before Exercise Eagle," Sterling said.

The return address read: Bates, Hensley and Woodard, Attorneys at Law, 300 Lincoln Square, Urbana, Illinois.

"No need to open it to have a pretty good idea what's inside, Sammy-boy."

Sam felt his anger rising in defense of his pal. "Why?"

Sterling shrugged. "She claims abandonment."

"Not possible." Sam handed the letter back. "There's a war on."

"And I joined it. Way too soon according to her. She thinks I might still be at the U of I if I'd waited for my number to come up."

"That's crazy!"

"Is it? Or does my own flawed logic call *my* sanity into question." Sterling lit his pipe. "Figured I'd have the rest of my life to be a husband and study history in the bowels of some musty old library. But only a small window of opportunity to actually participate in changing history." A cloud of vanilla-scented smoke hung thick inside the tent. "As it turns out, my marriage gets iced before my war even gets hot. And Adolph's little minions are preparing to do everything in their power to see that my life ends—well before the divorce is even final."

"I'm really sorry, Lloyd." Sam stared down at the plank floor and tried to think of something encouraging to say. "At least it wasn't some four-F, or a sailor."

"Nope. She went and found herself a physicist. Only twenty-three and already a PhD from MIT." Sterling exhaled a cloud of sweet smoke. "Working on some big hush-hush war department project at U of I. She said we were already over by the time she met him. Like that's supposed to comfort me."

"You don't need this hanging over you before the big jump. Couldn't she wait? The lawyers have to know this'll affect your morale and your platoon."

"Does it really matter?" Sterling's expression remained detached. "I've got this gut feeling that I'll never see the end of Neptune anyway."

Sam hurled his overseas cap across the tent and hit Sterling in the face. "Quit talking garbage. When you took that commission you gave up the right to just think of yourself. You'll have thirty-five lives depending upon your decisions. More than that, your platoon folds and my flank gets rolled. I'm not getting killed because some discontented grad student four-thousand miles away isn't getting her wifely needs met."

"Relax. I have no intention of letting my men *or* Able Company down." He stared at the floor. "I've heard some guys just know."

"Does the old man know?"

"About the divorce? You bet. Army has to get involved in the paperwork."

"Lloyd, you and I both need to get our heads back in the game. Too much time to do things the Army doesn't pay us to do. How about we get together? Study maps. Review objectives, tactics. Get our mission down. Any time leftover, we can discuss literature, history, philosophy. Anything but the fairer sex. How about it?"

"How about we just get this over with." Sterling slapped his pipe bowl into his hand. "I'm sick of the waiting."

Chapter 24

The Briefing

28 May 1944
Merryfield, England

Sam shifted his weight on the wooden folding chair, yet comfort still eluded him. Something other than the narrow chair was irritating him. He couldn't pinpoint what.

First Battalion, 501st commander, Lieutenant Colonel Crawford—looking a decade older than the average officer present and wearing his perpetual frown—stood in the musty canvas assembly tent and addressed his officers. "OK, gentlemen, get the big picture. It's essential that every officer knows how to accomplish the Operation Neptune objective of every platoon in your company, and of every company in our battalion, along with Second Battalion's objectives."

Colonel Crawford slapped the wall map with a long pointer. "We'll be holding the southeast flank for all Seven Corps. Especially critical are the N-Thirteen highway and the railway…"

A half-hour earlier the battalion S-3—operations officer—had distributed mimeographed copies of each platoon's objective, along with tactical maps. Sam was devouring the details, matching his Operation Neptune objectives to map names and symbols.

Sam studied the topographical map on his lap, glanced up, and squinted at the wall map between Colonel Crawford and Captain Young. Sam swung his head ninety-degrees right to reconcile the map's symbols with landmarks on the enlarged aerial photographs along the tent's olive-drab canvas sidewall. The aerial photos were overlapped and pieced together on plywood easels.

Pettigrew leaned close to Sam's left ear. "Pay attention, Henry."

Colonel Crawford turned the briefing over to Captain Young for the S-2 intelligence portion. Young stepped onto the makeshift crate and plywood platform.

"We've got a critical change, gentlemen. Scratch Drop Zone-B. Every Merryfield stick will now drop here at the *new* drop zone, designated D." He tapped the map with the long pointer. "Colonel Johnson convinced divisional HQ that DZ-B was too far from our Douve River objectives. You'll find DZ-D just south of Vierville and a bit east of St. Come-du-Mont. There'll be a few scattered farmhouses and outbuildings, labeled Les Drouries on your maps. On the northwest edge of D you'll find the village of Angoville au Plein. Now, don't be looking for any skyscrapers. Best landmark will be a church steeple. Just remember, little steeple, Angoville au Plein. Big steeple, you're two miles due west, in St. Come-Du-Mont."

Captain Young traced ovals with his pointer to the north and continued. "By the time it's our turn almost all other Hundred-'n-First serials will have already dropped on DZ-A and C. So as soon as you hit the coast count on every Kraut AA gunner to be hacked-off over us interrupting his sleep. Once on the ground, expect primary opposition from the Seven-O-Ninth Infantry Division. These are static troops, hardly the Kraut's first-string varsity. The Seven-O-Ninth also has a battalion or two of what they call *Ost* troops—Soviet Army turncoats. We're about as uncertain as Hitler over how much fight they have left in them. You might run into a variety of support troops, including Luftwaffe antiaircraft batteries."

Murmurs rolled through the tent. Colonel Crawford rose and glared at his officers. "Don't get cocky—it hardly takes an elite soldier to pull a MG Forty-two trigger from inside a bunker." He turned back to Captain Young. "Continue, Captain."

"Anticipate determined counterattacks from St. Come-du-Mont direction and points west courtesy of the Ninety-first Air Landing Division. The Ninety-first represents the best outfit the Krauts currently have on the Cotentin Peninsula. As far as the Five-O-First is concerned, tangling with them should fall upon the Second Battalion boys. St. Come-Du-Mont's their objective. But who knows where the Ninety-first will deploy when over twelve thousand Screaming Eagles and Eighty-Second Airborne troops drop in unannounced."

Captain Young lowered the pointer. "When Hitler figures out Seven Corps is going after the harbor at Cherbourg, he could deploy an assortment of veteran panzer, SS panzergrenadier, and parachute *fallschirmjager* units held in reserve throughout inland Normandy and Brittany to retake the Cotentin Peninsula and split our First Army beachhead. However, the straight-leg infantry and armor units will relieve us well before then. Any questions about the big picture?"

C-Company's commander stood. "We've only got First and Second Battalion and Regimental HQ Company here at Merryfield. So what's up with Third Battalion?"

"Just speculation, but being the S-Two, I'm paid to do that." Polite laughter scattered across the room. "In my estimation, it seems General Taylor wants part of the best with him, so Third will jump with division HQ up here at Drop Zone-C—just west of Saint Marie-du-Mont—acting as divisional reserve."

Murmurs and nods of approval rolled through the tent.

As Captain Young sat, the S-3—plans and operations officer—stood to deliver his briefing. "Getting back to DZ-D. Our friends from Third, Five-O-Sixth will be coming in on our tail and attacking due east to seize the two wooden bridges below us on the lower Douve, right about…" The S-3 tapped the map "…here in the Le Port and Brevands neighborhood. Get off the DZ ASAP so your men don't get mixed up with them. But those of you with airborne engineers attached for demolition…"

Sam didn't have any engineers attached, so he returned to comparing the topographical map and aerial reconnaissance photos. *Something's not right. What is it?*

Captain Young got back up and mentioned La Barquette—the key words for Able's Neptune objective. Sam's attention refocused. Young tapped the map's center. "The Douve River locks at La Barquette are critical. Expect moderate to heavy resistance and immediate counterattacks. All I know about tides is that they go in and they go out. But I'm told that combining the tides and rivers, these locks can be used to turn all this low ground," he circled a large area north of Carentan with his pointer, "into one shallow lake. It's all tidal—some even below sea level—up to the Merderet River.

"If we can hold the La Barquette locks we have the ability to flood the low ground and prevent German armored counterattacks from the south. That is, as long as we also succeed in blowing the causeway bridges. On the other hand, if we let the Krauts keep the locks they can keep us bottled up on the Cotentin Peninsula and our armor boys will have one heck of a time hooking up with V Corps coming in at Omaha Beach to our east. General Taylor has made it clear, we must capture the locks at once and intact. Questions concerning La Barquette?"

Sam bit his lower lip. The thing that had been bugging him had finally made its way into his consciousness. Now, he had one huge question. *How do I word it?*

"If not, let's look again at the bridges and causeways…" Young spoke of objectives not directly concerning 1st Platoon, so Sam focused on his own map for several minutes.

"Regimental S-Two has done one helluva job making us some highly detailed sand tables." Young's words recaptured Sam's attention. "We expect each platoon to study them, one squad at a time. You've been provided a schedule.

"For now, you can see that your maps and the aerial photos show irregular fields, especially on the high ground, separated by hedgerows. We have no reason to expect these hedgerows to be much different from the ones here in England. Shouldn't pose any problems. DZ-D is a smooth, clear pasture. No barbwire fences. A piece of cake. On the odd chance your stick misses the DZ, the worst hazard will be an apple orchard, or a little mud if you land in the lower ground near the river. Not to worry, though, our capable friends in the Four-Hundred-n'-Forty-First Troop Carrier Group assure us that we'll be on time and on target."

Young nodded to Colonel Crawford.

Sam raised his hand.

"Hold additional questions until after the operations briefing, Lieutenant Henry," Crawford said.

Sam felt Pettigrew's hot breath in his ear. "If you'd paid better attention you wouldn't have questions. Don't embarrass me again."

The S-3 stepped forward. "Able and Baker companies in serial number fourteen will be the first Geronimos to drop. You'll get the green light at zero-one-thirty hours. Assemble and advance on La Barquette locks, due south one mile. Division timetable calls for seizure no later than zero-six-thirty hours—the same time the Fourth ID is due to hit Utah Beach six miles to your northeast." The S-3 poked the map on each side of the river lock. "Able is to seize Carentan side, and Baker the near side."

The S-3 stepped away from the map. "Then get patrols out and hold against counterattacks. If needed, call fire support from div-arty and Navy tubs sitting offshore. Your mission is the embodiment of the parachute infantry motto—strike, seize, and hold."

The S-3 switched to C-Company's bridge destruction objective. Sam couldn't listen. His eyes darted back and forth from maps to aerial photographs. He fingered an elevation contour line. *No way! That can't be right.*

The plans and operations officer turned the briefing back over to the battalion commander. Colonel Crawford said, "See to it every man is fully briefed. Any questions?"

Sam's hand shot up. Crawford pointed to the third row. A Baker Company lieutenant asked, "Sir, we take our objectives and hold. Then what?"

"Seven Corps plans call for the Hundred-'n-First to take Carentan as soon as practicable," Crawford said. "That call will be made at the divisional HQ level. Since we'll already be in the neighborhood, I wouldn't be surprised if it fell to us. General Taylor is asking us for three days. Three days at the most, then we're slated to head back to jolly ol' England. Strike, seize, and hold. Three days." Crawford paused and Sam's hand shot up again. "I hadn't forgotten about you, Lieutenant Henry."

"Sir, I understand the strategic value of the locks. That much is obvious." Sam pointed at the center of the wall map in front. "So how can we be certain that Rommel hasn't already used the locks to flood all this lower ground?"

Crawford looked perplexed. "Captain Young, can you answer that?"

Young stepped forward and pointed toward the sidewall. "Answer's pretty clear once you look at the aerial reconnaissance photos."

Sam nodded. "I have, sir."

"Then you've seen all the grass and vegetation. This one was taken just two weeks ago." Young picked up the pointer, moved across the tent, and pointed at the photo nearest Sam. "Grass doesn't grow underwater, especially brackish water."

"Sir, it does if given enough time." Sam got up and moved closer to the photo. The assembled officers twisted in their seats. "Notice the cattle. None are grazing down here. None below this contour line on our topographical map, sir."

Lieutenant Pettigrew leaned forward. "Our photo analysis experts know a thing or two more than you, Henry. Just a coincidence."

Pettigrew's comment drew a frown from Colonel Crawford.

"A coincidence *if* just observed once. But look." Sam pointed at the enlarged series of overlapping photos. "When were those taken?"

Captain Young looked to the bottom right corner of the enlargement. "Let's see... last summer. Sixteen July. Same vegetation patterns. It wasn't flooded then, either."

"But look at what's going on. Looks like they're cutting hay. See the windrows?" Sam was so engrossed in pursuing his argument that he forgot military courtesy.

Pettigrew rose. "So what if they are, *Lieutenant* Henry?"

Captain Young studied the photos.

"Look." Sam pointed and squeezed around two officers sitting by the plywood easels. "Look at the shadowing from where the hay has been mowed and where it hasn't." He tapped the photo. "Follows the exact same contour line as on our topographical maps *and* matches the grazing pattern of the cattle in the other photo."

"Still, the time factor applies," Young said. "All photos taken during the past eighteen months are consistent."

"But haven't the Germans been there *since* nineteen-forty? A lot can change in four years."

"What do you know about cows and cutting hay?" Pettigrew said through his smug grin. "You're from Los Angeles."

"You know very well I wasn't always from Los Angeles. I know a thing or two about cattle and cutting hay along a river bottom. I want to make sure we get this one right. Look at the map."

Colonel Crawford stepped forward. "Excuse me, Lieutenant Henry, but are you trained in aerial reconnaissance photo analysis?"

"No, sir."

"Have you been qualified in military intelligence?"

Sam stood a little straighter. "No, sir, Colonel Crawford."

"Well, then, maybe I missed something, Lieutenant Henry. When did you get assigned to the S-Two?"

Sam looked at the ground.

"Have a seat, Lieutenant Henry. You too, Lieutenant Pettigrew. Everyone else is dismissed to brief your men."

As he walked by, Sterling gave Sam a confused look. Officers jammed the tent exit as half the men paused to light cigarettes. The metallic claps of cigarette lighters flipping shut punctuated the start of conversations.

"Captain Tarver, please remain here," Colonel Crawford said.

Topographical map in hand, Captain Young leaned forward, examining the aerial photographs. Colonel Crawford strode toward the row of folding chairs where Sam and Pettigrew remained seated. While staring ahead Sam pondered possible defenses. He rose and came to attention.

"Lieutenant Henry, don't you *ever* disrupt a briefing of mine again. Ask your question, if you find the answer not to your liking, deal with it in a military fashion, afterward!"

"Yes, sir. I was out—"

"What you managed to do, Lieutenant, was plant a seed of doubt in the minds of *my* men. Officers I'm counting on to lead my battalion into our first combat!" The colonel lit a cigarette and let it dangle from the corner of his mouth. "You know a paratrooper's two worst fears when jumping out the door of a C-Forty-seven?" The cigarette bounced with each syllable.

Sam gulped. "Yes sir, a streamer and a water landing."

"Exactly, so if you have concerns—founded or unfounded—that may damage the morale of my men, you keep your pie hole shut. Understood?"

"Yes, sir."

Colonel Crawford turned to Pettigrew. "And you mind your own business."

"Lieutenant Henry is my assistant platoon leader. Therefore I deemed it my—"

"Get off your high horse, Lieutenant. I was born on a Friday, but not last Friday. You jumped at the chance to take a jab at Lieutenant Henry." Colonel Crawford looked toward Captain Tarver. "I consider Able Company my best. That's why you got the La Barquette locks. I'll give you the benefit of the doubt and chalk today's little episode up to pre-invasion jitters. Need I remind you of the absolute necessity for unit cohesion?"

Captain Tarver snapped his basketball forward physique to attention and said in his Tennessee drawl, "It won't happen again, sir."

"See to it that it doesn't." Pulling the cigarette from the corner of his mouth, Colonel Crawford turned back to Sam. "Now, Lieutenant Henry, let's discuss your concerns. If they're founded, I'll send them up the ladder to the regimental S-Two."

"Well, sir, look at the photos and you'll note—"

"You're afraid of dropping in the damn water, aren't you?" Colonel Crawford said.

Pettigrew's perpetual smirk expanded.

Sam stood a little taller. "Not any more than the next paratrooper, sir. It's just that *if* the locks have already been used to flood the low ground, then I figure that would change the strategic value of the locks."

"Maybe, yes. Maybe, no," Colonel Crawford said. "Don't over-analyze, Henry. Just take your orders, execute the mission, and seize your objective. Besides, you've got to agree that even if you're right about the locks, just look at your map. Drop Zone-D is on a jutting piece of high ground. It'll be dry."

"If we get dropped where we're supposed to, sir," Sam said.

"The troop carrier flyboys did one helluva job dropping us right on target on Exercise Eagle," Captain Tarver said.

"Yes, sir. And if I recall, the weather was perfect and nobody was shooting at them." Sam took a deep breath. "Sir, fear is not the issue. The issue is being able to bring arms to bear against our objective in a timely manner." Sam realized he'd pushed the issue too far, but he had one more question. "Colonel Crawford, sir, has it been considered…? What if? How do we accomplish our mission if we're scattered—for any of a number of possible reasons—across the Cotentin Peninsula? Then what, sir?"

"Yeah, we've considered that possibility. Long and hard. And we consider such an outcome to be quite unfortunate for the Krauts." Colonel Crawford took a drag on his cigarette. "It's what we're calling the 'unleashing of a bunch of heavily armed and highly pissed-off nineteen-year-olds factor.'" He exhaled a stream of smoke. "We don't think it'll come down to that. But if it does, the Krauts will be worse off for it, not us."

Colonel Crawford's cavalier assessment stunned Sam. The expression on Captain Tarver's face looked like Sam felt. Even Pettigrew's perpetual smirk was erased.

"You're dismissed." Colonel Crawford dropped his cigarette and ground it under his boot's twisting toe.

Sam executed an about face and hurried out the tent behind Pettigrew and Tarver. Ducking through the exit, Sam observed Captain Young still bent close to the aerial photos, tracing lines with his finger while referring to the topographical map.

Captain Tarver walked alone. Sam trotted to alongside his company commander and said, "Sir, sorry if I embarrassed Able."

"We're all getting a little jumpy. Just think twice before you do stuff that might hack-off Colonel Crawford. OK?"

"Yes, sir." Captain Tarver's face reminded Sam that Able Company's *Old Man*—the traditional nickname for a company commander—only had two years on Sam. Sam let Tarver walk away.

With Tarver out of sight, Pettigrew swooped in. "Henry, how can you still fail to comprehend chain of command? I'm the platoon leader and you are the assistant platoon leader. Leader," he tapped his own chest, then tapped Sam's, "assistant. It's not a difficult concept."

Sam pushed Pettigrew's finger away from his chest. "Back in the Ozarks they say you don't put two herd-bulls in the same pasture."

"I don't speak hillbilly euphemisms, Henry, but I think you get the idea. Second, I want you to comprehend the bigger picture. Our nation's crisis requires the Army to adopt drastic measures—like making OCS ninety-day wonders out of draftee hillbilly boys. I spent my lifetime, plus four years at West Point to earn my commission. You, on the other hand, just got a notice in the mail, plus ninety days. Don't you imagine for a minute that we're even remotely close to being equals. Got it?"

Sam folded a piece of gum into his mouth because he knew it would irritate Pettigrew. Through smacks, he said, "I just wanted to be sure we have the best chance to seize our objective with the least cost of life."

Pettigrew forced a chortle. "Who you trying to kid, Henry? It's going to be a freakin' bloodbath. By dawn after the jump, we'll be damned lucky to have half our men walking. Remember the reasoning for putting us two bulls in the same pasture?" Pettigrew lit a Chesterfield. "And while we're talking about cattle, I guess you just blew your whole urbane-college-boy-from-California charade. Must point out that I'm not to blame." His smirk returned. "But since you let the cat out of the bag yourself, well, I might feel obliged to elaborate. After your farfetched analysis back there I'm sure there'll be a question or two headed my way."

"Then be sure you get your facts straight—it's Banta Springs, Missouri, along the Big Niangua River, on the Ozark Plateau, one hundred seventy miles southwest of St. Louis. Population two thousand one hundred and eighty." Sam locked gazes with Pettigrew. "That would be two thousand one hundred and eighty folks with more human decency than you."

A malevolence entered Pettigrew's eyes. "And I'm sure that sophisticated English dame of yours knows all about them."

"Drop dead, *sir.*" Sam walked away before he faced charges for striking a superior officer.

"That'll be the race, Henry." Pettigrew snickered. "And quite a race, to be sure. Get Springwater's squad up to the sand table. Only keep the hay and cows and grass-that-grows-underwater fantasies to yourself."

Chapter 25

The Atlas

31 May 1944
Overton, England

"Are you absolutely certain, Chloe?"

Maggie moved through the musty stacks of the Overton school library and stopped at a sloped table holding geographical reference books.

Chloe nodded. "Promised I'd ask if I ran into any RAF or Yank Air Corps chaps."

Maggie opened the broken binding of the United Kingdom atlas and flipped to the index of place names. "And you're *positive* he called it Merryfield?"

"Don't talk down to me, Maggie."

"I just want to be sure." Maggie feared offending her friend. "You were at this dance. The music could've been loud. He may have had too much to drink."

Chloe raised her hand. "You mean, *I* was probably drunk."

Maggie shook her head. "Please, Chloe, not at all."

"No need to fret, the evening was young. We popped out for a bit o' fresh air. Neither of us had downed more than a pint. When I mentioned Merryfield, you should've seen his face light up. 'Heard of Merryfield?' he says, 'it bloody well saved me bacon!'"

"When?"

"Early March. Returning in his Mosquito, a mission over Brittany—Rennes, I think—when he noticed his oil pressure dropping in both engines faster than a Yank can spend a quid. He radioed a distress call, spotted a runway, and put it down. His engines gave up the ghost before he could even taxi off the ruddy runway."

Maggie opened the atlas. "We've already established that there's no town or village in all Great Britain named Merryfield. I've checked every—"

"Merry-field. Perhaps *field* has nothing to do with a town name. Perhaps *field* just has to do with the fact that it's an *airfield*?"

"You may be onto something there, ol' girl," Maggie said. "But that would be no help at all, not without military maps."

"The mosquito pilot said Merryfield was new. Not even on his RAF map. He had to dodge runway construction."

Maggie turned to the map of southwest England. "And he was heading for…?"

"Said his squadron's stationed at Weston Zoyland. Here." Chloe poked northern Somerset County on the map. "Claimed he almost made it."

Maggie scurried to the librarian's desk, snipped a yard of string from a spool, and returned to the atlas. She flipped to an expanded map of the English Channel region. She pressed the string down on Rennes and stretched it to Weston Zoyland. "That could put him down somewhere between Taunton and Yeovil." Maggie flipped back to the detailed map of southwest England and squinted. "So I start my search in the Ilminster to Langport area." She etched an oval with her fingernail.

"I'd start with a better map. Perhaps something printed this century." Chloe put a hand on Maggie's shoulder. "Maggie?"

Maggie looked up. Chloe appeared concerned. Maggie recognized the look from when Ian's fate was unknown.

"Do you really want to go down this road again?" Chloe asked.

Maggie attempted to smile. "Far too late for that now, isn't it?"

Chapter 26

Eavesdropping

3 June 1944, Evening
Merryfield, England

"Think it'll be much longer?"

Sam sat in A-Company's grassy staging area among stacked A-5 para-packs and A-12 parachute cargo canisters. Riggers and ordinance men had stuffed each with crew-served weapons, associated ammo, explosives, rations, and medical supplies.

Sterling gazed at the sunset's last orange remnants. "Surprised they've kept us caged this long."

Sam turned toward the eastern horizon. "Full moon in a couple days."

Sterling huffed. "That mean you'uns aim to plant taters or cut boar pigs?"

"Look, Lloyd, a dozen times already, I'm sorry."

Sterling frowned. "Like our friendship depended on you being from Los Angeles, rather than Po-Dunk, Missouri." He slammed the cleaning rod down his M-1 barrel.

"Yeah, and how many weeks passed without you telling me about your wife stepping out on you?" Sam oiled his carbine bolt.

"Apples to oysters, Sammy-boy, apples to oysters." Sterling pulled a wire brush up the rifle's bore. "So which is it?"

Sam gave Sterling a questioning glance.

Sterling grinned. "Taters or pigs?"

Sam shook his head. "Seriously, I always thought we'd jump during a full moon. I bet it'd also give the swabbies and straight-legs the right tides to hit the beaches."

"Got to figure Rommel knows that, too. The only surprise we're springing on him is the exact location. Helen Keller could figure the rest out."

Sam folded the stock of his carbine and slid it into its canvas sheath—essentially an oversized holster. "Ike's not keeping us all cooped up 'til July." He hooked the carbine case onto his web belt. He stood and practiced drawing the folded carbine out as fast as he could without it snagging on the protruding fifteen-round magazine.

Sterling glanced around the para-packs. "Could you wait until it's darker? You look like Wyatt Earp playing with that peashooter."

"Yeah, when we jump you'll have fun putting your M-One together in the dark."

Sterling laid his M-1 aside and loaded the bowl of his root-burl pipe. "But you just said we'll have a full moon to light our way." Sterling's Ronson lighter illuminated his face before pipe smoke engulfed his head. "I can't get used to how long the days are now. Here it is almost twenty-three hundred hours and not even dark yet."

"Thank double daylight savings time." Sam shifted the gear on his belt to get the carbine sheath in the ideal position. "Sorry, this whole deal hasn't worked out how you'd envisioned."

Sterling puffed on his pipe. "You referring to my fairytale turned tragedy?"

"The end hasn't been written yet." The sweet tobacco again reminded Sam of his heady philosophy student days at UCLA. "Keep making choices—choices, my friend—and write your own story."

In one fluid motion Sam drew his carbine, adeptly snapped the stock in position, threw back the bolt to chamber an imaginary round, and shouldered it. He held his aim on a spot on the horizon.

"Hold it right there, my philosopher friend." Sterling pulled the pipestem from his mouth. "For one, you may have more jumps under your belt than most, but you're hardly fooling me. You're not cut out for the Army. Not the same way guys like Pettigrew or Jennings are. You're a scholar-athlete. Made to be a teacher."

Sterling jabbed his pipestem at Sam. "So, just cease your usual *authentic choices* ranting for a minute and just imagine it's the real McCoy right now. In your sights is the back of a helmet occupied by a fellow scholar from the University of Munich. Nicely illuminated by your full moon. What's going through your mind when you—as trained—exhale halfway and squeeze that trigger?"

Sam held his aim. "Doing my duty. Making a difference. That's the line of reasoning I used to keep that Five-O-Sixth sergeant from blowing his brains out. Ridding the world of despotism."

"Really? When did the UCLA scholar become the war bonds poster boy?" Sterling relit his pipe. The flare of light showed his solemnity.

"You're the one so quick to volunteer." Sam lowered his carbine. "So, why don't you tell me."

"I'm just here to get a job done," Sterling said.

Sam smirked. "So, ours is not to reason why—"

"Cut the baloney, Sam. I'm deadly serious. At this point I'm just frightened enough to stay on my toes. But something I have no idea about is what it'll be like to pull that trigger with another human filling my sights."

Sam reclined on the stacked para-packs. "Our training kicks in. Don't think too much—that's what they keep telling me. Accomplish the mission, without losing too many men."

Sterling sucked on his pipestem. The bowl glowed. "And exactly how many is *too* many? What have we been taught since weaned from our mothers' breasts?"

Sam grinned. "I bet you're about to tell me."

"Thou shalt not kill. Thou shalt not kill. Thou shalt not kill. For five years I studied history, which is just an arrangement of eons of time featuring men breaking the sixth commandment, with a liberal portion of breaking the other commandments—assorted idols, dishonoring parents, lying, stealing, coveting, and basic adultery—thrown in. Those are easily justified. But forever extinguishing the spark of human life? We better pause a moment before we get too cavalier about killing. It's irrevocable."

Sam pushed his hand back through his hair. "If ideas are worth dying for, they're worth killing for. It's got to be a two-way street."

"Sounds more like something spoken from the spit-and-whittle bench outside *your* Banta Springs general store. How about the hallowed halls of UCLA? What would your revered philosophers say about the sanctioned suspension of God's sacred commandments?"

Sam looked away. "I'm afraid they wouldn't place much credence in any sort of moral absolutes. *Sacred* isn't part of any equation. They pretty much managed to explain away the notion of God."

"Wasn't Kierkegaard a good Christian theist? Hegel was a practicing Lutheran, wasn't he?"

"They certainly weren't on the UCLA faculty, either. And what Hegel embraced at the end of his life wouldn't have met with Brother Martin's approval." Sam slid his carbine into the canvas case and snapped the flap shut. "I toyed with the professors' ideas. Some points had strong merit. Merit from a hypothetical standpoint, anyway."

Sterling raised his eyebrows. "Like…?"

"Ideas that Dostoevsky explored. Ideas Nietzsche took to their logical conclusion. Ideas with considerable historical support."

"Like…?"

Sam rubbed his chin. "*Like* the very concept of morality. Historically speaking, isn't it true that immorality can flourish only in proportion to the level of morality? Consider society's ever-expanding rulebook. You name the culture—the more laws, the more lawlessness. Wouldn't it hold true that the fewer the morality rules the less immorality to contend with? Hence, *less* guilt and *more* happiness?"

Grinning, Sterling shook his head. "You're playing word games. I haven't forgotten the lectures on Kant. Didn't he contend that moral codes weren't from us, but from God?"

"Sure, it's a classic argument for the existence of God. Nevertheless, where did it get him? Kant died pretty much an agnostic. In the end he doubted a transcendent God was even knowable."

"Whoa! Stop the presses—a philosopher changes his mind! Big deal. But this much you and I both do know: one, there *are* morals. And two, belief in God *is* the rule, not the exception. An innate concept, I think Descartes contended." Sterling reclined down the length of a para-pack and gazed at the darkening sky. "Who's going to argue that things like, say… cold-blooded murder and rape are morally acceptable acts?"

Sam leaned forward. "OK, but just suppose there is no God. And none of the professors I ran into at UCLA believed there was. Not in the biblical sense, anyway. Well, if there is no God, wouldn't everything be permitted? Man would be truly free. No ancient restraints. No taboos. No concern about final judgment. No ultimate accountability. Freedom to reach our full human potential."

"Come back to the real world, Sammy-boy," Sterling scoffed. "Freedom to—"

Sam heard a noise from behind and twisted around. "Who's there?"

A silhouette rose from the canisters and para-packs. "Just me, Lieutenant."

Sam stood. "That you, Private Morton?"

Morton sheepishly raised a hand.

"What are you doing there?"

"Uh…uh." Morton pointed at the cargo. "Lieutenant Pettigrew sent me to count para-packs."

Sam frowned and narrowed his eyes. "From on the ground?"

"Uh…" Morton averted his eyes. "Need inventory numbers, sir. Found them."

Sam gave him a dismissive wave. "Then go report back to Lieutenant Pettigrew."

"Sir," Morton said, "what you been talking about, it have anything to do with what you did with that Five-O-Sixth clown who was going to blow his head off back at Piccadilly?" Morton blinked rapidly. "Being free and making choices and all that?"

Sam shook his head. "You got your tag numbers, right? So quit your eavesdropping and go catch some sack time, Private."

"Yes, sir." Morton drifted into the shadows.

Sam turned to Sterling. "At times he can sure be one odd duck." He sat back down. "Anyway, historically, hasn't the concept of God been used to suppress, exploit, and enslave?"

"Can't argue that religious concepts haven't been used for wrongdoing. But I don't know, what you're saying is just going too far the opposite direction." Sterling sat up and looked Sam in the eye. "I'm not particularly religious. Even had a hard time deciding which letter to let them stamp on my dog tags. My father was raised Presbyterian. Mom, Roman Catholic. Ended up, rather than fight over it, they didn't practice any religion apart from your major holidays. But this much I do know for sure, what you're toying with is dangerous, Sammy-boy."

"No." Sam shook his head. "This war, that's what's dangerous."

Sterling reached over for his canvas web gear harness and removed a pineapple grenade. He gripped it as trained—one finger hooked in the ring, ready to pull the pin.

Sam stared at the grenade and gathered his feet under him.

"Relax, Sam. I haven't gone section-eight. Just need a teaching aid. Your philosophical musings. What Nietzsche said about God being dead. That's like pulling the pin on this grenade." Sterling jerked his finger out of the ring in an exaggerated imitation pull. "And then dropping the pin in the grass. In the dark. Only *after* pulling and dropping the pin do you realize you don't need the grenade, after all. How many times are you going to be able to find and replace that pin?"

Sterling looked at the grass as if trying to find something. "You're not always going to have your full moon and short grass to help out, either. Your hand won't always be steady and dry, undistracted, able to hold that fuse spoon down. Nope, time runs out. This grenade's guaranteed to blow sooner or later."

Sterling loosened his fingers, palm up, and let the grenade roll out off his hand. It came to rest against Sam's boot. "You remove God and you've pulled the *moral* pin. Sooner or later society will blow up. Kaboom!"

"No." Sam shook his head adamantly. "It doesn't have to work that way. Mankind can get it right through reasoning."

"If reasoning was enough, if philosophical thought didn't have real world consequences, then we wouldn't be sitting here right now, pal. And my marriage wouldn't have gone down the crapper. But, unfortunately one madman, Adolph Hitler, picked up a book by another madman, Friedrich Nietzsche, and decided it was convenient for God to be dead so he could be the global superman."

Sam frowned. "You history types find such great pleasure in taking a hundred years, summarizing, simplifying, and wrapping it all up in a neat little paragraph."

"Perhaps, but history tells me enough to prevent me from philosophizing about something that sounds like handing the insane asylum over to the inmates." Sterling snatched up his grenade, gear, and rifle and walked toward the tents.

"Geez. Lighten up, Lloyd. I'm just throwing out ideas."

Chapter 27

Postponed

4 June 1944, Late Morning
Merryfield, England

"The Old Man wants all Able Company personnel at chapel. And, yes, it's an order."

Sam looked up from packing his musette bag. "Attending religious services is a personal choice."

"That's right," Sterling said, popping his head inside the pyramidal tent, "and Captain Tarver is letting you choose."

Sam closed his eyes and pinched the bridge of his nose. "Then it's not an order."

"Oh, he made it crystal clear—it's an order. Your choice is Catholic or Protestant." Sterling displayed his wristwatch. "Services kick-off in three minutes."

Sam grabbed his helmet and ducked out the tent. "Which are you *choosing?*"

"Tarver is old-timey Tennessee Baptist, so I'll choose my dear Protestant dad."

"Good, that means I won't be the only hypocrite there." As they walked, Sam noticed the activity around Merryfield had dropped off. "Hope the good parson has something interesting prepared—this may be record attendance." He pushed his steel pot further down on his head. "Can't get my helmet to feel right."

Sterling flicked a strip of burlap scrim hanging from Sam's helmet. "You did a swell job weaving in the scrim. I'm impressed, Sammy-boy. It's certainly due to your vast experience with burlap. Ever make a dress out of flour sacks?"

"Like Danville, Illinois, is *so* cosmopolitan." Sam removed his helmet and ran his hand over the one-inch stubble. The sides and back were even shorter. "These haircuts make us all look right off the chain gang."

"Except those guys in HQ Company. They look like a bunch of lunatics with their Mohawks." Sterling looked him over as they rounded a row of tents. "So you're going to jump in Maggie's jacket?"

"Brought me great luck last time I jumped in it." Sam held up his sleeve to this nose. "I wish we didn't have to get it soaked in that anti-gas gunk. Gives me a headache."

"And it breathes like a mackinaw," Sterling said. "Three days and we're heading back. No need to lug a raincoat. Not with these jackets."

As they neared the ball-field, Sam spotted the Protestant chaplain on an ammo crate and plank platform. An expanded congregation of several hundred spread out before the makeshift altar. The chaplain wore a flowing black robe affixed with silver jump wings. Jump wings earned under Sam's tutelage. The service had begun.

Approaching from the left flank, Sam scanned the crowd. Captain Tarver knelt near the back. Jennings and Springwater were two rows behind Tarver's left shoulder. Pettigrew knelt right next to Tarver. Pettigrew interrupted his mock reference to smirk at Sam and tap his watch.

Sam leaned close to Sterling. "Go to the Catholic service if you want."

"Why?"

"See Pettigrew? Next to Captain Tarver."

"Yeah. So?"

"So now I'm not the biggest hypocrite here." Sam removed his helmet and knelt.

The chaplain—a major by rank and Episcopalian by trade—finished his call to worship and launched into a dramatic reading of the Twenty-third Psalm. In an intonation one might expect from a New England reverend, he proclaimed: "The Lord is my shepherd; I shall not want. He maketh me to lie down in green pastures: he leadeth me beside the still waters…"

Sam's mind drifted. *Shepherd, huh? I suppose the Army intends to comfort us lambs being led to slaughter. Too bad last time I heard this was at my kid brother's funeral, so it's not working, parson.*

"He restoreth my soul: he leadeth me in the paths of righteousness for his name's sake…"

The wind picked up. Several raindrops hit Sam's shorn head. A chill shot down his spine.

The chaplain gazed skyward. "Yea, though I *jump into* the valley of the shadow of death, I will fear no evil…"

Sam jerked his head up. *Did I hear that right?* He looked to his left and found the same look of uncertainty on Sterling's face. He looked toward the front.

Tarver was nodding his head and saying, "Amen. Amen, preacher. We're *jumping* into that valley. Amen. Jumping into the valley of the shadow."

He'd heard right. The chaplain now had Sam's full attention.

"…for thou art with me; thy rod and thy staff they comfort me."

I'd prefer the comfort of some good arty support.

"Thou preparest a table before me in the presence of mine enemies."

The Krauts may just decide to interrupt our little picnic.

"Thou anointest my head with oil; my cup runneth over."

A drop of rainwater rolled off his forehead and down the bridge of his nose, leaving an irritating tickle.

"Surely goodness and mercy shall follow me all the days of my life…"

How many days will that be? General Taylor says three days and we're out.

"…and I will dwell in the house of the Lord forever."

Today's Sunday, so maybe next weekend with Maggie in Kensington Gardens.

His attention on the sermon diminished in a downward spiral of mental drift. He fidgeted like an adolescent in a hot and crowded Baptist church made of Ozark flagstone—just like at his brother's funeral.

Three days and the straight-legs take over. Then it's back to England. Back to Maggie. And then what…? Then what? Weren't those Maggie's exact words? He knew what was next—another jump. And another jump. And yet another jump. Until Hitler's defeat, or Sam's death or maiming—whichever came first.

Another raindrop rolled off his head and came to rest in the corner of his eye.

The reverend roared, "May we, O Lord, not fail our brothers at arms in their hour of great and dire need…"

Now he's making some sense. He bit his lower lip until it hurt. *I can't let First Platoon down!*

"…as we embark upon this great crusade against the godless forces of evil. In our Lord's name, amen and amen!" The chaplain raised his head and held his arms over the assembled paratroopers. "Go with God's speed. Geronimo!"

Sam lingered long enough to assure that Captain Tarver noticed him.

"Glad I chose to be Protestant today," Sterling said. "The major's not as long-winded as that Catholic colonel. Let's grab a good spot in the chow line."

Sam arched a brow. "You really feel like eating?"

Sterling licked his lips. "Prime steak and ice cream today."

Sam frowned. The steak only reminded him of promises unkept. Desires unfulfilled. "What chalk number you in?"

Sterling held up three fingers. "Able's the tip of the spear on DZ-D. Cross your fingers. Hope our pathfinders have it secured and marked *before* we get the green light."

A gust of wind hit Sam's face. He looked northwest. Dark clouds rolled on the horizon. "What's the weather forecast?"

"Could be perfect in France." Sterling grinned. "Full moon and a front about to move through. Just about ideal for cutting boar pigs."

*　　　*　　　*

The tent's canvas sides billowed and popped like the sails of a clipper ship in a gale. Sam shut out the weather annoyances and focused on finishing stuffing his musette bag. Without removing the added D-ration box with its fortified chocolate bars, he tried squeezing in an extra paratrooper first aid kit—he'd already tied one kit to the front of his net-covered helmet.

A poncho-clad figure slid between the door-flaps, stood just inside the pyramidal tent, and removed his wet helmet. Sam recognized Captain Tarver and alerted his second lieutenant tent-mates.

"At ease," Captain Tarver said. "Relax men. And I mean, *relax*. School is out!"

Sam recognized the code phrase for Operation Neptune's cancellation and slammed a D-ration onto his cot. "They scrubbed our jump?"

"Not exactly. The entire invasion's been postponed," Captain Tarver said. "It's not just the air. The fellas going in from the sea wouldn't stand a chance. Weather lets up and we're on for tomorrow, exact same timetable. They've got a good movie for us, if anyone's interested."

Sam exhaled hard. His stomach did flip-flops. He couldn't identify his feelings. Relief. Disappointment. Frustration. He didn't know what to do, so he sat on his cot and reclined until flat on his back. He looked at his watch—now it was thirty hours until he had to board his C-47. Within five minutes, sleep overtook him.

*　　　*　　　*

Yeovil, England

Maggie sat in the Yeovil train station and studied her Royal Automobile Club map. She found herself in southern Somerset County—a district entirely unfamiliar to her—and on the eastern edge of where she had deduced Merryfield's proximity. It had taken half of Sunday just to get this far from Overton.

Rain lashed against the station windows. She had decisions to make. The time—8:30 P.M.—made it painfully evident she wouldn't find Merryfield today. Yet there couldn't be many tomorrows left. A friend working at the Ministry of Defense had recently whispered that over two-million Americans were in Southern England. *Yet I haven't seen one ruddy Yank in days.*

Every Yeovil resident she'd queried claimed total ignorance concerning Merryfield. One conductor advised her that proper English ladies did not go about seeking Yanks on military facilities.

From Yeovil, she had two options for launching off into the prime search area between Ilminster and Langport—both involved trains. She could head west to Chard, transfer and head north toward Ilminster. Or, she could go straight by rail to Langport, only about ten miles away.

At the ticket window she explained her plight and requested a schedule.

"If you'd be my daughter, I'd send you right home," the agent said.

Thank God I'm not your daughter. Maggie silently counted to five. "Thank you for your concern, sir. Could you please simply advise me on the best route?"

"Nary a train heading Chard way tonight. Only one Langport way."

The schedule dictating her choice, Maggie dug into her coin purse. "Fine, I'll take the Langport train. The fare?"

"I wouldn't do that either, miss. You'll find no lodging there. You should catch the first train from here in the morning."

"What time?"

"Nine o'clock. Stops in Langport on its way to Taunton."

"Fine, I'd like to buy a ticket." Maggie pushed bank notes across the counter. "And might you suggest lodging?"

"Certainly. Red Lion Inn, across the road."

Maggie thanked the man and pivoted to leave.

"Miss, it be none of my business, but…"

Maggie responded with a frustrated frown.

"Well, my brother has a wee dairy down at Upottery. About a fortnight ago they had several hundred Yank paras pour in with them fancy eagle-head shoulder flashes."

The mention of the 101st's emblem grabbed Maggie's interest. "And?"

"My brother figures his ship's come in. A new market of robust young men for his fresh Guernsey milk and butter. But to his chagrin, nary a soldier has been allowed outside the barbwire they strung up. And he's not allowed near the Yanks."

The news left Maggie crestfallen. She had suspected that her task wouldn't be easy, but the railway clerk's story painted it as impossible. *Yet, Sam is an officer. There're exceptions, certainly.*

"Sorry, lass. But there be no use getting your hopes up just to get them dashed."

I will find a way. You, sir, didn't land your position through creative thinking and grand ambition. Maggie departed.

She entered her room on the second floor of the Red Lion Inn. Crossing the street had left her drenched. Exhaustion overtook her. She didn't know what to do, so she sat on her bed and reclined until flat on her back. She looked at her watch—now it was twelve hours until she had to board her train. Within five minutes, sleep overtook her.

Chapter 28

Green Light

5 June 1944, Morning
Merryfield, England

Sam awoke without prompting. Three other lieutenants stirred. The wind no longer pumped the canvas sides in and out like a giant bellows. He rose and stuck his head outside the tent door. The clouds were breaking up and drifting eastward. "Too bad they can't just drop us right now."

"We'll still have your full moon tonight." Sterling stepped next to him, stretched and yawned. "Let's not rush things."

*   *   *

Langport, England

Maggie disembarked the train and glanced at her wristwatch. Eleven-thirty already. She hastened her pace. *I do hope Chloe remembered to cover for me.*

The hour stop in the village of Martock—one which the ticket clerk had failed to mention—had put Maggie behind on her self-imposed timetable. Inside the Langport train station, she inquired about Merryfield from a conductor, ticket clerk, and a banker-looking man in a bowler hat.

Only a cleaning lady offered more than a shrug or curt reply: "If I'd be you, I'd check at the Royal Mail, not some old bird working a mop."

After brisk five-minute walk from the train station she found the post office. It had a worktable, a wall covered in brass and glass postal boxes, and a counter separating patrons from the clerk. Patriotic posters and fly specks adorned the beige walls.

"Aye, I'm aware of a Merryfield." The postal clerk spoke without looking up from sorting letters. "Forwarded mail that way to some chaps doing a bit o' construction."

"Where exactly is Merryfield?"

"North edge of Ilton, on the road from Isle Abbotts."

Maggie unfolded her RAC map atop the postal counter. The clerk continued his letter sorting. She found Isle Abbotts. Her hope surged. An elderly gent entered and queued up. Ignoring the proper folds, she gathered the map and stepped away from the counter. The pensioner purchased stamps and shuffled out.

Maggie cleared her throat. "Do excuse me again, sir, but I'd be most grateful if you'd suggest the best route."

The clerk made a sour face and appraised her over the half-spectacles perched on the tip of his long nose. "You sound like a Londoner." He leaned forward over the counter and looked at her feet. "No bus service from here south. Not with the petrol shortage. And you don't look particularly dressed for a twelve-mile trek on bad road. Take the train. Here to Taunton. Taunton to Ilminster. From Ilminster you'll have a wee hike." He slammed a rubber stamp on four parcels. "I imagine if you got a good jump on it you might get to Merryfield a couple hours before dark."

"Oh, that simply won't do at all." She pouted. "You said it's only twelve miles."

"Aye, lass. And in Somerset County you won't be finding no ruddy Underground. No taxis. No trains departing every five minutes. Now if you'd kindly excuse me, I have the King's business to attend."

She departed, unenthused, contemplating the journey's next leg. She considered her valise and what clothes remained that would allow her to look presentable to Sam. She was wearing them. *I'll jolly well never last twelve miles in these shoes. Certainly, it can't take all day by train.* She examined her pocketbook to see if she had enough schillings for train fare and another night's lodging. Enough, but barely. *I can skip lunch.*

She clenched her jaw and fought the urge to swear.

*   *   *

Merryfield, England

Every 501st paratrooper at Merryfield crowded around the platform that the day before had served as a pulpit. Yet Sam had never witnessed the religious fervor Colonel Howard Johnson was whipping up. Not at a Banta Springs First Baptist brush-arbor revival meeting. Not at a UCLA football pep rally.

Anticipating the speech's climax, Sam pressed forward. Fellow paratroopers surged like the tide, jostling him from behind.

"Who's the best?" Colonel Johnson shouted.

"We are!" Sam shouted in practiced regimental unison.

"I *said*, who's the best?"

"We are!" the paratroopers screamed even louder.

"You know any one of you is worth three in any other army. But today, I look out and can say that four Nazis against one Geronimo would still be no contest!"

Sam grinned. *He's safe saying that now. Ike's unleashing us.*

"We've toiled together, sweated together." Colonel Johnson pointed at his men. "And tonight we will write history together!" He bent over to pull his trench knife from the scabbard lashed to his ankle.

Captain Tarver shifted his stance and blocked Sam's view. Sam craned his neck to see. Pinball tiptoed and asked Collins, "What gives?"

Holding a monstrous Randall Bowie knife, Colonel Johnson thrust his fist high above his head. "'Ere another dawn. Yes indeed, before I see another sunrise, I hope this knife is buried in the back of the foulest, black-hearted Nazi bastard in France!" Colonel Johnson twisted the blade in the air and scanned his men. "Are you with me?"

The roared response drowned out Sam's yell. He glanced to his right. Silva hollered and waved two knifes above his head. Sam might've even joined in with his own trench knife if the crush of bodies hadn't prevented him from reaching his ankle sheath.

"Then let's go get 'em! Good hunting, men!" Colonel Johnson jumped off the raised planks. "Line up now. I want to shake the hand of each and every man."

*   *   *

Taunton, England

Maggie gazed at her wristwatch. It did no good—the train remained motionless.

She exhaled hard and prayed.

Eight twenty-five in the evening. She tapped her foot and huffed. She caught herself reading the same paragraph in *Gone With the Wind*—a gift from Sam—for the third time. She sat stranded farther from Ilminster than she had been in the early afternoon at Langport. According to her RAC map, from Ilminster she had at least another two miles on foot to Merryfield. *I should've just trekked cross-country. Could've caught a ride on a farmer's wagon.*

She forced herself to return to Scarlett O'Hara's world. If the train departed on schedule, she'd be to Ilminster by ten o'clock. If not, no cause for panic, she'd simply find Merryfield in the morning. *Chloe will keep covering for me.*

Chapter 29

The Tarmac

5 June 1944, Evening
Merryfield, England

Sam paced around his assigned C-47. In the past forty-five minutes he'd inspected it from wingtip to wingtip, nose to tail-rudder, twice. Unlike his father, he knew nothing about inspecting a C-47—it just seemed more productive than tapping his toes on the tarmac, or chewing his tenth stick of Wrigley's Spearmint.

Sam noted the freshly painted invasion stripes—three white bands on a black base on each wing and encircling the fuselage near the tail. *So that's the clever plan to keep our own navy from blowing troop transports out of the sky like they did at Sicily.*

The large 3J painted near the cockpit designated this C-47 as being a part of the 99th Troop Carrier Squadron. An artist's cartoon-like rendition of a red fox—endowed with an exaggerated human female form—decorated the plane's nose. Aft of the fox the artist had scrolled the plane's name: The Voluptuous Vixen. Smaller script below the fox announced: Gentlemen may prefer blondes, but pilots prefer redheads.

Sam smiled. *You can keep your redheads, flyboy. This paratrooper prefers one particular blonde.*

Across Merryfield, groups of fifteen to twenty paratroopers—called *sticks*—clustered near their assigned Skytrains.

"Sarge, why we just sitting around, twiddling our thumbs?" Pinball patted the black curls atop his head, now almost entirely shorn off.

Springwater ignored him.

"Come on, Pinball." Silva lit a Lucky Strike. "You know Springwater doesn't take stupid questions right before we board."

"Do the math, Pinball." Lazeski stood and towered a good seven inches over Pinball. "We're Chalk Number-Two and they've got eighty-nine more after us. It takes time. Got someplace else you need to be?"

"Reckon we found the right dang plane, Laze?" Collins asked.

A jeep pulled up to the plane. An Air Corps tech sergeant jumped out holding a large chalk stick and scrawled a foot-high numeral 2 next to the C-47's door.

Silva pointed at the chalked number. "Any other brainy questions, you big hillbilly?"

Collins spit a brown stream Silva's direction.

Watching the chalk glide onto the plane's fuselage gave Sam an idea. The long-shot was worth it, if it concerned Maggie. "Hey, Sergeant, got any of that chalk to spare?"

The Air Corps tech sergeant tossed Sam a stick.

"How about a quick ride back to the tents, too, if you're heading that way."

"Hop in, sir."

"Springwater, the stick's yours." Sam jumped into the jeep. "I'll be back in ten."

*   *   *

Sam returned to the Voluptuous Vixen twenty minutes later. Paratroopers stood in groups of two or three, applying burnt cork to their faces. "Anyone got any to spare?"

Springwater lobbed him a chunk. "Have mine."

Sam caught the burnt cork. "Putting on warpaint?"

"Not the Crow way."

All men were supposed to blacken their faces for night camouflage. Sam wasn't going to press the issue. Springwater's copper skin would never give his position away in the dark.

Sam darkened his cheekbones. "What happened to the warpaint tradition?"

"Crow paint after battle. Black. I'll mark a band across my cheeks and eyes back to my hair."

"So that's why I got you that black shoe polish in London?"

Springwater looked down at his brown Corcorans. "Wasn't for my boots, sir."

Soot covered Sergeant Lazeski's fair skin surrounding where his wire-rimmed glasses had been, leaving him looking like the negative image of a raccoon.

"Come on, Silva," Private Morton said in a whiney voice. "Give me the password one more time."

"Listen this time. The challenge is *flash*. The response is *thunder*. Just like it happens in the sky. Lightning flashes, then comes the thunder. Then the first guy says, *welcome*. Three parts: flash, thunder, welcome. Got it?"

Morton nodded. "Thanks, buddy."

"Yeah, and they'll change it in about twenty-eight hours. Then what you going to do? We're doomed with you as our runner." Silva punctuated his opinion with a string of Portuguese oaths. "Some GI's going to blow your freakin' head clean off."

"Use your toy cricket. It's idiot-proof," Harrigan said. "If I don't get back a double..." The machinegunner pressed his brass cricket twice. Click-clack. Click-clack. "...whoever's on the other end gets a half-belt sprayed his way."

"Remember orders," Springwater said. "Just grenades tonight unless you've got no choice. Getting trigger-happy will just give away your position."

"This won't give away my position either, Sarge." Sneering, Silva brandished his black Fairbairn-Sykes British commando stiletto.

Sam looked Silva over. "Just how many knives you packing?"

"Sir, if'n you want to go 'n count that switchblade jackknife, that'd be six." Collins began pointing out blades attached to Silva. "He's done got that Limey pig-sticker on one ankle. An Army issue trench knife on the other. His bayonet on his left hip, and his daddy's dern Portagee Bowie on his right. And then there's one of them machetes. Reckon he thinks he's got him a genuine sword."

"What's it to you, hillbilly? Not counting the machete, that's only two more than you. And the Army says each squad must have a machete. Why shouldn't I be the one carrying it?" Silva took a drag on his cigarette and glared at Collins. "A big hayseed like yourself obviously can't appreciate the weaponry needs of the Latin male."

"And I ain't fixin' to let no Kraut close enough to this ol' boy to be needing no pig-sticker. Pappy didn't raise no fool." Collins gnawed off a chunk of his twisted braid of tobacco.

"Didn't he, now? Seems he forgot to warn you about jumping out of flying airplanes. Probably because he's never even seen one."

"Sorry I asked," Sam said. "Save some hostility for the Krauts." Sam finished blackening his forehead and chin. His sweat helped smear on the charred cork.

He spotted Pettigrew making a beeline for him. Pettigrew's face retained the greasy sheen despite the burnt cork camouflage. He handed Sam a sheet of paper. "The operation is a go. You're ordered to read this to your whole stick before embarkation."

"Will do, sir."

"Once on the DZ, don't be a cowboy, do it just like we rehearsed it. You and that Injun roll up your stick. Get Collins and Skinner out scouting the route. Then you find me. We'll advance on the locks, platoon diamond formation. I want First Platoon all under me and first to the locks. Got it, Lieutenant Henry?"

Sam nodded.

Pettigrew turned to leave, but pivoted back. "One more thing. Word is, do not, I repeat; *do not* bother with prisoners tonight. Focus on mission objective, period."

"Sir, I want to be clear on this. Are you ordering us to not take prisoners?"

Pettigrew scowled. "We've got a mission to execute on their turf. How do you propose we babysit EPWs? We won't have the time, facilities, nor inclination. Just strike, seize, hold." Pettigrew returned to Chalk Number-1.

Sam wondered why he hadn't considered the potential prisoner dilemma earlier. Sterling's somber, *thou shalt not kill* paradox came back into his mind. He took off his helmet and ran his fingers back through his hair. *Just disarm and move on. I won't…I can't shoot prisoners.*

Private Vigiano's face looked troubled. "Did I hear Lieutenant Pettigrew right?"

"Yep, Pinball. Geronimo don't take no prisoners," Silva said. "I'm liking this parachute infantry life more and more, boys."

Sam turned his attention to the page Pettigrew had delivered. SECRET dominated the top of the page in bold capital letters. Before being sequestered at Merryfield, he'd never seen a secret document. Now it seemed SHAEF was handing them out like Hershey bars. In unique Army grammatical construction, the top of the page stated that the document was from the Supreme Allied Commander and was to be read by an officer to all troops, but only when certain that there'd be no postponement of Operation Overlord. He read the notice through, reread it, then called his stick together.

The other twenty men of Chalk Number-2 congregated in an arc and took a knee on the grass adjacent the tarmac.

"Sergeant Springwater, Sergeant Phillips, did you hand out the invasion francs?"

Both men nodded.

Morton raised his hand. "Sir, what's a franc worth? More than a dollar or less than a dollar? I still don't have the pound, schilling thing figured—"

"What the Sam Hill does it matter to you?" Collins asked.

Silva sneered. "Yeah, you just keep forking it over until her *no* becomes *yes*." Nervous laughter erupted.

"That's *non* becomes *oui*," Pinball said. "Looks like you've been reading that little French phrasebook they passed out about like you read the VD pamphlets."

"You clowns just shut up," Sergeant Lazeski said. "Listen to the lieutenant!"

Sam held up the secret page. "What I'm about to read you deals with your question, Morton. We're not to make a bad situation worse for the French. If you have to take something from a Frenchman, you're to pay for it."

"Like his daughter?" Silva whispered too loudly. Subdued snickers followed.

Sam cleared his throat. "This is from General Eisenhower himself." He read aloud: "'You are about to be engaged in a great undertaking—the invasion of Europe. Our purpose is to bring about, in the company of our Allies, and our comrades on other fronts—'"

"Comrades? More like butchering Bolsheviks." Lazeski looked up. "Sorry, sir. Didn't mean to be heard."

Sam read several more lines outlining the political picture and increased his volume with one paragraph: "'As a representative of your country, you will be welcomed with deep gratitude by the liberated peoples who for years have longed for this deliverance—'"

"Mademoiselle, meet your very own Latin liberator." Silva's comment drew an elbow jab from Collins and more snickers.

Springwater rose to his full six-foot-two height. The squad leader's black-eyed gaze pierced each man in his squad starting and ending with Silva. "We're about to follow this man into the enemy's camp. I'll take the next joker who interrupts Lieutenant Henry out behind that plane, take off these stripes, and beat some respect into him." Springwater scowled and scanned the tops of the down-turned helmets. "Look up here. Let me see your eyes. I want to see eyes of proud warriors."

When every head was looking up Springwater knelt and nodded toward Sam.

Sam found his place on the page. "'The inhabitants of Nazi-occupied Europe have suffered great privations, and you will find that many of them lack even the barest necessities. You, on the other hand, have been, and will continue to be, provided adequate food, clothing, and other necessities.'"

Sam looked up from the paper. He had their full attention. "'You must not deplete the already meager local stocks of food and other supplies by indiscriminate buying, thereby fostering the black market, which can only increase the hardship of the inhabitants. The rights of individuals, as to their persons and property, must be scrupulously respected…'"

Sam read on for another minute about mutual respect, defeating a common enemy, and a lasting peace. The closing phrase struck him as odd: "…without which our great effort will have been in vain." He'd never considered that victory didn't lie in just defeating totalitarianism, but also—according to Eisenhower—in the moral climate and actions in which they achieved victory.

Sam mused over Eisenhower's philosophical last words. He couldn't let it end so awkwardly. He needed to say something—something meaningful, before there was no time for anything but orders shouted over the noise of over 180 Pratt & Whitney aircraft engines. He had prepared nothing.

"OK men, listen up." He winced at starting his speech like a bad Hollywood production selling war bonds. "We're all a little edgy. So I don't mind if…well, it's OK to stay a little loose. Before dawn, we're all going to experience sights and sounds none of us have ever experienced. We'll need each other. We're a team. We stick together no matter what. No one gets left behind. You each have a job to do on the team and I know every last one of you can do it with excellence. I've watched you with pride from the day I was lucky enough to get assigned to First Platoon." He scanned his stick and saw some grins of confidence return.

"You'll need to both take the initiative and execute orders without a second thought. I'm not going to sugarcoat this. I can offer you no assurances except my best effort to see the mission accomplished and every last one of us getting out of Normandy alive and in one piece. There'll be ninety-odd planes leaving here tonight, who knows how many hundreds more from the rest of Hundred-'n-First and Eighty-Second, but there's not a single plane I'd choose over this one right here, the one hauling Chalk Number-Two. Let's go get it done—done right—and get back."

In the background, aircrews—clustered in groups of three or four—moved in a wave toward the C-47s. "Here come our chauffeurs. Get geared up."

Solemn-faced, each man moved away to the scattered piles of weaponry and parachute harnesses.

"Hey!" Sam said. "Forget the SOP. Put the Mae West on last, over your chute harness."

"We're packin' over a hundred pounds each, Lieutenant," Skinner said. "Will them dang vests even float us?"

"A whole lot better than it will from under a T-Five harness," Sam said.

Sam marveled at the weight of his own load. Several times he'd practiced what were termed "full combat load" jumps, yet he'd never jumped with this much gear. Doing a visual inventory, he worked around his web-belt and harness shoulder straps.

First, he had a canvas pouch holding two clips for the 45-auto pistol. The big pistol itself he carried in a leather shoulder holster under his left arm. To the left of the pistol magazine pouch was a specially rigged lightweight canvas pouch made by the Air Corps that held two pineapple fragmentation grenades—the standard allotment. Yet orders specified to use grenades exclusively until dawn. The math didn't work, so he'd found additional places to stow grenades.

Next to the grenade pouch, he had attached a standard carbine ammo pouch that held two fifteen-round magazines. His canteen rested on the back of his left hip. Next to the canteen hung the rope coil all paratroopers carried. A folding shovel hung near the center of the belt. He'd cut four inches off the handle to make it more compatible with airborne missions. His canvas map case draped over his shoulder so it came to rest covering the back of his right hip. He slung his binocular case so it hung on his left side, just above the gasmask in its rubberized case.

The folding-stock 30-caliber carbine rested along his right leg in its canvas sheath. In front of it was the same specially rigged pouch that carried the grenades, only this one held four carbine magazines.

On his left suspender strap, high on his chest he slipped the spoon of a smoke grenade through a d-ring and held it in place with friction tape. On the right side of his harness, he strapped his first additional fragmentation grenade in a similar manner. His stuffed musette bag, normally carried on the small of the back, would ride on his lower belly, under his reserve chute, for the jump.

The weight carried below his waist made walking even more awkward. He'd strapped an M-3 fighting knife to his right ankle and a British Hawkins landmine on his left. Sam used the cargo pockets on each thigh to carry gifts for the French—extra rations, cigarettes and chocolate bars— and an extra hand grenade in each, making a total of five fragmentation grenades.

He'd stuffed the four jacket pockets with miscellaneous items he thought he might need. As part of the standard issue or small arms ammunition, he'd thrown over his shoulder a cotton bandoleer with six additional carbine magazines. Last to go on was the T-5 chute harness, main and reserve chutes, Mae West inflatable life vest, and helmet. His brass and tin toy cricket dangled from a string attached to the zipper of the collar pouch that held his paratrooper's emergency Schrade switchblade jackknife.

He ached for the one item he lacked for the jump—a picture of Maggie. In all their times together in London a simple photo had eluded him. A steak dinner he could explain away, but not a picture. He'd have to close his eyes to recall the honey-brown eyes and beautiful countenance he longed for.

Chapter 30

Embarkation

5 June 1944, Late Evening
Approaching Ilminster, England

Maggie sensed the train slowing. She gazed eastward, out the train's left side.

Blurred trees flashed by. Far off, she thought she spotted a jutting airplane tail. She twisted and pressed her head against the glass.

A gap in the trees revealed a field covered in planes, a half-mile distant. Clusters of men milled around. Her heart jumped. Trees blocked her view. Merryfield! She sighed. *Now what?*

She grabbed her belongings and moved into the aisle. A conductor, facing away, impeded her progress. Trying to squeeze past, her valise bumped his elbow.

"No need to make haste, miss. We'll be in Ilminster soon enough." The conductor gestured toward the interior of the car, empty but for three passengers. "You'll experience no delay."

"The airfield we just passed, is it Merryfield?"

"I'm employed by the Southwestern Railroad, not the RAF, miss."

Brakes squealed. She lost her balance and lurched forward.

The conductor grabbed her arm. "You best have a seat, miss."

*   *   *

Merryfield, England

Sam heaved Springwater's parachute pack high onto the tall Indian's back. With the slack out of the straps, Springwater clipped the T-5 harness across his chest and tightened the belly-band through his reserve chute until the Thompson submachine gun—slung upside-down over his right shoulder—became secured against his side. Springwater fastened the rest of the harness around his upper thighs.

Sam tapped the gun. "Why not carry your Thompson in the case?"

"A Crow warrior never carries his bow into battle unstrung."

"Makes sense." Sam picked up his main chute and reserve harness. "I've been meaning to tell you, you're jumpmaster."

Springwater helped Sam into the parachute harness. "If an officer's onboard, an officer serves as jumpmaster."

"What?" Sam grinned. "You don't have all the maps and landmarks leading to DZ-D memorized?"

"Lieutenant Pettigrew wouldn't approve."

"Well, I do believe we've seen the last of Lieutenant Pettigrew 'til we're on French soil. And I really don't think he'll know which of us went out the door first. I want the honor to be yours."

"This won't help me make chief. You're here, not me leading the war party."

"Too bad. You're still jumpmaster."

Springwater's focus shifted to past Sam. "Didn't you say we'd seen the last of Lieutenant Pettigrew?"

Sam turned. Pettigrew, burdened under a full combat load, waddled toward them. First platoon's medic—a short man with a wrestler's build—followed.

Pettigrew smirked. "Your stick get it backwards, Henry?"

"Afraid I don't follow you, sir."

"You're the only stick putting Mae Wests outside the parachute harness."

"Sir, most men are wearing over a hundred pounds of gear. They'd never get out of a T-Five harness before drowning."

"Once again, you decide you know more than your superiors. This have anything to do with your unfounded fear of a water landing?"

Sam frowned. "If legitimate concerns weren't warranted, the Army would've never issued the vests in the first place."

"I'm making note of this failure to follow SOPs." As Pettigrew's agitation grew so did the shrillness of his voice. "And as for you, Sergeant Springwater." Pettigrew shifted his disdainful gaze to the Thompson strapped to Springwater's side. "I've taken note that you have chosen to not use the issued equipment required to protect both your weapon and yourself. However, your independent attitudes are not why I'm here. Medical staff has something for us."

The medic, Doc Walters, stepped up and handed Sam a small manila envelope.

Sam opened the flap and squeezed the envelope open, revealing a pile of tiny white pills. "We already have halizone tablets for water."

"Seasick pills. They do the trick in the air, too," Doc Walters said. "Give each man one now. One more mid-flight."

Sam shook his head. "Never had to take these before."

Pettigrew smirked. "We've never jumped into combat before either, Henry."

"Expecting rough weather crossing the Channel?" Sam asked.

"Follow orders and quit trying to figure everything out." Pettigrew waddled off.

Doc Walters turned to follow, but Sam held him by the shoulder and leaned close to his ear. "Hey. Doc, shoot straight with me. Don't these pills knock a guy out?"

Doc Walters shrugged. "Some more than others, sir."

"Look, Doc, we've been running on adrenaline since before noon yesterday. Most only got twenty of their forty winks last night. In about three hours we'll be in our first combat. No prospect for sleep for at least a couple days. Whose bright idea was it to do this in a drugged stupor?"

"Preaching to the choir, sir." Doc Walters pointed to the two stripes on his sleeve. "These don't carry much weight. See you at the DZ, sir."

Sam waddled to the men lined up near the Voluptuous Vixen's door. Each forced step required exertion. "Chalk Number-Two, we've got one more item of business." He turned so his voice carried away from Pettigrew. "Who has trouble keeping his chow down when we fly?"

Phillips and Harrigan lifted an arm as high as they could under their burdens.

"I better see that hand, Phillips. You splashed all over my jump boots on Exercise Eagle," Sam said. "I want every man to take one pill out of this envelope. Only Phillips and Harrigan are to swallow the pill. The rest of you are to throw it back and miss your mouth. And don't ever mention it again. Am I clear?"

The men passed the envelope down the line. Each did as instructed.

Frantic coughing erupted, followed by rapid spitting. Morton bent forward, hacking. "It went in my mouth."

"Morton, you ignoramus," Collins said. "Can't even miss your dang mouth."

The laughter made Sam cringe. He cast a furtive glance toward Pettigrew.

A Troop Carrier Command tech sergeant stuck his head out the Voluptuous Vixen's door. "Time to load, sir."

*   *   *

Ilton, England

Daylight fading fast, Maggie hurried her pace up the railroad tracks.

Once off the train in Ilminster she had referred to her RAC map and noted that the most direct route took her straight back up the rail-bed. It would save her about a half-mile of farm road angles and odd turns, and lead her right to the spot where she'd spotted the C-47s. She also avoided meddlesome village folk offering unsolicited opinions.

She'd crossed the Ilton road ten minutes earlier. It felt like thirty. She gazed ahead, trying to recognize the spot where she'd spotted the airplanes. Nothing looked familiar.

She tripped on a railroad tie, again. This time she regained her balance before hitting the ground. She faced a bothersome dilemma. If she looked very far forward, she tripped on the ties. If she looked down, she made more rapid progress, but couldn't scan the distance for planes.

The rail-bed surface put her at least six feet below the view she had from the train window. She massaged her temples. Merryfield had to be close. Seeing no sign of airplanes, she stumbled on.

A distant engine coughed to life. She tiptoed and gazed in the direction of the noise. Nothing. She trotted to her right, down off the railroad bed, then back up a small embankment to a row of brush and small trees along an old fence.

She reached a gap in the vegetation. Her heart leapt at the vast panorama of C-47s in staggered rows. Yet she failed to find any clusters of khaki-clad soldiers.

She waded through the grass down the fence-line. Her pulse raced.

At a fence corner, she followed it left, toward the planes. She almost collided with a sign warning: CIVILIANS ARE FORBIDDEN TO LOITER OR TALK TO TROOPS!

In the gathering dusk she made out the central control-tower, scattered outbuildings, and a whole sea of pyramidal tents.

More engines ignited. The cacophony grew.

No! Her throat tightened. *Not now! I just found you!*

She dropped her valise and busted through waist-high grass as fast as her legs could carry her.

*   *   *

Hands under the main parachute pack, Sam boosted Springwater upward into the Voluptuous Vixen.

Wanting one last view of England's lush landscape, he pivoted and took in the distant silhouetted hills. He glanced toward the other C-47s transporting Able Company. Several had already started their engines.

Then a most welcome sight appeared. Lloyd Sterling stood in the door of Chalk Number-3 giving a thumbs-up. Sam returned the gesture.

However, Sam had a more specific message. Certain their gazes were locked, he attempted exaggerated hand signals. He stabbed at his chest with a repeated motion and then with forked fingers pointed at his own eyes. He then pointed directly back at Sterling. He ended the series of gestures by holding his point at the horizon toward France. *See you there, buddy.*

Sterling responded by holding his palms up and shrugging his shoulders. He faded backward into the darkness of Chalk Number-3's fuselage.

"Time to go, sir!"

The crew-chief's yell roused Sam. He looked up to the door. Two hands—one white and one copper—reached down. He struggled just to get one foot onto the first ladder step. With an upward lurch, he grabbed the hands that tugged him into the cabin.

"Enjoy the jumpmaster's view, Springwater." Sam worked his way up the sloping aisle toward the cockpit. The two door-bags and twenty-one overburdened paratroopers packed the cabin. The smokers had lit up, leaving a blue haze in the cabin. Collins had nowhere to spit, so he bummed a Chesterfield off Morton.

Sam nodded at the first man after Springwater, their Bazooka man, Private Craighead. Sam walked past Silva. "Stick one for me, Joe. You choose which knife."

Silva gave a cocky grin.

Vigiano fingered a set of Rosary beads, eyes closed, lips moving.

"Relax, Pinball. You'll do just fine."

Pinball looked up with eyes like an altar boy. Which reminded Sam, the teen had indeed been one a mere three years earlier. "I'll do my very best, sir."

"Of that, I have no doubt." Sam glanced left. Collins's bulk crowded Silva and Morton on each side. "Out of chew already, Collins?"

Collins patted his musette bag riding below his reserve chute.

Sam patted the Griswold bag holding the M-1 on Collins's chest. "When we hit the ground open this one first."

As Sam passed, Morton struggled to stand. "You need me, sir?"

"Have a seat. You're blocking the aisle."

"Sir, I got a question. If I'm your runner, why am I in the middle of the stick instead of next to you?"

"So if something happens to me you'll be just as close to Sergeant Springwater."

"Then why's Carter sitting next to you?"

"Can't afford to lose both runners all at once, now can we?" *And because he doesn't ask pestering questions every thirty seconds.* "Why don't you just try getting a little shut-eye before the red light comes on?"

"Yes, sir." Morton sat. "I'll just be right here if you need me."

As Sam waded through the knees and jump boots he overheard Pinball say, "Like where else would you be, Morton? Changing planes in midair?" Laughter followed. Sam glanced back. Morton flashed Pinball an obscene gesture and informed him where he could go.

"No doubt we'll all be there in about two and a half hours." Lazeski put his glasses in a hard case and stowed them in a special pocket he'd rigged near the collar of his jump jacket. "Dropped right smack-dab into Hell."

Sergeant Phillips, the mortar squad leader, was chewing gum with the jaw motion of a cow chewing her cud.

Sam tapped Phillips's knee. "You and your boys get on that yellow chute as soon as you can. We're going to need your tube." He looked at a round Irish face—freckles covered with burnt cork—sitting next to Phillips. "That goes double for you and your machinegun, Harrigan."

"Not leaving the DZ without finding the green chute, sir."

Sam moved through the mortar squad and past his empty bulkhead seat until he poked his head inside the cockpit. "No navigator?"

The pilot, copilot, and radio operator were conducting instrument checks. The copilot jerked his head around. "Not enough to go around. No problem. Chalk Number-One's got one and we plan on staying right on his wingtip."

"By the way, I'm Lieutenant Sam Henry. Glad you guys…" Obvious that the preoccupied pilots weren't listening, he quit talking.

The copilot fired up the starboard engine and spoke in technical aviation gibberish. The pilot glanced over his shoulder and gave Sam a get-out-of-my-business look. "Something bothering you, Lieutenant?"

"No, sir, Captain. It's just that my father makes these planes. The cockpit always reminds me of him. He worked at Douglas in Santa Mon—"

"That's just fine and dandy, Lieutenant." The pilot returned to his toggle switches and gauges. "Next time you drop Daddy a line perhaps you could mention that the port rudder pedal is too mushy to my liking, plus the starboard engine likes to blow gaskets." The pilot's comments drew a disrespectful chortle from the copilot. "Reminds me, how's the oil pressure?"

"Holding steady," the copilot said.

"Here we go then." The pilot threw his thumb over his shoulder. "Best grab your seat, Lieutenant. Chalk-One is already taxiing and we're supposed to be in the air five seconds behind her."

The C-47 lurched forward and threw Sam off balance. He grabbed the doorframe with both hands. He let go with his left hand and let the plane's momentum swing him back into his seat, next to the last mortar man, Private Perkowski, and across the aisle from Private Carter. The shovel handle dug into his thigh. The cockpit door slammed shut.

I wonder if Pa worked on this one. He closed his eyes. After thirty seconds of acceleration, he sensed the instant the landing gear lifted off English soil.

*   *   *

Maggie's mind convinced her heart that her mission was now futile. Gasping for breath, she stopped running.

The planes maneuvered into position. The roar of a multitude of propellers and scent of burnt aviation fuel assaulted her senses. She stared at the first plane racing down the tarmac and lifting off the ground. She remembered that Sam's favorite part of being a leader of a planeload of paratroopers was getting to gaze out the door. As the second plane took off, she waved toward the blackness of the plane's door.

Maggie continued the process with every plane. Tears flowed freely over her cheeks as each roared away. She lost count somewhere after forty.

The noise faded to silence. Darkness washed over the field.

She ran out of tears. Her legs burnt. Her aching arms hung limp. Her head throbbed. Her empty stomach twisted. She had experienced the sensation once before—at Ian's departure.

She blew her nose and turned to follow the fence into the darkness to recover her jettisoned valise.

She was quite certain she would never again see Sam.

Alone in the field, she gazed up at a darkening sky crowded with C-47s.

She cursed the war and questioned her God.

PART III

LET ALL THE WARRIORS DRAW NEAR.

Joel 3:9

Macbeth: If we should fail—
Lady Macbeth: We fail!
But screw your courage to the sticking place,
And we'll not fail.

WILLIAM SHAKESPEARE
Macbeth, 1606

Chapter 31

The Flight

6 June 1944, 0045 hours
English Channel

Sam poked his head out the C-47's portside door. Salty air blasted his face. Fingers locked onto the doorframe, his goggles allowed him to gaze upon the scene that had excited the unexcitable Springwater.

The panorama left Sam awestruck.

Illuminated by the full moon—less than two football fields below—sailed the invasion armada. Stretched across the English Channel as far as he could see, ships of every size and description held the same heading, each leaving a phosphorescent wake.

"Wow!" Sam yelled over the flight noise.

"Just *wow*?" Springwater yelled back into Sam's ear.

Sam pointed downward. "There're no English words for that."

Springwater said something Sam failed to catch. Sam cupped his hand behind his ear. The squad leader tried again, but to no avail. Springwater's lips seemed to form random syllables, mostly vowels. Sam cupped his hand again.

"The Crow have a word. The way *bishee*—you call buffalo—covered the Montana prairie." Springwater pointed out the door. "It looked like that."

Sam stared out at C-47s in flight level. He spotted chalks three, seven, nine and the nose of eight. Though his view prevented Sam from seeing it, he knew Chalk Number-1 flew the closest—just ahead of their port wingtip, setting the pace at 150 mph.

They'd been in the air well over an hour—most of that spent at higher altitudes forming up into their V formations. Every three planes formed a small V, which then joined with others to form a larger V-formation of three small Vs. These formations of nine planes would each pass over Drop Zone-D, wave after wave, until every C-47 had disgorged all human and munitions cargo.

Sam worked a gap on his left wrist between his jacket sleeve and glove and found himself trying to decipher the time from a wrist compass. He checked his right wrist—0047 hours. Forty-three minutes left. He headed back to his seat.

He got as comfortable as he could while sitting on his shovel handle and coiled rope. While folding a stick of Wrigley's Spearmint into his mouth, he recalled Springwater's comments about going into battle with an unstrung bow. Sam reached over his chest, past his reserve chute, and tried to unlatch his 45-auto from its shoulder holster. His first attempt came up short but he caught it on his second try. He pulled the 45's slide back and let it fly forward, loading a stubby cartridge from the seven-round clip. He gingerly lowered the hammer, thumbed it back to the half-cock safety position, then strained to holster the pistol.

Stretching out his right leg, he unsnapped the carbine case, and slid the weapon halfway out. He pulled back the carbine charging handle and let it fly forward. He double-checked the safety and slid it back into its sheath.

Safety SOP insisted on no chambered ammunition while in flight. Sam's violation didn't go unnoticed. His men went into a flurry of weapons checks and loading—primarily from men on crew-served weapons also carrying carbines. Most of the men carried M-1 rifles broken down into two pieces for transport in padded canvas Griswold bags strapped to their chests. Several packed personal pistols, usually gifts from concerned fathers. Silva and Collins had secured Army 45-autos by more creative means. Morton, armed with only one firearm—an M-1—gazed at his pistol-packing buddies, distress etched on his face.

The plane completed a wide ninety-degree turn, putting them over the Channel Islands of Jersey and Guernsey, now heading east-southeast on the last leg.

Sam's mind took him back to a Jersey cow. His boyhood chores had included milking Bessie before school. He recalled the odd sight of steam rising off her bony back on a frosty Ozark morn. She had a nasty habit of stepping in the bucket and spoiling the milk—seemingly in protest for the milk being taken against her will. His bizarre mental drift struck him as peculiar for a man about to be initiated in combat. However, his memory had no context for battle and only one for the name Jersey—so there his nervous mind wafted.

The crew-chief donned his steel pot and bulky flak-vest, and latched on his seat-pack emergency parachute. Pinball kissed his Rosary Beads and stuffed them away.

Sam glanced at the red and green jump lights by the door. *Come on, let's get this over with.* He leaned back to rest his head, but his protruding gear frustrated the effort. He leaned right and rested his helmet on the aluminum bulkhead.

Eyes closed, he soon found himself humming "Lili Marlene." Marlene Dietrich's sultry voice soon played in his mind:

> Bugler tonight don't play the call to arms
> I want another evening with her charms.
> Then we will say goodbye and part
> I always keep you in my heart
> With me, Lili Marlene
> With me, Lili Marlene

Yet Eisenhower did play the call to arms, free of romantic Hollywood partings. Sam needed a picture of Maggie. Eyes still closed, he settled on the best image his memory could conjure. Her large, honey-brown eyes were laden with tears.

Sam's stomach lurched upward. His eyes came wide open. The plane was gaining altitude fast and banking starboard. He glanced to the rear. The crew-chief shouted into an intercom headset. The crew-chief's agitated face prompted Sam to action. He struggled out of his seat, opened the cockpit door, and squeezed past the radio operator. The murky whiteness on the other side of the windshield stunned him.

"Level off at fifteen-hundred?" The copilot's voice cracked.

"No way," the pilot said. "We climb above this pea soup first."

"What about holding formation?" Sam cringed, certain the very next, and last, thing he would see through the windshield was another C-47.

"The wise guy who ordered that didn't know about this pea soup fog, buddy," the copilot said. "Our feet went dry and ten seconds later we hit this mess. We can hold formation and most likely die, or—"

"Hold on!" Sam's already racing pulse increased. "You mean we're over land?"

"Don't get your panties all in a bunch," the pilot said. "We'll drop you on DZ-D. Just won't be as pretty as we'd rehearsed."

After a couple minutes of silent tension, the plane popped above the fog.

"Twenty-five hundred feet," the copilot said in an aviator's deadpan tone—sweat beads rolling down his forehead betraying his actual mental state.

Sam leaned forward and craned his neck from side to side. "Where're the other planes?"

"Behind us, where they belong," the captain said. "Except Chalk-One. I suspect they stayed right on course."

The fogbank ended. Farther ahead, strings of crisscrossing tracers mesmerized Sam. Red glowing balls lanced upward. Small explosions flashed in the sky. Larger flames glowed stationary on the ground.

"Head on back, Lieutenant." The pilot wiped a palm on his pant leg. "We're about to earn all that hazardous-duty pay. And do shut the door on your way out. We prefer working in private." The pilot turned to the copilot. "I'm taking her back down to seven hundred. Find me some landmarks. And pronto."

Sam shut the cockpit door and looked down the cabin aisle. Anxious eyes begged for information. Sam fought to hide his own fear.

The C-47 began losing altitude and gaining airspeed. Knees buckling, he grabbed the cable for the static lines. All eyes were fixed upon him, except Springwater, who was hanging his head out the door.

Sam cupped his hands around his mouth. "Get ready for a little AA!"

An explosion off the starboard wing bucked the plane. Shrapnel peppered the fuselage. A string of machinegun bullets punctured the cabin. Collins dodged after the fact, squashing Morton.

The C-47 dipped and banked right. More bullets popped and pinged the port wing aluminum. The Voluptuous Vixen shuddered.

"Looks like them DZ-A and C boys done gave Jerry a wake-up call," Collins said over the engine noise and muffled explosions.

The crew-chief spoke into his intercom microphone, but Sam couldn't make out the words. Occupied by his duties, the crew-chief's face seemed to be the only one in the crowded cabin that Sam could see not etched with fear. Everyone else had nothing to do but wait. Wait for the jump light, or a high-velocity projectile to rip into his backside.

Springwater pulled his head back inside the door. Looking bewildered he adjusted his goggles and leaned his top-heavy body dangerously far out the door. A near miss jolted the plane. Springwater jerked back in, shook his left hand, and yanked off his glove. Blood blossomed on the back of his dark skin. He bit at the back of his hand, spit something out, and returned to hanging out the door.

The red light glowed—indicating they were four minutes out from the drop zone. And everyone knew it except the jumpmaster. The paratroopers stood and hooked their static lines.

The crew-chief tapped Springwater on the ankle and made exaggerated pointing thrusts toward the glowing red light. Springwater's expression changed from bewilderment to disgust.

"Stand up and hook up!" Springwater yelled out of habit as he hooked up himself and the two door-bags. "Check equipment!"

Each paratrooper made a flurry of final checks. "Sound off for equip—"

Slugs ripped into the tail section just aft of the cabin.

Springwater ducked.

Sam completed his check. "Twenty, OK!"

As the countdown shouts progressed, Springwater's alarmed eyes got Sam's attention. Something catastrophic was brewing. Sam could only guess at exactly what.

Private Craighead's voice cracked, "One, OK!"

"Shuffle to the door!" Springwater glanced outside.

The line of overburdened men contracted like a compressed spring.

Poised to shove the door bags, Springwater watched for the green light.

Sam pulled his goggles down over his eyes. "How about we break some records getting out of this tin can, Private Carter?"

"I'll be climbing up Perkowski's backside," Carter said.

Perkowski looked over his shoulder, face blanched. "You'll never catch me."

The starboard wing dipped hard and threw the packed paratroopers to their left. Arms flailed. Men scrambled and shoved off each other to recover balance.

The pilot overcorrected and launched those who had regained their feet over to their right side.

A door bag slid toward the exit. Springwater lunged, but the bag tumbled out.

Profanity filled the cabin.

"Captain, get your damn plane under control!" The crew-chief yelled loud enough to be heard in the cockpit without an intercom.

Feeling like an overturned turtle, Sam struggled to right himself. Carter offered a hand.

Harrigan heaved and puked down the back of Donovan's neck. Down on his knees, Donovan could do nothing but curse his best friend.

Don't give us the green light now! Sam braced himself on one knee. *What's this pilot's problem?*

Explosions erupted inside the cockpit. Screams and oaths followed.

As Sam opened his mouth to order an emergency evacuation, the light switched to green.

Chapter 32

The Drop

6 June 1944, 0130 hours
Over Normandy

"Go! Go! Go!"

Sergeant Springwater heaved the remaining door bag and threw himself out. Men followed like a torrent of rainwater through a twisted downspout.

Ten men jumped. The crew-chief hit the switch releasing the para-packs.

The floor exploded under Sam's feet.

A burning sensation seared his left cheek. He collapsed

*   *   *

Dazed, ears ringing like a fire alarm, he blinked his stinging eyes. *Where am I?*

The crew-chief sprayed a fire extinguisher across a smoking pile of bodies. Wind roared through the deck.

Sam forced his arms under his chest to push off the floor. His vision filled with a charred face. Private Carter's lifeless blue eyes stared back. An unnatural hissing crackle issued from Carter's chest.

Sam spotted the source, a ruptured smoke grenade. It had generated little smoke but enough white phosphorus to burn off half of Carter's face.

The bile rising in his throat forced Sam to look away.

A steady drip puddled under his face. He reached to his left cheek. His goggles were gone. Pain forced him to jerk his hand away. His tan leather glove came away dark.

The crew-chief unclipped static lines.

The ruptured smoke grenade started generating more smoke. Sam yanked it away from the dead soldier's chest and heaved it toward the door. The heat scorched through his glove. The crew-chief swept the smoke grenade out the door with his foot.

The crew-chief came back down the aisle, grabbed the nearest paratrooper by the parachute harness, and dragged him away from the pile. A wet red swath contrasted by white bone fragments marked the route. Sam recognized the mangled trooper—Schutte, mortar squad.

Sam regained his feet and went into a coughing fit. He stepped over Carter's corpse, yanked off his right glove and reached down to check Private Perkowski for a pulse. His hand sunk into a gapping neck wound. It wasn't bleeding.

Private Vickers—also of the mortar squad—regained consciousness. He reached for his buttocks and screamed in agony.

Sam stepped over Vickers and reached down to check Private Mason. Blood trickled out the unconscious paratrooper's nose and ears.

The plane shuddered and banked left. Sam remembered the mission. He rushed for the door as best he could under the burden of all his gear. He slipped in a slick of blood and vomit and crawled for the door.

He pulled himself upright and re-hooked his bloody static line. He glanced down as his hands braced to pull himself out the door. A beach, followed by open water passed a mere 200 feet below. He fought to stop his momentum.

A hand latched onto his shoulder. "Too late now, sir. Looks like you'll be returning to England with us."

"Like hell I am! Get me back to my men!"

"You're wounded, sir."

Sam marched back down the gory aisle. The whistling wind coming through the hole mixed the stench of burnt flesh, singed hair, blood, and cordite. Sam almost retched. He unhooked his static line and threw the cockpit door open.

A slumped body partially blocked the door. The back of the radio operator's ribcage had a hole large enough to accommodate the barrel end of a baseball bat. The radio smoked and sparked. Sam squeezed into the cockpit.

"Take me back to the drop zone! Now!"

The copilot's face twisted in agony as he fumbled to wrap a bandage around the bloody stumps that remained of his left thumb and index finger.

Cold air and smoke swirled through the cockpit.

"Blew your chance, Lieutenant," the pilot said.

"You don't have the guts, Captain. It only took some fog and a little AA."

The captain twisted to face his challenger. The pilot's expression changed from rage to concern. He turned back to his instruments and broken windscreen. "You're wounded, Lieutenant. I'll attribute your outburst to shock. Shut your yap and get the hell out of my cockpit."

Enraged, Sam reached over his reserve chute and pulled his 45-auto. He cocked the hammer and pointed it at the pilot's knee.

"I'll call your bluff," the pilot said. "You don't fly with those loaded."

Sam shifted his hand and pulled the trigger. The shot noise filled the cockpit. The slug punched through the floor by a rudder pedal.

Gasping, the pilot released the yoke and lunged left—only kept in his seat by the safety belts. The copilot grabbed for his shattered yoke and cursed in pain. A bloody bandage dangled from his hand.

Sam shoved the pistol's muzzle against the pilot's temple.

"OK! OK! You win. You airborne clowns are all nuts. You get one pass, so get out of here, you crazy—"

"I'm staying put until I see that compass heading change one-eighty degrees."

"I hope Krauts cut off your—"

Sam exerted more pressure on his pistol. "Turn this crate around! Now!"

The moonlit horizon changed. He looked back into the cabin and made eye contact with the crew-chief tightening a tourniquet on Schutte's thigh.

Why doesn't he shoot me?

The crew-chief moved to Vickers—laid out, chute harness removed, face down across the seats—and jabbed a morphine Syrette into the paratrooper's thigh.

Sam looked back at the compass. It had changed. Whether it had spun 180° or not, he couldn't tell.

"Two minutes." The pilot's face contorted into a snarl. "Get off my aircraft."

Sam glanced ahead through the pilot's windshield. Scattered machinegun tracers and antiaircraft probed the sky. He exited the cockpit and hooked his static line. He slid the 45-auto back into its holster and had trouble snapping it secure. His hand was trembling. He stepped around his wounded and dead men to stand in the door.

The crew-chief leaned into his ear. "Two should make it. Ain't so sure about the one with the thighbone all shot to hell. Too much blood."

"Look after him. I'll watch for the green light."

The crew-chief leaned closer. "Sir, for what it's worth, I would've played my cards the same way. At least I hope I'd have the guts to. And I ain't seen nothing of what went on up there. Didn't hear no gunshot, either. Good luck, sir."

Sam hoped the crew-chief didn't notice his shaking knees. "Let's just get this over with before I change my mind." He looked out the door, to the unlit green light, and back out the door again. *You idiot! Now you've done it. What were you thinking, pulling a pistol on a plane's captain? Mutiny. You stupid idiot!*

They were too low. He estimated only 400 feet and flying fast. Way too fast.

He mentally urged the pilot. *Come on, come on. Get some more altitude. Throttle back, feather the props, raise the tail, and let me jump.*

The ugly reality of the situation struck him—why would a terrified pilot who just had a gun stuck to his head take steps to assure a safe and comfortable jump for his tormentor?

Sam sucked in his breath. *This can't end well.*

Orange baseball-sized tracers streaked in front of the door like mini-comets. The green light went on. Yet Sam didn't need to jump. The C-47 dipped and pitched to the portside, flinging him out the door.

Chapter 33

The Far Flung

6 June 1944, 0148 Hours
Normandy

Springwater crouched in a weedy hedgerow, scanning the western horizon for the St. Come-du-Mont steeple.

He found nothing. Nothing but another hedgerow. And the hedgerows weren't right. The S-2 briefing had said to expect hedgerows like England—trimmed, interwoven bushes no more than five or six feet high. Yet the two he'd already experienced were rocky earthen mounds topped by tangles of brush, thorns, and full-grown trees.

He recognized nothing.

Distant aircraft noise reached his ears. Hardly the wave upon wave of C-47s dropping the 501st.

Equipment rattled to his right.

He pushed away the vegetation blocking his view. A stinging, almost electrical, pain shot through the back of his hand. Nettles! He bit his lip, reached for his metal cricket and signaled. Click-clack.

No response.

He reached for a grenade.

"That you, Sarge?"

"Stay put. Coming to you." Springwater dashed toward Silva's voice. Upon reaching the hedgerow corner, he rolled right. He landed among the blackened faces of Craighead, Jeffers, and Silva. "Wrong way. We need to roll up the stick the other way."

"Whichever way that is," Silva said, adding Portuguese oaths.

"Craighead, I found the door-bag with your bazooka. Pulled it up into cover just around the corner. You and Jeffers go get all you can carry." Springwater turned to Silva. "Find anyone else?"

"Pinball messed up an ankle. Skinner landed on his noggin. I thought he was dead. He came to, threw up, and thought he's in Tennessee. Collins is babysitting."

"Anyone else? Smitty jumped between you and Jeffers."

Silva nodded. "Found him hanging from a tree about seventy-five yards behind us. Collins and I went to get him down. Stepped in five gallons of blood under him. Left him there. Must've gotten hit on the way down." Silva looked around. "Where are we?"

"Nowhere near where we're supposed—"

A low flying C-47, racing east to west, interrupted Springwater. Moonlight allowed him to make out a 3J and well endowed fox.

"That's our ride!" Silva threw his M-1 up to his shoulder. "I ought to shoot the…" Two aircraft engines screaming at full throttle drowned out Silva's profanity.

"Heading the wrong way," Springwater said. "Maybe his compass got shot up."

"Flash!" Craighead and Jeffers came in huffing, burdened with a bazooka and rocket-carrying harness.

Springwater stood. "Let's roll up the stick to Lieutenant Henry."

He followed Silva into the shadows and dashed across a small pasture. The brown and white speckled cattle grazed unperturbed. He passed through a rickety wooden gate and down the darkened recesses of yet another hedgerow until finding Collins, Vigiano, and Skinner. Morton, Harrigan, Sergeant Lazeski, and Sergeant Phillips had joined the group. A bulky dressing wrapped Phillips's left bicep.

Springwater scanned the men. *Where's Lieutenant Henry?*

He pulled the sergeants to the side and conferred. "Any idea where we're at?"

"How should I know?" Phillips said.

Springwater reeled in the lanyard tethering his compass. "Watched a lot of ground pass under us. Too much to be west of the DZ. I'd say south, maybe southeast."

"Check the maps," Phillips said.

"And which hedgerow do you suggest we use as our reference point? We need a landmark—church, road intersection, village." Springwater strained his hearing. Distant small arms fire sounded from every point of the compass, but the faint rumble of a full battle came from the north. He pointed north. Lazeski nodded.

Springwater unfurled the friction tape securing a grenade. "Who've we got?"

"Smitty's dead. O'Connor, too. He caught a streamer and hit somewhere over there." Lazeski pointed out into the pasture. "No time for the reserve. Flew right past Morton."

"Not everyone jumped," Phillips said.

Springwater eyed Lazeski in disbelief.

Lazeski nodded confirmation. "Something way bigger than an MG slammed the plane's belly while I was going out the door."

"That's when I caught shrapnel," Phillips said. "But I wasn't the last out. Taylor was pushing me hard."

Springwater patted his web gear to locate more grenades. "Then where's Taylor?"

"You tell me. I looked back enough to see a pile of bodies, some fire. A lot of smoke. Taylor shoved me out."

"Lieutenant Henry hit?"

Phillips shrugged. "He wasn't standing when I looked back."

Not far to the north, two grenades exploded in close succession. A submachine gun and guttural shouts responded. Springwater collapsed to his belly.

Tormented screams and repeated automatic weapons bursts followed a third grenade explosion.

Tracers streaked overhead.

Springwater pointed his Thompson toward the north hedgerow and waited for the firefight to pour into their pasture.

Minutes passed without further action. Springwater huddled back with his fellow sergeants. "So we've got eight troopers a hundred-percent good to go, Pinball with a bum ankle, Skinner knocked loopy, and you with one arm."

"Found one para-pack with the sixty and half a dozen mortar rounds," Phillips said.

"And no mortar squad to man it." Springwater took a deep breath. "Our machinegun?"

"No such luck," Lazeski said. "Found some shredded para-pack pieces. AA must've blown it up. Besides, Harrigan's all we've got left from our all Mick crew."

Springwater wanted to scream curses. "Did you see the Voluptuous Vixen come back through?"

Lazeski nodded.

Phillips shook his head. "Thought we were getting strafed and went to ground."

Springwater cocked his Thompson's bolt. "What do you make of it, Laze?"

"Must've been some of our guys wanting off. Why else would *that* pilot make another pass?"

"He wouldn't do it for a private," Springwater said.

Phillips gave an exasperated sigh. "I know what I saw. No one was left standing."

"Better get moving." Springwater sighted down his pointing finger. "On the exact opposite vector the Voluptuous Vixen was flying."

"Why?" Phillips asked.

Lazeski answered for Springwater. "To find Lieutenant Henry."

Phillips pointed northwest. "How about those grenades?"

"Wrong direction for Lieutenant Henry." Lazeski rose to a crouch. "Could be Donovan. Maybe Taylor. Maybe some other unlucky saps, lost courtesy of Troop Carrier Command."

"First we make an effort to join up with the lieutenant and the rest of *your* mortar squad. Then we figure out where we are and make for the locks." Springwater turned to Lazeski. "Put Collins out front scouting. Moon's bright. Stay in the hedgerow shadows. Keep good intervals, but everyone keeps visual contact with the next guy in front and behind. You bring up the rear." He looked at his compass. "Let's try to stay on a ninety-five degree heading. Get a dog tag off Smitty and O'Connor. We move out in three."

Chapter 34

First Contact

6 June 1944, 0143 Hours
Normandy

The chute deployed with Sam's feet positioned above his head and behind him. The instant deceleration had the effect of cracking a bullwhip. His ankles knocked together with a sharp slap. The leg straps of the T-5 harness slammed into his crotch with the severity of a mule kick. Blood from his cut cheek blew into his eye.

Uniform seams tore loose.

Equipment broke away.

Sam grabbed for the risers, fighting to keep from blacking-out. He oscillated out of control—far to his right, then hard left, like a pendulum.

The earth rushed upward.

Swinging in the fourth oscillation, his feet dangled a mere twenty feet off the ground. The chute caught on tree branches and emptied of air.

With his body horizontal to the earth, he cascaded the final ten feet.

His helmet tangled in branches. Thorns and twigs lashed his face.

He slammed into the ground on his left side. A jolt shot through his hip.

Pulling his knees toward his chest, he rolled into a ball and gasped for air.

A wave of nausea crashed into him. He braced himself on his hands and knees and ejected his stomach contents with such force that vomit spewed out both his mouth and nose. Stomach acid stung his nostrils.

Blood dripping from his cheek mingled with the vomit. He looked up through the weeds and found himself in a road ditch.

His hip throbbed. His groin shot pain to his gut. Sam groaned and rolled so his back was resting on the slope of the ditch bank. He reached toward the pain radiating from the back of his left hip. The glove came away wet. Blood? He yanked the glove off and checked again. The fluid was cool and thin.

His probing hand bumped his canteen. The case was dripping and almost detached from his web belt. He pulled a misshapen canteen out. Jagged holes marked the entry and exit of shrapnel. He unscrewed the cap and rinsed the puke from his mouth. He drained the last swig of water into his mouth and tossed the ruined canteen aside.

He mustered the strength to free himself of the parachute harness. The leg straps unlatched, but he couldn't undo the chest. He tugged, pushed, and shifted to no avail. Any weight shift to his left side compounded his pain.

Why am I wasting my time? He unzipped the collar pouch and triggered the Schrade switchblade jackknife. The blade popped out and he commenced slicing.

While cutting canvas harness straps, he gained back his senses enough to realize something else was amiss. No airplane noise. No shouted orders. No racket of small arms fire and moving soldiers.

Sam's ears rang like one long chime from a church bell. *Maybe the explosion on the plane deafened me.* He strained to hear. His own heavy breathing dominated all sound. He held his breath.

The sound of boots crunching on gravel came from his right. Indistinct voices followed.

Frantically cutting at the harness, he tangled his hand in shroud-lines. His gaze followed the shroud-lines into the camouflage parachute canopy, hanging above from a tall hedge. He yanked the parachute down and wadded it into a ball.

Four armed men appeared in a road intersection a hundred yards away. Semidarkness and pain hindered Sam's vision.

He strained his eyes, hoping to find something distinguishing his men—Collins's hulking frame, Pinball's fireplug silhouette. The acrid scent of cordite filled his nostrils. He realized that a smoky haze was inhibiting his vision as much as darkness.

One man pointed to the right and another moved off in that direction. The leader then pointed to the left, toward Sam. Two men moved down the lane like hunters stalking prey. The leader rose and ventured straight.

Heart racing, Sam kept vigil on the hunters while cutting the chute harness. The hunters moved eighty yards away. Sweat stung his eyes.

At last, the blade cut through. He slid the reserve chute off his stomach and went to push the harness away from his shoulders. His hand felt rubber—his Mae West in all its bright yellow glory. The very color that would save his life on a darkened sea, now threatened it.

Bayonet fixed, one hunter stepped into a smoky shaft of moonlight seventy yards distant.

Sam unfastened the leather cupped-chinstrap and eased his helmet off. He slipped the life vest over his head and stuffed it in the weeds.

The cautious hunters stalked in half-steps, one on each side of the one-lane road, sixty yards away. Sam reached toward his toy cricket. A soldier's head swiveled. Sam's recognition of the coal bucket helmet shot a renewed surge of dread through his hurting body.

Pressing himself deeper into the weedy ditch, Sam put his helmet back on. His palm felt the helmet's bare metal, devoid of netting and canvas strips. He reached to unsnap his carbine sheath, but his discarded reserve chute blocked his hand.

Risking movement, he slid his fingers across his belt. Expecting hand grenades, he found only loose canvas flaps. *No!*

Fifty-yards separated him from the German hunters. Their heads and guns swung in searching arcs.

Sam flattened himself into the weedy ditch bottom. Each time the Germans looked away, he used his hands and elbows to scoot backward, away from the incriminating chute, harness, and Mae West.

Ten yards down the ditch, he paused. Still focused on pineapple grenades, he felt his right suspender. One was there! He began unraveling the friction tape, grew frustrated by the tangle, and reached for the Schrade jackknife. The collar pouch was empty. He'd left the switchblade with the harness.

He parted the grass with a hand. The Germans were thirty yards away—twenty from the discarded gear.

Sam resumed pawing at the friction tape as he pushed his way backward down the ditch. The grenade came free.

He glanced up. The Germans hunted only twenty-five yards away. One discovered the pile of paratrooper debris in the ditch. The other rushed to the pile, stiffened, turned back toward the intersection, and sounded an alarm.

Sam yanked the pin, released the spoon, and counted two full seconds. He rose to his knees and lobbed the grenade. The grenade skittered on the road and stopped behind the soldiers gawking at his gear.

He ducked. A sharp explosion accompanied the shrapnel ripping through the hedgerow foliage.

From his knees he peeked above the grass and weeds. Two crumpled heaps lay in the ditch. Sam's eyes transfixed on the men he'd killed.

POP!

A sharp crack sounded next to his ear. A rifle report followed. Down the road another enemy stood, weapon leveled. The second shot rang out and dug into the earth between Sam's legs.

He dropped and the third shot popped and cut grass overhead.

A foreign tongue renewed the alarm. Rapid footsteps moved toward him.

Sam leapt to his feet.

The enemy soldier halted and raised his rifle.

Sam turned and ran.

He cringed at the close report of the high-powered rifle.

He anticipated a sharp, searing pain in the center of his spine. Yet the only pain he felt was of the dull, throbbing variety—still coming from his hip and groin.

He caught an opening in the dense hedge and cut hard left to duck through a partially opened wooden gate, losing his footing in the muddy cow trail. His helmet flew off and tumbled ahead several yards.

On all fours he scrambled left for a darkened recess. Chest heaving, seated with his back against the earthen mound of the hedgerow base, he unsnapped his carbine case.

Footsteps and heavy breathing approached the gate. A huge German lumbered past, gravitating on Sam's helmet. The German picked it up, pivoted around, and opened his mouth as if to shout. A mere twenty feet away, the German spotted Sam.

Sam unsheathed his folded carbine and centered the sights on the German's enormous torso. He fingered the safety button and something hit his knee. He pulled a motionless trigger.

The weapon failed.

The German gasped.

A sense of absolute dread overwhelmed Sam—he'd hit the magazine release.

The German flung the helmet at Sam and raised his own rifle.

Sam rolled left as the German's rifle discharged.

Frantic, Sam pushed the actual safety, pointed his weapon, and jerked the trigger.

His carbine discharged.

Dust puffed from the German's tunic.

To Sam's astonishment, his adversary didn't drop. Instead, the German worked his rifle bolt and aimed at Sam's chest.

Sam groaned and cringed.

The German's rifle clicked.

Snarling, the German lunged forward. The Mauser bayonet glistened in the moonlight.

In a futile reaction, Sam pulled the trigger of his empty carbine. He closed his eyes and cowered.

A searing pain ripped through his left shoulder near his neck.

The bayonet pinned him to the hedgerow's earthen base.

Immobilized and desperate, he lashed out with his carbine and knocked the German's helmet off.

Cocking his folded carbine back to strike again, he noticed bright froth issuing from the German's mouth and nose. The man's eyes looked distant, yet he continued to shove the bayonet.

Sam pulled his right knee to his chest and launched his boot upward into his adversary's midsection. The solid impact forced air up the wounded German's throat and showered Sam in pinkish froth.

The German flew backward and landed flat on his back, unmoving, emitting wheezing gurgles.

The lurching kick also forced the bayonet pinning him to tear through flesh and fabric. Searing pain shot through his shoulder and neck. He rolled away from the bloody Mauser.

"Helmut? *Wo ist der Amerikaner?* Helmut?" The calls came from the area of Sam's discarded chute.

Warm blood flowed.

"Helmut?" a voice called from outside the gate.

Sam gritted his teeth and reached across his chest. He found his 45-auto where it belonged. He un-holstered it and thumb-cocked the hammer.

"Helmut? *Der Amerikaner es tot, ja?*" The voice grew nearer.

A moonlit shadow inched past the gate. The fourth hunter stepped into view.

Sam looked down the iron sights and pulled the trigger. The heavy pistol roared and bucked four times in rapid succession before Sam relaxed his finger.

The German crashed into the gate. Boards cracked and splintered. Dead.

Sam had seen four and had dispatched four. He sighed and relaxed his tensed muscles. He holstered his pistol, reached for the bayonet wound, and winced.

The propeller buzz of a C-47 approached. He got to his feet and strained his eyesight, hoping to spot a plane disgorging paratroopers.

An automatic cannon ripped a burst. Orange flames jutted upward.

Sam dropped and cowered.

The antiaircraft gun fired another burst. The muzzle flashes illuminated the four-barreled gun's position over the next hedgerow, eighty yards away. Oversized tracers lanced skyward.

He leapt up. His knees wobbled, then collapsed.

Shaking and panting, Sam crawled to the large German. The enemy's wheezing gurgle had stopped, but every few seconds a frothy pink bubble rose between his parted lips. The man appeared too old and overweight to be infantry. The uniform had a flying eagle sewn to the chest. *Luftwaffe?* The helmets weren't paratrooper. *Must be antiaircraft.*

Sam averted his eyes from the dying man's face. He retrieved his carbine and reached for the rigger's pouch over his right hip that had held four carbine magazines. Torn and empty! He scraped his hand across his chest for the ammo bandoleer. Nothing! He reached for the front of his belt. The two magazines in the standard issue pouch were still secure.

He limped back to where he had been pinned, dropped to his hands and knees, and patted the grass in search of the magazine he'd inadvertently released. *Idiot!*

Nothing! Breaths came in abbreviated gasps. He resisted the urge to scream. He swept his hands through more grass. Nothing! He took a deep breath and winced at the pain emanating from his left side—shoulder to hip.

Sam ceased searching. He had no idea where he was, but lingering would only invite death or capture. Scooping up his helmet, he refocused. *Time to find my stick and move on the locks at La Barquette.* He limped through the broken gate.

Staying in the darkened shadows near the road's edge, he unfolded the stock of his carbine and fed a fresh magazine into the bottom of the receiver. The blood dripping from the bayonet wound didn't strike him as life threatening and he could rotate his shoulder. But he needed to find a place to treat his wound. He glanced both directions. All clear. But which way? He pushed back his left sleeve to check his wrist compass. The compass face was shattered, the needle gone.

He looked to his right wrist for his watch. The second hand was moving, but something had to be wrong. The luminescent hands read 0158 hours. Sam tapped the watch face. *There's no way only twenty-eight minutes have passed since the first green light!*

He shifted his musette bag from his belly to the small of his back. A web gear strap dug into the bayonet wound. He almost cried out before he slipped the left shoulder strap off.

He gazed upward. *Where're all the planes? Where am I?* The adrenaline of the firefight was wearing off and turning to anger. Anger turned to resolve. Survival depended upon one task—finding Americans.

Chapter 35

Wet Feet

6 June 1944, 0207 Hours
Cotentin Peninsula, Normandy

The sloshing grew closer. The noise had a deliberate rhythm—as though made by a man on a mission.

The paratrooper tucked his submerged boots tighter into the willow brush island. He fingered a grenade, but feared that an exploding grenade would betray his position. The willow patch offered the lone refuge for 200 yards in any direction.

His shaking hand grabbed his metal cricket. He waited.

The sloshing slowed, then stopped altogether. Close.

Without warning, the hidden paratrooper was staring down the bore of a submachine gun. Warm fluid flowed down his leg.

"Flash."

"Flash, flash! I mean, thunder." His voice came out as a squeal. "Don't shoot."

"Welcome. That you, Lieutenant?"

"Get under here before the Krauts spot us."

Staff Sergeant Jennings ducked under the willow branches. "Time to get out of this here swamp, sir."

"Drop the *sirs*, real quick. They shoot officers first."

Jennings took the unlit stub of a cigar out of his mouth. "Got to be one SNAFU even beyond the scale the old regular Army could muster. I dang sure didn't need to volunteer for the parachute infantry for this."

"Not the Airborne's fault. The Air Corps did this to us."

"I reckon we got us plenty of blame to spread 'round. S-Two said nothing about our DZ being surrounded by no lake, *sir*." Jennings wrinkled his nose. "Smells like piss."

"We're not anywhere near Drop Zone-D."

"Didn't you hear all them other planes behind us?"

"I think the whole serial got it wrong. Must've been that fog. Maybe the pathfinders screwed it all up. No, we're misdropped, way off course."

Jennings parted the leafy canopy with his Thompson barrel and revealed the moonlit silhouette of a tall steeple a mile away. "Then I reckon that ain't the St. Come-du-Mont church steeple that I spent the past two weeks memorizing."

A burst of machinegun fire erupted from the high ground. Tracers probed the flooded lowland.

"Close that up, now! You'll expose us. That's an order."

Jennings held the gap open. "An' I suppose that ain't the railroad causeway that runs from behind St. Come-du-Mont on down to Carentan?"

Several C-47s rumbled across the horizon and disgorged paratroopers over the steeple. New lines of tracers stitched the sky. The racket of small arms fire increased.

"That would be the last of the Sink's boys. Right on schedule. Just dropped a tad short, I do believe. At least they'll have dry feet." Jennings lowered his barrel and allowed the gap to close. "I figure we got dropped a mile 'n a half, maybe two, shy."

"Where's the rest of the stick?"

"Mostly drowned, I suppose. Heard some splashing around and hollering. Couldn't find no one. And what did the S-Two say? If we miss the dern DZ, we might get a 'bit muddy'? So how the Sam Hill did your West Point buddies miss it this bad, Lieutenant?"

"Due to the circumstances, I won't hold you accountable for that insubordination," Pettigrew said.

Chapter 36

The Big Barn

6 June 1944, 0230 hours
"Normandy

Springwater knelt in the grass and studied the massive stone barn seventy yards ahead.

Mid-thigh down he was dripping wet from crossing one hundred thirty yards of flooded marshland. Silva knelt at water's edge a few yards behind. Collins lay prone in weedy grass five yards forward. Jeffers and Morton paused in knee-deep water, while the rest of the squad waited on the far side, not to cross until receiving relayed hand signals.

A stone cottage stood left of the barn. Between the cottage and barn, Springwater made out rows of fruit trees. Aside from a muffled horse whinny, the buildings showed no sign of life. Being in a war zone told him to anticipate otherwise—occupying troops utilized such prime shelter and concealment. His gut told him the barn might also attract misdropped paratroopers—like Lieutenant Henry.

The farmstead also represented a crucial piece of the puzzle. The building cluster had to have a lane. The lane had to lead to a road, the road to a village or river—all the ingredients needed to pinpoint their location on a map.

Scattered clouds drifted across the sky, blocking out a good portion of the moonlight. He signaled Silva forward. Leaning close to Silva's ear he said, "We bypass this place. But first we make sure no fellow Geronimos are holed up inside."

Silva nodded.

"Go to the barn's left corner." Springwater pointed. "On my signal, give one cricket click, no more. Listen for any response. Tell Collins to do the same, right corner."

Watching Silva and Collins creep into position—M-1s shouldered and ready—Springwater waved the next two forward. Jeffers reached his side. He pointed right. "Take an overwatch position behind Collins. Do *not* approach the barn."

Morton bumped into Springwater's shoulder.

"We're bypassing this place." Springwater pointed to the left. "First, go to that cottage. Do not go in. Cover Silva."

Springwater belly crawled half the distance to the barn. From behind a bush, he gazed at the double-doors left of center on the stone barn. One was open and appeared to lead into a courtyard. He glanced back. Pinball, supported by Skinner, limped at the water's edge.

Focused back on the barn door, Springwater tried to identify shadowy objects in the courtyard.

Yellow light flared in the courtyard. A struck match. Springwater's pulse raced. Darkness returned, except for a glowing cigarette tip.

The cigarette tip moved through the passageway. He signaled Collins to move around the corner. To Silva he signaled visual contact with one person walking their way. The last signal he flashed was a slashing motion across the throat.

Silva slid along the barn wall and hid behind the door. He set his M-1 aside and unsheathed the Portuguese knife.

The glowing cigarette drifted closer until a small man stood several yards outside the door. Facing the marsh, the man unbuttoned his trousers and urinated.

The man wore a sleeveless undershirt, tall boots, and baggy pants. Soldier or civilian? Springwater cringed, hoping Silva understood that his signal to slide cold steel along human flesh applied only to an enemy soldier.

Something slipped off the man's shoulder—a slung machine-pistol. The man muttered and adjusted his stance to avoid fouling his clothing and MP-40.

Bent in a crouch, Silva inched closer.

Bladder relieved, the German buttoned his fly and re-slung his weapon. He took a long drag on his cigarette and turned left.

The German was about to catch Silva in the open.

Silva knelt coiled to strike, yet remained out of knife range.

Springwater found the leather cord hanging from his collar and ran his hand down until finding the cricket. He pressed and released. The metallic *click-clack* shattering the silence.

The German spun to face the foreign sound.

Clouds thinned. Moonlight increased.

The German dropped his cigarette and stared forward. Seeming uncertain over what to make of the strange sound and clumps of shadows, the soldier shifted the machine-pistol from his shoulder to his hands.

Silva leapt, grabbed the man's face from behind, and—pushing his knee belt-high—yanked back. He struck with ferocity, drawing the heavy blade deep across a taut and exposed throat.

Silva failed to keep his grip on the soldier. The voiceless man twisted in an instinctive act of self-preservation.

Thick arterial spray flooded Silva's eyes and open mouth. Silva wiped frantically at his face and groaned.

The soldier convulsed, emptying his weapon in a long sweeping arc of orange muzzle blasts.

Silva collapsed.

Alarmed foreign voices arose from inside the barn.

Springwater dashed to rescue Silva. He caught movement—weapons being raised in the courtyard. A shot whip-popped past his ear. He dodged right and dashed until his back pressed against the barn where the stone and closed plank door joined.

Silva muttered Portuguese oaths as he scrambled on all fours back to the barn corner. The open door hid him from Springwater's view.

More foreign shouts. Now from the courtyard.

The first response came from the stone cottage. A half-dressed soldier rushed out the door. Crouched, Morton pivoted and shot from the hip, pointblank, knocking the alarmed German off his feet.

Hobnailed boots scraping stone sounded from inside the courtyard.

Rock fragments spattered Springwater's jump jacket. A rifle sounded.

He dropped to a knee. A muzzle flashed from the cottage's right corner window. More rock and masonry fragments stung his face. Blinking to clear the grit, he sprayed a burst from his Thompson at the muzzle flash.

Morton stayed down but held his M-1 above his head and fired three quick shots into the cottage, shattering the small window next to the door.

A cottage occupant answered with two shots.

Morton jerked his rifle down.

Springwater fired an aimed burst at the cottage window.

"Silva?"

No answer. *He's hit, I know it. And Sam's definitely not hiding here. No GIs are. Get Silva. Disengage.*

Springwater fired a long burst. Pinball dashed with an obvious limp and dove next to Morton. Pinball pressed his back against the cottage and slammed a grenade through the broken pane.

The grenade blast blew all remaining glass outward.

Springwater released his Thompson spent magazine. *I've got to get to Silva.* Sliding along the plank door, he pulled a fresh magazine out of the chest pouch.

Before he could slam the magazine home, a German brandishing a machine-pistol exited the barn, not an arm's length away.

Springwater dropped the magazine and thrust out the submachine gun stock in a hasty butt stroke.

The blow hit low, catching the enemy between the shoulder blades, sending him sprawling in the dirt.

The German rolled over.

Springwater leapt and stomped the German's groin. He grabbed the MP-40 out of the stunned man's hands and flung it away. He shifted his empty Thompson to his left hand and clawed for the pistol on his right hip.

Accented English commands, "Halt! Surrender!" stopped him.

He glanced over his shoulder. Two Germans stood fifteen yards away—a pistol and rifle leveled on him. He looked at the stunned German between his feet and gambled that the man's comrades would hesitate before shooting. Legs already poised to jump, he sprung to his left and rolled behind the door.

Pistol bullets slammed into the heavy plank door. Two high-powered rifle bullets left splintered exit holes.

Springwater rolled until he could again press himself to the stone wall.

The disarmed German crawled for the barn. Before the enemy reached safety, his head snapped sideways, hands and legs collapsing.

Springwater spun left. Collins knelt at the barn corner, M-1 sights locked on the head-shot enemy.

Springwater finished reloading his Thompson, grabbed a grenade, and edged his way along with his back pressed to the plank door. Near the door's edge, he pulled the pin and released the spoon. He flung the grenade with a firm backhand. Scooting back to the protection of the stone barn wall, he heard the grenade bang into something close.

The grenade exploded in the passage. The blast rattled the plank door.

Silence.

He repeated the procedure with a second grenade, this time releasing the grenade a split second sooner from his backhand toss. It flew further into the courtyard. As he got back to the stone wall a rapid string of at least a dozen bullet holes erupted waist high, splintering wood where he had just stood.

Muzzle flashes emanated from the water's edge. Suppressive fire whizzed by and hit rock and wood through the doorway.

He scooted away. "Silva? You there, Joe? Cover your corner. Pinball, cover Silva. Watch that orchard! Don't let—"

Something hard struck Springwater's helmet and bumped his boot.

A potato masher grenade hissed between his feet.

"Grenade!" He grabbed the wooden handle and hurled it toward the void between Collins and Jeffers. It exploded just above the grass.

He glanced up to a window in the loft and sprayed a burst into it before trotting along the wall toward Collins's corner.

A sustained volley of rapid M-1 fire went out from Morton and Pinball's cottage and Silva's corner.

From above came a burst of fire sounding like amplified ripping canvas. Springwater looked up to another rectangular void fifteen feet above. He flinched as another burst accompanied with a long finger of flame flashed out the dark window.

Collins swore. "MG-Forty-two!"

Muzzle flashes came from the far side of the marsh. The suppressive fire slugs hit high above. The enemy machinegun shifted its fire to across the marsh.

"Lazeski's still on the other side." Springwater readied another grenade. "We're too spread out."

The firefight intensified from Morton and Pinball's position. "They want to flank us from the left." Springwater looked up. "We'll never get back together with that MG-Forty-two there." Springwater readied another grenade.

Another burst left the window. Tracers stabbed the ground sixty yards away. Collins glanced up. "Mighty small strike zone. Miss and it drops right back on us."

Springwater pointed his Thompson at the window. "I'll crawl out. Cover me."

Three grenades exploded in the gap between Silva and Vigiano. A few seconds passed and three more exploded. Then two more.

"No time left." Springwater crawled out from the wall.

Collins grabbed his ankle. "I'm the pitcher, Sarge." Collins crept ten yards and rose to a crouch.

A burst from the MG-42 flattened the big scout.

The bullets terminated in the water's edge. Muddy geysers erupted five feet into the air.

Collins got back into a crouch and nodded. Springwater took three steps back and sprayed half a clip of heavy slugs into the inky blackness of the window. A grenade flew through the window in a perfect strike.

A German shouted. Boots scrambled on wood. The explosion sounded too far back in the barn.

"Another!" Springwater emptied the Thompson into the window.

The second grenade flew down the middle, lower than the first, collided with metal, and exploded. A man screamed.

The Norman farmstead fell into an eerie silence.

"Silva?" Springwater tried calling just loud enough for Silva to hear. He feared his voice's tenor might betray his terror.

"Silva."

Silence.

"Silva!" he shouted louder.

"He's not moving, Sarge," Pinball responded.

Springwater took a deep breath. "Coming over. Hold your fire."

Lazeski and Harrigan ran in saying, "Flash," and dropped with their backs to the barn wall. Both were soaking wet, gasping for air. Harrigan was carrying both the mortar bipod and the bazooka. Marsh water obscured Lazeski's glasses.

"Everyone across?" Springwater said.

Lazeski gave an exaggerated nod.

"I'm getting Silva. He's hit." Springwater touched his cheek where the stone fragments had hit. His fingers came away sticky wet. "Gather around the corner. Watch windows. Be ready to scoot. Got it?"

Lazeski nodded.

"Spread out in a defensive ring. Maintain visual contact."

"Got it, Ted."

Springwater slinked along the barn wall until nearing the open door. He gritted his teeth and sprinted across the opening.

No gunfire erupted from the courtyard.

He ducked around the open door and dropped next to Silva—huddled in a ball at the corner of the barn. "Joe, it's me. You OK, buddy?"

No response. Springwater placed a hand on Silva's shoulder. It felt wet and sticky. He yanked it away and held it before his face. Blood covered his palm.

"Where you hit?" He grabbed Silva's bloody jump jacket collar and pulled him back from his semi-exposed position. He laid Silva flat and ran his hands over Silva's torso and neck searching for the blood source. Silva trembled.

"OK. Stay with me Joe. Where'd he get you?" He yanked the paratrooper's first aid kit off the front of Silva's helmet and ripped it open.

Silva sat up. Terror filled his dark Latin eyes.

Springwater grabbed Silva's shoulders. Each hand landed in tacky blood. "You got to help me, Joe. Need to know where you're—"

"Leave me the hell alone, Sarge."

Silva's odd behavior suggested a head wound. Springwater lifted Silva's helmet.

Silva snatched his steel pot back and shoved it on. "Hey, watch it. A guy could get his melon hurt!"

"Where you hit?" Springwater reached to unzip Silva's jump jacket.

Batting Springwater's hands away, Silva said, "I'm not."

"There's blood. Now just take it easy."

"Not mine! Get lost, Sarge." Silva closed his eyes. "Just give me some time."

"No time. Krauts will counterattack."

Silva elbowed Springwater. "Then go. I'll cover our rear."

"No. You're going with us. I'll be back in a minute." Springwater stuffed the first aid kit away and looked toward the cottage. "Pinball, I'm coming in." He patted Silva on the back, sprinted the thirty yards to the cottage corner, and slid into Vigiano.

"Two more dead in there." Pinball jabbed his thumb over his shoulder toward the window and gave Springwater a German pay book. "Thought our G-Two might want to see that." He pointed to the gap between the stone buildings leading into the orchard. "They attacked in skirmish line through there. Had to be at least a squad. Grenades changed their mind." He met Springwater's eyes with a concerned look. "How bad did Silva catch it?"

"He'll be OK. I need you and Morton to go to the edge of the orchard and listen for the Krauts organizing a counterattack. Got it?"

"Got it, Sarge."

"You hear them coming, you hightail it past the far corner of the barn. Make sure you've got Silva. Be quick. Got it?"

Pinball nodded and limped away.

Springwater trotted back to where he'd instructed Lazeski to gather the rest of the squad. He looked around and, by body shape and weapon, did a mental roll call—Lazeski, Collins, Harrigan, Phillips, Skinner... Skinner looked asleep. He stepped over and nudged his boot toe into Skinner's side. "Get up."

"Let me sleep, Sarge."

"No! You got a concussion. Go to sleep and you might not wake up again." Springwater turned to Lazeski. "Craighead and Jeffers out on flank security?"

Lazeski shook his head.

Springwater frowned. "Not in the barn, are they? Barn's not secure."

Lazeski opened his hand to reveal two dog tags.

"How?"

"That machinegun up—"

BANG!

Chapter 37

The Shot

Springwater and Lazeski dropped.

Sniper?

Springwater rose to a stoop. "The orchard. Collins, come with me. Laze, if we're not back in ten, go south at least two hundred yards, find some cover. We rendezvous there." He trotted off with Collins.

At the far corner of the barn he found Silva—alert, rifle pointed toward the orchard.

"Sniper?" Springwater asked.

Silva shrugged. "Pinball and Morton went to the edge of the orchard, then I lost Morton."

"Stay on my right." Springwater moved away from the barn, cautiously, Collins ten yards to his left, Silva five yards to his right.

At the first row of apple trees Pinball gave a thumbs up and joined them.

The orchard smelled of an odd mixture of cordite and apple blossoms. Thirty yards in, Springwater made out the outline of a GI on his knees.

Collins clicked his toy cricket.

Morton pivoted, displaying a holster above his head. "Got me a Luger!"

Springwater knelt at Morton's side. "Did you shoot?" Springwater scanned the limits of his vision. Behind Morton, a gnarled apple trunk braced a German corpse.

"He asked for it. Bet I'm the first guy in Able to get a Luger." Morton grinned like a kid just visited by Santa Claus.

A bullet hole marked the center of the German's forehead. The back of the corpse's head was a gooey mass, missing about a quarter of its skull. A patch of hair and bone stuck to the oozing tissue covering the tree-trunk. Another dead German was sprawled on the orchard floor.

Springwater inched closer. Even in the moonlight he could make out a gunpowder ring tattooed into the pale skin surrounding the bullet hole. The dead man's hands clutched entrails over a yawning abdominal wound. Silva turned away and dry heaved.

"Land's sake, Morton, what did you go and do that for?" Collins asked. "This feller's war was done over."

"I told you he was begging for it."

Springwater took a deep breath. "You speak no German."

"I know what I'd want if I was left in some orchard with my guts hanging out."

Collins wagged his head. "You just don't go 'n blow a helpless feller's brains out."

"He wanted it. Saw it in his eyes."

Springwater leaned over the dead man and sniffed. "His bowels weren't cut." He picked up a bandage on the man's lap. "This man was trying to bandage himself. Decent chance he might've survived, but he'd never fight again."

Morton tilted his head back. "Lieutenant Pettigrew's orders. Geronimo don't take no prisoners tonight."

"There's a big difference between bypassing men who want to surrender and executing a wounded man," Springwater said. "You disarm him. Call for a medic if one's available. Then you move on. Got it!"

"Got it already, Sarge. No need to get all sore. Next time I'll do it your—"

"Forget next time! Right now you've messed the nest for all of us," Springwater said. "The Krauts come back and find their buddy like this and what do you think they'll do to the next wounded GI *they* capture? Think, Morton!"

Morton pouted like a scolded ten-year-old.

Springwater turned to Pinball. "You hear anything from over this way?"

"Faint moans. About loaded my drawers when he shot."

Collins crouched. "Sarge, I reckon we 'bout done wore out our welcome here."

Springwater looked down. The other corpse gripped an MG-42. "Two, maybe three MG-Forty-twos. Means they had at least two squads. Maybe a platoon. I want a good head start when the Krauts find their friend here."

Collins spit and said, "Sarge, them Krauts won't find him if'n we dump him in the swamp."

"Like we're covering up a crime?" Springwater pondered Collins's suggestion as long as he dared. "No choice. We dump the body with the Kraut machinegun. Now."

Collins carried the legs, a boot stuck under each arm. Morton struggled to keep a grip on the dead man's wrists while also keeping the bobbing, partial head away. "Gonna shoot me a Kraut with my Luger."

Silva kept his head turned away. "Just shut up about your stupid Luger."

Springwater ordered Morton to drag the corpse into the water and make sure the machinegun weighed it down. He watched the back-trail while making frequent glances to check Morton's progress.

"Dang it, Morton," Collins said, "get it in gear or we're ditching your sorry behind."

"No you won't. I'm the officers' runner."

"If you ain't noticed, we're fresh out of *officers*."

Morton ran back splashing and cursing.

Silva grimaced. "Keep it quiet, Morton."

Springwater leaned close to his men. "Collins, take Pinball and Morton back to Laze. Stay out of view of the upper barn windows. Joe and I'll cover—"

"Hey, Joe. Saw you cut that Kraut's throat." Morton sneered. "Nice. Wish I—"

Silva's face contorted.

Springwater grabbed Morton's jacket. "Morton! Pay attention! Collins, go."

The three took off. Springwater trained his Thompson on the barn.

Silva stepped into ankle deep water, unsheathed his father's Portuguese knife, and heaved it into the marsh. In quick succession he removed his trench knife, British Commando stiletto, and bayonet, hurling each one.

Reaching around his back, Silva grabbed the machete handle. Springwater clamped on Silva's trembling wrist.

"No, Joe. No. The squad might need that. Hold still. Just let me unhook it. There we go now. Come on, relax." He pulled the machete and scabbard away. "It'll be OK. You did fine. It was my order. My fault."

He put his arm around the young Portuguese soldier's shoulders. Silva was trembling. Springwater tugged him downward to reduce their profile.

"Ted, I…I saw his eyes." Silva sniffed and looked to the sky. "I saw his eyes. He was just a kid. I saw his eyes. He knew he was dead, but his eyes begged for life. I saw his eyes. Then his blood blinded me. I even swallowed some. It was hot." Silva spit. "Can't get rid of the taste."

"Come on, Joe. The squad needs you. Morton needs you. Pinball's ankle's messed up, he needs you. I need you, Joe."

"Not ever using a knife again. Never in a million years." Silva spouted profanity, grabbed the front of Springwater's jacket, and pulled him to within an inch of his face. "Don't you *ever* ask me again, because it won't happen. You can shoot me first, Sarge."

"No problem, Joe. You got it. But for now we need your rifle." He tapped the side of Silva's helmet. "And I really need you here."

The crazed look left Silva's eyes.

"Let's go," Springwater said, "before Laze follows my orders and leaves us behind."

As Springwater trotted, he pondered the tactical situation. *Desperate.* Just two hours and less than a mile from the drop and he'd already lost two more men. Chalk Number-2 remained disoriented, officer-less, and with only nine paratroopers gathered and semi-effective out of the packed stick of twenty-one that had boarded the Voluptuous Vixen.

The rest of Able Company had to be faring better.

Chapter 38

The Little Barn

6 June 1944, 0245 hours
St. Georges-de-Bohon, Normandy

Beyond the pasture loomed a cluster of darkened geometric silhouettes. A village.

A half-hour earlier Sam thought he'd heard gunfire from this direction. His pulse quickened. Perhaps other misdropped Americans—maybe even his men—had seized this village.

He crawled down the roadside ditch, pushing off with his right leg to lessen the lingering pain in his left hip. Every ten yards he listened and scanned the limits of his vision. A quarter-hour passed without incident. At the first building a white plank sign announced: St. Georges-de-Bohon.

Never heard of the place. Just how far off target did that clown drop me?

He snuck further down the ditch, pausing in front of a stuccoed farmhouse. A stone barn past the house caught his attention. He crawled on. The corral behind the barn held four calves, a trough, and water pump. His thirst drove him to crawl under a plank fence and through patches of muck.

Sidling along the concrete water trough, he paused to listen. Aside from the aggravating ringing in his ears, he heard nothing. He took off his helmet and splashed water on his face.

Sam checked his dark surroundings. The calves crowded in a corner watching him. He crouched next to the pump. Thirst overpowered caution. He worked the handle with long strokes. Feeling the resistance of rising water, he pumped more vigorously. When water gushed he stuck his mouth under the cascade and took hearty gulps. He reached for his canteen but found only an empty pouch. So he pumped the handle again and drank his fill of cool well water, then splashed his face a second time.

Out of the corner of his eye he noticed the glaring white officer's stripe on the back of his bare helmet. *No wonder they call that an aiming stake.* He picked up the helmet. The stenciled diamonds on each side—identifying him as a member of the 501st PIR—also glowed bright in the moonlight.

Sam reached down, grabbed a handful of mud, and slapped it onto the stripe, then rubbed mud on each white diamond.

The rattling scrape of hobnailed boots startled him. His heart rate jumped.

The barn! Get in the barn. On his third bounding step he slipped in an unseen, yet unmistakable, cow flop. His left shoulder collided into the barn wall. The bayonet wound reopened. He grimaced and bit his tongue.

Blood flowed. The hobnailed boots grew closer.

He moved along the barn wall toward the dark recess of a narrow door. He lifted a latch and ducked inside. The interior was pitch-black. He eased the door shut and waited for his eyes to adjust.

German voices came from just outside the far wall.

As his eyes grew accustomed to the darkness he found himself in an aisle—cow stalls to his right, a hayloft above. Moonlight pierced through the gap in the back doors.

An intense firefight broke out, maybe 150 yards into the village. Sam tried deciphering the fight through sound alone. German MP-40s issued chattering pops, versus the faster and louder Thompson. The rapid fire of the semi-auto M-1 rifles contrasted to the spaced, heavy crack of the Mausers. The solitary machinegun issued an unnatural ripping sound— the unmistakable audio signature of a German MG-42. He thought he picked out the quieter, rapid barking of an American carbine. Grenade explosions punctuated the small arms fire.

Fewer American weapons sounded. Grenades detonated. Germans shouted.

A long Thompson burst made him mentally picture Springwater— surrounded, desperate. Four rapid M-1 shots rang out, followed by a profane suggestion in English directed at the Nazis. *Silva?* He'd heard Silva use the expression countless times.

A renewed fusillade sounded. Even over the gunfire, Sam heard the shouts of fellow Americans in frantic English and accented German. "Don't shoot! We surrender! *Nicht schiessen!* Don't shoot! *Nicht schiessen!*"

As the firefight quieted, another erupted on the village's far side. German weapons spoke last at this firefight, too.

Feeling utterly useless, Sam's chin dropped to his chest.

Hobnailed boots again scraped the pavement outside the barn.

Sam moved to the moonlit crack in the far doors. Four Germans walked away, wearing baggy tunics and abbreviated helmets. *Nothing in the S-Two briefings mentioned Kraut paratroopers!*

One German limped, another clutched his shoulder. They stopped at the stucco farmhouse. One stepped forward and tapped his rifle butt on the doorframe. No response. The soldier drove the rifle butt into the door with greater vigor.

Sam shouldered his carbine. *Can I hit all four before taking return fire?* Bunched up, only forty yards away. Two appeared unarmed. *Start with the one banging the door.*

Centering the carbine's rear sight aperture and front post on the man's chest, he applied pressure to the trigger—and hesitated. The first use of his carbine had left his confidence shaken. The carbine failed to halt the big Luftwaffe soldier's attack despite a chest hit at pointblank range.

Sam shifted his aim to the silhouetted head and resumed squeezing the trigger.

More hobnails scraped on pavement. Sam released the trigger and yanked the exposed barrel back. A short *fallschirmjager* ran past holding up a bandaged hand.

The fourth soldier laughed and directed a comment toward his tardy comrade. The first soldier continued banging on the door.

This is insane. What can I gain from fighting here?

A dim glow appeared in the farmhouse window. The door opened. Shoving the cowering Frenchman aside, the soldiers barged into the house. The fourth soldier remained outside, lit a cigarette, and leaned against the wall.

Blood spread down Sam's ribcage.

More boots clattered up the road. A German wearing a white helmet and white smock, both displaying prominent red crosses, assisted another wounded soldier toward the farmhouse. Two heavily-armed German paratroopers followed.

Feeling trapped, Sam's breaths came in short gasps.

He gazed back into the barn's black interior and blinked to speed his vision's adjustment. He spotted a ladder leading to the hayloft and climbed it. Despite using his left leg only for balance, the dull pain in his hip sharpened with each rung.

He gravitated to a loft corner devoid of light, and collapsed.

Chapter 39

Scattered

6 June 1944, 0345 hours
Near St. Come-du-Mont, Normandy

German automatic weapons erupted from the northeast.

Pettigrew cringed in his willow brush refuge.

Staff Sergeant Jennings hurled his soggy cigar stub straight down into the water. "Lieutenant, ain't no way I aim to just sit here. Not while men counting on us are getting all chewed up."

"We wait. It'll be suicide to venture out."

"Daylight in a couple hours is what it'll be. Then we ain't going nowhere for quite a spell."

"You've got it all wrong, Sergeant. Second Battalion will have St. Come-du-Mont seized way before then. Then we walk right in."

Jennings jabbed his Thompson toward the village—unseen through the willow curtain. "So you finally admit that there's St. Come-du-Mont?"

Pettigrew busied himself, pretending to read his compass and map, in darkness.

"Well, my pa didn't raise no coward. I'm making for the locks. Gather *men* along the way." Jennings parted the foliage with his Thompson barrel and leaned outside the green canopy. "Got to be under two miles."

Pettigrew latched onto his platoon sergeant's musette bag and tugged Jennings back under the willows. "You're staying put. That's an order."

"You can bust me back to a buck private. Even take away my jump wings. I'm wagering it all on you not wanting me to testify about your time here hiding and shirking duty." Jennings's eyes shifted downward. "Or your wet britches."

Pettigrew released his grasp. The willow branches closed behind Jennings. Sloshing noise headed east—the direction he was now convinced held 1st Platoon, Able Company, 501st PIR's Operation Neptune objective. The La Barquette locks.

*   *   *

Near Meautis, Normandy

Hidden in yet another apple orchard, Springwater came out from under the shelter of his improvised jacket-tent. "Can't find it. You sure that's what it said, Collins?"

"It done said, Mew-tis, one and a half kilometers. And Car-fore des Che-mins, two and a half."

"Spell them."

"Can't the second one. I recollect the first was M-A-E...no...no, it was M-E-A-U-T-I-S."

Springwater ducked back under his jacket and switched his flashlight on. He searched for the right combination of terrain features and names—marshland, a large farmstead, orchards, and the road they were now hiding alongside. They had traveled about half a mile since the barn firefight.

He searched the tactical map titled Carentan. The map encompassed Able Company's intended drop zone and the La Barquette locks. The faint sounds of battle and his gut instinct told him they were well south of Drop Zone-D. *Be on this map. Please be on this map.*

His eyes scanned one grid at a time, hoping a landmark would leap out. None did. He gritted his teeth. Wanting to quit the futile exercise and get back to moving, he noted a finger of fine blue lines along the map's bottom edge. Marshland. The blue lines passed right behind a cluster of buildings and an orchard. Just east was a road. His flashlight beam traced the road to a hamlet labeled, Meautis. "Bingo!"

"Where are we?" Lazeski asked from outside the makeshift tent.

"Hang on. Got to do a little figuring." A minute later Springwater turned off his flashlight and popped out. He threw his jump jacket on and wrestled his web gear over his shoulders.

"Come on, Ted," Phillips said, "what's the skinny?"

"Good news, we're on the right map. Maybe four miles southwest of Carentan."

"Just wonderful…" Phillips muttered profanity. "May as well be four miles southwest of Berlin."

"Do you enjoy borrowing trouble, Phillips?" Lazeski said. "At least we're on the right map."

"Barely." Springwater buckled his web belt. "Forget making the locks by dawn."

"Brilliant deduction, Chief," Phillips said. "So, now what?"

Springwater grabbed the front of Phillips's jacket and cocked his fist back. "Don't call me that again."

Phillips raised his hands in surrender. "Relax, Ted. I've never been—"

"And who here has?" Springwater released the wadded fabric. "We stick to our plan. Head east. Try to find Lieutenant Henry, the rest of the stick. Then work our way north. Either avoid contact or hit targets of opportunity. Find more GIs."

"What's ahead?" Lazeski asked.

"The north-south Periers-Carentan highway. About a mile east. We cross it and turn northeast, parallel to the highway. Head for Carentan and hope our side holds it before we get there."

Yet if Chalk Number-2 was anywhere near typical of even a small fraction of the 501st, he couldn't bank on such an optimistic timetable. Springwater suspected each man harbored such thoughts, Phillips even more so. Yet he refused to let it become contagious. *A war chief shows hope.* He held his head high and gazed northward.

"We'll get there."

*   *   *

St. Georges-de-Bohon, Normandy

Sam drifted on the edge of consciousness. The noise of yet more hobnailed boots scraping pavement jolted him back to his desperate reality. He crawled to a ventilation slit in the barn's stone wall and peered out over the narrow road. He could just make out two teams of Germans carrying litters.

The sight reminded Sam of his own wound. It needed treatment. It required something more than his cotton undershirt to stem the bleeding.

Pulling his helmet off, the chinstrap bumped his face. The ensuing twinge made him reach for his left cheek. He found a small gash amidst the scratches from the hedge. He pressed his face again and felt cool moisture. Tracing his fingertips over his cheek, he sensed small bumps on crinkled skin. Blisters. He recalled the packed C-47 aisle. A searing flash. Carter's charred face.

Sam shook his head to erase the image. He unbuckled his web belt and let the web gear fall to the loose hay. He peeled through the layers—jump jacket, pants suspenders, wool shirt, undershirt and, at last, skin. Each progressive layer grew bloodier.

Despite straining and twisting, he couldn't view the wound. He'd have to explore the area with his fingers. Grimacing in anticipation, he forced his fingers on the wound. Rather than a stab-wound, his fingertips probed a gaping gash in the flesh leading from his neck to his shoulder. He shuttered and withdrew his hand.

He opened his musette bag and found the spare first aid kit. He ripped it open but tossed the morphine Syrette and tourniquet back into the bag. He dumped most of the sulfanilamide packet into the laceration. The intense stinging forced his eyes shut. Tears squeezed out the corners. He took the remaining yellow sulfa powder and dabbed it onto the small gash, popped blisters, and scratches on his face.

He shook out the Carlisle bandage and pressed the pad onto the bayonet wound. He struggled several minutes to tie off the bandage under his armpit. On the fifth attempt he realized he could do no better than a loose knot and began putting layers back on. He counted on light pressure from his pants suspender to help hold the bandage secure.

Outside, litter bearers labored past with yet another stretcher case. Sam moved to the end of the loft, got on his knees, and peered through another slit. Five fallschirmjager stood in front of the house. Most smoked. All talked loud enough for distinct, yet unintelligible German to reach inside the barn.

A sharp exchange of gunfire erupted on the far side of St. Georges-de-Bohon. The soldiers' attention shifted toward the firefight. One spoke and all five laughed.

Sam crawled to his gear and did a quick inventory of what remained to prosecute his war. No hand grenades. One smoke grenade. His 45-auto pistol had one round in the chamber and one left in the clip. He pushed the magazine release, dropped the near-empty clip and exchanged it for a full one from the pouch. That left him sixteen rounds for a weapon that, while saving his life once already, was nonetheless a weapon of desperation. He had a fresh magazine of fifteen rounds in his carbine, but only one left in his pouch, for a grand-total of thirty cartridges. The M-3 fighting knife strapped to his ankle completed his armament.

Panic surged through him. *Where's my map case?*

In the barn's darkness, he ran his hands through his gear and patted down the surrounding straw. No map case. He moaned. His breaths came in short gasps.

No grenades, almost out of ammo, lacking confidence in his primary weapon, lost, wounded, and gimpy, he wondered if he wouldn't be more a liability than an asset to any GIs he might encounter.

Acrid smoke drifted into the barn. He limped to the large hay-loading windows on the north end of the barn to investigate. As soon as he could see outside, he jerked his head back. Thirty feet away a trio of German paratroopers stood in the road.

He overcame his shock and inched his head back to the crack to get another look. Two Germans were setting up a heavy machinegun tripod. The third, a submachine gun hanging across his chest, examined a US Army Colt 45-auto pistol held up to the moonlight. An orange glow emanated from the other side of the village. Sam went to the other side of the barn to view the horizon. Dim hints of yellow and pink showed. Now he had a general idea of which way was east. The luminescent hand of his watch said 0548 hours. The 4th Infantry Division would be hitting Utah Beach in under an hour. Operation Neptune was merging into Operation Overlord.

He strained to hear sounds of the Air Corps and Navy hitting the bunkers and artillery positions behind Utah Beach. Northward, he could make out faint booming rumbles, like an Ozark thunderstorm off in the distance.

He decided to make himself at least feel useful by squaring away his gear. He removed the carbine sheath and all the ripped canvas pouches. He grabbed his coil of paratrooper's rope, started to toss it aside, but hesitated. Rope had more utility than just getting out of a tree. He kept it. He put his harness back on, but again let his left weight-bearing web gear suspender hang loose to keep it from digging into the bayonet wound.

A tuneless bell clanked. He looked again through the crack between the loft doors. A civilian herded a dozen white and brown mottled cows up the road past the German machinegun. Sam's mind returned to the chores of his youth. Cows in need of milking never took a holiday, indeed, not even in deference to the unprecedented armada waiting off the Norman shore.

He went over to the loose stack of hay and raked out a nest with the carbine's metal folding stock. He sat in the nest, haystack supporting his back. His position shielded him from the ground floor yet gave him a good view of the ladder's top. He pulled a D-ration fortified chocolate bar from a jacket pocket and ate breakfast.

Why did I go and duck into this death trap? Should've done a shoot-'n-scoot when I had the chance. He gnawed off a piece of the thick chocolate bar and moved it around in his mouth. *Pettigrew's probably sitting at the locks right now brown-nosing the brass. He'd have just one word for my mess—cowardice.*

Sam clung to a slim hope that the rest of the 501ˢᵗ Parachute Infantry Regiment might be faring better.

✶   ✶   ✶

Near Angoville-au-Plein, Normandy

"Get that machinegun set up to suppress the intersection!"

Lieutenant Lloyd Sterling shouted the orders even though unsure if anyone from the 506ᵗʰ G-Company machinegun team remained alive.

Bullets popped and clipped the hedgerow overhead. Twigs and leaves rained down. He ducked lower into the weedy ditch.

Mortar rounds crashed on the opposite side of the road.

Sterling held his helmet down and shoved his face into the grass. A body thumped into his side and groaned. Sterling rolled over. "You hit?"

"My...arrgh...my leg," the C-Company staff sergeant said through gritted teeth.

Sterling and the sergeant had repulsed a half-dozen attacks and moved their twenty-five-member force 400 yards off DZ-D. Yet Sterling had yet to learn the man's name.

He grabbed the sergeant's leg and in the half-light of dawn found dark moisture spreading from a rip in the pants between the knee and boot top. "Can you move your leg?"

The sergeant raised a German submachine gun and sprayed a burst at the road intersection. "Here they come!"

Sterling glanced toward the intersection and fired at a fleeting shadow. "Not too much bleeding." Tracers streaked overhead. "First aid kit?"

"Fresh out." The sergeant cursed. "It burns...burns like a...."

Sterling rolled over and snatched a first aid kit from a motionless paratrooper's load-bearing harness. Sterling averted his eyes so he didn't again have to witness the disgusting gore. The dead paratrooper's entire lower jaw, both sides, had been blown off. For eighteen months Sterling had led the likable teen. He recalled that the boy had joined the day after his seventeenth birthday out of his father's fear that his son would miss the war. *Dad deserves to know all about this, but for his mother's sake, I'll spare them the details.*

Sterling enlarged the rip in the sergeant's pants and dressed the leg wound. "What've we got left?"

The thirty-caliber machinegun fired a burst.

"Looks like the Five-O-Sixth machinegun. Five of your men from Able, two each from Dog and Charlie, maybe a half-dozen others from who knows where."

Sterling turned back toward the enemy and caught shadowy movement along a hedgerow fifty yards away. He yanked his M-1 trigger twice.

A metallic ping announced that his rifle needed reloading.

A scream came from the direction of his shots.

He patted his cartridge belt. Empty. He reached over, took the last bullet clip off the jawless teen and reloaded.

More German mortars rained down. The Five-O-Sixth's machinegun fell silent.

Sterling glanced over his shoulder. Smoking soil and tangled metal marked the machinegun position.

"We fall back two hundred yards. Rally at the Angoville au Plein church aid station. Anyone who can't fight *and* move stays there. We'll find a larger group or another route to the locks. You lead out. I'll delay these jokers a bit, then bring up the rear."

The staff sergeant crawled away, shouting orders. After twenty yards, he rose and trotted with a limp. Battered paratroopers rose from shallow foxholes and ditch bottoms, and followed.

Two Germans materialized in the road intersection and leveled black machine-pistols on the withdrawing Americans.

Sterling put two quick shots into each and scanned for more targets.

It had nothing to do with choosing to kill—it became irreducibly simplified to one thing. Survival. Kill or be killed.

Equipment rattled around the corner. He rose to his knees and chucked his last grenade high and hard over the hedge concealing his attackers.

The grenade exploded.

Miles away, naval guns boomed.

A German shouted orders.

Here they come! He rolled over in the ditch and rose to chase his patchwork parachute infantry force.

In the yellow light of dawn he watched two potato masher grenades arch through the sky, tumbling end-over-end, and land in his ditch.

He dropped and tucked into a ball.

The blasts flung him onto the road.

Pain paralyzed him.

He half-opened an eye. Jackboots charged toward him. Shots rang out so close that he felt the muzzle blasts. His body shuddered.

So it ends. So history is made.

Lieutenant Lloyd Sterling's world went dark.

Chapter 40

Pleas

6 June 1944, 0900 hours
Merryfield, England

"Pardon me, lassie, but I *officially* don't know a thing about what took place last night," the forty-ish sentry said in a thick Scottish brogue. "Nor can I ask after some Yank on your behalf. Still an active airfield." He lowered his voice to a whisper. "Even if all the Yank paratroopers be gone. And you didn't hear it from me."

The sentry stood just outside a black and white striped guard shack set in the gap between sandbags and concertina wire. Aircraft engines droned nearby. A pair of C-47s took off towing gliders.

"Can you just tell me this much—was it a training exercise?"

"Go home, lassie." The sentry squinted at the morning sun. "You be wasting your time here."

"Then you're quite certain, the invasion *is* on?"

"Afraid Monty and Ike don't invite me over to share a shot 'o whiskey and cigars. But it would be a right daft chap who'd wager otherwise."

"Can't you tell me anything more?"

"You miss me point, lassie—haven't told you a bloomin' thing."

Maggie crossed her arms and pleaded with her eyes. The Scot frowned and scanned around his post. "Will ye be gone if I do?"

"I suppose that depends..."

"My, but you be the persistent lass." He made a furtive glance over his shoulder. "Some of us stayed up. Didn't seem right to be all-cozy like in bed considering where the Yanks was heading. Ninety-one planes left. Counted each Dakota making its return. Eighty-eight come back. Aye, things must be going smashing. And I'll deny every word if—" The Scot came to attention and held his rifle out as an RAF officer passed through the gate. "Be gone now, lassie."

Maggie walked away following the fence that separated the restricted part of the airfield from other military buildings. She ventured south, past a temporary hospital and small car-park crowded with American ambulances. A soldier threw a wet mop into the back of an ambulance and pulled back a cascade of crimson water. She cringed at her close proximity to blood spilled on Sam's mission. She picked up her pace. The fence jutted west. She followed it in hopes of finding a talkative Yank she could ply for information.

Instead, she discovered a tent city and another plywood sign forbidding contact with troops. Beyond the sign soldiers scurried about—lowering tent poles, folding canvas, and loading lorries. What the Scot had speculated, the bloody ambulance and collapsing tents confirmed.

She gazed at the rows of tents. Which one had been Sam's?

A tent in the first row, fifty yards from the fence, captured her attention. Large, white handwritten block letters stood out against the olive drab canvas. She squinted and read: MAGGIE, UNDERNEATH THE LANTERN. STEAK DINNER. I WILL RETURN. SAM

Her pulse quickened. *Am I imaging it?* She bit her lower lip and read it again.

Her mind wasn't playing tricks. Perhaps nonsensical to anyone else—the reference to "Lili Marlene" lyrics, the steak, the promise—the impromptu billboard could have only one author. Her Sam. Focused on the words, she failed to notice the crew surrounding the tent. The soldiers pulled up stakes and lowered poles. The canvas message collapsed.

A spark of hope ignited in her heart. Sam had sought her, too, even up to the last moment.

A guard pacing the beaten path inside the fence spotted her. He yelled in Cockney thick enough to make her feel at home, "Miss, you can't ruddy well be standin' round 'ere a gawkin'. Be movin' on!"

She turned away, her head pounding. Nothing remained but to return to Overton. Return to her routine. Return to enduring an agonizing waiting game, one more time.

Several minutes of aimless meandering later, she found herself in central Ilton. The village center consisted of little more than a small pub and inn under one roof, a Royal Mail office, a merchant, and a few scattered brick or stone homes. She noticed a lych-gate in a stone wall. An ancient yew shaded a cobbled path that led to the door of an even more ancient stone chapel. She crossed the street and read the sign identifying St. Peter's Church. Glass protected the printed papers listing an agenda of church services, the churchwardens, and the vicar—a Dr. Simon Guard.

Her aching heart drew her through the gate and up the uneven, mossy cobbles. Time had arrayed old tombstones at haphazard angles on each side of the path. The chapel's size was befitting Ilton.

At the main double doors she pushed her thumb down on the latch. The doors held fast. *It's Tuesday. Shouldn't be all that surprised*, she thought and stepped away. She noticed steppingstones along the chapel's side and followed them to a side entrance. Pushing the handle, the door yielded. She stepped through a low arched doorway.

She reacted to the musty air with a sneeze. Moving into the small sanctuary, she went to the third pew and took a seat. The eastern light poured through a stained glass window depicting Christ as the Good Shepherd.

Overwhelmed with anguish, she went to her knees and pleaded with God.

*   *   *

Thouars, France
1330 Hours

Hauptscharfuhrer Helmut Behr trotted down the worn cobblestones, ushering thirty-six untested *panzergrenadieren* in full battle array.

The initial warning order—"Prepare for deployment to coastal districts"—had brought much relief. For almost two days the 17th SS Panzergrenadier Division had stood at alert. Helmut had mentally cursed Berlin when the invasion expected on 5 June failed to materialize. He ached for action—any action to get him out of this backwater burg.

"Helmut, please wait!" A frantic female voice called out in French. "Helmut!"

Behr glanced over his shoulder. Claudette hiked up her skirt and ran after him. Behr halted. "Keep moving! What are you *kinder* looking at?" He hooked a soldat by the arm and yanked him out of the ranks. "Sturmmann Henshel, take this platoon to the vehicle park. Mount all crew served weapons and assure each has a full complement of ammunition."

He pushed Henshel away as Claudette arrived.

Tears streamed down her cheeks. Wind blew wavy brunette strands across her face. "You mustn't leave. Not without a proper—"

"Which will you miss more? My demons or my dead soul?"

"Please, Helmut." Claudette brushed the hair out of her face. "I never expected it so soon."

"What? Not enough time to learn English?"

"Helmut, please." Her breath reeked of alcohol. "I am with child."

His head swooned. Claudette's German was poor on her best day. Maybe he'd heard wrong. "You're pregnant?" He pointed at her belly and tried French. "*Bebe?*"

"*Oui.*" Her tears returned.

He shrugged. "So why do you come to me?"

She slapped his cheek so hard his ear rang. He felt his cheek scar flush. He held Claudette by the shoulders and looked her in the eye. "I am a soldier. A *Deutschlander* soldier at war. You knew as much the day we met. Now I must go. Do not drink so much sherry and *calvados*." He embraced her and parted with a kiss on her cheek. "I will send francs."

Jogging after his young charges, he licked his lips and tasted her tears. Her sobs pleaded for him to turn back.

Behr picked up his pace.

*   *   *

Ilton, England
1347 Hours

"Perhaps I can help?"

A gentle, yet authoritative voice disrupted Maggie's prayers. She got off her knees.

"Terribly sorry, miss. I hadn't the slightest intention of frightening you, but you've been here at least an hour. I've been back that long." A plump middle-aged man in a clerical collar extended his hand and a warm smile. "I suppose it's high time to do what's expected of a good vicar. I'm Simon Guard and I know every soul in Ilton. And you'd be…?"

"Margaret Elliott. Visiting from Overton."

"And London before that, if my ear serves me correctly."

"As your voice also gives you away as a Londoner, too, *Doctor* Guard."

"Ah, so you read the propaganda the church wardens insist on posting. Ignore it, please. So, what brings you to Ilton, Miss Elliott?"

"Merryfield. And please call me Maggie."

"Aye, naturally it'd be Merryfield, Maggie. In its short life Merryfield has already managed to increase Ilton's population six-fold. I just came from there—the hospital, to be precise." He picked up a hymnal and slid it into its pew-back rack. "I can be of more use in the Lord's service at the hospital than sitting around here preparing sermons few choose to hear."

Maggie perked up. "You mean the sentries allow you past?"

"The American commanding surgeon—an Episcopalian chap from Virginia—is quite accommodating. They had extra need for me this morning. But I digress."

"Please, I must know. What happened last night, Vicar?"

"Actually in the wee hours of the morning. Some American paratroopers never jumped from their planes. Suffered wounds while still in flight. A number of crew members required medical assistance, too. The planes were instantly transformed into flying ambulances. Aye, a good thing, to be sure. Saved some from a horrible end."

"Were any of the wounded named Henry? Surname Henry, that is. Samuel Henry, a Yank second lef'tenant paratrooper."

"None that I recall." Dr. Guard moved his fingertips through his disheveled hair. "But I can be quite dreadful with names. Not exactly the setting for formal introductions. Most weren't in any shape for chitchat. A few succumbed to their wounds before the surgeons could operate."

His words tied Maggie's stomach in knots. Her eyes must have betrayed her fear.

"Oh, dear, I'm terribly sorry. Be assured, there was only one officer among the wounded paratroopers, a captain. Of that, I'm quite certain. Would I be too presumptuous to assume that you hold a special, personal interest in this lef'tenant?"

"He's the reason I'm here. Not just Merryfield, I mean here," Maggie pointed at the altar, "praying."

"Some consider me a professional listener. Care to tell me the tale of Maggie Elliot and this Lef'tenant Henry?"

Chapter 41

The Innocent

6 June 1944, 1540 Hours
St. Georges-de-Bohon, Normandy

Outside the barn a diesel engine idled, heightening Sam's already alerted state. Metallic noise and shouts forced him to investigate. He limped to the loft door and peered through the gap.

German paratroopers loaded the machinegun and folded tripod into a truck covered with cut tree limbs. The truck pulled away, taking men and weapons toward the faint rumbling detonations—the direction that Sam had deduced as north.

About seven hours earlier the Germans had evacuated their wounded and Sam's bayonet wound had stopped bleeding. However, his aching hip forced him to shift positions about every fifteen minutes.

The farmstead took on a surreal serenity. Furtive Frenchmen appeared on the roads and just as quickly returned to homes. *Time to scoot from this death trap.* But where to? Like the Civil War general—whose name escaped him—he would advance toward the sound of guns. North.

Standing in the same doorway he'd entered, he checked all approaches and made for the water trough. He pumped and drank his belly full.

Escaping the barnyard, he nearly collided with a hunched-over farmer herding several heifers. The farmer refused to make eye contact. The heifers weren't as discerning, balking at the sight of a battered and bloody American. The farmer used a shaft to prod the heifers.

Sam moved among the clustered buildings, casting furtive glances as he went. He noticed blackened pools of dried blood on the macadam pavement and splashes of brighter red on pockmarked stucco walls. Scattered debris identified the area he had heard the Americans corralled and captured like helpless livestock. Discarded paratrooper first aid kit wrappers, a bloody jump jacket sleeve—complete with screaming eagle patch—spent brass, and empty bullet clips littered the pavement. A ripped open Corcoran jump boot lay across the street. Grenade scorch marks scarred walls.

He found a helmet and pushed the net and burlap scrim aside. The stenciled diamond had a tick mark at the three o'clock position—First Battalion, Five-O-First. His fears affirmed, he turned the helmet to find a horizontal white stripe of a sergeant. Springwater's? Lazeski's?

Footfalls from behind interrupted his inspection. He sat the helmet down and scrambled for an escape route. He ducked into a narrow alley and found concealment in a recessed doorway. His soaring pulse rate descended when he realized that the footsteps had no hint of noisy hobnails.

A sobbing middle-aged woman and a Frenchman carrying a stack of blankets passed. Sam hid another five minutes before stepping out of the doorway. He massaged his hip joint while walking.

He ignored the helmet and other scattered American items. He couldn't bear learning details possibly confirming the demise of his men. He had to forget his own men and find a way to join up with any allied troops. Survival depended upon it.

In St. Georges-de-Bohon's market center, he rounded a cobblestoned bend. At a crossroads, two civilians gazed up into an ancient elm. Sam recognized them as the couple he'd seen ten minutes earlier. The massive tree-trunk blocked Sam's view of what captured their attention.

Limping around the bend, the view stunned him.

Three corpses hung from a sturdy limb, feet suspended at head height. On two, skirts and hair flapped in the breeze. Ropes elongated their necks and bent their heads askew. As Sam neared he noted a priest's collar on the third victim.

A Frenchman stood on a ladder propped on the limb. The man on the ground ducked and dodged the victims' feet as he laid blankets out.

Abandoning military caution, Sam crossed the intersection toward the atrocity. The sobs of the inconsolable reached his ears. The man spreading blankets spotted Sam. His expression contorted with hatred.

Speechless, Sam stood underneath the limb. The hung females appeared to be in their late teens. They wore bloodstained aprons. One had wavy brunette hair and a swollen tongue protruding in an unnatural shade of blue.

Sam took a deep breath. "Who did this?"

The man on the ladder scooted onto the limb. He gave Sam a dismissive look and muttered in French. The man on the ground babbled a staccato burst of angry words and spit at Sam's feet.

Sam felt feeble. "Do you need help?"

The middle-aged woman gained control over her sobs. "*Non*. You go."

"You speak English?"

The woman's face twisted in agony. "*Non. C'est peu.* You go!"

The man on the ground looked Sam in the eye and spewed more angry words. The woman attempted to interpret. "Man say, Americans few. *Le Boche beaucoup.* No good."

The man on the ground again sprayed a glob of white spittle, barely missing the blankets. "*Le Boche.*"

"Tell *monsieur* I'm terribly sorry. We weren't even supposed to drop here. This wasn't in the plan." Realizing the woman didn't comprehend his words, Sam heaved a frustrated sigh and sifted his gaze upward. "Who?"

"*Fille.*" She pointed to herself and the man spreading blankets. "How say English...? Daughter." She pointed at middle corpse. "Daughter friend." Sobbing, the woman made the sign of the cross. "*Pere.*"

"Why?"

"Aid Americans." The woman made the hand motions of bandaging an arm and head. "*Eglise.* You say, church."

The daughter resembled Sam's youngest sister. *What if the Japanese had invaded Santa Monica Bay, like expected? Would my sisters have been this brave?* The other executed girl's eyes remained wide-open, clouded, yet still honey-brown. *What if Hitler invaded England? Would this have been Maggie's fate?*

His questions ignited a fury in his gut. "Sorry, but I'd be one cold-blooded S-O-B to just stand ." He choked back his emotion. "Worse if I walked away."

The French had confused expressions. Sam leaned his carbine against the tree-trunk. He unraveled his coil of white rope. As Sam climbed the ladder, the father muttered on, but without such angry tones. Sam stopped a few inches above the first girl—the one identified as their daughter.

He leaned over and, as if the girl was injured rather than dead, looped his rope across her chest and under each arm, forming a harness. His cheek brushed against hers, already cold and stiff. The breeze blew her light brown hair into his face and tickled his nose. He caught traces of perfume on her stretched neck.

While knotting the rope behind her back the breeze ceased. The odor of feces and urine surrounding the three corpses assaulted him. He repressed the urge to gag—no reason to heap humiliation onto the parents' grief.

He draped the rope over the limb, reached to his right ankle to remove his fighting knife, and offered it to the man sitting on the limb.

Sam climbed down to the ground and looped the slack rope behind his rump. He leaned back until the rope was taut, bracing himself, careful to keep the pressure off his injured hip, and nodded. "Cut it."

The Frenchman may not have understood the words but he knew the next step. The razor-sharp knife touched the tight noose, releasing the body. The loosed weight surprised Sam. He fought to keep his balance as he lowered the dead mademoiselle with the dignity she deserved. As the body descended, the father guided it onto a blanket.

Sam stepped to the corpse and knelt next to her head. Wanting to spare the father the horrific task of removing the rope, Sam wedged his fingers between the braided fibers and neck flesh and tugged outward. A four-foot length of paratrooper rope came free in his hand. *How'd my rope get around her neck?*

A sickening realization hit him—the sadists had used American rope. He looked upward. American paratrooper rope pinched the necks of the other victims. Feeling like an accomplice, he flipped the rope away in disgust.

He helped arrange the couple's daughter in a dignified position on a blanket. Yet after repeated tries, concluded that he could achieve nothing dignified with the girl's neck. He spread a blanket over her face.

Sam and the Frenchman on the limb repeated the process until wrapping all three bodies in blankets. While lowering the priest, Sam felt his shoulder wound reopen, issuing a fresh flow of blood. He ignored it. His discomfort paled compared to the French parents' anguish.

The gruesome task complete, he gathered his gear and glanced at his watch. Almost eighteen hundred hours—time to get back to being a soldier. He held his helmet to his chest and bowed respectfully. "I'm terribly sorry. Please accept my deepest sympathy. I need to go now. But we *will* be back. Maybe not me exactly, but we'll be back. And next time with enough…" He shook his head. "I wish you could understand. I'll remember your daughter as a merciful angel. A heroic daughter of France."

The parents stared at the forms outlined under blankets.

As Sam backed away the father said, "*Merci, monsieur.*"

The other Frenchman rolled up Sam's rope and started toward Sam, extending it.

Sam backed away, waving a hand. "No. No. You keep it." *I don't want any reminder what that rope will forever represent to me.* He turned his back to the atrocity. Walking away he wanted to kick himself. *Like there's a chance the French will find the rope any less repulsive?*

He remembered something he did need. He turned to the Frenchman, pointed north, and named the closest town to his La Barquette locks objective. "Carentan?"

The Frenchman nodded.

Chapter 42

Desperation

Sam hadn't ventured two hundred yards before detecting a scorched paint and burnt wood odor tainting the air.

Atop a knoll he stumbled upon smoldering ruins. The church. Mere hours earlier it had served as a refuge for wounded Geronimos ministered to by the French angels of mercy. Now it was a roofless burned-out shell with a lingering stench—a monument to hideous death and wanton destruction. Sam leaned into a window. A half-dozen charred human remains lined where the altar had been. Corcoran jump boots identified them as paratroopers.

Bile rose in his throat. He pushed away from the window and busted though a tight poplar hedge—leaves on the church-side scorched brown.

The sight arrayed before him was staggering.

Floodwaters extended across the entire plain. The sun cast an annoying glare off the water.

"We didn't get the locks. We failed!" He slumped to the ground. *Or was I right? Had the German occupation flooded the lowlands long ago?*

It didn't matter. Everything he had witnessed, all the evidence he could gather, every indicator pointed to the same conclusion—Operation Neptune, perhaps even Overlord itself, was one colossal failure on historical proportions.

Nonetheless, lingering around St. Georges-de-Bohon invited death. To continue northward at least offered the possibility of survival. *The roads will be crawling with Krauts. Follow the water's edge as long as I can. After that…one step at a time.*

Rising, he reached for his canteen. It hadn't magically rematerialized. Disappointed and thirsty, he set off down the gentle slope toward water's edge.

After paralleling the water for about a mile, his pulse quickened at what he spotted in the cow trail mud. Fresh footprints. He picked up his own foot and looked down to be sure. A match. Corcoran jump boots had indeed made the prints. He moved fifteen yards and scanned the trail—more boot prints. Three, maybe four paratroopers.

Evening shadows lengthened. *Make contact before dark!* He picked up his pace.

He waded through a chest-deep weed patch to access a slight rise in the terrain.

Seventy-five yards ahead, a scrim-covered American helmet dipped out of sight. Adrenaline pumping, Sam tiptoed and craned his neck.

Another helmet bobbed above the weeds—accompanied by a distinct carbine barrel.

Ignoring his aching hip, Sam charged through the weeds back to the path.

He splashed through a wet drainage, ran up a short bank, and searched for the Americans.

Nothing.

He trotted forward to where the path jogged right and rose to his tiptoes. Movement ahead caught his attention. *Odd. Not where I expected them. How—?*

He spotted another helmet. A German helmet.

Broadside to Sam, two Germans dropped to an earthen brim overlooking the flooded area.

Sam threw his carbine to his shoulder. An MG-42 barrel protruded from the weeds, pointing at water's edge.

The machinegun fired a ripping burst.

Before the burst ended Sam fired three rounds into the patch of Wehrmacht gray-green fabric nearest him. The MG-42's ripping chatter concealed the sound of his diminutive carbine.

From the water's edge a single carbine returned fire.

Sam seized the opportunity, dashing left through the high weeds to get further on the enemies' flank.

The MG-42 fired another burst.

Running, he lost sight of the machinegun, so dropped in the weeds to listen.

Two carbine shots rang out in quick succession.

The German machinegunners responded with two short bursts.

Sam sprang to his feet and rushed the sound.

The tall weeds ended. He found himself ten yards from the prone loader and machinegunner's right rear flank.

A third soldier rose to his knees and pumped his hand toward the water.

Sam sighted on the gunner and felt the carbine buck twice before he was even aware he was pulling the trigger.

He shifted his aim right until gray-green filled his peep sights. He squeezed the trigger three times.

Three puffs of dust billowed from the spotter's wool-covered back.

Sam dropped to one knee and shifted his muzzle to the loader. The frantic enemy was trying to spin around and shoulder a Mauser rifle. Sam jerked the trigger three times without aiming.

Seeming unaffected, the loader dropped to the ground, pointing the Mauser at Sam.

Sam's next shots punched two neat holes in the front of the loader's helmet.

Sam rolled right and cringed. The Mauser remained silent.

He rose to his feet.

Motion near the MG-42 caught his attention. Sam swung his carbine back. The gunner groaned and collapsed as he reached for the loader's rifle. Sam rushed over and kicked the rifle away.

All enemy movement ceased.

Sam's knees commenced trembling. He yelled, "Flash."

No password came back.

"Flash! Able, Five-O-First." The trembling spread to his hands.

Still no response.

He caught a blur of movement to the northwest. He wiped sweat from his right eye and looked again. Two men came into focus two hundred yards out, splashing in ankle-deep water. Fleeing.

He squinted. Uniform color marked them as enemy.

He knelt for better stability, flipped the rear aperture sight for the increased distance, and took careful aim at the soldier to the right and trailing. He squeezed the trigger. The carbine gave its sharp report.

A fraction of a second later his target's hands flew outward. The German plunged face first into the shallow water. The lead German halted and turned back.

Sam aimed at the second target and squeezed the trigger.

The soldier was reaching down to aid his wounded comrade.

Sam let up on the trigger.

With flailing arms the wounded soldier regained his feet and draped an arm over his comrade's neck. The two stumbled toward the nearest hedgerow.

Sam mentally reentered the war and found the fleeing men in his sight aperture. He centered the front sight between the shoulders of the unwounded man. And again hesitated. The German soldiers were retreating—no longer posing an immediate threat. *Maybe they're the ones who hung the girls? Burned the wounded paratroopers alive.*

He released half a breath and squeezed the trigger.

A small white geyser spouted at the feet of his target.

Sam adjusted his aim to just above the Nazi's helmet and squeezed the trigger.

A dull metallic clap sounded.

With shaky hands he jerked the receiver open. No cartridge ejected. He stared into the top of an empty magazine. He pushed the magazine release, grabbed his last magazine, shoved it home, and racked a round.

He looked up as the last German disappeared through the distant hedgerow. *Just dandy! They'll find more Krauts and in short-order this whole area will be crawling with enemy troops.*

He trotted toward the ambushed GIs. "Flash. Coming in, hold your fire. Flash! All clear here."

He stepped onto the cow path. His face twisted at the grotesque sight of three paratroopers—mere seconds earlier, living, breathing, hopeful beings—now robbed of life. Multiple 8mm slugs had pierced and exited the torsos and arms of each body. He spotted the diamond stenciled on the side of a bullet pierced helmet, a tick mark at the bottom of the diamond. *So, Second Battalion got misdropped, too.*

Sam twisted to see back down the trail. A boot—toe jutting upward—appeared at the edge of the path. The boot led to a leg that disappeared, mid-calf, underwater. He rushed to the immersed soldier.

A swirl of pink spread in the dark water.

Tossing his carbine aside, he grabbed the boot and yanked. Sam's footing gave way in the mud and he flopped on the trail, landing on his bruised hip. Resisting the urge to scream, he bit his lip and writhed in the mud. Before the pain subsided he refocused on his task. The paratrooper's torso was out, but the man's head remained submerged.

He pulled both boots. The head cleared the water.

Sam scanned the limp body. A grazing wound gouged the man's right temple and sheared off the top of his ear. The body appeared free of other bullet wounds. Sam felt the man's neck under the jawbone and found a strong pulse.

Yet the paratrooper's chest remained motionless.

Sam rolled the limp paratrooper over onto his belly, straddled his back, and lifted him by the hips. Swamp water seeped from blue-tinged lips. Sam opened the man's mouth and strained to lift the hips higher. More water drained.

He reached under the man's belly and removed the load-bearing harness. He then positioned himself straddling the man's thighs, placed the heels of his hands in the small of the man's back, and rocking back and forth, began artificial respiration—applying and releasing pressure to the chest cavity from behind.

Five rapid M-1 shots distracted Sam from the drowned paratrooper. The shots sounded about a half-mile away. From the same direction the two Germans had fled.

Sam jumped up. The sound represented a live American. *Run to the sound. Go. This guy's a goner.* He looked down at the drowned paratrooper and hesitated.

He dropped and resumed artificial respiration. "Come on. Breathe already. Please breathe." Sam pushed on the limp paratrooper's ribs. "Don't die on me."

He continued leaning forward and back into strong compressions. He paused. The man wasn't breathing. He again checked the pulse. His fingers sensed nothing.

His hand shook. Exertion was making him pant. His heart still raced with adrenalin. Too much was happening, too fast. No pulse. *Or am I too shook up to feel it?* He held his breath and rechecked the carotid artery. Nothing.

Straddling the drowned man, Sam looked skyward and slammed the heel of his hand into the man's back.

The sting coming from Sam's popped blisters and cut cheek confirmed that he was crying. He let the salty tears stream over his abused face. He could bear no more. He rolled off to the side and slumped over on the drowned paratrooper's back. Fatigue permeated every muscle. His wounds rotated in their cry for attention. His head throbbed.

'*It won't be a bloomin' thing like training.*' The words of the Lambourn ironmonger and survivor of the Somme trenches rang in his head. The context of the meeting with Mr. Alvis came to mind—Maggie's pitchfork ring. *Focus on Maggie. Get my heart back in the war and my body will follow.* However, the image of Maggie that first surfaced was in Kensington Gardens. Maggie's troubled visage screamed, *I'm not enough!*

"You've got to be enough, Maggie. Our song says so." He slammed his hand on the back of the drowned paratrooper. His mind drifted to "Lili Marlene" lyrics:

> When we are marching in the mud and cold
> And when my pack seems more than I can hold

My love for you renews my might
It's warm again, my pack is light
It's you, Lili Marlene
It's you, Lili Marlene

He again slammed his fist into the drenched body. "Marlene Dietrich lied! The OCS cadre lied! Dr. Rosenfeld lied! UCLA lied! Everything's one big lie!"

Chapter 43

The Proximity

6 June 1944, 1913 Hours
Normandy

"Collins, keep an eye out front. Silva, watch our six."

Springwater knelt over the two Wehrmacht soldiers sprawled facedown. The sharp odor of male sweat hung in the shadows of the hedgerow. He lifted a corpse's shoulder until it rolled over. Decaying leaves stuck to the dead soldier's sweaty face.

"No Lugers, Sarge," Morton said. "Already checked."

"Not looking for souvenirs." Springwater probed inside the dead man's field jacket. "Need to know who we're going up against." He pulled out a document holder. Sorting through it, he discarded personal items onto the man's chest. A photograph fluttered down to cover side-by-side bullet holes.

Morton stared at the photograph and whistled. "A real dish. Bet she's a natural blonde. Fritz won't be getting anymore of that—"

"Hush up," Collins said over his shoulder. "Try 'n show some respect for the dead." He spit a stream of brown saliva in Morton's direction.

Springwater thumbed through a pay book. "You said they were running toward you. Attacking?"

"Never saw me. I let them get real close. Then I pop up and shoot them both. From the hip. Just like I did that Kraut charging out of that shack." Morton lit a Chesterfield and billowed out a cloud of smoke as if puffing a victory cigar. "Geronimo don't take no prisoners."

"That one wasn't running too fast." Springwater nodded toward the other corpse. "Not with a bullet in his calf."

"I might've hit him there." Morton flicked his cigarette ashes to fall onto the cheek of the dead soldier. "I'm getting pretty good at this."

Springwater pointed to a field-expedient bandage on the second German's lower leg. "Dead men don't apply bandages."

Silva pointed his rifle toward the southeast. "Remember that shooting 'bout fifteen minutes ago?"

Springwater nodded. "One MG-42. More than a full magazine's worth from a carbine and—"

"And then nothing." Silva raised an eyebrow. "And the way Morton says these guys were moving, I'd bet the good guys won that little shootout."

"Reckon we might go make our acquaintance with them boys?" Collins said.

"Exactly what we intend to do." Springwater shoved the German documents into his jacket pocket. "We go back east. Sit on that cow path heading north toward Carentan. The one near the water. Dig in and let them run into us."

"Sounds like a plan," Silva said. "I'm tired of ducking, dodging, hiding. Go a little this way, spot a damn Kraut patrol, then go back that way."

"We find more Americans, or we make a beeline for Carentan." Springwater stood. "This was just some Kraut helping his buddy back to their aid station."

He took in his men. Collins looked uneasy. Silva's eyes pleaded for relief. Morton sneered.

Chapter 44

Revived

6 June 1944, 1916 Hours
Normandy

The body seemed to spasm beneath Sam.

It's just me moving. This poor guy's long gone.

He looked at the paratrooper's face. The youthfulness was striking, yet wasted in death.

The body shuddered. Startled, Sam pushed away.

The young paratrooper's chest rose and he emitted a weak cough. The next cough triggered a coughing fit.

Sam rolled the paratrooper onto his back. The coughing intensified. Unsure what to do, he grabbed the paratrooper's shoulders and pulled until the limp body sat upright. The paratrooper braced himself on his right elbow. Watery phlegm drained from the paratrooper's mouth and nose as he shifted to his hands and knees, hung his head, and gasped between coughs.

Bending low, Sam rested a hand on the paratrooper's back. The paratrooper's youthful face contorted in agony. Semi-coagulated blood dripped from his scalp. Reminded of the bullet crease and chopped ear, Sam grabbed for the first aid kit he kept tied to the front of his helmet. His hand came away empty. He searched for the drowned paratrooper's helmet and failed to find it. He looked to the paratrooper's ankles and web gear. No first aid kits.

He glanced toward the three bullet-riddled GIs and spotted a helmet. He slipped in the mud, regained his footing, and rushed down the trail. Through the netting and scrim he saw the horizontal stripe identifying a sergeant. The front had an airborne first aid kit. He yanked it off and returned to the revived paratrooper.

Sam guided the paratrooper to a sitting position. "What do you need?"

Color was returning to the paratrooper's lips, but his eyes appeared vacant—seeing, yet uncomprehending. The paratrooper's teeth chattered. His body shivered. The head wound oozed blood through a smear of mud and algae. He started hacking again. More watery phlegm drained out of his mouth.

Sam grabbed the paratrooper's canteen. "Hang in there, pal." The heavy weight of the canteen elated him. He doused water on the wound, took a long swig himself, and doused the wound again—this time in a more controlled manner, with his thumb covering most of the canteen spout. The sprinkled water intensified the paratrooper's shivering.

Sam dumped a whole packet of sulfanilamide powder on the wound. The paratrooper winced and pulled away. Sam unfurled a Carlisle bandage and covered both the raw ear and grazing wound with the compress. He wrapped it tight around wet hair.

The paratrooper touched the bandage wrapping his skull. "Need a smoke."

Sam shook his head. "Sorry, don't smoke."

"Can't remember." The paratrooper coughed and wheezed. "Wha… what happened?"

"Kraut ambush. You got knocked out. Fell into the water." Sam patted a crammed jacket pocket. "Wait a minute, I've got some gift cigarettes." He stuck a Lucky Strike between lips that were blue just a couple of minutes earlier. "Sorry, no lighter."

The young paratrooper waved him off and reached into his own jacket pocket. He flipped his Zippo open and water flowed out. "Must've been under awhile." He looked around and, seeing the bodies on the trail, groaned. "Geez, not Sarge." His hand shook as he pointed at the nearest corpse. "Keeps a lighter in his collar pouch."

Sam retrieved the dead sergeant's lighter and tossed it back. The two bandoleers of M-1 ammo and hand grenade on the sergeant's perforated chest distracted him. It was time to act like an officer again. He pulled a useless M-1 from under the dead man. Machinegun hits had bent the receiver and shattered the stock.

Quick scavenging produced one functional M-1 rifle, four bandoleers of rifle ammo, three pineapple grenades, two first aid kits, and two full canteens. He found a spare jump jacket, dry socks, and a spare undershirt in the musette bag of the second dead GI. Sam handed the wad to the wet paratrooper. "Get into those. Should help warm you up. Did your sergeant carry any maps?"

"Inside his jump jacket." The paratrooper took a drag on his cigarette and went into a hacking fit.

Sam found two maps and a compass. The topographical map labeled "Carentan" included DZ-D and the La Barquette locks. He wiped blood off the second map and discovered a road and rail map of greater Normandy.

Somewhat dryer, the young paratrooper quit shivering yet remained seated in the trail, head between his knees. "Where's my carbine?"

"Carry mine. I'm switching back to a real rifle. Catch." Sam tossed his carbine. "Magazine's full. I've got half a mind to toss it in the swamp. Yours must already be there. Helmet, too. Couldn't fit a helmet over that bandage anyway." He tossed the paratrooper a grenade. "We need to get moving. You up to it?"

Frowning, the paratrooper gazed at his cigarette, then nodded.

"I assume you were making for Carentan. I'll lead. Keep an eye on our back-trail…" An awkward pause filled where name and rank belonged. "I'm Sam Henry. Army thought I should be a lieutenant. Able, Five-O-First." He reached out to shake hands.

"Private Wellston." He coughed and spit. "Excuse my manners, sir. Jimmy Wellston. Dog Company."

"How's your head?"

"Hurts like a son of…" Wellston rammed a finger in his right ear and twisted it. "Ear won't quit ringing like a siren. Still got a few cobwebs." He flicked the Lucky Strike into the water. "I quit breathing? Glad I don't remember." Wellston's gaze landed on Sam's bayonet wound. "Want me to take a look at that?"

Sam shook his head. "Not unless you've got a medical degree."

"Nope, just another dog-face who fell for the recruiter's extra jump-pay pitch." Wellston coughed into his fist. "Did I thank you?"

Sam waved him off. "I was getting pretty tired of fighting this war all alone anyway. What happened to your stick last night?"

"Got dropped along some road. Spent too long looking for my bazooka. Never did find the door-bags." Wellston coughed up more watery phlegm. "About half our stick gathered. Had no clue where we were. No officers. Squad leader took us up this road. Found a sign saying St. Georges-de… de…"

"De-Bohon. Coming from the south?'

"No." Wellston looked confused. "Memory's fuzzy. Just following some road. Lost. Hid out for awhile. A big firefight broke out in town. Buddy of mine, my loader, got hit. We left him with some wounded at the church and got the hell out of Dodge."

Sam just nodded, deciding the timing was all wrong to tell Wellston about the charred corpses in the torched church.

Wellston coughed, spit, and said, "We'd move and hide. Spot some Kraut patrol, move and hide. Zigzagged a lot. Started working north toward the sound of the big guns." He stood, testing his wobbly legs. "How come you're all alone, sir?"

Sam looked at the lowering clouds. "Where you from?"

"Alton, Illinois."

"My best buddy's from Danville."

"Clear the opposite side of the state, sir. Where—"

"Can you walk? We really need to put some distance between us and this spot before Fritz comes back. I didn't get them all."

"Where'd you come from? I mean, how'd you get the drop on that machinegun?"

Sam shrugged. "Just another misdropped Geronimo."

"Yeah, seems there's a lot of that going around. I've half a mind to shoot the next Troop Carrier Command pilot I see."

"Seems there's a lot of that going around, too." Sam's memory flashed to the Voluptuous Vixen. "Sure wouldn't recommend it while still in the air, though."

Wellston gave him a puzzled look. Sam marched northward down the cow path. Wellston followed, muffling coughs.

The drizzle tickled Sam's face.

Chapter 45

Departure

6 June 1944, 2030 Hours
Thouars, France

Behr wove his way through the jumble of trees veiling his vehicles. The lush elm and ash foliage confined and humidified the June air. The evening light was diminishing inside the grove.

His panzergrenadier reconnaissance *kompanie* had gained an additional SdKfz -231 eight-wheeled armored car, three more halftracks and four additional motorcycles—two BMWs with sidecars. A near miracle considering the severe shortage of vehicles the rest of the 17th SS was suffering. He'd heard an assault regiment senior sergeant complain that his panzergrenadier troops would deploy on bicycles.

Untried youths scurried about, stripped to their undershirts. Behr pointed at a teenager loading a halftrack. "Sturmmann Henshel, stow those ammo cans nearer your machinegun."

"Jawohl, Herr Hauptscharfuhrer Behr." Henshel ducked his glistening tan shoulders away from the MG-34 armor shield mounted atop a halftrack. The portrait of a striking blond maiden was dangling, partially pasted to the inside of the shield.

Behr suppressed a grin. "Is your little fraulein waiting back home like a dutiful Aryan sweetheart, Sturmmann Henshel?"

The corporal feigned innocence. "Are you talking to me, Hauptscharfuhrer?"

Behr pointed to the picture. "*Ja.*"

The corporal reached toward the picture. "I'll see to it that it's removed at once."

"Nein. First you answer the question, Henshel."

"We've been in love since we were both fifteen."

"But what kind of lasting love can be cultivated in a mere year, Henshel?"

Henshel looked indignant. "Pardon me, Herr Hauptscharfuhrer, but it's been almost two-and-a-half years."

Behr let his grin show. "Then pardon me, and by all means keep it posted. Just don't let her distract your marksmanship."

Henshel pivoted the steel shield and fingered the surface. "The paint's dry now." He dusted his artwork of an armored fist and gothic lettering. The armored fist—the 17th SS's divisional symbol—represented the prosthetic metal hand of the division's historical namesake, the Baron Gotz von Berlichingen. The gothic letters formed a quote attributed as the baron's response to his archenemy's surrender demand. The legendary three-word reply was crude yet straightforward: "*Lecken mein Arse!*" The youthful troops embraced their ribald rallying cry.

"A shame the Ami gangsters cannot read *Deustch.* Just send a few rounds up their backsides when we chase them back into the English Channel."

"Danke, Herr Hauptscharfuhrer."

Behr slapped the halftrack and departed to find the *kompanie* commander. A profusion of antennas identified Von Gremp's command halftrack—antennas that would serve as bullet and high explosive magnets the instant combat commenced. Behr preferred performing his duties from a less conspicuous vehicle.

Von Gremp nodded his head, absorbed with the squawking headphones covering his ears. Behr climbed in. Von Gremp said, "Jawohl, Herr *Oberstrumbannfuhrer,*" into the handset and pulled the headphones off. He handed the tangle of electronics to the radioman.

Behr took a papirosa out of his tarnished brass cigarette case and lit it. He took mild amusement in watching the radio operator suppress a cough and excuse himself on the pretext of checking batteries.

Behr removed his camouflaged canvas-covered helmet. His long hair tumbled over his brow. "We'll be ready to deploy within the hour. Any word on our destination?" He knew Von Gremp's Prussian pride tolerated his casual demeanor only as long as they were alone.

"An estimated three divisions of Ami paratroopers and glider troops have dropped across the Cotentin Peninsula." Von Gremp stabbed the folded section of map on his lap. "Scattered reports of contact from near Cherbourg clear to Periers. Started about zero-one-hundred hours. Followed at dawn by numerous beach landings across seventy kilometers. I can't get much more information other than what pertains to our mission."

Behr flipped the hair back to the top of his head. "Which is?"

"Proceed to Periers. Advance north toward Carentan." Von Gremp circled the town with his finger. "Probe for the Ami main line of resistance, which we might expect as early as just south of Carentan. Upon contact, conduct reconnaissance to locate weak spots for the assault regiments to exploit."

Behr grabbed his commander's map. "High Command has already conceded Carentan?" He studied the map. "The Carentan road and rail network is critical to the whole Cotentin Peninsula. What if our Seven Hundred Ninth Division holds?"

Von Gremp shrugged. "It's really of little consequence. A friend on divisional staff says Berlin still sees this as a mere sideshow. An elaborate feint."

Behr scowled and took one last drag on the papirosa—burned down to the width of his tobacco stained fingers.

"They remain convinced that the main invasion will be at the English Channel's narrowest point—the Pa-de-Calais. Led by their best—General Patton. Berlin's holding our best panzer divisions north." Von Gremp gave a frustrated sigh. "It has been deemed best to let the much-vaunted 17th SS *Gotz von Berlichingen* Panzergrenadier Division draw its first blood in a sideshow. A feint. A mere diversion."

Behr vehemently shook his head. "In Russia I lost as many men in feints and diversions as in main attacks. Regardless of who was attacking, defending, or feinting. To the dead, it makes no difference."

"You've lost me, Behr."

"You will have to write the young widow, the proud father, the mother grieving over her firstborn. Will you write that their beloved soldat was less heroic, less valued to the Reich because fate landed him someplace other than that one minuscule point decisive to the whole battlefield?"

Von Gremp seemed to ponder Behr's point for a moment. "Is it your contention that it's not where a soldier dies, but how?"

Behr gave an ironic chuckle. "It'd be nice if it was that simple. The soldier with the most promise in the *kompanie*—Sturmmann Henshel, for example—may die tomorrow from random artillery. Maybe even from our own artillery. Does that measure his value as a soldier?"

"You always find new ways to complicate my life, Hauptscharfuhrer."

Behr hopped out the rear of the armored personnel carrier. "Danke. A pleasure to be of service, Herr *Kompanie* Commander." He reached in to retrieve his helmet. "It's just a hypothetical exercise, anyway."

Von Gremp gave a puzzled expression. "What is?"

"The hasty assessment that our sector is merely an Anglo-American diversion from the real invasion," Behr said. "It's not. And our role will not be insignificant to the final outcome."

Von Gremp pulled on his lower lip. "What makes you so sure?"

"The bombings around my Frankfurt home. The Americans go out of their way to avoid old cathedrals, civilian neighborhoods. I doubt they'd sacrifice elite airborne troops on a mere diversion. The Russians, *ja*. Americans, *nein*. They'll not give a second thought to wasting mountains of precious material. In that regard they're spoiled by their own vast abundance. Nevertheless, they won't waste lives. The airborne troops are there on a vital mission."

"How vital?"

"Protecting the flanks of the main invasion force." Behr lit another Russian cigarette. "They need ports. Cherbourg would meet their needs quite nicely."

"You know I respect your vast combat experience, but I'm obligated to trust Berlin over a noncommissioned officer when it comes to the strategic analysis."

"Naturally, as a good Prussian officer should." Behr adjusted his SS pea-pattern summer camouflage *tarnjacke* smock. "The truth? That we'll discover soon enough. Too soon for some, much too late for others. Right, Hauptsturmfuhrer?" Behr strode away. His parting comment produced a bewildered expression on Von Gremp's face. Behr allowed a grin to spread across his scarred face.

He spent the next hour exhorting *panzergrenadieren* to hasten their mechanized departure. At last, engines roaring and exhaust fumes fouling the air, Behr climbed into his halftrack and stood with a dominant view down the road. He gave the order to advance out of Thouars in the dim light of dusk—the first elements of the 17th SS Panzergrenadier Division deploying for battle.

Mere anticipation of rejoining the war made his jagged cheek scar swell and throb.

Chapter 46

The Trail

6 June 1944, 2310 Hours
Normandy

Cloaked in darkness, Sam picked his way down the muddy cow trail. The steady drizzle had lightened to a mist. He'd lost sight of the floodwater on his right flank, so he kept glancing at the luminous needle on the dead sergeant's compass to assure that the trail headed north.

He paused to massage away the ache in his hip. Reeds rustled. Private Wellston coughed and spit, then went into a muffled coughing fit. Sam knelt.

Explosions rumbled far to the north. A rattling wheeze sounded from Wellston's direction.

The trail went silent.

A dull metallic click sounded. *A rifle safety?* He thought his weary mind was playing audio tricks on him. *I've got to be right on top of it.*

What's Wellston doing? Maybe he got knifed. Sam craned his neck to look down his back-trail. Nothing.

He raised his M-1 and placed his finger on the trigger. Sweat stung his eyes. He dared not move. *Are we surrounded?* He feared his pounding heart might give away his presence.

Click-clack.

He pointed his rifle toward the foreign noise, then remembered his toy cricket.

Keeping his rifle pressed back into his shoulder, he reached across his body for the toy cricket tied to his left collar. Finding it, he fumbled to answer. Something wasn't right. The cricket felt nearly flattened. Useless.

His sleep deprived brain scrambled for the password. His mind landed on *flash*, but his tongue refused to respond.

From behind, Wellston signaled a rushed, *click-clack, click-clack.*

Three yards forward a silhouetted helmet, torso, and rifle materialized out of the weeds.

Sam trained his M-1 on the center-mass of the dark silhouette.

Without warning, a Thompson muzzle pushed his M-1 barrel down.

"Flash. Able, Five-O-First." With each syllable, puffs of breath struck Sam's left ear. "Keep your weapon off my man."

Sam heaved a sigh and said, "Ted."

"Been hunting for you, Sam." Sergeant Springwater released the pressure depressing Sam's M-1 barrel.

"Relax, Pinball. It's the lieutenant."

"You mean, *our* Lieutenant Henry?" Vigiano limped onto the trail and got within inches of Sam's face. "Well, I'll be a…you must have a saint praying for you. When did you start carrying a real rifle, sir?"

Springwater's dark eyes probed the back-trail. "Who's behind you? Carter? Rest of the mortar squad?" His smile was so big that his white teeth shown in the darkness. "Glad to see you!"

Sam grinned. "You have no idea."

Wellston came forward, white head-bandage bobbing up the dark trail.

Pinball stepped close to Wellston. "Who's this?"

"PFC Wellston. A stray from Dog Company. We're all there is…" A flood of exhaustion washed over Sam. He collapsed.

*   *   *

Sam awoke to find himself lying tucked away in a copse of low trees and brush. Wellston slept five feet away, musette bag as a pillow. The misty drizzle had ceased.

Sam sat up and stretched. The stiffness in his hip made him wince. Springwater, Lazeski, Silva, Collins, and Pinball scooted close around him.

Lazeski whispered, "How'd you get that roller-coaster-operator-turned-pilot to make a u-turn?"

Sam yawned and rubbed his eyes. "Who's out on security?"

"You know ain't no way Springwater's gonna overlook security, sir." Collins leaned closer. "We done saw the Voluptuous Vixen fly right back over us. How'd you get that dang pilot to do an about-face?"

Sam grinned. "What? You think I'd let you clowns invade a continent without me? Who'd keep Silva from bedding all the French girls?" His comment failed to solicit any reaction from Silva.

"Phillips says he saw you down in the aisle, hit," Springwater said.

"Some AA knocked me off my feet." He remembered Carter's charred face, the smell of burned flesh, Perkowski's neck. Slippery gore. "I just felt some heat, got a scratch on the cheek. By the time I reached the door we were over the English Channel. Got turned around but about lost all my gear on the jump. Too fast and way too—"

"But your shoulder, sir?" Pinball said.

Sam surmised that darkness hadn't entirely hidden his shoulder wound. "That happened after I hit the ground."

"Kraut bullet?" Lazeski asked.

Sam lowered his voice. "Bayonet."

Collins let a quiet whistle pass over his lips. "Dang, sir!"

Springwater broke off a section of D-ration fortified chocolate and handed it to Sam. "You four go take security. Send the others back to sleep. The lieutenant and I got work to do."

Once alone, Springwater gave Sam a sketchy briefing on their movements, casualties, and enemy contact since the jump. Sam told what he knew about the men left on the Voluptuous Vixen.

The first yellow streaks of dawn showed on the northeast horizon. Sam mentally reviewed the first full day's nightmare. Operation Neptune had claimed half his stick—dead, maimed, or missing. They remained several miles behind enemy lines—if military lines even existed. All indicators screamed that the invasion was an unmitigated disaster. Dawn of D-Day-plus-one was fast approaching. *June seventh? Certainly it had to be at least the eighth, maybe the ninth.*

What next? His head throbbed. *What combination of near perfect choices, good fortune, and plain dumb luck will it take for me to get my men out of this mess?*

Chapter 47

The Canisters

7 June 1944, 1035 Hours
South of Carentan, Normandy

Sam stuffed another stick of Wrigley's Spearmint into his mouth as he kept vigil on the trail. *They should've been back half an hour ago.* An anxious knot grew in his gut.

At first light, he and Springwater had studied maps, taken inventory, and prioritized needs. The hand grenades were about depleted—six left between eleven paratroopers. Sam wasn't the only one to have had grenade pouches rip during the jump. Rifle ammo was adequate, but one prolonged firefight would turn that situation critical, too. The three Hawkins mines had the least utility of all their weaponry. They had the 60mm mortar with six rounds, but lacked a crew. Against armor, they possessed one bazooka with three rockets, and Private Wellston alone qualified to use it. They had one dandy machinegunner, Harrigan, but no machinegun.

Sam had considered three options: disregard firepower and continue without a machinegun; luck into a misdropped para-pack with an undamaged Browning LMG and ammo; or get one on loan from Hitler. None of the options held much appeal. Nevertheless, he did recall an unclaimed machinegun—right where he'd found Wellston.

After confirming that Harrigan had checked out on the MG-42 during enemy weapons orientation, Sam decided to scavenge the machinegun. He would lead a patrol with Harrigan and Morton. However, Springwater had pulled him aside and—while staring at his bloody shoulder—pointed out that while they wanted a machinegun, they *required* their lieutenant. Sam admitted to himself that he felt weak from exhaustion and loss of blood. Springwater convinced him to have a scout lead the patrol. Skinner—even not fully recovered from his concussion—had the best sense of direction in the platoon and could track a lone ant on cold asphalt.

Sam smacked his gum. In the daylight, he estimated he could've made the approximate three-mile roundtrip in a little over an hour, maybe two, tops. His estimation was proving too sanguine. He gazed down the trail. *Great, I want more firepower and it just cost me three men MIA.*

Another fifteen minutes ticked by, each one accentuated by Phillips fidgeting, Collins spitting tobacco, Lazeski cleaning glasses, Wellston muffling a cough. Only Springwater seemed calm.

Silva jotted a letter with a stubby pencil. His ankle sheath was missing and his treasured Portuguese fighting knife sheath was empty. "Private Silva, I guess you left a couple of blades in the backs of Nazis. Just don't go and cut more throats than Colonel Johnson. Don't need him jealous…" Sam tailed off as Silva's face contorted and the private jabbed pencil through paper.

Springwater cleared his throat. "Lieutenant Henry, can I see you? Now, sir."

Sam followed Springwater twenty-five yards into the trees. Springwater laid a map out on the ground. Sam knelt beside it.

"Sir, don't mention anything about knifes around Silva. Can't afford to have him—"

"Was he too eager with his knifes? I knew—"

"No. I should've told you hours ago." In detail, Springwater shared his take on Silva's throat cutting experience. He looked to the sky and sighed. "I need to get you up to speed on Morton, too."

Lazeski jogged up and said, "They're coming in."

Replenished adrenaline kicking in, Sam leapt up. He arrived at his shallow foxhole as the three-man patrol scampered in. Skinner and Harrigan sat and gasped for air—the Irish machinegunner cradling the sinister looking MG-42. Skinner had ammo belts draped around his neck. Morton lit a cigarette. A German gasmask canister hung from each of his shoulders.

"We…got it!" Harrigan said between gasps. "Only found about two hundred… rounds of ammo…though."

"Excellent." Sam was thrilled just to have all three men back. "Run into any trouble?"

"Took longer coming back." Harrigan's freckled face looked flushed. "More weight. Some farmers gathering—"

"Morton held us up," Skinner said, glaring at Morton. "Worse than a buzzard."

Morton sneered. "Like hell I did. I was gathering vital intelligence."

Skinner rose and took a step toward Morton. "You wouldn't know intelligence if it bit you on—"

"No backwoods hayseed who does a P-L-F headfirst tells me what to do." Morton turned to Harrigan. "And a couple stripes on some Mick's sleeve don't give him no right—"

"Shut up. Everyone!" Springwater held up his hand. "Morton, show us what intelligence you collected."

Morton patted a German gasmask canister. "Right in here, safe and sound."

"Show me," Springwater said.

Morton tugged a canister latch and pointed the open top toward Springwater and Sam.

"Dump it out," Springwater said.

Morton squatted, tilted the canister, and let the contents slide onto the ground in a jumbled line. Smirking, he lit another Chesterfield.

Sam knelt and raked his fingers through the German items. "Might have some intel value." He noted four pay books, a couple of wallets, tabs hacked from uniforms, some personal snapshots, letters, and a couple of identity disks. "Next time a *soldbuch* or two will be sufficient for the S-Two. Let's see what's in the other canister."

"Just more of the same, Lieutenant. I'll make sure—"

"How about you just show me, *Private*."

"It can wait, sir. Like I said, just more of the same."

"Can't be just more of the same." Sam pointed at the pile and looked Morton in the eye. "I shot four at the MG, and there's four soldbuchs."

Morton looked away. "And impressive shooting it was, sir. Tight little groups. One Kraut caught two square in the front of his noggin."

Sam narrowed his eyes. "Dump it now, soldier."

Morton flipped the lid latch and scattered the contents atop the first pile—a tangled assortment of medals, aluminum belt buckles, badges, French francs, a pocketknife, and wristwatches. A photo of a buxom nude slid off the top of the pile. Sam flipped it away and stirred the pile with his finger. He pulled out a blood-encrusted wedding ring. He held it up to Morton. "Explain this."

"Like I said, sir, you did some excellent shooting. There was blood everywhere."

Sam cringed and dropped the ring.

Skinner pointed at the ring. "See? Stinkin' buzzard."

Springwater picked out the pay books and slipped them into his chest pocket. He flipped the pocketknife toward Morton's feet, raked the rest of the contents back into the canisters, and fastened the tops. Rising to his full height, towering over Morton, Springwater flung the canisters right past Morton's helmet, into the mucky marsh grass.

Springwater lashed out with an open hand, boxing Morton's ear and knocking his helmet off. Morton held his ear and cowered.

Collins stepped up—just as tall as Springwater but adding fifty pounds of muscle and bone. Six inches from Morton's face, Collins said, "In case you ain't noticed, we're still a might behind enemy lines. Get nabbed with that crap and them Krauts will kill us all on the spot." Collins tapped Morton's skull repeatedly and hard. "Start using what little brains the good Lord done gave you or I'll give your scrawny behind a whupping you ain't soon forgettin'." Collins spit a stream of tobacco juice on Morton's Corcorans to seal the threat.

"Here, Morton, make yourself useful." Skinner draped two belts over Morton's shoulders. "Carry some ammo."

"You got it all wrong, chum. I'm a runner." Morton lifted the belt of 8mm bullets off his neck.

"We don't need a runner now," Springwater said. "You're Harrigan's loader and ammo bearer."

"Sorry, Sarge, but I ain't in your squad. I'm assigned—"

"You will follow Sergeant Springwater's orders as if they're mine, Morton," Sam said, picking up his M-1. "Let's get moving."

*   *   *

With a buzzing propeller roar and combined blasting chatter of sixteen fifty-caliber machineguns, two P-47 Thunderbolts strafed the highway. Wehrmacht troops abandoned vehicles and scrambled for cover. Two trucks erupted in flames. Draught horses pulling wagons and artillery pieces screamed and bucked to escape harnesses.

The Thunderbolts made another strafing pass, this time north to south, and departed. Ineffective tracers chased them.

Sam peered through the hedgerow toward the N-171 highway a half-mile distant.

"Maybe they'll report the good hunting to their buddies," Springwater said.

Sam sighed. "If only we had a radio. I'd contact a Navy tub sitting off Utah Beach and…"

Springwater pointed north. "That'd be happening now if we held the high ground in Carentan."

"Your point?"

"We don't hold Carentan. Not even close." The rumble of distant explosives carried from the north and confirmed Springwater's opinion. "I'd say four, five, maybe even six miles away."

Sam frowned. "So why keep heading for a town in the Kraut's grip?"

"Need a boat to go east."

"We've got another option. Not a great one, but... Get your map out." Sam stared at the highway as map paper rustled. "Find Baupte."

"Got it. Five miles northwest," Springwater said. "Wasn't it on the Eighty-Second's objective list?"

"So let's head there. Shouldn't need to swim. Then we break north until we meet some Eighty-Second troopers. Might run into fewer Krauts further from this road, too." Sam crawled over to Springwater and traced the proposed new route with a grass stem. "So we just find a clear spot, dash across N-171, and play another five mile game of hide-n-seek with Fritz."

Phillips approached from behind and peeked through the hedgerow. "Never figured on the Krauts using horses so much."

"What'd you find at that yellow parachute?" Sam asked.

"Just what there was supposed to be—a para-pack canister full of eighty-one millimeter mortar rounds. Couldn't find any other chutes or canisters."

Sam shook his head in disgust. "So we stumble on the one thing we don't need."

Phillips walked away.

"Lieutenant Henry, sir?" Springwater said.

Springwater's reversion to formal military address made Sam suspect bad news. "What now?"

"I was trying to tell you something when the patrol came back. Something's not right with Morton."

"He made a mistake."

"He keeps making mistakes."

"Look, you and Collins straightened him out." Sam pulled off his helmet and ran his hand back through his cropped hair. "Besides, everyone there wanted to pick through those souvenirs. Morton's timing just stunk."

Springwater shook his head. "Bloody wedding rings."

Sam held up a finger. "One ring."

"I saw two. And how did they get so bloody? I'd like to check his knife blades."

Sam exhaled hard. "Look, I'll keep an eye on him."

"Don't bother. I've already got one on him. What he did is *not* the Crow way."

"He's not a Crow."

"Not the US Army way, either." Springwater frowned. "Not since Custer's day anyway."

Chapter 48

The Apple Farmer

7 June 1944, 2150 Hours
Les Fevres, Normandy

Sam, Collins, and Springwater stretched out side-by-side on their bellies. The big scout stabbed the map with his muscular finger. "Them Krauts got checkpoints and machinegun nests packed tighter than shoats on a mama sow at suppertime, from this here bridge to—"

"You mean Canal d'Auvers?" Sam asked.

"Sorry, sir. Ain't no way this country boy gonna par-lay-vu these Frenchy names. Like I was saying, Krauts are crawling all over each other clear past the La Seves River stone bridge going into Baupte."

Sam pushed his fingers back through his hair. Skinner had used nearly the same terms—something about ticks on a hound—to describe the bridge at the railroad tracks and canal north of their position. The men needed rest and food. Sam didn't like the option of lingering in the apple orchard on the edge of Les Fevres—a collection of twenty houses plus assorted out buildings and barns of various shapes and sizes, yet all constructed from the same Norman stone.

The latest five-mile leg in the journey had taken ten hours to traverse—good time considering the delays, detours, and dodging wary Wehrmacht and curious French. Now, from the Germans holding Baupte and the distant rumble to the north, Sam deduced that the 82nd Airborne was faring no better than the 101st.

Darkness approached. Having his plan thwarted perturbed Sam. His physical pain hindered his decision-making. His bayonet wound throbbed. His left hip ached whenever he shifted weight onto it. Phillips had taken to complaining about the shrapnel in his arm. Pinball never complained, but it was obvious that trekking across irregular terrain had aggravated his ankle. Skinner's concussion had turned into a monster headache that required a regular feeding of aspirin. Wellston's occasional grimace betrayed his pain. The remaining men grew more sullen by the moment.

Sam mentally praised Colonel Johnson for the torturous parachute infantry training regime—starting with running up and down Mount Currahee—that they had all cursed. It now produced endurance when lesser soldiers would've succumbed.

A sharp pain in his left shoulder jarred him out of his melancholy thoughts.

"Sorry, Lieutenant." Morton crawled alongside Sam and pulled the muzzle of his cradled rifle out of Sam's injured shoulder. "Some Frog's making a beeline for us."

Sam bit the inside of his cheek to suppress the urge to scream. Without allowing the pain to subside, he crawled after Morton beneath the dark canopy of apple limbs.

A gaunt Frenchman carried a basket and wore a cap low over his eyes. His suspenders offered a distinct symmetrical contrast on his stained undershirt. He strolled toward the hidden paratroopers while humming a tune through his unlit cigarette. Sam recognized "La Marseillaise"—the French national anthem.

The middle-aged Frenchman rested the basket against his hip and pushed small branches aside. He whispered an accented, "*Bon jour* my American brothers. *Oui*, our liberators." In hushed tones, the man continued in his native tongue, occasionally glancing over his shoulder toward Les Fevres.

Sam started to respond, but instead tucked his lips over his teeth and bit down to end the temptation. *Who speaks French?* He knew he had one. Who was it? Then, with a flash of a charred face and vacant eyes, he remembered—Private Carter's mother was French-Canadian from Montreal.

The rustle of fabric and equipment told Sam someone was crawling up from behind. The muffled cough told him it was Private Wellston. Wellston inched next to Sam's right side and whispered into Sam's ear. "Says he's with the Résistance. Wants to help. They've been waiting ye—"

"You speak French?"

"Alton High French club president. If he slows down, I think I can catch most of it. I've got a French-English dictionary, not too wet—"

"Slow him down," Sam said. "Find out what he wants."

Wellston spoke. The Frenchman's ramblings ceased. When the Frenchman spoke again it was slower, almost as if an adult was addressing a toddler. The pair conversed in short phrases. Wellston frequently paused mid-phrase to mentally retrieve a French phrase.

Sam scanned his surroundings. Sweat rolled down his forehead.

At last, Wellston leaned over to Sam's ear. "Says he's associated with some Resistance cell, wants to help—"

"We've established that! How?"

"He's got some special hiding place. He can give us food, medical care, news about the invasion from his Resistance network. He says the Boche think Les Fevres is passive, just a good place to steal *calvados* from farmers. Not sure what he means. I think it's a local hard drink, from apples, like—"

"Doesn't matter! Where's this hiding place?"

Wellston and the farmer spoke a quick exchange.

"In his barn, in the village. He'll come back to guide us when it's dark. The Boche may be stupid, but even they know apples aren't picked in June."

"Tell him to prove he's Resistance."

The Frenchman's response, "*Impossible!*" required no interpretation.

"How do we know he isn't going to turn us over for a bounty?"

Wellston took extra time to communicate the concept. Sam wiped sweat out of his eyes, leveled his M-1 at the Frenchman's chest, and clicked the safety off. No fear showed in the Frenchman's eyes. He spoke and wagged his finger at Sam.

Morton leaned close to Sam. "Let me shoot the Frog, sir."

"Get back on your post, Morton," Sam said out the corner of his mouth.

Wellston said, "He claims just standing here now is enough for the Boche to execute him."

Sam remembered the hung girls and priest. "Tell him he waits right here with us until dark. If anything looks fishy, he's the first to die. We've got a knife-crazy Portagee who'll cut him a new ear-to-ear grin." He knew Silva couldn't follow through, but on short-order couldn't think of a better threat.

"Don't think I know how to say all that in French, sir."

"Then make it up as you go with words you do know. Just make sure he gets the gist—it's his neck."

Chapter 49

The Silo

7 June 1944, 2320 Hours
Les Fevres, Normandy

"Springwater. Flashlight."

Sam reached backward until he felt the flashlight in his palm. As he pushed the on-off switch, a match flared. The French farmer lit a lantern. The air smelled of musty straw and horse manure. Sam stepped over the top of a stone and mortar wall. Above, a slate roof peaked and sloped downward to each side. They crossed a hayloft. At an oak plank wall, the farmer twisted a couple of bent nails. A secret door swung open. The farmer stepped through.

Sam ventured through the disguised door, following Wellston onto a catwalk amidst the rafters. Ahead of Wellston, Silva held his M-1 muzzle to the Frenchman's kidneys. The catwalk—five yards above the barn's floor—consisted of two side-by-side planks. Bundles of dried herbs and empty poultry cages hung from the catwalk. Below, an array of plows and cultivators crowded the floor.

The catwalk widened. The farmer stopped at a curved stone wall that rose from ground level to past the roof's peak. Sam remembered seeing a grain silo attached to the end of the barn complex. The farmer set the lantern down and began removing stones, precisely stacking them on a plank platform. He made a two-foot-by-three-foot hole in the stone wall, picked up the lantern, and climbed through.

Sam inched his way past Wellston and Silva and poked his head through the hole. Ladder rungs led into a room. An oak plank wall split the silo down the center. Planks also formed the floor and ceiling. The room held a crude wooden table, several mismatched chairs, jugs, a crate, a stack of clothes, blankets, and two covered buckets.

The Frenchman waved for him to come down. Sam signaled Springwater forward.

Springwater ducked his head into the hole. "Box canyon."

"I was thinking fish in a barrel." Sam scowled. "We leave a sentry just this side of the hidden wood door. If there's trouble we can drop off this catwalk."

He assigned Pinball to the first watch at the secret wooden door and climbed down the ladder. Grain dust tickled his nose. The room filled with paratroopers shedding their burdens and stacking weapons in the corners.

The farmer chattered in hushed tones. Wellston translated. "He says we can see outside through the vent holes covered by that tarp. Just make sure no light shows. No smoking. The Germans have checked this silo before. Nothing but grain on all sides of us except where we came in. He's going now to talk with his Resistance cell."

The farmer lit a second lantern and hung it from a suspended hook. Before departing, he shook each paratrooper's hand.

Once settled in, Sam, Springwater, and Lazeski spread maps on the table. They lit a candle to spotlight important areas on the maps. Phillips slept holding his injured bicep, his back shaped to the curved stone wall. Others cleaned weapons or organized gear. Looking morose, Silva sat, knees tucked to his chest, continuing his letter.

Pinball poked his head through the hole. "We got company."

Sam jerked his head up. Collins and Harrigan pulled pistols.

"Relax, guys. It's just chow. Some French *vino,* too." Pinball lowered a basket, baguettes protruding out the top.

A petite, middle-aged woman in a long skirt followed Pinball down the ladder carrying a black leather satchel and chattering in hushed French. Wellston said, "Just small talk. Hate for *le* Boche. She's the farmer's wife."

She laid out bread, two hard salamis, and a soft cheese, then placed four bottles on the table that she declared as "*vin*" and a jug she called "calvados." She emptied the basket of seven glasses and four ceramic mugs. Tilting her head to the side, she passed a hand over the table. "*Voila. Bon appetite.*" The paratroopers rushed the table.

Sam tossed Harrigan a chunk of bread and portion of salami. "You're up on sentry duty."

The petite woman set her satchel on the table corner nearest the overhanging lantern. She folded the top open, revealing medical instruments and medicinal bottles. She scanned the group, her visual triage pausing on blood or bandages. She grabbed Wellston by the front of his jacket, forced him into a chair, and manipulated him until he was under the best light.

Sam grinned. "Looks like the doctor's in, gentlemen. And head wounds get top priority."

Wellston asked the farmer's wife a question and listened to a lengthy reply as she unwrapped the bandage from his head and made occasional clucking sounds of disapproval.

"During the Great War she was a surgical nurse near the front. A fact they've managed to keep hidden from the Krauts. She's patched up the local Résistance since—" Wellston winced as she pulled the dried compress off his chopped ear. "Ouch!" He sucked in a deep breath. "She's also a midwife. Delivered babies in Les Fevres and Baupte since nineteen-twenty."

"Won't have much need of those services. Give Silva a few days here and *Madame* could be awfully busy in nine months though." Sam's little joke drew a grin from Silva, the first he'd seen from the gregarious private since their reunion. "Don't get your hopes up, Joe. We won't be hanging around long enough."

The petite nurse muttered something as she pulled the remnants of Wellston's ear away from his head.

"Ouch!" Wellston gritted his teeth. "She wants more light. Says there's a better lantern in the crate."

Skinner found one with a reflective shield, lit it, and held it near Wellston's ear.

The scent of kerosene, grain, and dirty male bodies filled the confined space.

"She says she still needs more light." Wellston squinted from the lantern being so close to his eyes.

Collins and Springwater produced GI flashlights and focused the beams on Wellston's wound while stuffing their mouths with salami. The nurse picked minuscule debris from Wellston's ear and grazed scalp. Not satisfied with the results, she took the calvados jug and splashed a liberal dose over the wound.

"Is that the best she can do for disinfectant?" Sam asked.

"Don't fret, Lieutenant," Skinner said with bread crust sticking out his mouth. "Had me a swig. Reckon that stuff's got more alcohol than Uncle Versey's moonshine. Just smells a might apple-ie."

The nurse finished with a sprinkling of sulfa powder, dressed the ear and scalp wounds separately, then wrapped Wellston's head in a single bandage.

"Tell her you about drowned on floodwater," Sam said.

Wellston did and the nurse handed him three packets of GI sulfadiazine tablets.

The nurse turned to Sam. He pointed to Phillips. "He's next. Still has metal in him."

Without interpretation, the nurse pulled Phillips into the chair. She stripped him to the waist and shifted the makeshift surgical lighting. She examined his bicep, doused it with calvados, and poked around the cut. Phillips yelped a little too loud and drew disapproving looks. The nurse said something and pointed at the ladder.

"Look where she's pointing," Wellston said.

As soon as Phillips turned his head away, the petite nurse made a quick flick with a hidden scalpel, extending the shrapnel entry hole upward. He started to yell, caught himself, and bit his lip. The nurse blotted the wound with cotton gauze and darted in with tweezers. Smiling, she held a three-quarter-inch metal sliver up to the light. Her performance matched the showmanship of a magician pulling a rabbit from a hat. Sam almost applauded.

Seeming to relish the spotlight, the nurse dusted the inside of the wound with GI sulfanilamide powder, gave the wound four quick sutures, bandaged the bicep, and dismissed Phillips. Like a maître d' at a Parisian restaurant, the petite nurse motioned Sam into the chair.

He stripped himself to the waist—each layer progressively bloodier. The exposed bayonet wound made Silva grimace and turn away. The nurse made more clucks of disapproval as she shifted the chair to gain more light.

She doused the deep laceration with calvados and picked out foreign matter. She irrigated it a second time and sponged it. The calvados stung, but Sam refused to react beyond clenching his fists and an occasional hard exhale through pursed lips.

The nurse spoke. Wellston translated. "What did this?"

"Bayonet. Had a harder time coming out than going in."

Collins let out a soft whistle of admiration.

The nurse handed him a palm mirror. As he'd suspected, the bayonet had struck above his collarbone, cutting the muscle that connected his neck to his shoulder. He viewed the result of the bayonet tearing upward. The laceration looked more like a chop from an axe than a neat stab. It looked bad, yet he felt fortunate the bayonet hadn't dragged the decay at the base of a hedgerow back through the piercing.

He shifted the mirror to reflect his face. A mixture of thorn scratches, blood, dirt and the remnants of burnt cork covered both sides. A short but gaping cut and blistered skin marked his left cheekbone. Sweat and tears had traced paths on the surface.

The nurse spread the bayonet wound open. He squeezed his eyes shut and bounced his foot with a frenzied beat. She irrigated it with calvados a third time. He slapped his thigh and looked for something to bite on. Finding nothing, he bit the inside of his cheek until tasting blood.

She rinsed the wound with calvados once more, rolled a couple of cotton swabs through, and dusted the gash with a liberal portion of sulfa powder. She capped off her work with eleven well-spaced sutures and a secure bandage.

Wasting no time, she grabbed his face and twisted it to the lantern light. She swabbed the bare skin with a cloth saturated in what Sam surmised was the Norman cure-all—calvados. The nurse's touch felt unnatural on his crinkled, burnt skin. The cut on his cheek stung.

Saying something including the word *jour*, she pulled an ointment tin out of her bag and held up two fingers.

"She says—"

"Apply twice a day and call me in the morning."

"Close enough, sir."

The nurse pulled out a tiny hooked needle and a length of fine suture. Three stitches closed the cut on his cheekbone.

All wounds cleaned and closed, Sam pointed at his sore hip. "Can she check my hip?" Sam dropped his jump pants and inched the side of his skivvies down, revealing a grapefruit-sized area of purple, red, and yellow skin. "This is what happens when you do a hard parachute landing fall, canteen first."

The nurse asked something. "*Oui,*" Wellston answered and clarified, "Told her you can walk OK, sir."

The nurse pulled a brown medicinal bottle out of her satchel and handed it to Sam. The label pictured a horse. Sam unscrewed the cap and sniffed the contents. "Horse liniment? Ask her about Pinball's ankle."

Wellston spoke, having to pause and refer to his waterlogged dictionary. The nurse spoke. Wellston said, "Same stuff, four times a day. Keep the ankle supported."

Sam rubbed a generous portion of horse liniment on his colorful hip and tossed the bottle to Pinball. "You hang onto it."

Vigiano shook his head. "I know better than to take my boot off before we get back to England, sir."

"Just loosen your boot-top and let it seep down, Pinball." Sam looked the nurse in the eye. "*Merci beaucoup*, madame. Your generosity is greatly appreciated." He held out a fifty-franc note.

The nurse's face soured. She slapped her medical satchel shut and rattled French. Wellston said, "I'm afraid you've insulted her, sir. She's going on about hating *le* Boche. This is how she does her part. Even if it all ended today, she'd still be delivering little Boche bastards for another nine months. She's sick of it all."

"Tell her we're allies against the Boche. The money is just to replace what she used up tonight. No offense intended."

Wellston tried, but his words followed a flurry of a rustling skirt up the ladder.

Sam reached into his jacket cargo pocket, pulled out the partial carton of Lucky Strikes and tossed it against the wall by some jugs. He rummaged through his musette bag and added a carton of Camels. "Any of you clowns have similar gifts, this would be an appropriate place to leave a token of our appreciation."

The pile grew.

Silva tossed a pair of nylon stockings. "I was hoping to bed my first French broad in Paris with those."

Morton looked puzzled. "But Paris wasn't an objective."

Silva cocked his head. "So I won't be needing them for sure, genius, now will I?"

Sam checked his wristwatch. "What you need for sure is to relieve Harrigan."

"Yes, sir." Silva stepped toward the table. "Mind if I throw back a shot of that calvados, first?"

Morton stuck out his foot. Silva tripped and lunged to regain his balance. He knocked over the calvados jug and candle. The candle flame landed atop a spreading pool of spilled spirits. The table erupted in an inferno of blue and yellow flame.

Springwater grabbed the jug. Sam threw his jump jacket over the table, smothering the flames. Sam took a deep breath and lifted his jacket. A puff of smoke drifted to the ceiling.

A blue flame flickered from the mouth of the jug. "Now that's real firewater." Springwater corked the jug.

Sam fanned his jump jacket to dissipate the smoke.

Skinner shook his head. "Like I said, hotter than Uncle's Versey's moonshine."

"Nobody drinks another drop," Sam said.

"Afraid we'll go blind?" Skinner said. "A feller blamed Uncle Versey for that once."

Sam tapped the side of his head. "No, Skinner, I think we might've just found a home remedy for our hand grenade shortage. We'll make up some Molotov cocktails. Original recipe calls for high octane gasoline, but we're a little short on ethyl."

Lazeski lifted the maps off the smoldering table and inspected them.

"How'd the maps make it, Laze?" Sam said.

"Just need to dry out a little. Only lost the southwest corner on the big map."

"Didn't want to head that direction anyway." Sam rushed over to the stack of old clothes. "Skinner and Wellston, tear up one of these cotton shirts for fuses. We'll stuff them into the necks of wine bottles. What've we got? Four bottles?"

"Only three empties." Collins swirled the fourth. He turned it upside down, draining the contents into his mouth. "Now we got four."

Sam smiled. "Thank you for your contribution to the war effort, Private."

"Springwater, fill those bottles with calvados and cork them off good." He grabbed one of the jugs by the wall, uncorked it, and took a whiff. "Wow!" He pulled his head away. "Here's some more in case you run out." He unstopped a ceramic jug, smelled the spout, and took a long swig. "Drinking water." He stepped to his big scout and pushed the jug into his gut. "Here, Collins. You're so good at handling beverages—make sure all canteens are full."

He moved back to the pile of clothes and picked out a pair of slacks. "Morton and Pinball, tie off the legs of two pair. They'll be our Molotov carriers."

After organizing his little workshop of misdropped paratroopers, he looked at his watch. They'd passed into D-Day-plus-two—June 8th—and were no closer to their La Barquette objective than when they had dropped forty-eight hours earlier.

Sam's gut told him strategic military objectives no longer mattered. All that mattered was getting his men out alive.

Chapter 50

The Exodus

Prodding to his ribs awakened Sam. *Where am I?*

The rough-sawn oak floor and musty grain dust jogged his memory.

"Sam, you need to see this," Springwater said. "Not good." Springwater ducked back under the tarp.

Sam followed, careful not to let any light escape. Springwater moved aside to allow Sam a view through the ventilation slit. German infantry gathered on the main road just 120 yards east.

"Started with a squad ten minutes ago."

Sam looked at his watch: 0420 hours. "At least a reinforced platoon now."

"Shedding everything but weapons and ammo. Launching an operation," Springwater said. "Not fallschirmjager. Uniform and helmets aren't right."

Sam blinked and rubbed his eyes. "They're about to sweep this area."

"We get sold out? Just how bad did you offend that nurse?"

"Wake everyone." Sam moved aside, allowing Springwater one last peek. "Get geared up and ready to leave. Pronto."

"We've got five minutes, tops."

"If we're not out of here in the next hour, we're here another eighteen anyway. Double-up security on the false door."

Springwater slipped out. The sudden rattle of arms and clicking safeties confused Sam. Discovered already? He ducked out from under the tarp. Their French host appeared in the hole, hands raised. The Frenchman spotted Sam and pleaded with his eyes. Wellston said, "He needs your map. Says there's not much time."

Sam ran his fingers back through his hair. "Who sold us out?" Sam spread the map on the table and turned up the lantern. "Skinner, keep an eye on the Krauts."

Talking all the while, the farmer scrambled down the ladder and wriggled between Springwater and Sam over the scorched map.

Wellston said, "I can't catch it all. Mostly, we've got to hurry. He doesn't know why the Boche showed up. He overheard them say someone was hiding Americans. He knows nothing. Just more hurry, hurry, hurry."

Sam reached across his body and gripped his 45-auto. "Ask him where the other Americans are."

Wellston stammered through his French and got an immediate shrugging of the Frenchman's narrow shoulders. "Says such things would never be spoken of openly."

The Frenchman's voice grew agitated. Wellston said, "He talked to his Résistance network. Some of our paratroopers are getting back through the Catz area. Just east of Carentan."

"That's a lie. We've been over there." Sam unsnapped the strap holding his 45-auto in his shoulder holster. "It's all flooded."

The Frenchman shook his head. "*Non, non, non!*" He got within inches of Wellston's face and spoke in plaintive tones. "He says there is a way, sir. Skirt around Carentan on the south, head east to Catz, then north to Brevands. He claims Americans hold the wooden bridges at Brevands."

"That was Sink's Third Battalion objective. Reassuring to know someone got where they were supposed to." Sam released his pistol and ran his fingers back through his hair. "Find out if there's fighting in Carentan."

To the disappointment of all, they learned the battle remained north of the Douve and east of the Merderet rivers.

The French farmer brought the right map to the top of the stack and with his work-stained finger traced a route east along the railroad line, a straight shot all the way to Carentan, maybe four miles away. He then arched a route around the south of Carentan. He pointed at Carentan and shook his twig of a finger as if scolding a small child.

"That settles it, gentlemen, we depart for Catz," Sam said. "And we'd better hurry. We've only got 'til midnight to get back."

The men exchanged puzzled looks.

"You all *do* remember what General Taylor said, don't you?" Sam looked around to see that they'd bitten on his bait. "'Men, give me three days of hard fighting and I'll get you back to England.' Well today's the third day and I intend to hold him to his word." He made sure his grin was seen. A couple of men groaned.

"Good one, sir," Pinball said, smiling. "Have to write papa that one."

Sam shook his head. "Don't bother. No way it'll get past the censors."

Skinner ducked his head from behind the tarp. "Sir, here they come. Two platoons. Sweeping down the road, double-time."

"Everyone up on the catwalk!" Sam grabbed up the maps and ducked under the tarp. Before seeing anything he heard the angry chorus of scores of hobnailed boots on cobblestones, joined by alarmed village dogs barking.

A pair of Germans split off the main group and posted themselves fifty feet from the silo. The main group rounded a curve, leaving a pair of sentinels at every building. He thought he heard a pair of Germans run through the farm's courtyard and take up a position behind the house. An unintelligible feminine outburst confirmed his suspicion. The orchard route they'd entered the farmstead from was now blocked. The petite nurse showed great courage in issuing her covert warning.

Sam shifted to gain a view back to the east. Two officers in peaked caps stood in the road at the enemy's starting position.

Three shots rang out. Germans shouted orders. A fusillade of fire erupted and promptly waned. American semiautomatic weapons answered. The Germans responded with even greater firepower. The lethal mix included grenade explosions.

The two officers ran past, pistols drawn, a squad in tow. The two sentries by the silo ran after them.

The enemy had inadvertently opened Sam's window of opportunity. How long the window stayed open was dependent upon the other hapless Americans fighting for survival. *They've no idea they're buying us time.*

He departed the hiding place and wove his way through the paratroopers waiting on the catwalk, grabbing trusses to keep his balance. The catwalk reminded him of a C-47 aisle—all static lines hooked up, equipment checked, red light on. They all shuffled forward, across the barn loft and to the ground floor. He hoped the darkness concealed his surging fear.

Sam stuck his head out an arched entryway. The ground-level perspective limited visibility. The German assembly area still appeared vacated. He moved back down the line counting his men. The firefight slackened.

"We going to rescue them, Lieutenant?" Wellston said.

Sam shook his head. "They're rescuing us."

"How's that?" Vigiano asked.

"We're running this play right up the gut, Pinball. I found a huge hole in their D-line. Everyone run after the man in front, don't stop."

He made a final survey of the street, took a deep breath, and dashed for the cobbled street.

Fresh firing erupted from behind.

Sam ducked into the shadows and prepared to make a desperate last stand. He looked back. His men dove into the ditch and prepared to meet the onslaught. No one appeared hit.

The firing continued, but devoid of muzzle flashes, ricochets, or popping in the air from near misses. The gunfire wasn't intended for them. The enemy remained focused on the other Americans.

Sam shoved his helmet on tighter and sprinted, sticking to the darker recesses next to the trees and village buildings.

Adrenaline pumping, he dashed headlong through the German assembly area, passing a glowing cigarette tip.

Sam looked over his shoulder and almost tripped.

The German leapt from the ditch, the glowing cigarette tumbling as he opened his mouth to raise the alarm.

Without breaking stride, Pinball thrust his rifle stock into the back of the enemy's head, butt-stroking the man in textbook Army manual fashion. The German helmet skittered down the cobbles past Sam.

No shots or alarms followed.

Dashing another 150 yards, Sam slowed until he had visual contact with all ten men following. Just outside Les Fevres, he cut left off the road into a small orchard and jogged until finding the railroad. He turned right and used the elevated rail-bed to conceal their left flank. The terrain grew uneven and difficult to negotiate in the dark. He slowed the pace just enough to assure solid footing.

*   *   *

Half an hour later Sam halted and tried reading the shadowy terrain ahead. The eastern horizon was growing brighter, yellowish-orange.

A waterway flowed north, disappearing under a short span of wooden trestle bridge. Dark outlines of cattails sprang up on the far bank. They needed rest and to shift the heavy weapons burden around. This spot would suffice. In an emergency they could duck under the trestles. He took a knee.

His adrenaline subsided, yet the pain in his hip didn't come screaming back. *Maybe there's something to that horse liniment.*

He signaled for a scout. Skinner appeared at his side. Sam pointed to the tracks. "Get up top, check the other side. If it's clear, stay there, keep watch."

Skinner scurried up the rail-bed rock embankment. Reappearing twenty seconds later, he signaled all clear and disappeared back out of view. The men relaxed and bunched up. Except Lazeski—he retreated thirty yards to keep vigil on the back-trail. The men carrying the mortar components and Harrigan with the MG-42 pushed their loads aside and collapsed on the embankment, gasping for oxygen.

Collins stuffed his cheek with a wad of Beechnut tobacco. "Did you fellers see ol' Pinball butt-stroke that there Kraut?"

"My fault. Thought that position was clear," Sam said, turning an ear toward Les Fevres. He detected no more gunfire. "Need to get moving again before he tells them which way we went."

"I reckon he ain't tellin' his buddies squat, sir." Collins's toothy grin shown through dawn's dim light. "Expected to find his noggin still in that dern helmet a rollin' down the road."

"His body will tell them enough," Sam said.

"Dang, Pinball, you got skills you're keeping from us," Collins said.

Vigiano shook his head. "About like giving a linebacker a good forearm shimmy under the chin."

"Well then," Collins said, "I sure ain't playin' no football against the likes of you,"

"In case you hadn't noticed—you big hick—we're not playing football. We're playing for keeps," Silva said, slightly trilling the *r* letters. "Poor SOB was probably just some draftee with a momma and a papa and a girl back home."

"Thank you kindly for the reminder, Brother Silva." Collins glared at his buddy. "When did you go 'n turn Quaker on us?"

"Just cut the wise cracks about dead guys." Silva glared back. "Like *you* told Morton—show a little respect."

Collins sent a spray of brown saliva toward Silva's boots.

"Collins, go relieve Skinner," Sam said, and relaxed with his back propped against the rail embankment. "Pinball, that ankle must be on the mend."

"Magic of adrenaline, sir. Just like the Soldan High game my senior year. Couldn't hardly walk before the game. Never felt a thing after the kickoff. Ran in four touchdowns." He rubbed his ankle. "Just parking here's making it act up a little, though."

"Rub some more of that horse liniment on it." Sam leaned forward and looked for Springwater. "Ted, let's move back out in ten." He collapsed back and closed his eyes.

*   *   *

Something nudged his leg. Sam's eyes sprang open. Springwater stood over him. Sam leaped to his feet and stared at his watch. Twenty minutes had passed. Full morning light had arrived, revealing a cattail marsh across the creek. *Get your head back in the game!* He suppressed a yawn and blinked. "Let's use the rails to get around this swamp. One person at a time."

Springwater nodded and began issuing orders. He climbed the rail embankment and crossed the trestle bridge first. Collins followed, then Silva. Sam crossed fourth and joined the security perimeter on the far side.

A distant buzzing caught Sam's attention. A couple of miles north a glint of silver flashed in the sky. P-47 Thunderbolts on dawn patrol. *Still working over that highway. Go get some, flyboys.*

Two more men crossed. Sam scanned the perimeter and signaled for the next man.

Trotting down the tracks, Skinner crossed the bridge.

A screaming roar came out of the low morning sun. Sam jerked his head toward the sound. He shielded his eyes yet saw nothing in the intense glare.

Multiple machinegun blasts roared. The marsh erupted in a swath of brownish-white geysers. The last four paratroopers dove for cover under the trestle.

Skinner dropped and laid flat between the rails.

The geysers turned into dusty eruptions in the rail-bed rocks.

Heavy slugs struck the rails like amplified sledgehammer blows.

The plane zipped past and banked right, gaining altitude.

Skinner stuck his head up, scrambled to his feet, and lurched left for the protection of the embankment.

The wingman roared out of the sun, raucous machineguns spitting flames.

One slug caught Skinner square in the back.

Time seemed to slow. Sam watched Skinner's chest explode outward. An aura of red mist suspended in contrast to the dull dust and water vapor swirling in the air.

Sam pounded the ground with his fist.

Silva cursed. Pinball whispered Hail Marys.

The buzzing roar intensified.

"Stay down!" Sam screamed.

The fighter planes made their second pass right down the tracks. The first plane strafed the tracks. Skinner's body jerked and bounced.

The second plane didn't shoot at all, but skimmed the ground thirty yards to the side of the elevated railway. The pilot flashed an obscene gesture. A US Air Corps stripe and star adorned the fuselage behind the pilot.

Silva shot the gesture back. "Thunderbolts! They're ours!"

After five seconds the planes flew out of sight.

Collins and Silva rushed down the tracks toward Skinner.

Lazeski poked his head out from under the trestle. Springwater frantically signaled for them to cross.

Silva and Collins each grabbed Skinner under an arm. They returned running—dragging the limp body—their faces anguished. Skinner's head dangled backward unnaturally, while his boots danced in the air like a marionette each time a heel struck a railroad tie. One leg flopped higher— shattered shinbones showing through torn fabric.

Stomach contents rose in Sam's throat. He turned away.

"Find cover. They'll make another pass," Silva said as he and Collins dragged Skinner down the embankment.

"They're not coming back. Just finishing off ammo before flying back to England," Sam said while sliding down the steep slope. "Anyone else hit?"

"You mean Limeys killed Skinner?" Morton said.

"They were ours. Thunderbolts," Springwater said.

"You sure?" Lazeski asked as he arrived with the tail-end of the squad. His face twisted in a grimace as he looked down at Skinner's broken body.

"Krauts aren't putting white stars on the side of their fighters." Sam's gaze locked on Skinner. His nausea grew. He plopped down.

Phillips rubbed his thigh. "Can't they tell—?"

"Tell what?" Sam tossed his hands up. "Just how much can you *tell* at two thousand feet and three hundred miles per hour? Their S-Two is probably telling the flyboys that *anything* this side of the Douve River is the enemy. Kill it."

Collins shoved more chewing tobacco into his cheek. "I reckon our own Air Corps is doing us more harm than them Krauts is."

"You can bet they're flying home to their comfy barracks, beer, and English whores right now." Silva slapped his M-1 stock. "They'll report how they shot-up a whole Kraut platoon along some French railroad."

"Just like all those Troop Carrier Command pilots probably reported us parachute infantry patsies dropped on time and on target." Pinball took out his rosary beads and mouthed a prayer over Skinner.

"You'll get no argument from me." Sam picked up his M-1 and worked his way back up the embankment to Skinner. He silently eulogized a good paratrooper, an excellent scout, a fine young volunteer from the Volunteer State. After a moment, Sam forced himself to consider the valuable equipment. He bent over the body and smelled a mixture of copper and disrupted internal organs. *Smells like hog butchering.*

Sam pulled one of their six remaining pineapple grenades off Skinner's web gear and tossed it to Collins. He then popped eight-round clips of M-1 ammo out of the web belt and passed them around. Clenching his teeth, he lifted the ammo bandoleer off Skinner's ravaged chest. The exiting 50-caliber slug had missed the bandoleer, but covered it with frothed blood and tiny bone chips. He wanted to drop it in disgust, but they needed ammunition. He slid it over Skinner's head and draped it over his own neck and shoulder, careful to keep the gory side concealed.

Springwater stood over the body. "A brave warrior. A true friend. A man of his word." He walked away.

Sam reached down to perform his final responsibility. He yanked off one of Skinner's dog tags and pocketed it. The other he left on the chain but placed it on edge between Skinner's front teeth and lifted the corpse's lower jaw upward until the tag locked between the upper and lower teeth. The gruesome task completed, Sam stood.

Morton leaned closer to the body. "What you gotta do that for, sir?"

"Assures the guys from graves registration can identify the body later. Some say it's supposed to keep the body from bloating as much, too."

Lazeski—clothing dripping wet—reported his group's status. "Phillips caught a flying rock in the thigh. Nothing broken. Dropped three mortar shells in the water. Couldn't find them. Want me to go back, sir?"

Sam's muscles tensed. "No." He clenched his jaw to keep from screaming profanities. Instead, he turned and followed Springwater.

This exodus is far from over. But, where's the end? The sole Promised Land he could think of was back in England, with Maggie. Yet, as Maggie had pointed out—*then what?* The Army would always come up with a new mission. A new exodus. A new wilderness. Until they ran all out of the Children of Israel. He was almost convinced that Maggie was right. *Then what?*

As he worked to catch Springwater, Sam found himself doing something he couldn't remember doing since the day his brother drowned, something he considered irrelevant since his initiation to the lecture halls of UCLA.

Samuel George Henry lifted his eyes to the horizon and prayed.

Chapter 51

Accusation

8 June 1944, 1355 Hours
Near Auvers, Normandy

Reclining in the tall grass of yet another apple orchard, Sam half-closed his eyes. Late apple blossoms hung near his face. His mind tumbled through looming decisions and anticipated consequences.

Wellston cleared his throat. "Sir, can we talk?"

"What's on your mind?"

The security rotation had left Sam and Wellston alone, their shift to catch a catnap. A defensive ring of six surrounded them. Springwater and Collins were out conducting a recon patrol.

If Sam correctly identified the last village they had skirted, they were past Auvers and halfway to Carentan—making decent progress. Following the railway eliminated any chance of becoming disoriented in the maze of hedgerows. Regrettably, a company of Wehrmacht infantry marching down the tracks toward Baupte had put an end to using the path of least resistance. Springwater detected the German vanguard first and the American paratroopers faded southeast without incident.

Wellston coughed into his fist. "Permission to speak openly, sir?"

Sam held up his hand and wiggled his ring finger. "I'm no ring-knocker. Speak."

"No offense then, sir?"

Sam rolled off his helmet pillow and, leaning on his elbow, looked Wellston in the eye. "Say what you've got to, Wellston."

Wellston looked bewildered. "Early this morning, back at Les Fevres… why?"

"You've got to be more specific."

"Why did you…I mean…" Wellston fidgeted with a cigarette. "Why did we run?"

Sam sighed. "Simple. To save my men. The Krauts had us at least five to one. Besides, at OCS they don't call it running. It's referred to as a tactical withdrawal."

Wellston lit the cigarette using his dead sergeant's Zippo. "Call it what you like. We ran away."

Wellston's conclusion irritated Sam. After a moment, he held up a finger. "Look, first, we were vastly outnumbered and outgunned on a field of the enemy's choosing." Sam held up another finger. "Second, we had zero advance intelligence. We knew squat before and after the shooting started." He held up a third finger. "Third, it's wasn't our mission or objective."

Wellston took a long drag on his cigarette, said, "Neither was I," and coughed.

"What are you talking about?"

"Day before yesterday, sir." Wellston's eyes turned troubled. "You rescued me."

Sam swatted a low hanging apple blossom. "Comparing apples to oysters."

"I don't see it that way." Wellston gazed at the hazy Norman sky. "Six Krauts against only you. You with just a carbine, low on ammo, up against an MG-Forty-two. On ground *they* chose. You knew nothing about my unit. And none of it was a part of your mission or objective. Sounds like a situation your OCS instructors would say called for one of your tactical withdrawals." Wellston pointed his cigarette toward Sam. "But you didn't. And I'm here now only because you didn't. Wish we could've done the same for those other fellas."

A breeze rustled the orchard. Wellston's idealism seemed unarguable. The prolonged silence amplified the tension.

Sam heaved a sigh. "I'm afraid you've made me into something more than I really am. You set yourself up for disappointment. Given enough time, any man you look up to will disappoint you. Besides, there's a big difference."

"And that would be, sir?"

"I'm allowed to choose to throw away my own life. I was alone. Alone and desperate. I gambled. Or maybe I just reacted. Whichever—it makes no difference—I have no right to toss the dice like that with the lives of my men."

Wellston seemed to ponder Sam's point. "Maybe. But it still just doesn't feel right. Here I sit, and I shouldn't be. Why me and not them?"

Sam shook his head. "I've no idea, but I hope we're both still asking that question six months from now."

"Six months?" Wellston flicked his cigarette butt away and chortled. "Make it out of this mess and I'll still be asking that question sixty years from now."

Chapter 52

The Encounter

8 June 1944, 1520 Hours
Near Cantepie, Normandy

"Here they come! Those stupid…" Silva's profanity mixed English and Portuguese.

Shielding his eyes, Sam gazed toward the screaming buzz. The Thunderbolts again brought their attack from out of the sun. This time Silva spotted them before it was too late. Sam dove for concealment in the hedgerow.

Gritting his teeth, he pushed his helmet down tighter, and waited for the hedgerow to erupt. However, the two stout P-47s didn't open fire until directly overhead. Over the roar of the diving fighter-bombers came the whoosh of rockets and chatter of machineguns.

The rockets detonated in a rapid series of booms.

"At least these bums can't hit squat," Pinball said.

Sam untangled himself from the vegetation and dashed for a gap in the uncharacteristically low, thin hedgerow. "Springwater, on me! Everyone else, stay down." The planes climbed and banked eastward. Sooty smoke billowed from a patch of woods not quite a half-mile away. "What do you make of it?"

As usual, Springwater refrained from speculation.

"They hit something," Sam said. "Ours or theirs? Wish I had my binoculars."

The P-47s swooped for a second pass. Rockets expended, the Thunderbolts flew wingtip to wingtip strafing the woodlot with sixteen 50-caliber machineguns.

The woodlot erupted in an outgoing fusillade of small arms and machinegun fire, punctuated by a small automatic cannon. Like angry hornets, the tracers chased the Thunderbolts away.

"Fritz will be licking his wounds and keeping his eye on the sky for awhile," Springwater said. "Good time to get a better look."

"I'd wager on a supply dump." Sam pulled his map out. "A good thing to have marked on the map for the S-Two."

Springwater gathered Collins and the two disappeared through the hedgerow.

*   *   *

Hauptscharfuhrer Helmut Behr's temples pounded. He couldn't figure out how the American *jabo* pilots had spotted the vehicles. Every vehicle had been well camouflaged, off the road, and hidden in the woodlot. Yet the fighter-bombers had, and it cost Behr dearly—one halftrack, two motorcycle sidecars, and nine men killed. He had to get the working vehicles relocated before more Ami planes arrived.

The gangsters own the air! Where's our vaunted Luftwaffe? He muttered profanity. *We can't even travel in the daylight without constantly scanning the sky.*

Early that morning they'd neared the zone between Baupte and Carentan, where orders stipulated they recon and probe for the American main line of resistance. It was obvious to all but the biggest dummkopf that American ground forces were nowhere near, which perhaps explained why Hauptsturmfuhrer Von Gremp had insisted they commence executing their pointless orders to the letter.

The rest of SS Reconnaissance Battalion 17 lagged behind by at least eighteen hours. At least two days separated Behr's company from the 17th SS's lead assault regiments. *If we find any significant American presence, so what? We're powerless to do a thing about it.* In an odd way, Behr had become a victim of his own military prowess.

To hasten the end of their current exercise in futility, Behr had convinced Von Gremp to split the company. Von Gremp took half north along the paved road. That half remained hidden between the buildings, under trees, and in the barns of the sleepy Norman village of Cantepie. After another couple hours of wasted effort Behr would persuade Von Gremp that they'd fulfilled their orders.

However, at that moment, another *jabo* attack posed the immediate threat. He looked at his watch and cursed. He shielded his eyes and scanned the sky—certain more fighter-bombers would reappear at any moment.

"What about my dead, Hauptscharfuhrer Behr?" The teenaged squad leader's tear tracks contrasted against his dust and soot covered cheeks.

"Let the dead bury the dead." Behr hoped his eyes reflected the rage he felt. "And you all will be most decidedly dead if we loiter in this cursed woodlot another minute."

*   *   *

Springwater and Collins—wet with perspiration—had a look in their eyes that alarmed Sam.

"What's out there?" Sam knelt tucked into the shadows of the hedgerow.

Springwater removed his scrim-covered helmet and scratched his jet-black hair. "Mixture of light armor and motorcycles, Kraut jeep. Well camouflaged. I'd guess a reinforced platoon—forty-plus men. No tanks, but at least one big, eight-wheeled armored car."

Collins stuffed a wad of Beechnut chewing tobacco into his cheek. "I wouldn't think twice about calling the dern contraption a tank."

"Mostly halftracks," Springwater said. "One's burning. Krauts were pushing a damaged motorcycle sidecar out of the way."

"Like they're fixing to skedaddle, sir," Collins said. "Before them P-Forty-seven cowboys fetch their buddies."

Springwater wiped his brow. "Looks like they want to head this way."

"Sounds like elements of a mechanized recon outfit." Sam removed his helmet and ran his fingers back through his hair. "For a panzer division?"

Springwater shrugged. "S-Two didn't say anything about any this close."

"Then all the more reason to suspect they're exactly that." Sam realized he'd spoken too freely in front of Private Collins, so he said, "Besides, our last briefing was five days ago. In that time they could've driven from Berlin."

Engine noise drifted in on the breeze.

Sam's pulse rate jumped. "Get everyone on me, pronto." Sam spread out the map on the grass. The remnants of Chalk Number-2 huddled around. Sam felt like a quarterback in a sandlot football game. The sense in his gut told him he also had about as much time as a quarterback to call the next play.

"A whole lot more Kraut vehicles than we want to mess with will be passing right through here real quick. Picking a fight with them would be stupid, so we're not sticking round, but we might slow them down a tad." He jabbed a spot on the map. "This bridge is on the paved road running from Baupte to Carentan a quarter-mile due north. That's our rendezvous point. Follow the creek."

Springwater nodded. "Collins, Silva, and I will double-time it ahead to make sure they're no Krauts already there, and get security out."

"Good call." Sam looked around at the faces and picked men. "Phillips, Harrigan, Wellston, Pinball, and Sergeant Lazeski, carry the crew-served weapons. Give Springwater a three minute jump."

Morton leaned closer. "You forgot me, sir."

"No, I didn't," Sam said, gathering up his map. "How many Hawkins mines have we got?"

Lazeski held up three fingers.

"Morton, you and I are planting some surprises that'll make the Krauts think twice about using the road behind us for the next couple hours. Then we hoof it to catch up. Time it right and we should arrive at the bridge about the same time as the crew-served weapons."

Morton puffed up. "I'm your man, Lieutenant."

Silva rolled his eyes.

The growing engine noises made it clear that time for discussion or revision had ended. The paratroopers scrambled to redistribute equipment. Sam scooped up two Hawkins mines and rushed downhill toward the gate in the hedgerow. Morton followed with the third mine. Springwater, Collins, and Silva trotted northward, up a slight rise in the pasture.

The one-lane farm road wove on the other side of the sparse hedgerow. The road came from the south and abruptly turned east for a hundred yard stretch toward a plank bridge over a creek. Past the bridge and creek, the map showed the road curving to the northeast, eventually intersecting with the paved road.

Once on the road, Sam hunted for a place to plant the Hawkins mines.

Resembling an oversized tin flask, but stuffed with high explosive rather than liquor, the Hawkins mine didn't have the power to destroy even the lightest tank. However, it could blow off a tank tread or wreak a truck.

Morton ambled down the road fumbling with the triggering mechanism. His slung rifle slipped off his shoulder and the mine tumbled out of his hands.

Sam braced himself for an explosion.

None came.

Morton picked the mine up and resumed messing with the pressure trigger.

Sam cringed. "Give me that. Go up to the corner and watch for Krauts."

Just before the road joined the bridge, Sam spotted potholes. Using his entrenching tool, he scraped out a pothole. He placed the Hawkins mine, sprinkled the excess dirt and gravel around it, and set the trigger. He repeated the procedure in a pothole in the other tire path. With a growing sense of urgency, he planted the third on the bridge's far side where a bridge plank met road dirt.

Morton ran down the road, wide-eyed. "Motorcycles coming fast! A tank with wheels behind them!"

*   *   *

Standing atop the eight-wheeled armored car behind the turret, Behr surveyed the road through his binoculars. His ears stayed tuned for attacking aircraft.

He cursed. They'd failed to progress a half-kilometer before the Achtrad commander halted, reporting possible movement through the hedgerow where the road curved sharply right. Probably more cows. The teen feared an ambush. And with good reason—narrow roads, hedgerow cover, limited visibility. This district was nothing but a colossal armor ambush site.

Behr's experience and gut agreed—they were nowhere near the American lines, and the French lacked the audacity of Russian partisans. He considered it safe to proceed. However, rushing forward would teach his green troops bad habits. He needed to instill disciplined speed into his recon company. Yet, another *jabo* attack posed the greatest threat.

He waved a scout motorcycle forward. A BMW R75 motorcycle sidecar—carrying three men and mounted with an MG-42—struggled to get alongside the Achtrad on the narrow road. Behr looked down at the riders. "Go a hundred meters past the corner, check behind the hedgerows. There should be a bridge. Check it to assure it can accommodate the Achtrad." He waved them on.

He signaled a pair of motorcycles—solo-rider Gnome & Rhone DKW NZ350s— forward. The motorcycles roared up and skidded to a halt.

Behr frowned, yet longed to once more feel a motorcycle throttle in his hand. "Must I remind you? Motorcycle reconnaissance is not a race."

One goggled rider said, "Jawohl, Hauptscharfuhrer Behr."

Behr shook his head. "Reconnoiter two kilometers and return."

The teens gunned their engines, popped clutches, and sprayed gravel. The more nimble DKWs passed the BMW and rounded the curve, each rider skimming right boots on the dirt for balance.

Behr banged the Achtrad turret. "Advance at ten kilometers per hour. Halt at the curve. Provide cover for the motorcycle patrol."

Staying perched atop the Achtrad, Behr waved his arm for the line of halftracks, *kublewagon*, and motorcycles to follow.

*   *   *

Sam dashed through the pasture gate and dove left, under cover of the hedgerow. Morton landed next to him.

The rattling roar of motorcycle engines grew closer. Two unseen motorcycles roared past. A third arrived, slowed, then the engine sound became stationary, idling just yards away. Sam estimated just this side of the bridge.

The motorcycles had thrown him an unanticipated curve. They'd never conducted a field problem involving reconnaissance motorcycles. *And what happened to the Hawkins mines? Didn't I arm them right?*

Feeling vulnerable, Sam belly-crawled to where they'd huddled before planting the mines. He caught movement out of the corner of his eye. Lazeski's crew-served weapons group was jogging across the pasture. Forty more yards and they'd drop down a slope and be out of sight.

Sam frantically waved them forward. *Go! Go! Run!*

Phillips—lugging the mortar tube—lagged behind the group.

The throaty rumble of a large diesel engine grew closer. Sam heard guttural German shouts.

Automatic cannon fire erupted. The muzzle blasts reverberated through Sam's chest.

*   *   *

From atop the Achtrad, Behr lost sight of the DKW motorcycles roaring off past the bridge. The BMW sidecar stopped on the bridge. A scout jumped off and began stomping his foot on the heavy planks. The scout walked to each end and took an occasional look over the side at the supporting beams and pylons. Seemingly satisfied, he moved to check behind the hedgerow.

The Achtrad reached the curve. Through a gap in the hedgerow vegetation Behr caught movement in the pasture. Four or five foreign soldiers retreating.

He banged on the turret. "Enemy infantry. Due north. One hundred fifty meters."

The turret slewed about fifteen-degrees left.

The gunner loosed a five-shot burst from the 20mm cannon.

The last retreating man dropped like a giant scythe had struck him at the ankles.

No targets remained visible. "Sweep the area with machinegun fire."

The Achtrad commander sprayed a long burst with the coaxially mounted MG-34.

The DKW motorcyclists flashed back into view in Behr's right peripheral vision, racing across the bridge, back toward the recon convoy.

BOOM!

An explosion erupted under a DKW, launching the motorcycle and rider eight meters high and ten meters forward. The other DKW rider swerved into the ditch and flew over the handlebars.

Behr cursed. Mines! He leapt off the Achtrad.

The turret slewed back right, toward the explosion.

The BMW sidecar driver backed his vehicle off the bridge.

A second explosion lifted the BMW four meters over the bridge. The blast plunged the driver into the creek. The machinegunner crammed into the sidecar wasn't so fortunate. The sidecar flipped at its apex and landed upside down, driving the machinegunner's head into the bridge planks.

Behr cursed again. His jagged cheek scar throbbed and became engorged.

A whooshing noise reached his ears just before a massive blast wave slammed him into the roadside ditch.

He rolled over. Heat scorched his face. The Achtrad was ablaze.

*   *   *

The first Hawkins mine explosion startled Sam.

The second mine eruption encouraged him.

He looked toward where he'd last seen his men. Nothing. He caught movement to the right, darting among scattered walnut trees. He recognized Wellston's bandaged head. Half-shielded by a walnut trunk, Wellston knelt and shouldered his bazooka.

A hundred seventy-five yards. *You better be good, Wellston.*

Flame and smoke shot out of the back of the bazooka. The rocket whooshed mere feet over Sam's head and connected with metal with a resounding blast. The shockwave washed over him.

"Time to go, Morton!" He leapt up and sprinted away.

His hip forced him to lag. Seventy yards from the hedgerow, he glanced back. A fireball shot skyward as the armored car's ammo cooked off all at once. He pushed himself to run faster.

At the high spot in the pasture, Lazeski lifted a body out of the grass. Morton ran past Lazeski. Sam stopped and threw the wounded man's arm over his shoulder. He recognized Phillips. A mangled 60mm mortar tube lay in the grass. Phillips held one foot high. An explosive 20mm shell had sheared away the back of his foot like a giant snapping turtle bite, boot heel and all.

Lazeski and Sam rushed for the bridge. Phillips groaned and stumbled along.

Sam cringed, expecting a bullet to sever his spine.

Chapter 53

The Bridge

Sam wrapped another compress bandage around Phillips's mangled foot. The bleeding was heavy—both oozing and spurting.

"Don't unlace his boot." Sam feared the Corcoran was the only thing holding the remains of the foot together. His blood-drenched hands fumbled the bandage. He caught it before it hit the ground, and resumed wrapping.

Lazeski unfurled a first aid kit tourniquet and tightened it around Phillips's ankle. The bleeding slowed.

Two minutes earlier Sam had arrived at the bridge rally point. He ordered his men to jettison the now useless mortar base-plate, bipod, and mortar rounds into the creek.

The squad congregated on a grass flat on the south side of the twenty-five foot concrete bridge over the ten-foot wide, north-flowing creek. A man could stand erect under the bridge. The creek bottom on either side of the bridge had scattered trees, brush, and cattails along the water. From the west, a paved two-lane road passed down a sunken lane lined with mature elm trees. East of the bridge the elevated roadway climbed and after ninety yards curved right. Springwater had sent Collins out to observe the road from the west. Silva watched from the east. The rest of the men formed a security perimeter around Sam and Lazeski, tending Phillips just a few feet from underneath the bridge.

"Ted, we've about got Phillips ready to move." Sam's heart felt like it was going to burst out his chest. "Pull Collins and Silva in. We've got to move, *pronto*. Take us northeast."

Phillips groaned and pounded the ground with his fist. "It hurts. Hurts like a—"

A faint whistle sounded. Sam looked skyward.

*   *   *

The inferno that was once an Achtrad blocked Behr's column from advancing. Even without the flaming armored car, the minefield around the bridge kept his vehicles jammed.

He set security out on the flanks and climbed into his halftrack.

A smooth-faced *Untersturmfuhrer* wearing a radio headset looked to him with questioning eyes. "Are we under attack?"

"Hardly. I saw a mere squad running away. A stronger force would've stayed right here and wiped us out." Behr grabbed the map off the junior lieutenant's lap and let his mind absorb the map's features. "We hit one. They'll stop to tend his wounds. It will be close. It will be easy to find…like this patch of woods, here. Or *this* bridge." Helmut stabbed the map with his finger. "That's where I'd choose. Walk a mortar barrage back onto that bridge. At least 25 rounds. I'll follow the barrage with two squads sweeping down the creek. Did you radio a contact report to Hauptsturmfuhrer Von Gremp?"

The Untersturmfuhrer gulped. "*Ja.*"

"Get back on the radio. Tell the Hauptsturmfuhrer that I strongly advise that he advance his entire force on that bridge immediately. Beware of anti-tank teams. I'll take two dismounted squads and meet him there. You clear the road of mines, then meet us with all your vehicles where this road intersects the paved road."

Nodding, the junior lieutenant jotted notes. Behr leapt over the side. He shouted orders for two squads to join him and trotted toward the spot he'd seen the enemy troops.

Three minutes later, he stood over a damaged light mortar tube. Fresh blood added a splash of color on the olive green tube. A blood trail went northward, downhill toward the creek.

He pivoted toward the rattle of equipment. Fifteen panzergrenadieren jogged toward him. Behr grinned and looked back north. "You will regret such audacity, whoever you are."

A hollow, metallic pop drew his attention back to the vehicles. Through the hedgerow he saw smoke puff from the halftrack-mounted mortar. Two additional mortars joined the action. If he had deduced correctly, in a few seconds 81mm parcels of high explosives and razor sharp steel splinters would rain down on his tormentors.

*   *   *

A mortar round hit the creek forty yards beyond the bridge and raised a murky fount of water and reeds into the air.

"Under the bridge, now!" Sam grabbed Phillips around the knees, while Lazeski hooked his arms under Phillips's armpits. They lifted and rushed for cover. Sam tripped and dropped the wounded man's legs. Phillips screamed.

The next six rounds walked back toward the bridge.

"Everyone stay down!" Sam stabbed a morphine Syrette into Phillips's thigh.

A faint whistle announced nine additional shells dropping straight down and landing just outside the bridge. Muck showered down.

The next rounds exploded on the road surface, knocking sand and debris on the paratroopers. The mortar barrage walked south. Shrapnel whistled between the bridge bottom and the paratroopers hugging the mud below.

As abruptly as the barrage had started, it stopped. Smoke and the scent of high explosives hung heavy in the air.

"Troops will follow," Springwater said. "Need to move."

Breathing hard, Collins slid down the bank. "We got us another of them eight-wheeled little tanks a movin' down the road like he's hunting something. One halftrack trailing him. Sounded like more following—dern screeching that don't come from no tires."

Fifty yards east, six shots rang out in rapid two-shot bursts. A few seconds later Silva arrived huffing. "More than a squad of Krauts. Got one of them, I think. A hundred fifty yards south. Moving up both sides of the creek." Blood mingled with sweat ran down the back of Silva's hand.

Sam grabbed Silva's forearm and pulled back the sleeve to reveal a gash that the petite French nurse would've closed with four or five stitches.

"Just a scratch, sir. Got nicked by a piece of mortar right before it ran out of gas."

"Dress it as we go." Sam turned to Springwater. "Lead out. Keep bearing northeast. Five yard intervals."

German shouts came from the south. Creek bottom vegetation and smoke limited visibility.

"Sir, them Krauts in that panzer aim to be here right quick." Collins scrambled up the embankment and popped his head up to observe the sunken lane.

"Let's move it," Sam said. "Collins, Morton, carry Phillips."

"Too dang late." Collins slid down the bank. "They're here."

The sunken lane funneled the rumblings of an approaching diesel engine to everyone under the bridge.

*   *   *

The tracks showed three boot prints, thick smears of blood, then two boot prints, all side-by-side. Two soldiers rescuing a wounded comrade. *How touching. I do enjoy hunting valiant men.* He grinned and touched his engorged cheek scar.

Rifle shots rang out in pairs. A picket. Behr dropped and rolled behind a bush.

With a mixture of cajoling and threats, Behr got the two squads back up and advancing. The low hanging smoke from the mortar barrage and thick vegetation impaired visibility.

His men blended in well in their SS summer dot pattern camouflaged tunics. He set the pace and advanced in the center, a squad on each flank.

Behr heard a low rumble and grinding of gears. Through the trees he caught a glimpse of the top of the Achtrad—hatches closed, creeping forward. The turret rotated in sweeping motions.

Behr knelt and signaled the skirmish line to do the same. *Never trust half-blind and paranoid panzer crews in a combat zone.*

He could just make out the west abutment of the bridge. The Achtrad grew more visible. The turret swept to its right and halted—its coaxially mounted 20mm gun and MG-34 pointed at two panzergrenadieren along the opposite creek bank.

The Achtrad stopped.

Behr sunk lower. Sweat rolled off his temples.

The Achtrad belched a cloud of black exhaust and lurched forward. Behr raised his Bergmann into the air and pushed himself back up. His young SS men in visible contact followed his example.

Flame spurted from the Achtrad MG-34 muzzle. Two scouts across the creek jerked from multiple hits.

Behr dropped. Slugs made supersonic snaps over his head.

He rolled to his right as the MG-34 traversed to his left. "Cease fire, dummkopf!"

A man screamed.

Behr cursed, rolled right again into a shallow depression and buried his face into the ground.

A sharp explosion silenced the Achtrad machinegun. He risked a glance. The turret sat askew. Flames erupted from every Achtrad hatch.

He caught a flicker of movement under the bridge and rose to his feet.

Yellow smoke billowed between him and the bridge.

Before the smoke hid the bridge, muzzles flashed. A bullet popped past his ear.

So, I was right. And this time the enemy probably saved my life.

Squeaking halftrack treads advanced from the west.

An MG-42 opened up from the bridge. *What is going on?*

*   *   *

"Nobody panic," Sam said, shifting to under the south edge of the bridge. *Yeah, right. Armor approaching from the west, infantry pinching our south flank.* "Everyone stays put. Wellston, let the armor pass, then put one up its tail."

Wellston wired a rocket to the bazooka tube and shifted to the north edge, ready to spring out.

The sound of the eight-wheeled panzer grew nearer, but at a slower rate. Sam looked around. Men readied themselves. Collins, Harrigan, and Pinball gazed upward at the bridge bottom.

Sam realized he needed to quit reacting and anticipate the next action. "Collins, how far behind the armor were the other vehicles?"

"Hundred yards, I reckon."

"OK, we can expect less than that now." Sam turned to Springwater. "Get the Molotov cocktails ready. If needed, you and Collins do the throwing."

Silva stared at him—apprehension in his dark eyes.

"Relax, Silva. We're not attacking. We're checking out of this hotel without paying." Sam tossed him an orange smoke grenade. "When I say, I want you popping two smoke grenades in the road on the west side of the bridge. Pinball, you pop two on the south side to blind the infantry coming down the creek."

The sound of the armored car grew closer.

"Give me all the hand grenades." Sam collected all six and straightening pins, said, "Harrigan, set up that MG-Forty-two to pour suppressive fire down the road. You and I'll cover our retreat."

Sam heard the panzer stop. Close. He took a deep breath. "Ready?"

His men shuffled position. Springwater stuffed cloth fuses into the calvados-filled wine bottles. Harrigan double-checked the MG-42 belt.

The sound of grinding gears reached Sam's ears. The armored car moved onto the bridge. Its machinegun opened fire.

Mesmerized, Sam watched tracers probe the creek bottom south of the bridge.

"What's that crazy Kraut doing?" Silva held a smoke grenade ready.

"Now, Wellston, kill it!" Sam shouted.

Wellston stepped out from under the north side of the bridge and aimed his bazooka upward at almost a forty-five degree angle. Flame shot out the back of the tube. The rocket collided with the German armor almost instantly. The armored car exploded, knocking Wellston back into the creek.

Sam lunged out, reached underwater, and grabbed a handful of jacket. Wellston came up sputtering water but still clutching his bazooka.

"Pop smoke!" Sam grabbed his M-1.

Silva tossed smoke grenades into the road as Harrigan climbed to just shy of road level and propped the MG-42 on its bipod. Sam joined Pinball—tossing smoke grenades—on the south side of the bridge.

Yellow smoke billowed in the creek bottom. Sam caught movement about 125 yards distant. A camouflaged German rose out of the weeds.

Sam centered the M-1 sight aperture on the German's sizable chest. A doubt forced him to hesitate. He had yet to shoot the M-1. It wasn't zeroed in for him.

He pulled the trigger anyway. The German dropped. But not like a man hit. More Germans advanced. He and Pinball emptied their eight-shot clips to delay the infantry.

Harrigan opened up with a burst from the MG-42.

Over the noise of a blazing armored car, Sam heard the sound of screeching sprockets.

"Springwater, light the Molotovs. Then lead the way out of here. Now!"

Scrambling back to the north side of the bridge, he noticed Phillips and could've kicked himself for almost forgetting his wounded man. Only one man could carry Phillips at the speed needed. "Collins! Forget the rest of the Molotovs. Grab Phillips and get out of here. Harrigan, suppressive fire! Go, go, go!"

Harrigan fired short bursts westward down the lane. Slugs pinged and ricocheted off steel armor.

Collins tossed Phillips over his shoulder in a fireman's carry with the ease he would a sack of feed.

Shielded by thick smoke, Springwater splashed across the creek, leading the escaping men on the north side of the bridge. The elevated roadway east of the bridge shielded them.

Sam grabbed two lit calvados Molotov cocktails and ducked out the south side.

A halftrack loomed on them just fifteen yards away. Sam could see only the top half of the armored personnel carrier. A painted armored fist and German gothic lettering caught his attention. He tossed the first

Molotov cocktail. It broke on the hood and splashed blue flame into the driver's vision slit.

The second calvados bomb burst on the painted fist. Flaming alcohol surged into the troop compartment.

Screaming men in flaming tunics jumped over the side.

A string of bullets popped by Sam's head, chipping the concrete abutment.

Ducking under the bridge, he collided with Wellston. "I ordered everyone out of here!"

Wellston held up his bazooka. "Got one rocket left."

Harrigan kept firing controlled bursts from the MG-42.

The screeching sound of another approaching halftrack approached. Wellston stood where Sam had thrown the Molotovs. He craned his neck and took two steps up the embankment. His eyes lit up. He shouldered the bazooka and squeezed the trigger.

A burst of automatic fire hit the concrete abutment around Wellston's head. He flinched just as the rocket ignited.

The rocket shot over the road and struck two-thirds of the way up one of the elms lining the lane. The entire treetop crashed onto the road.

Sam emptied his M-1 into the smoke to suppress the dismounted German infantry.

Both men scrambled for cover under the bridge.

"That's it for the rockets." Wellston tossed the bazooka tube into the creek.

Sam grabbed a third Molotov cocktail and stood below Harrigan. "Time to bug-out."

Harrigan fired a sustained burst and let himself slide back down with the MG-42. "Out of ammo, anyway."

"Toss it in the creek and catch up with Springwater." Sam heaved the Molotov cocktail through the wall of orange smoke.

He grabbed three grenades. Wellston grabbed the other three. In rapid succession, they tossed every grenade, then splashed across the creek, heading northeast. Ducking and dodging through trees and brush.

Screams intermingled with the cacophony of hand grenade detonations.

A frenzy of small arms fire splashed in the creek or ricocheted off the bridge.

Two German grenades exploded at the bridge.

*   *   *

Incoming rifle fire coming through the yellow smoke slackened. Behr grew irritated with shooting at shadows. He crossed the creek and gathered a half-dozen men around him.

He shouted to his left, "Cover fire. Under the bridge. On three." He rose and made sure the six young SS men around him were ready to follow his example. "*Eins, drei…*"

He bent forward and launched himself into a sprint for the bridge. His angle and smoke prevented anyone under the bridge from observing his advance. Covering fire from several guns opened up and ceased as he passed through the smoke and reached the bridge.

His shoulder banged into the southeast concrete bridge abutment. He unscrewed the caps at the end of two stick grenades, let the porcelain ball and string fall out, and yanked both at once, igniting the five second fuses. He leisurely tossed one across the elevated roadway and blindly flicked the other under the bridge.

The grenades exploded.

He ducked around the bridge abutment spraying full-auto Bergmann fire.

No movement. No human forms. He ran through the water toward drifting orange smoky haze and scanned for targets on the north side of the road. Nothing.

At his feet he found a bloody bandage and waxed paper wrappers. He grabbed a wrapper and recognized one word, Chicago. *As I expected— Americans.*

His men swept in and took positions under the bridge.

Behr picked up a helmet out of the mud. A net with shredded strips of coarse green and brown fabric covered it. He flipped it over and found an extra, cupped-leather chinstrap. Something a fallschirmjager might need when jumping from a plane. The owner had scrawled his name inside the helmet. Behr read aloud, "Phil-lips."

The Teutonic warrior in him scowled as he thought, *Today, Herr Phillips, we hit you, ja? Why else would I be holding your precious helmet? Your comrades were more fortunate. This will not be the case should we meet again.* He tossed the helmet into the creek. It landed upside down, twirled, and floated downstream several meters before sinking.

A flickering flame caught his attention. Remaining under the bridge, he crossed the creek and found a cracked wine bottle laying on its side, a smoldering rag stuffed in it. He picked it up, yanked the rag out, and smelled the contents. Calvados?

Behr lit a papirosa. The harsh Russian tobacco soothed his frayed nerves.

Chapter 54

The Mess

Ammunition in the burning Achtrad cooked-off in random explosions, pops, and whistling fragments.

Behr walked out from under the bridge standing erect, ignoring the 20mm and 8mm ammo detonations. The stench of burning human flesh reached his nostrils. Behr spat a foul taste from his mouth and savored his Russian makhorka tobacco. Urgent shouts reached his ears as green squad leaders tried to reorganize and account for men.

Anger welled up in Behr's gut. *Just how many ways can the Americans find to humiliate my boys?* He had taken reasonable precautions. He had used proven tactics. Yet for the past hour, fate had served his warriors as banquet dishes feeding war's insatiable appetite. *Soon I will find an opportunity to turn the tables.* He climbed the embankment and walked down the sunken lane.

Four wounded men occupied the south ditch. Orange flame and black smoke poured from under the hood of their abandoned halftrack. The heat withered the cut small branches and leaves camouflaging the armored troop carrier.

He recognized half of Sturmmann Henshel's handsome face. The other half was a reddened mass of blisters and sloughing skin. Behr turned away and examined the halftrack troop compartment. A bluish flame burned on the padded bench seats. The pasted portrait of Henshel's Aryan sweetheart was also half-burned and crinkled.

A treetop had fallen atop the second halftrack. The tree had snapped three of the five antennas. Behr pushed through the fallen foliage and climbed on the treads. Grabbing the upper edge of the armor-plated side, he launched himself into the command halftrack.

The radio operator's face blanched and emitted a sound bordering on a squeal. Raising a P-38 pistol, Von Gremp recognized Behr and returned his attention to the long-range radio. The odor in the tight confines betrayed the nature of the dark patch spreading down the radioman's trouser leg.

Wearing headphones, Von Gremp flicked a toggle switch and shouted into a microphone. "Repeat. Encountered American main line of resistance. Experiencing heavy casualties. Attacked by coordinated air, infantry, and anti-tank artillery. Over." Von Gremp bit his lip and renewed his report. "Engaging entrenched infantry. We require ambulances. Breaking contact and withdrawing two kilometer west. Over."

Behr reached across and tugged Von Gremp's headset off.

Von Gremp's face went ashen. "What are you doing, Behr! I was—"

Behr looked at the incontinent radioman. "Get out of here!"

The radioman scrambled out the back.

Behr looked his commander in the eye. "Your long range antenna is broken, Herr Hauptsturmfuhrer. As fate would have it, a fortunate malfunction for you. The SS has zero tolerance for grossly inaccurate or exaggerated reports from their reconnaissance units. In Russia heads rolled for less than what you just did. This is hardly the Ami main line—"

"You're wrong. This is exactly where we were told to look."

"Suit yourself. Repair your antenna. Radio your report. At best, you will find yourself transferred to Byelorussia. It's quite lovely this time of year."

Von Gremp's angry expression softened.

"Did you take fire from an MG-Forty-two?" Behr asked.

Von Gremp pondered for a moment, then nodded.

Behr tapped the side of his helmet. "Think! Has the Reich contracted to provide Roosevelt with our machineguns?"

Behr handed Von Gremp the wine bottle half-filled with calvados. "Smell!" Behr tilted the bottled in Von Gremp's hand until liquid splashed out. "Do Ami factories manufacture Molotov cocktails from apple brandy? Even as potent as calvados?"

Von Gremp switched the radio off. "Partisans?"

"Nein. We were informed of concentrated Ami fallschirmjager drops north of Carentan. I suspect a band of wandering paratroopers, separated from their parent unit. And each minute we sit without putting vehicles in pursuit, we permit their escape to report on us." Behr sneered. "You stay here and change diapers. I'll take a platoon and chase the vermin down."

Chapter 55

The Comeaux Farm

8 June 1944, 1650 Hours
Near Carentan, Normandy

Seeking concealment in the shadows of an overgrown hedgerow, Sam retightened Phillips's tourniquet.

He turned an ear toward the bridge. The random explosions had ceased. He heard no advancing vehicles. He estimated they'd fled about half a mile. The squad fanned out, forming a security perimeter in waist-high grass as he and Lazeski tended to Phillips's mangled foot. Bandages had worked loose. Sam had never imagined attending to such gore.

A cowbell clanked. Sam turned toward the noise. Nothing. The cowbell clanked again, closer. Over a slight rise a white and brown speckled cow approached, saw Sam, and halted. Within seconds, five cows balked, all staring at Sam.

A short civilian carrying a long cane approached. The Frenchman— appearing to be in his early forties—gave the cows admonishing taps with his cane. They refused to budge. He looked ahead of his cows and made eye contact with Sam. "*Sacré bleu!*"

Wellston rose to one side, Silva on the other, rifles leveled on the Frenchman.

The Frenchman's expression became troubled. He raised his hands, yet approached Sam.

"Let him," Sam said.

The farmer chatted away as he leaned over Phillips. Wellston trotted over and translated. "He's asking what we need."

The Frenchman removed his cap and knelt. He made the sign of the cross over his chest, seemed to pray for a moment, and then crossed himself again.

"Does he have something we can make into a stretcher? Clean bandages." Sam listened for pursuing enemy. "Is he alone?"

Wellston stammered in high school French and listened. "He's alone. Something about his wife. Medical stuff I couldn't understand. He can help. His home is close."

Sam feared Phillips was slipping into shock. "We need a blanket, too." He ran his fingers back through his hair and motioned Springwater to join him. "I'm taking Morton, Silva, and Wellston to the farmhouse. Keep Phillips's foot elevated." Sam pulled out the Carentan map and examined it. "If we're not back in thirty minutes, or if there's a firefight, rendezvous here." He poked a road intersection on the map a half-mile nearer Carentan.

Springwater studied the map and nodded.

Sam extended his hand to the Frenchman. "Sam Henry."

The Frenchman shook hands. "Jacques Comeaux."

Sam looked into Comeaux's brown eyes and saw genuine concern. "Tell Monsieur Comeaux we'd be grateful for any help. We won't burden him long."

Comeaux led them up cow trials through a maze of hedgerows. After about a quarter-mile, Sam spotted a gray-stone, two-story Norman farmhouse with matching barns.

Inside the farmhouse, Comeaux led them to a large kitchen with an open-beamed ceiling and sturdy oak table. An ornate crucifix hung on the plaster wall. Comeaux exited though a side door. Upon returning he shoved a wheel of cheese into Wellston's midsection.

A radiant girl carrying a pitcher entered the kitchen from the same side door and distributed mugs to each American. Her hair—the same shade of blond as Maggie's—represented a genetic echo of when Vikings ruled Normandy. The Frenchman pointed to the girl and spoke with an air of obvious pride.

"Monsieur Comeaux would like to introduce his youngest daughter, Raquel," Wellston translated. "Only fourteen and already the very image of her beautiful mother. May God rest her soul."

Raquel poured milk into Morton's mug and moved on to Wellston.

Morton elbowed Silva. "You catch the way she smiled at me? I think she likes me." Morton's eyes roamed up and down Raquel's adolescent figure.

"What planet do you live on? She's smiling at everyone." Silva scowled. "Besides, are you blind on top of being just plain stupid? She's just a kid."

Comeaux motioned Sam to stay and left the kitchen.

Another teenage girl entered the room—this one appearing three or four years older than Raquel. She handed Sam a folded sheet, gray wool blanket, and unused cheesecloth.

A sense of dread rose in Sam's gut. The image of the two French girls hanging from a limb flashed before him—girls executed for no reason other than aiding Americans. "We've got to get out of here. Now!"

Silva and Wellston looked puzzled. Morton kept ogling Raquel.

"Leave nothing." Sam stuffed the sheet and cheesecloth inside his jacket and tucked the blanket under his arm. "I've seen what they do to civilians that help us. Back at a village near where I was dropped, they lynched two French girls and a priest for aiding wounded paratroopers."

Wellston's jaw dropped. "At St. Georges?"

"Yeah, they helped at that church the Nazis torched."

"Torched? They patched up my bazooka loader. I left him in that church." Wellston looked troubled and coughed. "Those girls were just kids."

"They're dead kids now. I won't condemn these girls to the same fate." Sam scowled at Wellston. "You said Comeaux was alone."

Wellston nodded and coughed. "I thought he said he was, sir."

Comeaux returned carrying two wooden poles, a canvas tarp, and coil of twine.

"Silva, Morton, grab that stuff. We can rig the stretcher back where we left Phillips." Sam stopped in front of Comeaux. "*Merci.*" He looked to Wellston. "Tell him we would've never come here if I'd known about his daughters. If we forget anything, he's to destroy it immediately. They should all hide for at least twenty-four—"

"Hold on, sir. I can't remember all that." Wellston fumbled through the waterlogged French-English dictionary's stuck pages.

"Just get the idea across. Let's go!"

Wellston stammered in faltering French.

"Let's go, Private!" Sam slapped forty francs worth of invasion currency on the oak table and led the Americans out the house. They ran north past a garden and through a pasture gate. He halted to check their back-trail and waved his men past. Road dust billowed beyond the farmhouse. He sprinted on and rounded the cover of a hedgerow just as sounds of heavy vehicles reached his ears.

I sure hope you're a convincing liar, Monsieur Comeaux.

*   *   *

Behr jumped out of the halftrack troop compartment and scanned the Norman farmstead from over his Bergmann sights. Only cows moved among the gray stone structures. At his hand signals, panzergrenadieren swept out to his left and right.

He pumped his fist and flashed three fingers. A teenaged squad leader arrived at Behr's side like a well-trained, eager pup. Behr said, "Search the barns."

"Jawohl, Herr Hauptscharfuhrer."

Behr strode toward the two-story farmhouse. Ten men followed.

A smiling farmer in knee-high rubber boots and a cream-colored apron stood in the doorway holding a cheese wheel. *"Bon jour!"*

Behr shoved the farmer aside and entered the house. Hobnailed boots sounded on the flagstone floor. "Search every room." Weapons ready, panzergrenadieren filed past. Behr examined the floor for blood drops. His task took him into a kitchen. A small statue of the crucified Christ overlooked the room. He looked for anything American. Several French franc bills lay on an oak table. He picked them up and studied them—a twenty, ten and two fives. Folded, damp, yet appearing new to circulation.

The sound of stomping boots and shouts rang throughout the house.

Babbling something about a cheese market, the middle-aged farmer took the francs out of Behr's hand. Behr thought, *Who markets cheese during an invasion?*

The farmer held out a cheese wedge and said something cheery, including the word for gift.

A panzergrenadier poked his head into the kitchen. "The house is clear, Hauptscharfuhrer."

"We take the road east to Douville then." Behr took the cheese, reached in his pocket, and dropped a tattered ten-franc note on the table.

Exiting the house a squad leader asked, "Shouldn't we question the little Frog?"

"Nein. If he knows anything, he'll lie for at least the first hour. Meanwhile the Ami gangsters escape. Take your squad and sweep north on foot."

*   *   *

2230 Hours

In a darkening pasture corner, sheltered by intersecting hedgerows, Sam and Lazeski tended Phillips's wound. Using the sheet and cheesecloth, they redressed the wound and loosened the tourniquet.

Sam's melancholy funk grew as nightfall approached. The lack of landmarks left him uncertain of their exact location, but he and Springwater concurred that they had put enough distance between themselves and the bridge. It seemed that the Germans hadn't pressed the pursuit into the maze of hedgerows.

Northward, the rumble of distant artillery sounded like an approaching thunderstorm. Phillips's groans grew louder and more frequent. Sam jabbed another precious morphine Syrette into Phillips's thigh. "We run out of morphine, and he gets loud. Then we're sunk."

Lazeski rose. "I'll ask around again. Just one Syrette per first aid kit though."

Sam hovered over Phillips on the makeshift stretcher. *Sleep, Phillips. Just sleep. We'll get you back.*

Having looked after his men, Sam turned to his own needs. He found the bandage on his shoulder secure enough. *Good thing. We've got none left.* He applied the salve to his scorched and cut face. He'd forgotten the sutures high on his cheek until his fingers bumped the bristled knots. He turned to Pinball. "You keeping that horse liniment on your ankle?"

"Rubbed some in five minutes ago."

"Good. Mind if I borrow some for my hip?"

As Sam rubbed horse medicine into his skin, he considered their food situation. The last of the three-day supply of D-ration fortified chocolate bars was being devoured. *Have we been here only three days? More like three lifetimes. What did General Taylor say? 'Give me three days of hard fighting and then back to England.' Maybe they'll pay overtime. Add it to our jump-pay.* He had a small chuckle, then recalled a visit to a Fort Benning watering hole where a half-drunk OCS cadre had referred to jump-pay as blood money. Sam's mirth ceased. Operation Neptune had proven the cynical major a prophet.

The cheese wheel circulated. Using his trench knife, Sam cut himself a wedge. The cheese's soft texture and strong mushroomy aroma offered an unappetizing contrast to the chocolate.

Around 0130 hours the sounds of singing drifted into their impromptu bivouac. The words were foreign, yet there was no mistaking the melody of "Lili Marlene." The singers drifted eastward. *Troops expecting combat don't sing.* Sam's sense of dread grew.

What's Maggie doing tonight? How much does she know? Probably not enough...and way too much. He sat a mere hundred miles from Overton. Yet it might as well have been thousands of miles—like North Africa, where she'd lost her first love. Did he even have the right to consider himself her second?

He longed for a photo of Maggie.

"Maggie, Maggie, what have I done to you?" he mumbled. *Time to face facts—odds are stacked way against me getting out of this mess. I can't leave her like Ian did. I can at least spare her that pain.*

Darkness prevented him from putting thoughts to paper. Yet he had to write. He had to tell Maggie that she was right. He'd been wrong—a wrongheadedness born out of naiveté and intellectual pride. What a selfish fool he'd been to promise he would return. He wasn't choosing his fate. Not here in this endless maze of Norman hedgerows and marshes. Here he was merely reacting to the unrelenting and ugly circumstances hurled at him like un-hittable screwballs.

Sam reflected back on the heady days at UCLA. Surely, something there would help him get his bearings. Yet, try as he might, he failed to get the academic philosophical propositions to make sense amidst the maelstrom of war. He hadn't given up on reconciling the two. Never. He just needed three ingredients—time, sleep, and a respite from the chaos. He smirked. *Like I'll live long enough to see that day.*

*   *   *

9 June 1944, 0915 Hours

Sam studied the Carentan map. The direct rays of the morning sun warmed his back as he listened to his scouts' recon report.

"Don't like it," Springwater said. "We're backed up along the railroad tracks again. Other side's all water. There's this little village just northeast of us." Springwater pointed at a collection of tiny black rectangles on the map.

Sam read, Pommenauque. "Puts us real close to Carentan." Sam ran his fingers back through his dirty hair. "Could you see Carentan?"

Collin spit a brown stream. "A dern hill blocked us."

"How about across the river valley?"

Springwater shrugged. "Smoke, haze, glare. It's all flooded."

"Troop movement?"

"Reckon there's enough arty spotters and snipers both sides of the valley," Collins said. "Ain't no one fixin' to get caught out in the open in broad daylight."

Sam looked Springwater in the eye. "Can't just sit here."

Springwater shifted his Thompson to his other arm. "Wait for cover of darkness."

"But Phillips?"

"Move out there in the daylight and a lot more could die."

Focused on the map, Sam tried to gauge the distance to the Douve River crossing. "What then? Make a mad dash for Catz?"

Springwater shrugged. "Or maybe…" He slid his long finger along a map line depicting the railroad connecting Carentan to Cherbourg. "The causeway seemed abandoned. We can move hidden, low along the west bank."

"Shortest route, no doubt." Sam jabbed his finger into the map. "But Second Battalion was supposed to blow those rail bridges."

"If the Second got dropped anything like us, I doubt they got the job done. If so, we rig a way to float Phillips across."

Sam frowned. "We're shy on choices."

"We're dang close, Lieutenant," Collins said.

"We've only got about sixteen hours worth of morphine left. Maybe eighteen if we stretch it thin. Infection has me concerned. Can't see us carrying Phillips clear to Catz. Krauts will be concentrated there, too." Sam removed his helmet and ran his fingers back through his hair. "OK, we use the rail causeway and cross under cover of darkness."

*   *   *

1350 Hours

Sam rummaged through his musette bag until he found a writing tablet. Words flew onto paper, yet failed to satisfy his intent. He wadded the page into a tight ball.

How do I write that I chose to play this deadly game and lost? How do I express regret for dragging her in? How do I say, goodbye, forever? Oh, and P.S., please remember me. How do I write this while I fight to avoid death with every shrinking ounce of mental and physical energy? What good is potential love when life is extinguished?

No great philosopher's teaching filled the void. No logical arguments—constructed like mathematical formulas—came to mind. Maybe life was, indeed, as Dr. Rosenfeld had proposed—absurd, meaningless.

Everyone dies. Did I really think I could choose the when, where, and how? There's only one way to do that. Dr. Rosenfeld's way. Suicide. Sam recalled his arguments against that at the Piccadilly cathouse.

Maggie deserved closure. He transferred his thoughts and love onto paper, and stuffed the letter in an envelope. He wrote "Miss Margaret Elliott" across the front, and paused. Where to address it? Overton or London? He settled on 47 Albert Street. She'd need the comfort of home.

He sought out the only messenger he trusted unconditionally. Springwater was cleaning his Thompson. Sam held out the envelope. The Crow warrior looked up with questioning eyes.

"If I don't make it, see to it Maggie gets this."

Expressionless, Springwater took the letter and slipped it into a waterproof pouch hidden in a secure pocket inside his jacket.

Sam shrugged. "The Army won't notify her. Can't leave her hanging in limbo. It wouldn't be right."

"Is it right for our warriors to get wind of their lieutenant singing his death song?" Springwater's dark eyes were penetrating. "Do *not* quit on them, Sam. They need you."

Chapter 56

The Causeway

10 June 1944, 0023 Hours
Near Carentan, Normandy

Sam sloshed through knee-deep floodwater. The moon had not yet risen. With each step into the inky void he strained to see the deeper darkness of the elevated causeway contrasted against the night sky.

To the north, the battle for the Cotentin Peninsula had quieted. Only the occasional explosion or machinegun burst sounded in the far distance.

The plan called for them to hit the causeway at the first bridge outside the hamlet of Pommenauque and head north along the railroad causeway. Their progress in the flooded marsh was slower than he'd plotted on the map. They crossed three submerged drainage ditches. Each time, without warning, the water became chest-deep. Passing Phillips over the ditches had proven troublesome. Keeping Phillips's wound dry had proven impossible. Sam refused to dwell on what the stagnant water might do to Phillips's haphazardly dressed wound. Sam found his own struggle in keeping his bayonet gash dry and his weapons and ammo from becoming waterlogged.

He slogged forward at the tip of the squad diamond formation. Lazeski took position on Sam's left flank, Springwater on the right. Collins and Harrigan served as stretcher-bearers in the diamond's center. Silva brought up the rear.

None too soon, the rail embankment loomed ahead. Sam discerned geometric shadows indicating a bridge. If so, his navigation had put them right on target. His pulse rate quickened.

He raised his hand to signal a halt. Water lapped against his thighs. Sloshing noises diminished while men relayed the signal back. Sam stared into shades of darkness and strained his ears.

Nothing.

The moon was brightening the thin clouds on the eastern horizon. He wanted out of the open water flats—devoid of all cover—before moonlight exposed them.

He motioned Springwater forward. The Crow warrior advanced, lightly sloshing.

A guttural German challenge broke the silence.

Sam crouched.

Atop the embankment a muzzle flashed. An automatic weapon chattered. Water geysers erupted around Springwater. He disappeared.

Sam cringed. *So, this is how it all ends.*

A disembodied voice shouted more German. A flat pop sounded. An illumination flare arched and hissed across the sky. In the artificial light he caught a glimpse of movement on the rails.

Prevent the slaughter! Sam opened his mouth to order surrender.

Two muffled shots stopped him.

Burning magnesium cast eerie light. The nightmarish scene fell silent. The rails seemed abandoned.

Sam dashed through water for the minimal cover the embankment offered. His men followed. He dove against the packed earth and rocks. Excruciating pain from his hip and shoulder forced his eyes shut. White flashes exploded behind his eyelids.

"Bunker, left!" Lazeski said.

Sam opened his eyes and raised his head.

"Got sandbags, south flank too!" Pinball said.

"Phillips is clear." Silva flopped next to Sam and scanned the tracks for targets.

The flare cast flickering shadows, making movement appear jittery, like a silent movie.

"Cover me. Ted's still out there." Sam pivoted toward the water. A hand hooked on his web belt. "Let go! I saw where he went under."

Silva yanked him back and pointed under the bridge.

Sam raised his rifle, expecting to see an attacking German squad. His sights landed on Springwater standing under the bridge—Thompson ready, searching for threats.

The flare sputtered and dimmed.

A voice called out. *"Kamerad! Bitte! Kamerad!"*

Their faces inches apart, Sam and Silva exchanged bewildered looks. Sam pushed up on his elbows and stretched his neck.

A pale rag waved on a rifle barrel. The voice, not sounding German, called out. "*Pazhalsta!* Vee vant sur-een-durr! *Amerikansky* good! *Roos-see-velt khar-a-sho-ye! Ghitler kaput! Stal-een ochen ploh-kha-ye! Pazhalsta!*" Additional unintelligible, yet subdued voices reached Sam.

The flare died.

Lazeski yelled a string of incomprehensible words. A voice answered in a compliant tone. Lazeski responded.

Lazeski plopped down next to Sam. "Lieutenant, they want to surrender. Give the word they'll lay down their weapons. He claims there's eight of them."

"I want to see eight men, no guns, side-by-side, *hande hoch*, standing facing us."

Lazeski rattled in the foreign tongue. More than a dozen hands appeared, followed by frightened faces, then bodies. Bodies draped in Wehrmacht greatcoats.

Sam rose, staring over his M-1 barrel. "Order them to all turn about-face."

Lazeski relayed the command. The captives refused. Lazeski shouted the order again. The surrendering soldiers fidgeted. One stepped forward and spoke.

"They're afraid we'll pop them in the back," Lazeski said. "He expected better treatment from Americans."

Sam raised his head from his rifle. "Tell them they're my prisoners and will do as I say. We won't shoot."

Lazeski translated and one-by-one the enemy soldiers pivoted. Some hunched their shoulders or bowed their heads.

Flanking the captives, Springwater inched his way up the embankment.

Sam glanced south toward Pommenauque, anticipating enemy troops coming to investigate the commotion. "Laze, have them walk backwards, hands up, nice and slow, one at a time." Sam turned to Harrigan. "Get up top. You and Springwater look for anything we can use." Sam looked around. "Collins, Silva, go a hundred yards south and listen."

"How about me, sir?" Morton appeared at Sam's side.

"You, Wellston, and Pinball hold the prisoners right here until we get this mess sorted out." The first two prisoners reached the bottom of the embankment. "Lazeski, keep them quiet."

Sam couldn't tell much in the dark, yet his first good look at his prisoners told him that something wasn't ringing true. *Don't look very Aryan.* Pushing paranoia aside, he climbed the embankment.

He found Harrigan checking a pile of weapons stacked between the tracks. Scattered helmets and assorted kit littered the ground. An obese German was slumped over sandbags. Sam rolled the body over and noted two dark holes over the man's heart. An MP-40 hung from the man's neck. Sam picked it up, smelled the ejection port, and felt the barrel. It was warm. *The guy shooting at Springwater?* Yet, that failed to explain the two holes in his chest.

Something felt odd underfoot. He reached under his boot and picked up a revolver with a small grip. *I've never seen one like this before.* He fumbled around and pushed, but the cylinder refused to swing open. So he sniffed where the cylinder met the barrel. Sam dropped the revolver in his jacket pocket and walked to Springwater. "One of those clowns down there shot that dead ape pointblank with a revolver. What'd you find?"

"An MG-Forty-two. Another light machinegun with a pan magazine on top. Seven old bolt-action rifles. Not Mausers." Springwater held up a wooden-stocked, submachine gun with a drum magazine. "And this."

The submachine gun jogged Sam's memory. He remembered an S-2 briefing about the possibility of encountering Red Army turncoats. Germans called them *Ost*—for east—battalions. He slid down the embankment. "Laze, exactly who are these soldiers?"

"Red Army POWs. They joined what they're calling the R-O-A. Short for Russian Liberation Army. They were all captured in forty-one near the Polish frontier."

"Laze, what are you doing speaking Russian? Aren't you Polish?"

"My family has zero use for Poles, sir. I grew up speaking about as much Russian as English."

"You told me you didn't speak any other languages."

"Beg to differ, sir. You asked who spoke French or German. I don't."

"Be a little less literal and more forthcoming in the future, Laze. Now, I need to know which one shot the guy they left up there."

Lazeski pulled his glasses off and wiped away the splashed water as Russian flowed off his lips. Before Lazeski finished, a barrel-chested soldier with a drooping mustache stepped forward and spoke. Even in the dim moonlight, pronounced lines fanned out from the corner of the man's narrow eyes. The ROA man slapped the back of his fingers into his palm to punctuate his words.

Sam feared he was leaving his men exposed, vulnerable. "We don't have all night. Give me the bottom line, Laze."

Lazeski turned to Sam. "Sergeant Shevchenko says he killed the, and I quote, 'fat fascist pig.' As a group, they decided a month ago to kill their Nazi minder and surrender to the first Allied troops they saw. Says they signed on to liberate *Rodina Mat*—that's the Motherland—from the butcher Stalin. Not to fight Americans. They like Americans. Now they're excited to go to America."

Sam sighed and looked upward to the dark sky. "His surrender's a tad premature." Sam took off his helmet and ran his fingers back through his hair. "We need to get far away from here. Get them to the top."

Lazeski put six of the prisoners to work getting Phillips and the rickety stretcher up the embankment.

On the tracks, Sam sent Morton to retrieve Collins and Silva. He kept four prisoners carrying the stretcher. Phillips moaned. Sam looked at his watch and took out the last Syrette of morphine. He jabbed the injection into the semiconscious paratrooper's thigh and patted Phillips's good leg. "Not long now, Phillips. Just across this causeway. You'll be in England for afternoon tea." He turned to Lazeski. "Do they have any morphine?"

Lazeski translated. Shevchenko laughed and said, "*Nyet.*"

Sam faced north. "I want absolute noise discipline. Laze, make sure our Russian friends know what that means."

A knot of anticipation grew in Sam's gut. Just one more mile, two at the most—free of confounding hedgerow mazes—and they'd cross American lines.

He'd walked fifteen yards when a hand tugged his left shoulder. He grimaced and ducked out from under the hand.

"Sorry, sir. That your hurt shoulder?" Morton said. "I was afraid of making noise."

"What's the problem?"

"Sergeant Lazeski, sir. Well, not actually him, it's the Rooskies."

"And...?"

"They refuse to budge, sir."

Sam stomped back and shot Lazeski an angry glance. The Russians were all squatting on their haunches. "What's the problem, Sergeant?"

"Sergeant Shevchenko says they won't go that way."

"Douve River Bridge out? We expect that. We're going that way anyway. Moving out, now."

Lazeski translated and listened. He waved a hand and stopped Shevchenko mid-sentence. Lazeski's face looked alarmed. "All the bridges are up. Looks like Second Battalion didn't—"

"A little hard when we're flung all the hell over France," Wellston said in defense of his battalion.

Lazeski shushed Wellston. "The problem's bigger than that. According to Shevchenko, what's left of the Sixth Fallschirmjager Regiment is retreating from St. Come-du-Mont down these tracks sometime in the next hour or two. That's why they were here. To make contact with the Kraut paratroopers and cover their retreat. They thought we were the lead elements of an American force sent to cut off the Sixth. They now realize they're badly mistaken."

Sam's jaw dropped. Springwater sent Silva and Collins north a hundred yards as a listening post for the approaching German paratroopers.

Sam scowled. "I think he's lying. Tell him."

Lazeski spoke and listened to Shevchenko's retort. "He says, think whatever you want. You can lead your men to certain death. He won't. He knows another way."

"How?"

"Through Catz." Lazeski interpreted as the Russian spoke. "There's a way across held by Americans. Near Brevands."

"So we've heard," Sam said and gave Springwater a questioning look.

Springwater shrugged. "So we go back to Plan A."

"And the Russians?" Sam asked.

"Take them with us," Springwater said. "They know the area. Might help us, because as of ten minutes ago they're all as good as dead if they stay."

Morton leaned close to Sam. "Sir, they're just lousy Reds. Geronimo takes no prisoners. May I suggest we just—"

"No, you may not, Morton." Springwater cocked back his fist. "You can shut your pie hole and go relieve Collins. We need a scout."

Morton glowered and backed away into the darkness.

"Can we risk trusting them?" Sam walked to Shevchenko before Springwater could answer. Shevchenko rose off his haunches. Sam stepped to within inches of the weathered face. "Why should I trust a traitor? Changing sides every chance he gets."

Lazeski translated. "Do you have a choice? You also have no idea what a butcher Roosevelt's ally, Stalin, is. He's murdered millions for his precious revolution." Lazeski swallowed hard. "And he's right sir. Half my father's family was killed by—"

"I don't need your editorial commentary or family history." Sam expected bullets or artillery to shower them at any moment. "Not the time or place. Just translate, Laze."

"Fine, sir. He also says you have no idea what it's like to starve as a lice-ridden slave. He says you've never lived in the squalor of some camp called Bergen-Belsen, so you're in no position to pass moral judgment."

"He exaggerates. The Soviet Union is our ally. The Germans are signatories to the Geneva Convention."

Lazeski translated. Shevchenko spit through his long mustache whiskers and spoke in staccato bursts.

"I'll spare you a word-for-word translation, Lieutenant. Let's just say our prisoner wants to know if all American officers are—his words, not mine, sir—so naïve. I think you hit a raw nerve."

Shevchenko stepped back and changed his tone.

"He thinks he knows how to get his men and us to our lines. But we must hurry and get off this causeway. He also thinks carrying Phillips will draw attention and keep us from reaching Brevands before dawn."

"I'll hear him out," Sam said.

Huddling together, Sam, Springwater, Lazeski, and Shevchenko outlined a hasty plan.

Sam broke the huddle. "Harrigan, grab the MG-Forty-two. Have some Russians carry ammo cans and that Russian machinegun, unloaded. Silva, remove the bolts out of the rifles but hang on to them. Give the other Russians a disabled rifle. Wellston, gather up any grenades. Everyone, be quick about it."

Lazeski carried the submachine gun after Shevchenko gave a rapid lesson on its operation. The Russians donned their German helmets and ammo belts, returning to a combat ready appearance. Silva and Collins dumped the dead Nazi minder under the bridge.

They had to reach Brevands before sunrise.

Chapter 57

Restlessness

A green signal flare streaked across the northern horizon.

A look of vindication on his face, Shevchenko informed Sam that the lead elements of the 6th Fallschirmjager were crossing the causeway.

"I hope he's not just making this all up as we go." Sam took off his helmet and ran his fingers back through his hair. His hand came away dripping sweat.

They hid in the darker recesses of a pasture occupied by speckled cows. Sam had advanced the anxious band of misdropped Americans and displaced Russians along the rails, past Pommenauque. From there, Shevchenko had guided them south down a dirt road. Collins and Springwater were scouting the route Shevchenko had suggested. The perpetual presence of Sam's 45-auto pointed at Shevchenko's barrel chest didn't seem to perturb the Russian.

Metallic crickets announced the scouts' return.

Springwater reported, "Just like the Russian described it. Long stone stables. Right at the base of Hill Thirty on the map, by La Billonnerie. It's quiet. No one moving around but a couple sentries."

"Russians?" Sam asked.

"Couldn't tell. But there're wagons. And I could smell many horses,"

Assigning Morton to guard the Russians, Sam pulled the rest of his men into a huddle. "OK, everything rides on this roll of the dice. Springwater, Collins, Lazeski, and I are taking our Russian friend to borrow some wheels. Should be back within the hour. Harrigan, while we're gone you've got rank. You hear *any* shooting within a quarter-mile east, forget the Russians and make a break for Brevands. Got it?"

"Yes, sir."

Sam slipped out the hedgerow gate, following Springwater and Collins toward the wagon yard. Lazeski and Shevchenko trailed. Within fifteen minutes, they crawled up a slight rise in a pasture. Sam made out a long, one-story stable in a glen. Shevchenko claimed the stable housed his ROA company. Behind the stable rose a small hill with scattered buildings. At least a dozen wagons were parked in the pasture between them and the stable. A sentry patrolled.

The group quick-crawled to the wagons while Lazeski covered them with the Russian submachine gun. They halted at a cargo wagon with hard-rubber tires. Lazeski rejoined them. Springwater and Collins snuck off on their mission.

Sam inspected the wagon. The wooden sides were two feet high. The bed was about the size of his Uncle's Ford logging truck. A canvas tarp lay folded in the center of the bed. The leather harness riggings and horse collars were laid out on top the tarp.

He leaned close to Lazeski. "This one will do. Big enough. Has a tarp." He ducked under the wagon. Lazeski and Shevchenko followed.

A sentry passed. Shevchenko claimed the man was ROA.

Ten minutes later Springwater and Collins crawled up, empty-handed.

A queasy feeling grew in Sam's stomach. "Where are the freakin' horses?"

Springwater's dark eyes remained calm. "Not there."

Sam felt ready to explode. "You said you smelled them."

"I did. Found the picket line. Horses were gone."

Sam ran his fingers through his hair. "Lazeski, find out where the horses are."

Lazeski whispered foreign syllables in the Shevchenko's ear, listened, and translated. "Sometimes they're hobbled in the orchard behind the stable. Be careful. Shevchenko says not all ROA men are as eager to surrender."

Springwater and Collins crawled into the darkness.

A sentry sneezed. Minutes passed. Through the jumble of wagon wheels Sam watched sentry boots patrol.

Staying propped up on his elbows made his bayonet laceration ache. Dropping flat to his belly offered some relief, but forced him to crane his neck to see anything. Soon his bruised hip ached, too. He needed more horse liniment. Foreign whispers distracted him from his restlessness.

Lazeski leaned close to Sam's ear. "Shevchenko wants to know what you did before the war. I told him you were a student. He wants to know what of."

"Literature and philosophy. I wanted to be a teacher." Sam shook his head at the absurdity of the question. "Why does it matter now?"

Lazeski and Shevchenko exchanged whispers.

"He says you have a poet's eyes. That's a great compliment from a Slav."

Two sneezes came from their right. Sam twisted toward the noise and pointed his M-1 at a pair of boots forty feet away.

Something rustled. He twisted back left. Shevchenko had vanished.

The sentry challenged. Shevchenko replied in Russian. The sentry trotted away.

"I knew it! I'm not dying like a trapped rat." Sam pushed himself forward and crouched between the rows of wagons. "Should've never been conned by that traitor."

Lazeski followed Sam's example. The Russian submachine gun gave Lazeski a foreign silhouette. It also gave Sam an idea. "Lose the helmet. If we're challenged, stand up with that gun and bluff our way out in Russian."

Heavy hoofbeats vibrated the ground. Sam looked under the wagon. On the opposite side eight enormous hoofs appeared. He moved toward them.

Springwater rode bareback astride a massive chestnut horse. The horse's flaxen mane and tail glowed in the moonlight. Paratrooper rope trailed from Springwater's hand and led to another mammoth horse. The second horse's dapple-gray coloring gave it a ghost-like appearance.

Collins jogged up and jumped into the wagon bed. He lifted the bridle and blinders and placed them over the dapple-gray's head. Lazeski harnessed the chestnut.

Dismounting, Springwater slid down the Chestnut's side. He paused, gripping a fistful of flaxen mane while his feet searched for the ground, and dropped off.

Sam stepped beside Springwater. "Our Russian guide skipped out."

Springwater scowled and nodded, before helping Lazeski with the collar and hames.

Expecting to hear the alarm raised at any instant, Sam joined in on the dapple-gray and hooked the traces. The beast dwarfed his Missouri mule, yet the memory in his hands operated without flaw despite his years in Los Angeles.

The rushed harnessing finished, Collins checked the traces and gave Sam a bewildered look. Collins climbed onto the bench seat, gave the reins a light flick, and made quiet clucking noises to get the wagon rolling. Lazeski stood in the wagon bed, brandishing the Russian submachine gun.

Sam jumped into the wagon bed as the wheels broke out of their compressed ruts. He and Springwater dropped flat. Across the dark wagon-lot he caught glimpses of men bobbing and darting toward them. He aimed his M-1 out the back. Springwater joined with his heavy-slugged Thompson.

The bobbing heads gained on them.

Sam whispered over his shoulder, "We've got company coming up our six. Collins, keep it slow. Laze, bluff first." The advancing men perplexed Sam. *Why aren't they raising the alarm?*

The lead man threw up his hands. Sam recognized the walrus mustache centered above the barrel chest.

"*Tovarish, stoityeh, pazhalsta!*"

Lazeski knelt down. "He wants us to wait."

Shevchenko turned around and raised his hands higher. His entourage followed his example. While some carried rifles slung behind shoulders, not a single man brandished a weapon.

"Stop," Sam said. Weapons ready, he and Lazeski leapt out the wagon.

Shevchenko smiled. The moonlight revealed gaps in his teeth. He spoke in hushed tones. Lazeski translated. "How could I leave comrades who also dream of freedom? We're done with Stalin and Hitler. We must hurry before these men are missed."

Sam restrained himself from ramming his rifle butt into Shevchenko's gut. "Tell them to hop on." He took a deep breath. "Springwater, take the bolts out of every rifle. Pat each man down. No grenades. No bayonets"

"*Spaceeba bolshoiye,*" Shevchenko said and rattled on.

"He says thank you very much but he thinks you chose the wrong horses. They call the gray, Adolph, after Hitler. And the chestnut, Joseph, after Stalin. They refuse to work together. Both insist on being the dominant horse. Neither knows when he's beat."

Sam exhaled hard. "I'm afraid we're stuck with Adolph and Joseph."

As if on cue, the dapple-gray bit the chestnut's neck. Joseph whinnied and kicked. Collins tried to calm the pair.

As Shevchenko brushed past to climb on the wagon, Sam grabbed his arm and yanked him close. Sam's anger overpowered the repulsion he found in the garlic, stale tobacco, and tooth rot on Shevchenko's breath. "Try to leave us again and I will blow your freakin' head off. Translate, Laze!" Lazeski translated with passion.

"*Koneshna, Gospodin.*" Shevchenko grinned. "*Koneshna!*"

"Of course, Master. Of course!" Lazeski translated.

Yet the mischievous glimmer in the Russian's eyes told Sam that he didn't believe he'd do it. Sam's mind flashed back to the Voluptuous Vixen cockpit. "You don't want to try me, Sergeant Shevchenko."

Sam counted sixteen Russians before he and Lazeski jumped into the back of the overloaded wagon and departed.

*   *   *

10 June 1944, 0430 Hours
Overton, England

Muffled footfalls distracted Maggie from reading the 139th Psalm.

Mrs. Weatherall appeared across the darkened sitting room in Overton. Maggie turned her face away and wiped tear tracks from her cheeks.

"Maggie?"

"Couldn't sleep. I've this dreadful feeling." Maggie couldn't elaborate on the lump in her stomach that had nagged at her for hours.

Mrs. Weatherall turned up the lantern and took Maggie's chin in hand. She applied gentle upward pressure until they were face-to-face. "A lass your age shouldn't have dark circles under her eyes. You need your sleep."

Maggie turned her head away from Mrs. Weatherall's grasp. "I felt prompted…like something was terribly amiss with—"

"Please take no offense, Maggie, but there's simply no way you can know. Perhaps you should stop listening to the BBC. Our appointed lot is to endure. We'll hear enough in due time."

Maggie closed her Bible and thought, *Just like I heard from Ian.*

Chapter 58

The Bakery

10 June 1944, 0500 Hours
Catz, Normandy

The clatter of exchanged small arms and mortars grew closer.

Aside from Adolph and Joseph's constant jostling for dominance, the four-mile roundabout route to Catz had proven uneventful.

Phillips was lying in the center of the wagon bed. Silva, Wellston, Pinball, and Morton surrounded the wounded trooper. Springwater and Harrigan faced backward, prone—automatic weapons trained on the twenty-two ROA soldiers marching behind. Sixteen Russians carried disabled rifles and one an empty light machinegun, thus reinforcing the façade of a deploying military unit.

Collins and Lazeski had draped ROA greatcoats over their shoulders and wore Russian caps. Shevchenko sat next to Collins on the teamster's bench seat. Lazeski stood behind them, Russian submachine gun slung across his chest. A canvas tarp covered the other paratroopers. Only Sam, in front, or Springwater and Harrigan, in the rear, could peer outward. Sam hid in the front of the wagon-bed, below and behind Shevchenko.

They had encountered scattered groups of Germans, including walking wounded. Aside from their wagon, all traffic was going one-way—southwest, away from Catz. Some Germans tried to engage in conversation, however all interaction ceased when they discovered the platoon was Russian Liberation Army. The ruse was holding.

Sam peeked out from under the tarp and frowned. Traces of yellow and pink on the northeastern horizon announced the coming dawn. The silhouetted outline of Catz stood a good 400 yards away. *How do I get us across the front lines from Catz to Brevands?* Sam gnawed his lower lip. *How'd I fail to even consider that 'til now?* The prospect of crossing the front lines before sunrise was ebbing fast. *You're rounding third, heading for home. Don't get desperate. Don't get tagged out now.*

A wagon wheel dropped into a pothole. Phillips emitted a long moan.

Sam ducked further under the tarp. "Somebody gag him." He laid his palm flat on Phillips's forehead. Even his untrained hand recognized a raging fever. The putrid-sweet smell told Sam that the early stages of gas gangrene had set in. Yet that hardly represented the most urgent cause for alarm. A dose of morphine was past due. The supply was exhausted. Silva gently tied a gag. Phillips squirmed and mumbled gibberish through the cloth. Sam stuck his head out from under the tarp and gulped fresh air.

Shevchenko hand-rolled and lit a cigarette. The smoke drifted back. Sam almost gagged on the Russian's rank tobacco. The Russian chatted.

Lazeski whispered in Sam's direction. "A couple Kraut MPs ahead. Directing traffic. Shevchenko doesn't like the looks of it."

The wagon rolled another minute and stopped. A German spoke with the air of authority universal to police. Shevchenko conversed in faltering German.

Pointing his 45-auto at Shevchenko's back, Sam glanced out below the bench seat and through the Russian's legs. He caught sight of a heavy chained gorget displayed outside a dark leather coat. Below the oversized badge hung a menacing MP-40.

The German MP chuckled and waved the wagon forward.

Anxious to escape scrutiny, Collins snapped the reins with too much vigor. In their competition to lead, the chestnut and dapple gray lurched. The wagon jolted forward. Phillips cried out.

The German threw up a hand and grabbed the pistol grip of his MP-40. "*Hahlt!*"

Collins yanked the reins.

"*Wer da?*" the MP demanded.

Sam tensed his muscles, ready to leap out blasting away.

Shevchenko laughed and flicked his middle finger against his throat three times—making a hollow slapping sound—as he conversed. Sam understood one word. Vodka.

The German shook his head and waved them on.

Collins clicked his tongue and jiggled the reins.

Sam collapsed. He hoped the others couldn't feel his knees shaking.

Rolling into the village of Catz, the sound of hobnailed boots passed along both sides of the wagon. A nearby MG-42 ripped a long burst. Outgoing mortars popped leaving their tubes. The wagon turned right onto rough cobblestones. They rolled for thirty seconds and jerked into a left turn up a short incline.

Phillips groaned through his gag.

The wagon sat motionless. Shevchenko disappeared. Without explanation, Lazeski shed the ROA greatcoat and jumped off.

It seemed like minutes passed without any sound, apart from faint hobnailed boots on pavement and small arms fire.

Sam couldn't stand the mental fog another instant. He holstered his pistol and gripped his M-1. Before he could rid himself of the tarp shroud, someone yanked it away.

He leveled his M-1 in the direction the tarp was pulled. His sights landed on Lazeski. Springwater was already out and moving toward the corner of a light-colored stucco building. Sam found himself in a narrow alley sandwiched between three-story structures. The eastern horizon was brightening.

"First door on the right." Lazeski's eyes looked frantic. "Someone give me a hand with Phillips. Let's go! Move it!"

Sam vaulted over the sideboards. Despite the painful jolt to his hip, he ran in the direction he'd seen Springwater disappear. He rounded the corner and saw the Russians in loose groups, some pretending to work on equipment or loading their disabled rifles. The wall they formed and predawn darkness screened the view from the main road just sixty yards away.

He caught a glimpse of heavily armed Germans retreating down the main road. *What's going on?* He trotted past a shop window labeled *Boulangerie* and ducked into the first door, finding himself standing in a bare-shelved bakery. The scent of bread and flour clung to the vacant interior.

"Heads up! Coming through!"

He moved aside. Lazeski and Wellston rushed past carrying Phillips on the makeshift stretcher. Pinball limped in carrying Lazeski's M-1 and the Russian submachine gun. Sam's ignorance of what was going on planted a seed of fear in him.

Harrigan and Silva ducked through the front door. Harrigan toted the MG-42.

Springwater appeared bounding down a stairway from the second floor. "Collins, get up on the third floor to keep an eye on the main road. Harrigan and Wellston on the second floor with the machinegun, cover all approaches to the front."

Sam snagged Springwater's arm. "What's going on, Ted?"

"Shevchenko says we need to hole up right here."

Sam glared. "When did Shevchenko start giving orders?"

"There's a whole Kraut company right outside. Building's deserted. We need to set up a defense." Springwater shook his head. "Morton, get out of that window. Go downstairs. You're guarding the Russians. Silva, I want you and Pinball on the front door. Keep out of sight and keep Pinball off that ankle."

The ROA platoon, led by Shevchenko, paraded past Sam and disappeared into the back. Morton tried putting on an intimidating scowl as he waved each Russian past with his rifle barrel. More than one Russian looked at him and snickered.

"If you need me, sir, I'll be in the basement keeping the Reds under control," Morton said.

Lazeski moved back down the hall. "Shevchenko wants to talk, Lieutenant."

Sam's head pounded. "What for?" He squeezed the bridge of his nose. "Does he have orders for me?"

Lazeski looked puzzled. "He just wants to give an explanation. If you ask me, sir, he's sure pulled our fat out of the fire."

Sam took his helmet off and ran trembling fingers back through his hair. "Our fat won't be out of this fire 'til we're all across our lines."

Lazeski shrugged and led the way through a backroom of commercial ovens. He pushed a door open. Morton stood on the other side smoking a Chesterfield while perched on a wooden landing atop the basement stairs.

A layer of blue cigarette smoke floated above the crowded Russians. None sat, rather they all squatted on their haunches—arms resting thrust forward on knees. The disabled rifles were propped in a corner.

Sam and Lazeski descended wooden stairs into the olfactory cocktail of dank basement mildew, Phillips's putrefied wound, unwashed male bodies, damp wool, and Russian tobacco. Shevchenko carried one of the three lanterns lighting the basement and leaned over Phillips.

Sam wove through the ROA men. Shevchenko spoke in normal conversational tones. After days of using a hushed voice, normal conversation sounded like shouts. Sam signaled Morton to close the door.

Morton bounced down the stairs like a puppy summoned by its master. "You need me, sir?"

"Just shut the door." Sam pressed his temples. "Wait. You got any aspirin?"

"No, sir. Gave mine to Skinner." Shoulders sagging, Morton returned to his post.

Shevchenko rambled on during Sam's exchange with Morton. Lazeski held up his hand to stop the Russian and turned to Sam. "That Kraut MP told him that they were pulling out of Catz, we should turn around."

Sam continued rubbing his temples. "Good thing to know."

"Shevchenko told him that we were an ROA heavy weapons platoon hauling machineguns and mortars. We had orders to fight a rearguard delaying action. The MP said he hadn't heard anything about an ROA rearguard. Which Shevchenko pointed out was just business as usual. They both had a good laugh, and the MP wished the ROA better luck than the Krauts were having." Lazeski extended his hand. Four white tablets lay in his palm. "Aspirin, sir?"

"Thanks, Laze." Sam popped all four tablets and took a swig from his canteen. "How about when that MP heard Phillips?"

Lazeski chuckled. "Shevchenko told him it was just some backward *muzhiek* who, fearing American gangsters, drank too much vodka."

"None of that explains why we're holed up here."

Lazeski translated and the Russian smiled.

"Too many Fascists on the road. It's getting light. Our masquerade couldn't last much longer. Like he said, Krauts are pulling out of Catz. Now we only need to wait. Our troops will come to us."

Sam shook his head. "Yeah, and they'll prep it with an artillery barrage first."

"That's exactly why he put his men down here in the basement."

"So now we wait. I guess it makes more sense than crossing two hostile lines."

Lazeski heaved a big sigh and touched Sam on the arm. "You got us out, Lieutenant Henry. After that FUBAR drop… Well, I figured my number was up. But now we're out of it."

"Not yet. And it's far from over for Phillips." He took another swig from his canteen. "Thank Shevchenko for me."

"You can, sir. It's easy. Just say, *spaceeba.*"

Sam looked at Shevchenko and stuck out his right hand. "Spah-cee-bah."

Shevchenko pumped his hand with a firm grip. "Pazhalsta, pazhalsta!"

"Sir, how come we got Japs fighting for the damn Nazis, with the Rooskies?"

Sam spun. Morton stood next to him. Sam said, "What the heck you talking about? And who said you could leave your post?"

Morton pointed across the basement and retreated up the stairs.

Sam followed Morton's point. The faces of the Russian troops, seen now for the first time in any real light, could have come out of the pages of his University High School, West Los Angeles yearbook. Round eyes and slanted eyes. Blond curls and straight black hair. Occidental and Oriental features, and many somewhere in between. One ROA man could've passed for Springwater's shorter brother. "These guys get easier to tell from the Krauts once you get them in the light."

Shevchenko gave a questioning glance and Lazeski offered a loose translation.

Shevchenko replied through Lazeski. "Says Russia is vast, hundreds of nationalities. Just in this basement we've got White Russians, an ethnic Finn, Kalmucks, Siberian nomads he calls *Chu-Chies*, Tartars, and, of course, Greater Russians. His mother was Russian, his father a Ukrainian in the Tsar's army. He grew up on the steppes between Kharkov and Belgorod." Lazeski smiled. "Not far from my relatives."

Sam noticed that Shevchenko had a leather case slung over his shoulder. "What's in the case?" Before Lazeski could interpret, Sam opened the latch and pulled out a pair of binoculars. "Do we ever need these!" He touched the Soviet hammer and sickle stamped opposite the 6x30. "Tell him they won't let POWs keep these."

Sam rummaged through his musette bag. "How about a trade? Two Lucky Strikes and a pack of Camels. One of the Lucky Strikes might've gotten a little damp. He's in serious need of a change of brands anyway. That stuff he smokes is pretty rank."

Shevchenko pulled the case over his head and handed it to Sam.

Pleased over the trade and waiting for the aspirin to kick in, Sam leaned back against the wall and let his back slide down. He came to rest sitting on the damp floor, his knees bent up to his chest.

Lazeski settled beside Sam, examined his wire-rimmed glasses by lantern light, and blew off dust specks. "Is now the right time and place, sir?"

Sam didn't move his head from resting on his forearm. "You've lost me."

"Back at the tracks. When Shevchenko refused to move. You said that wasn't the time or place for my family history."

"Is it that important to you?"

"Might put some perspective on what you've done for these ROA men."

Sam raised his head. "How's that?"

"Germany *will* lose the war. Every man in this basement knows that by now. Then Stalin will kill all these ROA soldiers. Either by summary execution for officers and NCOs, like Shevchenko, or twenty years in Siberia—same as a death sentence."

"Go on," Sam said.

"Well, sir, the Bolsheviks killed over half of my father's relatives. He was lucky to escape Russia with his life. Most had fought for the Whites. Those who survived stayed to farm the *chernozem*—that's rich black soil that would make any American farmer drool." Lazeski spit as if he was trying to get something bitter out of his mouth. "Stalin's a butcher. Roosevelt and Churchill are both fools for trusting the Bolsheviks."

"Tough choices, Sergeant Lazeski. Politics is a game of perpetual dilemmas, rife with compromise." Sam shook his head. "Sometimes we must choose compromise to achieve a greater good."

"Easy for you to say. My grandfather, father, and uncles were all labeled *kulaks*—enemies of the Revolution. In a kangaroo court the village Soviet tried them for exploitation of the proletariat, because during planting and harvest they hired some drunken *muzhiekie*. One uncle committed the high crime of owning three milk cows. Any more than one cow was a capitalistic exploitation of the masses. Cost him ten years in Siberia. My father escaped through Romania before his turn for a sham trial. And now we give that Georgian butcher trucks, tanks, planes, food."

"I've read Sholokhov's *And Quiet Flows the Don* series." Sam raised his head. "What you say sheds new—"

"Sholokhov?" Laze chortled. "Nothing but Red propaganda."

Shevchenko perked up. He asked a question and Lazeski explained. Shevchenko's response grew animated and harsh. He slapped the back of his fingers into his palm as he spoke.

"Shevchenko says Mikhail Sholokhov is both a liar and a thief. His books should be banned in a great and free nation like America. On the steppes it's common knowledge that Sholokhov stole the manuscript for the first two books from a dead White officer. It might be funny if it weren't so tragic. So Russian."

Phillips thrashed and groaned. Sam put a hand to Phillips's forehead. The fever had worsened.

Crackling roars pierced the air. A series of explosions shook the bakery. Dust rained down from the underside of the plank and beam floor.

Lazeski put his helmet back on and shielded his glasses from the falling dust.

The basement door flew open. The paratroopers rushed past Morton. Pinball trailed the group, limping. Springwater entered last, unhurried. More roars and explosions sounded. Morton took it upon himself to descend the stairs.

Springwater approached Sam. "Krauts hightailed it south. Main Street emptied. No reason to risk it up there."

More explosions rocked the basement.

"Not sure which is deadlier, the high explosives up there or the stench down here." Pinball frowned and fanned his hand in front of his face. "Makes me regret dumping my gas mask."

The explosions intensified. Dirt and dust particles cascaded. The lantern light flickered.

Silva lit a cigarette. "Pack seventy-fives. Mortars. Bigger than sixties."

Collins shoved chewing tobacco into his cheek. "When did you go 'n become a dang arty expert?"

"When I got hit by some, you big hillbilly."

Five more explosions in quick succession rocked the bakery. More debris dusted them. Men coughed.

The explosions ceased. Phillips moaned. Sam gazed up at the planks and beams. "That it?"

"Boys, I'm kinda new at all this," Wellston said, "but that sure sounded like artillery prep much lacking in enthusiasm."

"Everyone back to your posts." Sam got to his feet. "Morton, keep the Russians down here."

Morton unsheathed and fixed his bayonet.

"Ted, come with me." Sam said, bounding up the stairs three at a time, ignoring the ache in his hip. He slipped running through shattered window glass on the ground floor. Regaining his balance, he negotiated stairwells to the third floor. He ducked into a bedroom. Springwater pointed Sam toward the dormer with the best view.

Sam craned his neck to see about sixty yards away where the main road intersected with the bakery's side street. "Need a better view. Can we get on the roof?"

Movement flashed across the intersection.

Sam twisted and pressed the side of his head against the cracked glass to gain a better perspective.

A patch of greenish cloth streaked by.

Sam looked through the Russian field-glasses to try to find something more definitive—a helmet, M-1 rifle, musette bag, anything.

More olive-drab darted down the street.

A GI with a BAR took up a firing position at a corner. "Yes!" The automatic rifleman covered more GIs advancing into Catz.

Sam focused his binoculars on the net-covered helmet and made out the white stenciling of a playing-card club.

"The Three-Twenty-Seventh glider-riders! They're Screaming Eagles!"

PART IV

...INTO THE HAND OF BRUTISH MEN, SKILLFUL TO DESTROY.
Ezekiel 21:31

There should be nothing agreeable about warfare. God forbid that I should recommend brutality, but we face facts like men. It is not a trade for a philosopher.

CHARLES-JOSEPH LaMORAL
Prince De Linge, Belgium, 1735-1814

Chapter 59

Harsh Reality

10 June 1944, 0908 Hours
Catz, Normandy

"What you're saying about the Krauts quitting this berg sounds legit. But we're just a combat patrol. I'll have to pass it up the ladder to our S-two." The 327th Glider Infantry Regiment lieutenant spoke around a dangling, unlit cigarette. "Got no orders to hold this real estate. Maybe tomorrow. Today we're pulling back ASAP."

Sam refused to let the glider-rider's negativity squelch his elation. *From his accent, I'd bet he's a Brooklyn Dodger fan, too.*

Under an overcast morning sky, Sam stood on the cobblestone street outside the bakery. His men mingled with glider infantrymen and accepted K-ration breakfasts in exchange for stories about their misdropped misadventures.

An angry whinny came from around the corner.

The glider infantry lieutenant cringed. "So where'd you get dropped? We're hearing some wild tales."

A pimply-faced medic jogged out of the bakery. "Sorry to interrupt, sirs." He turned to Sam. "I've done all I can for your wounded guy. Morphine's kicked in, but he ain't got much longer if he don't get to a real doctor in a real hospital, real quick. They'll want to take that foot off, toot sweet."

The glider lieutenant frowned. "Then quit your yakking. Take four men and double-time the poor SOB to the battalion aid station."

The medic shook his head. "They won't be able to do nothing more for him, sir. I suggest we skip battalion aid and find him a jeep straight to Utah Beach. They'll tag him for the next LST sailing back to England"

"Your call, Doc. Just make it happen. These guys have been through holy hell already."

The medic called four names and reentered the bakery.

"How we doing?" Sam asked.

"The big picture?" The glider lieutenant shrugged. "My platoon, maybe my company, that much I can tell you about. We got off lucky, came in by sea through Utah with the Fourth ID. Beyond that?" He shrugged again. "Scuttlebutt has it the Five-O-Sixth and you Geronimos caught the brunt of it. You paratroopers got the Fourth off the beach on time. From what I hear, today is SUSFU—situation unchanged, still *fouled* up."

Four stretcher-bearers exited the bakery carrying Phillips. The medic walked alongside holding a plasma bottle high above Phillips.

"Excuse me, Lieutenant." Sam trotted to the stretcher. "Hang tough, Phillips. You chose parachute infantry. You didn't let Mount Currahee stop you, this won't—"

"He's all doped up, sir." The medic shook his head. "Can't talk."

"Doesn't mean he can't hear." Sam touched Phillips's shoulder. "I'll look you up in England." Sam backed away from the stretcher. Springwater, Lazeski, and Pinball got near Phillips and spoke encouraging words. Back with the glider infantry lieutenant, Sam said, "Forget the right drop zone, they didn't even get us on the right map."

"You think *you* had a bad pilot?" The glider lieutenant narrowed his eyes and loosed a string of creative profanity. "The parachute artillery battalion had a couple dozen to match yours. They got scattered from here to Cherbourg. Can't find the pack howitzers. Can't find the crews. So lots of luck getting much friggin' arty support." He lit his cigarette. "Oh, yeah, I hear the Eighty-Second boys got one tough fight going west of St. Mare Eglise. At least we pretty much own the skies."

"Did we get La Barquette in time?"

"Got it from my S-two that your Colonel Johnson personally took the locks. But hardly in time. About three years late! How intelligence missed that one—"

Sam rolled his eyes. "The best-laid plans of mice and men often go awry."

"Huh?"

"Where's the First of the Five-O-First now? La Barquette?"

"Got pulled out. Two days ago, I think. Might've been yesterday. Some of Sink's boys hold it now. That's where they butt up with our right flank." The glider lieutenant took a drag on his cigarette. "Haven't a clue where your unit's at. Get your prisoners to the POW cage they got at Divisional HQ at Hiesville. They'll get you squared away."

"Divisional HQ? What happened to General Taylor's, give me three days hard fighting and he'd get us back to England?"

The glider lieutenant chuckled. "You didn't actually buy that line, did you?"

A loud whinny and irregular hoof beats echoed from around the corner.

The glider lieutenant shuddered. "Wish someone would do something about that friggin' horse. Gives me the willies." He crushed his half-smoked cigarette under his combat shoe. "So how many Rooskies you bag?"

Walking away, Sam said, "Excuse me." He turned left at the corner onto the main road. Brick shops and houses lined each side of the road for seventy-five yards. Windows were shattered. One building had a gaping hole in the roof and a half-collapsed wall. Broken masonry and glass littered the road.

A horse lay on the street in a pool of blood and gore. It was Adolph. Intestines trailed for five-yards behind the massive dapple-gray's inert body. Dark, thickening blood flowed into the gutter. Fright remained locked in the horse's huge eyes, though he was clearly dead.

An eerie whinny reverberated down the street. Sam pivoted. Joseph, the chestnut, struggled down the street dragging the broken harness. A quarter of his flaxen mane was crimson and dripping blood. A pot-roast sized flap of flesh hung from his hindquarters. Artillery had shattered the horse's left front leg. The Chestnut's massive hoof was swinging from a strap of tissue holding it to the fetlock.

Sam looked back over his shoulder. "Collins! Give me a handful of chewing tobacco. Some of the moist stuff."

Collins approached slowly. He moaned, gave Sam the tobacco, and backed away.

Sam held out his hand and inched toward Joseph. He spoke softly. "Easy, boy. That's OK. Easy, now…"

Joseph's eyes communicated betrayal. He hobbled toward Sam.

Keeping soothing words flowing, Sam extended his hand. Joseph nibbled chewing tobacco out of Sam's flattened palm. The velvet touch and nimble action of the horse's muzzle on his palm reminded Sam of innocent days in Banta Springs.

The massive hoof hanging by shreds of sinew drew Sam's attention back to his task. "Easy, boy. Easy. That's OK." He reached up and stroked the horse's thick neck. "I'm not going to let you hurt anymore." He drew the 45-auto from his shoulder holster.

He cocked the hammer, making a metallic click. Joseph jerked his head up.

Sam stroked the horse's neck again. "Easy, boy. Let me do this for you."

Joseph lowered his head and let a rumbling nicker pass through his nostrils. Sam sensed a hundred eyes on his back. He touched his pistol's muzzle to a spot slightly above the chestnut's eyes. Hand quivering, he squeezed the trigger.

The single blast echoed off the empty street's masonry walls.

Joseph's ton-and-a-quarter of horseflesh dropped with a pounding thud.

The warring Adolph and Joseph were dead.

If only the solution was just that easy.

*   *   *

1200 Hours

Each labored step northward took Sam nearer Hiesville and farther from the flooded river valley. He guided his force of nine Americans—escorting twenty-three Russians—down hedgerow-lined farm roads on rolling low hills. Along the way they asked GIs for directions, invasion news, and chow.

The relaxed atmosphere felt alien. Soldiers went about their duties without ducking and dodging. Men spoke aloud and even dared to yell. Scarred and broken trees, parachutes hanging on branches, burned-out vehicles, broken crates, and ruptured parachute canisters gave testimony to recent violent clashes.

A sickly-sweet smell of ripening death filled the air. Bloated carcasses of speckled Norman cows were the chief contributors to fouling the air. However, an occasional German corpse left unclaimed by graves registration gave testimony to the human element. Morton prodded a German corpse in the ditch and swore. "All the good souvenirs are picked over."

To cover the stench, smokers chain-smoked. Some American nonsmokers bummed a cigarette, broke it in half, and shoved an unlit portion up each nostril. Sam wanted relief. However, as an officer he drew the line at stuffing cigarettes up his nose. Like the Russians, he endured the stench unaided.

Nearing Hiesville he caught glimpses of busted up gliders and debris-strewn fields through gates and gaps in the hedgerows. Ten-foot-high poles connected at the top by barbed wire dotted the larger, more level fields. One pole had split a glider down the center, end-to-end. Collins said, "Hey, Lieutenant, we dang sure weren't never briefed 'bout them there poles."

Sam wanted to recite a litany of items the S-2 staff had failed to mention. He wondered whether the intelligence failure originated in oversight, ignoring unpopular opinions, or falling asleep at their post. All possible excuses failed to justify the end result—by Sam's estimation, hundreds of dead American airborne soldiers. The absolute best troops America had to offer. Three-to-one better than any others. Hundreds thrown away before they even had the chance to prove themselves in combat. Forever nineteen.

Sheer negligence. He kept his thoughts to himself. Why undermine his men's hope of surviving future operations? He turned to Collins. "Just be thankful for your fifty bucks a month extra jump pay."

"Amen to that, Lieutenant. Reckon it sets a feller to thinking. Them glider boys ain't even getting no extra pay."

"Write your congressman," Pinball said.

"You're making a big assumption there," Silva said.

Pinball grinned. "What's that?"

"You assume the big hillbilly's congressman can read."

A concentrated stench wafted over the paratroopers. Every man kept his mouth shut. Some pinched their nostrils closed. All walked a little faster. Sam coughed. Silva deposited his stomach contents in the ditch. The Russians chattered and looked upset.

To their right, from the opposite side of the hedgerow, came the sound of spades and picks striking earth.

Upon reaching the upwind side, Sam gasped for air. At a gate, he ducked into the pasture, seeking an explanation for the stench.

Two dozen masked German POWs dug graves. Several airborne MPs observed. Rows of corpses lined the hedgerow three deep for fifty yards. All were German. Most wore baggy paratrooper tunics.

Sam turned away. His eight men stood behind him, dumbfounded. "Doesn't look like the whole Sixth Fallschirmjager crossed that causeway last night, now does it?"

"Varsity on varsity. Airborne on airborne." Morton sneered and flicked his Chesterfield butt on the nearest corpse. "Looks like we came out ahead. Huh, Sarge?"

Springwater frowned. "Haven't seen our own burial ground yet."

Lazeski said, "Yeah, our stick took off with twenty-one. Now I'm counting nine."

"And we aren't on a boat back to England quite yet, boys," Pinball said.

Morton kept staring. The corpses held the runner transfixed.

Silva snorted and shook his head. "Come on. Let's get moving before our Rooskie buddies make a break for it."

*   *   *

Hiesville—where the 101st Airborne had established divisional headquarters—wasn't much more than a rutted crossroads, with tents staked on dank soil and a couple of expansive, cut-limestone chateaus. The constant motion of the division's vehicles and soldiers kept exhaust fumes and dust suspended in the air.

Escorting the ROA soldiers, Sam and his small band sauntered into the mix, heads held high. A tech sergeant directed Sam to the POW processing cage across the road from a half-destroyed, smoldering chateau.

Sam approached an MP sitting at a table in front of the barbed wire enclosure. Men wearing assorted Wehrmacht field-gray and green milled about inside the stockade. The caged POWs reminded Sam of lions and bears viewed through the safety of a zoo's cage bars. Some captives wore relieved smiles, others defiant scowls. Some paced. Many displayed professionally applied bandages.

"Corporal, I've got twenty-three arriving guests to check in." Sam looked around to assure no German POWs were eavesdropping. "And cut them some slack. They're ROA. Gave up without firing a shot, except into their Nazi babysitter. Saved our bacon, for sure. We'd still be wandering around other side of the Douve if it hadn't been for these guys."

The MP looked up from his paperwork. His sleepy eyes jumped to life. "Will do…" The MP looked Sam over for name or rank.

"Second Lieutenant Samuel Henry. Able, Five-O-First. Reporting in with what's left of my stick."

"Yes sir, Lieutenant. How long you been out?"

"Since Neptune Zero-Hour. Got dropped south of Carentan."

"Then welcome home, sir." The corporal pumped Sam's hand. "Guys have been pouring in from all over, but it's tailed off considerably today. Can't remember any that hauled in so many Krauts."

"Not Krauts. Russians. Just some misguided ROA guys. Like I said, they really helped us. You might want to search them, we didn't exactly…"

The MP smirked. "We know how to take care of them, sir."

"We also need to find our First and Second Battalions."

"Division reserve. Been in Vierville since…a day or so. I was down there yesterday picking up some Kraut paratroopers." The MP shoved a form in front of Sam. "Sign, please, sir."

As the Russians passed into the stockade, Sam dug into his musette bag and gave his remaining gift cigarettes to Shevchenko's men. Springwater and Pinball followed Sam's example.

Sam grabbed Lazeski so he could verbalize his thanks to Sergeant Shevchenko. The mustached Russian was all smiles.

"Shevchenko thinks maybe he'll see you in New York," Lazeski translated.

"Don't count on it." Sam chuckled. "Tell him I live in California."

Shevchenko pointed to his head as if a better idea had just struck him and spoke. "He says we'll meet again. After Hitler's gone. Americans, Brits, ROA, all free men just keep rolling east and we don't stop until Stalin's dead, too."

"Tell him I'd be honored to serve alongside him again."

Water pooled in Shevchenko's eyes as he spoke. Lazeski translated. "And he would proudly fight under your leadership. He says it's clear that you care for your men. Unlike the Communist and Fascist, or even Tsarist, officers. God bless you, Lieutenant Henry."

"God bless you, too," Sam muttered, fearing his parroted reply came off as insincere as it felt awkward on his tongue. "Tell me again, how do you say, thank you?"

Lazeski sounded it out. "Spa-cee-ba."

Sam extended his hand. "Spa-cee-ba, Sergeant Shevchenko! Spaceeba very much."

Shevchenko's rough hands wrapped around Sam's hand. Shevchenko pulled away and entered the initial stockade pen. Sam felt something in his palm and looked down to discover the white, blue, and red ROA patch. He jerked his head up. An MP was patting Shevchenko down and turning the Russian's pockets inside-out. A shield shaped portion of clean cloth stood out on the Russian's ragged greatcoat shoulder. Shevchenko looked back over his shoulder in a broken-toothed smile.

"A little souvenir to remember him by until you meet again, in New York," Lazeski said.

"As if I could ever forget him." Sam swallowed hard, turned away, and took a few aimless steps.

"Lieutenant Henry. Sir."

Sam acknowledged the MP behind the table.

"Sir, it looks like you may want to get checked out at the divisional hospital."

"And where might that be, Corporal?"

"Up until last night—when the Luftwaffe decided to pay us a little visit—it was right there." The MP pointed to the smoking chateau ruins across the road. "Just head northeast a couple hundred yards. All in tents now. Can't miss it, sir."

*   *   *

Sam let the canvas tent walls shut out the flurry of activity outside. He looked over his men. Redeemed men. Men with fight left in them. Despite all odds, victors. They sprawled across all available surface—four folding cots and the ground. Pinball slumped in a chair, soaking his ankle in Epsom salts. All slept. Collins snored.

An hour earlier doctors had cleaned and stitched Silva's wrist, and inspected and rewrapped Wellston's head wound. A surgeon with dark bags under his eyes examined Sam's shoulder and face and commented on the French nurse's superb suture work. In a neighboring tent, a chest surgeon had listened to Wellston's lungs, injected him with a dose of penicillin, and replenished his sulfadiazine tablets to ward off pneumonia.

Through Sam's five-day whisker growth a medic had cleansed the blisters and cuts and prescribed another salve tube. The medic told Sam where he might find a replacement jump jacket behind the triage tent. Without going into detail, Sam informed the medic that there was no chance he'd ever part with his lucky jacket. Rolling his eyes, the medic made his opinion clear—Sam was just another section-eight parachute infantry nutcase.

While the 101st medical staff attended to Sam, Silva, Pinball, and Wellston, the remaining five paratroopers had hunted hot chow and restocked K-rations, cigarettes, gum, and chocolate. Springwater, Harrigan, Collins, Morton, and Lazeski returned, sharing their newfound affluence. For the first time in more than five days, they relaxed. Sam informed them they had time for two hours of shut-eye before heading for Vierville.

His men cared for, Sam released himself to slumber.

Chapter 60

The Debrief

10 June 1944, 1635 Hours
Hiesville, Normandy

"Looking for a Lieutenant Henry."

Sunlight poured past a soldier standing in the tent flap. Sam shielded his eyes.

"Is there a Lieutenant Henry, Able, Five-O-First, in here?"

Silva cussed in Portuguese. "Take a powder, pal. He got evacuated back to England." More men stirred and grumbled.

Sam rubbed his eyes. "I'm him. Who are you?"

"Corporal Schifrin, Divisional HQ Company. Major Sinclair's been wanting you. He's not one to keep waiting, sir."

Fear seized Sam's gut. He found Springwater on the ground and shook his shoulder. "Ted, wake up. I need a word with you."

Springwater followed him out the tent. Sam turned to the HQ corporal. "Would you excuse us for a minute, Corporal?"

"Make it quick, sir. The major…"

Sam pulled Springwater aside. "I may not be coming back. If I don't… well…if you don't see me again, don't tell the men everything, but…"

Springwater shot him an alarmed glance. Sam told what really happened on the Voluptuous Vixen.

*   *   *

Chewing a fat cigar, Major Sinclair gazed up at the chateau chandelier. "Right out of a dime-store novel, Lieutenant Henry."

Sam had spent over an hour in an ornate French chair, reciting in great, yet non-incriminating, detail, hour-by-hour events starting with the English Channel crossing. Concerning the Voluptuous Vixen cockpit episode, he'd hedged his bets—telling the G-2 that he'd made remarks that, in the heat of the moment, and combined with an accidental pistol discharge, might've been mistakenly interpreted as threats. The staff officers seemed more interested in his time since escaping the grain silo. The officers shot questions and jotted notes. At times an answer prompted an inquisitor to dash out, only to reappear with a follow-up question.

"We've got to be damn certain about one thing," Major Sinclair—divisional G-Two intelligence officer—said. "Lieutenant, please describe again the markings on that halftrack."

"Like I said, sir, looked like a knight's armored fist, a gauntlet, held upward." Sam looked at the fists around the table. The four blue-stoned West Point class rings annoyed him. He felt he had one sympathetic ear in the bunch—Captain Young.

"Seventeenth SS Panzergrenadier," Captain Young said. An S-2 briefing had called him to Hiesville. HQ staff used Young to confirm the identity of the soldier who had crawled out of the swamps claiming to be 2nd Lieutenant Samuel George Henry.

"And this was on the eighth, approximately sixteen-hundred hours?" Major Sinclair tapped his pencil eraser on the table. "Let's hope it's a *very* advance recon unit. Our goose is sure-as-hell cooked if the Krauts get an SS Panzergrenadier division deployed at Carentan."

"Seven Corps would be forced to divert armor from the push to Cherbourg," an intelligence captain said. "Any link-up with Omaha would become near impossible."

"What'll happen if we pass it up the ladder? They'll move up our attack on Carentan. Push harder on the flanks. Wish you'd picked up a *soldbuch* from some Seventeenth SS SOB, Henry. It would sure make for an easier sell." Major Sinclair chomped down on his unlit cigar. "No offense, Lieutenant Henry, but it's hard to go to General Taylor and suggest pushing divisional sized operations forward based upon what a sleep-deprived, wounded butter-bar thinks he might've seen."

Captain Young cleared his throat. "Sir, I've worked with Lieutenant Henry awhile. He's got a cool head under pressure and keen observation skills."

Major Sinclair raised his eyebrows.

"This is the same lieutenant that picked apart our aerial photo analysis on the locks," Young said. "He figured out that the low ground had already been flooded."

Side conversations and note jotting ceased. Every ring-knocker stared at Sam. Sam squirmed in the chair.

"So he got lucky once." Major Sinclair bit off the soggy end of his cigar and spit it on the marble tile floor. "OK. The Seventeenth SS is making for Carentan. We've been expecting such a reaction from Berlin. Yeah, we'll pass it on up. All the way up. We should've been in Carentan two days ago anyway. The Five-O-Second's getting all chewed up trying to get into Carentan down that N-Thirteen causeway even as we speak. We must pressure the flanks. Nevertheless, we're not the plans and operations shop. We can only pass the intel on. You're dismissed, Henry."

Sam advanced on the exit, his mind dwelling on the Voluptuous Vixen. *How'd they let me off the hook that easy? Get out the door before—*

"One more thing, Lieutenant," Major Sinclair said.

Sam cringed and turned back facing the ring-knockers.

"You did one helluva job out there. Took a lot of guts." Major Sinclair stuck a fresh cigar in his mouth. "Have you seen a doctor yet?"

"Yes, sir." Sam wanted to expound. *How do I describe the terror? The desperation? The sheer chaos?* He walked out.

Captain Young walked up alongside him. "Great to have you back, Henry. You brought eight men out, plus prisoners?" He pointed left to guide Sam out the chateau's labyrinth.

"Nine, if my mortar squad leader makes it. The credit goes to Sergeant Springwater."

"It's amazing you hooked back up with your stick."

"Springwater's doing, too."

They stepped out into the sunlight and walked across a wheel-rutted lawn.

"You hit the bulls-eye on the La Barquette locks." Young shielded his eyes. "I should've pushed harder. Might've saved a lot of men from drowning."

Sam shook his head. "How bad off's First Battalion?"

"Colonel Crawford bought it before dawn on D-Day, trying to organize some officers. We're critically short on line officers. First Battalion lost every single company commander and most of the execs."

Sam stopped walking. "Captain Tarver?"

"Sorry. I might need to slow down. I got all the bad news in small doses over several days." Young lit a cigarette. "They found Tarver hanging from a tree, still in his parachute harness. Bullet holes stitched across his chest, a few bayonet thrusts in the groin for good measure. The guys who found him quit accepting surrenders."

Sam tried to work up the nerve to ask about others in Able Company. He failed. Walking through the flurry of paratroopers and scattered equipment, he said, "Heard that Colonel Johnson took the locks personally."

"You heard right. He got misdropped real close to La Barquette, gathered a mishmash of over a hundred Geronimos, and took the locks at first light. I got there midmorning. Krauts had used some big planks years ago to flood the whole valley. But we struck, we seized, and we held."

"Did it even matter?" Sam asked.

Young took a deep drag on his cigarette. "In the end, it paid off. Got the whole First Battalion of the Kraut's Sixth Parachute to walk right into an ambush. It was a slaughter. Counted over a hundred-fifty dead, over three-hundred-fifty wounded or captured. All in about five minutes. They were just sloshing through the ankle-deep water making a beeline for Carentan." He exhaled smoke. "Staff Sergeant Jennings caught it later that afternoon. Wasn't he your platoon sergeant?"

Sam nodded and shoved a stick of Wrigley's Spearmint in his mouth. Back in England, Sam couldn't imagine an old trooper like Jennings getting killed. He sighed. Operation Neptune had crushed just about every such idealistic notion.

"An Eighty-eight dead-centered his foxhole." Young snapped his fingers. "Gone like that. Better than suffering and knowing you're dying, if you ask me. Shame, too. Before that, Jennings had waded out of a swamp and fought his way toward the locks. Organized ten paratroopers—no two from the same stick. He hooked-up with Colonel Johnson and was the first man to cross the locks."

"Waded? Where'd Chalk Number-One get dropped?"

"A flooded marsh near St. Come-du-Mont. Over a mile short of DZ-D, but better off than most of Able."

"So the rest of my platoon made it?"

"Not likely. I know Pettigrew made it. Let's just say, as close as he landed to La Barquette, it still took him a bit *longer* than Jennings to find his way out of that swamp." Young stepped out of the path of an oncoming jeep. "He's Able's acting commander."

Shoving bitter thoughts of Pettigrew aside, Sam thought about his buddy. He swallowed back the lump in his throat and said, "How about Lloyd Sterling?"

Young tossed his cigarette butt on the path and stomped on it. "Sure you're ready for all this?"

Sam's heart sunk. He nodded.

"Conflicting reports. His stick actually hit Drop Zone-D. One account claims he was severely wounded. Last seen getting patched up by a couple of medics in the Angoville au Plein church. But the medics have no official record. Another trooper said he saw Sterling knocked out cold from a potato masher blast and dragged off by some Krauts. Then again, one of his sergeants swears he saw Sterling, dead in a ditch just south of Vierville. Graves registration hasn't recovered his remains, yet. He's listed as MIA."

Sam heaved a sigh. He remembered the mock Purple Heart Sterling had fashioned. The trout. Trying to bluff his way out of their Overton charade. Long philosophical discussions. He cleared his throat. "What's battalion strength?"

"Roughly sixty-percent. That's up from thirty-six hours ago. Then we were just at forty-five percent. Men keep wandering in. Sorry I don't have better news. *You're* the best news we've had in awhile."

They arrived among the hospital tents. Sam wove his way through to where he'd left his men.

"We should get headed to Vierville." Captain Young looked Sam over and grimaced. "You need to see a doctor first, Henry?"

"I've been treated, sir. Let's get my men and head on down the road."

A weariness unlike any he'd felt since his brother's funeral penetrated Sam's bones.

Chapter 61

The Weighing

10 June 1944, 2030 Hours
Vierville, Normandy

"You sure, Wellston? I could pull a few strings."

Sam and Private Wellston stood in a gravel lane at the stone pillar gate leading to the majestic Vierville chateau serving as 501st PIR HQ.

"No, thanks, Lieutenant Henry. You got some swell guys. Hell, I wouldn't even be standing here if it wasn't for you. But my home's in Dog Company." Wellston coughed twice. "That doctor-captain back at Hiesville ordered me hospitalized. When he stepped out the front of the tent to start the paperwork and I slipped out the back."

Sam stuck out his hand to shake. "I'll be letting your CO know what you did back at our bridge fight. I'm putting you in for a silver star."

"Hey, I'd rather shoot rockets then lug them all over creation." Wellston shook Sam's hand. "It was an honor serving under you, sir."

Sam grinned. "Even after I ran at Les Fevres?"

"Even after we executed that masterful tactical withdrawal, don't you mean?" Wellston shook Sam's hand and departed to find D-Company.

A corporal jogged up from the chateau. "That you, Lieutenant Henry? Lieutenant Pettigrew says I'm not to return without you, sir."

Sam glared at the corporal. "He waited five days. He can wait five more minutes."

The corporal backed away like Sam was a rabid dog.

Sam cut across the expansive lawn covered with crates, jeeps, trailers, and a couple of duce-and-a-half trucks. He found an isolated spot along the west side and sat with his back against the chateau's cut-limestone wall. The low sun appeared as a darkened, smoke-obscured orb. Allowing his eyes to close, he nodded off.

*   *   *

"Can't sleep here, trooper. Where's your unit?"

Sam jerked awake. Reaching for his pistol he knocked his helmet off his lap. His head throbbed. "Tell Pettigrew I'm on my way."

The paratrooper who'd awakened Sam looked at the mud-smeared vertical bar on the helmet. His gaze shifted to Sam's face. "Lieutenant Henry? That you, sir? Sorry to disturb you. I was just stepping out for a smoke break. Glad to have you back." The sergeant held out a pack of Lucky Strikes. Sam declined with a wave of his hand. "Heard from the radio room you found your way back. The scuttlebutt has it you really managed to do some damage in Jerry's rear. Brought a whole platoon of EPWs back with you."

Sam stood up and braced himself against the cut stone. "You make it sound more glorious—ow!"

The sergeant's eyes held genuine concern. "You seen a doctor yet, Lieutenant?"

Sam nodded.

"Don't know if you heard yet or not, but your platoon lost one helluva staff sergeant."

"Jennings will be tough to replace."

"Tough? Can't replace him. We got stationed together at Fort Sill. Good man. My foxhole was not thirty feet from his at La Barquette. Never seen him so mad."

"Nothing fazed him in training," Sam said. "What got him all bent out of shape?"

The sergeant looked away. Half under his breath he said, "His platoon leader. Makes me worried for Able." The sergeant looked Sam in the eye. "Don't want no trouble, Lieutenant." The sergeant flicked his cigarette away and reached for the doorknob. Sam grabbed the sergeant's arm. "Look, sir, I'm done talking. Been in eleven years. Don't want to get busted."

Sam tried to look sympathetic. "Look, I'm no fan of Pettigrew. If it affects Able, it affects me. Plus some outstanding paratroopers deserving a fair shake."

The sergeant looked at Sam's ring-less right hand and quit trying to pull away.

"Sergeant, I honestly can't even remember your name and my vision isn't the greatest just now. No one will ever know the source. But I need to know."

The sergeant nodded. "Some things have got to be worth putting my neck on the chopping block for. But I'll deny we ever had this talk, sir."

Sam winked. "What talk?"

"I run into Jennings about dawn. He's still soaking wet and angrier than a mama grizzly robbed of her cubs. So we take the locks. I think Jennings and Colonel Johnson could've done it all by their lonesome. Things settle down, but Jennings doesn't. We talk. He's got a few choice words of the four-letter variety for Lieutenant Pettigrew, but the one word that really caught my attention was *coward*." The sergeant recited, in detail, the story of Sergeant Jennings's time in the swamp.

*   *   *

Eyes straight ahead Sam marched down the carpeted hallway on the chateau's third floor. He bypassed the company clerk sitting behind an end table.

The clerk stood. "Excuse me, sir, but I'll need to inform Lieutenant Pettigrew—"

Sam's glare once again forced the corporal to yield. Sam twisted the doorknob and barged into what had been a bedroom. Pettigrew sat behind an ornate mahogany desk.

Sam shut the door more enthusiastically than needed. He dropped his helmet and leaned his M-1 in the corner. Almost coming to attention, he held a sloppy salute. "Second Lieutenant Henry reporting as ordered, *sir*."

Pettigrew appeared far removed from any combat zone—hair combed, face shaven, uniform stain-free. Cigarette smoke hung heavily in the air. An empty pack of Chesterfields and full ashtray sat on the desk. Pettigrew returned the salute and added a condescending smirk.

"Mind if I sit, sir? Got a sore hip." Sam pulled an antique chair underneath himself before Pettigrew could answer.

"I'd written you off, Henry."

"Thank you. I was beginning to have doubts, myself."

Pettigrew scanned Sam. A look of disgust came over his face. "If you're going to report so late, you could've at least cleaned up."

"Had things to square away. Looking after my men first."

Pettigrew blew a stream of smoke at Sam. "In the future look after yourself first. An officer can't lead looking like you. You're an unholy mess."

"Personal appearance was the least of my concerns over the last five days."

"You aren't telling me one thing I don't already know, Henry. I had to make my way out of a swamp and back to our lines, too." Pettigrew flipped his hand dismissively toward Sam. "You didn't find me looking like that."

Sam made an exaggerated show of looking himself over. "Most of it's my own blood. Could be blood from one or two others mixed—"

"I hold little interest for your embellished comic book exploits. As far as I'm concerned you merely performed your duty, nothing above or beyond." Pettigrew crushed out his Chesterfield. "Have you seen a doctor?"

"Funny that I keep hearing that. Yes. More than one back at Hiesville. They declared me a little worse for wear but fit for military service, nonetheless."

"Strictly limited to a medical opinion from where I sit. I want you cleaned up. Get some new clothes and shave. Good grief, Henry, can't you even keep both your web-gear shoulder straps fastened?"

"I'd love to, but a bayonet left a sizable gap right where that strap wants to dig in. Did you get close enough to the enemy to get bayoneted, *sir*?"

Pettigrew averted his gaze to the corner. "The Army authorized you one primary weapon. Turn in the M-One. Account for the carbine."

"If it's all the same, I'll keep the M-One. My peashooter is rusting underwater." Sam didn't consider it a complete fabrication. "Underwater where there was supposed to be dry land."

"You want to be a rifleman?" Pettigrew's eyes danced with malevolence. "I can arrange that. But for now I have an acute officer shortage, so I guess I'm stuck with—"

"Excuse me, but isn't that how you got command of Able Company? Because of an acute officer shortage?"

The pencil in his Pettigrew's hands snapped in two.

Sam took a deep breath. *Don't play your hand too soon.*

Pettigrew rose, stomped across the room, and picked up Sam's steel pot. "Where's the netting you were issued?"

"A hedgerow wanted it worse."

Pettigrew banged the helmet on the floor then brushed off some of the mud with his hand. "Funny how the mud just seems to cover your officer's stripe. Almost looks intentional."

"Maybe you haven't heard—they call it an aiming-stake."

"Ashamed to be an officer? Only a coward would shed symbols of leadership. That stripe is on the back of every officer's helmet so when you lead from up front—where you're supposed to be—the men will know where their leader is and follow."

"At the time there was no front and I had no men to lead. I was alone."

"And so was I. So was I, Henry. But I didn't—"

"No you weren't."

"How dare you contradict me! I was alone and—"

"No, you most certainly were *not* alone, Lieutenant Pettigrew! Jennings was with you. Staff Sergeant Jennings. I'm sure you remember him. I heard he was first to cross the locks. Our *sole* First Platoon trooper to reach the objective on time. I'm sure every man had a good view of the back of his helmet."

Sam folded a piece of Wrigley's Spearmint into his mouth. "But where were you? How much longer did it take you to work up the nerve to leave your willow hideout? Seems you weighed in considerably deficient of West Point standards." Sam stuck his nose out and gave a couple of exaggerated sniffs. "Do I smell piss?"

Despite the dim light, he watched Pettigrew's face turn crimson. Sam rose to his feet and clenched his fists, afraid that at any moment he might need to defend himself. *Keep your hand off your pistol this time.*

Pettigrew's perpetual smirk vanished.

Sam's legs trembled.

"Get out of my sight." Pettigrew sat back at the desk "We're moving on Carentan tomorrow. We're going to need every last soldier. First Platoon's yours. Yet, as far as you're concerned, the handwriting's on the wall, Henry. So, enjoy it while you can. I'll see to it you're relieved of command soon enough."

Chapter 62

New Problems

2210 Hours

Sam shaved in a chateau bathroom. The razor stung the burned and scraped half of his face. He attempted washing his matted hair. Sergeant Jennings's Ft. Sill buddy found Sam a clean undershirt and OD wool shirt, and disposed of the foul shirts—stiff with a mixture of dried blood and perspiration. Sam pulled fresh socks, clean skivvies, and spare jump pants from his musette bag. He stepped out into the Norman evening feeling refreshed for the first time in days.

After beef stew and coffee, he found the supply section and collected needed items—first aid kits, another bandoleer of M-1 ammo, three clips for the 45-auto, and four pineapple grenades.

After a couple of inquiries he located A-Company's enlisted men. They were billeted at a farm compound on Vierville's northwest corner, across the road from a centuries-old Roman Catholic chapel. Darkness had fallen when he crossed the road and turned into a farm's cobblestoned courtyard. A paratrooper stoked a fire beneath a huge kettle. Sparks flew upward. Another paratrooper poured a bucket of water into the kettle. Their faces glowed in the firelight.

"What's cooking?" Sam asked.

"That stinkin' anti-gas crap out of our jackets and pants. Hitler ain't gonna gas us."

"Mind if I throw mine in?" Sam started shedding gear. "I'll give you five francs." He stepped closer to the firelight.

The paratrooper smiled. "Welcome back, Lieutenant Henry. Your money's no good here, sir."

Sam shook out his jacket, cleared the pockets, and tossed it toward the kettle. The paratrooper caught it over the water. "I can find you a better one."

"That bad, huh? Even in the dark?"

The private nodded.

"If it's all the same to you, wash it anyway. It's my lucky jacket."

"Pardon me, sir, but I'd sure hate to think what would've happened if you jumped wearing your *unlucky* jacket."

Sam laughed. "That's the jacket I was wearing when I met the most special girl in the world. You might say she even added a few personal touches and—"

"That's right! You're the one who got stuck by that Limey school teacher." The trooper grabbed the jacket and held it close to the firelight. "Can't promise I'll get all that blood out. I can sew that rip in the shoulder and get a new epaulet button. Should be ready midmorning." The paratrooper pushed the jacket under the water. "Glad you're back, sir. We could use some *good* officers."

"You're in second platoon, right?" Sam swallowed hard. "What happened to Lieutenant Sterling?"

"Wish I knew. Never hooked up. One says this, another that. Whoever's version you hear, he didn't go down easy. Took out a passel of Krauts. Sorry, though. I know you two were buddies."

Sam walked toward a water pump next to the gray-stone Norman barn. Holding his helmet under the spigot, he pumped the handle several strokes until water ran over the dried mud that had incensed Pettigrew. Sam's anger reignited. *I could've brought Field Marshall Erwin Rommel in as my personal prisoner and Pettigrew still would've declared me a failure.*

Laughter erupted from inside the barn. Carrying his web-gear in one hand and M-1 in the other, he entered the barn. Tucked in the corner, under yellow lantern light, more than a dozen paratroopers sat or reclined in loose hay. Donovan sat next to Harrigan. Sam smiled. *So, we weren't the only ones on the Voluptuous Vixen to find our way back.*

Collins launched into a story. Not wanting to put an officer's damper on the enlisted men's reunion party, Sam leaned against a post in the dark recesses.

"That may be, boys, but y'all didn't see Sarge here at that big ol' barn." Collins spit a brown stream into the straw. "Sarge is standing at this barn door dropping an empty mag out his Thompson when this Kraut comes a bustin' out. And the two meet like they's at a square dance. Well, doseydoe, this Kraut meets his Geronimo dance partner and his eyes get as big as a hoot owl's. So, Sarge here just cracks him but good with the butt of his Tommy gun. Then this Kraut tries getting' the drop on him with a burp-gun. Sarge here, he just kicks Fritz in the nuts and yanks that burp-gun out of his hands." Collins shoved more chewing tobacco into his cheek.

Donovan leaned forward. "Then what happened?"

"Seems Sarge got a might busy doing somethin'. Fritz tries to crawl back into the barn and I put some copper-jacketed lead right here." Collins tapped a finger to his temple.

Morton waved his hand. "Tell about Silva slitting that Kraut's throat."

Silva grimaced and departed. "I need a smoke."

Pinball shook his head. "Morton, you just don't get it."

Morton furrowed his brow. "Get what?"

"Dumber than a fence post." Collins spit toward Morton's feet.

"Don't forget, that's the place I pulled a Luger off this Nazi officer I killed." Morton unzipped his jacket halfway and pulled out a black pistol. "Yep, eat your heart out, boys. Got me the *first* Luger."

Sam heard muffled chuckles.

Collins laughed aloud. "Morton, I got me a mule back home with more brains. What you got is a dang P-Thirty-eight."

Morton's face flushed. He looked at the gun, to Collins, then back to the gun. He flipped the safety off, grabbed the slide, and threw it back. A live round ejected and landed on Pinball. Morton grabbed the bullet. He looked at the gun and back at Collins. Paratroopers sat up. Morton shoved the pistol back inside his jacket, held up the bullet, and examined it. "Lugers shoot a nine millimeter. This is a nine millimeter. German officers carry Lugers. I got this off a Kraut officer. So, it's a Luger."

Springwater rose and stood over Morton. "OK, Morton. Can't argue with that logic. You got yourself one dandy Kraut pistol and you're the first one."

"That's right, Morton," Pinball said, "and you might want to make your one-of-a-kind *Luger* safe. You just put it in your jacket hammer cocked, safety off." He muttered Italian and exited through same door Silva had.

Sam pushed his fingers back through his hair. *Morton's already killed this party.* He stepped out of the shadows.

Morton jumped to his feet and shouted, "Atten—"

"Relax. Nobody needs to get up." Massive shells roared overhead and crashed like rolling thunder on the outskirts of Carentan. "From the sound of things I'd say we're still very much in a combat zone. Sounds like we're getting a little assistance from the Navy, too." Sam scanned his platoon in a mental roll call he'd been dreading. "Glad to see you made it back,

Donovan." Sam shook the Irish machinegunner's hand. "Looks like you two Micks can actually get by without each other after all."

"Glad you got all these guys back, sir." Donovan pointed to a darkened corner. "Made it back with Taylor. He's half Irish, so we got along just fine."

Sam stepped over and shook Taylor's hand.

"Got back yesterday, sir," Taylor, the only remaining mortarman, said. "Never thought I'd see you again after that ack-ack hit us."

Sam spotted Doc Walters. "Good to see you, Doc. We could've used you."

"I hear you got patched up by someone better looking."

"Better looking? Maybe, but a bit old for the discriminating paratrooper—with the possible exception of Silva."

Everyone laughed.

Sam shook hands with the other survivors. It didn't take long. "What's platoon strength, Sergeant Springwater?"

"Fifteen, counting you, sir. We need to lend Taylor to Second Platoon for Able to deploy one mortar squad."

Quick mental math put platoon strength at forty percent. He suppressed a frown. "No problem. We've proven it takes three Krauts to match one of us. Haven't we, men?"

However, in his mind he knew the principal lesson he'd learned over the past five days was that death arrived suddenly, randomly, and was no respecter of persons. Tomorrow would be no different.

"We have new orders," Sam said. "Seems the Army has once again postponed our one-way luxury cruise to England."

Lazeski raised his hand. "No disrespect, Lieutenant, but I think you might be the only guy I know who bought the general's 'give me three days hard fighting and I'll get you back to England' crock."

Sam grinned. "In the future feel free to burst my bubble a little sooner, Laze." He looked his men over. None looked distraught. "Seems they need all the straight-legs pushing north for Cherbourg. The southern flank is all ours. We'll be crossing the Douve—or I should say re-crossing the Douve for most of us. Probably paying Catz another visit. For now just get a good night's sleep. Relax. Be ready to assemble no later than ten-hundred hours." Sam walked out to the cobblestoned courtyard to check the laundry kettle.

Springwater caught up to him. "We need to talk. Alone."

Sam drifted away from the paratroopers stewing uniforms. "What's on your mind, Ted?"

"Morton. I want him gone."

"Not sure we can just transfer a guy in the middle of an operation. Especially one this FUBAR. No replacements 'til we get back to England." Sam removed his helmet and ran his fingers back through his short hair. "I caught what happened in there with his pistol. Do you think he was threatening Collins?"

Springwater frowned. "You need to stop that in front of the men."

Sam scrunched his brow. "Stop what?"

"Raking your fingers through your hair. You do it when you face a tough decision. Or if you're bothered. Makes you look unsure, indecisive. The men will pick up on it."

Sam's anger flared. "Sorry we can't all be stoic Indians."

"I meant no offense, Sam." Springwater pointed back at the barn. "Right now those men almost worship you. I don't know when you walked in, but most of the stories they told were about you. Not flying back to England, when you had every right to. Taking on that MG-Forty-two, alone. Saving Wellston. Getting us out of Les Fevres. The calvados bombs. Killing some Kraut armor. The bridge, ducking that walking mortar barrage. The Russians. How you had the guts to show mercy on that horse. Getting Phillips out. Getting us all out as fighting warriors."

Sam waved dismissively. "If anyone deserves the credit, it's you."

Springwater shook his head. "Back at Hiesville I told them that you might be arrested. Pinball cried. Collins and Silva grabbed their rifles and headed for the chateau to break you out. I had to physically restrain them." He put a hand on Sam's shoulder. "Sam, right now they'd jump into Hades wearing gasoline suits, if you're leading. Don't give them a chance to doubt. Lieutenant Pettigrew will do enough of that." Springwater looked at his boots. "We've got to do something about Morton."

"Was he threatening Collins or not?"

"I don't think so." Springwater shrugged. "I'm still bothered by those bloody rings. And a couple other incidents before we got back together."

Another implication from the rings struck Sam like a fist to his gut. Morton had taken the rings from soldiers Sam had killed. Sam was responsible for making two new German widows. Young women like Maggie. A wave of nausea distracted him from Springwater's argument. He forced himself to refocus.

"…then something happened this evening that convinced me that he's got to go," Springwater said. "Pinball filled in some blanks."

Sam leaned against the barn's stone wall. "The problem?"

Springwater spoke a string of vowel-laden syllables.

"What?" Sam shook his head. "More buffalo covering the prairie?"

Springwater enunciated each syllable in his native tongue. "A Crow term. Means a warrior who's lost his moral compass. Can no longer separate right from wrong. Represents a great danger. He must be put outside the warrior society."

"What merits this excommunication?"

"I had Laze out looking for Able. We're sitting along the road. A French mailman in uniform rides through on a bicycle. He gets about fifty yards off and Morton raises his rifle and draws a careful bead on the guy. I was about to tell him to quit goofing off. Then I see his trigger finger go forward and push the safety off. I yell Morton's name. He looks my way but starts squeezing the trigger, gun rock-steady. Pinball leans over and pushes the barrel down. Morton glares at Pinball and cusses him out. I ask Morton what he's thinking and he says he thought the postman was going to tell the Krauts our position."

Sam sighed. "OK, a stretch. But not totally out of the realm of possibility—"

"And when did the French ever betray us?" Springwater glared. "No. I'm convinced Morton was making up an excuse."

"Why?"

"Pinball told me that right when the Frenchman rode through, he heard Morton cussing the guy out for no reason." Springwater looked up to the starry sky. "Then right before Morton leveled his rifle he says, 'Why the hell does that Frog get a bicycle when we've got to walk everywhere?'"

Sam tilted his head back and did some stargazing of his own. "OK. You want him out, he's out. As soon as we're pulled back to England, I'll see to it that he's transferred to a support unit. Make him a rigger or something." He yawned. "No, that wouldn't be such a good idea. I sure wouldn't want to jump with any chute he'd packed." He yawned again. "All right, Ted, I'll give it some thought." He looked at the barn. "Any more stalls with straw left in them?"

"Officers can sleep in the chateau."

"But my men are here." His mind spinning, Sam dragged his weary body back to the barn. "Something else, Ted. I overheard some things that were news to me. That barn firefight. I think you and I need to talk some more. First we sleep."

*   *   *

11 June 1944, 0935 Hours
Overton, England

"Fine, Maggie, you're hardly obliged to tell me a bloomin' thing." Chloe tossed her head back. "I was under the impression that good mates shared their concerns…like why the headmaster might be so insistent upon seeing you late on a Friday afternoon."

Walking down the road, nearing central Overton, Maggie kept her eyes locked forward. "And I was under the impression that good mates didn't harp, pester and pry into sensitive matters. I told you Friday *and* yesterday, I couldn't bring myself to talk about it."

More people seemed to be out than on a typical Sunday morning. *Might have something to do with this being the first Sabbath since the invasion. We Brits are quick to evoke God during times of national crisis. I wonder; might it put Him off a bit?* Her head buzzed courtesy of a week of incessant anxiety interrupted by negligible sleep.

The sun was already warming the air. Jackdaws and house sparrows darted in and out lush tree canopies. The air smelled of flowerbeds and flourishing gardens. An elderly gentleman walking a Welsh Corgi tipped his hat. A horse-drawn milk cart rolled up the road. From happenings in Overton, one would never guess that a mere hundred miles away over a million men clashed in the greatest continental invasion in history.

Her single-paged copy of the special delivery letter weighed heavy in her purse. Headmaster Hampton had personally handed it to her. It heaped professional anguish atop her personal torment. *That pig-eyed ogre failed to find even an ounce of compassion over my 'inability to sort out the personal from the professional.'* A tear rolled off Maggie's chin.

"Do forgive me, Maggie." Chloe offered a handkerchief. "It's none of my ruddy business."

Maggie dabbed her eyes and barely checked for cross traffic before stepping into the highway connecting Whitchurch and Basingstoke. Closer to the River Test a toddler sporting a frilly dress picked wild flowers. Maggie pointed out a bench along the river. "Shall we sit?" Leaning back into the bench, Maggie relaxed her tense muscles. A pair of white swans paddled up the shallow river. In singles, pairs, and family groups, people made their way toward the stone church across the river.

Maggie regained her composure. "When we met at Birkbeck I was seventeen and you were eighteen."

"An introductory course into pedagogical theory, if I remember correctly." Chloe chuckled. "You sat in the front-row center, raising your hand *ad nauseam*, putting us laggards to shame."

"All I jolly well ever wanted was to be a teacher and some handsome bloke's doted-over wife. Looks like accomplishing either may prove beyond my ability." She reached into her purse and pulled out the letter. "This is why Headmaster Hampton required my immediate presence."

Chloe took the envelope and read the notation on front. "Carbon Copy: certified letter to Ministry of Education, Office of Relocated and Evacuee Children. What the bloody…?"

"Just read it."

As Chloe read, Maggie watched the toddler present the handpicked bouquet to her mother. Maggie smiled. *I wonder where her father is. Normandy?* She closed her eyes and took a deep breath.

"I'd appeal." Chloe handed the letter back. "Take it all the way to Whitehall."

Maggie shrugged. "Could be worse, I suppose. Second official reprimand and a year extension to my probationary period."

"But the accusation of 'unorthodox and unfounded teaching methodology' is pure poppycock," Chloe said. "Your pupils can actually read. You got thirteen-year-old boys to ruddy well enjoy Jane Austen. They love you, Maggie."

"My favorite part was about the two unexcused absences 'to pursue a morally dubious dalliance and illicit rendezvous with a foreign army officer.' That sentence alone probably cost Hampton a couple hours in a thesaurus."

"The pig-eyed old goat. You, morally dubious? Poppy-cock! I'm sure his opinion wasn't the slightest bit influenced by his tart daughter-in-law. I hear she's shacking up with some Yank bomber mechanic up Suffolk County way, while her officer hubby fights both malaria and the Japanese in Burma."

"Don't go about repeating rumors, Chloe." Maggie held out her hand and gazed at the pitchfork ring. "Headmaster Hampton had a particular distaste for the way I handled Sam dropping in on us. I do believe he felt he should've been the one wielding the pitchfork. That accounted for my first official reprimand."

"What now?"

"Go to church. Pray. Get through today." Maggie lifted herself off the bench. "I've never desired a profession outside of education. Now I'm the recipient of quite *the* education. I guess I'll just have to keep my record spotless from here on out. He was quite clear—one more incident and I'm sacked. Unemployable as an educator by any school in the UK." The church bell chimed. "I shan't dwell on it. I'm certain the cross I must now bear is nothing compared to what Sam must be enduring."

Chapter 63

Worth Fighting For

11 June 1944, 1005 Hours
Vierville, Normandy

"Did the best I could, sir." The 2nd Platoon private held up Sam's jump jacket. "Afraid that blood stain left a border."

Sam examined it. "A huge improvement."

The private had used black thread and a mismatched epaulet button. Not even in the same league as Maggie's workmanship. *But, hey, we're in a war zone. Maybe Maggie can redo the repairs when I get back to England.* Sam shook his head. Very bad idea. *Best she never sees the bayonet damage, nor the remnants of my spilled blood.* He put the jump jacket on. It fit like a well-worn work glove.

Exploring the farm buildings, he found Springwater at a shop workbench cleaning his Thompson and talking ranching with Lazeski.

A smile spread across Lazeski's face. "Your jacket cleaned up real nice, Lieutenant. This should go well with it." Lazeski produced a one-foot-by-three-foot strip of camouflage parachute material. "For you, sir. Parachutes are scattered all over. Latest fashion trend is to wear them like a neck scarf."

"Thanks, Laze." Sam looked at Lazeski's neck and noted a strip of camouflage parachute worn like an English lord's silk ascot. "But since when's a South Dakota State animal husbandry major interested in fashion?"

"Since I saw an English lit and philosophy student from Los Angeles harness up a horse team like an old muleskinner. And how'd you know horses fancied chewing tobacco?"

Sam looked away. "I'm here to speak to Springwater, Laze. Thanks for the gift, but now if you'd please excuse us." As soon as Lazeski departed, Sam said, "Any problems this morning, Ted?"

Springwater didn't look up from his well-oiled Thompson parts. "Silva bellyaches about no girls in the village. Morton found some dead Krauts, but carps about souvenirs being picked over. Collins is about out of chew. Pinball, Harrigan, and Donovan were late for mass across the road with the locals."

Sam bent over to inspect the Thompson receiver. "I do believe you're going to be the first man ever to wear out a weapon from cleaning it."

"Take care of my weapon; my weapon takes care of me. And—"

"And it's the Crow way?" Sam said.

Springwater gave a subtle nod.

"I'm having some difficulty discerning the Crow way. How's the progress on making war chief going?"

Springwater shrugged.

"Let's see, we can cross horse theft from an enemy camp off the list. In fact Adolph and Joseph were so big I think I'll send your tribal council credit for four horses."

Springwater held up two long fingers. "Only two *illichi*."

"Anything else?"

Springwater examined the Thompson's firing pin.

"I think there is, Ted. Last night I overheard Collins tell about the barn firefight. You hitting a German with the butt of that Thompson and wresting an MP-40 out of his hands. That gives you three out of four requirements. Why didn't you tell me?"

"You need to hear it from someone else."

"I did."

"Makes no difference. I lost four from my war party."

"Smith and O'Connor don't count. You weren't leading then. Technically, I was."

"OK, then two. Jeffers and Craighead. That's still two too many." Springwater slapped the Thompson back together and rammed a clip into the bottom of the receiver. "I got them killed looking for you in that barn. And this isn't about me making chief."

Sam put a hand on his friend's shoulder. "You don't have to tell me that."

∗   ∗   ∗

1530 Hours

The Geronimos moved out to reenter the Normandy Campaign as a reduced, yet more rested, reorganized, and refitted light infantry regiment. Their mission was to get into position to hit Carentan from the rear, via the left flank, so the 506th could relieve the 502nd and finish clearing Carentan from the northwest. It was the first time all three of the division's parachute infantry regiments would maneuver together in a coordinated effort on a common objective.

It was taking all afternoon for the remaining 501st paratroopers to weave their way south-by-southeast through the hedgerows, pastures, and marshes. Third Battalion led, followed by Second. First Battalion—in reserve—brought up the rear. Sam played the Army's favorite game: hurry up and wait.

First Platoon lounged in cool grass along a shady lane behind the Vierville church. Not a single paratrooper grumbled about not being on the point of the 501st's attack. All day long the cacophony of an intense battle two miles distant reached Vierville. The 502nd PIR was still catching it from their frontal assault of Carentan along the N-13 causeway. Yet nesting birds chirped in the tree limbs above Sam.

He took a swig from his canteen. Silva, Morton, Collins and Pinball played gin rummy. Springwater caught a catnap.

A man with an unsure walk and a middle-aged spread to his torso made his way down the lane. His olive drab uniform lacked insignia. His shiny-new helmet carried no markings. He held a pad of paper in one hand and a pencil in the other. A freckle-faced paratrooper escorted him.

"Hello there, Lieutenant." The man extended his hand. "Hubert McNeil. Associated Press war correspondent."

Without getting up, Sam leaned forward and shook the soft hand. Springwater opened his dark eyes and sat up.

"Heard you Five-O-First, First Battalion boys had a rough go of it over the past few days." The reporter's lead-in statement came across as flippant. It solicited a frown from every paratrooper within hearing range.

The card game halted. "Pretty much impossible for you to know," Silva mumbled.

All smiles, the correspondent said, "Mind if I ask your platoon a few questions?"

Sam extended his hand toward his men. "Ask away."

"Marvelous. This won't take long, Lieutenant." The correspondent eyed Springwater. "What're you fighting for, Sergeant?"

"My nation."

"And that would be?" The correspondent squinted and studied Springwater. "No, don't tell me, let me guess. Cherokee? Navajo?"

Springwater stood, clenched his fists, and looked down at the reporter. "Same as you. United States of America." He strode away.

Undeterred the correspondent turned to Sam and said, "How about you, Lieutenant? A handsome fella like yourself. Fighting for that special girl back home?"

The card-playing quartet failed to suppress their chuckles.

The reporter whipped around. "What's so funny? Did I—?"

"Never mind them," Sam said. "It's just that my special girl back home happens to call London home. Probably not something you'll want to publish to bolster the morale of the gals waiting back on the home front."

The reporter made a sour face and scanned the paratroopers. He stopped on Lazeski. "How about you, Sergeant? What're you fighting for?"

"Doing my part to put an end to tyranny," Lazeski said.

"Excellent. Your name and where you're from."

Lazeski wagged a finger at the AP correspondent. "We start with Hitler, then keep right on rolling east until we kill that Georgian butcher Stalin, too."

The reporter stopped writing. Collins laughed and almost choked on his chewing tobacco. Hearing the noise, the AP correspondent turned to the card players. "How about you, soldier? You look big enough to fight your way through any scrape. Have things been pretty rough?"

"I reckon near tolerable from them there Germans. We can whup them. We just need to figure out a way to keep our own Air Corps from a killin' us. Between getting dropped in swamps to drown and our own fighter pilot boys strafing us, well, I reckon they kilt near as many of us as the dang Krauts."

The reporter tapped his pencil on the paper. "I don't think we can print that." The correspondent looked at Morton. "How about you, Private?"

"Sir, that's PFC Stephen Morton. That's with a *ph*, not a *v*. Joliet, Illinois. I'm Able Company's runner."

"Thank you, Private Morton." The correspondent scribbled notes. "And what are you fighting for?"

"To kill as many damn Nazi S-O-Bs as I can before they kill me. They're just a bunch of…" Morton launched into a string of profanity.

The correspondent's pencil froze. He cleared his throat to stop Morton and looked at Vigiano, "What's a good Italian kid like you fighting for, son?

How about letting folks back at the home parish read about you. Fighting for God and country? Mama?"

Sam smiled at the reporter's accurate spot appraisal of Pinball.

Pinball said nothing. He pointed first at Silva, then Collins, and continued pointing until he'd pointed out every member of his squad. He ended by including Sam. "These guys right here. My buddies. Squad-mates. When the bullets start flying, they're really all that matters. I know they've got me covered, and I cover them. If I get home to mama it'll be because of them."

The AP correspondent smiled. "Great, great. I think I can fashion that into some good copy. What's your name and hometown, son?"

"PFC Vincenzo Vigiano. St. Louis, Missouri."

Jotting Vigiano's comments, the reporter's zeal seemed renewed. He glanced toward Silva. "How about you, Private?"

Silva stood and turned his back to the correspondent. He dropped his pants, bent over, and lifted the tail of his jump jacket—revealing hairy butt cheeks. "Right there, mister reporter." He slapped a cheek. "That's what I'm fighting for, right there. And you can kiss—"

Sam leapt to his feet. "Silva! Pull your pants up!"

Silva complied and smirked. "That's Joseph Silva, with a *ph*. Merced, California. The Silvas read the *Merced Sun-Star*."

The reporter slammed his notebook shut and waddled off in a huff. The freckled paratrooper followed, covering his mouth to suppress laughter. Sam's platoon hooted and rolled in the grassy alley. Lazeski wiped tears away.

Sam worked hard to suppress his own laughter. "Silva, you take the cake. You're never making corporal with antics like that."

Silva cinched his belt. "Could you please put that in writing, sir?"

"What drove you to do that?" Sam asked.

"Are you kidding me, sir?" Silva gave Pinball a mock punch to the arm. "After Pinball's sappy answer someone needed to bring us back to reality."

Morton stood and gazed down the road. "You went and got Lieutenant Henry in trouble. Here comes Lieutenant Pettigrew. And he don't look none too happy."

Sam pivoted. Pettigrew rode shotgun in a jeep speeding their way.

Collins stood. "Aw, he ain't no different than usual. He always looks like he's been sucking green persimmons."

Sam shot Collins a disapproving look.

The jeep skidded to a halt where the lane joined the road. Pettigrew grabbed the windshield to pull himself upright. "Moving out, boys! Lieutenant Henry, I want your platoon in formation and on the road." Pettigrew scanned 1st Platoon. "Where's that Indian? He won't be platoon sergeant long if I can't find him when he's needed."

"What do you need him for, sir?" Sam asked. "I sent him to find us a few more boxes of K-rations."

"I don't need him." Pettigrew flipped his Chesterfield butt away while gazing over Sam's head. "I need him here doing his job. You could've sent someone else."

The smoldering butt came to rest between Sam's boots.

Pettigrew struck a general-like pose. "Sorry boys, today we're in reserve. But, I sure as hell hope Able gets to take it to the Nazi scum tomorrow. And take it to them like wild Apaches we will, because you're not going to see twenty-one anyway. So take as many of those Nazi S-O-Bs with you as you can. What do you say, boys?"

Wearing his condescending smirk, Pettigrew dropped to his seat. The jeep driver whipped a gravel spraying u-turn.

Chapter 64

Recon Patrols

12 June 1944, 1115 Hours
Hill 30, La Billonnerie, Normandy

Nearby mortar tubes popped. Distant MG-42s ripped burst after burst. Not ten yards away a paratrooper fired three carbine rounds into some unseen threat. Sam flinched and tucked his body tighter behind the overturned German scout car before returning his attention to Captain Young's map.

"Sink's boys are sitting in Carentan. It's secure." Young jabbed the map. "Item Company is dug-in along the Periers highway, right here. Pass through them." He spoke with uncharacteristic urgency. "Then cut west. Recon the area up to a half-mile south and just west of Douville. You know this area, right?"

"Spent time there on...I believe on the eighth." Sam tapped the position on the map. "Spent the ninth up by the tracks."

"Forget north of this paved east-west road." Young pointed out the road where Sam had fought from under the bridge. "I'm still not sure where regimental boundaries will fall, but for sure that sector belongs to the Five-O-Sixth. Reconnaissance-wise, it's usually the regimental boundaries that get overlooked. But we won't let that happen."

Incoming artillery landed a couple hundred yards south. A firefight erupted along Item Company's line. The acrid odor of cordite and white phosphorus hung heavy on the late morning air. Dead American paratroopers—yet un-recovered by graves registration—gave silent testimony to the ferocity of 3rd Battalion's early morning battle for Hill 30 and La Billonnerie. Numerous enemy corpses, many sporting ROA patches, littered enemy strong points. Artillery had reduced the stables that had served as Shevchenko's barracks to stone rubble and broken timbers.

Heavy footsteps and the rattle of equipment made Sam tighten the grip on his M-1. Three lightly wounded paratroopers and a medic jogged past the bloated remains of a team of draft horses still hitched to a smashed wagon.

"Sir, this sounds like a job for you S-Two guys. Springwater and Collins are my only men trained in reconnaissance." Sam reached under his helmet and started running his hand back through his hair. Remembering Springwater's admonition, he stopped.

"Listen, Henry, the divisional G-Two selected you. Your debrief impressed the brass." Young took a deep breath and sighed. "Besides, we've barely got enough men left in battalion S-Two to mount even one patrol. You already know this ground."

The knot in Sam's gut grew. "What exactly do you want us to find out?"

"First, where the Krauts are massing and how ready they might be to counterattack. Second, who they are and what they've got to hit us with. We're expecting the Seventeenth SS Panzergrenadier. But, we need confirmation. If it's the Seventeenth, well…apart from your skirmish no allied unit has fully engaged them yet. We need to know what kind of heavy armor they've got."

Nausea washed over Sam. "Heavy armor?"

Young nodded. "I don't like pitting paratrooper against panzer either. That's why this intel is so critical. We must know where to best deploy our anti-tank assets. And we'll have one tank outfit on loan from the straight-legs."

"The hedgerows should confine armor to the roads." Sam pointed at the map where they'd tangled with the 17th SS Panzer recon unit. "I doubt many of the bridges will support heavy armor. This creek bottom's too mucky."

"That's thinking like a good S-Two already, Lieutenant. Check likely approaches and existing funnels. You won't have to cover nearly as much ground. What's your platoon strength?"

"Only fifteen, sir."

"You can knock that in half and still get this job done. It won't be tidy out there. Disregard German stragglers. You could run into remnants of the Sixth Fallschirmjager, Ost battalions, and the Wehrmacht Three-Fifty-Second Infantry. I suspect the Seventeenth SS will be sending out recon patrols of their own. The SS boys will be wearing that distinct camouflage pattern, like pea-sized dots. And that armored fist will be painted on their vehicles. You've already seen it. Make sure your scouts have binoculars."

"We need a couple more pair."

"No problem." Young folded up his map. "You may bump into recon units from the Five-O-Sixth. Tell your men not to get trigger-happy. You're a recon patrol, not a combat patrol. You'll serve us absolutely no good if you let yourself get bogged down in a firefight. Gather intel and get back pronto. Go."

Rising above the overturned vehicle, Sam hunched his shoulders and trotted back to where he'd left 1st Platoon.

Briefing his men on their new role, he tried to assess morale. "Go as light as possible. Ammo and grenades only." Their poker faces frustrated his effort. "Stash your musette bags at company HQ. Machinegun teams stay put."

The four machinegunners quit stripping themselves of excess gear. Donovan plopped down and lit a cigarette with a shaking hand.

"Collins and Springwater will be up front, I'll be right behind them. Lazeski brings up the rear. Laze, keep an eye peeled for Kraut stragglers running up our six. Everyone watch for patrols from Sink's boys on our north side. Silva, you're in." He looked around until his eyes landed on the barrel-chested Italian. "Pinball, how's that ankle holding up?"

Vigiano hooked a grenade to his web gear. "Good to go, sir."

Sam surveyed his men. "Ogden, we won't need rifle grenades. You're staying. Diaz, you're in. Ames, has your French improved any since last week?"

"Every day I find out more about the French language that I don't know, sir."

Sam nodded. "If we run into any French stupid enough to still be hanging around, I want you at my side, toot sweet. I think I know right where we need to go." He looked around as he doffed his musette bag. "Where's Morton?"

Springwater muttered something in Crow.

"Right here, sir," Morton said, walking up with a Luger held up as a trophy for all to admire. "You need me?"

Sam clenched his jaw. *Got to keep a shorter leash on him.* "Yeah. You're coming with us on a recon patrol. Rifle, ammo, and grenades. Everything else stays."

"But sir, I just got me some dandy souvenirs." Morton pouted. "Some clown will steal it all."

"No, they won't. Harrigan will watch."

Morton stuffed the pistol into his musette bag, secured the fastening straps extra tight, and handed it to Harrigan. "Don't let anyone near that Luger."

Morton's Luger reminded Sam of the arrangement he'd made with the Lambourn clerk, Mazooti. He called Morton over. "You want to help me out?" Sam asked in a hushed tone as he handed Morton a stick of Wrigley's Spearmint.

"You name it, sir." Morton stuffed the gum into his mouth.

"I need a Luger, too. If you happen to get your hands on another, I'll trade you Shevchenko's Russian revolver."

"Deal, sir." Morton stuck his hand out to seal the agreement.

Sam pivoted and found Springwater only a couple of feet away.

Springwater shoved a pair of binoculars into a jacket pocket. "Take Doc Walters."

"It's a recon patrol. We're to avoid contact."

"Eight men nosing around in no-man's-land." Springwater arched a brow. "Contact may find us. Take Doc Walters."

*   *   *

Sam's nine-man patrol maintained a vigorous pace as they moved south and slipped through what remained of Item Company dug in astride Highway N-171 connecting Carentan and Periers. He took a compass heading of 270 degrees and headed west.

In a large pasture just outside I-Company's field of fire, Sam pushed through a hedgerow, finding Collins and Springwater crouched, staring at a half-dozen dead cows. Two agitated cows moved along the far hedge. A third stretched out its neck and bellowed.

"Mines or artillery?" Springwater asked.

"Arty," Sam said. "These are dairy cows with full udders. A farmer would be with them at least twice a day. He'd know if it was mined."

Springwater and Collins exchanged puzzled glances. Collins asked, "Where'd you get your learning 'bout cows from, sir?"

Movement from their right interrupted the riddle. They shouldered weapons. A hunched-over Frenchman came into view. The show of firepower failed to deter the man. The farmer scurried past, spouting angry syllables and shaking his walking stick.

Ames arrived at Sam's side. "They never taught those words in school, but—"

Sam waved him off. "Give me the general idea."

"He says even the Boche can tell men from cows. He wants to know why. How should I answer, sir?"

"Ignore him. He just told us what we need to know. The field's not mined."

Sam led his patrol across the pasture, running in single file. French curses chased each man.

Fifteen uneventful minutes later, they veered southwest on a secondary road. If Sam was reading his map right they were 500 yards south of Douville. He planned to use the meandering farm-road network to work their way toward the creek they were all too familiar with.

*   *   *

1213 Hours
West of Douville, Normandy

Behr bounced on the balls of his feet, checking his gear for betraying rattles. The eight men of his recon patrol followed his example—except the radio-telephone operator hauling a wireless on his back.

With any luck, Behr would find clues to the American paratroopers' next move and call in harassing artillery fire. He also decided to drag along his plump sniper. One shot from a sniper was sufficient to delay an advancing company for one hour. Behr reveled in the power he wielded with just nine men.

"*Ja*, my young *jager*, time to move out. Really not all that different from a Black Forest roebuck hunt." He slapped his youthful sniper on the back. "But for one minor difference—now the roebuck shoot back." Behr laughed and the recon party joined in. The sniper grinned nervously and fumbled with a riflescope lens cap.

Behr took out his compass and set a heading of ninety degrees. Due east.

*   *   *

1357 Hours

Sam raised his 6x30 Soviet binoculars and focused on enemy guarding a decrepit bridge.

He had maneuvered his patrol through the Norman countryside to the first bridge he had picked out on the map. It was less than a quarter of a mile south of the plank bridge he had mined on the eighth. The difference being that this particular wooden bridge didn't appear capable of supporting even a hay wagon and team of horses, much less a panzer.

He estimated fifty Germans were milling about the bridge. An aggregate of fallschirmjager, regular Wehrmacht, and SS. Two German paratroopers—one carrying an arm in a belt sling—showed their papers to a man in a peaked cap. A shiver went up Sam's spine when he realized that the two Germans had to have passed within twenty-five yards mere minutes ago.

He leaned close to Springwater's ear. "Looks like that SS officer is trying to sort out this mess. My guess is just a bunch of stragglers, walking wounded." Sam slid the binoculars back into the case. "Nothing heavy can cross here. Let's move downstream."

He took the patrol on a course parallel to the creek. They moved in short spurts and stuck to terrain that hid their movement from the west side of the creek. Crossing a dirt track he came across discarded bandages and a bloody green-gray tunic. Feeling exposed and vulnerable he checked the tunic's inside breast pocket, pocketed some papers bearing official Nazi stamps, and dashed off the farm road.

After thirty minutes and a quarter-mile, he caught a glimpse of a wood-plank bridge. The wrecked motorcycles piled into the ditch confirmed it as the bridge he'd mined. Vegetation limited his view, yet through his binoculars, he found the spot where Phillips got hit. *Phillips. He'd be back in England by now. I need to get all these guys back to England, but not like Phillips.*

The damaged mortar tube poked above the grass. It summoned up images of blood gushing from the remnants of Phillips's foot. Sam's heart rate jumped. *This recon thing is insanity. We've got to run into someone sooner or later!*

He crouched and waited for Springwater to glance back. They needed to find a better view of this bridge.

The surrounding silence was overpowering.

If you ever prayed for me, pray now, Maggie.

He was certain his heart was going to burst. Stinging sweat rolled into his eyes.

*   *   *

Behr positioned his sniper on a grassy knoll and returned to his binoculars. He had been catching glimpses of the Americans for a couple of minutes.

The American reconnaissance patrol had penetrated deeper than expected. *So, they waste no time in exploiting their morning gains.* This was information the 17th SS planners would be eager to learn.

He panned his binoculars, searching for the Ami leader. It was proving more difficult with the Americans than the Russians. There seemed to be little in the Americans' dress or demeanor to distinguish the leaders from the followers. He noticed that the front two soldiers, both tall, would advance, scan surroundings, and wait or backtrack a few meters to make contact with the third American.

Behr again found the third American. The man twisted, revealing two things that distinguished him: a leather binocular case under his arm and a vertical stripe on the back of his helmet.

"See the third one? Crouched. By the pasture gate," Behr said, keeping his binoculars pressed to his eyes.

"Jawohl, Herr Hauptscharfuhrer."

"Take him. Now." Behr felt his disfigured cheek twitch.

The Mauser's sharp crack shattered the temporary serenity of the Norman countryside.

Through his 8x50 Zeiss binoculars, Behr watched the back of the American's head erupt in a red mist. He seemed to hang suspended in midair, balanced on his knees. Behr enjoyed the sounds of metallic sliding and clicks as the sniper ejected a shell casing and re-chambered a live round in his customized Mauser. The spent cartridge casing struck Behr's arm as the Ami paratrooper's face struck the ground.

Behr shifted his field-glasses. "Next one forward, right. Tall. Thin. Spade painted—"

"Half in the ditch. Got him, Herr Hauptscharfuhrer."

"Take him."

The Mauser cracked again. A millisecond later, the copper-jacketed slug punched an 8mm black hole into the white mark on the side of the helmet.

Behr scooted backward. The sniper reloaded. Behr grabbed his heel and tugged. "One more shot and the roebucks will return fire. Never get greedy. That patrol is *kaputt*. You took out a junior officer and a lead scout. We should find a new place to hunt."

He cradled his Bergmann in the crook of his elbows and belly-crawled out of the pasture. Upon reaching the concealment of an overgrown hedge, he lit a papirosa and offered it to his huffing sniper. The plump teen drew hard on the Russian cigarette.

"Your first two shots, two confirmed kills. Excellent marksmanship, I might add. Do you hand-load your own cartridges?"

Being doubled over and puking up his lunch prevented the sniper from answering.

*   *   *

The shot sent a jolt through Sam's jumpy nerves. He gasped and dropped face first.

A second shot echoed between the hedgerows.

He crawled down the ditch toward Springwater. He found his sergeant prone, half in the ditch. Unmoving.

Sam sprinted the last fifteen yards and slid in next to Springwater.

"Ted, you hit?"

Springwater shifted his weight and raised his head. "Not shooting at us. We're in range, though. Two hundred yards. I'm not feeling good about this one."

"Let's get this done," Sam said. "We need a better view west, up the road."

He shuffled the patrol north—downstream another 75 yards—found the observation point he wanted and positioned his men to provide broader security for the patrol's flanks and rear.

A scorched black spot in the curve marked the spot where Wellston had destroyed the first armored car. German troop movement seemed more purposeful. All the soldiers wore Waffen SS camouflage smocks. No tanks, but over the rise Sam made out the barrels of artillery pieces protruding among the branches of an apple orchard. "S-Two should be interested. Wish we had a way to call down some arty."

Springwater let his binoculars drop. "Next time we bring a radio."

"Next time they send real S-Two guys. We're out of our league. Time for the last bridge." Using hand signals, Sam summoned the whole patrol.

Lazeski trotted in and pulled Sam aside. "When I first got up in that hedgerow by that little knoll, I smelled makhorka."

"What?"

"Shevchenko's brand. That rank Russian tobacco every muzhiek smokes."

"We were warned that Ost troops might be retreating this way. Keep an eye out. I don't think the rest of the ROA boys are quite as keen on surrendering as Shevchenko. Take Morton as an extra set of eyes. Keep him close, though."

From the German position, a howitzer boomed. Sam dove and tucked himself against the earthen base of a hedgerow. And waited.

A distant explosion sounded.

He regained his feet. Another howitzer fired. The round roared overhead. He hunched down and gazed skyward as if expecting to see the flying projectile. The sun blinded him. He scrunched his eyes shut. The second shell found the earth and exploded well to the east.

The whole battery opened up in a booming chorus.

*   *   *

Gazing through his binoculars, Behr licked his lips. Arrayed before him on a hillside pasture—large by Norman standards—at least a company of khaki-clad soldiers were digging fighting positions. His cheek scar inflamed and twitched.

After sniping the American patrol and enjoying Russian tobacco, he'd led his reconnaissance patrol to the paved road and traded exposure risk for rapid movement. Once past the 38th SS Panzergrenadier Regiment's most forward observation post at Douville, he had cut southeast until finding the enemy.

Prone, he pulled out his map and jotted coordinates. Extending his hand behind him, he said, "Radio." The radio-telephone operator crawled to Behr's side and slapped the handset into Behr's palm. The radioman's jaw dropped at the sight of Americans digging in.

"Impressive, no?" Behr said.

The sniper crawled alongside. The youth's eyes radiated a sense of dread. Behr guessed that the dread originated in the youth's first killings. *Only one way to cure that—kill some more.* Behr put a hand on the sniper's shoulder. "Relax, my little *jager*, too many eyes. You'd shoot two and then we'd take fire. Nein, we'll use all the tools at our disposal. One call and many more will suffer, and at no risk to ourselves."

The sniper's gifted eyes showed a measure of relief. Behr thought, *I must get him some trigger time soon or he'll be as worthless as a Gypsy night watchman.*

A faint voice crackled in the receiver. Behr's attention shifted to the radio handset. "Fire mission. Exposed infantry. Company strength. Coordinates *eins, sieben, null. Vier, drei, eins.* Repeat *eins…*"

After two minutes a quick whistle sounded.

A deafening explosion jolted the earth under his belly. Dirt clods and clumps of grass rained down.

The sniper scrunched into a ball, facedown, with his precious scope tucked under his body. The radioman spit soil. A gaping hole smoked just twenty-five meters forward.

Behr cursed. "So much for the element of surprise. Dummkopf artillerymen!"

The Americans ducked into unfinished foxholes.

Behr grabbed the handset. "Up two hundred meters."

The next round roared overhead and blew a hole in the hedgerow just behind the Americans.

"Drop thirty. Fire for effect."

The full artillery barrage roared overhead.

"Time to leave." Behr trotted back to the remainder of his patrol. Squatting in a huddle, he spoke in his teacher's voice. "We have the information we came for, and managed to punch the gangsters in the nose, twice. We need not tempt fate. No reconnaissance patrol remains undetected for long."

Chapter 65

The Scattered Herd

The German artillery barrage lifted. Sam thought it sounded like it struck southwest of Carentan He guided his recon patrol to high ground just east of the last bridge.

The June foliage again frustrated his view. He turned to Collins and Springwater. "Spread out to the right." He looked at his watch—1535 hours. "Find the best view you can and report back in fifteen. Don't cross the paved road."

Sam methodically examined terrain through the Russian binoculars. He could pick out most of the concrete bridge and part of the burned-out armored car—shoved off the bridge and overturned. Though the view told him little, the sounds that soon arose alarmed him—multiple engines and screeching sprockets. Armor! Belches of black diesel exhaust billowed through the tree canopy. He already knew that the bridge could accommodate any weight panzer.

Springwater appeared at his side. "SS digging in around the bridge."

Seven minutes later Collins plopped down holding his helmet on. "Can't see squat from this here side of the road, so I done crossed..." Collins paused to catch his breath.

Sam exhaled hard. "I told you *not* to."

"Found a little herd of them speckled cows loose in the road. Hid me right nicely as I crossed amongst them." Collins stuffed a wad of tobacco in his cheek. "Got me a might better view, too. Field-glasses came in handy."

"What'd you see?"

"Six funny lookin' tanks. No turret. Just a flat top and a big ol' cannon sticking out front, machinegun up top."

"Assault guns," Sam said. "Krauts call them *stugs*. For infantry support and tank destroyers."

"Halftracks, too." Collins loosed a stream of tobacco juice. "I seen that armored fist you told us about painted on them, too."

"Sounds like an assembly area." Sam cased his binoculars. "We've got more than enough for the S-Two to chew on for awhile." He assembled his patrol and headed back east on a direct ninety degree heading.

At the second hedgerow, he ducked through a gate and encountered a short Frenchman gathering cows. Monsieur Comeaux? Sam waved Ames forward. "Stay right on my hip." He advanced toward the Frenchman, M-1 shouldered, scanning the small pasture.

The Frenchman's face lit up with recognition. He called out, "Bon jour!" way too loud.

Sam cringed and crouched beside a cow with a full udder. "Bon jour, Monsieur Comeaux," he said in a hushed tone.

Comeaux took the hint and whispered. Ames spoke in halting French, then turned to Sam. "Wanted to know how Phillips is. Said he lit a candle for him."

"What's he still doing here?"

Ames and Comeaux conversed. Ames said, "He says he's trying to gather his cows. Something about the Boche leaving all the gates open."

Sam shook his head. "That's not what I meant. Tell him he must leave." Sam tapped his rifle. "He's about to get caught in a big battle."

Sam looked back at Springwater. The sergeant's dark eyes looked nervous. Comeaux rattled on. Springwater tensed and shifted his Thompson muzzle. Sam jerked around. Comeaux's eldest daughter rounded the hedgerow corner herding two cows.

Ames leaned close to Sam. "He says cows must be milked, regardless of politics. He thinks the fighting won't be here. Nothing to fight over. If so, they have a cellar." Ames glanced at the daughter. "With a daughter that gorgeous he should keep her locked up in the cellar from the Krauts."

"I won't sit here arguing with some stubborn farmer while a Panzergrenadier division prepares a counterattack right behind us." Sam looked Comeaux in the eye. "*Merci beaucoup*, Monsieur Comeaux." He signaled the patrol forward and took a step.

Comeaux grabbed Sam's sleeve and babbled, eyes wide in alarm.

"He says don't go that way," Ames said. "Groups of Boche are moving back and forth all over and south side of the road. They also have an observation post in Douville. But he's seen only Americans north."

Sam gave Springwater a questioning look.

Springwater nodded. "Sounds like the Five-O-Sixth might be getting ahead of the timetable. We know that way back, too. The quicker we find our lines, the better."

Adopting Collins's method, the patrol crossed the paved road using the cows as cover. Thirty yards off the road, Raquel—Comeaux's younger daughter—walked toward the group. Raquel and her father exchanged words. She made a point greeting each paratrooper with cheery bon jour and genuine smile.

Sam leaned toward Ames. "Tell her we're in a hurry."

Comeaux and the eldest daughter passed seven cows off to Raquel before heading down the paved road west, toward the German assembly area where Collins reported seeing the rest of their scattered herd.

Sam moved the patrol mixed among the cows, north down a tree-lined lane. Bending low at the knees and waist, the patrol kept pace with fourteen-year-old Raquel.

The Comeaux dairy barns and two-story, gray-stone house came into view, catching Sam by surprise. *What am I doing? Comeaux has helped us twice now. I won't tempt fate. Get away from here!*

*   *   *

Behr adjusted the binocular focus. Nein. Not even the Russians would attempt such a stunt. He caught patches of tan jackets and American helmets moving among cattle. He signaled his sniper forward and pointed west. "That lane."

The cherub-faced sniper gazed through his six-power riflescope. "Americans mixed in with cattle, Herr Hauptscharfuhrer."

"*Ja!* Shoot one."

"An officer?"

"Any!"

The sniper dropped prone. "Can't see." He took a kneeling position, and repeatedly raised and lowered his head to the scope. "Still too low."

"Rest the barrel on my shoulder. Quickly, soldat. They're getting away." Behr squatted and felt the rifle rest on his shoulder.

"Hold still, Hauptscharfuhrer—"

"Shoot, boy!" Behr plugged his ears.

The rifle barrel shifted. "Herr Hauptscharfuhrer, they're gone."

Behr pushed the barrel off his shoulder and panned his binoculars, following the lane north until his field of view landed on slate rooftops. Perhaps they took refuge there.

Switching to hand signals, he motioned his patrol to follow and advanced northwest, Bergmann shouldered and ready.

Chapter 66

The Crime

Sam advanced at the point position—anxious to get his men far from the Comeaux farm as quickly as possible.

Before darting around a hedgerow corner, he glanced back. Collins signaled him to halt. Sam scowled. Collins motioned his thumb over his shoulder. After trotting back forty yards bent low at the waist, Sam found his sergeants huddled. "What's the holdup?"

Anger etched on his face, Springwater nodded toward Lazeski.

"Lost Morton." Lazeski averted his eyes. "Is he up front with you?"

"What do you mean, *lost?* A man just doesn't disappear, Laze!"

"Told me he had a bad case of the runs." Lazeski yanked his wire-rimmed glasses off. "Said he wouldn't let us get out of sight."

"So?" Sam said.

Lazeski's eyes blazed. "That was almost ten minutes ago."

"Gather everyone on me." Sam reached for his helmet and caught Springwater's disapproving glance. Gritting his teeth, he suppressed the urge to run his hand through his hair. The rattle of gear announced the arrival of his patrol.

Springwater broke the silence. "Who saw Morton last?"

Ames raised a hand. "Back near the barns, he moved up on my shoulder and said he and Silva were going to help the French girl pen the cattle. Said they knew the way, he'd catch up."

Sam's gaze flashed to Silva.

"He told me he liked the way Raquel smiled at him. He wanted to know if I'd ask you to stop at the farm. Give him a chance to get to know

-403-

her a little better. I told him he was sick, that we're on a freakin' patrol. I told him to shut his yap and get back in formation. Thought he did, sir. If that…" Silva cursed in Portuguese.

Collins spit. "I'm gonna wring the little turd's neck."

"Shut up, all of you." Sam scanned the circled paratroopers. "Ames, come with me, might need your French. Pinball, you, too. You're least likely to shoot Morton on sight." He looked at Springwater. "If we're not back in fifteen, leave without us. It's critical we get what we've learned back to the S-Two, ASAP."

*   *   *

Behr advanced with a purposeful pace, enjoying the stalk. *Perhaps I'll take a prisoner.* He grinned. Intelligence officers always craved an enemy tongue.

Among a line of scattered trees and brush one hundred forty meters southeast of the farmhouse he found a suitable location for concealed observation. He surveyed the farmstead through his binoculars. Several cows were corralled along a stone barn.

Panting sounded close to his ear. Behr leaned toward the sniper. "Catch your breath, my jager. I expect a trophy roebuck for you at any moment."

Behr suspected he was hunting another recon patrol—one that had penetrated deeply. He had to admit that the American paratroopers were well trained and audacious. He used the company frequency to radio in the farmstead map coordinates. He felt certain the regimental artillery battery would refuse a fire mission request on a mere recon patrol. However, Hauptsturmfuhrer Von Gremp would refuse him nothing. All company 81mm mortars were dialed in and standing by. A mere five-second radio call would unleash sufficient hell.

Behr panned his binoculars, pausing at each window, door, and building corner. He caught a flash of tan and a helmet in the gap between the penned cattle and house. "Between the house and cows."

"Jawohl," the sniper said from his prone firing position.

"One just went through that gap. Shoot the next. He'll be angling left to right."

Minutes passed without an Ami following.

An eerie howl came from the house. A fraulein? His cheek scar throbbed.

*   *   *

The scream rattled Sam worse than a burst of incoming MG-42 fire. He stood upright and sprinted the final sixty yards, hurdling both sides of the garden fence on a direct line to the house. He reached for the handle of the double French doors, pushed, and pulled. Locked! Ames and Pinball arrived.

Another scream pierced the air. *"A l'aide! A l'aide!"*

Ames translated the obvious. "She's calling for help."

"Upstairs." Sam rammed his shoulder where the doors joined. Wood cracked. Glass shattered. He stumbled into the great-room. "Pinball, door security."

Sam dashed down a hallway and stumbled into the kitchen. Christ on the Cross still watched over the room. Yet now, a helmet, M-1 rifle, and web gear were strewn across the table. Ames trailing right behind, Sam scrambled around the table, turned into a hall, and found a staircase.

He bounded up the stairs, stopping three steps short of the top. A breeze billowed the hallway curtains inward. The silence set him even more on edge. He turned to Ames and whispered, "Hang back. Cover me."

Sam inched down the white plaster hallway. He opened the first door on the left. Linen closet.

The second door stood open wide. Sam ducked his head into an empty bedroom. Two beds. A feminine motif. A portrait held a prominent place on the wall. The woman pictured had a striking resemblance to Raquel.

The third door faced the length of the hall. Sam twisted the knob. Locked. He removed his helmet and pressed his ear flat against the door. Muffled moans and grunts came from the other side.

Stepping back, he dropped his helmet, raised his foot, and crashed a boot into the door just above the knob. The jamb shattered. The door flew open with such force that it rebounded off the wall and flew back in his face. He barged though into a large bedroom.

The duvet atop the bed was disheveled and splotched with bright crimson.

Sam stepped left and scanned the room. Morton's flushed face popped up from the far side of the high bed. Fingernail scratches marked the private's left cheek.

Sam sidestepped the width of the bedroom. Raquel struggled underneath Morton.

Morton clutched a trench knife in his right hand while pressing his left hand on Raquel's mouth. The girl's eyes were wide with terror. With each frantic breath, blood bubbled out her nose and popped across Morton's hand. Morton's jump pants gathered around his ankles.

Sam aimed his M-1 at Morton's head.

Morton's eyes flashed defiance. He turned back to Raquel, dug his jump boot toes into the rug, and renewed the assault, thrusting forward with his hips.

Afraid of hitting Raquel, Sam lowered his rifle.

Raquel clutched her attacker's ear and yanked. Morton cursed and grabbed for her wrist, leaving her mouth uncovered.

"*Arretez-le!*" she screamed.

"Drop the knife! Get off her, Morton! That's an order!"

Morton released her wrist and groped at Raquel's exposed chest.

Sam tossed his M-1 onto the bed, drew his 45-auto, and fired three quick rounds into the ceiling. Plaster chips and dust rained down.

Morton paused.

Sam rushed forward and straddled Morton. Grabbing a handful of jump jacket collar, he yanked back and rammed the muzzle of the big pistol into Morton's temple. "Drop the knife!"

Morton complied.

Pistol pressed to the private's skull, Sam dragged Morton backward by the collar. In a fury, he flung Morton backward. Pants at his ankles, Morton crashed into a chest of drawers.

Sam couldn't help but look at Raquel. The sight left him aghast.

Violent grunts and curses made Sam spin around, pistol ready. Ames smashed his fist into Morton's mouth.

Raquel crab-walked into the corner. Her blouse was ripped open to her waist. Her pure white breasts bore bruises. The fruit of Morton's perversity disgusted and shamed Sam.

Wearing an expression more like an uncomprehending and helpless animal than human, Raquel squeezed herself into the corner under an open window and repeatedly tried to rearrange a skirt that wasn't there. Her throat emitted little whimpering rasps.

The sound of groans and fists striking flesh drew Sam's attention. He pivoted. Ames continued to pummel Morton's face. Pinball stood in the door, dumbfounded.

"Enough!" Sam dropped the 45 hammer and holstered it.

Morton collapsed. Ames stomped Morton's crotch and backed away.

"Private Vigiano, I ordered you to guard the door. You abandoned your post. Get back down there. Now!"

Pinball turned and ran, feet echoing down the hardwood hall and stairway.

Sam looked to Raquel. "Tell her I won't let anyone hurt her anymore."

Ames stammered with long pauses in his French.

"Tell her I'm sorry. Tell her..." Sam searched for appropriate words. "Tell her Morton will be punished."

Raquel exploded into wracking sobs. She drew her knees up to her chest and tried to rearrange her torn blouse.

Sam pulled the duvet off the bed and covered her. "It's OK. It's OK. It's over now. We'll protect you, Raquel."

Ames translated in the same soothing tone as Sam.

"Ames, get Raquel a jacket or…something. First door."

Morton spit a glob of blood and piece of tooth as he struggled to pull his pants up. Ames's fists had reduced one eye to a blood-engorged slit.

Raquel whimpered, "*Non, non, non. A l'aide. A l'aide.*" Locking her frightened gaze on Morton, she drew the duvet tighter and exposed a blood-smeared inner thigh.

Sam averted his gaze. Morton leered at Raquel's leg.

What am I thinking? Morton sitting there has got to be torture for her. Sam un-holstered his pistol. "What're you staring at?" He pointed the big-bored 45-auto at Morton. "Get out of here."

Sam kicked Morton in the seat to hasten his exit out the door. It propelled Morton into Ames. Ames threw a right-hook and knocked Morton into the Comeaux sisters' room. Ames held up an old tan raincoat.

"Good. Find her a wet washcloth. Tell her we'll get her some help." Sam stepped into the doorway of the sisters' room. "Then stay away. The less you know the better."

"Sir, this goes down however you say."

Sam bent down to pick his helmet off the hallway floor and stepped into the sisters' bedroom. Morton sat on the floor, his back slouched against the opposite wall, rubbing the ear that just took Ames's right hook. Mournful sobs came from down the hall, intensifying Sam's rage. "Eyes on me, Morton!"

Morton straightened slightly and tilted his head back.

"You're going to tell me why." Sam exhaled hard through his nostrils. "Why…why such brutality? Why risk your buddies?"

Morton broke eye contact.

"Why?" Sam pointed his 45-auto at Morton's scrawny center mass. "Why such a heinous act? Such unadulterated, vile barbarism!"

Morton wiped blood off his upper lip. "Don't be using none of your college-boy words on me."

"You idiot! She's just an innocent girl, not some Piccadilly whore."

Morton pouted. "I need a cigarette."

"You need to tell me why!"

Morton gave an obscene gesture and let his head droop.

"You pitiful and…and deplorable little piece…" Sam thumbed the pistol's hammer back two metallic clicks and stepped closer. "Look at me, Morton. *Why?*"

Morton jerked his head back, flinging blood. "That jerk, Pettigrew, for starters."

"That's asinine!" Sam said. "How could Pettigrew have anything to do with you raping a girl?"

"Him always yelling in that whiny voice that none of us was ever making it to twenty-one. Last week sure proved him right. It's just a friggin' matter of time. Every last one of us suckers is just a dead man walking. What the hell's left to hope for?" Morton spit a mixture of clotted blood and mucus. "Been too long since I had a woman. Figured if I'm dead tomorrow, today's my last chance. Of all people, *you* got to understand."

Sam blinked. "Me? What am I supposed to understand about you acting like a vicious animal?" Sam's hand trembled. He raised the pistol.

"No sir, you ain't getting off that easy." Morton glowered at Sam. "Pettigrew's just part of the reason. You officers always talking down to me like I were just some punk kid, or worse, like a dog. Like I don't know nothin'. But you officers—you college-boy officers—you know everything. You know everything but you keep it from us so we'll stay your little *peons*. Jump at your orders."

"Morton, now you're making zero sense."

"No? Well how about that time back at Merryfield. Just a few days ago. You and your butter-bar buddy was having one of your college-boy chats. Sharing your college-boy secrets. But you blew it. You didn't figure on me hearing. But I heard you—loud and clear. You said there's no God, so we can do as we damn well please. No God to make the rights *right* and the wrongs *wrong*. We're free to make our own rules. You said that! Remember? I thought about it long and hard. It made sense."

Morton's shattered nose forced him to pause to catch his breath. "So maybe I die today. Or, I die tomorrow. If not, it'll just be next week. In the end I don't have to answer to no God, so what the hell difference does anything make?"

Sam clenched his teeth together. "What you did is wrong."

"Why? Because you don't like it and you've got the gun? So end it right here, right now." Morton spread his arms open. "I really don't give a damn who made the bullet—Kraut or the good ol' US of A—it's all the same in the end. Just know that when you pull that trigger, you carry some blame. Raquel ain't all on me."

Sam's pistol grew heavy beyond what he could bear. He holstered it and scanned the room for a belt, length of cord, or anything to tie Morton's hands. Sam's stomach turned. Bile surged up his throat. He gagged and put his hand to his mouth. "I should tie you up, give her your trench knife, and let her have her way with you!"

"Like you said, '*all* things are permitted.'"

Morton's hand darted inside his jump jacket and came out gripping his P-38.

Sam reached for his own pistol, knowing he could never bring it to bear in time.

Morton shoved the P-38 muzzle into his mouth. His whole body trembled.

Sam's instincts told him that Morton's eyes were pleading for life. *Just like Billy back at that Piccadilly cathouse.* "Do it, Morton…pull that trigger."

Morton scrunched his face and yanked the trigger. Sam's muscles convulsed. Crimson gore splashed the white plaster wall.

Chapter 67

Target of Opportunity

Ames burst in, M-1 shouldered.

Sam stared at Morton's lifeless body. "It's OK."

"Didn't sound like no Forty-five."

"Shot himself. Forgot about his Kraut pistol." Sam's knees started shaking. "Let's get out of here before any more of us have to die."

"The girl?"

"We're messing around on Kraut turf. Can't sit here waiting for her father to round up all the cows. We can't just leave her here, either." Sam ran his fingers back through his hair. "Raquel needs a doctor. She'll know someone in Carentan who can look after her."

Feeling queasy, Sam approached Morton's corpse and pulled out the dog tag chain. "For his mother's sake, he died on a vital mission behind enemy lines." He removed a dog tag. "Took a German nine-millimeter to the head. Didn't feel a thing."

"Went down just like you said, sir," Ames said. "Mamas don't need to know nothing about this kind of crap."

Sam grabbed Morton's corpse by the ankles started dragging him out. "Take Raquel downstairs. Keep talking to her. Comfort her. Have Pinball collect Morton's gear."

"Just like she's my kid sister." Ames left and Sam soon heard less-than-fluent French spoken kindly. This day would forever traumatize Raquel's memories and terrorize her soul. Everything was happening way too fast. *This has zero resemblance to warfare taught at OCS. Nothing but pure existential chaos.* Choices had to be made before possible consequences could even be anticipated.

He looked at Morton's head and the trailing blood swath. A wave of nausea washed over him. He dropped Morton's feet. All that blood. *I can't just drag him out of here.* It struck him that they couldn't leave without telling Comeaux something, either. The Frenchman would see the blood, not find his daughter, and become frantic. He ducked his head out the door. "Ames!"

Ames stopped at the top of the stairs and looked back. Three steps behind, Raquel also paused and looked over her shoulder.

"Write Monsieur Comeaux a note—"

The hall exploded in a red mist followed by the ringing report of a rifle.

*   *   *

What Behr was witnessing left him both curious and annoyed. Following the scream, three Americans ran to the farmhouse displaying zero discretion of reconnaissance troops. It was as if the scream had served as a signal to dash forward. In addition, they came from an unexpected direction—right to left, from the northeast. Before he could alert his sniper to the new targets, the Americans disappeared behind the house. "Fence. Right of the house. Three just jumped it. Shoot the next."

The sniper shifted. "Jawohl!"

Behr detected the faint tinkling of breaking glass. Why break into the house? The Ami actions defied reason. He shifted his binoculars back to the cattle pen and panned to the corner of the house. Nothing. He moved the binoculars upward and across the second story of the house. Tan flashed across the left window. There! He caught movement in the right window, too. "Target! Second story. Right window."

The drapes billowed inward with the breeze. He spotted a white stripe on the back of the helmet. "Officer. Upstairs. Right window. Hurry!"

"Got him…wait…he's gone."

"Don't take your scope off that window," Behr said. "Patience, my jager, patience. If you have a sure shot, take it. We'll get another with only a little patience."

He waited.

Three pistol shots rang out from inside the house. Another American streaked by the window.

"Patience. Only a little more patience." Behr refused to allow his voice to betray his confusion over the shots. *Why risk discovery so far from your own lines, Ami?* "We now have at least three cornered upstairs. One officer. Patience."

Another flash of tan went by the right window.

"The staircase must be between the two windows. Patience."

More movement across the window frame, but no American paused.

Minutes passed. "Have patience."

A muffled pistol shot came from within the house.

Most puzzling. Behr kept his binoculars centered on the window. "Patience. We may yet solve this little riddle."

An American crossed the window frame twice, too fast for a sure shot.

A patch of tan filled the window.

This American paused.

"Take him!"

A gust of breeze lifted the curtains upward. The Mauser fired with a sharp report.

As the bullet struck, Behr saw flowing blond locks.

He dropped his binoculars. "Nein! Nein! Nein! A fraulein? How?" He slammed his fist into the ground. Sounds came from his sniper's throat as if the teen was about to vomit. Behr glanced left. The sniper's face was ashen.

"Get back on that scope! Shoot all you see."

The sniper fired again.

Behr turned toward the rest of his reconnaissance patrol and raised his voice. "Baum, Stroh, Werner, follow me. It's time you learn to clear a house." Behr jabbed the toe of his jackboot into the radio operator. "You see an orange flare, call in the mortar barrage."

"Jawohl, Herr Hauptscharfuhrer." The radioman readied his machine-pistol.

Behr found a corporal behind a tree-trunk, clutching an MP-40. "Sturmmann, you spot any movement, give us cover fire. When we duck behind the house, cease-fire. You see the orange flare, break contact and rally at the concrete bridge."

Behr bent low and trotted southwest, three young panzergrenadieren in tow.

Chapter 68

Close Combat

The shot ringing in his head, Sam dropped prone. He blinked and focused on the hallway wall. The bloody mist stained the plaster a muted crimson around a bullet hole.

Below the crimson stain, Raquel struggled for breath like a catfish out of water. The girl's eyes remained open wide, while her mouth opened and closed, opened and closed.

The breeze carried faint German shouts.

Raquel's blood expanded across the hardwood floor. With each silent gasp for breath, pink froth issued from her mouth.

Sam rose and rushed to her side. A bullet whip-cracked by his ear and slammed into the plaster wall. He went flat.

Raquel's breaths came in gurgles and wheezes. She was drowning in her own blood. Her panicked eyes begged for help.

"Sniper." Ames hugged the floor. "Hey, Pinball! We've got us a sniper this side, straight out."

Footsteps sounded below. "Got movement." Pinball fired two shots. "Four running to right flank. Tree line. Hundred fifty yards out."

A fusillade of rifle and submachine gun fire erupted and struck the ground floor.

Ames popped up in the window to the right of the stairway. As fast as he could pull the trigger, he emptied his M-1 to suppress the fire pouring in on Pinball.

The incoming fire shifted. Second floor window frames splintered. Shattered glass sprayed inward. Plaster chips and dust showered down.

Ames spewed oaths as he hunched below the window and shoved another clip into his rifle. "We sure stepped in it now, Lieutenant."

Sam was fixated on getting Raquel away from the window without exposing himself to the flurry of bullets. He hooked his arm under her armpit, and pushed off with his heels. It worked. He pulled his legs back under him and tried it again. His boots slipped in the pool of Raquel's blood. He strained again. After several attempts, he got Raquel clear of the window.

Pinball fired three more rapid shots. The incoming fire concentrated back on the first floor.

Sam ripped apart a first aid kit, opened Raquel's raincoat and pulled back her ripped blouse. He slapped a bandage compress over the entry hole in her ribcage just behind her left arm. The hole wheezed and bubbled with each gasp for air she attempted.

Sam opened another first aid kit and further spread the front of the raincoat and blouse open to locate the exit wound. The contrast of bright blood and pale feminine flesh sickened him further. He swallowed hard. "Don't die, Raquel."

He found the exit wound just under Raquel's right armpit. Blood gurgled and bubbled from the gaping exit wound. The bullet had then passed through her tiny bicep. In obvious futility, he covered the ribcage exit hole with a military dressing, tied it around her chest, and closed the blouse.

Ames popped up and got off two well-aimed shots before the hallway again erupted in bullet-shattered debris. He crawled to the window where Raquel had dropped.

Sam took a morphine Syrette and jabbed it into Raquel's thigh. He picked up the second Syrette and paused with it poised over her leg. *Do I dare?* Raquel was petite—two doses might prove lethal.

He refused to allow her to die in pain—not physical pain, anyway. He jabbed the second morphine injection into Raquel's flesh and wrapped her in his arms. She would die knowing someone cared, someone held her to the end. He swayed back and forth and tried to hum a lullaby he remembered singing to his baby sister.

His gaze landed on Morton's jump boots, toes up, protruding out the doorway. *It's my fault. All my fault.* "Forgive me, Raquel. Please, please, forgive me." Tears plowed furrows through plaster dust on his cheeks. *This wasn't supposed to happen. It was just ideas. Just philosophy.*

Ames fired again.

The wheezing stopped. Sam rocked Raquel until all life faded from her tormented eyes.

Pinball fired three evenly spaced shots.

A burst of submachine gun fire erupted from the first floor.

*   *   *

Behr approached the stone Norman farmhouse from the flank, through the barnyard. The modest firefight on the opposite side raged on. This side of the house seemed abandoned.

The shattered double doors stood wide open. He turned to his entry team. "Never fully trust comrades firing guns—stay out of windows."

He paused to try to gain an accurate assessment on the location of every firearm in the house. One downstairs. Not sure about upstairs—maybe three. He snuck into the house, Bergmann submachine gun at the ready.

He remembered the route through the great-room, with its open beamed ceiling, down a hall leading to the kitchen. He made each step lightly to silence his hobnailed boots. Reaching the end of the hall, he halted.

He heard movement in the next room—the kitchen, if he remembered correctly.

Behr bent at the knees, poised like a coiled spring.

Three evenly spaced rifle shots rang out, followed by a distinct metallic ping.

His mind flashed to American weapons orientation at the Thouars range. *The American wonder-rifle is empty.*

He leapt into the kitchen and pivoted left.

Three meters away, under a window, a short American was cramming a clipped bundle of bullets into the top of his rifle.

The American's eyes locked onto Behr's and widened in fear—reflecting a realization that his death was a blink away.

Behr jerked the trigger all the way back and released. A four-round burst impacted the American's broad chest.

Behr scanned the room. An American rifle and combat harness on the oak table struck him as odd. His disfigured cheek twitched and grew hotter. The close combat aroused all his senses. He was once again fighting in Russia.

Now came the tricky part. His burst of fire no doubt aroused the suspicion of the Americans upstairs. He had to act fast to retain the initiative. He barged through his men and rushed for the stairwell. He pointed to the man carrying a Mauser rifle. "Baum, stay down here, cover our rear." He let his slung Bergmann hang loose from his neck and pulled two stick grenades out from under his belt. He armed the grenades and nodded to the two men carrying MP-40 machine-pistols. "Follow me."

Foreign shouts came from upstairs.

At the base of the stairway, he jerked the porcelain knob hanging out of one wooden handled grenade, counted to three, and tossed it up the stairway.

The grenade bumped the floor. A man shouted the English word for *handgranate.*

The grenade blast sent masonry particles and wood debris falling down the stairs.

Behr went halfway up the stairs and, seeing that the upstairs hall extended back the opposite direction, tossed the second hand grenade that way.

He dropped back two steps for cover.

The second grenade exploded.

*   *   *

The burst of automatic fire downstairs had the effect of a slap to Sam's face. "Pinball! What's going on down there? Vigiano!"

Hobnailed boots sounded from below.

Ames's eyes widened. "We've got to find—"

A potato masher grenade landed next to Ames's ribcage.

Sam shouted a warning.

An explosion erupted.

The concussion left Sam stunned. His ears rang like he was standing in a bell tower. He still held Raquel against his chest. Her raincoat had smoking rips. Her body had shielded Sam from the deadly fragments.

Ames lay broken, bleeding. Motionless.

My rifle! Where's my rifle? On the bed. He crawled into the master bedroom and grabbed his M-1.

Another grenade blasted the opposite end of the hall.

He dove between the bed and the wall. Despite the ringing in his ears, he recognized the sound of hobnailed boots rushing up the stairway. He pivoted on his knees and whipped his M-1 around toward the doorway.

*   *   *

Leading with his Bergmann, Behr craned his neck to catch a glimpse of the second floor. A soldier crumpled on the floor and a pair of boots—toes up—sticking out a doorway. The female was slumped in the far corner. He ducked his head back and then looked again. Nothing had moved.

Behr dashed up the stairs. Two storm troopers followed.

He fired a short burst into the crumpled body and doubled back to a door at the end of the hall, behind the stairway. His second grenade had blown it open. He signaled Stroh to cover the blown door Behr stood beside, and Werner to cover the hall toward the bodies.

Back to the wall, Behr pulled his last stick grenade from the top of his jackboot, armed it and, exposing nothing more than his hand and forearm, tossed the grenade into the room.

The hand grenade blast blew black smoke and debris out the door.

Weapon ready, Behr entered the room.

Nothing but crates and trunks.

He moved back down the hallway, past a linen closet, and halted next to the doorway with the protruding boots. "Grenade." He held out his hand. Werner placed a grenade in it. Behr armed the grenade and flicked it around the doorjamb.

BOOM!

Smoke and debris dust still billowing out the door, Behr ducked into the room. He stepped over an inert body and almost slipped in a trail of blood. A broken-framed portrait of a beautiful woman lay in the floor. The dead American had a massive head wound on the back of his skull, yet his face looked pummeled.

This whole episode is too odd. Behr's internal survival alarm—honed by years surviving Russia—was going off in his head. *This is a charnel house. All are dead. Finish teaching the drill and get out.*

Exiting the bedroom, he yanked Werner's last grenade out of his belt. Behr moved to the last door and took up a position opposite the dead female. *She's just a child.* He averted his gaze. *Why another fraulein?*

Behr grimaced and tossed a grenade around the doorjamb.

Two rapid rifle shots greeted his hand. He jerked it back, untouched.

*   *   *

My room's next, Sam thought as he centered his M-1 on the doorway.

A large hand swung around the doorjamb and released a potato masher grenade. The long grenade flipped end-over-end, seemingly flying toward Sam in slow motion.

Sam jerked the trigger twice.

He dropped to the floor. Through the gap under the bed he saw the grenade, just a few feet away, smoking and hissing. In reflex reaction, he kicked out and connected with a bedpost. The foot of the bed collapsed. Sam shoved his shoulder into the bed.

The head of the bed collapsed as the grenade exploded.

The blast lifted the massive bed and deposited it onto Sam. The explosive concussion left him even more woozy and disoriented.

His hearing abandoned him.

The smell of cordite filled the air. Smoke and feathers clouded the bedroom.

His rifle lost, Sam fumbled at his shoulder holster as he struggled to free himself from the smothering weight of the mattress.

A silhouette filled the doorway, already firing as it advanced through the smoke and feather filled air. Sam's focus sharpened on the epitome of an Aryan warrior. A giant of a man. A disfigured face.

He ceased wrestling the ripped and smoking mattress and found a grip on his Colt pistol. He'd just cleared leather when more orange flames spurt from the enemy soldier's gun muzzle.

An intense burning sensation engulfed his left side.

He fought to hang on to reality. His will failed to overpower his concussed and pierced body. "Maggie. Maggie…" He couldn't take in air. His senses faded.

*   *   *

Behr barged into the room firing bursts into blind corners. Swirling feathers and smoke dominated his vision.

Across the room, a pathetic creature struggled to free itself from under a smoldering mattress. The American's eyes begged for life, but his hand came up brandishing a big pistol.

Behr loosed a string of 9mm bullets across the mattress and into the man.

I read the eyes wrong. He still had fight in him.

"Clear!" Behr lit a papirosa and shoved a fresh magazine into his empty Bergmann. "Stroh, get downstairs with Baum. Make sure our exit is secure." His engorged cheek throbbed. "Werner, collect Ami papers." Behr took a long drag and let the Russian tobacco sooth his nerves. Boots pounded down the stairs. Behr sighed. In a shattered mirror he watched smoke billow out his nostrils like a dragon.

Werner leaned inside the door. "What about the girl, Herr Hauptscharfuhrer?"

"Maggie. Maggie…" the dying American moaned.

A roar of rifle and submachine gun fire erupted on the first floor, accompanied by foreign shouts. Behr dashed for the door.

Werner rushed toward the stairway.

"Nein!" Behr shouted just as his green soldat peeked down the stairway.

Werner jerked his MP-40 up to fire. An American submachine gun fired first. A bullet struck Werner's throat.

Werner stumbled back down the hall, mouth opened in a silent scream, spraying arterial blood on both walls. He died before reaching Behr.

Shouted pleas came from the first floor. Behr made out the English word for *leutnant*. "Lieutenant? Lieutenant Henry!"

He glanced back into the bedroom. Escape through the window. But first… He patted his belt. Nothing. He felt his boot top. No grenades. He scrambled across the ruined bed and stepped on the bullet-riddled American. He stuck a leg out the window and looked below to gauge the drop.

Heavy footfalls came up the stairs.

"Mag…" the dying American moaned.

He heard shuffling behind him and turned to face the door. An American crouched in the doorway, his big-bored submachine gun pointed toward Behr. The American also spotted the dying American beside Behr's leg, and hesitated.

Behr and the squinting American made eye contact. The man was the very visage of the American Frontier aboriginal warrior he had admired in his boyhood books.

Behr pushed off to drop out the windowsill.

The big-bored submachine gun belched flame. A bullet plowed across his shoulder and Behr tumbled out the window. His mind flashed to an image of a Russian beauty, a mixture of East and West. *Anya!*

He slammed to the ground. All the air whooshed out of his lungs. Pain shot through his ankle. His vision filled with cobalt Russian sky.

Chapter 69

Consequences Compounded

Behr bit his lower lip and limped through the penned cows. His ankle protested each step. He opened a gate and ducked around the corner of a stone barn. Gasping for air, he fumbled for the holster holding his flare pistol. He broke open the single-shot pistol and confirmed the flare color—orange.

He pointed the pistol skyward and jerked the trigger. A star cluster flare burst a hundred meters overhead. He grimaced. *I will have the last say in this insignificant corner of the war, my Ami friends.*

He limped downhill, toward the bridge, careful not to slip on the cow trail. His swelling ankle filled his boot. He snapped a dead limb out of a hedgerow to use as a cane.

A hundred meters down the trail, he rounded a corner and almost collided with a huffing, middle-aged farmer. Behr recognized the alarmed farmer. The fraulein behind the farmer was an older version of the girl his sniper had shot.

Behr refused eye contact and hobbled on downhill. He glanced over his shoulder. The dairy farmer and girl dashed up the trail. "Raquel!"

For the first time, he felt disgrace over a combat operation.

*   *   *

Sam regained consciousness in the middle of the bedroom floor. Springwater ripped Sam's jump jacket and shirt sleeves open and wrapped a Carlisle bandage around his left forearm. Sam lifted his head. Additional battle dressings wrapped his torso. He let his head loll to the side. Down feathers stuck to blood on the floor. "Get the intel back across our lines."

Springwater pulled Sam's shirt and jacket closed. "Can you breathe?"

"It hurts." Sam closed his eyes and grimaced. "But not as much as my head."

"No air coming out. I think they missed your lung." Springwater placed Sam's helmet on his head.

Sam rose to a crouch and vomited. His head swooned. "Pinball?"

Bracing Sam's arm, Springwater guided him out the bedroom and down the hall. Sam averted his eyes from the carnage—a dead SS trooper, Ames, Morton, Raquel.

Rapid footsteps sounded up the stairway. Lazeski's head popped up. "Tree line's clear. Krauts are long gone. High time we cleared out."

Sam resisted Springwater's grasp. "Can't just leave Raquel."

Lazeski headed back up the stairs. "I'll get her."

A mortar round faintly whistled.

The blast collapsed the ceiling and knocked Sam flat at the top of the stairs.

Sam rose to his hands and knees. Lath, broken chunks of plaster, and slate roof tiles slid off his back. Through the dust and smoke he saw Lazeski and Springwater tangled together at the bottom of the stairs. Lazeski pushed off Springwater and climbed up the stairs. Springwater went into a coughing fit.

A mortar barrage exploded around the farmstead. Smoke roiled up the stairway.

Sam stood on wobbly legs, descended four steps, and looked back over his shoulder. The pool of blood had disappeared, yet through the shattered building materials he could make out patches of tan cloth and blond hair. Raquel—viciously robbed of her innocence and her life—remained slumped in the corner. An overwhelming sense of culpability immobilized him.

Two mortar rounds struck the opposite pitch of the roof. The house shuddered.

Another round hit the kitchen. The concussion wave slammed Sam. His ears rang.

He felt a tug on his baggy pants and turned. Lazeski's lips were moving but no words registered. It didn't matter. The next action was obvious.

Sam leapt to the base of the stairs. Pain shot through his left side.

Flames were engulfing the kitchen. Jagged crucifix pieces lay spread across the table. Going down the hall, he raised a forearm to shield his face from the flames. He followed Lazeski away from the fire, toward the front doors.

Silva trotted by, Pinball's body draped over his back in a fireman's carry.

"We need to move fast, Silva." Springwater coughed. "Pinball's gone. Nothing you can do."

"Not leaving him to burn!" Silva neared the double doors.

Two mortar rounds exploded alongside the house. Flying glass and debris showered the paratroopers as they dropped.

The mortar barrage walked toward the barns. Cows bellowed frantically.

Shrapnel still striking the wall and windows above them, Sam and the other paratroopers stayed prone. The room was filling with acrid smoke. Flames licked around an interior door. Sam inhaled and choked on the fumes.

"Can you run?" Springwater said. Blood trickled from small gashes on his brow and cheek.

More faint whistles warned of incoming mortar rounds.

Sam felt his head for his helmet, found nothing, and dropped to the floor.

More German 81mm mortar rounds showered the farmstead.

Dark smoke lowered. Flames grew closer. The crackling roar of burning ceiling beams and dry flooring dominated Sam's hearing. The heat was becoming unbearable.

"Now!" Springwater grabbed Sam's arm and ran.

Sam's lungs couldn't find the air he needed, but with Springwater keeping a grip on his arm, he pushed on. Lazeski scanned ahead for threats. Silva carried Pinball's body.

Dashing straight for the cover of a stone barn, they wove through dead cows. Among the cattle, Sam spotted human bodies. Monsieur Comeaux and Raquel's older sister. *No! No! They did nothing to deserve this! I brought this hell upon them.* His legs faltered and stumbled.

Springwater dragged him around the corner of a barn.

Sam fought for breaths. His chest hurt.

Silva eased Pinball's body to the ground. Tears streamed down his face.

Mortars struck on the other side of the barn. Springwater studied his compass, looked up, and pointed. He grabbed Sam's arm and trotted along the barn. Springwater opened a gate. "Can you run?"

Sam nodded.

Pumping his legs, half-stumbling, he tried to keep up with Springwater. A hedgerow grew nearer.

A faint whine was gaining on them from above.

BLAM!

The explosive force swept him forward. He landed in a headfirst slide. Pain shot through his left side.

Except for a horrific ringing, Sam's hearing was again lost.

He rolled over and sat up. A twisted pair of wire-rimmed glasses lay between his boots. One lens was missing, the other was cracked and dripping bloody goo.

Covering his ears in an effort to stop the ringing, he lolled his head back. A piece of camouflage parachute fluttered across the pasture. Sam reached for his neck. His parachute scarf was there.

His throat constricted. He looked back at the mangled glasses at his feet.

"Lazeski!" he screamed. "Laz-es-ki!"

A forearm slid under his armpit and dragged him away.

"Lazeski's glasses. Get... He needs his..."

He looked to see who was dragging him. Springwater's lips were moving, yet Sam heard nothing. He pointed to his ears.

Springwater leaned close. "Laze is gone!"

Sam jerked away from Springwater and yelled over the ringing in his head, "Laze needs his glasses!"

He ran to the spot where the mortar had knocked him down, went to his knees, and searched the grass. Another mortar hit the house and sent a thick shower of sparks skyward as if a giant had stirred a colossal campfire.

He spotted the glasses, seized them, and lofted them high in his left hand. "Found them!" He sensed warm liquid spurting down his side.

Springwater grabbed Sam's arm. "Lazeski's dead. We've got to leave now, sir!" Springwater lifted him to his feet.

Sam caught a glimpse of jump boots and tan fabric in the grass. The top of the baggy pants terminated in a smoking, bloody mass. Nothing remained above mid-torso.

Silva staggered past, still carrying Pinball's body.

Springwater held Sam's elbow as if guiding an elderly aunt. Sweat traced tracks down Springwater's sooty face. "Sam, you're bleeding. Bad."

Sam followed Springwater's gaze. Blood was pouring out a rip in his left armpit.

He grew woozy, yet kept his grip on Lazeski's wire-rimmed glasses. The world dimmed. He sensed Springwater tossing him over his shoulder in the fireman's carry. The world went dark.

*   *   *

Regaining consciousness, flat on his back, Sam sensed something unfamiliar in his grip. He opened his palm and looked. Lazeski's mangled glasses. Rising bile seared his throat. With a swift backhand he flung the glasses away.

It didn't help. He couldn't keep the images of Lazeski's half-corpse, Raquel's pleading eyes, or Morton's condemning words from replaying in his mind.

"Stop moving, Lieutenant! You're making the bleeding worse. Someone hold him down."

Gazing into the overcast Norman sky, the coppery odor of blood filled Sam's nostrils. He closed his eyes. Pinball. Ames. The Comeaux family. All dead. He twisted his neck right and opened his eyes. Grass filled his vision. He groaned.

"Come on, Doc," Springwater pleaded, "stop the bleeding."

Sam looked left. Doc Walters hovered over his side. "Got to find the source."

The sound of scissors snipping fabric reached through the ringing in Sam's ears.

"Stay with us, Lieutenant Henry. Let's see where you caught that shrapnel." Doc Walters gingerly lifted Sam's left arm up and outward.

With detached repulsion, Sam watched his blood spurt into Doc Walters's face.

Doc Walters thrust his index finger into the hole. In a clinical voice he said, "Brachial artery. Too high for a tourniquet. If it retracts... Not good. We've got to stem the bleeding." Doc Walters pivoted on his knees, pressed his thumb into the skin between the collarbone and muscle that ran from the neck, and squeezed hard.

Sam screamed and twisted as the sutures tore out of his half-healed bayonet wound.

"Morphine, Sergeant." Doc Walters maintained his grip and pulled his finger out of the shrapnel wound. The artery quit spurting.

Springwater grabbed a Syrette from Doc's bag and jabbed Sam's thigh.

"Now, you've got to squeeze hard right here." Doc Walters and Springwater changed places. "Just like I am, Sergeant."

Sam bit his lip and slapped his hand down into the grass. "Ted, listen." Sam gritted his teeth. "Maggie. The letter—"

"Shut up!" Springwater said and mumbled something in Crow.

"English, Ted. English."

Springwater glanced toward the distance as if he was expecting someone. "We've got some of Sink's Five-O-Sixth boys coming with a stretcher and plasma."

Heavy footsteps and profanity distracted Sam.

"They kilt Pinball. Them lousy Nazi bastards done kilt Pinball."

"Just shut up, Collins, and help," Springwater said.

"Hold those compresses to his side and stay out of the way," Doc Walters said. "Sorry, Lieutenant Henry. This could get a little ugly, but I've got to get a clamp on that artery. Means I've got to do some cutting."

Sam nodded. He'd never envisioned his last lingering moments of existence to be spent laid out helpless in a Norman cow pasture, in pool of his own blood, mourning a girl he'd helped kill, longing to salvage a love affair he'd caused to fail, and grieving over men who'd become closer than brothers.

He felt the scalpel slice the taut skin of his armpit.

He rolled his head away and focused on his wadded up jump jacket—covered with a mixture of his and Raquel's blood. *Damn jacket.* He closed his eyes and cried.

"Can't see." Doc Walters shifted his position. "Too much blood."

"Find it, Doc! Find it now. Come on, Doc, stop the bleeding."

Sam found no comfort in Springwater's frantic tone.

"There! I think I got it. Sergeant, let go…slowly."

Sam felt the pressure released on his bayonet wound. A spray of arterial blood hit Doc Walters in the forehead.

Springwater clamped back down. "Do your job, Doc!"

Doc Walters went back to work. Scalpel slicing. Hemostat clamp probing. "I think…let up…slowly."

Springwater released the pressure point.

Sam tried to look. His position limited his view, but no blood spurted.

"Got it! He needs plasma, pronto." Doc Walters wiped the blood from his eyes and gazed beyond the huddle. "What the hell's taking Sink's boys?"

Springwater swiped his bloody hands across his pants and slid his fingers between Sam's head and the pasture. "He's going to make it now. Right, Doc?"

Doc Walters busied himself in his medic's bag. "Dump some sulfa on his forearm."

Sam pounded his right fist into the ground. He got Springwater's attention. Sam's lips moved but no audible sounds came out. Reaching deep inside to muster the strength, he raised his head slightly. Springwater brought his head down to Sam's mouth.

"Get Maggie the letter. The platoon is yours. Take care of our men… the Crow…"

"Here come Sink's boys! Move out of the way," Doc Walters commanded. "He's going into shock. Damn it, we're losing him! Get that plasma in…"

Sam's vision blurred. He faded into darkness.

Chapter 70

Luxury to Priority

12 June 1944, 1810 Hours
Carentan, Normandy

"We're wasting our time. There's no way we can perform the kind of surgery he needs."

In the *Hotellerie Centrale* kitchen, two surgeons conferred over the bloody body. A medic carrying a transfusion bottle entered through the swinging double doors connecting the kitchen to the hotel dining room. "You order O-positive?"

The younger surgeon glanced up. "Excellent, Corporal. Plasma's not doing the trick anymore." He unhooked the plasma I.V. and began transfusing whole blood. "Good timing on the lieutenant's part. Much earlier and we wouldn't have had the luxury to even consider his case. Still, I hate to admit that you're right, Major. No possibility of saving him. Not here." He checked the pulse—weak and thready. "This is the guy who taught me to jump. Not a bad egg, either—even for a UCLA ballplayer. I patched him up when that English dame stuck a pitchfork through his forearm."

"This is *that* lieutenant?" The major shook his head. "A crying shame. Scuttlebutt had it those two had quite the romance going."

"Yeah, so let's see if we can't get them back together." The young surgeon frowned. "I just wish we had that brachial clamped better."

The major looked at the hemostat sticking out the lieutenant's armpit. "We can transfer him to Utah Beach for evac, but no way he'd survive any boat ride across the Channel. Especially on a slow LST."

The younger surgeon forced his sleep-deprived mind to focus. *Air Corps just opened an airstrip behind Omaha Beach a couple of days ago. Vital supplies come in. Severely wounded go out.* He rubbed his temples. *A farther drive than Utah. Falls under Five Corps. But…what do I care about military protocol?*

The USC pitcher-turned-Army-surgeon pulled down his surgical mask and wiped his hands on his bloody apron. "Priority cases can now be air evacuated. I'm making Lieutenant Henry a top priority. With any luck he'll be back in England in two or three hours."

He stuck his head out the swinging door. "Corporal, I want this paratrooper rushed to that new airstrip behind Omaha. Get me the ambulance driver with the heaviest lead-foot. Driver gets a bottle of aged scotch if he delivers the lieutenant in less than an hour, and alive. Keep O-positive going into him. And whatever you do, don't bump that hemostat sticking out of his armpit."

*   *   *

1945 Hours
Near Omaha Beach, Normandy

Aviation fuel. Hydraulic fluid.
Dad's fedora. I smell it.
Where am I?
Aircraft engine noise increased to a frenzied pitch.
C-47. *My dad makes C-Forty-sevens.* He squirmed and twisted his
    body. *How did I…?*
Are you here, Pa?
Sam's eyes jerked open. *Another jump, so soon?* Through blurred vision he watched two Negro GIs work to lift his stretcher.

He closed his eyes and drifted. *Maggie, oh, Maggie, I'm so sorry. Don't listen to Morton. Raquel wasn't my fault. Maggie, forgive…*

His eyes jerked open. He raised his right arm and found a red tube running into it. A dark-haired nurse with matching bags under her eyes, silver bars on her collar, and a dour expression on her ruby-red lips held a half-empty bottle of blood over him. He tried to speak, but words refused to form. His abused left side shot pain to his brain. He moaned.

"We need some more morphine in this one," the nurse said in a southern belle accent. "There now, slide him into that lower rack. We have to keep that I.V. up high, boy. Gently now. Gently. Thank you, boy."

Sam groaned.

"Where's that morphine?"

He felt a needle slide into his right arm. The pain subsided. The Pratt & Whitney engines howled. He sensed the plane rolling. He reached for his reserve chute and panicked. "Wait! I can't jump! Where's my chute?"

The nurse appeared at his side. "It'll be just fine, trooper. No one's making you jump out this time. We'll have ya'll back in England in no time at'all. You don't go n' worry your little ol' head."

"No! My men, they…"

He sensed consciousness fading, yet was impotent to do anything about it.

*   *   *

The nurse checked the I.V. bottle for the fourth time in fifteen minutes. The paratrooper lieutenant had nearly emptied it. His pulse was weakening. She shook her head. *We need to start flying with at least some plasma.*

Moving up the aisle, she had to grab for support as the plane hit another air pocket. She entered the cockpit and leaned over the napping copilot to catch the view out his window. English Channel whitecaps pitched 5,000 feet below.

The nurse stepped back and handed the radioman a list of names, wounds, and conditions. "Twenty minutes advance notice might save the life of these eight soldiers." She tapped the name Lieutenant Samuel Henry. "Tell them we need at least two units of O-positive to stabilize the airborne lieutenant. He won't make it off the table unless we get more whole blood in him first. Have them get their cracker-jack vascular surgeon standing by, too." She turned back toward the pilot and laid a flirtatious hand on his shoulder. "Any way ya'll might speed this flight up a little?"

The pilot scowled and shifted his unlit cigar.

"Please do oblige me this once, sir. We haven't lost a patient yet. Please, sir, let's not make that paratrooper our first."

The pilot nudged the throttle forward and added thirty knots to the airspeed.

PART V

---

*FOR MY INIQUITIES HAVE GONE
OVER MY HEAD. AS A HEAVY BURDEN,
THEY ARE TOO HEAVY FOR ME.*

Psalm 38:4

Is there any blame attached because somebody took Nietzsche's philosophy seriously and fashioned his life on it…? Your Honor, it is hardly fair to hang a nineteen-year-old boy for the philosophy that was taught him at the university.

CLARENCE DARROW
1924

Chapter 71

Unwelcome Discoveries

14 June 1944, Wednesday
Merryfield, England

Reverend Simon Guard paced down the hospital ward aisle. Beds lined each side, with only narrow gaps between. The opening of the Omaha Beach airstrip had filled the Merryfield hospital to capacity. The US Army Medical Corps had packed this ward with over thirty critically wounded patients. Elevated electric fans circulated the antiseptic and testosterone tainted air. White dominated everything above the gray concrete floor—sheets, walls, casts, patient gowns, bandages, and bedpans.

He made his best effort to match names with faces. The beds he moved between experienced rapid turnover. He updated his notes on missing soldiers. If they ended up at another part of the growing Merryfield medical complex, he would be sure to pay them a follow-up visit. He sighed. *Too many of these poor lads are going from here to a grave.*

He stopped at the foot of a bed. The new patient was lying unconscious, his left side bandaged from neck to waist, including the arm. Rev. Guard lifted the patient's chart from the hook at the foot of the bed. Despite his educational deficiency in the healing arts he could tell that this soldier's prognosis was poor. He skimmed the chart, noting a shrapnel wound requiring a resection of the brachial artery, three bullet wounds, a collapsed lung, and a deep laceration to the trapezius muscle…

A nurse came alongside, administering morphine.

"Excuse me, nurse. This lad?" Rev. Guard referred to the chart. "Second Lef'tenant Samuel Henry. Perhaps he needs a wee bit extra…" He guarded his words around comatose patients—just because they couldn't respond, didn't mean they couldn't hear.

The nurse pulled the needle out her patient's arm. "This one's already had his miracle, Reverend."

"Oh? I hold a professional interest in the miraculous."

The nurse took the clipboard out of his hand. "Either that or these paratroopers are the toughest customers the Army has. I've never seen a man survive the blood loss he had. The textbooks say he should've died." She made a notation on the chart. "But textbooks don't account for darn— pardon my French, Reverend—good medics, lots of plasma, doctors going above and beyond—"

"Or perhaps a praying mother or wife?"

"Mother, maybe. No wedding ring listed among his personal effects." The nurse scurried off to her next patient.

Rev. Guard let his hand hover over the soldier's head and prayed.

*   *   *

Walking through Ilton en route to his parsonage, an uneasiness kept nagging at the back of Rev. Guard's mind. He had missed something in the day's events. Something significant. He narrowed it down to the lef'tenant paratrooper. *Scott Henry… Oh, bother! Not Scott, you senile old fool. It was Samuel. Lef'tenant Samuel Henry.*

He retired that night still troubled, yet convinced he'd never met the Samuel Henry barely hanging onto life a half-mile away.

Over breakfast, the name was still nagging him. *Samuel Henry. Not all that uncommon. Could just as well be an Englishman's name.* He swallowed a spoonful of oatmeal porridge. *Samuel Henry… Perhaps a chap I made an acquaintance with in London? Weymouth? Oxford?*

Following morning devotionals, he decided the time had come to sweep the dried mud out of the sanctuary. The first Sunday after the invasion had seen the worship service attendance triple to forty-four souls. It hardly bothered him that about half the parishioners had tracked in mud.

Sweeping the third row he remembered the tall lass he'd found praying more than a week earlier. What was her name? He reached the broom under the pew. *Maggie. Miss Margaret Elliott. There, you're not as daft as all that. You can still jolly well remember a name. And not just a name. What a story that lass had. I do hope she's faring better. Got herself all involved—in love, I dare say—with a Yank paratrooper. An officer at that. What was his name?* He swept dirt into a pile. *Oh, yes, his name was Sam Henry.*

Rev. Guard dropped his broom. "Oh, good Lord, no."

*   *   *

15 June 1944, Thursday
Overton, England

"This past term we read some marvelous tales, inhabited by fascinating characters. Of all the characters, who has a favorite?"

Maggie turned from writing novel titles on the slate chalkboard and scanned the classroom. Students' hands shot up. Her gaze landed on Jeremy. He leaned forward, waving his hand. "Jeremy?"

Jeremy stood next to his desk. "Mr. Darcy, Miss Elliott."

She smiled. *And to think, ten months ago he bragged, 'I jolly well ain't never read no ruddy sissy books.'* "A favorite of mine, too. Do tell us why. Might he remind you of someone you know?"

"Not hardly like a mate, but that Yank lef'tenant you stuck with the pitchfork seems like a bloke a lot like Mr. Darcy."

A lump lodged in Maggie's throat. She tried to swallow. "Interesting choice. Please explain yourself, Jeremy. His name's Lef'tenant Henry."

"Well, Lef'tenant 'Enery did the right thing, even when you had the wrong idea 'bout him. Reckon he could've shot you and no bobby could've pinched him."

"Lef'tenant Henry was unarmed. It was my fault. I made wrong presumptions."

"Aye, you was prejudiced, just like Elizabeth Bennet. But like Mr. Darcy, Lef'tenant 'Enery was a gentleman." Jeremy's face beamed. "He must've told you something like Mr. Darcy told Elizabeth. I seen you holdin' his hand back Easter weekend, over at Laverstoke Woods."

Giggles rippled through the classroom. Maggie blushed.

Headmaster Hampton stuck his head into the classroom. "Miss Elliott, may I have a word with you?"

Maggie's pulse rate jumped. *Spying again? There was nothing unorthodox in my teaching this time.* She stepped into the hallway and tried gauging the situation. However, Headmaster Hampton's little pig-eyes refused to make contact. He held out an opened telegram envelope.

"It's addressed to me." Maggie wrinkled her brow. "With all due respect, sir, you have no right—"

"I shall grant you special leave for the remainder of today and tomorrow." Headmaster Hampton gazed at the ceiling. "I'm quite certain Miss Hamlin will agree to substitute for your weekend duties. However, I fully expect you to be present Monday morning. If not, I'll be forced to consider it a violation of—"

"Pardon me, but you're making no sense."

Headmaster Hampton nodded toward the envelope.

Maggie noted that the telegram originated from Ilton. It identified the sender as Reverend Guard.

Before she could finish reading, tears were splashing on the telegram.

*   *   *

18 June 1944, Sunday
Merryfield, England

You must be strong. Find it in yourself, Maggie.

She stroked the back of Sam's hand. She hadn't left his bedside for more than a ten-minute span in nearly forty-eight hours. She glanced at her watch. Her train departed within the hour. Reverend Guard had arranged a jeep ride to the Ilminster train station. By the time her train reached Overton she'd need to walk straight to her classroom.

Sam remained unconscious. Yet, on occasion, he had screamed, panted for air, and convulsed. More than once he'd called out scrambled names.

The medical staff refused to venture an opinion for when Sam might regain consciousness. One nurse—a captain with a deplorable bedside manner—seemed to take pleasure in pointing out that Lieutenant Henry shouldn't even be alive, much less engaging his English girlfriend in lucid conversation. The more tactful medical staff attributed his persistent semi-comatose state to massive blood loss, shock, morphine, and enduring a week of combat with little sleep. A surgeon confided to Maggie that it was yet too early to speculate on permanent disability, including possible brain damage. The doctors even declined to rule out the dreadful military designation, DOW—died of wounds.

Rev. Guard's influence in the hospital provided a degree of tolerance for her highly irregular stay. Fortunately, the nurses—the ill-tempered captain excepted—welcomed the personal care and attention she paid Sam. From time to time Maggie had even assisted with Sam's neighbors.

She placed a folded note atop the small nightstand. The nightstand held the small display she'd made with the contents of the parcel she had twice tried, yet failed, to deliver. *When* Sam did awaken he would see her gifts, old and new—a framed portrait, a soldier's pocket New Testament, and a rose with a lock of her golden hair tied to it.

"Sam?" She swallowed back the lump in her throat. "I must leave now or I may never be allowed to teach again. Seems we all have our Lef'tenant Pettigrews." She wiped away a tear. "You know how much teaching means to me. It makes me feel alive. Like…like, I feel with you. Sam, I love…" The empty ache in her stomach prevented her from finishing. She lovingly placed his hand back at his side and pulled herself away.

She held herself together until outside the ward before bursting into tears.

*   *   *

21 June 1944, Wednesday

Sam regained consciousness in a panicked start. "Sergeant Springwater, I ordered…where's Laze? Pinball's hit! Grenade!"

He panted rapidly. His left side ached. His heart raced. He felt feverish, claustrophobic. Reaching for his canteen, his hand collided with a mattress. Semi-darkness cloaked the room. He distinguished silhouettes—beds, elevated I.V. bottles, arms and legs in traction. His sense of smell awakened to an odd mixture—antiseptic, males, plaster, urine, a hint of feces. A hospital? *How'd I get here?*

He lifted his right arm. A tube protruded from it. He attempted raising his left arm. It didn't respond. Amputated? In horror, he grabbed across his body and sighed with relief. His left arm was present and accounted for.

A surge of pain cleared his head like smelling salts. He tried sitting up. Intense pain emanated from his ribs. He collapsed back.

Propping himself up on his right elbow, he tried to gain his bearings. A female form scurried by. "Excuse me, ma'am." His voice croaked. "But… but, where am I?"

"A US Army hospital, Lieutenant Henry. So please keep your voice down," the nurse said. "We've been doing our danged-est to get you back among the living for over a week now."

Sam collapsed into his pillow. "Hospital. Obviously. But where?"

"England. Some out of the way airfield you wouldn't know. Merryfield."

"Geronimo." His voice was devoid of emotion. "Flew out of here."

"OK, Mr. Geronimo. Now that you can speak for yourself, how's your pain?"

"Nothing I can't handle. Why am I here?"

"Three bullet wounds, all through-and-through. Two to your distal left side. Exiting, one caught a rib. Another bullet wound, left forearm, also through-and-through. Shrapnel fragment cut the brachial artery and nicked the upper humerus. One collapsed lung. Deep laceration to the left trapezius—"

Sam held up his hand and closed his eyes.

"Don't care for me to continue?"

"I get the idea." The litany of wounds triggered memories of the Comeaux farm. He closed his eyes. The scene played back like a movie. Certain scenes froze, yet the film refused to melt and burn away from his memory.

A hand gripped his arm. Before he could jerk away the soothing numbness of the morphine surged through his body. He hoped a drug-induced stupor would take away the appalling images—Raquel, Morton, what remained of Lazeski.

*   *   *

By dawn, Sam had endured horrific memories of all his Normandy tragedies. Sweat soaked his hospital gown. He grew agitated and morose. Morton's accusing voice haunted him. The weight of Raquel's brutal rape and subsequent death rested upon his shoulders. Apart from his folly, Lazeski's dismembered body wouldn't be scattered across a Norman pasture. Pinball was dead. Ames was dead. Monsieur Comeaux and his eldest daughter…all dead.

His self-loathing surpassed his increasing physical pain. He refused morphine.

Mid-morning, a nurse came through and pulled the blinds, flooding the ward with sunlight. Sam scrunched his eyes shut tighter and shifted his head to face left.

Upon opening his eyes he thought he was hallucinating. He blinked three times to refocus. Fourteen inches from his face, the visage of an angel smiled down upon him. Even in black-and-white the studio photo captured both Maggie's beauty—her radiant complexion, large eyes, light hair—and her passion for life. Her subdued smile hinted at her spunk and quick wit. *I'm unworthy of her beauty. Normandy proved as much.*

He recalled naively proclaiming Maggie as his purpose for living. Yet now, just as she had predicted, he had discovered that she was not enough. Not enough to remove his anguish, his guilt. "You managed to find me. Again."

"What's that, Lieutenant?" The nurse looked up from his chart. "Oh, I see you found your gifts. She left a note, too."

"She was actually *here?*"

"Oh, yes. Stayed as long as she could. Quite a gal." The nurse unfolded the note. "Want me to read it to you?"

"No. Give it here." He grabbed at the note. Pain shot through his body.

"Do you need more morphine? You look like—"

"Just give me my note." He gritted his teeth. "What is today?"

"Wednesday, June twenty-first." The nurse handed him the note and departed.

He held the paper before his eyes and almost called the nurse back. He couldn't distinguish words. He rubbed his eyes and squinted. The letters weren't crisp, but just legible.

> *18 June 1944, Sunday*
>
> *My Dearest Sam,*
>
> *I stayed as long as I dared, but not long enough. I can't bear to leave, but I must. I'll explain later.*
>
> *Twice I tried getting the photograph to you before the invasion. The pocket Testament, too.*
>
> *I never wanted you to return this way, but return you did, as you promised.*
>
> *I long to be at your side. And I pray it'll be soon. Until then, to quote Miss Dietrich's version of "Lili Marlene" you Yanks favor: "Give me a rose to show how much you care, Tie to the stem a lock of golden hair."*
>
> *I will return. I promise. Underneath the lantern. You still owe me a steak dinner.*
>
> *Love, Maggie*
>
> *PS – A Rev. Guard informed me that you were here. He's a marvelous man. I do hope you two become acquainted. This was my second trip to Merryfield. My first was on the evening of June 5th—another thing I shall explain later.*

He gazed back at the picture and noticed a glass of water. Through the glass he made out a thorny stem. His eyes followed the stem upward. Below the red rose petals, a pink ribbon tied a lock of Maggie's blond hair to the stem.

His head collapsed into his pillow. *Why offer hope? I deserve none.*

The nurse returned with a bald surgeon. The surgeon's lab coat displayed the gold oak leaves of a major. Sam stared at the ceiling. The surgeon examined him for several minutes and jotted on the charts. "Lieutenant Henry, I had to work some magic to keep you among the living. Even so, completing your recovery's still going to take a concerted effort on your part. Listen, son, you airborne boys are tough, but it's obvious you're in considerable pain."

Sam stared upward, refusing to acknowledge the surgeon.

"Have it your way then." The surgeon shrugged. "Though I'd wager my next leave to London that you'll be begging for morphine before my shift's over."

Sam closed his eyes, knowing sleep would only bring hideous images from that Norman farmstead.

Chapter 72

Logical Deductions

22 June 1944, Thursday

Sam discovered a distinctly nonmilitary man standing at the foot of his bed. He blinked several times to clear his sleep-blurred vision. The middle-aged man was somewhat pear-shaped—thickening in the middle and narrowing toward the top. His wild gray hair was sparse. Yet, the most noteworthy aspect was his clerical collar.

Sam squinted. "Reverend Guard, I presume."

"A pleasure to meet you, too, Lef'tenant Henry." Rev. Guard's face radiated a genuine smile. "I've already heard so much about you, though. I suggest we dispense with formalities. May I call you Sam?"

Sam turned away and stared across the ward. "Sounds swell, Reverend."

"Please, call me Simon. I do grow weary of formal titles, especially since we share much in common."

Sam snorted. "Yeah, sure. Like what?"

"Oh, I do believe I'll let you make that discovery. But to show you that I'm not just blowing smoke, well…suffice it to say that I too found the father-son struggle in *The Yearling* exceptionally insightful, at times painfully so. Odd, wouldn't you say, seeing that the author has never experienced being either a father or a son."

Sam let his eyes sag closed. "You've been talking to Maggie."

"Simply an incredible lass, if ever there was one."

Sam pinched the bridge of his nose and grimaced. "Preaching to the choir."

"I dare say, shave thirty years off my age and I'd jolly well give you a good run for your money. A lad might fish a whole lifetime and not land a catch like Maggie."

Sam turned to face Rev. Guard, hoping his scowl would discourage conversation. "What would you know about—?"

"Oh, this blasted collar confounds so many of you Yanks. I'm Anglican. Allowed to marry and all associated God ordained pleasures. I have three daughters. I suspect the youngest would be nearest your age."

"Why're you here? They've got a chaplain surplus in the British Army?"

Rev. Guard scratched his thinning hair. "I'm without official duties. You might say I'm here on behalf of our mutual friend, Maggie. Which we've already established. So, shall we move on to more engaging conversation?"

"I've talked to you people before. Chaplains and such. Never got past their pat answers and spiritual platitudes. Did me zero good." Sam closed his eyes, hoping Rev. Guard would catch the hint.

"Amen to that sentiment, Sam! I dare say I've bumped into such boorish louts more times than I dare mention."

Sam let his eyes open, but gazed out the window. The sky had a heavy overcast, explaining the humidity in the ward. "With all due respect, Reverend, you have no idea of the depth of the *valley of the shadow of death* I jumped into."

"Perhaps you paint me with brushstrokes too broad. A twenty-three-year-old grenadier in the mud of Passchendaele comes to mind. I'm dreadful with names, but if I recall, those around him addressed him as Lef'tenant Guard."

Sam bit his lower lip and sighed. "How's Maggie?"

"Oh, I imagine she's aged several years the past fortnight. But she'll—"

"It stinks in here." Sam scrunched up his nose. "Need some fresh air."

"Perhaps I can be of some assistance with that, too. As soon as we get a doctor's consent you can come visit me. It's really just a wee trek."

Sam closed his eyes.

"Must pop out," Rev. Guard said. "I'll inform Maggie that you're—"

Sam jerked up. "No! Don't." He tried to calm his voice. "I'm not ready."

"Duly noted." Rev. Guard put on a black bowler hat. "And, Sam, refusing medication won't erase whatever happened over there."

Sam tossed his head to the side. "That's got nothing—"

"I've heard enough of your nightmares to suspect otherwise. Self-flagellation becomes a downward spiral solving nothing, son." Rev. Guard removed his spectacles and slid them into his vest pocket.

"Can you...find out where my men are?" Sam fought the lump constricting his throat. "Able Company, Five-O-First Parachute Infantry Regiment, Hundred-'n-First Airborne Division."

"I'll do my best." Rev. Guard placed a hand on Sam's good shoulder. "Before I leave, do you mind if I pray for you?"

"*Yes.* Please don't."

Reverend Guard prayed anyway.

*   *   *

27 June 1944, Tuesday

"You aren't going to like what I overheard this morning."

Sam grimaced and shifted his torso to gain a semblance of comfort from the hospital bed. "If you say so, Simon."

Rev. Guard examined Sam's chart. "What's a section-eight?"

"Medical discharge for psychological reasons. The Army doesn't like keeping nutcases, even if they're responsible for making them."

"I dare say, given context, that's precisely what I'd deduced."

"Your point?"

"I don't pretend to know anything about the American educational system, but I suspect a young teacher might find employment rather difficult to secure—entrusted with a community's children and all—with a section-eight discharge on his record. But what do I know?"

Sam ran his hand back through his unkept hair. "I'm not crazy."

"No argument here. We've had some marvelous and very lucid conversations over the past week. But..."

Sam scowled. "So the wonderful medical staff likes to tattle."

Rev. Guard extended his index finger. "First, you refuse to communicate. Not a word. Not even grunts or gestures."

Sam shrugged. "Nothing I say would help them do their job any better."

Rev. Guard held up another finger. "Second, you refuse food and scarcely drink any fluids."

"I detest the bedpan. Just adds insult to injury."

"Sam, you're free to get up and walk." Rev. Guard extended a third finger. "Third, you continue to refuse pain medication."

Sam looked away. "It's tough for a drug addict to get a teaching job, too."

"Sam, there's absolutely no self-inflicted punishment that can change what happened."

"Something I'll have to live with."

"And Maggie?"

Sam looked back to get a read on Rev. Guard's face.

"Maggie is very concerned," Rev. Guard said. "Distraught might be a more appropriate description."

"What've you told her?"

"Here I am, an ordained minister of the Church of England, and I let some Yank convince me to break our Lord's holy commandment about bearing false witness. Not a complete fabrication, mind you. I tell her that you aren't even communicating with the medical staff. You're in considerable pain, but the physical prognosis is looking better each day. I've about reached my limit, Sam."

"But she wants to come see me?"

"She'd be here right now if not for my little deception and the matter of her unjust probation. The poor lass is crushed and torn. She dares not put her teaching career at grave risk without some assurance that you can communicate." Rev. Guard pointed to the unopened letters next to Maggie's portrait. "You could jolly well at least read what she's written."

Sam looked away and bit his lower lip—still dried and chapped from his comatose days on morphine. Three beds to the right a fan buzzed. Four beds to the left a GI thrashed and shrieked through a nightmare. A nurse scurried to sedate the man. Sam gazed at Maggie's picture, then to the wilting rose and lock of golden hair.

"I must be off." Rev. Guard put on his bowler. "Oh, I almost forgot. As best as I can ascertain, your regiment remains in Normandy. I'm unable to learn any more than that. Mind if I pray for you?"

Sam closed his eyes. "Not me, I'm safe. Pray for First Platoon, Able Company." He felt a tear slide down his cheek.

*　　*　　*

Sam pushed the food tray away and tried to sleep. His body refused. Three weeks ago, hunted night and day behind enemy lines, he'd convinced himself he'd never catch up on lost sleep. *I was wrong about that, too.*

He felt the tray being lifted away, and opened his eyes. A male orderly with corporal stripes frowned disapprovingly. "You've got to start getting some chow down, sir. If you won't listen to me, I'll get a particularly disagreeable captain in here and have her order you to eat."

Sam glared at the straight-leg orderly. *It would take jump wings on her chest for me to obey her.*

He gazed at Maggie's picture, the wilted rose, the unopened letters. He reached over his battered and perforated left side, groaned at the weight shift on his wounds, and tilted Maggie's picture to lie face down. His hand bumped the pocket Testament. *I remember Sunday school. A little hellfire and damnation is what I've earned.* He picked up the Testament. *Bet I can find some in there.*

He flipped open the front cover. Below an elaborate British crest, he found the typeset words, "Presented to." On a line under that, Maggie's feminine hand had written: 2ⁿᵈ Lt. Samuel Henry, 501ˢᵗ PIR. The printing press had printed, "By the British Bible Society," which Maggie had crossed out and added, "Love, Margaret Elliott." Below her name the publisher inscribed, "Be strong and of a good courage."

Easy to say from behind a printing press. *Bet my jump pay he never led a recon patrol into enemy territory.*

The facing page had a regal imprint of a crown and below that in bold, capital letters: A MESSAGE FROM HIS MAJESTY THE KING. *So his royal highness, King George the VI, himself, has a special message just for me?* Back in the U.S., a straight-legged chaplain had handed Sam a similar pocket Bible, except President Franklin Delano Roosevelt had signed that one. *Why do rulers want to appeal to God so badly?*

And not just the allied democracies. His mind flashed to a bloated Wehrmacht corpse in the swamp near Catz. A protruding aluminum belt buckle proclaiming: *"GOTT MIT UNS"*—God is for us.

He tossed in bed. *But it can't work for both sides! Evil is evil. Certain things must be good.* His deductions did nothing to decrease his discomfort. *Morality must go beyond mere personal preference. Beyond cultural boundaries. Moral truth must transcend national mandates. Or, I can't judge anything. Not even what Morton did to Raquel.*

Then, almost as if a veil had been lifted, illumination. *Kant was right— moral absolutes require a Moral Giver. A God who, somehow, cares about what destruction we might wreak on Earth.* He sighed deeply, his existential angst finding a measure of relief.

Yet, his immediate situation posed a more practical crisis. He considered Rev. Guard's section-eight comments. He had to get a handle on reality. He closed his eyes and drifted.

*   *   *

A nurse scurrying past awoke Sam from a shallow nap.

"Nurse, pardon me, could I get some chow?"

The nurse spun mid-stride and smirked. "So, the deaf-mute speaks. One of Reverend Guard's miracles?"

He averted his eyes. "How about a cheeseburger and a Coke?" He shifted his hips to sit up straighter. "Sorry for acting like a jerk. Could you get me something for my arm and side? They're a bit sore. But I still want to lay off the hard stuff, so hold the morphine, please."

Writing on Sam's chart, she said, "Pain we can handle. The cheeseburger and Coke might prove a little tricky."

"Then how about the daily special and a cup of joe?"

Her smirk softened to a smile. "Coming right up."

"And, nurse, I really am sorry. Please note on my chart that I was just being a jackass. I'm not losing my marbles. Please, no section-eight."

"Who mentioned any section-eight? No medical staff has questioned your sanity."

Sam shook his head and almost smiled. Simon Guard.

*   *   *

June 30, Friday

Sam rose early and rounded up enough clothing to venture outside. He felt self-conscious wearing *straight-leg* regular infantry pants, shirt, and overseas cap. At least he was able to get his jump boots. Someone had cleaned the blood and polished them. He'd walk out as a paratrooper.

He got a shave and a haircut to tame his wild re-growth. His left arm in a sling didn't prevent him from returning a smart salute and handing his pass to the RAF sentry manning Merryfield's main gate.

Having been twice confined to Merryfield, he finally entered Ilton. The village's pronounced insignificance came as a surprise to him—a few houses, pub, small hotel, and post office. An ancient chapel stood across the road from the Royal Mail.

A sunken footpath led him to the stone church. A yew tree dominated the obligatory English churchyard cemetery. While working the lych-gate latch, the glass-covered church notice-board caught his attention. It outlined the weekly schedule and listing of religious services offered. At the bottom, skillful calligraphy proclaimed, "Dr. Simon Guard; Vicar."

Sam furrowed his brow. Doctor?

He passed through the lych-gate and ventured up a path with weeds encroaching on the cobblestones. He tried to read tombstones. Erosion had long since rendered most illegible. He sensed growing rings of perspiration under his arms. He spent several minutes attempting to decipher colonial-era grave markers. "You're just stalling," he said to himself. He focused on the church entrance and took deliberate steps toward it. *Here's one more chance for a refusal at the door. Jump school all over again.* He thumbed the latch on the main doors.

Locked.

He heaved a sigh of relief and walked around under the shade of the imposing yew. Lichen covered the church's wall. He discovered another door and thumbed the latch. It released. He pushed the door inward and stepped into a hallway. The chilly air smelled musty. Overseas cap in hand, he moved down the hall and peered into the first door on the left.

Rev. Guard looked up from a book, his eyes radiating joy. Rising from behind his desk, he pulled his spectacles off and waved Sam inside. Rev. Guard extended his hand. Sam found comfort in the firm handshake.

"Do have a seat, Sam. I'm so glad you dropped by." Rev. Guard placed a teakettle on an electric hotplate. "Care for a cup of tea?"

"Yes, please, *Doctor* Guard."

Rev. Guard chuckled. "My, but you are the observant lad."

Sam cocked his head and held an index finger in front of his face. "So let me guess. A doctorate in theology?"

Rev. Guard shook his head. "Hardly."

"Church history?"

"Wrong again. Though I do enjoy—"

"Psychology. Have I been your little project?"

Rev. Guard frowned. "Heavens no, Sam."

"Then what? I know it's not medical."

"Philosophy," Rev. Guard said without looking up from tea preparation.

The casual pronouncement silenced Sam. At once, every conversation over the past week both made more sense and baffled him. "I wasn't aware seminaries offered philosophy degrees."

"Oh? It's rather irrelevant in my case. Oxford conferred mine."

"*The* Oxford University?" Grinning, Sam shook his head. "You're pulling my leg."

"I did tell you I'd leave much for you to discover on your own. It tends to leave a deeper impression that way."

"But Ilton? I mean no disrespect, but I find it hard to believe that an Oxford University doctor of philosophy would choose a backwater like Ilton as his parish."

"You assume the choice was mine. Certainly you can't believe you're the only chap with a superior akin to your Lef'tenant Petrilew."

"That's Pettigrew."

"Precisely!" Rev. Guard handed Sam a steaming cup. "There was this certain bishop... Let's just say I chose to cross swords with him once too often. It was over an ecclesiastical direction I deemed crucial at the time. I refused to yield. He informed me that I was to consider his leadership decisions as directly from God."

"A common ploy used by leaders throughout history." Sam took a sip of tea. It burned his tongue. "It's why I contend that human potential must—"

"Abuse is not ample reason to throw the proverbial baby out—" Rev. Guard waved off his own comment. "But we digress. May we return to my story?"

"Sure. I want to hear about Oxford."

"Well, I informed the bishop that *I* was Anglican and as such parted ways with the concept of papal infallibility about four centuries ago."

"Good point." Sam blew on his tea and took another sip.

"Good enough to land me in an Oxfordshire parish just a wee bit larger than Ilton. I was angry, bored, and a short bicycle ride from Oxford University. In the end, it was a blessing. I thrived. Like Joseph sold into Egyptian slavery, what the good bishop meant for evil..." Rev. Guard pushed a tin of condensed milk and bowl of sugar toward Sam. "I landed precisely where the good Lord intended."

"The university pretty much shipwrecked my faith, Dr. Guard." Sam scooped sugar into his cup. "I questioned it all and failed to find satisfying answers in traditional Christian theism."

"Failed to find satisfying answers?" Rev. Guard took a long sip of tea. "Or perhaps you didn't find the implications personally convenient?"

Sam frowned. "So what made your experience at Oxford different?"

"Enough maturity to avoid becoming too enamored with the professors, nor the futile hamster wheel of academia. I was also well enough acquainted with my own ego to recognize other inflated egos. Care for a biscuit?" Rev. Guard offered a plate with assorted cookies. "Don't confuse good critical thinking with the deconstruction of good thought. Academicians—especially philosophical types—all too often think they must either deconstruct or add to truth. It's quite necessary for one to get published, tenured, or a department chair."

"Interesting." Sam took a shortbread. "I haven't seen your cynical side before. So, you found academia self-serving and futile. So what? Futility is everywhere."

"Absolutely! Found everywhere, yet not in everything. A vibrant faith must—as just one key consideration—possess meaning, purpose. Such theism was embodied in two dear friends, about my age, but professors. *Literature* professors, no less! I met with them each week, just off campus at St. Giles. A small pub—the Eagle and Child. We nicknamed it the Bird and Baby." Rev. Guard's smile expanded. "What invigorating discussions. What simply marvelous fellowship. Oh, but I jolly well do miss them. I looked to each Tuesday evening with great expectancy. Just like I held a great expectancy concerning our meeting, here, today."

Sam smirked. "No way you could've been expecting me."

"My good lad, the life of faith is lived out in expectancy."

"Sounds more like hope to me."

"I find hope nearly synonymous with faith. Just add conviction and you have it. Nevertheless, *faith* must have an object. What I've yet to figure out is this, Sam, what is your object?"

Sam shifted in his chair. "You're sounding like Maggie. How about today I get to ask all the questions?"

Rev. Guard waved a dismissive hand. "As you wish."

Sam leaned forward. "What happened between Oxford and here?"

"Long story short, my *gracious* bishop—the closet papist—moved up the hierarchy. He managed to learn about my great joy found in Oxford. On the same day Oxford conferred upon me a doctorate, he exiled me to Ilton. Not that Ilton is all so dreadful, the people are quite admirable, the very salt of the earth. But…" Rev. Guard sighed.

"I'd expect better from a bishop—a man who claims to represent Christ."

"Again, Sam, faith must have an object. You mustn't miss that point, lad. If I placed my hope in man, I'd end up bitter and oft disappointed." Rev. Guard extended the teakettle. "Care for more?"

Sam rose, trying to balance the teacup and saucer with just one hand. "I should go now, Dr. Guard. May I call you *Doctor* Guard? It seems the most natural way to address you at this point."

"Please, refrain from overuse. It tends to play to my vain side."

Sam extended his hand. "And that was one slick trick you played."

"Oh?" Rev. Guard arched his eyebrows as they shook hands. "I'm afraid you lost—"

"Yeah, go ahead, play dumb like a fox." Sam chuckled. "The section-eight ploy. It worked."

Rev. Guard feigned innocence, then his face turned solemn. "You forgot to inquire about Maggie."

"I didn't forget." The lingering knot in Sam's gut intensified.

"Sam, must I remind you once again? Punishing yourself will wind up crushing that dear lass, too." Rev. Guard frowned and perched the reading spectacles back on the end of his nose. "Do attend Sunday services. Ten o'clock sharp, or when a dozen souls show up. I'll be speaking on the gift of divine forgiveness."

"Maybe." Sam shrugged. "I'll let you finish your sermon preparations now."

"Oh, gracious no, Sam. I finished days ago." Rev. Guard held up the book. "Indulging myself in a good novel. *The Brothers Karamazov,* to be precise. Dostoevsky makes a powerful argument for a theist morality. Much along the same lines as Kant."

The comment halted Sam at the door. "That's not how I was taught Dostoevsky."

"Then perhaps it's high time to again question what you've been taught. Employ a little critical thinking."

"Can we discuss Dostoevsky?"

"What a breath of fresh air you've become, lad. I can't recall a more appealing proposal since my arrival in Ilton."

*   *   *

On the walk back to Merryfield, Sam enjoyed both the fresh air and his first stick of Wrigley's Spearmint since Normandy. Back within the expanding hospital complex, he went in search of fellow Screaming Eagles. Of those he found, only two had been wounded after June 12th–the worst day of his life. Yet, he took that as a good sign. In the records office he learned that Privates Schutte, Mason, and Vickers had all recovered enough from wounds received on the Voluptuous Vixen to be transferred to other facilities. Though, surgeons had amputated Schutte's leg.

Crossing through Merryfield's jumble of permanent and temporary structures, Anne Shelton singing "Lili Marlene"—Maggie's favored version—drifted out a window. Sam paused, savoring the melody to the last note.

> Resting in our billet just behind the line
> Even tho' we're parted, your lips are close to mine
> You wait where the lantern softly gleams
> Your sweet face seems to haunt my dream
> My Lili of the lamplight

My own Lili Marlene

That night it wasn't Lili haunting his dreams. He wrestled his demons. He'd fade into slumber, only to be startled awake by Lazeski's abbreviated remains. Or, Morton thrusting a pistol into his mouth. Or, Raquel's mouth bubbling bloody, yet soundless words as she cowered naked in the corner of the supposed sanctity of her own house. Or, the wood handled hand grenade coming to rest against Ames's ribcage. Or, Pinball's bullet-riddled chest. Or, Monsieur Comeaux and his eldest daughter sprawled among dead cows. Or, a pair of mangled wire-rimmed glasses…

Chapter 73

Thought and Action

2 July 1944, Sunday
Ilton, England

Sam sat in the second row of the undersized St. Peter's Church sanctuary. Considering the calendar, the air retained a chill. Above the altar, a stained-glass window depicted The Good Shepherd. It took Sam back to the pre-Operation Neptune 501st PIR chapel service. *Jumping into the valley of the shadow, I sure didn't feel shepherded…or a good enough shepherd to my men.*

An elderly couple sat in front of him. Their wool jackets carried the sweetly malodorous scent that originated only within a dairy milking parlor. The scent took his mind back to the Ozarks. Back to memories of milking while getting swatted in the face with a urine-saturated, cocklebur-imbedded tail-switch. *How did I ever go from an ignorant hillbilly kid to here in just six short years?*

The service began. Unfamiliar with when to stand, when to sit, or when to kneel, he felt self-conscious. Not recognizing a single hymn, he felt ignorant. Being the sole GI, he felt foreign. Yet, when Rev. Guard delivered the sermon, Sam felt captivated. He hung on every word as if the man in the pulpit was Dr. Guard of the Oxford University philosophy department delivering an extraordinary lecture.

The service concluded, Sam moved to the last pew and waited while all eighteen parishioners filed out exchanging pleasantries with their vicar.

Rev. Guard plopped down next to him and heaved a sigh.

"Seems like about every Anglican service I attend is themed around forgiveness." Sam stared at the stained glass. "Coincidence?"

Rev. Guard chuckled. "Hoping to maintain a semblance of consistency to my theism, I must say I reject the concept of mere coincidence." Rev. Guard placed a hand on Sam's good shoulder. "So there must be another reason. Wouldn't you agree?"

Sam shrugged. "We can wish esoteric meaning into events that may not be there."

"Perhaps. Nevertheless, many coincidences defy randomness and stretch credulity. Don't you find that, indeed, too often truth *is* stranger than fiction? There must be a writer on a cosmic scale." Rev. Guard tugged Sam's sling away from his chest. "Where's your new medal? I believe you Yanks call it a Purple Heart."

"How'd you know?"

"Popped by for a chat yesterday. You weren't home. However, your pillow displayed that purple medal with two oak leaves pinned to it—representing three separate incidents of enemy inflicted wounds."

"I was just trying to survive."

Rev. Guard rose and took off his priestly robe. "Have I recounted the time—October, nineteen seventeen—when Lef'tenant Guard caught a leaden gift from the Kaiser in his nether regions?"

Sam couldn't resist a chuckle. "No, but I think I'm destined to hear about it."

"Oddest thing. One bullet, yet four holes. My platoon sergeant warned about crawling with an elevated bum…"

*   *   *

5 July 1944, Wednesday

"It sounds like, on a visceral level, our wars weren't all that different," Sam said, strolling with Rev. Guard through the valley holding Merryfield. "You lost men entrusted to you. Buddies closer than brothers. You got close enough to have the enemy's blood splashed on you. But…but…"

Sam gazed southeast. The Blackdown Hills dominated the horizon. The English Channel waters washed ashore on the other side of those hills. The Cotentin Peninsula jutted out into that same channel. Sam had learned that the 101st Airborne Division held the base of that peninsula. The 501st fought to hold the division's line. Sam's platoon struggled somewhere on the 501st's periphery.

Looking into Rev. Guard's eyes, Sam found compassion.

"But…" Rev. Guard sighed. "No one ever blamed me for the unthinkable?"

Sam shook his head. "I'd let a hundred bayonets get run through my shoulder if it would've stopped Morton." He grimaced. "It hurts. Oh, how it hurts. It would be easier to stomach if it just resulted from a military tactical decision. You choose to engage the enemy. The Krauts just execute a maneuver better. That's war. You do your best and men may still die. But not a single one of my men got killed that way." Sam's eyes got misty. "I can't sort out the whole deal with Morton."

"Giving voice to your thoughts may help, lad."

Sam returned his gaze to the Blackdown Hills. He removed his overseas cap and ran his fingers back through his hair. He stopped, then remembered that Springwater wasn't there to scold him for exhibiting indecisiveness. Anger climbed up his throat. "It's not fair. I can understand Pettigrew catching some blame for dashing their hope. He did it maliciously and repeatedly. But, come on. How can I be blamed just because Morton overheard a private conversation? A philosophical discussion between two guys longing for their university days. I was just voicing ideas, hypothetical thoughts, possibilities. Stuff we'd been taught—"

"Taught and perhaps embraced?" Rev. Guard's tone implied no accusation. "At the very least, toyed with?"

"Yeah, sure. But it was still just ideas we'd learned at the university." Sam waved his good arm in the air. "No one at UCLA followed a lecture on Nietzsche by raping a sorority girl, or shooting at his postman."

"Perhaps only because all the right ingredients weren't present."

Sam glared at Rev. Guard and stomped away down the farm lane.

Rev. Guard caught up as three C-47s approached Merryfield for landing. The vicar remained silent until the aircraft engine and propeller noises faded. "Certainly now you realize that thought will eventually result in action. Actions have consequences. Someone is bound to live out a philosophy to its logical endpoint."

Sam stopped walking. "Not everyone."

"No, not everyone. But it only takes one." Rev. Guard found a stick and tossed it high into the air. As it came down he said, "And one will, as sure as the law of gravity." The stick bounced in the pasture. "It's common knowledge that Nietzsche's teachings led to fascism. Every Hitler requires a Nietzsche. Every Joseph Stalin requires a Karl Marx. Every Apostle Paul requires a Jesus of Nazareth."

Sam shot Rev. Guard a skeptical glance.

"Oh, so I make mention of Christ and you think I've stepped out of bounds, lad?"

They resumed walking.

"Not to trivialize your anguish, Sam, but your sticky wicket brings to mind a portion of *The Brothers Karamazov* I read just yesterday. Ivan Karamazov touted atheism as mankind's door to freedom. Dostoevsky spent much of the rest of the book showing it as a way paved with death and destruction. If there's no God, then there is no ultimate source of absolute moral truth."

Sam held up his hand and stopped Rev. Guard. "Now you're preaching to the choir again. Stuck in that hospital bed—my mind replaying the whole unholy mess at the Comeaux farm about every time I closed my eyes—I reached some discoveries on my own. You did say those were the best discoveries, right, those you make on your own?"

Rev. Guard grinned and nodded.

They stepped aside to allow a hay wagon to pass.

Sam heaved a big sigh. "In one case, if we have no Moral Giver, then we have moral anarchy. The individual gets to decide all that's right and wrong—which obviously can't work. If that were the case, then no moral judgments could be made against *any* individual action, including what Morton did."

"Quite right. Well spoken," Rev. Guard said. "Yet there is another possible source of truth."

"Sure. The group, the nation, the tribe decides what's morally true." Sam stopped walking. "Without a healthy democracy, such thinking leads to nothing more than might-makes-right. Tyranny through power. Your garden-variety thug dictators. Hitler. Mussolini."

"Aye, but democracies are far from immune from the error of might-makes-right," Rev. Guard said. "A free majority can, and oft does get it wrong. Both our nations' wretched history with slavery gives ample witness to that fact."

Sam's expression grew troubled. "If truth is determined through power, then only the strong can determine what's right. If that's the case, then we can only be right if we win through might. Which means…"

"Which means that if the Nazis win, they are morally right," Rev. Guard said.

A shiver went through Sam's body. "And then we have no absolute basis for judging anything as evil. Which is rubbish." He resumed walking. "So, my metaphysical dilemma seems resolved… which does nothing for all the guilt I'm wrestling with."

A half-dozen C-47s labored into the sky and faded away to the southeast. A pair of rooks glided down the road, cawing.

"Sam, do hear me out. You're a bright and conscientious infantry officer. I don't say this to condemn you, but—"

"Shoot straight. I've already condemned myself."

"But this Private Martin—"

"That's *Morton.*"

"Precisely. This Private Morton—a man, albeit with a wretched past and robbed of his hope—he just put into action what you seemingly held forth as an acceptable and valid philosophy."

"So, I *am* to blame."

"Not a single court in the Realm would convict you. Yet. I cannot pronounce you free of culpability. You didn't force Morton's actions. He was a moral free agent. Nor is Nietzsche fully responsible for all the evils of the Third Reich. However, academia does not operate in a moral void. Thought leads to action. Action has consequences."

"Consequences I'll carry with me to the grave."

Rev. Guard mopped the sweat off his brow with a handkerchief. "Have you given any thought to my sermon?"

Sam kicked at a loose rock in the roadway. "About every ten minutes for the past three days. It seems too easy."

"Grace often does…to the recipient. Nevertheless, it always seems to cost the giver quite dearly."

Sam let his shoulders sag. "I'm exhausted. I wasn't as ready for this walk as I thought."

*   *   *

6 July 1944, Thursday, 0210 Hours

Sam tossed and turned in his hospital bed. He would sleep twenty minutes, then awaken—guilt overwhelming him—staring at the ceiling until drifting back to sleep. The cycle repeated itself until dawn's light shone through the windows.

Chest aching, he struggled dressing with just one good arm. Ignoring an orderly's questions, he departed the ward.

*   *   *

0950 Hours

Rev. Guard hadn't seen Sam for twenty-four hours. This struck him as odd considering the two had spent at least a dozen hours together over the previous three days. The mere thought of Sam Henry's turmoil caused Rev. Guard's gut to ache. Sam's physical wounds were healing with remarkable speed. He had his doubts about the lad's emotional wounds.

A sudden flood of 2nd Infantry Division casualties had kept Rev. Guard occupied from dawn until midmorning. He stopped by Sam's ward and found him absent. He noted that Maggie's picture was upright. Her letters were ripped open. Sam?

Rev. Guard's mind played with the possibilities as he walked toward his office to retrieve a commentary on Ecclesiastes. He strode up the stone path, past the headstones and domineering yew, and opened the backdoor route to his office. He noticed a lightbulb on in the sanctuary. *Odd. I'm certain I turned off every light*, he thought, venturing down the hall and into the sanctuary. A figure in an olive drab uniform knelt in the muted red, blue, yellow, and orange light cast by the stained glass window. A sling cradled the man's left arm.

Sam Henry's shoulders convulsed.

Ecclesiastes could wait. Rev. Guard knelt beside the broken paratrooper and put a comforting arm around him.

"Dr. Guard, I think…" Sam wiped the tears away from his eyes. "I think I'm forgiven. But, I'm not so sure I can *ever* forgive myself. Think you could pray for me?"

Chapter 74

Underneath the Lantern

7 July 1944, Friday
Ilton, England

Sam gazed at the gray belly of a low flying C-47 as he meandered down one of the farm roads branching out from Ilton.

Rev. Guard waited until the propeller and engine noise had diminished. "Did I mention that Maggie will arrive this evening?"

Sam ran his fingers back through his hair. The aching knot in his gut grew.

"We were actually able to connect on the telephone at the Royal Mail early this morning. I gave her fair warning. The whole untidy business of your wounds healing. You tire easily, so on and so forth. Nevertheless, your status is rather irrelevant. She's been granted a weekend leave. A regiment of Nazi storm troopers couldn't keep her away."

A farm dog challenged their approach. A calf bellowed.

"Did you tell her anything else?"

Rev. Guard's face broke into a mischievous grin. "Now, Sam, do I strike you as a bloke who might meddle?"

"Thankfully, yes."

*　　*　　*

Sam waited on Ilminster train station's sole platform, a lamppost supporting his battered body. He chewed Wrigley's Spearmint like a chain-smoker smoking cigarettes. He hoped the perspiration rings on his shirt weren't too obvious. He'd wanted to meet Maggie in a class-A airborne uniform, but that had proven impossible. *If it weren't for the slung arm and jump boots, I'd look just like another sad-sack Air Corps clerk.*

Dusk was gathering. Using the street lantern light he looked at his watch for the fourth time in ten minutes. The station's PA system had announced Maggie's train as running twenty minutes behind schedule. That was twenty-seven-and-a-half minutes ago.

Anne Shelton's "Lili Marlene" sounded from the nearby ticket window:

> Underneath the lantern, by the barrack gate
> Darling I remember the way you used to wait
> T'was there that you whispered tenderly
> That you loved me, you'd always be
> My Lili of the lamplight,
> My own Lili Marlene

The train clanged into the station, engulfing the platform with the smell of coal-tainted steam. He searched every window rolling by, trying to catch a glimpse of Maggie. Failing to find her, he nearly panicked.

The train halted and hissed.

He scanned back and forth, end to end.

Maggie stepped off the train, fifteen feet from Sam's lamppost.

His gaze met hers.

Maggie dropped her valise and rushed the final steps.

Their bodies collided. He couldn't suppress a groan. Maggie pulled away, alarm evident on her face.

"It's OK." He held out his slung arm. "The left side's still a bit tender." He reached out with his right arm and pulled her close. "At least this time I know you're here." He buried his face into her hair and inhaled her sweet essence.

Her sobs triggered his tears. "I told you I'd return." He pulled her tighter. "But I was wrong to promise I would."

Maggie shook her head and buried it deeper into his shoulder.

"Maggie, Maggie...Maggie, please forgive me. You were right. Right about everything. You're not enough. I'm not enough. But...you *are* enough to convince that I'm hopelessly in love with you. I can't imagine life without you."

Maggie's shoulders heaved. He pulled his face out of her hair to catch her expression. She wouldn't allow him.

"Nothing to say? That's not like you. You always—"

Maggie raised her left hand and held it in front of his face.

His gaze locked on the pitchfork ring. Joy swept through him. "Feels more like three years than three months." He pulled her back in tight to his right side. "You were also right about Reverend Guard. One incredible man. We share so much in common."

"It's no accident, Sam."

"No need to convince me."

Maggie pulled away just enough to retrieve her handkerchief and dab her eyes. She sniffled. "Think we might find a proper steak in this thriving metropolis? You jolly well still owe me one."

He held out his sling. "Might need some help cutting mine."

"I'm handier with pitchforks." She traced her fingers over the left side of his face. "Your face is all healed."

"Yeah. Got a couple of new character scars. A real good one to go alongside your pitchfork work."

Maggie gave a mock pout. "How dare you allow another. I'm jealous."

"I'll have to keep that in mind next time."

Maggie's countenance dropped. "What do you mean, next time?" Her eyes pleaded. "You've done your part. You were dreadfully wounded. They can't send—"

He pressed his index finger to her lips. "Don't say it."

"No, Sam." Her eyes looked desperate. "No, please no."

"Maggie, please. Not here. Not yet. We're together now. It's a gift."

Maggie moved her lips, kissing his finger.

He took the same finger and wiped a rolling tear from Maggie's cheek.

They leaned together until lips met, and they kissed—a passionate first kiss of ill-timed love.

Underneath the lantern.

Chapter 75

Aftermath

14 July 1944, 0057 Hours
Hungry Hill, near St. Lo, Normandy

Cold liquid crashed into his face. Sputtering and coughing, he swiped his finger across his cheek. He didn't have to look at his hand to recognize the filth that came away stuck to his hand. The stench was sufficient to tell him the goons had tossed the latrine bucket contents to revive him.

He rolled over on the rough concrete and lifted himself to his hands and knees. A tooth fell out his swollen mouth as a jackboot thrust his midsection upward. He collapsed and tucked himself into the fetal position. A kick landed in his kidney. *Not good. I've been passing blood for what, two...three days? What is today?*

He moaned, then retched. The remains of the watery turnip greens soup the POWs called "whispering grass" soup gushed out his mouth and nose.

"Might we engage in a more, shall we say, *intellectually* stimulating conversation, Lieutenant Sterling?"

Brutish hands jerked him up and shoved him onto a milking stool. Sterling looked up. The bare lightbulb above his tormentor's head made him squint. *Doesn't this monster ever sleep?*

Wire-rimmed glasses highlighted the Nazi's bony face. He wore a long leather coat and kept his hair shorn to a uniform peach-fuzz length—the fuzz being sparser on top. He spoke grammatically perfect, almost unaccented English. The Nazi refrained from soiling his own dainty hands and stylish shoes. Sterling figured the man as *Gestapo*.

Airplane engine noise droned through the brick walls. Distant bombs detonated in concussive strings. The ancient French city of St. Lo was receiving yet another pounding.

"Come now, Lieutenant Sterling, your identification tag has my curiosity piqued. Your place of residence is stamped right there—Urbana, Illinois—so what harm can come from us having a little chat?" The Gestapo monster smirked. "Urbana. What you Americans call a college town. Am I not correct? So, perhaps you are a scholar? My colleague completed his doctorate at the University of Illinois. Perhaps you two met?"

The Gestapo monster flicked his finger. A goon made a sweeping kick at a stool leg. Sterling dropped into the filthy wet floor. Pain shot up his spine.

"The University of Cologne conferred a master's degree upon me— philosophical history." The Gestapo absentmindedly spun his wedding band around his finger. "But, alas, the war interrupted. I concluded, why merely study history, when one can make history? Why merely interpret the world when one can shape it? My dear wife and precious daughters can wait. My doctorate can wait. I am certain that a man of letters, such as I assume you to be, can relate to such sentiments. Am I not right, Lieutenant Sterling?" The Gestapo turned away.

A cupped hand slammed over Sterling's ear. His inner ear seemed to explode. He howled in pain.

"Friedrich Nietzsche said..." The Gestapo monster turned back around. "Pardon me for being rather presumptuous. Certainly they taught Nietzsche at the University of Illinois, did they not, Lieutenant Sterling?" He shrugged. "Regardless, the point remains the same. Nietzsche said, 'He who has a *why* to live for can bear almost any *how*.'" He lit his pipe. "I must admit I am having a hard time discovering your *why*." He gave a dismissive wave of his hand.

The goons dragged Lloyd Sterling away.

"Shall we resume our conversation tomorrow evening, Lieutenant Sterling. One scholar to another."

*   *   *

1035 Hours
Evreux, France

Behr smoked the last of his loose Russian tobacco. The hand-rolled cigarette held equal parts makhorka and American Velvet pipe tobacco. He savored each drag. A lung-shot *soldat* in the adjoining bed coughed and hacked. An orderly scurried by, took a sideways glance, but once again declined to admonish Behr for smoking in a zone labeled: *Rauchen verboten!*

The Wehrmacht had recently converted the Evreux girl's school into a hospital. Nothing within the overcrowded classroom pleased Behr. Not the stench of infection and disinfectant hanging in the unmoving air. Not the medical notations for each patient on the slate chalkboard. Not the whimpering and screams heard each night. Not the lumpy bed. Not his leg in traction. Not the grazing bullet wound across his shoulder blade. He took a long drag and closed his eyes. His mind carried him back to the breezes blowing across the Russian steppes. He inhaled the fragrance of buckwheat, ripe barley, and radiant sunflower fields.

Pain shot up his leg. His eyes jerked open. A white-frocked surgeon held a fountain pen above Behr's elevated toes.

The orthopedic surgeon gave a disapproving look. "No military award—Knight's Cross included—exempts one from hospital regulations, *Hauptscharfuhrer* Behr."

Behr took a drag from the cigarette burned down to the width of his nicotine stained fingers. "Get me out of traction and I will gladly smoke outside, Herr *Oberstleutnant.*" He tossed the butt into a bedpan.

"Nein, I'll do better than that. It seems the screws and plates held this time. Your ankle should fully recover." The surgeon looked toward the chalkboard and squinted. "Your bullet wound and broken rib have healed satisfactorily. *Ja*, today we will remove the traction. This evening I shall assign you to a truck heading east along the Seine. By midnight you'll arrive in Paris to complete you convalescence, forever out of my hair."

"Danke *schön.*" Behr grinned. "I look forward to rejoining my unit."

The surgeon snorted. "Little of the Seventeenth SS remains to rejoin. Your division—along with the Twelfth SS Hitler Youth—demands most of my surgical time."

*   *   *

1415 Hours
Newbury, England

Sam jogged through Hamstead Park Estate—the 501st Parachute Infantry Regiment's new home—anxious to reach the field where the buses would offload. *Who'll get off?* His aching bullet wounds slowed him to a brisk walk.

The first buses had just popped over the crest of the hill. On the other side of the hill were the Enborne crossroads. Two miles' distance from Enborne—east, past the Roman ruins—was Newbury. And a principal highway from Newbury ran southward to the coast and Southampton. The members of the 101st Airborne Division still able to fight had crossed the English Channel on naval landing ships and docked at Southampton yesterday. He knew his 1st Battalion had seen more combat, but had scant details.

Who'll get off the buses? What if Springwater doesn't? The knot in his stomach tightened.

Dust billowed as the first buses disgorged their human cargo. Air brakes hissed. Diesel exhaust fouled the air. Sam recognized nobody. He moved among the first arrivals. "Where's Able Company, sir?"

"We're Easy Company," a captain said and shouted over his shoulder, "Hey, any of you clowns know where Able is?"

A tech sergeant threw his thumb over his shoulder. "First Battalion starts somewhere about the eleventh bus, sir, I think."

Sam withdrew clear of the crowd and tried to count incoming buses. He failed and trotted toward where he guessed the eleventh bus should be. He recognized faces—faces that looked like they'd aged five years in five weeks. Faces from Baker Company, Charlie Company, Battalion HQ Company.

The crowd engulfed him. A trooper bumped his sore ribs. Sam winced. Sergeants barked orders. Sam stepped away from the offloading mob to gain a better view.

Forty yards away more buses pulled in.

One of his machinegun teams—Clarkson, Wade, and Porcelli—stepped off a bus. His heart raced as he jostled toward them. *That's three.*

Ogden, Diaz, and Taylor exited the bus. *That's six!*

Harrigan and Donovan came off together. Doc Walters followed them. *That's nine!* Sam moved closer, craning his neck. His vision grew misty.

Doc Walter's spotted Sam. The medic's jaw dropped. Grinning, Sam moved closer. Arriving paratroopers moved between them.

Silva paused at the bottom step in the bus door and scanned the area. *Scouting for women already,* Sam thought. Collins shoved Silva off. "Dern diesel fumes. I'm fixin' to puke. Out of my way, Portagee."

Sam's smile expanded. *Eleven!*

"What you gawking at, Doc?" Silva lit a cigarette. "Look like you saw a ghost."

Nobody else got off. Sam's throat constricted, erasing his smile. *No!*

A musette bag sailed out the door, striking Collins in the back. "You forgot personal gear, Collins." Springwater ducked into the door. In the

Crow way, he had painted a band across his high cheeks and eyes, back to his temples.

That's twelve! The number of men left when Sam turned 1ˢᵗ Platoon over to Springwater. Tears streamed down Sam's face. *Ted got them all back.*

Sam stepped forward.

Collins's eyes bugged out. "Well, I'll be danged and horse-whipped."

Springwater spotted him and reacted as if expecting Sam to be standing there. The Crow warrior stepped off the bus and snapped a perfect salute.

Sam swallowed back the lump in his throat. "Welcome back, *Chief* Springwater."

Epilogue

June 6, 2008

I heaved a sigh. "So, that pressed rose in *Crime and Punishment*…that was *the* rose from the Merryfield hospital?"

Eyes sparkling like someone who'd just shared a long treasured secret, she nodded.

My book-buying trip now seeming rather insignificant, I pushed myself out of the overstuffed recliner and approached a bookshelf section I had yet to peruse. "You must be incredibly proud. I never served."

"And you should thank the good Lord that your service wasn't required." With considerable effort, she pushed herself out of her recliner before I could help. "I dare say you won't find *All Quiet on the Western Front* there, either. That shelf holds nonfiction."

A book spine imprinted with C. S. Lewis's name caught my attention. I pointed it out. "May I?"

My hostess nodded her approval. I wiped my hand on my pants leg and carefully extracted *The Problem of Pain*. I flipped it open and discovered a 1940 copyright. "First printing? Pretty rare."

In flowing penmanship, an inscription on the front flyleaf read:
To my fellow Inkling, Dr. Simon Guard,
With many fond Bird & Baby memories.
All my best,
Jack

"That particular book is jolly well *not* for sale. At any price." She ran her fingertips over the inscription and let them pause on *Dr. Simon Guard* before pulling her wrinkled hand away.

Once again feeling like an intruder, I shelved the book and turned my attention back to the table—to the waxed envelope holding the brittle rose and lock of golden hair. "Call me a romantic, but I love a story with a happy ending."

Her gaze remained locked on the C. S. Lewis book. "I'm not sure how that applies to *The Problem of Pain*, but I agree."

"No, I'm sorry." I pointed at the envelope. "I meant—"

"Oh dear, no. Life is rarely so sanguine. Heavens, no." Moisture pooled in the corner of her eyes. "Where I left off, the war was far, far from over."

Author's Historical Notes

I have made a concerted effort to assure the overarching historical accuracy and authenticity of this novel—including, as far as possible, physically visiting every setting and visiting with airborne veterans. However, it remains, nonetheless, a work of fiction. On the larger scale, the military units, dates, locals, tactics, and strategic battles represent historical fact. Yet, the interaction of all characters, all scenes, and all combat actions described are entirely the product of my imagination—with one exception. Colonel Howard Johnson's brief cameo appearance and references to his extraordinary exploits, while fictitiously used, are documented historical fact. For the sake of story continuity, I have also taken slight liberties with certain minor historical details.

In no way do I intend for this fictional story to represent the collective nor individual experience of the heroic Normandy paratroopers, to whom all who cherish liberty will forever be indebted. Their sacrificial service—too many remain forever nineteen—defended the Truths we hold to be self-evident.

If You Enjoyed *The Great Hour Struck,* You Can Look Forward to More

"Where I left off, the war was far, far from over."

Yes, this last line from the epilogue is a veiled promise. Indeed, the saga of Lt. Sam Henry, Maggie Elliott, and Helmut Behr continues. Watch for *Where Valor Lies; On Eagles' Wings: Part II.*

In the midst of the overly ambitious military debacle codenamed Operation Market Garden, tragedy puts Sam and Maggie's young love to the ultimate test. While within the Reich's borders, Behr discovers unprecedented horrors—of both Allied and Nazi origin. Destined to clash again, Sam and Behr face off across Bastogne's frozen hell.

Whether seeking shelter in a hastily dug foxhole or London's Underground, survival of war's maelstrom becomes more than physical—these new battlegrounds test sanity and define valor.

Please visit *www.garyvarner.net* to check out setting and research photos, author's thoughts, discussion questions, book news, and more.

Breinigsville, PA USA
10 December 2010
251092BV00001B/19/P